Graham Greene

THE HUMAN FACTOR

Simon and Schuster · New York

c.15

A novel based on life in any Secret Service must necessarily contain a large element of fantasy, for a realistic description would almost certainly infringe some clause or other in some official secrets Act. Operation Uncle Remus is purely a product of the author's imagination (and I trust it will remain so), as are all the characters, whether English, African, Russian or Polish. All the same, to quote Hans Andersen, a wise author who also dealt in fantasy, "out of reality are our tales of imagination fashioned."

To my sister Elisabeth Dennys,
who cannot deny some responsibility

I only know that he who forms a tie is lost. The germ of corruption has entered into his soul.

—Joseph Conrad

Part One

Incidents of deceit and betrayal in British Intelligence prompt several members to plot the entrapment of the surprising suspect, trusted and respected veteran agent Castle, but only after they have murdered the wrong man.

Chapter I

Castle, ever since he had joined the firm as a young recruit more than thirty years ago, had taken his lunch in a public house behind St. James's Street, not far from the office. If he had been asked why he lunched there, he would have referred to the excellent quality of the sausages; he might have preferred a different bitter from Watney's, but the quality of the sausages outweighed that. He was always prepared to account for his actions, even the most innocent, and he was always strictly on time.

So by the stroke of one he was ready to leave. Arthur Davis, his assistant, with whom he shared a room, departed for lunch punctually at twelve and returned, but often only in theory, one hour later. It was understood that, in case of an urgent telegram, Davis or himself must always be there to receive the decoding, but they both knew well that in the particular sub-division of their department nothing was ever really urgent. The difference in time between England and the various parts of Eastern and Southern Africa, with which the two of them were concerned, was usually large enough—even when in the case of Johannesburg it was little more than an hour—for no one outside the department to worry about the delay in the delivery of a message: the fate of the world, Davis used to declare, would never be decided on their continent, however many embassies China or Russia might open from Addis Ababa to Conakry or however many Cubans landed. Castle wrote a memorandum for Davis: "If Zaire replies to No. 172 send copies to Treasury and FO." He looked at his watch. Davis was ten minutes late.

Castle began to pack his briefcase—he put in a note of what he had to buy for his wife at the cheese shop in Jermyn Street and of a present for his son to whom he had been disagreeable that morning (two packets of Maltesers), and a book, *Clarissa Harlowe*, in which he had never read further than Chapter LXXIX of the first volume. Directly he heard a lift door close and Davis's step in the passage he left his room. His lunchtime with the sausages had been cut by eleven minutes. Unlike Davis he always punctually returned. It was one of the virtues of age.

Arthur Davis in the staid office was conspicuous by his eccentricities. He could be seen now, approaching from the other end of the long white corridor, dressed as if he had just come from a rather horsy country weekend, or perhaps from the public enclosure of a racecourse. He wore a tweed sports jacket of a greenish overall color, and he displayed a scarlet spotted handkerchief in the breast pocket: he might have been attached in some way to a tote. But he was like an actor who has been miscast: when he tried to live up to the costume, he usually fumbled the part. If he looked in London as though he had arrived from the country, in the country when he visited Castle he was unmistakably a tourist from the city.

"Sharp on time as usual," Davis said with his habitual guilty grin.

"My watch is always a little fast," Castle said, apologizing for the criticism which he had not expressed. "An anxiety complex, I suppose."

"Smuggling out top secrets as usual?" Davis asked, making a playful pretense at seizing Castle's briefcase. His breath had a sweet smell: he was addicted to port.

"Oh, I've left all those behind for you to sell. You'll get a better price from your shady contacts."

"Kind of you, I'm sure."

"And then you're a bachelor. You need more money than a married man. I halve the cost of living . . ."

"Ah, but those awful leftovers," Davis said, "the joint remade into shepherd's pie, the dubious meatball. Is it worth it? A married man can't even afford a good port." He went into the room they shared and rang for Cynthia. Davis had been trying to make Cynthia for two years now, but the daughter of a major-general was after bigger game. All the same Davis continued to hope; it was always safer, he explained, to have an affair inside the department—it couldn't be regarded as a security risk, but Castle knew how deeply attached to Cynthia Davis really was. He had the keen desire for monogamy and the defensive humor of a lonely man. Once Castle had visited him in a flat, which he shared with two men from the Department of the Environment, over an antique shop not far from Claridge's—very central and W.1.

"You ought to come in a bit nearer," Davis had advised Castle in the overcrowded sitting-room where magazines of different tastes—

the *New Statesman, Penthouse* and *Nature*—littered the sofa, and where the used glasses from someone else's party had been pushed into corners for the daily woman to find.

"You know very well what they pay us," Castle said, "and I'm married."

"A grave error of judgment."

"Not for me," Castle said, "I like my wife."

"And of course there's the little bastard," Davis went on. "I couldn't afford children and port as well."

"I happen to like the little bastard too."

Castle was on the point of descending the four stone steps into Piccadilly when the porter said to him, "Brigadier Tomlinson wants to see you, sir."

"Brigadier Tomlinson?"

"Yes. In room A.3."

Castle had only met Brigadier Tomlinson once, many years before, more years than he cared to count, on the day that he was appointed—the day he put his name to the Official Secrets Act, when the brigadier was a very junior officer, if he had been an officer at all. All he could remember of him was a small black moustache hovering like an unidentified flying object over a field of blotting paper, which was entirely white and blank, perhaps for security reasons. The stain of his signature after he had signed the Act became the only flaw on its surface, and that leaf was almost certainly torn up and sent to the incinerator. The Dreyfus case had exposed the perils of a wastepaper basket nearly a century ago.

"Down the corridor on the left, sir," the porter reminded him when he was about to take the wrong route.

"Come in, come in, Castle," Brigadier Tomlinson called. His moustache was now as white as the blotting paper, and with the years he had grown a small pot-belly under a double-breasted waistcoat—only his dubious rank remained constant. Nobody knew to what regiment he had formerly belonged, if such a regiment indeed existed, for all military titles in this building were a little suspect. Ranks might just be part of the universal cover. He said, "I don't think you know Colonel Daintry."

"No. I don't think . . . How do you do?"

Daintry, in spite of his neat dark suit and his hatchet face, gave a more genuine out-of-doors impression than Davis ever did. If Davis at his first appearance looked as though he would be at home in a bookmakers' compound, Daintry was unmistakably at home in the expensive enclosure or on a grouse moor. Castle enjoyed making lightning sketches of his colleagues: there were times when he even put them on to paper.

"I think I knew a cousin of yours at Corpus," Daintry said. He spoke agreeably, but he looked a little impatient; he probably had to catch a train north at King's Cross.

"Colonel Daintry," Brigadier Tomlinson explained, "is our new broom," and Castle noticed the way Daintry winced at the description. "He has taken over security from Meredith. But I'm not sure you ever met Meredith."

"I suppose you mean my cousin Roger," Castle said to Daintry. "I haven't seen him for years. He got a first in Greats. I believe he's in the Treasury now."

"I've been describing the setup here to Colonel Daintry," Brigadier Tomlinson prattled on, keeping strictly to his own wavelength.

"I took Law myself. A poor second," Daintry said. "You read History, I think?"

"Yes. A very poor third."

"At the House?"

"Yes."

"I've explained to Colonel Daintry," Tomlinson said, "that only you and Davis deal with the Top Secret cables as far as Section 6A is concerned."

"If you can call anything Top Secret in our section. Of course, Watson sees them too."

"Davis—he's a Reading University man, isn't he?" Daintry asked with what might have been a slight touch of disdain.

"I see you've been doing your homework."

"As a matter of fact I've just been having a talk with Davis himself."

"So that's why he was ten minutes too long over his lunch."

Daintry's smile resembled the painful reopening of a wound. He had very red lips, and they parted at the corners with difficulty. He said, "I talked to Davis about you, so now I'm talking to you about Davis. An open check. You must forgive the new broom, I have to learn the ropes," he added, getting confused among the metaphors. "One has to keep to the drill—in spite of the confidence we have in both of you, of course. By the way, *did* he warn you?"

"No. But why believe me? We may be in collusion."

The wound opened again a very little way and closed tight.

"I gather that politically he's a bit on the left. Is that so?"

"He's a member of the Labour Party. I expect he told you himself."

"Nothing wrong in that, of course," Daintry said. "And you . . . ?"

"I have no politics. I expect Davis told you that too."

"But you sometimes vote, I suppose?"

"I don't think I've voted once since the war. The issues nowadays so often seem—well, a bit parish pump."

"An interesting point of view," Daintry said with disapproval. Castle could see that telling the truth this time had been an error of judgment, yet, except on really important occasions, he always preferred the truth. The truth can be double-checked. Daintry looked at his watch. "I won't keep you long. I have a train to catch at King's Cross."

"A shooting weekend?"

"Yes. How did you know?"

"Intuition," Castle said, and again he regretted his reply. It was always safer to be inconspicuous. There were times, which grew more frequent with every year, when he daydreamed of complete conformity, as a different character might have dreamt of making a dramatic century at Lord's.

"I suppose you noticed my gun-case by the door?"

"Yes," Castle said, who hadn't seen it until then, "that was the clue." He was glad to see that Daintry looked reassured.

Daintry explained, "There's nothing personal in all this, you know. Purely a routine check. There are so many rules that sometimes some of them get neglected. It's human nature. The regulation, for example, about not taking work out of the office . . ."

He looked significantly at Castle's briefcase. An officer and a gentleman would open it at once for inspection with an easy joke, but Castle was not an officer, nor had he ever classified himself as a gentleman. He wanted to see how far below the table the new broom was liable to sweep. He said, "I'm not going home. I'm only going out to lunch."

"You won't mind, will you . . . ?" Daintry held out his hand for the briefcase. "I asked the same of Davis," he said.

"Davis wasn't carrying a briefcase," Castle said, "when I saw him."

Daintry flushed at his mistake. He would have felt a similar shame, Castle felt sure, if he had shot a beater. "Oh, it must have been that other chap," Daintry said. "I've forgotten his name."

"Watson?" the brigadier suggested.

"Yes, Watson."

"So you've even been checking our chief?"

"It's all part of the drill," Daintry said.

Castle opened his briefcase. He took out a copy of the *Berk-hamsted Gazette*.

"What's this?" Daintry asked.

"My local paper. I was going to read it over lunch."

"Oh yes, of course. I'd forgotten. You live quite a long way out. Don't you find it a bit inconvenient?"

"Less than an hour by train. I need a house and a garden. I have a child, you see—and a dog. You can't keep either of them in a flat. Not with comfort."

"I notice you are reading *Clarissa Harlowe?* Like it?"

"Yes, so far. But there are four more volumes."

"What's this?"

"A list of things to remember."

"To remember?"

"My shopping list," Castle explained. He had written under the printed address of his house, 129 King's Road, "Two Maltesers. Half pound Earl Grey. Cheese—Wensleydale? or Double Gloucester? Yardley Pre-Shave Lotion."

"What on earth are Maltesers?"

"A sort of chocolate. You should try them. They're delicious. In my opinion better than Kit Kats."

Daintry said, "Do you think they would do for my hostess? I'd like to bring her something a little out of the ordinary." He looked at his watch. "Perhaps I could send the porter—there's just time. Where do you buy them?"

"He can get them at an ABC in the Strand."

"ABC?" Daintry asked.

"Aerated Bread Company."

"Aerated bread . . . what on earth . . . ? Oh well, there isn't time to go into that. Are you sure those—teasers would do?"

"Of course, tastes differ."

"Fortnum's is only a step away."

"You can't get them there. They are very inexpensive."

"I don't want to seem niggardly."

"Then go for quantity. Tell him to get three pounds of them."

"What is the name again? Perhaps you would tell the porter as you go out."

"Is my check over then? Am I clear?"

"Oh yes. Yes. I told you it was purely formal, Castle."

"Good shooting."

"Thanks a lot."

Castle gave the porter the message. "Three pounds did 'e say?"

"Yes."

"Three pounds of Maltesers!"

"Yes."

"Can I take a pantechnicon?"

The porter summoned the assistant porter who was reading a girlie magazine. He said, "Three pounds of Maltesers for Colonel Daintry."

"That would be a hundred and twenty packets or thereabouts," the man said after a little calculation.

"No, no," Castle said, "it's not as bad as that. The weight, I think, is what he means."

He left them making their calculations. He was fifteen minutes late at the pub and his usual corner was occupied. He ate and drank quickly and calculated that he had made up three minutes. Then he bought the Yardley's at the chemist in St. James's Arcade, the Earl Grey at Jackson's, a Double Gloucester there too to save time, although he usually went to the cheese shop in Jermyn Street, but the Maltesers, which he had intended to buy at the ABC, had run out by the time he got there—the assistant told him there had been an unexpected demand, and he had to buy Kit Kats instead. He was only three minutes late when he rejoined Davis.

"You never told me they were having a check," he said.

"I was sworn to secrecy. Did they catch you with anything?"

"Not exactly."

"He did with me. Asked what I had in my macintosh pocket. I'd got that report from 59800. I wanted to read it again over my lunch."

"What did he say?"

"Oh, he let me go with a warning. He said rules were made to be kept. To think that fellow Blake (whatever did he want to escape for?) got forty years freedom from income tax, intellectual strain and responsibility, and it's we who suffer for it now."

"Colonel Daintry wasn't very difficult," Castle said. "He knew a cousin of mine at Corpus. That sort of thing makes a difference."

Chapter II

Castle was usually able to catch the six-thirty-five train from Euston. This brought him to Berkhamsted punctually at seven twelve. His bicycle waited for him at the station—he had known the ticket collector for many years and he always left it in his care. Then he rode the longer way home, for the sake of exercise—across the canal bridge, past the Tudor school, into the High Street, past the gray flint parish church which contained the helmet of a crusader, then up the slope of the Chilterns toward his small semi-detached house in King's Road. He always arrived there, if he had not telephoned a warning from London, by half-past seven. There was just time to say goodnight to the boy and have a whisky or two before dinner at eight.

In a bizarre profession anything which belongs to an everyday routine gains great value—perhaps that was one reason why, when he came back from South Africa, he chose to return to his birthplace: to the canal under the weeping willows, to the school and the ruins of a once-famous castle which had withstood a siege by Prince John of France and of which, so the story went, Chaucer had been a Clerk of Works and—who knows?—perhaps an ancestral Castle one of the artisans. It consisted now of only a few grass mounds and some yards of flint wall, facing the canal and the railway line. Beyond was a long road leading away from the town bordered with hawthorn hedges and Spanish chestnut trees until one reached at last the freedom of the Common. Years ago the inhabitants of the town fought for their right to graze cattle upon the Common, but in the twentieth century it was doubtful whether any animal but a rabbit or a goat could have found provender among the ferns, the gorse and the bracken.

When Castle was a child there still remained on the Common the remnants of old trenches dug in the heavy red clay during the first German war by members of the Inns of Court OTC, young lawyers who practiced there before they went to die in Belgium or France as members of more orthodox units. It was unsafe to wander there without proper knowledge, since the old trenches had been dug several feet deep, modeled on the original trenches of the Old Contemptibles around Ypres, and a stranger risked a sudden fall and a broken leg. Children who had grown up with the knowledge of their whereabouts wandered freely, until the memory began to fade. Castle for some reason had always remembered, and sometimes on his days off from the office he took Sam by the hand and introduced him to the forgotten hiding-places and the multiple dangers of the Common. How many guerrilla campaigns he had fought there as a child against overwhelming odds. Well, the days of the guerrilla had returned, daydreams had become realities. Living thus with the long familiar he felt the security that an old lag feels when he goes back to the prison he knows.

Castle pushed his bicycle up King's Road. He had bought his house with the help of a building society after his return to England. He could easily have saved money by paying cash, but he had no wish to appear different from the schoolmasters on either side—on the salary they earned there was no possibility of saving. For the same reason he kept the rather gaudy stained glass of the Laughing Cavalier over the front door. He disliked it; he associated it with dentistry—so often stained glass in provincial towns hides the agony of the chair from outsiders—but again because his neighbors bore with theirs, he preferred to leave it alone. The schoolmasters in King's Road were strong upholders of the aesthetic principles of North Oxford, where many of them had taken tea with their tutors, and there too, in the Banbury Road, his bicycle would have fitted well, in the hall, under the staircase.

He opened his door with a Yale key. He had once thought of buying a mortise lock or something very special chosen in St. James's Street from Chubb's, but he restrained himself—his neighbors were content with Yale, and there had been no burglary nearer than Boxmoor in the last three years to justify him. The hall was empty; so seemed the sitting room, which he could see through the open door: there was not a sound from the kitchen. He noticed at once that the whisky bottle was not standing ready by the siphon on the sideboard. The habit of years had been broken and Castle felt anxiety like the prick of an insect. He called, "Sarah," but there was no reply. He stood just inside the hall door, beside the umbrella stand, taking in with rapid glances the familiar scene, with the one essential missing—the whisky bottle—and he held his breath. He had always, since they came, felt certain that one day a doom would catch up with them, and he knew that when that happened he must not be betrayed by panic: he must leave quickly, without an attempt to pick up any broken piece of their life together. "Those that are in Judea must take refuge in the mountains . . ." He thought for some reason of his cousin at the Treasury, as though he were an amulet, which could protect him, a lucky rabbit's foot, and then he was able to breathe again with relief, hearing voices on the floor above and the footsteps of Sarah as she came down the stairs.

"Darling, I didn't hear you. I was talking to Doctor Barker."

Doctor Barker followed her—a middle-aged man with a flaming strawberry mark on his left cheek, dressed in dusty gray, with two fountain pens in his breast pocket; or perhaps one of them was a pocket torch for peering into throats.

"Is anything wrong?"

"Sam's got measles, darling."

"He'll do all right," Doctor Barker said. "Just keep him quiet. Not too much light."

"Will you have a whisky, Doctor?"

"No, thank you. I have still two more visits to make and I'm late for dinner as it is."

"Where could he have caught it?"

"Oh, there's quite an epidemic. You needn't worry. It's only a light attack."

When the doctor had gone Castle kissed his wife. He ran his hand over her black resistant hair; he touched her high cheekbones. He felt the black contours of her face as a man might who has picked out one piece of achieved sculpture from all the hack carvings littering the steps of a hotel for white tourists; he was reassuring himself that what he valued most in life was still safe. By the end of a day he always felt as though he had been gone for years leaving her defenseless. Yet no one here minded her African blood. There was no law here to menace their life together. They were secure—or as secure as they would ever be.

"What's the matter?" she asked.

"I was worried. Everything seemed at sixes and sevens tonight when I came in. You weren't here. Not even the whisky . . ."

"What a creature of habit you are."

He began to unpack his briefcase while she prepared the whisky. "Is there really nothing to worry about?" Castle asked. "I never like the way doctors speak, especially when they are reassuring."

"Nothing."

"Can I go and see him?"

"He's asleep now. Better not wake him. I gave him an aspirin."
He put Volume One of *Clarissa Harlowe* back in the bookcase.
"Finished it?"

"No, I doubt whether I ever shall now. Life's a bit too short."

"But I thought you always liked long books."

"Perhaps I'll have a go at *War and Peace* before it's too late."

"We haven't got it."

"I'm going to buy a copy tomorrow."

She had carefully measured out a quadruple whisky by English
pub standards, and now she brought it to him and closed the glass
in his hand, as though it were a message no one else must read. Indeed, the degree of his drinking was known only to them: he usually drank nothing stronger than beer when he was with a colleague or even with a stranger in a bar. Any touch of alcoholism
might always be regarded in his profession with suspicion. Only
Davis had the indifference to knock the drinks back with a fine
abandon, not caring who saw him, but then he had the audacity
which comes from a sense of complete innocence. Castle had lost
both audacity and innocence forever in South Africa while he was
waiting for the blow to fall.

"You don't mind, do you," Sarah asked, "if it's a cold meal tonight? I was busy with Sam all evening."

"Of course not."

He put his arm round her. The depth of their love was as secret
as the quadruple measure of whisky. To speak of it to others would
invite danger. Love was a total risk. Literature had always so proclaimed it. Tristan, Anna Karenina, even the lust of Lovelace—he
had glanced at the last volume of *Clarissa*. "I like my wife" was the
most he had ever said even to Davis.

"I wonder what I would do without you," Castle said.

"Much the same as you are doing now. Two doubles before dinner at eight."

"When I arrived and you weren't here with the whisky, I was
scared."

"Scared of what?"

"Of being left alone. Poor Davis," he added, "going home to
nothing."

"Perhaps he has a lot more fun."

"This is my fun," he said. "A sense of security."

"Is life outside as dangerous as all that?" She sipped from his
glass and touched his mouth with lips which were wet with J & B.

He always bought J & B because of its color—a large whisky and soda looked no stronger than a weak one of another brand.

The telephone rang from the table by the sofa. He lifted the receiver and said "Hello," but no one replied. "Hello." He silently counted four, then put the receiver down when he heard the connection break.

"Nobody?"

"I expect it was a wrong number."

"It's happened three times this month. Always when you are late at the office. You don't think it could be a burglar checking up to see if we are at home?"

"There's nothing worth a burglary here."

"One reads such horrible stories, darling—men with stockings over their faces. I hate the time after sunset before you come home."

"That's why I bought you Buller. Where *is* Buller?"

"He's in the garden eating grass. Something has upset him. Anyway, you know what he's like with strangers. He fawns on them."

"He might object to a stocking mask all the same."

"He would think it was put on to please him. You remember at Christmas . . . with the paper hats . . ."

"I'd always thought before we got him that boxers were fierce dogs."

"They are—with cats."

The door creaked and Castle turned quickly: the square black muzzle of Buller pushed the door fully open, and then he launched his body like a sack of potatoes at Castle's fly. Castle fended him off. "Down, Buller, down." A long ribbon of spittle descended Castle's trouser leg. He said, "If that's fawning, any burglar would run a mile." Buller began to bark spasmodically and wriggle his haunches, like a dog with worms, moving backward toward the door.

"Be quiet, Buller."

"He only wants a walk."

"At this hour? I thought you said he was ill."

"He seems to have eaten enough grass."

"Be quiet, Buller, damn you. No walk."

Bullet slumped heavily down and dribbled onto the parquet to comfort himself.

"The meter man was scared of him this morning, but Buller only meant to be friendly."

"But the meter man knows him."

"This one was new."

"New. Why?"

"Oh, our usual man has got the flu."

"You asked to see his card?"

"Of course. Darling, are *you* getting scared of burglars now? Stop it, Buller. Stop." Buller was licking his private parts with the gusto of an alderman drinking soup.

Castle stepped over him and went into the hall. He examined the meter carefully, but there seemed nothing unusual about it, and he returned.

"You *are* worried about something?"

"It's nothing really. Something happened at the office. A new security man throwing his weight about. It irritated me—I've been more than thirty years in the firm, and I ought to be trusted by this time. They'll be searching our pockets next when we leave for lunch. He *did* look in my briefcase."

"Be fair, darling. It's not their fault. It's the fault of the job."

"It's too late to change that now."

"Nothing's ever too late," she said, and he wished he could believe her. She kissed him again as she went past him to the kitchen to fetch the cold meat.

When they were sitting down and he had taken another whisky, she said, "Joking apart, you *are* drinking too much."

"Only at home. No one sees me but you."

"I didn't mean for the job. I meant for your health. I don't care a damn about the job."

"No?"

"A department of the Foreign Office. Everyone knows what that means, but you have to go around with your mouth shut like a criminal. If you told me—me, your wife—what you'd done today, they'd sack you. I wish they would sack you. What *have* you done today?"

"I've gossiped with Davis, I've made notes on a few cards, I sent off one telegram—oh, and I've been interviewed by that new security officer. He knew my cousin when he was at Corpus."

"Which cousin?"

"Roger."

"That snob in the Treasury?"

"Yes."

On the way to bed, he said, "Could I look in on Sam?"

"Of course. But he'll be fast asleep by now."

Buller followed them and laid a bit of spittle like a bonbon on the bedclothes.

"Oh, Buller."

He wagged what remained of his tail as though he had been praised. For a boxer he was not intelligent. He had cost a lot of money and perhaps his pedigree was a little too perfect.

The boy lay asleep diagonally in his teak bunk with his head on a box of lead soldiers instead of a pillow. One black foot hung out of the blankets altogether and an officer of the Tank Corps was wedged between his toes. Castle watched Sarah rearrange him, picking out the officer and digging out a parachutist from under a thigh. She handled his body with the carelessness of an expert, and the child slept solidly on.

"He looks very hot and dry," Castle said.

"So would you if you had a temperature of 103." He looked more African than his mother, and the memory of a famine photograph came to Castle's mind—a small corpse spread-eagled on desert sand, watched by a vulture.

"Surely that's very high."

"Not for a child."

He was always amazed by her confidence: she could make a new dish without referring to any cookbook, and nothing ever came to pieces in her hands. Now she rolled the boy roughly on his side and firmly tucked him in, without making an eyelid stir.

"He's a good sleeper."

"Except for nightmares."

"Has he had another?"

"Always the same one. We both of us go off by train and he's left alone. On the platform someone—he doesn't know who—grips his arm. It's nothing to worry about. He's at the age for nightmares. I read somewhere that they come when school begins to threaten. I wish he hadn't got to go to prep school. He may have trouble. Sometimes I almost wish you had apartheid here too."

"He's a good runner. In England there's no trouble if you are good at any sort of games."

In bed that night she woke from her first sleep and said, as though the thought had occurred to her in a dream, "It's strange, isn't it, your being so fond of Sam."

"Of course I am. Why not? I thought you were asleep."

"There's no 'of course' about it. A little bastard."

"That's what Davis always calls him."

"Davis? He doesn't know?" she asked with fear. "Surely he doesn't know?"

"No, don't worry. It's the word he uses for any child."

"I'm glad his father's six feet underground," she said.

"Yes. So am I, poor devil. He might have married you in the end."

"No. I was in love with you all the time. Even when I started Sam I was in love with you. He's more your child than his. I tried to think of you when he made love. He was a tepid sort of fish. At the University they called him an Uncle Tom. Sam won't be tepid, will he? Hot or cold, but not tepid."

"Why are we talking about all that ancient history?"

"Because Sam's ill. And because you are worried. When I don't feel secure I remember what it felt like when I knew I had to tell you about him. That first night across the border in Lourenço Marques. The Hotel Polana. I thought, 'He'll put on his clothes again and go away forever.' But you didn't. You stayed. And we made love in spite of Sam inside."

They lay quietly together, all these years later, only a shoulder touching a shoulder. He wondered whether this was how the happiness of old age, which he had sometimes seen on a stranger's face, might come about, but he would be dead long before she reached old age. Old age was something they would never be able to share.

"Aren't you ever sad," she asked, "that we haven't made a child?"

"Sam's enough of a responsibility."

"I'm not joking. Wouldn't you have liked a child of ours?"

This time he knew that the question was one of those which couldn't be evaded.

"No," he said.

"Why not?"

"You want to look under stones too much, Sarah. I love Sam because he's yours. Because he's not mine. Because I don't have to see anything of myself there when I look at him. I see only something of you. I don't want to go on and on forever. I want the buck to stop here."

Chapter III

1

"A good morning's sport," Colonel Daintry remarked halfheartedly to Lady Hargreaves as he stamped the mud off his boots before entering the house. "The birds were going over well." His fellow guests piled out of cars behind him, with the forced joviality of a football team trying to show their keen sporting enjoyment and not how cold and muddy they really felt.

"Drinks are waiting," Lady Hargreaves said. "Help yourselves. Lunch in ten minutes."

Another car was climbing the hill through the park, a long way off. Somebody bellowed with laughter in the cold wet air, and someone cried, "Here's Buffy at last. In time for lunch, of course."

"And your famous steak-and-kidney pudding?" Daintry asked. "I've heard so much about it."

"My pie, you mean. Did you really have a good morning, Colonel?" Her voice had a faint American accent—the more agreeable for being faint, like the tang of an expensive perfume.

"Not many pheasants," Daintry said, "but otherwise very fine."

"Harry," she called over his shoulder, "Dicky" and then "Where's Dodo? Is he lost?" Nobody called Daintry by his first name because nobody knew it. With a sense of loneliness he watched the graceful elongated figure of his hostess limp down the stone steps to greet "Harry" with a kiss on both cheeks. Daintry went on alone into the dining room where the drinks stood waiting on the buffet.

A little stout rosy man in tweeds whom he thought he had seen somewhere before was mixing himself a dry martini. He wore silver-rimmed spectacles which glinted in the sunlight. "Add one for me," Daintry said, "if you are making them really dry."

"Ten to one," the little man said. "A whiff of the cork, eh? Always use a scent spray myself. You are Daintry, aren't you? You've forgotten me. I'm Percival. I took your blood pressure once."

"Oh yes. Doctor Percival. We're in the same firm more or less, aren't we?"

"That's right. C wanted us to get together quietly—no need for all that nonsense with scramblers here. I can never make mine work, can you? The trouble is, though, that I don't shoot. I only fish. This your first time here?"

"Yes. When did you arrive?"

"A bit early. Around midday. I'm a Jaguar fiend. Can't go at less than a hundred."

Daintry looked at the table. A bottle of beer stood by every place. He didn't like beer, but for some reason beer seemed always to be regarded as suitable for a shoot. Perhaps it went with the boyishness of the occasion like ginger beer at Lord's. Daintry was not boyish. A shoot to him was an exercise of strict competitive skill —he had once been runner-up for the King's Cup. Now down the center of the table stood small silver sweet bowls which he saw contained his Maltesers. He had been a little embarrassed the night before when he had presented almost a crate of them to Lady Hargreaves; she obviously hadn't an idea what they were or what to do with them. He felt that he had been deliberately fooled by that man Castle. He was glad to see they looked more sophisticated in silver bowls than they had done in plastic bags.

"Do you like beer?" he asked Percival.

"I like anything alcoholic," Percival said, "except Fernet-Branca," and then the boys burst boisterously in—Buffy and Dodo, Harry and Dicky and all the silver and the glasses vibrated with joviality. Daintry was glad Percival was there, for nobody seemed to know Percival's first name either.

Unfortunately he was separated from him at table. Percival had quickly finished his first bottle of beer and begun on a second. Daintry felt betrayed, for Percival seemed to be getting on with his neighbors as easily as if they had been members of the old firm too. He had begun to tell a fishing story which had made the man called Dicky laugh. Daintry was sitting between the fellow he took to be Buffy and a lean elderly man with a lawyer's face. He had introduced himself, and his surname was familiar. He was either the Attorney-General or the Solicitor-General, but Daintry couldn't remember which; his uncertainty inhibited conversation.

Buffy said suddenly, "My God, if those are not Maltesers!"

"You know Maltesers?" Daintry asked.

"Haven't tasted one for donkey's years. Always bought them at the movies when I was a kid. Taste wonderful. There's no movie house around here surely?"

"As a matter of fact I brought them from London."

"You go to the movies? Haven't been to one in ten years. So they still sell Maltesers?"

"You can buy them in shops too."

"I never knew that. Where did you find them?"

"In an ABC."

"ABC?"

Daintry repeated dubiously what Castle had said, "Aerated Bread Company."

"Extraordinary! What's aerated bread?"

"I don't know," Daintry said.

"The things they do invent nowadays. I wouldn't be surprised, would you, if their loaves were made by computers?" He leaned forward and took a Malteser and crackled it at his ear like a cigar.

Lady Hargreaves called down the table, "Buffy! Not before the steak-and-kidney pie."

"Sorry, my dear. Couldn't resist. Haven't tasted one since I was a kid." He said to Daintry, "Extraordinary things computers. I paid 'em a fiver once to find me a wife."

"You aren't married?" Daintry asked, looking at the gold ring Buffy wore.

"No. Always keep that on for protection. Wasn't really serious, you know. Like to try out new gadgets. Filled up a form as long as your arm. Qualifications, interests, profession, what have you." He took another Malteser. "Sweet tooth," he said. "Always had it."

"And did you get any applicants?"

"They sent me along a girl. Girl! Thirty-five if a day. I had to give her tea. Haven't had tea since my mum died. I said, 'My dear, do you mind if we make it a whisky? I know the waiter here. He'll slip us one.' She said she didn't drink. Didn't drink!"

"The computer had slipped up?"

"She had a degree in Economics at London University. And big spectacles. Flat-chested. She said she was a good cook. I said I always took my meals at White's."

"Did you ever see her again?"

"Not to speak to, but once she waved to me from a bus as I was coming down the club steps. Embarrassing! Because I was with Dicky at the time. That's what happened when they let buses go up St. James's Street. No one was safe."

After the steak-and-kidney pie came a treacle tart and a big Stilton cheese and Sir John Hargreaves circulated the port. There was a faint feeling of unrest at the table as though the holidays had been going on too long. People began to glance through the windows at the gray sky: in a few hours the light would fail. They drank their port rapidly as if with a sense of guilt—they were not really there for idle pleasure—except Percival, who wasn't concerned. He was telling another fishing story and had four empty bottles of beer beside him.

The Solicitor-General—or was it the Attorney-General?—said heavily, "We ought to be moving. The sun's going down." He certainly was not here for enjoyment, only for execution, and Daintry sympathized with his anxiety. Hargreaves really ought to make a move, but Hargreaves was almost asleep. After years in the Colonial Service—he had once been a young District Commissioner on what was then the Gold Coast—he had acquired the knack of snatching his siesta in the most unfavorable circumstances, even surrounded by quarreling chiefs, who used to make more noise than Buffy.

"John," Lady Hargreaves called down the table, "wake up."

He opened blue serene unshockable eyes and said, "A catnap." It was said that as a young man somewhere in Ashanti he had inadvertently eaten human flesh, but his digestion had not been impaired. According to the story he had told the Governor, "I couldn't really complain, sir. They were doing me a great honor by inviting me to take pot luck."

"Well, Daintry," he said. "I suppose it's time we got on with the massacre."

He unrolled himself from the table and yawned. "Your steak-and-kidney pie, dear, is *too* good."

Daintry watched him with envy. He envied him in the first place for his position. He was one of the very few men outside the services ever to have been appointed C. No one in the firm knew why he had been chosen—all kinds of recondite influences had been surmised, for his only experience of intelligence had been gained in Africa during the war. Daintry also envied him his wife; she was so rich, so decorative, so impeccably American. An American marriage, it seemed, could not be classified as a foreign marriage: to marry a foreigner special permission had to be obtained and it was often refused, but to marry an American was perhaps to confirm the special relationship. He wondered all the same whether Lady Hargreaves had been positively vetted by MI5 and been passed by the FBI.

"Tonight," Hargreaves said, "we'll have a chat, Daintry, won't we? You and I and Percival. When this crowd has gone home."

2

Sir John Hargreaves limped round, handing out cigars, pouring out whiskies, poking the fire. "I don't enjoy shooting much myself," he said. "Never used to shoot in Africa, except with a camera, but my wife likes all the old English customs. If you have land, she says, you must have birds. I'm afraid there weren't enough pheasants, Daintry."

"I had a very good day," Daintry said, "all in all."

"I wish you ran to a trout stream," Doctor Percival said.

"Oh yes, fishing's your game, isn't it? Well, you might say we've got a bit of fishing on hand now." He cracked a log with his poker. "Useless," he said, "but I love to see the sparks fly. There seems to be a leak somewhere in Section 6."

Percival said, "At home or in the field?"

"I'm not sure, but I have a nasty feeling that it's here at home. In one of the African sections—6A."

"I've just finished going through Section 6," Daintry said. "Only a routine run-through. So as to get to know people."

"Yes, so they told me. That's why I asked you to come here. Enjoyed having you for the shoot too, of course. Did anything strike you?"

"Security's got a bit slack. But that's true of all other sections too. I made a rough check for example of what people take out in their briefcases at lunchtime. Nothing serious, but I was surprised at the number of briefcases . . . It's a warning, that's all, of course. But a warning might scare a nervous man. We can't very well ask them to strip."

"They do that in the diamond fields, but I agree that in the West End stripping would seem a bit unusual."

"Anyone really out of order?" Percival asked.

"Not seriously. Davis in 6A was carrying a report—said he wanted to read it over lunch. I warned him, of course, and made him leave it behind with Brigadier Tomlinson. I've gone through all the traces too. Vetting has been done very efficiently since the Blake case broke, but we still have a few men who were with us in the bad old days. Some of them even go back as far as Burgess and Maclean. We *could* start tracing them all over again, but it's difficult to pick up a cold scent."

"It's possible, of course, just possible," C said, "that the leak came from abroad and that the evidence has been planted here. They would like to disrupt us, damage morale and hurt us with the Americans. The knowledge that there was a leak, if it became public, could be more damaging than the leak itself."

"That's what I was thinking," Percival said. "Questions in Parliament. All the old names thrown up—Vassall, the Portland affair, Philby. But if they're after publicity, there's little we can do."

"I suppose a Royal Commission would be appointed to shut the stable door," Hargreaves said. "But let's assume for a moment that they are really after information and not scandal. Section 6 seems a most unlikely department for that. There are no atomic secrets in Africa: guerrillas, tribal wars, mercenaries, petty dictators, crop failures, building scandals, gold beds, nothing very secret there. That's why I wonder whether the motive may be simply scandal, to prove they have penetrated the British Secret Service yet again."

"Is it an important leak, C?" Percival asked.

"Call it a very small drip, mainly economic, but the interesting thing is that apart from economics it concerns the Chinese. Isn't it possible—the Russians are such novices in Africa—that they want to make use of our service for information on the Chinese?"

"There's precious little they can learn from us," Percival said. "But you know what it's always like at everybody's Center. One thing no one can ever stand there is a blank white card."

"Why don't we send them carbon copies, with our compliments, of what we send the Americans? There's supposed to be a *détente*, isn't there? Save everyone a lot of trouble." Percival took a little tube from his pocket and sprayed his glasses, then wiped them with a clean white handkerchief.

"Help yourself to the whisky," C said. "I'm too stiff to move after that bloody shoot. Any ideas, Daintry?"

"Most of the people in Section 6 are post-Blake. If their traces are unreliable then no one is safe."

"All the same, the source seems to be Section 6—and probably 6A. Either at home or abroad."

"The head of Section 6, Watson, is a relative newcomer," Daintry said. "He was very thoroughly vetted. Then there's Castle—he's been with us a very long time, we brought him back from Pretoria seven years ago because they needed him in 6A, and there were personal reasons too—trouble about the girl he wanted to marry. Of course, he belongs to the slack vetting days, but I'd say he was clear. Dullish man, first-class, of course, with files—it's generally the brilliant and ambitious who are dangerous. Castle is safely married, second time, his first wife's dead. There's one child, a house on mortgage in Metroland. Life insurance—payments up to date. No high living. He doesn't even run to a car. I believe he bicycles every day to the station. A third class in history at the House. Careful and scrupulous. Roger Castle in the Treasury is his cousin."

"You think he's quite clear then?"

"He has his eccentricities, but I wouldn't say dangerous ones. For instance he suggested I bring those Maltesers to Lady Hargreaves."

"Maltesers?"

"It's a long story. I won't bother you with it now. And then there's Davis. I don't know that I'm quite so happy about Davis, in spite of the positive vetting."

"Pour me out another whisky, would you, Percival, there's a good chap. Every year I say it's my last shoot."

"But those steak-and-kidney pies of your wife's are wonderful. I wouldn't miss them," Percival said.

"I daresay we could find another excuse for them."

"You could try putting trout in that stream . . ."

Daintry again experienced a twitch of envy; once more he felt left out. He had no life in common with his companions in the world outside the borders of security. Even as a gun he felt professional. Percival was said to collect pictures, and C? A whole social existence had been opened up for him by his rich American wife. The steak-and-kidney pie was all that Dainty was permitted to share with them outside office hours—for the first and perhaps the last time.

"Tell me more about Davis," C said.

"Reading University. Mathematics and physics. Did some of his military service at Aldermaston. Never supported—anyway openly—the marchers. Labour Party, of course."

"Like forty-five percent of the population," C said.

"Yes, yes, of course, but all the same . . . He's a bachelor. Lives alone. Spends fairly freely. Fond of vintage port. Bets on the tote. That's a classic way, of course, of explaining why you can afford . . ."

"What does he afford? Besides port."

"Well, he has a Jaguar."

"So have I," Percival said. "I suppose we mustn't ask you how the leak was discovered?"

"I wouldn't have brought you here if I couldn't tell you that.

Watson knows, but no one else in Section 6. The source of information is an unusual one—a Soviet defector who remains in place."

"Could the leak come from Section 6 abroad?" Daintry asked.

"It could, but I doubt it. It's true that one report they had seemed to come direct from Lourenço Marques. It was word for word as 69300 wrote it. Almost like a photostat of the actual report, so one might have thought that the leak was there if it weren't for a few corrections and deletions. Inaccuracies which could only have been spotted here by comparing the report with the files."

"A secretary?" Percival suggested.

"Daintry began his check with those, didn't you? They are more heavily vetted than anyone. That leaves us Watson, Castle and Davis."

"A thing that worries me," Daintry said, "is that Davis was the one who was taking a report out of the office. One from Pretoria. No apparent importance, but it did have a Chinese angle. He said he wanted to reread it over lunch. He and Castle had got to discuss it later with Watson. I checked the truth of that with Watson."

"What do you suggest we do?" C asked.

"We could put down a maximum security check with the help of 5 and Special Branch. On everyone in Section 6. Letters, telephone calls, bug flats, watch movements."

"If things were as simple as that, Daintry, I wouldn't have bothered you to come up here. This is only a second-class shoot, and I knew the pheasants would disappoint you."

Hargreaves lifted his bad leg with both hands and eased it toward the fire. "Suppose we did prove Davis to be the culprit—or Castle or Watson. What should we do then?"

"Surely that would be up to the courts," Daintry said.

"Headlines in the papers. Another trial *in camera*. No one outside would know how small and unimportant the leaks were. Whoever he is he won't rate forty years like Blake. Perhaps he'll serve ten if the prison's secure."

"That's not our concern surely."

"No, Daintry, but I don't enjoy the thought of that trial one little bit. What cooperation can we expect from the Americans afterwards? And then there's our source. I told you, he's still in place. We don't want to blow him as long as he proves useful."

"In a way," Percival said, "it would be better to close our eyes like a complaisant husband. Draft whoever it is to some innocuous department. Forget things."

"And abet a crime?" Daintry protested.

"Oh, crime," Percival said and smiled at C like a fellow conspirator. "We are all committing crimes somewhere, aren't we? It's our job."

"The trouble is," C said, "that the situation *is* a bit like a rocky marriage. In a marriage, if the lover begins to be bored by the complaisant husband, he can always provoke a scandal. He holds the strong suit. He can choose his own time. I don't want any scandal provoked."

Daintry hated flippancy. Flippancy was like a secret code of which he didn't possess the book. He had the right to read cables and reports marked Top Secret, but flippancy like this was so secret that he hadn't a clue to its understanding. He said, "Personally I would resign rather than cover up." He put down his glass of whisky so hard that he chipped the crystal. Lady Hargreaves again, he thought. She must have insisted on crystal. He said, "I'm sorry."

"Of course you are right, Daintry," Hargreaves said. "Never mind the glass. Please don't think I've brought you all the way up here to persuade you to let things drop, if we have sufficient proof . . . But a trial isn't necessarily the right answer. The Russians don't usually bring things to a trial with their own people. The trial of Penkovsky gave all of us a great boost in morale, they even exaggerated his importance, just as the CIA did. I still wonder why they held it. I wish I were a chess player. Do you play chess, Daintry?"

"No, bridge is my game."

"The Russians don't play bridge, or so I understand."

"Is that important?"

"We are playing games, Daintry, games, all of us. It's important not to take a game too seriously or we may lose it. We have to keep flexible, but it's important, naturally, to play the same game."

"I'm sorry, sir," Daintry said, "I don't understand what you are talking about."

He was aware that he had drunk too much whisky, and he was aware that C and Percival were deliberately looking away from each other—they didn't want to humiliate him. They had heads of stone, he thought, stone.

"Shall we just have one more whisky," C said, "or perhaps not. It's been a long wet day. Percival . . . ?"

Daintry said, "I'd like another."

Percival poured out the drinks. Daintry said, "I'm sorry to be difficult, but I'd like to get things a little clearer before bed, or I won't sleep."

"It's really very simple," C said. "Put on your maximum security check if you like. It may flush the bird without more trouble. He'll soon realize what's going on—if he's guilty, that is. You might think up some kind of test—the old marked fiver technique seldom fails. When we are quite certain he's our man, then it seems to me we will just have to eliminate him. No trial, no publicity. If we can get information about his contacts first, so much the better, but we mustn't risk a public flight and then a press conference in Moscow. An arrest too is out of the question. Granted that he's in Section 6, there's no information he can possibly give which would do as much harm as the scandal of a court case."

"Elimination? You mean . . ."

"I know that elimination is rather a new thing for us. More in the KGB line or the CIA's. That's why I wanted Percival here to meet you. We may need the help of his science boys. Nothing spectacular. Doctor's certificate. No inquest if it can be avoided. A suicide's only too easy, but then a suicide always means an inquest, and that might lead to a question in the House. Everyone knows now what a 'department of the Foreign Office' means. 'Was any question of security involved?' You know the kind of thing some back-bencher is sure to ask. And no one ever believes the official answer. Certainly not the Americans."

"Yes," Percival said, "I quite understand. He should die quietly, peacefully, without pain too, poor chap. Pain sometimes shows on the face, and there may be relatives to consider. A natural death . . ."

"It's a bit difficult, I realize, with all the new antibiotics," C said. "Assuming for the moment that it *is* Davis, he's a man of only just over forty. In the prime of life."

"I agree. A heart attack might just possibly be arranged. Unless . . . Does anyone know whether he drinks a lot?"

"You said something about port, didn't you, Daintry?"

"I'm not saying he's guilty," Daintry said.

"None of us are," C said. "We are only taking Davis as a possible example . . . to help us examine the problem."

"I'd like to look at his medical history," Percival said, "and I'd like to get to know him on some excuse. In a way he would be my patient, wouldn't he? That is to say if . . ."

"You and Daintry could arrange that somehow together. There's no great hurry. We have to be quite sure he's our man. And now—it's been a long day—too many hares and too few pheasants—sleep well. Breakfast on a tray. Eggs and bacon? Sausages? Tea or coffee?"

Percival said, "The works, coffee, bacon, eggs and sausages, if that's all right."

"Nine o'clock?"

"Nine o'clock."

"And you, Daintry?"

"Just coffee and toast. Eight o'clock if you don't mind. I can never sleep late and I have a lot of work waiting."

"You ought to relax more," C said.

3

Colonel Daintry was a compulsive shaver. He had shaved already before dinner, but now he went over his chin a second time with his Remington. Then he shook a little dust into the basin and touching it with his fingers felt justified. Afterward he turned on his electric water-pick. The low buzz was enough to drown the tap on his door, so he was surprised when in the mirror he saw the door swing open and Doctor Percival pass diffidently in.

"Sorry to disturb you, Daintry."

"Come in, do. Forgot to pack something? Anything I can lend you?"

"No, no. I just wanted a word before bed. Amusing little gadget, that of yours. Fashionable, too. I suppose it really is better than an ordinary toothbrush?"

"The water gets between the teeth," Daintry said. "My dentist recommended it."

"I always carry a toothpick for that," Percival said. He took a little red Cartier case out of his pocket. "Pretty, isn't it? Eighteen carat. My father used it before me."

"I think this is more hygienic," Daintry said.

"Oh, I wouldn't be so sure of that. This washes easily. I was a general consultant, you know, Harley Street and all, before I got involved in this show. I don't know why they wanted me—perhaps to sign death certificates." He trotted around the room, showing an interest in everything. "I hope you keep clear of all this fluoride nonsense." He paused at a photograph which stood in a folding case on the dressing table. "Is this your wife?"

"No. My daughter."

"Pretty girl."

"My wife and I are separated."

"Never married myself," Percival said. "To tell you the truth I never had much interest in women. Don't mistake me—not in boys either. Now a good trout stream . . . Know the Aube?"

"No."

"A very small stream with very big fish."

"I can't say I've ever had much interest in fishing," Daintry said, and he began to tidy up his gadget.

"How I run on, don't I?" Percival said. "Never can go straight to a subject. It's like fishing again. You sometimes have to make a hundred false casts before you place the fly."

"I'm not a fish," Daintry said, "and it's after midnight."

"My dear fellow, I really am sorry. I promise I won't keep you up a minute longer. Only I didn't want you to go to bed troubled."

"Was I troubled?"

"It seemed to me you were a bit shocked at C's attitude—I mean to things in general."

"Yes, perhaps I was."

"You haven't been a long time with us, have you, or you'd know how we all live in boxes—you know—boxes."

"I still don't understand."

"Yes, you said that before, didn't you? Understanding isn't all that necessary in our business. I see they've given you the Ben Nicholson room."

"I don't . . ."

"I'm in the Miró room. Good lithographs, aren't they? As a matter of fact it was my idea—these decorations. Lady Hargreaves wanted sporting prints. To go with the pheasants."

"I don't understand modern pictures," Daintry said.

"Take a look at that Nicholson. Such a clever balance. Squares of different color. And yet living so happily together. No clash. The man has a wonderful eye. Change just one of the colors—even the size of the square, and it would be no good at all." Percival pointed at a yellow square. "There's your Section 6. That's your square from now on. You don't need to worry about the blue and the red. All you have to do is pinpoint our man and then tell me. You've no responsibility for what happens in the blue or red squares. In fact not even in the yellow. You just report. No bad conscience. No guilt."

"An action has nothing to do with its consequences. Is that what you're telling me?"

"The consequences are decided elsewhere, Daintry. You mustn't take the conversation tonight too seriously. C likes to toss ideas up into the air and see how they fall. He likes to shock. You know the cannibal story. As far as I know, the criminal—if there is a criminal

—will be handed over to the police in quite the conservative way. Nothing to keep you awake. Do just try to understand that picture. Particularly the yellow square. If you could only see it with my eyes, you would sleep well tonight."

Part Two

Chapter I

1

An old-young man with hair which dangled over his shoulders and the heaven-preoccupied gaze of some eighteenth-century *abbé* was sweeping out a discotheque at the corner of Little Compton Street as Castle went by.

Castle had taken an earlier train than usual, and he was not due at the office for another three-quarters of an hour. Soho at this hour had still some of the glamor and innocence he remembered from his youth. It was at this corner he had listened for the first time to a foreign tongue, at the small cheap restaurant next door he had drunk his first glass of wine; crossing Old Compton Street in those days had been the nearest he had ever come to crossing the Channel. At nine in the morning the strip-tease clubs were all closed and only the delicatessens of his memory were open. The names against the flat-bells—Lulu, Mimi and the like—were all that indicated the afternoon and evening activities of Old Compton Street. The drains ran with fresh water, and the early housewives passed him under the pale hazy sky, carrying bulging sacks of salami and liverwurst with an air of happy triumph. There was not a policeman in sight, though after dark they would be seen walking in pairs. Castle crossed the peaceful street and entered a bookshop he had frequented for several years now.

It was an unusually respectable bookshop for this area of Soho, quite unlike the bookshop which faced it across the street and bore the simple sign "Books" in scarlet letters. The window below the scarlet sign displayed girlie magazines which nobody was ever seen to buy—they were like a signal in an easy code long broken; they indicated the nature of private wares and interests inside. But the shop of Halliday & Son confronted the scarlet "Books" with a window full of Penguins and Everyman and second-hand copies of World's Classics. The son was never seen there, only old Mr. Halliday himself, bent and white-haired, wearing an air of courtesy like an old suit in which he would probably like to be buried. He wrote all his business letters in longhand: he was busy on one of them now.

"A fine autumn morning, Mr. Castle," Mr. Halliday remarked, as he traced with great care the phrase "Your obedient servant."

"There was a touch of frost this morning in the country."

"A bit early yet," Mr. Halliday said.

"I wonder if you've got a copy of *War and Peace?* I've never read it. It seems about time for me to begin."

"Finished *Clarissa* already, sir?"

"No, but I'm afraid I'm stuck. The thought of all those volumes to come . . . I need a change."

"The Macmillan edition is out of print, but I think I have a clean second-hand copy in the World's Classics in one volume. The Aylmer Maude translation. You can't beat Aylmer Maude for Tolstoy. He wasn't a mere translator, he knew the author as a friend." He put down his pen and looked regretfully at "Your obedient servant." The penmanship was obviously not up to the mark.

"That's the translation I want. Two copies of course."

"How are things with you, if I may ask, sir?"

"My boy's sick. Measles. Oh, nothing to worry about. No complications."

"I'm very glad to hear that, Mr. Castle. Measles in these days can cause a lot of anxiety. All well at the office, I hope? No crises in international affairs?"

"None I've been told about. Everything very quiet. I'm seriously thinking of retiring."

"I'm sorry to hear that, sir. We need traveled gentlemen like you to deal with foreign affairs. They will give you a good pension, I trust?"

"I doubt it. How's your business?"

"Quiet, sir, very quiet. Fashions change. I remember the 1940s, how people would queue for a new World's Classic. There's little demand today for the great writers. The old grow old, and the young—well, they seem to stay young a long time, and their tastes differ from ours . . . My son's doing better than I am—in that shop over the road."

"He must get some queer types."

"I prefer not to dwell on it, Mr. Castle. The two businesses remain distinct—I've always insisted on that. No policeman will ever come in here for what I would call, between you and me, a bribe. Not that any real harm can be done by the things the boy sells. It's like preaching to the converted I say. You can't corrupt the corrupt, sir."

"One day I must meet your son."

"He comes across in the evening to help me go over my books. He has a better head for figures than I ever had. We often speak of you, sir. It interests him to hear what you've been buying. I think he sometimes envies me the kind of clients I have, few though they are. He gets the furtive types, sir. They are not the ones to discuss a book like you and I do."

"You might tell him I have an edition of *Monsieur Nicolas* which I want to sell. Not quite your cup of tea, I think."

"I'm not so sure, sir, that it's quite his either. It's a sort of classic you must admit—the title is not suggestive enough for *his* customers, and it's expensive. It would be described in a catalogue as *erotica* rather than *curiosa*. Of course he might find a borrower. Most of his books are on loan, you understand. They buy a book one day and change it the next. His books are not for keeps—like a good set of Sir Walter Scott used to be."

"You won't forget to tell him? *Monsieur Nicolas*."

"Oh no, sir. Restif de la Bretonne. Limited edition. Published by Rodker. I have a memory like an encyclopedia, so far as the older books are concerned. Will you take *War and Peace* with you? If you'll allow me a five-minute search in the cellar."

"You can post it to Berkhamsted. I shan't have time for reading today. Only do remember to tell your son . . ."

"I've never forgotten a message yet, sir, have I?"

After Castle left the shop he crossed the street and peered for a moment into the other establishment. All he saw was one young spotty man making his way sadly down a rack of *Men Only* and *Penthouse* . . . A green rep curtain hung at the end of the shop. It probably held more erudite and expensive items as well as shyer customers, and perhaps young Halliday too whom Castle had never yet had the good fortune to meet—if good fortune were the right term, he thought, to employ.

2

Davis for once had arrived at the office ahead of him. He told Castle apologetically, "I came in early today. I said to myself—the new broom may still be sweeping around. And so I thought . . . an appearance of zeal . . . It does no harm."

"Daintry won't be here on a Monday morning. He went off somewhere for a shooting weekend. Anything in from Zaire yet?"

"Nothing at all. The Yanks are asking for more information about the Chinese mission in Zanzibar."

"We've nothing new to give them. It's up to MI5."

"You'd think from the fuss they make that Zanzibar was as close to them as Cuba."

"It almost is—in the jet age."

Cynthia, the major-general's daughter, came in with two cups of coffee and a telegram. She wore brown trousers and a turtleneck sweater. She had something in common with Davis, for she played a comedy too. If faithful Davis looked as untrustworthy as a bookie, Cynthia, the domestic-minded, looked as dashing as a young commando. It was a pity that her spelling was so bad, but perhaps there was something Elizabethan about her spelling as well as about her name. She was probably looking for a Philip Sidney, and so far she had only found a Davis.

"From Lourenço Marques," Cynthia told Castle.

"Your pigeon, Davis."

"Of absorbing interest," Davis said. "'Your 253 of September 10 mutilated. Please repeat.' That's *your* pigeon, Cynthia. Run along and code it again like a good girl and get the spelling right this time. It helps. You know, Castle, when I joined this outfit, I was a romantic. I thought of atom secrets. They only took me on because I was a good mathematician, and my physics were not too bad either."

"Atom secrets belong to Section 8."

"I thought I'd at least learn some interesting gadgets, like using secret ink. I'm sure you know all about secret ink."

"I did once—even to the use of bird shit. I had a course in it before they sent me on a mission at the end of the war. They gave me a handsome little wooden box, full of bottles like one of those chemistry cabinets for children. And an electric kettle—with a supply of plastic knitting needles."

"What on earth for?"

"For opening letters."

"And did you ever? Open one, I mean?"

"No, though I did once try. I was taught not to open an envelope at the flap, but at the side, and then when I closed it again I was supposed to use the same gum. The trouble was I hadn't got the right gum, so I had to burn the letter after reading it. It wasn't important anyway. Just a love letter."

"What about a Luger? I suppose you had a Luger. Or an explosive fountain pen?"

"No. We've never been very James Bond minded here. I wasn't allowed to carry a gun, and my only car was a secondhand Morris Minor."

"We might at least have been given one Luger between us. It's the age of terrorism."

"But we've got a scrambler," Castle said in the hope of soothing Davis. He recognized the kind of embittered dialogue which was always apt to crop up when Davis was out of sorts. A glass of port too many, a disappointment with Cynthia . . .

"Have you ever handled a microdot, Castle?"

"Never."

"Not even an old wartime hand like you? What was the most secret information you ever possessed, Castle?"

"I once knew the approximate date of an invasion."

"Normandy?"

"No, no. Only the Azores."

"*Were* they invaded? I'd forgotten—or perhaps I never knew. Oh well, old man, I suppose we've got to set our teeth and go through the bloody Zaire bag. Can you tell me why the Yanks are interested in our forecast for the copper crop?"

"I suppose it affects the budget. And that could affect aid programs. Perhaps the Zaire Government might be tempted to supplement its aid from elsewhere. You see, here we are—Report 397—someone with a rather Slavic name had lunch on the 24th with the President."

"Do we have to pass even that on to the CIA?"

"Of course."

"And do you suppose they will give us one little guided missile secret in return?"

It was certainly one of Davis's worst days. His eyes had a yellow tint. God only knew what mixture he had drunk the night before in his bachelor pad in Davies Street. He said glumly, "James Bond would have had Cynthia a long while ago. On a sandy beach under a hot sun. Pass me Philip Dibba's card, would you?"

"What's his number?"

"59800/3."

"What's he been up to?"

"There's a rumor that his retirement as director of the Post Office in Kinshasa was compulsory. He had too many stamps misprinted for his private collection. There goes our most high-powered agent in Zaire." Davis put his head in his hands and gave a doglike howl of genuine distress.

Castle said, "I know how you feel, Davis. Sometimes I would like to retire myself . . . or change my job."

"It's too late for that."

"I wonder. Sarah always tells me I could write a book."

"Official Secrets."

"Not about us. About apartheid."

"It's not what you'd call a best-selling subject."

Davis stopped writing Dibba's card. He said, "Joking apart, old man, please don't think of it. I couldn't stand this job without you. I'd crack up if there wasn't someone here with whom I could laugh at things. I'm afraid to smile with any of the others. Even Cynthia. I love her, but she's so damned loyal, she might report me as a security risk. To Colonel Daintry. Like James Bond killing the girl he slept with. Only she hasn't even slept with me."

"I wasn't really serious," Castle said. "How *could* I leave? Where would I go from here? Except retire. I'm sixty-two, Davis. Past the official age. I sometimes think they've forgotten me, or perhaps they've lost my file."

"Here they are asking for traces of a fellow called Agbo, an employee in Radio Zaire. 59800 proposes him as a sub-agent."

"What for?"

"He has a contact in Radio Ghana."

"That doesn't sound very valuable. Anyway Ghana's not our territory. Pass it on to 6B and see if they can use him."

"Don't be rash, Castle, we don't want to give away a treasure. Who knows what might spring from agent Agbo? From Ghana we might even penetrate Radio Guinea. That would put Penkovsky in the shade. What a triumph. The CIA have never penetrated as far as that into darkest Africa."

It was one of Davis's worst days.

"Perhaps we only see the dullest side of things in 6A," Castle said.

Cynthia returned with an envelope for Davis. "You have to sign here and acknowledge receipt."

"What's in it?"

"How would I know? It's administration." She collected a single piece of paper from the out-tray. "Is this all?"

"We are not exactly overworked at the moment, Cynthia. Are you free for lunch?"

"No, I have things to get for dinner tonight." She closed the door firmly.

"Oh well, another time. Always another time." Davis opened the envelope. He said, "What will they think up next?"

"What's wrong?" Castle asked.

"Haven't you received one of these?"

"Oh, a medical checkup? Of course. I don't know how many times I've been checked in my time. It's something to do with insurance—or pension. Before they sent me to South Africa, Doctor Percival—perhaps you haven't met Doctor Percival—tried to make out I had diabetes. They sent me to a specialist who found I had too little sugar instead of too much . . . Poor old Percival. I think he was a bit out of practice in general medicine, being mixed up with us. Security is more important than a correct diagnosis in this outfit."

"This chit *is* signed Percival, Emmanuel Percival. What a name. Wasn't Emmanuel the bringer of good tidings? Do you think they might be sending me abroad too?"

"Would you like to go?"

"I've always dreamt of being sent one day to Lourenço Marques. Our man there is due for a change. The port should be good, shouldn't it? I suppose even revolutionaries drink port. If only I could have Cynthia with me . . ."

"I thought you favored a bachelor life."

"I wasn't talking about marriage. Bond never had to marry. I like Portuguese cooking."

"It's probably African cooking by now. Do you know anything about the place apart from 69300's cables?"

"I collected a whole file on the nightspots and the restaurants before their damned revolution. Perhaps they are all closed now. All the same I don't suppose 69300 knows the half of what I do about what goes on there. He hasn't got the files, and anyway he's so damned serious—I think he takes his work to bed. Think what the two of us could put down on expenses."

"The two of you?"

"Cynthia and me."

"What a dreamer you are, Davis. She'll never take you on. Remember her father, the major-general."

"Everybody has his dream. What's yours, Castle?"

"Oh, I suppose sometimes I dream of security. I don't mean Daintry's sort of security. To be retired. With a good pension. Enough for me and my wife . . ."

"And your little bastard?"

"Yes, and my little bastard too, of course."

"They aren't very generous with pensions in this department."

"No, I don't suppose either of us will realize his dream."

"All the same—this medical checkup *must* mean something, Castle. That time I went over to Lisbon—our man there took me to a sort of cave beyond Estoril, where you could hear the water washing up under your table . . . I've never eaten any lobsters as good as those were. I've read about a restaurant in Lourenço Marques . . . I even like their green wine, Castle. I really ought to be there—not 69300. He doesn't appreciate good living. You know the place, don't you?"

"I spent two nights there with Sarah—seven years ago. At the Hotel Polana."

"Only two nights?"

"I'd left Pretoria in a hurry—you know that—just ahead of BOSS. I didn't feel safe so near the frontier. I wanted to put an ocean between BOSS and Sarah."

"Oh yes, you had Sarah. Lucky you. At the Hotel Polana. With the Indian Ocean outside."

Castle remembered the bachelor flat—the used glasses, *Penthouse* and *Nature*. "If you are really serious, Davis, I'll talk to Watson. I'll put you up for an exchange."

"I'm serious enough. I want to escape from here, Castle. Desperately."

"Is it as bad as all that?"

"We sit here writing meaningless telegrams. We feel important because we know a little bit more than someone else about the groundnuts or what Mobutu said at a private dinner . . . Do you know I came into this outfit for excitement? Excitement, Castle. What a fool I was. I don't know how you've stood it all these years . . ."

"Perhaps being married helps."

"If I ever married I wouldn't want to live my life here. I'm tired to death of this damned old country, Castle, electricity cuts, strikes, inflation. I'm not worried about the price of food—it's the price of good port which gets me down. I joined this outfit hoping to get abroad, I've even learned Portuguese, but here I stay answering telegrams from Zaire, reporting groundnuts."

"I always thought you were having fun, Davis."

"Oh, I have fun when I get a little drunk. I love that girl, Castle. I can't get her out of my head. And so I clown to please her, and the more I clown the less she likes me. Perhaps if I went to

Lourenço Marques . . . She said once she wanted to go abroad too."

The telephone rang. "Is that you, Cynthia?" but it wasn't. It was Watson, the head of Section 6. "Is that you, Castle?"

"It's Davis."

"Give me Castle."

"Yes," Castle said, "I'm here. What is it?"

"C wants to see us. Will you pick me up on the way down?"

3

It was a long way down, for C's office was one floor underground, established in what during the 1890s had been a millionaire's wine cellar. The room where Castle and Watson waited for a green light to go on above C's door had been the adjoining cellar for the coal and wood, and C's office had housed the best wines in London. It was rumored that, when the department had taken over the house in 1946 and the architect started to reconstruct the building, a false wall was discovered in the wine cellar and behind it lay like mummies the millionaire's secret treasure of fabulous vintages. They were sold—so the legend went—by some ignorant clerk in the Office of Works to the Army and Navy Stores for the price of common table wines. The story was probably untrue, but whenever a historic wine came up at a Christie auction, Davis would say with gloom, "That was one of ours."

The red light stayed interminably on. It was like waiting in a car for a traffic accident to be cleared away.

"Do you know what the trouble is?" Castle asked.

"No. He just asked me to introduce all the Section 6 men whom he's never met. He's been through 6B and now it's your turn. I'm to introduce you and then leave you. That's the drill. It sounds like a relic of colonialism to me."

"I met the old C once. Before I went abroad the first time. He had a black eyeglass. It was rather daunting being stared at by that black O, but all he did was shake hands and wish me good luck. They aren't thinking of sending me abroad again by any chance?"

"No. Why?"

"Remind me to speak to you about Davis."

The light turned green.

"I wish I'd shaved better this morning," Castle said.

Sir John Hargreaves, unlike the old C, was not daunting at all. He had a brace of pheasants on his desk and he was busy on the telephone. "I brought them up this morning. Mary thought you might like them." He waved his hand toward two chairs.

So that's where Colonel Daintry spent the weekend, Castle thought. To shoot pheasants or report on security? He took the smaller and harder chair with a due sense of protocol.

"She's fine. A bit of rheumatism in her bad leg, that's all," Hargreaves said and rang off.

"This is Maurice Castle, sir," Watson said. "He's in charge of 6A."

"In charge sounds a little too important," Castle said. "There are only two of us."

"You deal with Top Secret sources, don't you? You—and Davis under your direction?"

"And Watson's."

"Yes, of course. But Watson has the whole of 6 in his care. You delegate, I suppose, a good deal, Watson?"

"I find 6C the only section which needs my full attention. Wilkins hasn't been with us long. He has to work himself in."

"Well, I won't keep you any longer, Watson. Thanks for bringing Castle down."

Hargreaves stroked the feathers of one of the dead birds. He said, "Like Wilkins I'm working myself in. As I see it things are a bit like they were when I was a young man in West Africa. Watson is a sort of Provincial Commissioner and you are a District Commissioner left pretty well to yourself in your own territory. Of course, you know Africa too, don't you?"

"Only South Africa," Castle said.

"Yes, I was forgetting. South Africa never seems quite like the real Africa to me. Nor the north either. That's dealt with by 6C, isn't it? Daintry has been explaining things to me. Over the weekend."

"Did you have a good shoot, sir?" Castle asked.

"Medium. I don't think Daintry was quite satisfied. You must come and have a go yourself next autumn."

"I wouldn't be any good, sir. I've never shot anything in my life, not even a human being."

"Ah, yes, they are the best target. To tell you the truth, birds bore me too."

C looked at a paper on his desk. "You did very good work in Pretoria. You are described as a first-class administrator. You reduced the expenses of the station considerably."

"I took over from a man who was brilliant at recruiting agents, but he hadn't much idea of finance. It came easily to me. I was in a bank for a while before the war."

"Daintry writes here that you had some private trouble in Pretoria."

"I wouldn't call it trouble. I fell in love."

"Yes. So I see. With an African girl. What those fellows call Bantu without distinction. You broke their race laws."

"We're safely married now. But we did have a difficult time out there."

"Yes. So you reported to us. I wish all our people when they are in a bit of trouble would behave as correctly. You were afraid the South African police were getting on to you and would try to tear you in pieces."

"It didn't seem right to leave you with a vulnerable representative."

"You can see I've been looking pretty closely through your file. We told you to get out at once, though we never thought that you'd bring the girl with you."

"HQ had had her vetted. They found nothing wrong with her. Wasn't I right from your point of view to get her out too? I had used her as a contact with my African agents. My cover story was that I was planning a serious critical study of apartheid in my spare time, but the police might have broken her. So I got her away through Swaziland to Lourenço Marques."

"Oh, you did quite right, Castle. And now you're married with a child. All well, I hope?"

"Well, at the moment my son has measles."

"Ah, then you must pay attention to his eyes. The eyes are the weak spot. The thing I really wished to see you about, Castle, was a visit we are going to have in a few weeks' time from a certain Mr. Cornelius Muller, one of the head boys in BOSS. I think you knew him when you were in Pretoria."

"I did indeed."

"We are going to let him see some of the material you deal with. Of course, only enough to establish the fact that we *are* cooperating —in a sort of way."

"He'll know more than we do about Zaire."

"It's Mozambique he's most interested in."

"In that case Davis is your man, sir. He's more abreast of things there than I am."

"Oh yes, of course, Davis. I haven't yet met Davis."

"Another thing, sir. When I was in Pretoria, I didn't get on at all well with this man Muller. If you look further back in my file—it was he who tried to blackmail me under the race laws. That was why your predecessor told me to get out as fast as I could. I don't think that would help our personal relations. It would be better to have Davis deal with him."

"All the same you are Davis's superior, and you are the natural officer to see him. It won't be easy, I know that. Knives out on both sides, but he'll be the one who's taken by surprise. You know exactly what not to show him. It's very important to guard our agents—even if it means keeping some important material dark. Davis hasn't your personal experience of BOSS—and their Mr. Muller."

"Why do we have to show him anything, sir?"

"Have you ever wondered, Castle, what would happen to the West if the South African gold mines were closed by a racial war? And a losing war perhaps, as in Vietnam. Before the politicians have agreed on a substitute for gold. Russia as the chief source. It would be a bit more complicated than the petrol crisis. And the diamond mines . . . De Beers are more important than General Motors. Diamonds don't age like cars. There are even more serious aspects than gold and diamonds, there's uranium. I don't think you've been told yet of a secret White House paper on an operation they call Uncle Remus."

"No. There have been rumors . . ."

"Like it or not, we and South Africa and the States are all partners in Uncle Remus. And that means we have to be pleasant to Mr. Muller—even if he did blackmail you."

"And I have to show him . . . ?"

"Information on guerrillas, blockade-running to Rhodesia, the new chaps in power in Mozambique, Russian and Cuban penetration . . . economic information . . ."

"There's not much left, is there?"

"Go a bit carefully on the Chinese. The South Africans are too much inclined to lump them with the Russians. The day may come when we need the Chinese. I don't like the idea of Uncle Remus any more than you do. It's what the politicians call a realistic policy, and realism never got anyone very far in the kind of Africa I used to know. My Africa was a sentimental Africa. I really loved Africa, Castle. The Chinese don't, nor do the Russians nor the Americans—but we have to go with the White House and Uncle Remus and Mr. Muller. How easy it was in the old days when we dealt with chiefs and witch doctors and bush schools and devils and rain queens. My Africa was still a little like the Africa of Rider

Haggard. It wasn't a bad place. The Emperor Chaka was a lot better than Field Marshal Amin Dada. Oh well, do your best with Muller. He's the personal representative of the big BOSS himself. I suggest you see him first at home—it would be a salutary shock for him."

"I don't know if my wife would agree."

"Tell her I asked you to. I leave it to her—if it's too painful . . ."

Castle turned at the door, remembering his promise. "Could I have a word with you about Davis, sir?"

"Of course. What is it?"

"He's had too long at a London desk. I think that at the first opportunity we ought to send him to Lourenço Marques. Exchange him for 69300, who must need a change of climate by now."

"Has Davis suggested that?"

"Not exactly, but I think he'd be glad to get away—anywhere. He's in a pretty nervous state, sir."

"What about?"

"A spot of girl trouble, I expect. And desk fatigue."

"Oh, I can understand desk fatigue. We'll see what we can do for him."

"I *am* a little anxious about him."

"I promise you I'll bear him in mind, Castle. By the way, this visit of Muller's is strictly secret. You know how we like to make our little boxes watertight. This has got to be your personal box. I haven't even told Watson. And you shouldn't tell Davis."

Chapter II

In the second week of October Sam was still officially in quarantine. There had been no complication, so one less danger menaced his future—that future which always appeared to Castle as an unpredictable ambush. Walking down the High Street on a Sunday morning he felt a sudden desire to give a kind of thanks, if it was only to a myth, that Sam was safe, so he took himself in, for a few minutes, to the back of the parish church. The service was nearly at an end and the congregation of the well-dressed, the middle-aged and the old were standing at attention, as they sang with a kind of defiance as though they inwardly doubted the facts, "There is a green hill far away, without a city wall." The simple precise words, with the single *tache* of color, reminded Castle of the local background so often to be found in primitive paintings. The city wall was like the ruins of the keep beyond the station, and up the green hillside of the Common, on top of the abandoned rifle butts, had once stood a tall post on which a man could have been hanged. For a moment he came near to sharing their incredible belief—it would do no harm to mutter a prayer of thanks to the God of his childhood, the God of the Common and the castle, that no ill had yet come to Sarah's child. Then a sonic boom scattered the words of the hymn and shook the old glass of the west window and rattled the crusader's helmet which hung on a pillar, and he was reminded again of the grown-up world. He went quickly out and bought the Sunday papers. The *Sunday Express* had a headline on the front page—"Child's Body Found in Wood."

In the afternoon he took Sam and Buller for a walk across the Common, leaving Sarah to sleep. He would have liked to leave Buller behind, but his angry protest would have wakened Sarah, so he comforted himself with the thought that Buller was unlikely to find a cat astray on the Common. The fear was always there since one summer three years before, when providence played an ill trick by providing suddenly a picnic party among the beech woods who had brought with them an expensive cat with a blue collar round its neck on a scarlet silk leash. The cat—a Siamese—had not even time to give one cry of anger or pain before Buller snapped its back and tossed the corpse over his shoulder like a man loading a sack onto a lorry. Then he had trotted attentively away between the trees, turning his head this way and that—where there was one cat there ought surely to be another—and Castle was left to face alone the angry and grief-stricken picnickers.

In October, however, picnickers were unlikely. All the same Castle waited till the sun had nearly set and he kept Buller on his chain all the way down King's Road past the police station at the corner of the High Street. Once beyond the canal and the railway bridge and the new houses (they had been there for a quarter of a century, but anything which had not existed when he was a boy seemed new to Castle), he let Buller loose, and immediately, like a well-trained dog, Buller splayed out and dropped his *crotte* on the edge of the path, taking his time. The eyes stared ahead, inward-looking. Only on these sanitary occasions did Buller seem a dog of intelligence. Castle did not like Buller—he had bought him for a purpose, to reassure Sarah, but Buller had proved inadequate as a watchdog, so now he was only one responsibility more, though with canine lack of judgment he loved Castle more than any other human being.

The bracken was turning to the dusky gold of a fine autumn, and there were only a few flowers left on the gorse. Castle and Sam searched in vain for the rifle butts which had once stood—a red clay cliff—above the waste of Common. They were drowned now in tired greenery. "Did they shoot spies there?" Sam asked.

"No, no. What gave you that idea? This was simply for rifle practice. In the first war."

"But there are spies, aren't there—real spies?"

"I suppose so, yes. Why do you ask?"

"I just wanted to be sure, that's all."

Castle remembered how at the same age he had asked his father whether there were really fairies, and the answer had been less truthful than his own. His father had been a sentimental man; he wished to reassure his small son at any cost that living was worthwhile. It would have been unfair to accuse him of dishonesty: a fairy, he might well have argued, was a symbol which represented something which was at least approximately true. There were still fathers around even today who told their children that God existed.

"Spies like 007?"

"Well, not exactly." Castle tried to change the subject. He said,

"When I was a child I thought there was a dragon living here in an old dugout down there among those trenches."

"Where are the trenches?"

"You can't see them now for the bracken."

"What's a dragon?"

"You know—one of those armored creatures spitting out fire."

"Like a tank?"

"Well, yes, I suppose like a tank." There was a lack of contact between their two imaginations which discouraged him. "More like a giant lizard," he said. Then he realized that the boy had seen many tanks, but they had left the land of lizards before he was born.

"Did you ever see a dragon?"

"Once I saw smoke coming out of a trench and I thought it was the dragon."

"Were you afraid?"

"No, I was afraid of quite different things in those days. I hated my school, and I had few friends."

"Why did you hate school? Will I hate school? I mean *real* school."

"We don't all have the same enemies. Perhaps you won't need a dragon to help you, but I did. All the world hated my dragon and wanted to kill him. They were afraid of the smoke and the flames which came out of his mouth when he was angry. I used to steal out at night from my dormitory and take him tins of sardines from my tuck-box. He cooked them in the tin with his breath. He liked them hot."

"But did that *really* happen?"

"No, of course not, but it almost seems now as though it had. Once I lay in bed in the dormitory crying under the sheet because it was the first week of term and there were twelve endless weeks before the holidays, and I was afraid of—everything around. It was winter, and suddenly I saw the window of my cubicle was misted over with heat. I wiped away the steam with my fingers and looked down. The dragon was there, lying flat in the wet black street, he looked like a crocodile in a stream. He had never left the Common before because every man's hand was against him—just as I thought they were all against me. The police even kept rifles in a cupboard to shoot him if he ever came to town. Yet there he was, lying very still and breathing up at me big warm clouds of breath. You see, he had heard that school had started again and he knew I was unhappy and alone. He was more intelligent than any dog, much more intelligent than Buller."

"You are pulling my leg," Sam said.

"No, I'm just remembering."

"What happened then?"

"I made a secret signal to him. It meant 'Danger. Go away,' because I wasn't sure that he knew about the police with their rifles."

"Did he go?"

"Yes. Very slowly. Looking back over his tail as though he didn't want to leave me. But I never felt afraid or lonely again. At least not often. I knew I had only to give a signal and he would leave his dugout on the Common and come down and help me. We had a lot of private signals, codes, ciphers . . ."

"Like a spy," Sam said.

"Yes," Castle said with disappointment, "I suppose so. Like a spy."

Castle remembered how he had once made a map of the Common with all the trenches marked and the secret paths hidden by ferns. That was like a spy too. He said, "Time to be going home. Your mother will be anxious . . ."

"No, she won't. I'm with you. I want to see the dragon's cave."

"There wasn't really a dragon."

"But you aren't quite sure, are you?"

With difficulty Castle found the old trench. The dugout where the dragon had lived was blocked by blackberry bushes. As he forced his way through them his feet struck against a rusty tin and sent it tumbling.

"You see," Sam said, "you did bring food." He wormed his way forward, but there was no dragon and no skeleton. "Perhaps the police got him in the end," Sam said. Then he picked up the tin. "It's tobacco," he said, "not sardines."

That night Castle said to Sarah as they lay in bed, "Do you really think it's not too late?"

"For what?"

"To leave my job."

"Of course it isn't. You aren't an old man yet."

"We might have to move from here."

"Why? This place is as good as any."

"Wouldn't you like to go away? This house—it isn't much of a house, is it? Perhaps if I got a job abroad . . ."

"I'd like Sam to stay put in one place so that when he goes away he'll be able to come back. To something he knew in childhood. Like you came back. To something old. Something secure."

"A collection of old ruins by the railway?"

"Yes."

He remembered the bourgeois voices, as sedate as the owners in their Sunday clothes, singing in the flinty church, expressing their weekly moment of belief. "A green hill far away, without a city wall."

"The ruins are pretty," she said.

"But *you* can never go back," Castle said, "to your childhood."

"That's different, I wasn't secure. Until I knew you. And there were no ruins—only shacks."

"Muller is coming over, Sarah."

"Cornelius Muller?"

"Yes. He's a big man now. I have to be friendly to him—by order."

"Don't worry. He can't hurt us anymore."

"No. But I don't want you troubled."

"Why should I be?"

"C wants me to bring him here."

"Bring him then. And let him see how you and I . . . and Sam . . ."

"You agree?"

"Of course I agree. A black hostess for Mr. Cornelius Muller. And a black child." They laughed, with a touch of fear.

Chapter III

"How's the little bastard?" Davis asked as he had done every day now for three weeks.

"Oh, everything's over. He's quite well again. He wanted to know the other day when you were going to come and see us. He likes you—I can't imagine why. He often talks of that picnic we had last summer and the hide-and-seek. He seems to think no one else can hide like you can. He thinks you are a spy. He talks about spies like children talked about fairies in my day. Or didn't they?"

"Could I borrow his father for tonight?"

"Why? What's on?"

"Doctor Percival was in yesterday when you were away, and we got talking. Do you know, I really think they may be sending me abroad? He was asking if I'd mind a few more tests . . . blood, urine, radio of the kidneys, et cetera, et cetera. He said they had to be careful about the tropics. I liked him. He seems to be a sporting type."

"Racing?"

"No, only fishing as a matter of fact. That's a pretty lonely sport. Percival's a bit like me—no wife. Tonight we thought we'd get together and see the town. I haven't seen the town for a long while. Those chaps from the Department of the Environment are a pretty sad lot. Couldn't you face being a grass widower, old man, just for one evening?"

"My last train leaves Euston at 11:30."

"I've got the flat all to myself tonight. The Environment men have both gone off to a polluted area. You can have a bed. Double or single, whichever you prefer."

"Please—a single bed. I'm getting to be an old man, Davis. I don't know what plans you and Percival have . . ."

"I thought dinner in the Café Grill and afterward a spot of striptease. Raymond's Revuebar. They've got Rita Rolls . . ."

"Do you think Percival likes that sort of thing?"

"I sounded him out, and can you believe it? He's never been to a striptease in his life. He said he'd love to take a peek with colleagues he can trust. You know how it is with work like ours. He feels the same way. Nothing to talk about at a party for reasons of security. John Thomas doesn't even have a chance to lift his head. He's morose—that's the word. But if John Thomas dies, God help you, you might as well die too. Of course it's different for you—you are a married man. You can always talk to Sarah and . . ."

"We're not supposed to talk even to our wives."

"I bet you do."

"I don't, Davis. And if you are thinking of picking up a couple of tarts I wouldn't talk to them either. A lot of them are employed by MI5—oh, I always forget they've changed our names. We are all DI now. I wonder why? I suppose there's a Department of Semantics."

"You sound a bit fed up too."

"Yes. Perhaps a party will do me good. I'll telephone to Sarah and tell her—what?"

"Tell her the truth. You are dining with one of the big boys. Important for your future in the firm. And I'm giving you a bed. She trusts me. She knows I won't lead you astray."

"Yes, I suppose she does."

"And, damn it all, that's true too, isn't it?"

"I'll ring her up when I go out to lunch."

"Why not do it here and save money?"

"I like my calls private."

"Do you really think they bother to listen in to us?"

"Wouldn't you in their position?"

"I suppose I would. But what the hell of a lot of dreary stuff they must have to tape."

2

The evening was only half a success, though it had begun well enough. Doctor Percival in his slow unexciting fashion was a good enough companion. He made neither Castle nor Davis feel he was their superior in the department. When Colonel Daintry's name arose he poked gentle fun at him—he had met him, he said, at a shooting weekend. "He doesn't like abstract art and he doesn't approve of me. That's because I don't shoot," Doctor Percival explained, "I only fish."

They were at Raymond's Revuebar by that time, crushed at a small table, just large enough to hold three whiskies, while a pretty young thing was going through curious antics in a hammock.

"I'd like to get my hook into *her*," Davis said.

The girl drank from a bottle of High and Dry suspended above the hammock on a string, and after every swallow she removed a piece of clothing with an air of ginny abandon. At long last they could see her naked buttocks outlined by the net like the rump of a chicken seen through a Soho housewife's string bag. A party of businessmen from Birmingham applauded with some violence, and one man went so far as to wave a Diners Club card above his head, perhaps to show his financial standing.

"What do you fish?" Castle asked.

"Mainly trout or grayling," Percival said.

"Is there much difference?"

"My dear fellow, ask a big-game hunter if there's a difference between lion and tiger."

"Which do you prefer?"

"It's not really a question of preference. I just love fishing—any fly fishing. The grayling is less intelligent than the trout, but that doesn't mean he's always easier. He demands a different technique. And he's a fighter—he fights until there's no fight left in him."

"And the trout?"

"Oh, he's the king, all right. He scares easily—nail boots or a stick, any sound you make and he's off. Then you must place your fly exactly, the first time. Otherwise . . ." Percival made a gesture with his arm as though he were casting in the direction of yet another naked girl who was striped black and white by the lights like a zebra.

"What a bottom!" Davis said with awe. He sat with a glass of whisky halfway to his lips, watching the cheeks revolve with the same precision as the wheels of a Swiss watch: a diamond movement.

"You aren't doing your blood pressure any good," Percival told him.

"Blood pressure?"

"I told you it was high."

"You can't bother me tonight," Davis said. "That's the great Rita Rolls herself. The one and only Rita."

"You ought to have a more complete checkup if you are really thinking of going abroad."

"I feel all right, Percival. I've never felt better."

"That's where the danger lies."

"You almost begin to scare me," Davis said. "Nail boots and a stick. I can see why a trout . . ." He took a sip of whisky as though it were a disagreeable medicine and laid his glass down again.

Doctor Percival squeezed his arm and said, "I was only joking, Davis. You're more the grayling type."

"You mean I'm a poor fish?"

"You mustn't underestimate the grayling. He has a very delicate nervous system. And he's a fighter."

"Then I'm more of a cod," said Davis.

"Don't talk to me about cod. I don't go in for that sort of fishing."

The lights went up. It was the end of the show. Anything, the management had decided, would be an anticlimax after Rita Rolls. Davis lingered for a moment in the bar to try his luck with a fruit machine. He used up all the coins he had and took two off Castle. "It's not my evening," he said, his gloom returning. Obviously Doctor Percival had upset him.

"What about a nightcap at my place?" Doctor Percival asked.

"I thought you were warning me off the drink."

"My dear chap, I was exaggerating. Anyway whisky's the safest drink there is."

"All the same I begin to feel like bed now."

In Great Windmill Street prostitutes stood inside the doorways under red shades and asked, "Coming up, darling?"

"I suppose you'd warn me off that too?" Davis said.

"Well, the regularity of marriage is safer. Less strain on the blood pressure."

The night porter was scrubbing the steps of Albany as Doctor Percival left them. His chambers in Albany were designated by a letter and a figure—D.6—as though it were one more section of the old firm. Castle and Davis watched him pick his way carefully toward the Ropewalk so as not to wet his shoes—an odd precaution for someone accustomed to wading knee-deep in cold streams.

"I'm sorry he came," Davis said. "We could have had a good evening without him."

"I thought you liked him."

"I did, but he got on my nerves tonight with his damned fishing stories. And all his talk about my blood pressure. What's my blood pressure to do with him? Is he really a doctor?"

"I don't think he's practiced much for years," Castle said. "He's C's liaison officer with the bacteriological warfare people—I suppose someone with a medical degree comes in handy there."

"That place Porton gives me the shivers. People talk so much about the atom bomb, but they quite forget our little country establishment. Nobody has ever bothered to march there. Nobody wears an anti-bacterial button, but if the bomb were abolished, there'd still be that little deadly test-tube . . ."

They turned the corner by Claridge's. A tall lean woman in a long dress climbed into a Rolls Royce followed by a sullen man in a white tie who looked furtively at his watch—they looked like actors from an Edwardian play: it was two in the morning. There was a yellow lino worn into holes like a gruyère cheese on the steep stairs up to Davis's flat. With W.1. on the notepaper no one bothered about small details like that. The kitchen door was open, and Castle saw a stack of dirty dishes in the sink. Davis opened a cupboard door; the shelves were stacked with almost empty bottles—the protection of the environment did not begin at home. Davis tried to find a whisky bottle containing enough for two glasses. "Oh well," he said, "we'll mix them. They're all blends anyway." He combined what remained of a Johnnie Walker with a White Horse, and obtained a quarter bottle.

"Does no one here ever wash up?" Castle asked.

"A woman comes in twice a week, and we save it all for her."

Davis opened a door. "Here's your room. I'm afraid the bed's not made. She's due tomorrow." He picked a dirty handkerchief off the floor and stuffed it in a drawer for tidiness sake. Then he led Castle back into the sitting room and cleared some magazines off a chair onto the floor.

"I'm thinking of changing my name by deed poll," Davis said.

"What to?"

"Davis with an e. Davies of Davies Street has a certain classy ring." He put his feet up on the sofa. "You know, this blend of mine tastes quite good. I shall call it a White Walker. There might be a fortune in the idea—you could advertise it with the picture of a beautiful female ghost. What did you really think of Doctor Percival?"

"He seemed friendly enough. But I couldn't help wondering . . ."

"What?"

"Why he bothered to spend the evening with us. What he wanted."

"An evening out with people he could talk to. Why look further? Don't you get tired of keeping your mouth closed in mixed company?"

"He didn't open his very far. Even with us."

"He did before you came."

"What about?"

"That establishment at Porton. Apparently we are far ahead of the Americans in one range of goods and they've asked us to concentrate on a deadly little fellow suitable for employment at a certain altitude which at the same time can survive desert conditions . . . All the details, temperature and the like, point to China. Or perhaps Africa."

"Why did he tell you all that?"

"Well, we are supposed to know a bit about the Chinese through our African contacts. Ever since that report from Zanzibar our reputation stands quite high."

"That was two years ago and the report's still unconfirmed."

"He said we mustn't take any overt action. No questionnaires to agents. Too secret for that. Just keep our eyes open for any hint in any report that the Chinese are interested in Hell's Parlour and then report direct to him."

"Why did he speak to you and not to me?"

"Oh, I suppose he would have spoken to you, but you were late."

"Daintry kept me. Percival could have come to the office if he wanted to talk."

"What's troubling you?"

"I'm just wondering if he was telling you the truth."

"What earthly reason . . . ?"

"He might want to plant a false rumor."

"Not with us. We aren't exactly gossips, you and I and Watson."

"Has he spoken to Watson?"

"No—as a matter of fact—he gave the usual patter about watertight boxes. Top Secret, he said—but that can't apply to you, can it?"

"Better not let them know you told me all the same."

"Old man, you've caught the disease of the profession, suspicion."

"Yes. It's a bad infection. That's why I'm thinking of getting out."

"To grow vegetables?"

"To do anything non-secret and unimportant and relatively harmless. I nearly joined an advertising agency once."

"Be careful. They have secrets too—trade secrets."

The telephone rang at the head of the stairs. "At this hour," Davis complained. "It's anti-social. Who can it be?" He struggled off the sofa.

"Rita Rolls," Castle suggested.

"Give yourself another White Walker."

Castle hadn't time to pour it out before Davis called to him. "It's Sarah, Castle."

The hour was nearly half-past two and fear touched him. Were there complications which a child might get so late in quarantine as this?

"Sarah?" he asked. "What is it? Is it Sam?"

"Darling, I'm sorry. You weren't in bed, were you?"

"No. What's the matter?"

"I'm scared."

"Sam?"

"No, it's not Sam. But the telephone's rung twice since midnight, and no one answers."

"The wrong number," he said with relief. "It's always happening."

"Somebody knows you're not in the house. I'm frightened, Maurice."

"What could possibly happen in King's Road? Why, there's a police station two hundred yards away. And Buller? Buller's there, isn't he?"

"He's fast asleep, snoring."

"I'd come back if I could, but there are no trains. And no taxi would take me at this hour."

"I'll drive you down," Davis said.

"No, no, of course not."

"Not what?" Sarah said.

"I was talking to Davis. He said he'd drive me down."

"Oh no, I don't want that. I feel better now I've talked to you. I'll wake Buller up."

"Sam's all right?"

"He's fine."

"You've got the police number. They'd be with you in two minutes."

"I'm a fool, aren't I? Just a fool."

"A beloved fool."

"Say sorry to Davis. Have a good drink."

"Good night, darling."

"Good night, Maurice."

The use of his name was a sign of love—when they were together it was an invitation to love. Endearments—dear and darling—were everyday currency to be employed in company, but a name was strictly private, never to be betrayed to a stranger outside the tribe. At the height of love she would cry aloud his secret tribal name. He heard her ring off, but he stayed a moment with the receiver pressed against his ear.

"Nothing really wrong?" Davis asked.

"Not with Sarah, no."

He came back into the sitting room and poured himself a whisky. He said, "I think your telephone's tapped."

"How do you know?"

"I don't. I have an instinct, that's all. I'm trying to remember what gave me the idea."

"We aren't in the Stone Age. Nobody can tell nowadays when a phone's tapped."

"Unless they're careless. Or unless they want you to know."

"Why should they want me to know?"

"To scare you perhaps. Who can tell?"

"Anyway, why tap *me?*"

"A question of security. They don't trust anyone. Especially people in our position. We are the most dangerous. We are supposed to know those damned Top Secrets."

"I don't feel dangerous."

"Put on the gramophone," Castle said.

Davis had a collection of pop music which was kept more carefully than anything else in the apartment. It was catalogued as meticulously as the British Museum library, and the top of the pops for any given year came as readily to Davis's memory as a Derby winner. He said, "You like something really old-fashioned and classical, don't you?" and put on *A Hard Day's Night*.

"Turn it louder."

"It shouldn't be louder."

"Turn it up all the same."

"It's awful this way."

"I feel more private," Castle said.

"You think they bug us too?"

"I wouldn't be surprised."

"You certainly have caught the disease," Davis said.

"Percival's conversation with you—it worries me—I simply can't believe it . . . it smells to heaven. I think they are on to a leak and are trying to check up."

"OK by me. It's their duty, isn't it? But it doesn't seem very clever if one can spot the dodge so easily."

"Yes—but Percival's story might be true just the same. True and already blown. An agent, whatever he suspected, would feel bound to pass it on in case . . ."

"And *you* think *they* think we are the leaks?"

"Yes. One of us or perhaps both."

"But as we aren't who cares?" Davis said. "It's long past bed-time, Castle. If there's a mike under the pillow, they'll only hear my snores." He turned the music off. "We aren't the stuff of double agents, you and me."

Castle undressed and put out the light. It was stuffy in the small disordered room. He tried to raise the window, but the sash cord was broken. He stared down into the early morning street. No one went by: not even a policeman. Only a single taxi remained on a rank a little way down Davies Street in the direction of Claridge's. A burglar alarm sent up a futile ringing from somewhere in the Bond Street area, and a light rain had begun to fall. It gave a black glitter to the pavement like a policeman's raincoat. He drew the curtains close and got into bed, but he didn't sleep. A question mark kept him awake for a long while: had there always been a taxi rank so close to Davis's flat? Surely once he had to walk to the other side of Claridge's to find one? Before he fell asleep another question troubled him. Could they possibly, he wondered, be using Davis to watch him? Or were they using an innocent Davis to pass him on a marked bank note? He had small belief in Doctor Percival's story of Porton, and yet, as he had told Davis, it might be true.

Chapter IV

1

Castle had begun to be really worried about Davis. True, Davis made a joke of his own melancholy, but all the same the melancholy was deeply there, and it seemed a bad sign to Castle that Davis no longer chaffed Cynthia. His spoken thoughts too were becoming increasingly irrelevant to any work they had in hand. Once when Castle asked him, "69300/4, who's that?" Davis said, "A double room at the Polana looking out to sea." All the same there could be nothing seriously wrong with his health—he had been given his checkup recently by Doctor Percival.

"As usual we are waiting for a cable from Zaire," Davis said. "59800 never thinks of us, as he sits there on a hot evening swilling his sundowners without a care in the world."

"We'd better send him a reminder," Castle said. He wrote out on a slip of paper, "Our 185 no repeat no answer received," and put it in a tray for Cynthia to fetch.

Davis today had a regatta air. A new scarlet silk handkerchief with yellow dice dangled from his pocket like a flag on a still day, and his tie was bottle-green with a scarlet pattern. Even the handkerchief he kept for use which protruded from his sleeve looked new—a peacock blue. He had certainly dressed ship.

"Had a good weekend?" Castle asked.

"Yes, oh yes. In a way. Very quiet. The pollution boys were away smelling factory smoke in Gloucester. A gum factory."

A girl called Patricia (who had always refused to be known as Pat) came in from the secretaries' pool and collected their one cable. Like Cynthia she was army offspring, the niece of Brigadier Tomlinson: to employ close relations of men already in the department was considered good for security, and perhaps it eased the work of tracing, since many contacts would naturally be duplicated.

"Is this *all?*" the girl asked as though she were accustomed to work for more important sections than 6A.

"I'm afraid that's all we can manage, Pat," Castle told her, and she slammed the door behind her.

"You shouldn't have angered her," Davis said. "She may speak to Watson and we'll all be kept in after school writing telegrams."

"Where's Cynthia?"

"It's her day off."

Davis cleared his throat explosively—like a signal for the regatta to begin—and ran up a Red Ensign all over his face.

"I was going to ask you . . . would you mind if I slipped away at eleven? I'll be back at one, I promise, and there's nothing doing. If anyone wants me just say that I've gone to the dentist."

"You ought to be wearing black," Castle said, "to convince Daintry. Those glad rags of yours don't go with dentists."

"Of course I'm not really going to the dentist. The fact of the matter is Cynthia said she'd meet me at the Zoo to see the giant pandas. Do you think she's beginning to weaken?"

"You really are in love, aren't you, Davis?"

"All I want, Castle, is a serious adventure. An adventure indefinite in length. A month, a year, a decade. I'm tired of one-night stands. Home from the King's Road after a party at four with a bloody hangover. Next morning—I think oh, that was fine, the girl was wonderful, I wish I'd done better though, if only I hadn't mixed the drinks . . . and then I think how it would have been with Cynthia in Lourenço Marques. I could really *talk* to Cynthia. It helps John Thomas when you can talk a bit about your work. Those Chelsea birds, directly the fun's over, they want to find out things. What do I do? Where's my office? I used to pretend I was still at Aldermaston, but everyone now knows the bloody place is closed down. What am I to say?"

"Something in the City?"

"No glamor in that and these birds compare notes." He began arranging his things. He shut and locked his file of cards. There were two typed pages on his desk and he put them in his pocket.

"Taking things out of the office?" Castle said. "Be careful of Daintry. He's found you out once."

"He's finished with our section. 7 are catching it now. Anyway this is only the usual bit of nonsense: For your information only. Destroy after reading. Meaning damn all. I'll 'commit it to memory' while I'm waiting for Cynthia. She's certain to be late."

"Remember Dreyfus. Don't leave it in a rubbish bin for the cleaner to find."

"I'll burn it as an offering in front of Cynthia." He went out and then came quickly back. "I wish you'd wish me luck, Castle."

"Of course. With all my heart."

The hackneyed phrase came warm and unintended to Castle's tongue. It surprised him, as though, in penetrating a familiar cave, on some holiday at the sea, he had observed on a familiar rock the primeval painting of a human face which he had always mistaken before for a chance pattern of fungi.

Half an hour later the telephone rang. A girl's voice said, "J.W. wants to speak to A.D."

"Too bad," Castle said. "A.D. can't speak to J.W."

"Who's that?" the voice asked with suspicion.

"Someone called M.C."

"Hold on a moment, please." A kind of high yapping came back to him over the phone. Then Watson's voice emerged unmistakably from the canine background, "I say, is that Castle?"

"Yes."

"I must speak to Davis."

"He's not here."

"Where is he?"

"He'll be back at one."

"That's too late. Where is he now?"

"At his dentist," Castle said with reluctance. He didn't like being involved in other men's lies: they complicated things.

"We'd better scramble," Watson said. There was the usual confusion: one of them pressing the right button too soon and then going back to normal transmission just when the other scrambled. When their voices were at last sorted out, Watson said, "Can you fetch him back? He's wanted at a conference."

"I can't very well drag him out of a dentist's chair. Anyway I don't know who his dentist is. It's not in the files."

"No?" Watson said with disapproval. "Then he ought to have left a note with the address."

Watson had tried once to be a barrister and failed. His obvious integrity perhaps offended judges; a moral tone, most judges seemed to feel, should be reserved for the Bench and not employed by junior counsel. But in "a department of the Foreign Office" he had risen quickly by the very quality which had served him so ill at the Bar. He easily outdistanced men like Castle of an older generation.

"He ought to have let me know he was going out," Watson said.

"Perhaps it was a very sudden toothache."

"C specially wanted him to be present. There's some report he wanted to discuss with him afterward. He received it all right, I suppose?"

"He did mention a report. He seemed to think it was the usual average nonsense."

"Nonsense? It was Top Secret. What did he do with it?"

"I suppose he left it in the safe."

"Would you mind checking up?"

"I'll ask his secretary—oh, I'm sorry, I can't, she's off today. Is it all that important?"

"C must think so. I suppose you'd better come to the conference if Davis isn't there, but it was Davis's pigeon. Room 121 at twelve sharp."

2

The conference did not seem of pressing importance. A member of MI5 whom Castle had never seen before was present because the main point on the agenda was to distinguish more clearly than in the past between the responsibilities of MI5 and MI6. Before the last war MI6 had never operated on British territory and security there was left to MI5. The system broke down in Africa with the fall of France and the necessity of running agents from British territory into the Vichy colonies. With the return of peace the old system had never been quite re-established. Tanzania and Zanzibar were united officially as one state, a member of the Commonwealth, but it was difficult to regard the island of Zanzibar as British territory with its Chinese training camps. Confusion had arisen because MI5 and MI6 both had representatives in Dar-es-Salaam, and relations between them had not always been close or friendly.

"Rivalry," C said, as he opened the conference, "is a healthy thing up to a point. But sometimes there has been a lack of trust. We have not always exchanged traces of agents. Sometimes we've been playing the same man, for espionage and counter-espionage." He sat back to let the MI5 man have his say.

There were very few there whom Castle knew except Watson. A lean gray man with a prominent Adam's apple was said to be the oldest man in the firm. His name was Chilton. He dated back to before Hitler's war and surprisingly he had made no enemies. Now he dealt principally with Ethiopia. He was also the greatest living authority on tradesmen's tokens in the eighteenth century and was often called in for consultation by Sotheby's. Laker was an ex-guardsman with ginger hair and a ginger moustache who looked after the Arab republics in North Africa.

The MI5 man stopped talking about the crossed lines. C said, "Well, that's that. The treaty of Room 121. I'm sure we all understand our positions better now. It was very kind of you to look in, Puller."

"Pullen."

"Sorry, Pullen. Now, if you won't think us inhospitable, we have a few little domestic things to discuss . . ." When Pullen had closed the door he said, "I'm never quite happy with those MI5 types. Somehow they always seem to carry with them a kind of police atmosphere. It's natural, of course, dealing as they do with counterespionage. To me espionage is more of a gentleman's job, but of course I'm old-fashioned."

Percival spoke up from a distant corner. Castle hadn't even noticed that he was there. "I've always rather fancied MI9 myself."

"What does MI9 do?" Laker asked, brushing up his moustache. He was aware of being one of the few genuine military men among all the MI numerals.

"I've long forgotten," Percival said, "but they always seem more friendly." Chilton barked briefly—it was the way he always laughed.

Watson said, "Didn't they deal with escape methods in the war, or was that 11? I didn't know they were still around."

"Oh well, it's true I haven't seen them in a long time," Percival said with his kindly encouraging doctor's air. He might have been describing the symptoms of flu. "Perhaps they've packed up."

"By the way," C asked, "is Davis here? There was a report I wanted to discuss with him. I don't seem to have met him in my pilgrimage around Section 6."

"He's at the dentist's," Castle said.

"He never told me, sir," Watson complained.

"Oh well, it's not urgent. Nothing in Africa ever is. Changes come slowly and are generally impermanent. I wish the same were true of Europe." He gathered his papers and slipped quietly away, like a host who feels that a house party will get on much better without him.

"It's odd," Percival said, "when I saw Davis the other day his crackers seemed to be in good shape. Said he never had any trouble with them. No sign even of tartar. By the way, Castle, you might get me the name of his dentist. Just for my medical files. If he's having trouble we like to recommend our own men. It makes for better security."

Part Three

Part Three

Chapter I

1

Doctor Percival had invited Sir John Hargreaves to lunch with him at his club, the Reform. They made a habit of lunching alternately at the Reform and the Travellers once a month on a Saturday, when most members had already gone into the country. Pall Mall, a steely gray, like a Victorian engraving, was framed by the long windows. The Indian summer was nearly over, the clocks had all been altered, and you could feel the approach of winter concealed in the smallest wind. They began with smoked trout which led Sir John Hargreaves to tell Doctor Percival that he was now seriously thinking of trying to stock the stream which divided his park from the agricultural land. "I'll need your advice, Emmanuel," he said. They were on Christian-name terms when they were safely alone.

For a long while they talked of fishing for trout, or rather Doctor Percival talked—it was a subject which always appeared a limited one to Hargreaves, but he knew Doctor Percival would be quite capable of enlarging on it until dinner. However, he was shifted from trout to another favorite topic by a chance diversion to the subject of his club. "If I had a conscience," Doctor Percival said, "I would not remain a member here. I'm a member because the food—and the smoked trout too if you will forgive me, John—is the best in London."

"I like the food at the Travellers just as much," Hargreaves said.

"Ah, but you are forgetting our steak-and-kidney pudding. I know you won't like me saying so, but I prefer it to your wife's pie. Pastry holds the gravy at a distance. Pudding absorbs the gravy. Pudding, you might say, cooperates."

"But why would your conscience be troubled, Emmanuel, even if you had one—which is a most unlikely supposition?"

"You must know that to be a member here I had to sign a declaration in favor of the Reform Act of 1866. True, that Act was not so bad as some of its successors, like giving the vote at eighteen, but it opened the gates to the pernicious doctrine of one man one vote.

Even the Russians subscribe to that now for propaganda purposes, but they are clever enough to make sure that the things they can vote for in their own country are of no importance at all."

"What a reactionary you are, Emmanuel. I do believe, though, there's something in what you say about pudding and pastry. We might try out a pudding next year—if we are still able to afford a shoot."

"If you can't, it will be because of one man one vote. Be honest, John, and admit what a hash that stupid idea has made of Africa."

"I suppose it takes time for true democracy to work."

"That kind of democracy will never work."

"Would you really like to go back to the householder's vote, Emmanuel?" Hargreaves could never tell to what extent Doctor Percival was really serious.

"Yes, why not? The income required for a man to vote would be properly adjusted, of course, each year to deal with inflation. Four thousand a year might be the proper level for getting a vote today. That would give the miners and dockers a vote, which would save us a lot of trouble."

After coffee they walked, by common consent, down the great Gladstonian stairs out into the chill of Pall Mall. The old brickwork of St. James's Palace glowed like a dying fire through the gray weather, and the sentry flickered scarlet—a last doomed flame. They crossed into the park and Doctor Percival said, "Returning for a moment to trout . . ." They chose a bench where they could watch the ducks move with the effortlessness of magnetic toys across the surface of the pond. They both wore the same heavy tweed overcoats, the overcoats of men who live by choice in the country. A man wearing a bowler hat passed them; he was carrying an umbrella and he frowned at some thought of his own as he went by. "That's Browne with an e," Doctor Percival said.

"What a lot of people you know, Emmanuel."

"One of the PM's economic advisers. I wouldn't give him a vote whatever he earned."

"Well, let's talk a little business, shall we? Now we are alone. I suppose you are afraid of being bugged at the Reform."

"Why not? Surrounded by a lot of one man one vote fanatics. If they were capable of giving the vote to a bunch of cannibals . . ."

"You mustn't run down cannibals," Hargreaves said, "some of my best friends have been cannibals, and now that Browne with an e is out of earshot . . ."

"I've been going over things very carefully, John, with Daintry, and personally I'm convinced that Davis is the man we are looking for."

"Is Daintry convinced too?"

"No. It's all circumstantial, it has to be, and Daintry's got a very legalistic mind. I can't pretend that I like Daintry. No humor but naturally very conscientious. I spent an evening with Davis, a few weeks ago. He's not an advanced alcoholic like Burgess and Maclean, but he drinks a lot—and he's been drinking more since our check started, I think. Like those two and Philby, he's obviously under some sort of strain. A bit of a manic depressive—and a manic depressive usually has that touch of schizoid about him essential for a double agent. He's anxious to get abroad. Probably because he knows he's being watched and perhaps they've forbidden him to try and bolt. Of course he'd be out of our control in Lourenço Marques and in a very useful spot for them."

"But what about the evidence?"

"It's a bit patchy still, but can we afford to wait for perfect evidence, John? After all we don't intend to put him on trial. The alternative is Castle (you agreed with me that we could rule out Watson), and we've gone into Castle just as thoroughly. Happy second marriage, first wife killed in the blitz, a good family background, the father was a doctor—one of those old-fashioned GPs, a member of the Liberal Party, but not, please note, of the Reform, who looked after his patients through a lifetime and forgot to send in bills, the mother's still alive—she was a head warden in the blitz and won the George Medal. A bit of a patriot and attends Conservative rallies. Pretty good stock, you'll admit. No sign of heavy drinking with Castle, careful about money too. Davis spends a good deal on port and whisky and his Jaguar, bets regularly on the tote—pretends to be a judge of form and to win quite a lot—that's a classic excuse for spending more than you earn. Daintry told me he was caught once taking a report from 59800 out of the office. Said he meant to read it over lunch. Then you remember the day we had the conference with MI5 and you wanted him to be present. Left the office to see his dentist—he never went to his dentist (his teeth are in perfect condition—I know that myself) and then two weeks later we got evidence of another leak."

"Do we know where he went?"

"Daintry was already having him shadowed by Special Branch. He went to the Zoo. Through the members' entrance. The chap who was following him had to queue up at the ordinary entrance and lost him. A nice touch."

"Any idea whom he met?"

"He's a clever one. Must have known he was followed. It turned out that he'd confessed to Castle that he hadn't gone to the dentist. Said he was meeting his secretary (it was her day off) at the pandas. But there was that report you wanted to talk to him about. It was never in the safe—Daintry checked that."

"Not a very important report. Oh, it's all a bit shady, I admit, but I wouldn't call any of it hard evidence, Emmanuel. Did he meet the secretary?"

"Oh, he met her all right. He left the Zoo with her, but what happened in between?"

"Have you tried the marked note technique?"

"I told him in strict confidence a bogus story about researches at Porton, but nothing's turned up yet."

"I don't see how we can act on what you've got at present."

"Suppose he panicked and tried to make a bolt for it?"

"Then we'd have to act quickly. Have you decided on how we should act?"

"I'm working on rather a cute little notion, John. Peanuts."

"Peanuts!"

"Those little salted things you eat with cocktails."

"Of course I know what peanuts are, Emmanuel. Don't forget I was a Commissioner in West Africa."

"Well, they're the answer. Peanuts when they go bad produce a mold. Caused by *aspergillus flavus*—but you can forget the name. It's not important, and I know you were never any good at Latin."

"Go on, for heaven's sake."

"To make it easy for you I'll concentrate on the mold. The mold produces a group of highly toxic substances known collectively as aflatoxin. And aflatoxin is the answer to our little problem."

"How does it work?"

"We don't know for certain about human beings, but no animal seems immune, so it's highly unlikely that we are. Aflatoxin kills the liver cells. They only need to be exposed to the stuff for about three hours. The symptoms in animals are that they lose their appetites and become lethargic. The wings of birds become weak. A postmortem shows hemorrhage and necrosis in the liver and engorgement of the kidneys, if you'll forgive me my medical jargon. Death usually occurs within a week."

"Damnation, Emmanuel, I've always liked peanuts. Now I'll never be able to eat them again."

"Oh, you needn't worry, John. Your salted peanuts are hand

picked—though I suppose an accident might just possibly happen, but at the rate you finish a tin they are not likely to go bad."

"You seem to have really enjoyed your researches. Sometimes, Emmanuel, you give me the creeps."

"You must admit it's a very neat little solution to our problem. A postmortem would show only the damage done to the liver, and I expect the coroner would warn the public against the danger of overindulgence in port."

"I suppose you've even worked out how to get this aero—"

"Aflatoxin, John. There's no serious difficulty. I have a fellow at Porton preparing some now. You only need a very small quantity. Point 0063 milligrams per kilogram bodyweight. Of course I've weighed Davis. 0.5 milligrams should do the trick, but to be quite sure let's say .75. Though we might test first with an even smaller dose. One side advantage of all this, of course, is that we should gain valuable information on how aflatoxin works on a human being."

"Do you never find that you shock yourself, Emmanuel?"

"There's nothing shocking about this, John. Think of all the other deaths Davis might die. Real cirrhosis would be much slower. With a dose of aflatoxin he'll hardly suffer at all. Increasing lethargy, perhaps a bit of leg trouble as he doesn't have wings, and of course a certain amount of nausea is to be expected. To spend only a week dying is quite a happy fate, when you think what many people suffer."

"You talk as though he were already condemned."

"Well, John, I'm quite convinced he's our man. I'm only waiting for the green light from you."

"If Daintry were satisfied . . ."

"Oh, Daintry, John, we can't wait for the kind of evidence Daintry demands."

"Give me one piece of *hard* evidence."

"I can't yet, but better not wait for it too long. You remember what you said that night after the shoot—a complaisant husband is always at the mercy of the lover. We can't afford another scandal in the firm, John."

Another bowler-hatted figure went by, coat collar turned up, into the October dusk. The lights were coming on one by one in the Foreign Office.

"Let's talk a little more about the trout stream, Emmanuel. "

"Ah, trout. Let other people boast about salmon—gross oily stupid fellows with that blind urge of theirs to swim upstream which

makes for easy fishing. All you need are big boots and a strong arm
and a clever gillie. But the trout—oh, the trout—he's the real king of
fish."

2

Colonel Daintry had a two-roomed flat in St. James's Street which
he had found through the agency of another member of the firm.
During the war it had been used by MI6 as a rendezvous for inter-
viewing possible recruits. There were only three apartments in the
building, which was looked after by an old housekeeper, who lived
in a room somewhere out of sight under the roof. Daintry was on
the first floor above a restaurant (the noise of hilarity kept him
awake until the small hours when the last taxi ground away). Over
his head were a retired businessman who had once been connected
with the rival wartime service SOE, and a retired general who had
fought in the Western Desert. The general was too old now to be
seen often on the stairs, but the businessman, who suffered from
gout, used to get as far as the Carlton Club across the road. Daintry
was no cook and he usually economized for one meal by buying
cold chipolatas at Fortnum's. He had never liked clubs; if he felt
hungry, a rare event, there was Overton's just below. His bedroom
and his bathroom looked out on a tiny ancient court containing a
sun dial and a silversmith. Few people who walked down St.
James's Street knew of the court's existence. It was a very discreet
flat and not unsuitable for a lonely man.

For the third time with his Remington Daintry went over his
face. Scruples of cleanliness grew with loneliness like the hairs on a
corpse. He was about to have one of his rare dinners with his
daughter. He had suggested giving her dinner at Overton's where
he was known, but she told him she wanted roast beef. All the same
she refused to go to Simpson's where Daintry was also known because she said the atmosphere was too masculine. She insisted on
meeting him at Stone's in Panton Street, where she would expect
him at eight. She never came to his flat—that would have shown
disloyalty to her mother, even though she knew there was no
woman sharing it. Perhaps even Overton's was tainted by the prox-
imity of his flat.

It always irritated Daintry to enter Stone's and to be asked by a
man in a ridiculous topper if he had booked a table. The former
old-fashioned chophouse which he remembered as a young man
had been destroyed in the blitz and been rebuilt with an expense-
account décor. Daintry thought with regret of the ancient waiters

in dusty black tails and the sawdust on the floor and the strong beer specially brewed at Burton-on-Trent. Now all the way up the stairs there were meaningless panels of giant playing cards more suited to a gambling house, and white naked statues stood under the falling water of a fountain which played beyond the plate glass at the end of the restaurant. They seemed to make the autumn strike colder than the air outside. His daughter was already waiting there.

"I'm sorry if I'm late, Elizabeth," Daintry said. He knew he was three minutes early.

"It's all right. I've given myself a drink."

"I'll have a sherry too."

"I've got news to give you. Only Mother knows as yet."

"How is your mother?" Daintry asked with formal politeness. It was always his first question and he was glad when he had disposed of it.

"She's quite well considering. She's spending a week or two at Brighton for a change of air."

It was as if they were speaking of an acquaintance whom he hardly knew—it was odd to think there had ever been a time when he and his wife were close enough to share a sexual spasm which had produced the beautiful girl who sat so elegantly opposite him drinking her Tio Pepe. The sadness which was never far away from Daintry when he met his daughter descended as always—like a sense of guilt. Why guilt? he would argue with himself. He had always been what was called faithful. "I hope the weather will be good," he said. He knew that he had bored his wife, but why should that be a cause of guilt? After all she had consented to marry him knowing all; she had voluntarily entered that chilling world of long silences. He envied men who were free to come home and talk the gossip of an ordinary office.

"Don't you want to know my news, Father?"

Over her shoulder he suddenly noticed Davis. Davis sat alone at a table laid for two. He was waiting, drumming with his fingers, his eyes on his napkin. Daintry hoped he wouldn't look up.

"News?"

"I told you. Only Mother knows. And the other, of course," she added with an embarrassed laugh. Daintry looked at the tables on either side of Davis. He half expected to see Davis's shadow there, but the two elderly couples, well advanced in their meal, certainly didn't look like members of the Special Branch.

"You don't seem in the least interested, Father. Your thoughts are miles away."

"I'm sorry. I just saw someone I know. What is the secret news?"

"I'm getting married."

"Married!" Daintry exclaimed. "Does your mother know?"

"I've just said that I told her."

"I'm sorry."

"Why should you be sorry that I'm getting married?"

"I didn't mean that. I meant . . . Of course I'm not sorry if he's worthy of you. You are a very pretty girl, Elizabeth."

"I'm not up for sale, Father. I suppose in your day good legs put up the market price."

"What does he do?"

"He's in an advertising agency. He handles the Jameson's Baby Powder account."

"Is that a good thing?"

"It's very good. They are spending a huge amount trying to push Johnson's Baby Powder into second place. Colin's arranged wonderful television spots. He even wrote a theme song himself."

"You like him a lot? You're *quite* sure . . . ?"

Davis had ordered a second whisky. He was looking at the menu —but he must have read it many times already.

"We are both quite sure, Father. After all, we've been living together for the past year."

"I'm sorry," Daintry said again—it was turning into an evening of apologies. "I never knew. I suppose your mother did?"

"She guessed, naturally."

"She sees more of you than I do."

He felt like a man who was departing into a long exile and who looks back from the deck of a ship at the faint coastline of his country as it sinks below the horizon.

"He wanted to come tonight and be introduced, but I told him this time I wanted to be alone with you." "This time": it had the sound of a long goodbye; now he could see only the bare horizon, the land had gone.

"When are you getting married?"

"On Saturday the twenty-first. At a registry office. We aren't inviting anybody, except of course Mother. And a few of our friends. Colin has no parents."

Colin, he wondered, who's Colin? But of course he was the man at Jameson's.

"You'd be welcome—but I always have the feeling that you're frightened of meeting Mother."

Davis had given up whatever hope he may have had. As he paid for the whiskies, he looked up from the bill and saw Daintry. It was as though two emigrants had come on deck for the same purpose, to look their last on their country, saw each other and wondered whether to speak. Davis turned and made for the door. Daintry looked after him with regret—but after all there was no need to get acquainted yet, they were sailing together on a long voyage.

Daintry put his glass sharply down and spilled some sherry. He felt a sudden irritation against Percival. The man had no evidence against Davis which would stand up in a court of law. He didn't trust Percival. He remembered Percival at the shoot. Percival was never lonely, he laughed as easily as he talked, he knew about pictures, he was at ease with strangers. He had no daughter who was living with a stranger in a flat he had never seen—he didn't even know where it was.

"We thought afterwards we'd have some drinks and sandwiches at a hotel or perhaps at Mother's flat. Mother has to get back to Brighton afterward. But if you'd like to come . . ."

"I don't think I can. I'm going away that weekend," he lied.

"You do make engagements a long time ahead."

"I have to." He lied again miserably, "There are so many of them. I'm a busy man, Elizabeth. If I'd known . . ."

"I thought I'd give you a surprise."

"We ought to order, oughtn't we? You'll take the roast beef, not the saddle of mutton?"

"Roast beef for me."

"Are you having a honeymoon?"

"Oh, we'll just stay at home for the weekend. Perhaps when the spring comes . . . At the moment Colin's so busy with Jameson's Baby Powder."

"We ought to celebrate," Daintry said. "A bottle of champagne?" He didn't like champagne, but a man must do his duty.

"I'd really rather just have a glass of red wine."

"There's a wedding present to think about."

"A check would be best—and easier for you. You don't want to go shopping. Mother's giving us a lovely carpet."

"I haven't got my checkbook on me. I'll send the check round on Monday."

After dinner they said goodbye in Panton Street—he offered to take her home in a taxi, but she said she preferred to walk. He had no idea where the flat was that she shared. Her private life was as closely guarded as his own, but in his case there had never been anything much to guard. It was not often that he enjoyed their meals together because there was so little for them to talk about, but now, when he realized that they would never again be alone, he felt a sense of abandonment. He said, "Perhaps I could put off that weekend."

"Colin would be glad to meet you, Father."

"Could I perhaps bring a friend with me?"

"Of course. Anyone. Who will you bring?"

"I'm not sure. Perhaps someone from the office."

"That would be fine. But you know—you really needn't be scared. Mother likes you." He watched as she made her way east in the direction of Leicester Square—and after?—he had no idea—before he turned west for St. James's Street.

Chapter II

1

The Indian summer had returned for a day, and Castle agreed to a picnic—Sam was growing restive after the long quarantine and Sarah had a fanciful notion that any lingering last germ would be whisked away among the beech woods with the leaves of autumn. She had prepared a thermos of hot onion soup, half a cold chicken to be dismembered in the fingers, some rock buns, a mutton bone for Buller, and a second thermos of coffee. Castle added his flask of whisky. There were two blankets to sit on, and even Sam had consented to take an overcoat in case the wind rose.

"It's crazy to have a picnic in October," Castle said with pleasure at the rashness of it. The picnic offered escape from office caution, a prudent tongue, foresight. But then, of course, the telephone rang, clanging away like a police alarm while they packed the bags on their bicycles.

Sarah said, "It's those men with masks again. They'll spoil our picnic. I'll be wondering all the time what's happening at home."

Castle replied gloomily (he had his hand over the receiver), "No, no, don't worry, it's only Davis."

"What does he want?"

"He's at Boxmoor with his car. It was such a fine day he thought he'd look me up."

"Oh, damn Davis. Just when everything's prepared. There's no other food in the house. Except our supper. And there's not enough of that for four."

"You go off alone if you like with Sam. I'll lunch at the Swan with Davis."

"A picnic wouldn't be any fun," Sarah said, "without you."

Sam said, "Is it Mr. Davis? I want Mr. Davis. We can play hide-and-seek. We aren't enough without Mr. Davis."

Castle said, "We could take Davis with us, I suppose."

"Half a chicken among four . . . ?"

"There are enough rock buns already for a regiment."

"He won't enjoy a picnic in October unless he's crazy too."

But Davis proved as crazy as the rest of them. He said that he loved picnics even on a hot summer's day when there were wasps and flies, but he much preferred the autumn. As there was no room in his Jaguar he met them at a chosen rendezvous on the Common, and at lunch he won the wishbone of the half chicken with an agile turn of the wrist. Then he introduced a new game. The others had to guess his wish by asking questions, and only if they failed to guess could he expect his wish to be granted. Sarah guessed it with a flash of intuition. He had wished that one day he would become "top of the pops."

"Oh well, I had little hope of my wish coming true anyway. I can't write a note."

By the time the last rock buns had been eaten the afternoon sun was low above the gorse bushes and the wind was rising. Copper leaves floated down to lie on last year's mast. "Hide-and-seek," Davis suggested, and Castle saw how Sam gazed at Davis with the eyes of a hero-worshipper.

They drew lots to decide which of them should hide first, and Davis won. He went loping away among the trees huddled deep in his camel-hair overcoat, looking like a strayed bear from a zoo. After counting sixty the rest set off in pursuit, Sam toward the edge of the Common, Sarah toward Ashridge, Castle into the woods where he had last seen Davis go. Buller followed him, probably in hope of a cat. A low whistle guided Castle to where Davis hid in a hollow surrounded by bracken.

"It's bloody cold hiding," Davis said, "in the shade."

"You suggested the game yourself. We were all ready to go home. Down, Buller. Down, damn you."

"I know, but I could see how much the little bastard wanted it."

"You seem to know children better than I do. I'd better shout to them. We'll catch our death . . ."

"No, don't do that yet. I was hoping you'd come by. I want a word with you alone. Something important."

"Can't it wait till tomorrow at the office?"

"No, you've made me suspicious of the office. Castle, I really think I'm being followed."

"I told you I thought your phone was tapped."

"I didn't believe you. But since that night . . . On Thursday I took Cynthia out to Scott's. There was a man in the lift as we went down. And later he was in Scott's too drinking Black Velvet. And then today, driving down to Berkhamsted—I noticed a car behind me at Marble Arch—only by chance because for a moment I thought I knew the man—I didn't, but I saw him again behind me at Boxmoor. In a black Mercedes."

"The same man as at Scott's?"

"Of course not. They wouldn't be as stupid as that. My Jaguar's got a turn of speed and there was Sunday traffic on the road. I lost him before Berkhamsted."

"We're not trusted, Davis, nobody is, but who cares if we're innocent?"

"Oh yes, I know all that. Like an old theme song, isn't it? Who cares? 'I'm innocent. Who cares? If they take me unawares, I'll say I only went, To buy some golden apples and some pears . . .' I might be top of the pops yet."

"Did you really lose him before Berkhamsted?"

"Yes. As far as I can tell. But what's it all about, Castle? Is it just a routine check, like Daintry's seemed to be? You've been in this bloody show longer than any of us. You ought to know."

"I told you that night with Percival. I think there must have been a leak of some kind, and they suspect a double agent. So they're putting on a security check, and they don't much mind if you notice it. They think you may lose your nerve, if you are guilty."

"Me a double agent? You don't believe it, Castle?"

"No, of course not. You don't have to worry. Just be patient. Let them finish their check and they won't believe it either. I expect they're checking me too—and Watson."

In the distance Sarah was calling out, "We give up. We give up." A thin voice came from further away, "Oh no, we don't. Keep hiding, Mr. Davis. Please, Mr. Davis . . ."

Buller barked and Davis sneezed. "Children are merciless," he said.

There was a rustle in the bracken around their hiding-place and Sam appeared. "Caught," he said, and then he saw Castle. "Oh, but you cheated."

"No," Castle said, "I couldn't call out. He held me up at the point of a gun."

"Where's the gun?"

"Look in his breast pocket."

"There's only a fountain pen," Sam said.

"It's a gas gun," Davis said, "disguised as a fountain pen. You see this knob. It squirts what looks like ink—only it's not really ink, it's nerve gas. James Bond was never allowed one like this—it's too secret. Put up your hands."

Sam put them up. "Are you a real spy?" he asked.

"I'm a double agent for Russia," Davis said, "and if you value your life, you must give me fifty yards start." He burst through the bracken and ran clumsily in his heavy overcoat through the beech woods. Sam pursued him up one slope, down another. Davis reached a bank above the Ashridge road where he had left his scarlet Jaguar. He pointed his fountain pen at Sam and shouted a message as mutilated as one of Cynthia's cables, "Picnic . . . love . . . Sarah," and then he was gone with a loud explosion from his exhaust.

"Ask him to come again," Sam said, "please ask him to come again."

"Of course. Why not? When the spring comes."

"The spring's a long way off," Sam said. "I'll be at school."

"There'll always be weekends," Castle replied but without conviction. He remembered too well how slowly time limps by in childhood. A car passed them, heading toward London, a black car—perhaps it was a Mercedes, but Castle knew very little about cars.

"I like Mr. Davis," Sam said.

"Yes, so do I."

"Nobody plays hide-and-seek as well as he does. Not even you."

2

"I find I'm not making much headway with *War and Peace*, Mr. Halliday."

"Oh dear, oh dear. It's a great book if you only have the patience. Have you reached the retreat from Moscow?"

"No."

"It's a terrible story."

"It seems a lot less terrible to us today, doesn't it? After all, the French were soldiers—and snow isn't as bad as napalm. You fall asleep, so they say—you don't burn alive."

"Yes, when I think of all those poor children in Vietnam . . . I wanted to join some of the marches they used to have here, but my son would never let me. He's nervous of the police in that little shop of his, though what harm he does with a naughty book or two I can't see. As I always say—the men that buy them—well, you can't very well do much harm to them, can you?"

"No, they are not clean young Americans doing their duty like the napalm bombers were," Castle said. Sometimes he found it impossible not to show one splinter of the submerged iceberg life he led.

"And yet there wasn't a thing any of us could have done," Halliday said. "The Government talk about democracy, but what notice did the Government ever take of all our banners and slogans? Except at election time. It helped them choose which promises to break, that's all. Next day we used to read in the paper how another innocent village had been wiped out in error. Oh, they'll be doing the same thing in South Africa before long. First it was the little yellow babies—no more yellow than we are—and then it will be the little black babies . . ."

"Let's change the subject," Castle said. "Recommend me something to read that isn't about war."

"There's always Trollope," Mr. Halliday said. "My son's very fond of Trollope. Though it doesn't really go with the kind of things he sells, does it?"

"I've never read Trollope. Isn't he a bit ecclesiastical? Anyway, ask your son to choose me one and post it home."

"Your friend didn't like *War and Peace* either?"

"No. In fact he got tired of it before I did. Too much war for him too perhaps."

"I could easily slip across the road and have a word with my son. I know he prefers the political novels—or what he calls the sociological. I've heard him speak well of *The Way We Live Now*. A good title, sir. Always contemporary. Do you want to take it home tonight?"

"No, not today."

"It will be two copies as usual, sir, I suppose? I envy you having a friend with whom you can discuss literature. Too few people nowadays are interested in literature."

After Castle had left Mr. Halliday's shop he walked to Piccadilly Circus station and went to find a telephone. He chose an end box and looked through the glass at his only neighbor: she was a fat spotty girl who giggled and sucked a gum while she listened to something gratifying. A voice said, "Hello," and Castle said, "I'm sorry, wrong number again," and left the box. The girl was parking her gum on the back of the telephone directory while she got down to a long satisfactory conversation. He waited by a ticket machine and watched her for a little while to make sure she had no interest in him.

3

"What are you doing?" Sarah asked. "Didn't you hear me call?"

She looked at the book on his desk and said, "*War and Peace*. I thought you were getting tired of *War and Peace*."

He gathered up a sheet of paper, folded it and put it in his pocket.

"I'm trying my hand at an essay."

"Show me."

"No. Only if it comes off."

"Where will you send it?"

"The *New Statesman . . . Encounter . . .* who knows?"

"It's a very long time since you wrote anything. I'm glad you are starting again."

"Yes. I seem doomed always to try again."

Chapter III

Castle helped himself to another whisky. Sarah had been upstairs a long time with Sam, and he was alone, waiting for the bell to ring, waiting . . . His mind wandered to that other occasion when he had waited for at least three-quarters of an hour, in the office of Cornelius Muller. He had been given a copy of the *Rand Daily Mail* to read—an odd choice since the paper was the enemy of most things that BOSS, the organization which employed Muller, supported. He had already read that day's issue with his breakfast, but now he reread every page with no other purpose than just to pass the time. Whenever he looked up at the clock he met the eyes of one of the two junior officials who sat stiffly behind their desks and perhaps took it in turn to watch him. Did they expect him to pull out a razor blade and slit open a vein? But torture, he told himself, was always left to the Security Police—or so he believed. And in his case, after all, there could be no fear of torture from any service— he was protected by diplomatic privilege; he was one of the untorturables. No diplomatic privilege, however, could be extended to include Sarah; he had learned during the last year in South Africa the age-old lesson that fear and love are indivisible.

Castle finished his whisky and poured himself another small one. He had to be careful.

Sarah called down to him, "What are you doing, darling?"

"Just waiting for Mr. Muller," he replied, "and drinking another whisky."

"Not too many, darling." They had decided that he should welcome Muller first alone. Muller would no doubt arrive from London in an embassy car. A black Mercedes like the big officials all used in South Africa? "Get over the first embarrassments," C had said, "and leave serious business, of course, for the office. At home you are more likely to pick up a useful indication . . . I mean of what we have and they haven't. But for God's sake, Castle, keep your cool." And now he struggled to keep his cool with the help of a third whisky while he listened and listened for the sound of a car, any car, but there was little traffic at this hour in King's Road—all the commuters had long since arrived safely home.

If fear and love are indivisible, so too are fear and hate. Hate is an automatic response to fear, for fear humiliates. When he had been allowed at last to drop the *Rand Daily Mail* and they interrupted his fourth reading of the same leading article, with its useless routine protest against the evil of petty apartheid, he was deeply aware of his cowardice. Three years of life in South Africa and six months of love for Sarah had turned him, he knew well, into a coward.

Two men waited for him in the inner office: Mr. Muller sat behind a large desk of the finest South African wood which bore nothing but a blank blotting pad and a highly polished pen-stand and one file suggestively open. He was a man a little younger than Castle, approaching fifty perhaps, and he had the kind of face which in ordinary circumstances Castle would have found it easy to forget: an indoors face, as smooth and pale as a bank clerk's or a junior civil servant's, a face unmarked by the torments of any belief, human or religious, a face which was ready to receive orders and obey them promptly without question, a conformist face. Certainly not the face of a bully—though that described the features of the second man in uniform who sat with his legs slung with insolence over the arm of an easy chair as though he wanted to show he was any man's equal; *his* face had not avoided the sun: it had a kind of infernal flush as though it had been exposed too long to a heat which would have been much too fierce for ordinary men. Muller's glasses had gold rims; it was a gold-rimmed country.

"Take a seat," Muller told Castle with just sufficient politeness to pass as courtesy, but the only seat left him to take was a hard narrow chair as little made for comfort as a chair in a church—if he should be required to kneel, there was no hassock available on the hard floor to support his knees. He sat in silence and the two men, the pale one and the heated one, looked back at him and said nothing. Castle wondered how long the silence would continue. Cornelius Muller had a sheet detached from the file in front of him, and after a while he began to tap it with the end of his gold ball-point pen, always in the same place, as though he were hammering in a pin. The small tap tap tap recorded the length of silence like the tick of a watch. The other man scratched his skin above his sock, and so it went on, tap tap and scratch scratch.

At last Muller consented to speak. "I'm glad you found it possible to call, Mr. Castle."

"Yes, it wasn't very convenient, but, well, here I am."

"We wanted to avoid making an unnecessary scandal by writing to your ambassador."

It was Castle's turn now to remain silent, while he tried to make out what they meant by the word scandal.

"Captain Van Donck—this is Captain Van Donck—has brought the matter to us here. He felt it would be more suitably dealt with by us than by the Security Police—because of your position at the British Embassy. You've been under observation, Mr. Castle, for a long time, but an arrest in your case, I feel, would serve no practical purpose—your embassy would claim diplomatic privilege. Of course we could always dispute it before a magistrate and then they would certainly have to send you home. That would probably be the end of your career, wouldn't it?"

Castle said nothing.

"You've been very imprudent, even stupid," Cornelius Muller said, "but then I don't myself consider that stupidity ought to be punished as a crime. Captain Van Donck and the Security Police, though, take a different view, a legalistic view—and they may be right. He would prefer to go through the form of arrest and charge you in court. He feels that diplomatic privileges are often unduly stretched as far as the junior employees of an embassy are concerned. He would like to fight the case as a matter of principle."

The hard chair was becoming painful, and Castle wanted to shift his thigh, but he thought the movement might be taken as a sign of weakness. He was trying very hard to make out what it was they really knew. How many of his agents, he wondered, were incriminated? His own relative safety made him feel shame. In a genuine war an officer can always die with his men and so keep his self-respect.

"Start talking, Castle," Captain Van Donck demanded. He swung his legs off the arm of his chair and prepared to rise—or so it seemed—it was probably bluff. He opened and closed one fist and stared at his signet ring. Then he began to polish the gold ring with a finger as though it were a gun which had to be kept well oiled. In this country you couldn't escape gold. It was in the dust of the cities, artists used it as paint, it would be quite natural for the police to use it for beating in a man's face.

"Talk about what?" Castle asked.

"You are like most Englishmen who come to the Republic,"

Muller said, "you feel a certain automatic sympathy for black Africans. We can understand your feeling. All the more because we are Africans ourselves. We have lived here for three hundred years. The Bantu are newcomers like yourselves. But I don't need to give you a history lesson. As I said, we understand your point of view, even though it's a very ignorant one, but when it leads a man to grow emotional, then it becomes dangerous, and when you reach the point of breaking the law . . ."

"Which law?"

"I think you know very well which law."

"It's true I'm planning a study on apartheid, the Embassy have no objection, but it's a serious sociological one—quite objective—and it's still in my head. You hardly have the right to censor it yet. Anyway it won't be published, I imagine, in this country."

"If you want to fuck a black whore," Captain Van Donck interrupted with impatience, "why don't you go to a whorehouse in Lesotho or Swaziland? They are still part of your so-called Commonwealth."

Then it was that for the first time Castle realized Sarah, not he, was the one who was in danger.

"I'm too old to be interested in whores," he said.

"Where were you on the nights of February 4th and 7th? The afternoon of February 21st?"

"You obviously know—or think that you know," Castle said. "I keep my engagement book in my office."

He hadn't seen Sarah for forty-eight hours. Was she already in the hands of men like Captain Van Donck? His fear and his hate grew simultaneously. He forgot that in theory he was a diplomat, however junior. "What the hell are you talking about? And you?" he added to Cornelius Muller, "You too, what do you want me for?"

Captain Van Donck was a brutal and simple man who believed in something, however repugnant—he was one of those one could forgive. What Castle could never bring himself to forgive was this smooth educated officer of BOSS. It was men of this kind—men with the education to know what they were about—that made a hell in heaven's despite. He thought of what his Communist friend Carson had so often said to him—"Our worst enemies here are not the ignorant and the simple, however cruel, our worst enemies are the intelligent and the corrupt."

Muller said, "You must know very well that you've broken the Race Relations Act with that Bantu girl friend of yours." He spoke in a tone of reasonable reproach, like a bank clerk who points out to an unimportant customer an unacceptable overdraft. "You must be aware that if it wasn't for diplomatic privilege you'd be in prison now."

"Where have you hidden her?" Captain Van Donck demanded and Castle at the question felt immense relief.

"Hidden her?"

Captain Van Donck was on his feet, rubbing at his gold ring. He even spat on it.

"That's all right, Captain," Muller said. "I will look after Mr. Castle. I won't take up any more of your time. Thank you for all the help you've given our department. I want to talk to Mr. Castle alone."

When the door closed Castle found himself facing, as Carson would have said, the real enemy. Muller went on, "You mustn't mind Captain Van Donck. Men like that can see no further than their noses. There are other ways of settling this affair more reasonably than a prosecution which will ruin you and not help us."

"I can hear a car." A woman's voice called to him out of the present.

It was Sarah speaking to him from the top of the stairs. He went to the window. A black Mercedes was edging its way up the indistinguishable commuters' houses in King's Road. The driver was obviously looking for a number, but as usual several of the street lamps had fused.

"It's Mr. Muller all right," Castle called back. When he put down his whisky he found his hand shaking from holding the glass too rigidly.

At the sound of the bell Buller began to bark, but, after Castle opened the door, Buller fawned on the stranger with a total lack of discrimination and left a trail of affectionate spittle on Cornelius Muller's trousers. "Nice dog, nice dog," Muller said with caution.

The years had made a noticeable change in Muller—his hair was almost white now and his face was far less smooth. He no longer looked like a civil servant who knew only the proper answers. Since they last met something had happened to him: he looked more human—perhaps it was that he had taken on with promotion greater responsibilities and with them uncertainties and unanswered questions.

"Good evening, Mr. Castle. I'm sorry I'm so late. The traffic was bad in Watford—I think the place was called Watford."

You might almost have taken him now for a shy man, or perhaps it was only that he was at a loss without his familiar office and his desk of beautiful wood and the presence of two junior colleagues in an outer room. The back Mercedes slid away—the chauffeur had gone to find his dinner. Muller was on his own in a strange town, in a foreign land, where the post boxes bore the initials of a sovereign E II, and there was no statue of Kruger in any market place.

Castle poured out two glasses of whisky. "It's a long time since we met last," Muller said.

"Seven years?"

"It's good of you to ask me to have dinner at your own home."

"C thought it was the best idea. To break the ice. It seems we have to work closely together. On Uncle Remus."

Muller's eyes shifted to the telephone, to the lamp on the table, to a vase of flowers.

"It's all right. Don't worry. If we are bugged here it's only by my own people," Castle said, "and anyway I'm pretty sure we are not." He raised his glass. "To our last meeting. Do you remember you suggested then I might agree to work for you? Well, here I am. We are working together. Historical irony or predestination? Your Dutch church believes in that."

"Of course in those days I hadn't an idea of your real position," Muller said. "If I'd known I wouldn't have threatened you about that wretched Bantu girl. I realize now she was only one of your agents. We might even have worked her together. But, you see, I took you for one of those high-minded anti-apartheid sentimentalists. I was taken completely by surprise when your chief told me you were the man I was to see about Uncle Remus. I hope you don't bear me any grudge. After all you and I were professionals, and we are on the same side now."

"Yes, I suppose we are."

"I do wish though that you'd tell me—it can't matter any longer, can it?—how you got that Bantu girl away. I suppose it was to Swaziland?"

"Yes."

"I thought we had that frontier closed pretty effectively—except for the real guerrilla experts. I never considered you were an expert, though I realized you did have some Communist contacts, but I assumed you needed them for that book of yours on apartheid which was never published. You took me in all right there. Not to speak of Van Donck. You remember Captain Van Donck?"

"Oh, yes. Vividly."

"I had to ask the Security Police for his demotion over your affair. He acted very clumsily. I felt sure that, if we had the girl safe in prison, you'd consent to work for us, and he let her slip. You see—don't laugh—I was convinced it was a real love affair. I've known so many Englishmen who have started with the idea of attacking apartheid and ended trapped by us in a Bantu girl's bed. It's the romantic idea of breaking what they think is an unjust law that attracts them just as much as a black bottom. I never dreamt the girl—Sarah MaNkosi, I think that was the name?—all the time was an agent of MI6."

"She didn't know it herself. She believed in my book too. Have another whisky."

"Thank you. I will." Castle poured out two glasses, gambling on his better head.

"From all accounts she was a clever girl. We looked pretty closely into her background. Been to the African University in the Transvaal where Uncle Tom professors always produce dangerous students. Personally, though, I've always found that the cleverer the African the more easily he can be turned—one way or another. If we'd had that girl in prison for a month I'm pretty sure we could have turned her. Well, she might have been useful to both of us now in this Uncle Remus operation. Or would she? One forgets that old devil Time. By now she'd be getting a bit long in the tooth, I suppose. Bantu women age so quickly. They are generally finished —anyway to a white taste—long before the age of thirty. You know, Castle, I'm really glad we are working together and you are not what we in BOSS thought—one of those idealistic types who want to change the nature of human beings. We knew the people you were in touch with—or most of them, and we knew the sort of nonsense they'd be telling you. But you outwitted *us*, so you certainly outwitted those Bantu and Communists. I suppose they too thought you were writing a book which would serve their turn. Mind you, I'm not anti-African like Captain Van Donck. I consider myself a hundred percent African myself."

It was certainly not the Cornelius Muller of the Pretoria office who spoke now, the pale clerk doing his conformist job would never have spoken with such ease and confidence. Even the shyness and the uncertainty of a few minutes back had gone. The whisky had cured that. He was now a high officer of BOSS, entrusted with a foreign mission, who took his orders from no one under the rank of a general. He could relax. He could be—an unpleasant thought— himself, and it seemed to Castle that he began to resemble more and more closely, in the vulgarity and brutality of his speech, the Captain Van Donck whom he despised.

"I've taken pleasant enough weekends in Lesotho," Muller said, "rubbing shoulders with my black brothers in the casino at Holiday Inn. I'll admit once I even had a little—well, encounter—it somehow seemed quite different there—of course it wasn't against the law. I wasn't in the Republic."

Castle called out, "Sarah, bring Sam down to say goodnight to Mr. Muller."

"You are married?" Muller asked.

"Yes."

"I'm all the more flattered to be invited to your home. I brought with me a few little presents from South Africa, and perhaps there's something your wife would like. But you haven't answered my question. Now that we are working together—as I wanted to before, you remember—couldn't you tell me how you got that girl out? It can't harm any of your old agents now, and it does have a certain bearing on Uncle Remus, and the problems we have to face together. Your country and mine—and the States, of course—have a common frontier now."

"Perhaps she'll tell you herself. Let me introduce her and my son, Sam." They came down the stairs together as Cornelius Muller turned.

"Mr. Muller was asking how I got you into Swaziland, Sarah."

He had underestimated Muller. The surprise which he had planned failed completely. "I'm so glad to meet you, Mrs. Castle," Muller said and took her hand.

"We just failed to meet seven years ago," Sarah said.

"Yes. Seven wasted years. You have a very beautiful wife, Castle."

"Thank you," Sarah said. "Sam, shake hands with Mr. Muller."

"This is my son, Mr. Muller," Castle said. He knew Muller would be a good judge of color shades, and Sam was very black.

"How do you do, Sam? Do you go to school yet?"

"He goes to school in a week or two. Run along up to bed now, Sam."

"Can you play hide-and-seek?" Sam asked.

"I used to know the game, but I'm always ready to learn new roles."

"Are you a spy like Mr. Davis?"

"I said go to bed, Sam."

"Have you a poison pen?"

"Sam! Upstairs!"

"And now for Mr. Muller's question, Sarah," Castle said. "Where and how did you cross into Swaziland?"

"I don't think I ought to tell him, do you?"

Cornelius Muller said, "Oh, let's forget Swaziland. It's all past history and it happened in another country."

Castle watched him adapting, as naturally as a chameleon, to the color of the soil. He must have adapted in just that way during his weekend in Lesotho. Perhaps he would have found Muller more likable if he had been less adaptable. All through dinner Muller made his courteous conversation. Yes, thought Castle, I really would have preferred Captain Van Donck. Van Donck would have walked out of the house at the first sight of Sarah. A prejudice had something in common with an ideal. Cornelius Muller was without prejudice and he was without an ideal.

"How do you find the climate here, Mrs. Castle, after South Africa?"

"Do you mean the weather?"

"Yes, the weather."

"It's less extreme," Sarah said.

"Don't you sometimes miss Africa? I came by way of Madrid and Athens, so I've been away some weeks already, and do you know what I miss most? The mine dumps around Johannesburg. Their color when the sun's half set. What do you miss?"

Castle had not suspected Muller of any aesthetic feeling. Was it one of the larger interests which came with promotion or was it adapted for the occasion and the country like his courtesy?

"My memories are different," Sarah said. "My Africa was different to yours."

"Oh come, we are both of us Africans. By the way, I've brought a few presents for my friends here. Not knowing that you were one of us, I brought you a shawl. You know how in Lesotho they have those very fine weavers—the Royal Weavers. Would you accept a shawl—from your old enemy?"

"Of course. It's kind of you."

"Do you think Lady Hargreaves would accept an ostrich bag?"

"I don't know her. You must ask my husband."

It would hardly be up to her crocodile standard, Castle thought, but he said, "I'm sure . . . coming from you . . ."

"I take a sort of family interest in ostriches, you see," Muller explained. "My grandfather was what they call now one of the ostrich millionaires—put out of business by the 1914 war. He had a big house in the Cape Province. It was very splendid once, but it's only a ruin now. Ostrich feathers never really came back in Europe, and my father went bankrupt. My brothers still keep a few ostriches though."

Castle remembered visiting one of those big houses, which had been preserved as a sort of museum, camped in by the manager of all that was left of the ostrich farm. The manager was a little apologetic about the richness and the bad taste. The bathroom was the high spot of the tour—visitors were always taken to the bathroom last of all—a bath like a great white double bed with gold-plated taps, and on the wall a bad copy of an Italian primitive: on the haloes real goldleaf was beginning to peel off.

At the end of dinner Sarah left them, and Muller accepted a glass of port. The bottle had remained untouched since last Christmas—a present from Davis. "Seriously though," Muller said, "I wish you would give me a few details about your wife's route to Swaziland. No need to mention names. I know you had some Communist friends—I realize now it was all part of your job. They thought you were a sentimental fellow traveler—just as we did. For example, Carson must have thought you one—poor Carson."

"Why poor Carson?"

"He went too far. He had contacts with the guerrillas. He was a good fellow in his way and a very good advocate. He gave the Security Police a lot of trouble with the pass-laws."

"Doesn't he still?"

"Oh no. He died a year ago in prison."

"I hadn't heard."

Castle went to the sideboard and poured himself yet another double whisky. With plenty of soda the J & B looked no stronger than a single.

"Don't you like this port?" Muller asked. "We used to get admirable port from Lourenço Marques. Alas, those days are over."

"What did he die of?"

"Pneumonia," Muller said. He added, "Well, it saved him from a long trial."

"I liked Carson," Castle said.

"Yes. It's a great pity he always identified Africans with color. It's the kind of mistake second-generation men make. They refuse to admit a white man can be as good an African as a black. My family for instance arrived in 1700. We were early comers." He looked at his watch. "My God, with you I'm a late stayer. My driver must have been waiting an hour. You'll have to excuse me. I ought to be saying goodnight."

Castle said, "Perhaps we should talk a little before you go about Uncle Remus."

"That can wait for the office," Muller said.

At the door he turned. He said, "I'm really sorry about Carson. If I'd known that you hadn't heard I wouldn't have spoken so abruptly."

Buller licked the bottom of his trousers with undiscriminating affection. "Good dog," Muller said. "Good dog. There's nothing like a dog's fidelity."

2

At one o'clock in the morning Sarah broke a long silence. "You are still awake. Don't pretend. Was it as bad as all that seeing Muller? He was quite polite."

"Oh yes. In England he puts on English manners. He adapts very quickly."

"Shall I get you a Mogadon?"

"No. I'll sleep soon. Only—there's something I have to tell you. Carson's dead. In prison."

"Did they kill him?"

"Muller said he died from pneumonia."

She put her head under the crook of his arm and turned her face into the pillow. He guessed she was crying. He said, "I couldn't help remembering tonight the last note I ever had from him. It was waiting at the Embassy when I came back from seeing Muller and Van Donck. 'Don't worry about Sarah. Take the first possible plane to L.M. and wait for her at the Polana. She's in safe hands.'"

"Yes. I remember that note too. I was with him when he wrote it."

"I was never able to thank him—except by seven years of silence and . . ."

"And?"

"Oh, I don't know what I was going to say." He repeated what he had told Muller, "I liked Carson."

"Yes. I trusted him. Much more than I trusted his friends. During that week while you waited for me in Lourenço Marques we had time for a lot of argument. I used to tell him he wasn't a real Communist."

"Why? He was a member of the Party. One of the oldest members left in the Transvaal."

"Of course. I know that. But there are members and members, aren't there? I told him about Sam even before I told you."

"He had a way of drawing people to him."

"Most of the Communists I knew—they pushed, they didn't draw."

"All the same, Sarah, he was a genuine Communist. He survived Stalin like Roman Catholics survived the Borgias. He made me think better of the Party."

"But he never drew you that far, did he?"

"Oh, there were always some things which stuck in my throat. He used to say I strained at a gnat and swallowed a camel. You know I was never a religious man—I left God behind in the school chapel, but there were priests I sometimes met in Africa who made me believe again—for a moment—over a drink. If all priests had been like they were and I had seen them often enough, perhaps I would have swallowed the Resurrection, the Virgin birth, Lazarus, the whole works. I remember one I met twice—I wanted to use him as an agent as I used you, but he wasn't usable. His name was Connolly—or was it O'Connell? He worked in the slums of Soweto. He said to me exactly what Carson said—you strain at a gnat and you swallow . . . For a while I half believed in his God, like I half believed in Carson's. Perhaps I was born to be a half believer. When people talk about Prague and Budapest and how you can't find a human face in Communism I stay silent. Because I've seen—once—the human face. I say to myself that if it hadn't been for Carson Sam would have been born in a prison and you would probably have died in one. One kind of Communism—or Communist—saved you and Sam. I don't have any trust in Marx or Lenin any more than I have in Saint Paul, but haven't I the right to be grateful?"

"Why do you worry so much about it? No one would say you were wrong to be grateful, I'm grateful too. Gratitude's all right if . . ."

"If . . . ?"

"I think I was going to say if it doesn't take you too far."

It was hours before he slept. He lay awake and thought of Carson and Cornelius Muller, of Uncle Remus and Prague. He didn't want to sleep until he was sure from her breathing that Sarah was asleep first. Then he allowed himself to strike, like his childhood hero Allan Quatermain, off on that long slow underground stream which bore him on toward the interior of the dark continent where he hoped that he might find a permanent home, in a city where he could be accepted as a citizen, as a citizen without any pledge of faith, not the City of God or Marx, but the city called Peace of Mind.

Chapter IV

1

Once a month on his day off Castle was in the habit of taking Sarah and Sam for an excursion into the sandy conifered countryside of East Sussex in order to see his mother. No one ever questioned the necessity of the visit, but Castle doubted whether even his mother enjoyed it, though he had to admit she did all she could to please them—according to her own idea of what their pleasures were. Invariably the same supply of vanilla ice cream was waiting for Sam in the deep freeze—he preferred chocolate—and though she only lived half a mile from the station, she ordered a taxi to meet them. Castle, who had never wanted a car since he returned to England, had the impression that she regarded him as an unsuccessful and impecunious son, and Sarah once told him how *she* felt—like a black guest at an anti-apartheid garden party too fussed over to be at ease.

A further cause of nervous strain was Buller. Castle had given up arguing that they should leave Buller at home. Sarah was certain that without their protection he would be murdered by masked men, though Castle pointed out that he had been bought to defend them and not to be defended himself. In the long run it proved easier to give way, though his mother profoundly disliked dogs and had a Burmese cat which it was Buller's fixed ambition to destroy. Before they arrived the cat had to be locked in Mrs. Castle's bedroom, and her sad fate, deprived of human company, would be hinted at from time to time by his mother during the course of the long day. On one occasion Buller was found spread-eagled outside the bedroom door waiting his chance, breathing heavily like a Shakespearian murderer. Afterward Mrs. Castle wrote a long letter of reproach to Sarah on the subject. Apparently the cat's nerves had suffered for more than a week. She had refused her diet of Friskies and existed only on milk—a kind of hunger strike.

Gloom was apt to descend on all of them as soon as the taxi entered the deep shade of the laurel drive which led to the high-gabled Edwardian house that his father had bought for his retirement because it was near a golf course. (Soon after he had a stroke and was unable to walk even as far as the clubhouse.)

Mrs. Castle was invariably standing there on the porch waiting for them, a tall straight figure in an outdated skirt which showed to advantage her fine ankles, wearing a high collar like Queen Alexandra's which disguised the wrinkles of old age. To hide his despondency Castle would become unnaturally elated and he greeted his mother with an exaggerated hug which she barely returned. She believed that any emotions openly expressed must be false emotions. She had deserved to marry an ambassador or a colonial governor rather than a country doctor.

"You are looking wonderful, Mother," Castle said.

"I'm feeling well for my age." She was eighty-five. She offered a clean white cheek which smelled of lavender water for Sarah to kiss. "I hope Sam is feeling quite well again."

"Oh yes, he's never been better."

"Out of quarantine?"

"Of course."

Reassured, Mrs. Castle granted him the privilege of a brief kiss. "You'll be starting prep school soon, I suppose, won't you?"

Sam nodded.

"You'll enjoy having other boys to play with. Where's Buller?"

"He's gone upstairs looking for Tinker Bell," Sam said with satisfaction.

After lunch Sarah took Sam into the garden along with Buller so as to leave Castle alone with his mother for a little while. That was the monthly routine. Sarah meant well, but Castle had the impression that his mother was glad when the private interview was over. Invariably there was a long silence between them while Mrs. Castle poured out two more unwanted coffees; then she would propose a subject for discussion which Castle knew had been prepared a long time before just to cover this awkward interval.

"That was a terrible air crash last week," Mrs. Castle said, and she dropped the lump sugar in, one for her, two for him.

"Yes. It certainly was. Terrible." He tried to remember which company, where . . . TWA? Calcutta?

"I couldn't help thinking what would have happened to Sam if you and Sarah had been on board."

He remembered just in time. "But it happened in Bangladesh, Mother. Why on earth should we . . . ?"

"You are in the Foreign Office. They could send you anywhere."

"Oh no, they couldn't. I'm chained to my desk in London, Mother. Anyway you know very well we've appointed you as guardian if anything ever happened."

"An old woman approaching ninety."

"Eighty-five, Mother, surely."

"Every week I read of old women killed in bus crashes."

"You never go in a bus."

"I see no reason why I should make a *principle* of not going in a bus."

"If anything should ever happen to you be sure we'll appoint somebody reliable."

"It might be too late. One must prepare against simultaneous accidents. And in the case of Sam—well, there are special problems."

"I suppose you mean his color."

"You can't make him a Ward in Chancery. Many of those judges —your father always said that—are racialist. And then—has it occurred to you, dear, if we are all dead, there might be people—out there—who might claim him?"

"Sarah has no parents."

"What you leave behind, however small, might be thought quite a fortune—I mean by someone out there. If the deaths are simultaneous, the eldest is judged to have died first, or so I'm told. My money would then be added to yours. Sarah must have *some* relations and they might claim . . ."

"Mother, aren't you being a bit racialist yourself?"

"No, dear. I'm not at all racialist, though perhaps I'm old-fashioned and patriotic. Sam is English by birth whatever anyone may say."

"I'll think about it, Mother." That statement was the end of most of their discussions, but it was always well to try a diversion too. "I've been wondering, Mother, whether to retire."

"They don't give you a very good pension, do they?"

"I've saved a little. We live very economically."

"The more you've saved the more reason for a spare guardian— just in case. I hope I'm as liberal as your father was, but I would hate to see Sam dragged back to South Africa . . ."

"But you wouldn't see it, Mother, if you were dead."

"I'm not so certain of things, dear, as all that. I'm not an *atheist.*"

It was one of their most trying visits and he was only saved by Buller, who returned with heavy determination from the garden and lumbered upstairs looking for the imprisoned Tinker Bell.

"At least," Mrs. Castle said, "I hope I will never have to be a guardian for Buller."

"I can promise you that, Mother. In the event of a fatal accident in Bangladesh which coincides with a Grandmothers' Union bus crash in Sussex I have left strict directions for Buller to be put away—as painlessly as possible."

"It's not the sort of dog that I would personally have chosen for my grandson. Watchdogs like Buller are always very color-conscious. And Sam's a nervous child. He reminds me of you at his age —except for the color of course."

"Was I a nervous child?"

"You always had an exaggerated sense of gratitude for the least kindness. It was a sort of insecurity, though why you should have felt insecure with me and your father . . . You once gave away a good fountain pen to someone at school who had offered you a bun with a piece of chocolate inside."

"Oh well, Mother. I always insist on getting my money's worth now."

"I wonder."

"And I've quite given up gratitude." But as he spoke he remembered Carson dead in prison, and he remembered what Sarah had said. He added, "Anyway, I don't let it go too far. I demand more than a penny bun nowadays."

"There's something I've always found strange about you. Since you met Sarah you never mention Mary. I was very fond of Mary. I wish you had had a child with her."

"I try to forget the dead," he said, but that wasn't true. He had learned early in his marriage that he was sterile, so there was no child, but they were happy. It was as much an only child as a wife who was blown to pieces by a buzz bomb in Oxford Street when he was safe in Lisbon, making a contact. He had failed to protect her, and he hadn't died with her. That was why he never spoke of her even to Sarah.

2

"What always surprises me about your mother," Sarah said, when they began to go over in bed the record of their day in the country, "is that she accepts so easily the fact that Sam's your child. Does it never occur to her that he's very black to have a white father?"

"She doesn't seem to notice shades."

"Mr. Muller did. I'm sure of that."

Downstairs the telephone rang. It was nearly midnight.

"Oh hell," Castle said, "who would ring us at this hour? Your masked men again?"

"Aren't you going to answer?"

The ringing stopped.

"If it's your masked men," Castle said, "we'll have a chance to catch them."

The telephone rang a second time. Castle looked at his watch.

"For God's sake answer them."

"It's certain to be a wrong number."

"I'll answer if you won't."

"Put on your dressing gown. You'll catch cold." But as soon as she got out of bed the telephone stopped ringing.

"It's sure to ring again," Sarah said. "Don't you remember last month—three times at one o'clock in the morning?" But this time the telephone remained silent.

There was a cry from across the passage. Sarah said, "Damn them, they've woken up Sam. Whoever they are."

"I'll go to him. You're shivering. Get back into bed."

Sam asked, "Was it burglars? Why didn't Buller bark?"

"Buller knew better. There are no burglars, Sam. It was just a friend of mine ringing up late."

"Was it that Mr. Muller?"

"No. He's not a friend. Go to sleep. The telephone won't ring again."

"How do you know?"

"I know."

"It rang more than once."

"Yes."

"But you never answered. So how do you know it was a friend?"

"You ask too many questions, Sam."

"Was it a secret signal?"

"Do you have secrets, Sam?"

"Yes. Lots of them."

"Tell me one."

"I won't. It wouldn't be a secret if I told you."

"Well, I have my secrets too."

Sarah was still awake. "He's all right now," Castle said. "He thought they were burglars ringing up."

"Perhaps they were. What did you tell him?"

"Oh, I said they were secret signals."

"You always know how to calm him. You love him, don't you?"

"Yes."

"It's strange. I never understand. I wish he were really your child."

"I don't wish it. You know that."

"I've never really understood why."

"I've told you many times. I see enough of myself every day when I shave."

"All you see is a kind man, darling."

"I wouldn't describe myself that way."

"For me a child of yours would have been something to live for when you are not there anymore. You won't live forever."

"No, thank God for that." He brought the words out without thinking and regretted having spoken them. It was her sympathy which always made him commit himself too far; however much he tried to harden himself he was tempted to tell her everything. Sometimes he compared her cynically with a clever interrogator who uses sympathy and a timely cigarette.

Sarah said, "I know you are worried. I wish you could tell me why—but I know you can't. Perhaps one day . . . when you are free . . ." She added sadly, "If you are ever free, Maurice."

Chapter V

Castle left his bicycle with the ticket collector at Berkhamsted station and went upstairs to the London platform. He knew nearly all the commuters by sight—he was even on nodding terms with a few of them. A cold October mist was lying in the grassy pool of the castle and dripping from the willows into the canal on the other side of the line. He walked the length of the platform and back; he thought he recognized all the faces except for one woman in a shabby rabbity fur—women were rare on this train. He watched her climb into a compartment and he chose the same one so as to watch her more closely. The men opened newspapers and the woman opened a paperbound novel by Denise Robins. Castle began reading in Book II of *War and Peace*. It was a breach of security, even a small act of defiance, to read this book publicly for pleasure. "One step beyond that boundary line, which resembles the line dividing the living from the dead, lies uncertainty, suffering and death. And what is there? Who is there—there beyond that field, that tree . . ." He looked out of the window and seemed to see with the eyes of Tolstoy's soldier the motionless spirit-level of the canal pointing toward Boxmoor. "That roof lit up by the sun? No one knows, but one wants to know. You fear and yet long to cross that line . . ."

When the train stopped at Watford, Castle was the only one to leave the compartment. He stood beside the list of train departures and watched the last passenger go through the barrier—the woman was not among them. Outside the station he hesitated at the tail of the bus queue while he again noted the faces. Then he looked at his watch and with a studied gesture of impatience for any observer who cared to notice him walked on. Nobody followed him, he was sure of that, but all the same he was a little worried by the thought of the woman in the train and his petty defiance of the rules. One had to be meticulously careful. At the first post office to which he came he rang the office and asked for Cynthia—she always arrived half an hour at least before Watson or Davis or himself.

He said, "Will you tell Watson I shall be in a little late? I've had to stop at Watford on the way to see a vet. Buller's got an odd sort of rash. Tell Davis too." He considered for a moment whether it would be necessary for his alibi actually to visit the vet, but he decided that taking too much care could sometimes be as dangerous as taking too little—simplicity was always best, just as it paid to speak the truth whenever possible, for the truth is so much easier to memorize than a lie. He went into the third coffee bar on the list which he carried in his head and there he waited. He didn't recognize the tall lean man who followed him, in an overcoat which had seen better days. The man stopped at his table and said, "Excuse me, but aren't you William Hatchard?"

"No, my name's Castle."

"I'm sorry. An extraordinary likeness."

Castle drank two cups of coffee and read *The Times*. He valued the air of respectability that paper always seemed to lend the reader. He saw the man tying up his shoelace fifty yards down the road, and he experienced a similar sense of security to that which he had once felt while he was being carried from his ward in a hospital toward a major operation—he found himself again an object on a conveyor belt which moved him to a destined end with no responsibility, to anyone or anything, even to his own body. Everything would be looked after for better or worse by somebody else. Somebody with the highest professional qualifications. That was the way death ought to come in the end, he thought, as he moved slowly and happily in the wake of the stranger. He always hoped that he would move toward death with the same sense that before long he would be released from anxiety forever.

The road they were now in, he noticed, was called Elm View, although there were no elms anywhere in sight or any other trees, and the house to which he was guided was as anonymous and uninteresting as his own. There were even rather similar stained glass panels in the front door. Perhaps a dentist had once worked there too. The lean man ahead of him stopped for a moment by an iron gate to a front garden which was about the size of a billiard table, and then walked on. There were three bells by the door, but only one had an indicating card—very worn with illegible writing ending in the words "ition Limited." Castle rang the bell and saw that his guide had crossed Elm View and was walking back on the other side. When he was opposite the house he took a handkerchief from his sleeve and wiped his nose. It was probably an all-clear signal, for Castle almost immediately heard a creak-creak descending the stairs inside. He wondered whether "they" had taken their precautions in order to protect him from a possible follower or to protect themselves against his possible treachery—or both of course. He didn't care—he was on the conveyor belt.

The door opened on a familiar face he had not expected to see—eyes of a very startling blue over a wide welcoming grin, a small scar on the left cheek which he knew dated from a wound inflicted on a child in Warsaw when the city fell to Hitler.

"Boris," Castle exclaimed, "I thought I was never going to see *you* again."

"It's good to see you, Maurice."

Strange, he thought, that Sarah and Boris were the only people in the world who ever called him Maurice. To his mother he was simply "dear" in moments of affection, and at the office he lived among surnames or initials. Immediately he felt at home in this strange house which he had never visited before: a shabby house with worn carpeting on the stairs. For some reason he thought of his father. Perhaps when a child he had gone with him to see a patient in just such a house.

From the first landing he followed Boris into a small square room with a desk, two chairs and a large picture on rollers which showed a numerous family eating in a garden at a table laden with an unusual variety of food. All the courses seemed to be simultaneously displayed—an apple pie stood beside a joint of roast beef, and a salmon and a plate of apples beside a soup tureen. There was a jug of water and a bottle of wine and a coffeepot. Several dictionaries lay on a shelf and a pointer leaned against a blackboard on which was written a half-obliterated word in a language he couldn't identify.

"They decided to send me back after your last report," Boris said. "The one about Muller. I'm glad to be here. I like England so much better than France. How did you get on with Ivan?"

"All right. But it wasn't the same." He felt for a packet of cigarettes which was not there. "You know how Russians are. I had the impression that he didn't trust me. And he was always wanting more than I ever promised to do for any of you. He even wanted me to try to change my section."

"I think it's Marlboros you smoke?" Boris said, holding out a packet. Castle took one.

"Boris, did you know all the time you were here that Carson was dead?"

"No. I didn't know. Not until a few weeks ago. I don't even know the details yet."

"He died in prison. From pneumonia. Or so they say. Ivan must surely have known—but they let me learn it first from Cornelius Muller."

"Was it such a great shock? In the circumstances. Once arrested —there's never much hope."

"I know that, and yet I'd always believed that one day I would see him again—somewhere in safety far away from South Africa— perhaps in my home—and then I would be able to thank him for saving Sarah. Now he's dead and gone without a word of thanks from me."

"All you've done for us has been a kind of thanks. He will have understood that. You don't have to feel any regret."

"No? One can't reason away regret—it's a bit like falling in love, falling into regret."

He thought, with a sense of revulsion: The situation's impossible, there's no one in the world with whom I can talk of everything, except this man Boris whose real name even is unknown to me. He couldn't talk to Davis—half his life was hidden from Davis, nor to Sarah, who didn't even know that Boris existed. One day he had even told Boris about the night in the Hotel Polana when he learned the truth about Sam. A control was a bit like a priest must be to a Catholic—a man who received one's confession whatever it might be without emotion. He said, "When they changed my control and Ivan took over from you, I felt unbearably lonely. I could never speak about anything but business to Ivan."

"I'm sorry I had to go. I argued with them about it. I did my best to stay. But you know how it is in your own outfit. It's the same in ours. We live in boxes and it's they who choose the box." How often he had heard that comparison in his own office. Each side shares the same clichés.

Castle said, "It's time to change the book."

"Yes. Is that all? You gave an urgent signal on the phone. Is there more news of Porton?"

"No. I'm not sure I trust their story."

They were sitting on uncomfortable chairs on either side of the desk like a master and a pupil. Only the pupil in this case was so much older than the master. Well, it happened, Castle supposed, in the confessional too that an old man spoke his sins to a priest young enough to be his son. With Ivan at their rare meetings the dialogue had always been short, information was passed, questionnaires were received, everything was strictly to the point. With Boris he had been able to relax. "Was France promotion for you?" He took another cigarette.

"I don't know. One never does know, does one? Perhaps coming back here may be promotion. It may mean they took your last report very seriously, and thought I could deal with it better than Ivan. Or was Ivan compromised? You don't believe the Porton story, but have you really hard evidence that your people suspect a leak?"

"No. But in a game like ours one begins to trust one's instincts and they've certainly made a routine check on the whole section."

"You say yourself *routine*."

"Yes, it could be routine, some of it's quite open, but I believe it's a bit more than that. I think Davis's telephone is tapped and mine may be too, though I don't believe so. Anyway we'd better drop those call-signals to my house. You've read the report I made on Muller's visit and the Uncle Remus operation. I hope to God that's been channeled differently on your side if there *is* a leak. I have a feeling they might be passing me a marked note."

"You needn't be afraid. We've been most careful over that report. Though I don't think Muller's mission can be what you call a marked note. Porton perhaps, but not Muller. We've had confirmation of that from Washington. We take Uncle Remus very seriously, and we want you to concentrate on that. It could affect us in the Mediterranean, the Gulf, the Indian Ocean. Even the Pacific. In the long term . . ."

"There's no long term for me, Boris. I'm over retirement age as it is."

"I know."

"I want to retire now."

"We wouldn't like that. The next two years may be very important."

"For me too. I'd like to live them in my own way."

"Doing what?"

"Looking after Sarah and Sam. Going to the movies. Growing old in peace. It would be safer for you to drop me, Boris."

"Why?"

"Muller came and sat at my own table and ate our food and was polite to Sarah. Condescending. Pretending there was no color bar. How I dislike that man! And how I hate the whole bloody BOSS outfit. I hate the men who killed Carson and now call it pneumonia. I hate them for trying to shut Sarah up and let Sam be born in prison. You'd do much better to employ a man who doesn't hate, Boris. Hate's liable to make mistakes. It's as dangerous as love. I'm doubly dangerous, Boris, because I love too. Love's a fault in both our services."

He felt the enormous relief of speaking without prudence to someone who, he believed, understood him. The blue eyes seemed to offer complete friendship, the smile encouraged him to lay down for a short time the burden of secrecy. He said, "Uncle Remus is the last straw—that behind the scenes we should be joining with the States to help those apartheid bastards. Your worst crimes, Boris, are always in the past, and the future hasn't arrived yet. I can't go on parroting, 'Remember Prague! Remember Budapest!'—they were years ago. One has to be concerned about the present, and the present is Uncle Remus. I became a naturalized black when I fell in love with Sarah."

"Then why do you think you're dangerous?"

"Because for seven years I've kept my cool, and I'm losing it now. Cornelius Muller is making me lose it. Perhaps C sent him to me for that very reason. Perhaps C wants me to break out."

"We are only asking you to hold on a little longer. Of course the early years of this game are always the easiest, aren't they? The contradictions are not so obvious and the secrecy hasn't had time to build up like hysteria or a woman's menopause. Try not to worry so much, Maurice. Take your Valium and a Mogadon at night. Come and see me whenever you feel depressed and have to talk to someone. It's the lesser danger."

"I've done enough, haven't I, by now to pay my debt to Carson?"

"Yes, of course, but we can't lose you yet—because of Uncle Remus. As you put it, you're a naturalized black now."

Castle felt as though he were emerging from an anesthetic, an operation had been completed successfully. He said, "I'm sorry. I made a fool of myself." He couldn't remember exactly what he had said. "Give me a shot of whisky, Boris."

Boris opened the desk and took out a bottle and a glass. He said, "I know you like J & B." He poured out a generous measure and he watched the speed with which Castle drank. "You are taking a bit too much these days, aren't you, Maurice?"

"Yes. But no one knows that. Only at home. Sarah notices."

"How are things there?"

"Sarah's worried by the telephone rings. She always thinks of masked burglars. And Sam has bad dreams because soon he will be going to prep school—a white school. I'm worried about what will happen to both of them if something happens to me. Something always does happen in the end, doesn't it?"

"Leave all that to us. I promise you—we've got your escape route very carefully planned. If an emergency . . ."

"*My* escape route? What about Sarah's and Sam's?"

"They'll follow you. You can trust us, Maurice. We'll look after them. We know how to show our gratitude too. Remember Blake— we look after our own." Boris went to the window. "All's clear. You ought to be getting on to the office. My first pupil comes in a quarter of an hour."

"What language do you teach him?"

"English. You mustn't laugh at me."

"Your English is nearly perfect."

"My first pupil today is a Pole like myself. A refugee from *us*, not from the Germans. I like him—he's a ferocious enemy of Marx. You smile. That's better. You must never let things build up so far again."

"This security check. It's even getting Davis down—and he's innocent."

"Don't worry. I think I see a way of drawing their fire."

"I'll try not to worry."

"From now on we'll shift to the third drop, and if things get difficult signal me at once—I'm only here to help you. You do trust me?"

"Of course I trust you, Boris. I only wish your people really trusted *me*. This book code—it's a terribly slow and old-fashioned way of communicating, and you know how dangerous it is."

"It's not that we don't trust you. It's for your own safety. Your house might be searched any time as a routine check. At the beginning they wanted to give you a microdot outfit—I wouldn't let them. Does that satisfy your wish?"

"I have another."

"Tell me."

"I wish the impossible. I wish all the lies were unnecessary. And I wish we were on the same side."

"We?"

"You and I."

"Surely we are?"

"Yes, in this case . . . for the time being. You know Ivan tried to blackmail me once?"

"A stupid man. I suppose that's why I've been sent back."

"It has always been quite clear between you and me. I give you all the information you want in my section. I've never pretended that I share your faith—I'll never be a Communist."

"Of course. We've always understood your point of view. We need you for Africa only."

"But what I pass to you—I have to be the judge. I'll fight beside you in Africa, Boris—not in Europe."

"All we need from you is all the details you can get of Uncle Remus."

"Ivan wanted a lot. He threatened me."

"Ivan has gone. Forget him."

"You would do better without me."

"No. It would be Muller and his friends who would do better," Boris said.

Like a manic depressive Castle had had his outbreak, the recurrent boil had broken, and he felt a relief he never felt elsewhere.

2

It was the turn of the Travellers, and here, where he was on the Committee, Sir John Hargreaves felt quite at home, unlike at the Reform. The day was much colder than at their last lunch together and he saw no reason to go and talk in the park.

"Oh, I know what you are thinking, Emmanuel, but they all know you here only too well," he said to Doctor Percival. "They'll leave us quite alone with our coffee. They've learned by this time that you talk about nothing except fish. By the way, how was the smoked trout?"

"Rather dry," Doctor Percival said, "by Reform standards."

"And the roast beef?"

"Perhaps a little overdone?"

"You're an impossible man to please, Emmanuel. Have a cigar."

"If it's a real Havana."

"Of course."

"I wonder if you'll get them in Washington?"

"I doubt whether *détente* has got as far as cigars. Anyway, the question of laser beams will take priority. What a game it all is, Emmanuel. Sometimes I wish I was back in Africa."

"The old Africa."

"Yes. You are right. The old Africa."

"It's gone forever."

"I'm not so sure. Perhaps if we destroy the rest of the world, the roads will become overgrown and all the new luxury hotels will crumble, the forests will come back, the chiefs, the witch doctors—there's still a rain queen in the northeast Transvaal."

"Are you going to tell them that in Washington too?"

"No. But I shall talk without enthusiasm about Uncle Remus."

"You are against it?"

"The States, ourselves and South Africa—we are incompatible allies. But the plan will go ahead because the Pentagon want to play war games now that they haven't got a real war. Well, I'm leaving Castle behind to play it with their Mr. Muller. By the way, he's left for Bonn. I hope West Germany isn't in the game too."

"How long will you be away?"

"Not more than ten days, I hope. I don't like the Washington climate—in all senses of the word." With a smile of pleasure he tipped off a satisfactory length of ash. "Doctor Castro's cigars," he said, "are every bit as good as Sergeant Batista's."

"I wish you weren't going just at this moment, John, when we seem to have a fish on the line."

"I can trust you to land it without my help—anyway it may be only an old boot."

"I don't think it is. One gets to know the tug of an old boot."

"I leave it with confidence in your hands, Emmanuel. And in Daintry's too, of course."

"Suppose we don't agree?"

"Then it must be your decision. You are my deputy in this affair. But for God's sake, Emmanuel, don't do anything rash."

"I'm only rash when I'm in my Jaguar, John. When I'm fishing I have a great deal of patience."

Chapter VI

Castle's train was forty minutes late at Berkhamsted. There were repairs to the line somewhere beyond Tring, and when he arrived at the office his room seemed empty in an unaccustomed way. Davis wasn't there, but that hardly explained the sense of emptiness; Castle had often enough been alone in the room—with Davis at lunch, Davis in the lavatory, Davis off to the Zoo to see Cynthia. It was half an hour before he came on the note in his tray from Cynthia: "Arthur's not well. Colonel Daintry wants to see you." For a moment Castle wondered who the hell Arthur was; he was unused to thinking of Davis as anyone but Davis. Was Cynthia, he wondered, beginning to yield at last to the long siege? Was that why she now used his Christian name? He rang for her and asked, "What's wrong with Davis?"

"I don't know. One of the Environment men rang up for him. He said something about stomach cramps."

"A hangover?"

"He'd have rung up himself if it had been only that. I didn't know what I ought to do with you not in. So I rang Doctor Percival."

"What did he say?"

"The same as you—a hangover. Apparently they were together last night—drinking too much port and whisky. He's going to see him at lunchtime. He's busy till then."

"You don't think it's serious, do you?"

"I don't think it's serious but I don't think it's a hangover. If it was serious Doctor Percival would have gone at once, wouldn't he?"

"With C away in Washington I doubt if he's got much time for medicine," Castle said. "I'll go and see Daintry. Which room?"

He opened the door marked 72. Daintry was there and Doctor Percival—he had the sense of interrupting a dispute.

"Oh yes, Castle," Daintry said. "I did want to see you."

"I'll be pushing off," Doctor Percival said.

"We'll talk later, Percival. I don't agree with you. I'm sorry, but there it is. I can't agree."

"You remember what I said about boxes—and Ben Nicholson."

"I'm not a painter," Daintry said, "and I don't understand abstract art. Anyway, I'll be seeing you later."

Daintry was silent for quite a while after the shutting of the door. Then he said, "I don't like people jumping to conclusions. I've been brought up to believe in evidence—real evidence."

"Is something bothering you?"

"If it was a question of sickness, he'd take blood tests, X-rays . . . He wouldn't just *guess* a diagnosis."

"Doctor Percival?"

Daintry said, "I don't know how to begin. I'm not supposed to talk to you about this."

"About what?"

There was a photograph of a beautiful girl on Daintry's desk. Daintry's eyes kept returning to it. He said, "Don't you get damned lonely sometimes in this outfit?"

Castle hesitated. He said, "Oh well, I get on well with Davis. That makes a lot of difference."

"Davis? Yes. I wanted to talk to you about Davis."

Daintry rose and walked to the window. He gave the impression of a prisoner cooped up in a cell. He stared out morosely at the forbidding sky and was not reassured. He said, "It's a gray day. The autumn's really here at last."

" 'Change and decay in all around I see,' " Castle quoted.

"What's that?"

"A hymn I used to sing at school."

Daintry returned to his desk and faced the photograph again. "My daughter," he said, as though he felt the need of introducing the girl.

"Congratulations. She's a beautiful girl."

"She's getting married at the weekend, but I don't think I shall go."

"You don't like the man?"

"Oh, I dare say he's all right. I've never met him. But what would I talk to him about? Jameson's Baby Powder?"

"Baby powder?"

"Jameson's are trying to knock out Johnson's—or so she tells me." He sat down and lapsed into an unhappy silence.

Castle said, "Apparently Davis is ill. I was in late this morning. He's chosen a bad day. I've got the Zaire bag to deal with."

"I'm sorry. I'd better not keep you then. I didn't know that Davis was ill. It's nothing serious?"

"I don't think so. Doctor Percival is going to see him at lunch-time."

"Percival?" Daintry said. "Hasn't he a doctor of his own?"

"Well, if Doctor Percival sees him the cost is on the old firm, isn't it?"

"Yes. It's only that—working with us—he must get a bit out of date—medically, I mean."

"Oh well, it's probably a very simple diagnosis." He heard the echo of another conversation.

"Castle, all I wanted to see you about was—you *are* quite satisfied with Davis?"

"How do you mean 'satisfied'? We work well together."

"Sometimes I have to ask rather silly questions—oversimple ones —but then security's my job. They don't necessarily mean a great deal. Davis gambles, doesn't he?"

"A little. He likes to talk about horses. I doubt if he wins much, or loses much."

"And drinks?"

"I don't think he drinks more than I do."

"Then you *have* got complete confidence in him?"

"Complete. Of course we are all liable to make mistakes. Has there been a complaint of some kind? I wouldn't want to see Davis shifted unless it's to L.M."

"Forget I asked you," Daintry said. "I ask the same sort of thing about everyone. Even about you. Do you know a painter called Nicholson?"

"No. Is he one of us?"

"No, no. Sometimes," Daintry said, "I feel out of touch. I wonder if—but I suppose at night you always go home to your family?"

"Well, yes . . . I do."

"If, for some reason, you had to stay up in town one night . . . we might have dinner together."

"It doesn't often happen," Castle said.

"No, I suppose not."

"You see, my wife's nervous when she's left alone."

"Of course. I understand. It was only a passing idea." He was looking at the photograph again. "We used to have dinner together now and then. I hope to God she'll be happy. There's nothing one can ever do, is there?"

Silence fell like an old-fashioned smog, separating them from each other. Neither of them could see the pavement: they had to feel their way with a hand stretched out.

Castle said, "My son's not of marriageable age. I'm glad I don't have to worry about that."

"You come in on Saturday, don't you? I suppose you couldn't just stay up an hour or two longer . . . I won't know a soul at the wedding except my daughter—and her mother, of course. She said—my daughter, I mean—that I could bring someone from the office if I wanted to. For company."

Castle said, "Of course I'd be glad . . . if you really think . . ." He could seldom resist a call of distress however it was encoded.

2

For once Castle went without his lunch. He didn't suffer from hunger—he suffered only from a breach in his routine. He was uneasy. He wanted to see that Davis was all right.

As he was leaving the great anonymous building at one o'clock, after he had locked all his papers in the safe, even a humorless note from Watson, he saw Cynthia in the doorway. He told her, "I'm going to see how Davis is. Will you come?"

"No, why should I? I have a lot of shopping to do. Why are *you* going? It's nothing serious, is it?"

"No, but I thought I'd just look in. He's all alone in that flat except for those Environment types. And they never come home till evening."

"Doctor Percival promised to see him."

"Yes, I know, but he's probably gone by now. I thought perhaps you might like to come along with me . . . just to see . . ."

"Oh well, if we don't have to stay too long. We don't need to take flowers, do we? Like to a hospital." She was a harsh girl.

Davis opened the door to them wearing a dressing gown. Castle noticed how for a moment his face lit up at the sight of Cynthia, but then he realized that she had a companion.

He commented without enthusiasm, "Oh, *you* are here."

"What's wrong, Davis?"

"I don't know. Nothing much. The old liver's playing it up."

"I thought your friend said stomach cramps on the telephone," Cynthia said.

"Well, the liver's somewhere near the stomach, isn't it? Or is it the kidneys? I'm awfully vague about my own geography."

"I'll make your bed, Arthur," Cynthia said, "while you two talk."

"No, no, please no. It's only a bit rumpled. Sit down and make yourself comfortable. Have a drink."

"You and Castle can drink, but I'm going to make your bed."

"She has a very strong will," Davis said. "What'll you take, Castle? A whisky?"

"A small one, thank you."

Davis laid out two glasses.

"You'd better not have one if your liver's bad. What did Doctor Percival say exactly?"

"Oh, he tried to scare me. Doctors always do, don't they?"

"I don't mind drinking alone."

"He said if I didn't pull up a bit I was in danger of cirrhosis. I have to go and have an X-ray tomorrow. I told him that I don't drink more than anyone else, but he said some livers are weaker than others. Doctors always have the last word."

"I wouldn't drink that whisky if I were you."

"He said 'Cut down,' and I've cut this whisky down by half. And I've told him that I'd drop the port. So I will for a week or two. Anything to please. I'm glad you looked in, Castle. D'you know, Doctor Percival really did scare me a bit? I had the impression he wasn't telling me everything he knew. It would be awful, wouldn't it, if they had decided to send me to L.M. and then *he* wouldn't let me go. And there's another fear—have they spoken to you about me?"

"No. At least Daintry asked me this morning if I was satisfied with you, and I said I was—completely."

"You're a good friend, Castle."

"It's only that stupid security check. You remember the day you met Cynthia at the Zoo . . . I told them you were at the dentist, but all the same . . ."

"Yes. I'm the sort of man who's always found out. And yet I nearly always obey the rules. It's my form of loyalty, I suppose. You aren't the same. If I take out a report once to read at lunch, I'm spotted. But I've seen you take them out time after time. You take risks—like they say priests have to do. If I really leaked something—without meaning to, of course—I'd come to you for confession."

"Expecting absolution?"

"No. But expecting a bit of justice."

"Then you'd be wrong, Davis. I haven't the faintest idea what the word 'justice' means."

"So you'd condemn me to be shot at dawn?"

"Oh no. I would always absolve the people I liked."

"Why, then it's you who are the real security risk," Davis said. "How long do you suppose this damned check is going on?"

"I suppose till they find their leak or decide there was no leak after all. Perhaps some man in MI5 has misread the evidence."

"Or some woman, Castle. Why not a woman? It could be one of our secretaries, if it's not me or you or Watson. The thought gives me the creeps. Cynthia promised to dine with me the other night. I was waiting for her at Stone's, and there at the table next door was a pretty girl waiting for someone too. We half smiled at each other because we had both been stood up. Companions in distress. I'd have spoken to her—after all, Cynthia had let me down—and then the thought came—perhaps she's been planted to catch me, perhaps they heard me reserve the table on the office phone. Perhaps Cynthia kept away under orders. And then who should come in and join the girl—guess who—Daintry."

"It was probably his daughter."

"They use daughters in our outfit, don't they? What a damn silly profession ours is. You can't trust anyone. Now I even distrust Cynthia. She's making my bed, and God knows what she hopes to find in it. But all she'll get are yesterday's breadcrumbs. Perhaps they'll analyze those. A crumb could contain a microdot."

"I can't stay much longer. The Zaire bag is in."

Davis laid down his glass. "I'm damned if whisky tastes the same, since Percival put ideas in my head. Do *you* think I've got cirrhosis?"

"No. Just go easy for a while."

"Easier said than done. When I'm bored, I drink. You're lucky to have Sarah. How's Sam?"

"He asks after you a lot. He says nobody plays hide-and-seek like you do."

"A friendly little bastard. I wish I could have a little bastard too —but only with Cynthia. What a hope!"

"The climate of Lourenço Marques isn't very good . . ."

"Oh, people say that it's OK for children up to six."

"Well, perhaps Cynthia's weakening. After all, she *is* making your bed."

"Yes, she'd mother me, I daresay, but she's one of those girls who are looking all the time for someone to admire. She'd like someone serious—like you. The trouble is that when I'm serious I can't *act* serious. Acting serious embarrasses me. Can you picture anyone ever admiring me?"

"Well, Sam does."

"I doubt if Cynthia enjoys hide-and-seek."

Cynthia came back. She said, "Your bed was in an unholy mess. When was it made last?"

"Our daily comes in on Mondays and Fridays and today is Thursday."

"Why don't you make it yourself?"

"Well, I do sort of pull it up around me when I get in."

"Those Environment types? What do they do?"

"Oh, they're trained not to notice pollution until it's brought officially to their notice."

Davis saw the two of them to the door. Cynthia said, "See you tomorrow," and went down the stairs. She called over her shoulder that she had a lot of shopping to do.

> "'She should never have looked at me
> If she meant I should not love her,'"

Davis quoted. Castle was surprised. He would not have imagined Davis reading Browning—except at school, of course.

"Well," he said, "back to the bag."

"I'm sorry, Castle. I know how that bag irritates you. I'm not malingering, really I'm not. And it's not a hangover. It's my legs, my arms—they feel like jelly."

"Go back to bed."

"I think I will. Sam wouldn't find me any good now at hide-and-seek," Davis added, leaning over the banisters, watching Castle go. As Castle reached the top of the stairs he called out, "Castle!"

"Yes?" Castle looked up.

"You don't think, do you, this might stop me?"

"Stop you?"

"I'd be a different man if I could get to Lourenço Marques."

"I've done my best. I spoke to C."

"You're a good chap, Castle. Thank you, whatever happens."

"Go back to bed and rest."

"I think I will." But he continued to stand there looking down while Castle turned away.

Chapter VII

Castle and Daintry arrived last at the registry office and took seats in the back row of the grim brown room. They were divided by four rows of empty chairs from the other guests of whom there were about a dozen, separated into rival clans as in a church marriage, each clan regarding the other with critical interest and some disdain. Only champagne might possibly lead to a truce later between them.

"I suppose that's Colin," Colonel Daintry said, indicating a young man who had just joined his daughter in front of the registrar's table. He added, "I don't even know his surname."

"Who's the woman with the handkerchief? She seems upset about something."

"That's my wife," Colonel Daintry said. "I hope we can slip away before she notices."

"You can't do that. Your daughter won't even know you've come."

The registrar began to speak. Someone said "Shhh," as though they were in a theater and the curtain had risen.

"Your son-in-law's name is Clutters," Castle whispered.

"Are you sure?"

"No, but it sounded like that."

The registrar gave the kind of brief Godless good wishes which are sometimes described as a lay sermon and a few people left, looking at watches as an excuse. "Don't you think we could go too?" Daintry asked.

"No."

All the same no one seemed to notice them as they stood in Victoria Street. The taxis came winging in like birds of prey and Daintry made one more effort to escape.

"It's not fair to your daughter," Castle argued.

"I don't even know where they're all going," Daintry said. "To a hotel, I suppose."

"We can follow."

And follow they did—all the way to Harrods and beyond through a thin autumnal mist.

"I can't think what hotel . . ." Daintry said. "I believe we've lost them." He leaned forward to examine the car ahead. "No such luck. I can see the back of my wife's head."

"It's not much to go by."

"All the same I'm pretty sure of it. We were married for fifteen years." He added gloomily, "And we haven't spoken for seven."

"Champagne will help," Castle said.

"But I don't like champagne. It's awfully good of you, Castle, to come with me. I couldn't have faced this alone."

"We'll just have one glass and go away."

"I can't imagine where we are heading. I haven't been down this way for years. There seem to be so many new hotels."

They proceeded in fits and starts down the Brompton Road.

"One generally goes to the bride's home," Castle said, "if it's not to a hotel."

"She hasn't got a home. Officially she shares a flat with some girlfriend, but apparently she's been living quite a while with this chap Clutters. Clutters! What a name!"

"The name may not have been Clutters. The registrar was very indistinct."

The taxis began to deliver the other guests like gift-wrapped parcels at a small too-pretty house in a crescent. It was lucky there were not many of them—the houses here had not been built for large parties. Even with two dozen people one felt the walls might bend or the floors give way.

"I think I know where we are—my wife's flat," Daintry said. "I heard she'd bought something in Kensington."

They edged their way up the overloaded stairs into a drawing room. From every table, from the bookshelves, the piano, from the mantel, china owls gazed at the guests, alert, predatory, with cruel curved beaks. "Yes, it *is* her flat," Daintry said. "She always had a passion for owls—but the passion's grown since my day."

They couldn't see his daughter in the crowd which clustered before the buffet. Champagne bottles popped intermittently. There was a wedding cake, and a plaster owl was even balanced on the top of the pink sugar scaffolding. A tall man with a moustache trimmed exactly like Daintry's came up to them and said, "I don't know who you are, but do help yourselves to the champers." Judging by the slang he must have dated back nearly to the First World

War. He had the absent-minded air of a rather ancient host. "We've saved on waiters," he explained.

"I'm Daintry."

"Daintry?"

"This is my daughter's marriage," Daintry said in a voice as dry as a biscuit.

"Oh, then you must be Sylvia's husband?"

"Yes. I didn't catch *your* name."

The man went away calling, "Sylvia! Sylvia!"

"Let's get out," Daintry said in desperation.

"You must say hello to your daughter."

A woman burst her way through the guests at the buffet. Castle recognized the woman who had wept at the registrar's, but she didn't look at all like weeping now. She said, "Darling, Edward told me you were here. How nice of you to come. I know how desperately busy you always are."

"Yes, we really have to be going. This is Mr. Castle. From the office."

"That damned office. How do you do, Mr. Castle? I must find Elizabeth—and Colin."

"Don't disturb them. We really have to be going."

"I'm only up for the day myself. From Brighton. Edward drove me up."

"Who's Edward?"

"He's been awfully helpful. Ordering the champagne and things. A woman needs a man on these occasions. You haven't changed a bit, darling. How long is it?"

"Six—seven years?"

"How time flies."

"You've collected a lot more owls."

"Owls?" She went away calling, "Colin, Elizabeth, come over here." They came hand in hand. Daintry didn't associate his daughter with childlike tenderness, but she probably thought hand-holding a duty at a wedding.

Elizabeth said, "How sweet of you to make it, Father. I know how you hate this sort of thing."

"I've never experienced it before." He looked at her companion, who wore a carnation and a very new pin-stripe suit. His hair was jet black and well combed around the ears.

"How do you do, sir. Elizabeth has spoken such a lot about you."

"I can't say the same," Daintry said. "So you are Colin Clutters?"

"Not Clutters, Father. Whatever made you think that? His name's Clough. I mean *our* name's Clough."

A surge of latecomers who had not been at the registry office had separated Castle from Colonel Daintry. A man in a double-breasted waistcoat told him, "I don't know a soul here—except Colin, of course."

There was a smash of breaking china. Mrs. Daintry's voice rose above the clamor. "For Christ's sake, Edward, is it one of the owls?"

"No, no, don't worry, dear. Only an ashtray."

"Not a soul," repeated the man with the waistcoat. "My name's Joiner, by the way."

"Mine's Castle."

"You know Colin?"

"No, I came with Colonel Daintry."

"Who's he?"

"The bride's father."

Somewhere a telephone began to ring. No one paid any attention.

"You ought to have a word with young Colin. He's a bright lad."

"He's got a strange surname, hasn't he?"

"Strange?"

"Well . . . Clutters . . ."

"His name's Clough."

"Oh, then I heard it wrong."

Again something broke. Edward's voice rose reassuringly above the din. "Don't worry, Sylvia. Nothing serious. All the owls are safe."

"He's quite revolutionized our publicity."

"You work together?"

"You might say I *am* Jameson's Baby Powder."

The man called Edward grasped Castle's arm. He said, "Is your name Castle?"

"Yes."

"Somebody wants you on the telephone."

"But no one knows I'm here."

"It's a girl. She's a bit upset. Said it was urgent."

Castle's thoughts went to Sarah. She knew that he was attending this wedding, but not even Daintry knew where they were going to end up. Was Sam ill again? He asked, "Where's the telephone?"

"Follow me," but when they reached it—a white telephone beside a white double bed, guarded by a white owl—the receiver had been put back. "Sorry," Edward said, "I expect she'll ring again."

"Did she give a name?"

"Couldn't hear it with all this noise going on. Had an impression that she'd been crying. Come and have some more champers."

"If you don't mind, I'll stay here near the phone."

"Well, excuse me if I don't stay here with you. I have to look after all these owls, you see. Sylvia would be heartbroken if one of them got damaged. I suggested we tidy them away, but she's got more than a hundred of them. The place would have looked a bit bare without them. Are you a friend of Colonel Daintry?"

"We work in the same office."

"One of those hush-hush jobs, isn't it? A bit embarrassing for me meeting him like this. Sylvia didn't think he'd come. Perhaps I ought to have stayed away myself. Tactful. But then who would have looked after the owls?"

Castle sat down on the edge of the great white bed, and the white owl glared at him beside the white telephone as if it recognized him as an illegal immigrant who had just perched on the edge of this strange continent of snow—even the walls were white and there was a white rug under his feet. He was afraid—afraid for Sam, afraid for Sarah, afraid for himself—fear poured like an invisible gas from the mouth of the silent telephone. He and all he loved were menaced by the mysterious call. The clamor of voices from the living room seemed now no more than a rumor of distant tribes beyond the desert of snow. Then the telephone rang. He pushed the white owl to one side and lifted the receiver.

To his relief he heard Cynthia's voice. "Is that M.C.?"

"Yes, how did you know where to find me?"

"I tried the registry office, but you'd left. So I found a Mrs. Daintry in the telephone book."

"What's the matter, Cynthia? You sound odd."

"M.C., an awful thing has happened. Arthur's dead."

Again, as once before, he wondered for a moment who Arthur was.

"Davis? Dead? But he was coming back to the office next week."

"I know. The daily found him when she went to—to make his bed." Her voice broke.

"I'll come back to the office, Cynthia. Have you seen Doctor Percival?"

"He rang me up to tell me."

"I must go and tell Colonel Daintry."

"Oh, M.C., I wish I'd been nicer to him. All I ever did for him

was—was to make his bed." He could hear her catch her breath, trying not to sob.

"I'll be back as soon as I can." He rang off.

The living room was as crowded as ever and just as noisy. The
cake had been cut and people were looking for unobtrusive places
to hide their portions. Daintry stood alone with a slice in his fingers
behind a table littered with owls. He said, "For God's sake, let's be
off, Castle. I don't understand this sort of thing."

"Daintry, I've had a call from the office. Davis is dead."

"Davis?"

"He's dead. Doctor Percival . . ."

"Percival!" Daintry exclaimed. "My God, that man . . ." He
pushed his slice of cake among the owls and a big gray owl toppled
off and smashed on the floor.

"Edward," a woman's voice shrieked, "John's broken the gray
owl."

Edward thrust his way toward them. "I can't be everywhere at
once, Sylvia."

Mrs. Daintry appeared behind him. She said, "John, you damned
old boring fool. I'll never forgive you for this—never. What the hell
are you doing anyway in *my* house?"

Daintry said, "Come away, Castle. I'll buy you another owl,
Sylvia."

"It's irreplaceable, that one."

"A man's dead," Daintry said. "He's irreplaceable too."

2

"I had not expected this to happen," Doctor Percival told them.

To Castle it seemed an oddly indifferent phrase for him to use, a
phrase as cold as the poor body which lay in crumpled pajamas
stretched out upon the bed, the jacket wide open and the bare
chest exposed, where no doubt they had long since listened and
searched in vain for the least sound of a heartbeat. Doctor Percival
had struck him hitherto as a very genial man, but the geniality was
chilled in the presence of the dead, and there was an incongruous
note of embarrassed apology in the strange phrase he had uttered.

The sudden change had come as a shock to Castle, when he
found himself standing in this neglected room, after all the voices
of strangers, the flocks of china owls and the explosion of corks at
Mrs. Daintry's. Doctor Percival had fallen silent again after that
one unfortunate phrase and nobody else spoke. He stood back from
the bed rather as though he were exhibiting a picture to a couple of

unkind critics, and was waiting in apprehension for their judgement. Daintry was silent too. He seemed content to watch Doctor Percival as if it were up to him to explain away some obvious fault which he was expected to find in the painting.

Castle felt an urge to break the long silence.

"Who are those men in the sitting room? What are they doing?"

Doctor Percival turned with reluctance away from the bed. "What men? Oh, those. I asked the Special Branch to take a look around."

"Why? Do you think he was killed?"

"No, no. Of course not. Nothing of that kind. His liver was in a shocking state. He had an X-ray a few days ago."

"Then why did you say you didn't expect . . . ?"

"I didn't expect things to go so rapidly."

"I suppose there'll be a postmortem?"

"Of course. Of course."

The "of courses" multiplied like flies round the body.

Castle went back into the sitting room. There was a bottle of whisky and a used glass and a copy of *Playboy* on the coffee table.

"I told him he had to stop drinking," Doctor Percival called after Castle. "He wouldn't pay attention."

There were two men in the room. One of them picked up *Playboy* and ruffled and shook the pages. The other was going through the drawers of the bureau. He told his companion, "Here's his address book. You'd better go through the names. Check the telephone numbers in case they don't correspond."

"I still don't understand what they are after," Castle said.

"Just a security check," Doctor Percival explained. "I tried to get hold of you, Daintry, because it's really your pigeon, but apparently you were away at some wedding or other."

"Yes."

"There seems to have been some carelessness recently at the office. C's away but he would have wanted us to be sure that the poor chap hadn't left anything lying about."

"Like telephone numbers attached to the wrong names?" Castle asked. "I wouldn't call that exactly carelessness."

"These chaps always follow a certain routine. Isn't that so, Daintry?"

But Daintry didn't reply. He stood in the doorway of the bedroom looking at the body.

One of the men said, "Take a squint at this, Taylor." He handed the other a sheet of paper. The other read aloud, "Bonne chance, Kalamazoo, Widow Twanky."

"Bit odd, isn't it?"

Taylor said, "Bonne chance is French, Piper. Kalamazoo sounds like a town in Africa."

"Africa, eh? Might be important."

Castle said, "Better look in the *Evening News*. You'll probably find that they are three horses. He always bet on the tote at the weekend."

"Ah," Piper said. He sounded a little discouraged.

"I think we ought to leave our friends of the Special Branch to do their job in peace," Doctor Percival said.

"What about Davis's family?" Castle asked.

"The office has been seeing to that. The only next of kin seems to be a cousin in Droitwich. A dentist."

Piper said, "Here's something that looks a bit off-color to me, sir." He held out a book to Doctor Percival, and Castle intercepted it. It was a small selection of Robert Browning's poems. Inside was a book plate with a coat of arms and the name of a school, the Droitwich Royal Grammar School. Apparently the prize had been awarded in 1910 to a pupil called William Davis for English Composition and William Davis had written in black ink in a small finicky hand, "Passed on to my son Arthur from his father on his passing First in Physics, June 29, 1953." Browning and physics and a boy of sixteen certainly seemed a bit strange in conjunction, but presumably it was not this that Piper meant by "off-color."

"What is it?" Doctor Percival asked.

"Browning's poems. I don't see anything off-color about them."

All the same he had to admit that the little book didn't go with Aldermaston and the tote and *Playboy*, the dreary office routine and the Zaire bag; does one always discover clues to the complexity even of the most simple life if one rummages enough after death? Of course, Davis might have kept the book from filial piety, but it was obvious that he had read it. Hadn't he quoted Browning the last time Castle saw him alive?

"If you look, sir, there are passages marked," Piper said to Doctor Percival. "You know more about book codes than I do. I thought I ought to draw attention."

"What do you think, Castle?"

"Yes, there *are* marks." He turned the pages. "The book belonged to his father and of course they might be his father's marks—except that the ink looks too fresh: he puts a 'c' against them."

"Significant?"

Castle had never taken Davis seriously, not his drinking, not his gambling, not even his hopeless love for Cynthia, but a dead body could not be so easily ignored. For the first time he felt real curiosity about Davis. Death had made Davis important. Death gave Davis a kind of stature. The dead are perhaps wiser than we are. He turned the pages of the little book like a member of the Browning Society keen on interpreting a text.

Daintry dragged himself away from the bedroom door. He said, "There isn't anything, is there . . . in those marks?"

"Anything what?"

"Significant." He repeated Percival's question.

"Significant? I suppose there might be. Of a whole state of mind."

"What do you mean?" Percival asked. "Do you really think . . . ?" He sounded hopeful, as if he positively wished that the man who was dead next door might have represented a security risk and, well, in a way he had, Castle thought. Love and hate are both dangerous, as he had warned Boris. A scene came to his mind: a bedroom in Lourenço Marques, the hum of an air conditioner, and Sarah's voice on the telephone, "Here I am," and then the sudden sense of great joy. His love of Sarah had led him to Carson, and Carson finally to Boris. A man in love walks through the world like an anarchist, carrying a time bomb.

"You really mean there is some evidence . . . ?" Doctor Percival went on. "You've been trained in codes. I haven't."

"Listen to this passage. It's marked with a vertical line and the letter 'c.'

> *Yet I will but say what mere friends say,*
>   *Or only a thought stronger:*
> *I will hold your hand but as long as all may . . .'*"

"Have you any idea what 'c' stands for?" Percival asked—and again there was that note of hope which Castle found irritating. "It could mean, couldn't it, 'code,' to remind him that he had already used that particular passage? In a book code I suppose one must be careful not to use the same passage twice."

"True enough. Here's another marked passage.

'Worth how well, those dark gray eyes,
  That hair so dark and dear, how worth,
  That a man should strive and agonize,
    And taste a veriest hell on earth . . .'"

"It sounds to me like poetry, sir," Piper said.

"Again a vertical line and a 'c,' Doctor Percival."

"You really think then . . . ?"

"Davis said to me once, 'I can't be serious when I'm serious.' So I suppose he had to go to Browning for words."

"And 'c'?"

"It only stands for a girl's name, Doctor Percival. Cynthia. His secretary. A girl he was in love with. One of us. Not a case for the Special Branch."

Daintry had been a brooding restless presence, silent, locked in thoughts of his own. He said now with a sharp note of accusation, "There should be a postmortem."

"Of course," Doctor Percival said, "if his doctor wants it. I'm not his doctor. I'm only his colleague—though he did consult me, and we have the X-rays."

"His doctor should be here now."

"I'll have him called as soon as these men have finished their work. You of all people, Colonel Daintry, will appreciate the importance of that. Security is the first consideration."

"I wonder what a postmortem will show, Doctor Percival."

"I think I can tell you that—his liver is almost totally destroyed."

"Destroyed?"

"By drink, of course, Colonel. What else? Didn't you hear me tell Castle?"

Castle left them to their subterranean duel. It was time to have a last look at Davis before the pathologist got to work on him. He was glad that the face showed no indication of pain. He drew the pajamas together across the hollow chest. A button was missing. Sewing on buttons was not part of a daily woman's job. The telephone beside the bed gave a small preliminary tinkle which came to nothing. Perhaps somewhere far away a microphone and a recorder were being detached from the line. Davis would no longer be under surveillance. He had escaped.

Chapter VIII

1

Castle sat over what he meant to be his final report. Davis being dead the information from the African section must obviously cease. If the leaks continued there could be no doubt whose was the responsibility, but if the leaks stopped the guilt would be attributed with certainty to the dead man. Davis was beyond suffering; his personal file would be closed and sent to some central store of records, where no one would bother to examine it. What if it contained a story of treachery? Like a Cabinet secret it would be well guarded for thirty years. In a sad way it had been a providential death.

Castle could hear Sarah reading aloud to Sam before packing him off for the night. It was half an hour after his usual bedtime, but tonight he had needed that extra childish comfort for the first week of school had passed unhappily.

What a long slow business it was transcribing a report into book code. He would never now get to an end of *War and Peace*. The next day he would burn his copy for security in a bonfire of autumn leaves without waiting for the Trollope to arrive. He felt relief and regret—relief because he had repaid as far as he could his debt of gratitude to Carson, and regret that he would never be able to close the dossier on Uncle Remus and complete his revenge on Cornelius Muller.

When he had finished his report he went downstairs to wait for Sarah. Tomorrow was Sunday. He would have to leave the report in the drop, that third drop which would never be used again; he had signaled its presence there from a call box in Piccadilly Circus before he caught his train at Euston. It was an inordinately slow business, this way of making his last communication, but a quicker and more dangerous route had been reserved for use only in a final emergency. He poured himself a triple J & B and the murmur of voices upstairs began to give him a temporary sense of peace. A door was closed softly, footsteps passed along the corridor above;

the stairs always creaked on the way down—he thought how to some people this would seem a dull and domestic, even an intolerable routine. To him it represented a security he had been afraid every hour he might lose. He knew exactly what Sarah would say when she came into the sitting room, and he knew what he would answer. Familiarity was a protection against the darkness of King's Road outside and the lighted lamp of the police station at the corner. He had always pictured a uniformed policeman, whom he would probably know well by sight, accompanying the man from the Special Branch when the hour struck.

"You've taken your whisky?"

"Can I give *you* one?"

"A small one, darling."

"Sam all right?"

"He was asleep before I tucked him in."

As in an unmutilated cable, there was not one numeral wrongly transcribed.

He handed her the glass: he hadn't been able to speak until now of what had happened.

"How was the wedding, darling?"

"Pretty awful. I was sorry for poor Daintry."

"Why poor?"

"He was losing a daughter and I doubt if he has got any friends."

"There seem to be such a lot of lonely people in your office."

"Yes. All those that don't pair off for company. Drink up, Sarah."

"What's the hurry?"

"I want to get both of us another glass."

"Why?"

"I've got bad news, Sarah. I couldn't tell you in front of Sam. It's about Davis. Davis is dead."

"Dead? *Davis?*"

"Yes."

"How?"

"Doctor Percival talks of his liver."

"But a liver doesn't go like that—from one day to another."

"It's what Doctor Percival says."

"You don't believe him?"

"No. Not altogether. I don't think Daintry does either."

She gave herself two fingers of whisky—he had never seen her do that before. "Poor, poor Davis."

"Daintry wants an independent postmortem. Percival was quite ready for that. He's obviously quite sure his diagnosis will be confirmed."

"If he's sure, then it must be true?"

"I don't know. I really don't know. They can arrange so many things in our firm. Perhaps even a postmortem."

"What are we going to tell Sam?"

"The truth. It's no good keeping deaths from a child. They happen all the time."

"But he loved Davis so much. Darling, let me say nothing for a week or two. Until he finds his feet at school."

"You know best."

"I wish to God you could get away from all those people."

"I shall—in a few years."

"I mean now. This minute. We'd take Sam out of bed and go abroad. The first plane to anywhere."

"Wait till I've got my pension."

"I could work, Maurice. We could go to France. It would be easier there. They're used to my color."

"It isn't possible, Sarah. Not yet."

"Why? Give me one good reason . . ."

He tried to speak lightly. "Well, you know a man has to give proper notice."

"Do *they* bother about things like notice?"

He was scared by the quickness of her perception when she said, "Did they give Davis notice?"

He said, "If it was his liver . . ."

"You don't believe that, do you? Don't forget that I worked for you once—for them. I was your agent. Don't think I haven't noticed the last month how anxious you've been—even about the meter man. There's been a leak, is that it? In your section?"

"I think they think so."

"And they pinned it on Davis. Do you believe Davis was guilty?"

"It may not have been a deliberate leak. He was very careless."

"You think they may have killed him because he was careless."

"I suppose that in our outfit there's such a thing as criminal carelessness."

"It might have been you they suspected, not Davis. And then you'd have died. From too much J & B."

"Oh, I've always been very careful," and he added as a sad joke, "except when I fell in love with you."

"Where are you going?"

"I want a breath of air and so does Buller."

2

On the other side of the long ride through the Common known for some reason as Cold Harbour the beech woods began, sloping down toward the Ashridge road. Castle sat on a bank while Buller rummaged among last year's leaves. He knew he had no business to linger there. Curiosity was no excuse. He should have made his drop and gone. A car came slowly up the road from the direction of Berkhamsted and Castle looked at his watch. It was four hours since he had made his signal from the call box in Piccadilly Circus. He could just make out the number plate of the car, but as he might have expected it was just as strange to him as the car, a small red Toyota. Near the lodge at the entrance to Ashridge Park, the car stopped. No other car was in sight and no pedestrian. The driver turned off his lights, and then as though he had second thoughts turned them on again. A noise behind Castle made his heart leap, but it was only Buller bumbling through the bracken.

Castle climbed away through the tall olive-skinned trees which had turned black against the last light. It was over fifty years since he had discovered the hollow in one trunk . . . four, five, six trees back from the road. In those days he had been forced to stretch almost his full height to reach the hole, but his heart had knocked in the same erratic fashion as it did now. At ten years old he was leaving a message for someone he loved: the girl was only seven. He had shown her the hiding place when they were together on a picnic, and he had told her he would leave something important there for her the next time he came.

On the first occasion he left a large peppermint humbug wrapped in greaseproof paper, and when he revisited the hole it had gone. Then he left a note which declared his love—in capital letters because she had only just begun to read—but when he came back the third time he found the note was still there but disfigured by a vulgar drawing. Some stranger, he thought, must have discovered the hiding place; he wouldn't believe that she was responsible until she put her tongue out at him, as she went by on the other side of the High Street, and he realized she was disappointed because she had not found another humbug. It had been his first experience of sexual suffering, and he never returned to the tree until almost fifty years later he was asked by a man in the lounge of the Regent Palace, whom he never saw again, to suggest another safe drop.

He put Buller on his lead and watched from his hiding place in the bracken. The man from the car had to use a torch to find the hole. Castle saw his lower half outlined for a moment as the torch descended the trunk: a plump belly, an open fly. A clever precaution—he had even stored up a reasonable amount of urine. When the torch turned and lit the way back toward the Ashridge road, Castle started home. He told himself, "This is the last report," and his thoughts went back to the child of seven. She had seemed lonely at the picnic, where they had first met, she was shy and she was ugly, and perhaps he was drawn to her for those reasons.

Why are some of us, he wondered, unable to love success or power or great beauty? Because we feel unworthy of them, because we feel more at home with failure? He didn't believe that was the reason. Perhaps one wanted the right balance, just as Christ had, that legendary figure whom he would have liked to believe in. "Come unto me all ye that travail and are heavy laden." Young as the girl was at that August picnic she was heavily laden with her timidity and shame. Perhaps he had merely wanted her to feel that she was loved by someone and so he began to love her himself. It wasn't pity, any more than it had been pity when he fell in love with Sarah pregnant by another man. He was there to right the balance. That was all.

"You've been out a long time," Sarah said.

"Well, I needed a walk badly. How's Sam?"

"Fast asleep, of course. Shall I give you another whisky?"

"Yes. A small one again."

"A small one? Why?"

"I don't know. Just to show I can slow up a bit perhaps. Perhaps because I'm feeling happier. Don't ask me why, Sarah. Happiness goes when you speak of it."

The excuse seemed good enough to both of them. Sarah, during their last year in South Africa, had learned not to probe too far, but in bed that night he lay awake a long time, repeating to himself over and over again the final words of the last report which he had concocted with the aid of *War and Peace*. He had opened the book at random several times, seeking a *sortes Virgilianae*, before he chose the sentences on which his code was to be based. "You say: I am not free. But I have lifted my hand and let it fall." It was as if, in choosing that passage, he were transmitting a signal of defiance to both the services. The last word of the message, when it was decoded by Boris or another, would read "goodbye."

Part Four

Chapter I

The nights after Davis died were full of dreams for Castle, dreams formed out of broken fragments of a past which pursued him till the daylight hours. Davis played no part in them—perhaps because the thought of him, in their now reduced and saddened sub-section, filled many waking hours. The ghost of Davis hovered over the bag from Zaire and the telegrams which Cynthia encoded were now more mutilated than ever.

So at night Castle dreamt of a South Africa reconstructed with hatred, though sometimes the bits and pieces were jumbled up with an Africa which he had forgotten how much he loved. In one dream he came on Sarah suddenly in a litter-strewn Johannesburg park sitting on a bench for blacks only: he turned away to find a different bench. Carson separated from him at a lavatory door and chose the door reserved for blacks, leaving him on the outside ashamed of his lack of courage, but then quite another sort of dream came to him on the third night.

When he woke he said to Sarah, "It's funny. I dreamt of Rougemont. I haven't thought of him for years."

"Rougemont?"

"I forgot. You never knew Rougemont."

"Who was he?"

"A farmer in the Free State. I liked him in a way as much as I liked Carson."

"Was he a Communist? Surely not if he was a farmer."

"No. He was one of those who will have to die when your people take control."

"My people?"

"I meant of course 'our people,'" he said with sad haste as though he had been in danger of breaking a promise.

Rougemont lived on the edge of a semi-desert not far from an old battlefield of the Boer War. His ancestors, who were Huguenot, had fled from France at the time of the persecution, but he spoke no French, only Afrikaans and English. He had been, before he was born, assimilated to the Dutch way of life—but not to apartheid. He stood aside from it—he wouldn't vote Nationalist, he despised the United Party, and some undetermined sense of loyalty to his ancestors kept him from voting for the small band of progressives. It was not a heroic attitude, but perhaps in his eyes, as in his grandfather's, heroism began where politics stopped. He treated his laborers with kindness and understanding, with no condescension. Castle listened to him one day as he debated with his black foreman on the state of the crops—they argued with each other as equals. The family of Rougemont and the tribe of the foreman had arrived in South Africa at much the same time. Rougemont's grandfather had not been an ostrich millionaire from the Cape, like Cornelius Muller's: when he was sixty years old grandfather Rougemont had ridden with De Wet's commando against the English invaders and he had been wounded there on the local *kopje*, which leaned with the winter clouds over the farm, where the Bushmen hundreds of years earlier had carved the rocks with animal forms.

"Fancy climbing up that under fire with a pack on your back," Rougemont had remarked to Castle. He admired the British troops for their courage and endurance far from home rather as though they were legendary marauders in a history book, like the Vikings who had once descended on the Saxon coast. He had no resentment against those of the Vikings who remained, only perhaps a certain pity for a people without roots in this old tired beautiful land where his family had settled three hundred years ago. He had said to Castle one day over a glass of whisky, "You say you are writing a study of apartheid, but you'll never understand our complexities. I hate apartheid as much as you do, but you are much more a stranger to me than any of my laborers. We belong here—you are as much an outsider as the tourists who come and go." Castle felt sure that, when the time for decision came, he would take the gun on his living-room wall in defense of this difficult area of cultivation on the edge of a desert. He would not die fighting for apartheid or for the white race, but for so many *morgen* which he called his own, subject to drought and floods and earthquakes and cattle disease, and snakes which he regarded as a minor pest like mosquitoes.

"Was Rougemont one of your agents?" Sarah asked.

"No, but oddly enough it was through him that I met Carson." He might have added, "And through Carson I have joined Rougemont's enemies." Rougemont had hired Carson to defend one of his laborers accused by the local police of a crime of violence of which he was innocent.

Sarah said, "I sometimes wish I was still your agent. You tell me so much less than you did then."

"I never told you much—perhaps you thought I did, but I told you as little as I could, for your own safety, and then it was often lies. Like the book I intended to write on apartheid."

"I thought things would be different," Sarah said, "in England. I thought there would be no more secrets." She drew in her breath and was again immediately asleep, but Castle lay awake a long time. He had at such moments an enormous temptation to trust her, to tell her everything, much as a man who has had a passing affair with a woman, an affair which is finished, wants suddenly to trust his wife with the whole sad history—to explain once and for all the unexplained silences, the small deceptions, the worries they haven't been able to share, and in the same way as that other man he came to the conclusion, "Why worry her when it's all over?" for he really believed, if only for a while, that it was over.

2

It seemed very strange to Castle to be sitting in the same room he had occupied for so many years alone with Davis and to see, facing him across the table, the man called Cornelius Muller—a Muller curiously transformed, a Muller who said to him, "I was so sorry to hear the news when I got back from Bonn . . . I hadn't met your colleague, of course . . . but to you it must have been a great shock . . ." a Muller who began to resemble an ordinary human being, not an officer of BOSS but a man whom he might have met by chance in the train on the way to Euston. He was struck by the note of sympathy in the tone of Muller's voice—it sounded oddly sincere. In England, he thought, we have become increasingly cynical about all deaths which do not concern us closely, and even in those cases it is polite to fit on quickly a mask of indifference in the presence of a stranger; death and business don't go together. But in the Dutch Reformed Church to which Muller belonged, a death, Castle remembered, was still the most important event in family life. Castle had attended a funeral once in the Transvaal, and it was not the sorrow which he recalled but the dignity, even the protocol, of the occasion. Death remained socially important to Muller, even though he was an officer of BOSS.

"Well," Castle said, "it was certainly unexpected." He added, "I've asked my secretary to bring me in the Zaire and Mozambique files. For Malawi we have to depend on MI5, and I can't show you their material without permission."

"I'll be seeing them when I've finished with you," Muller said. He added, "I enjoyed so much the evening I spent at your house. Meeting your wife . . ." He hesitated a little before he continued, "and your son."

Castle hoped that these opening remarks were only a polite preparation before Muller took up again his enquiries about the route Sarah had taken into Swaziland. An enemy had to remain a caricature if he was to be kept at a safe distance: an enemy should never come alive. The generals were right—no Christmas cheer ought to be exchanged between the trenches.

He said, "Of course Sarah and I were very happy to see you." He rang his bell. "I'm sorry. They're taking the hell of a long time over those files. Davis's death has a bit upset our routine."

A girl he didn't know answered the bell. "I telephoned five minutes ago for the files," he said. "Where's Cynthia?"

"She isn't in."

"Why isn't she in?"

The girl looked at him with stone-cold eyes. "She's taken the day off."

"Is she sick?"

"Not exactly."

"Who are you?"

"Penelope."

"Well, will you tell me, Penelope, what exactly you mean by not exactly?"

"She's upset. It's natural, isn't it? Today's the funeral. Arthur's funeral."

"Today? I'm sorry. I forgot." He added, "All the same, Penelope, I would like you to get us the files."

When she had left the room he said to Muller, "I'm sorry for all this confusion. It must give you a strange impression of the way we do things. I really had forgotten—they're burying Davis today—they're having a funeral service at eleven. It's been delayed because of the postmortem. The girl remembered. I forgot."

"I'm sorry," Muller said, "I would have changed our date if I'd known."

"It's not your fault. The fact is—I have an official diary and a private diary. Here I have you marked, you see, for 10 Thursday. The private diary I keep at home, and I must have written the funeral down in that one. I'm always forgetting to compare the two."

"All the same . . . forgetting the funeral . . . isn't that a bit odd?"

"Yes, Freud would say I wanted to forget."

"Just fix another date for me and I'll be off. Tomorrow or the next day?"

"No, no. Which is more important anyway? Uncle Remus or listening to prayers being said over poor Davis? Where was Carson buried by the way?"

"At his home. A small town near Kimberley. I suppose you'll be surprised when I tell you that I was there?"

"No, I imagine you had to watch and observe who the mourners were."

"Someone—you're right—someone had to watch. But I chose to go."

"Not Captain Van Donck?"

"No. He would have been easily recognized."

"I can't think what they are doing with those files."

"This man Davis—perhaps he didn't mean very much to you?" Muller asked.

"Well, not as much as Carson. Whom you people killed. But my son was fond of him."

"Carson died of pneumonia."

"Yes. Of course. So you told me. I had forgotten that too."

When the files at last came Castle went through them, seeking to answer Muller's questions, but with only half of his mind. "We have no reliable information about that yet," he found himself saying for the third time. Of course it was a deliberate lie—he was protecting a source from Muller—for they were approaching dangerous ground, working together up to that point of non-cooperation which was still undetermined by either of them.

He asked Muller, "Is Uncle Remus really practicable? I can't believe the Americans will ever get involved again—I mean with troops in a strange continent. They are just as ignorant of Africa as they were of Asia—except, of course, through novelists like Hemingway. He would go off on a month's safari arranged by a travel agency and write about white hunters and shooting lions—the poor half-starved brutes reserved for tourists."

"The ideal that Uncle Remus has in mind," Muller said, "is to make the use of troops almost unnecessary. At any rate in great numbers. A few technicians, of course, but they're already with us. America maintains a guided missile tracking station and a space tracking station in the Republic, and they have over-flying rights to support those stations—you certainly know all that. No one has protested, no one has marched. There have been no student riots in Berkeley, no questions in Congress. Our internal security so far has proved excellent. You see, our race laws have in a way been justified: they prove an excellent cover. We don't have to charge anyone with espionage—that would only draw attention. Your friend Carson was dangerous—but he'd have been more dangerous still if we had had to try him for espionage. A lot is going on now at the tracking stations—that's why we want a close cooperation with your people. You can pinpoint any danger and we can deal with it quietly. In some ways you're much better placed than we are to penetrate the liberal elements, or even the black nationalists. Take an example. I'm grateful for what you've given me on Mark Ngambo—of course we knew it already. But now we can be satisfied that we've missed nothing important. There's no danger from that particular angle—for the time anyway. The next five years, you see, are of vital importance—I mean for our survival."

"But I wonder, Muller—can you survive? You've got a long open frontier—too long for minefields."

"Of the old-fashioned kind, yes," Muller said. "It's as well for us that the hydrogen bomb made the atom bomb just a tactical weapon. Tactical is a reassuring word. No one will start a nuclear war because a tactical weapon has been used in almost desert country very far away."

"How about the radiation?"

"We are lucky in our prevailing winds and our deserts. Besides, the tactical bomb is reasonably clean. Cleaner than the bomb at Hiroshima and we know how limited the effect of that was. In the areas which may for a few years be radioactive there are few white Africans. We plan to canalize any invasions there are."

"I begin to see the picture," Castle said. He remembered Sam, as he remembered him when he looked at the newspaper photograph of the drought—the spread-eagled body and the vulture, but the vulture would be dead too of radiation.

"That's what I came here to show you—the general picture—we needn't go into all the details—so that you can properly evaluate any information you obtain. The tracking stations are at this moment the sensitive point."

"Like the race laws they can cover a multitude of sins?"

"Exactly. You and I needn't go on playing with each other. I know you've been instructed to keep certain things from me, and I quite understand. I've received just the same orders as you have.

The only important thing is—we should both look at identically the same picture; we shall be fighting on the same side, so we've got to see the same picture."

"In fact we're in the same box?" Castle said, making his private joke against them all, against BOSS, against his own service, even against Boris.

"Box? Yes, I suppose you could put it that way." He looked at his watch. "Didn't you say the funeral was at eleven? It's ten to eleven now. You'd better be off."

"The funeral can go on without me. If there's an after-life Davis will understand, and if there isn't . . ."

"I'm quite sure there is an after-life," Cornelius Muller said.

"You are? Doesn't the idea frighten you a bit?"

"Why should it? I've always tried to do my duty."

"But those little tactical atomic weapons of yours. Think of all the blacks who will die before you do and be there waiting for you."

"Terrorists," Muller said. "I don't expect to meet them again."

"I didn't mean the guerrillas. I mean all the families in the infected area. Children, girls, the old grannies."

"I expect they'll have their own kind of heaven," Muller said.

"Apartheid in heaven?"

"Oh, I know you are laughing at me. But I don't suppose they'd enjoy our sort of heaven, do you? Anyway I leave all that to the theologians. You didn't exactly spare the children in Hamburg, did you?"

"Thank God, I didn't participate as I'm doing now."

"I think if you aren't going to the funeral, Castle, we should get on with our business."

"I'm sorry. I agree." Indeed he was sorry; he was even afraid, as he had been in the office of BOSS that morning in Pretoria. For seven years he had trodden with unremitting care through the minefields, and now with Cornelius Muller he had taken his first wrong step. Was it possible that he had fallen into a trap set by someone who understood his temperament?

"Of course," Muller said, "I know that you English like arguing for the sake of arguing. Why, even your C pulled my leg about apartheid, but when it comes to Uncle Remus . . . well, you and I have to be serious."

"Yes, we'd better get back to Uncle Remus."

"I have permission to tell you—in broad lines, of course—how things went with me in Bonn."

"You had difficulties?"

"Not serious ones. The Germans—unlike other ex-colonial powers —have a lot of secret sympathy for us. You could say that it goes back as far as the Kaiser's telegram to President Kruger. They are worried about South-West Africa; they would rather see us control South-West Africa than a vacuum there. After all they ruled the South-West more brutally than we have ever done, and the West needs our uranium."

"You brought back an agreement?"

"One shouldn't talk of an agreement. We are no longer in the days of secret treaties. I only had contact with my opposite number, not with the Foreign Secretary or the Chancellor. Just the same way as your C has been talking with the CIA in Washington. What I hope is that we've all three reached a clearer understanding."

"A secret understanding instead of a secret treaty?"

"Exactly."

"And the French?"

"No trouble there. If we are Calvinist they're Cartesian. Descartes didn't worry about the religious persecution of his time. The French have a great influence on Senegal, the Ivory Coast, they even have a fair understanding with Mobutu in Kinshasa. Cuba won't seriously interfere in Africa again (America has seen to that), and Angola won't be a danger for a good many years. No one is apocalyptic today. Even a Russian wants to die in his bed, not in a bunker. At the worst, with the use of a few atomic bombs—small tactical ones, of course—we shall gain five years of peace if we are attacked."

"And afterward?"

"That's the real point of our understanding with Germany. We need a technical revolution and the latest mining machines, although we've gone further than anyone realizes on our own. In five years we can more than halve the labor force in the mines: we can more than double wages for skilled men and we can begin to produce what they have in America, a black middle class."

"And the unemployed?"

"They can go back to their homelands. That is what the homelands were for. I'm an optimist, Castle."

"And apartheid stays?"

"There'll always be a certain apartheid as there is here—between the rich and the poor."

Cornelius Muller took off his gold-rimmed glasses and polished the gold till it gleamed. He said, "I hope your wife liked her shawl.

You know you will always be welcome to come back now that we realize your true position. With your family too, of course. You may be sure they will be treated as honorary whites."

Castle wanted to reply, "But I am an honorary black," but this time he showed a little prudence. "Thank you."

Muller opened his briefcase and took out a sheet of paper. He said, "I have made a few notes for you on my meetings in Bonn." He produced a ball-point pen—gold again. "You might have some useful information on these points when we next meet. Would Monday suit you? The same time?" He added, "Please destroy that when you've read it. BOSS wouldn't like it to go on even your most secret file."

"Of course. As you wish."

When Muller had gone he put the paper in his pocket.

Chapter II

There were very few people at St. George's in Hanover Square when Doctor Percival arrived with Sir John Hargreaves, who had only returned from Washington the night before.

A man with a black band around his arm stood alone by the aisle in the front row; presumably, Doctor Percival thought, he was the dentist from Droitwich. He refused to make way for anyone—it was as though he were safeguarding his right to the whole front row as the nearest living relative. Doctor Percival and C took their seats near the back of the church. Davis's secretary, Cynthia, was two rows behind them. Colonel Daintry sat beside Watson on the other side of the aisle, and there were a number of faces only half known to Doctor Percival. He had glimpsed them once perhaps in a corridor or at a conference with MI5, perhaps there were even intruders —a funeral attracts strangers like a wedding. Two tousled men in the last row were almost certainly Davis's fellow lodgers from the Department of the Environment. Someone began to play softly on the organ.

Doctor Percival whispered to Hargreaves, "Did you have a good flight?"

"Three hours late at Heathrow," Hargreaves said. "The food was uneatable." He sighed—perhaps he was remembering with regret his wife's steak-and-kidney pie, or the smoked trout at his club. The organ breathed a last note and fell silent. A few people knelt and a few stood up. There was a lack of certainty about what to do next.

The Vicar, who was probably known to nobody there, not even to the dead man in the coffin, intoned "Take Thy plague away from me; I am even consumed by means of Thy heavy hand."

"What plague was it that killed Davis, Emmanuel?"

"Don't worry, John. The postmortem was all in order."

The service seemed to Doctor Percival, who had not attended a funeral for many years, full of irrelevant information. The Vicar had begun reading the lesson from the First Epistle to the Corinthians: "All flesh is not the same flesh: but there is one kind of flesh of men, another flesh of beasts, another of fishes, and another of birds." The statement was undeniably true, Doctor Percival thought. The coffin did not contain a fish; he would have been more interested in it if it had—an enormous trout perhaps. He took a quick look round. There was a tear caged behind the girl's lashes. Colonel Daintry had an angry or perhaps a sullen expression which might bode ill. Watson too was obviously worried about something —probably he was wondering whom to promote in Davis's place. "I want to have a word with you after the service," Hargreaves said, and that might be tiresome too.

"Behold I show you a mystery," the Vicar read. The mystery of whether I killed the right man? Doctor Percival wondered, but that will never be solved unless the leaks continue—that would certainly suggest he had made an unfortunate mistake. C would be very upset and so would Daintry. It was a pity one couldn't throw a man back into the river of life as one could throw a fish. The Vicar's voice, which had risen to greet a familiar passage of English literature, "O Death, where is thy sting?" as a bad actor playing Hamlet picks out from its context the famous soliloquy, fell to a drone again for the dull and academic conclusion, "The sting of death is sin, and the strength of sin is the law." It sounded like a proposition of Euclid.

"What did you say?" C whispered.

"Q.E.D.," Doctor Percival replied.

2

"What exactly did you mean by Q.E.D.?" Sir John Hargreaves asked when they managed to get outside.

"It seemed a more suitable response to what the Vicar was saying than Amen."

They walked after that in a near silence toward the Travellers Club. By a mute consent the Travellers seemed a spot more suited for lunch that day than the Reform—Davis had become an honorary traveller by this voyage of his into unexplored regions and he certainly had lost his claim to one man one vote.

"I don't remember when I last attended a funeral," Doctor Percival said. "An old great-aunt, I think, more than fifteen years ago. A rather stiff ceremony, isn't it?"

"I used to enjoy funerals in Africa. Lots of music—even if the only instruments were pots and pans and empty sardine tins. They made one think that death after all might be a lot of fun. Who was the girl I saw crying?"

"Davis's secretary. Her name is Cynthia. Apparently he was in love with her."

"A lot of that goes on, I imagine. It's inevitable in an outfit like ours. Daintry checked on her thoroughly, I suppose?"

"Oh yes, yes. In fact—quite unconsciously—she gave us some useful information—you remember that business at the Zoo."

"The Zoo?"

"When Davis . . ."

"Oh yes, I remember now."

As usual at the weekend, the club was almost empty. They would have begun lunch—it was an almost automatic reflex—with smoked trout, but it was not available. Doctor Percival reluctantly accepted as a substitute smoked salmon. He said, "I wish I had known Davis better. I think I might have come to like him quite a lot."

"And yet you still believe he was the leak?"

"He played the role of a rather simple man very cleverly. I admire cleverness—and courage too. He must have needed a lot of courage."

"In a wrong cause."

"John, John! You and I are not really in a position to talk about cause. We aren't Crusaders—we are in the wrong century. Saladin was long ago driven out of Jerusalem. Not that Jerusalem has gained much by that."

"All the same, Emmanuel . . . I can't admire treachery."

"Thirty years ago when I was a student I rather fancied myself as a kind of Communist. Now . . . ? Who is the traitor—me or Davis? I really believed in internationalism, and now I'm fighting an underground war for nationalism."

"You've grown up, Emmanuel, that's all. What do you want to drink—claret or burgundy?"

"Claret, if it's all the same to you."

Sir John Hargreaves crouched in his chair and buried himself deep in the wine list. He looked unhappy—perhaps only because he couldn't make up his mind between St. Emilion and Médoc. At last he made his decision and his order. "I sometimes wonder why you are with us, Emmanuel."

"You've just said it, I grew up. I don't think Communism will work—in the long run—any better than Christianity has done, and I'm not the Crusader type. Capitalism or Communism? Perhaps God is a Capitalist. I want to be on the side most likely to win during my lifetime. Don't look shocked, John. You think I'm a cynic, but I just don't want to waste a lot of time. The side that wins will be able to build the better hospitals, and give more to cancer research—when all this atomic nonsense is abandoned. In the meanwhile I enjoy the game we're all playing. Enjoy. Only enjoy. I don't pretend to be an enthusiast for God or Marx. Beware of people who believe. They aren't reliable players. All the same one grows to like a good player on the other side of the board—it increases the fun."

"Even if he's a traitor?"

"Oh, traitor—that's an old-fashioned word, John. The player is as important as the game. I wouldn't enjoy the game with a bad player across the table."

"And yet . . . you did kill Davis? Or didn't you?"

"He died of his liver, John. Read the postmortem."

"A happy coincidence?"

"The marked card—you suggested it—turned up, you see—the oldest trick of all. Only he and I knew of my little fantasy about Porton."

"You should have waited till I came home. Did you discuss it with Daintry?"

"You had left me in charge, John. When you feel the fish on the line you don't stand waiting on the bank for someone else to advise you what to do."

"This Château Talbot—does it seem to you quite up to the mark?"

"It's excellent."

"I think they must have ruined my palate in Washington. All those dry martinis." He tried his wine again. "Or else it's your fault. Does nothing ever worry you, Emmanuel?"

"Well, yes, I am a little worried about the funeral service—you noticed they even had an organ—and then there's the interment. All that must cost a lot, and I don't suppose Davis left many pennies behind. Do you suppose that poor devil of a dentist has paid for it all—or did our friends from the East? That doesn't seem quite proper to me."

"Don't worry about that, Emmanuel. The office will pay. We don't have to account for secret funds." Hargreaves pushed his glass on one side. He said, "This Talbot doesn't taste to me like '71."

"I was taken aback myself, John, by Davis's quick reaction. I'd calculated his weight exactly and I gave him what I thought would be less than lethal. You see, aflatoxin had never been tested before on a human being, and I wanted to be sure in case of a sudden emergency that we gave the right dose. Perhaps his liver was in a bad way already."

"How did you give it to him?"

"I dropped in for a drink and he gave me some hideous whisky which he called a White Walker. The flavor was quite enough to drown the aflatoxin."

"I can only pray you got the right fish," Sir John Hargreaves said.

3

Daintry turned gloomily into St. James's Street, and as he passed White's on the way to his flat a voice hailed him from the steps. He looked up from the gutter in which his thoughts had lain. He recognized the face, but he couldn't for the moment put a name to it, nor even remember in what circumstances he had seen it before. Boffin occurred to him. Buffer?

"Got any Maltesers, old man?"

Then the scene of their encounter came back to him with a sense of embarrassment.

"What about a spot of lunch, Colonel?"

Buffy was the absurd name. Of course, the fellow must certainly possess another, but Daintry had never learned it. He said, "I'm sorry. I've got lunch waiting for me at home." This was not exactly a lie. He had put out a tin of sardines before he went to Hanover Square, and there remained some bread and cheese from yesterday's lunch.

"Come and have a drink then. Meals at home can always wait," Buffy said, and Daintry could think of no excuse not to join him.

As it was still early only two people were in the bar. They seemed to know Buffy a thought too well, for they greeted him without enthusiasm. Buffy didn't seem to mind. He waved his hand in a wide gesture that included the barman. "This is the Colonel." Both of them grunted at Daintry with weary politeness. "Never caught your name," Buffy said, "at that shoot."

"I never caught yours."

"We met," Buffy explained, "at Hargreaves's place. The Colonel is one of the hush-hush boys. James Bond and all that."

One of the two said, "I never could read those books by Ian."

"Too sexy for me," the other one said. "Exaggerated. I like a good screw as much as the next man, but it's not all that important, is it? Not the way you do it, I mean."

"What'll you have?" Buffy asked.

"A dry martini," Colonel Daintry said, and, remembering his meeting with Doctor Percival, he added, "very dry."

"One large very dry, Joe, and one large pink. Really large, old chap. Don't be stingy."

A deep silence fell over the little bar as though each one was thinking of something different—of a novel by Ian Fleming, of a shooting party, or a funeral. Buffy said, "The Colonel and I have a taste in common—Maltesers."

One of the men emerged from his private thoughts and said, "Maltesers? I prefer Smarties."

"What the hell are Smarties, Dicky?"

"Little chocolate things all different colors. They taste much the same, but, I don't know why, I prefer the red and yellow ones. I don't like the mauve."

Buffy said, "I saw you coming down the street, Colonel. You seemed to be having quite a talk with yourself, if you don't mind my saying so. State secrets? Where were you off to?"

"Only home," Daintry said. "I live near here."

"You looked properly browned off. I said to myself, the country must be in serious trouble. The hush-hush boys know more than we do."

"I've come from a funeral."

"No one close, I hope?"

"No. Someone from the office."

"Oh well, a funeral's always better to my mind than a wedding. I can't bear weddings. A funeral's final. A wedding—well, it's only an unfortunate stage to something else. I'd rather celebrate a divorce— but then that's often a stage too, to just another wedding. People get into the habit."

"Come off it, Buffy," said Dicky, the man who liked Smarties, "you thought of it once yourself. We know all about that marriage bureau of yours. You were damned lucky to escape. Joe, give the Colonel another martini."

Daintry, with a feeling of being lost among strangers, drank the first down. He said, like a man picking a sentence from a phrase book in a language he doesn't know, "I was at a wedding too. Not long ago."

"Hush-hush again? I mean, one of your lot?"

"No. It was my daughter. She got married."

"Good God," Buffy said, "I never thought you were one of those —I mean one of those married fellows."

"It doesn't necessarily follow," Dicky said.

The third man, who had hardly spoken up till then, said, "You needn't be so damned superior, Buffy. I was one of those too once. Though it seems the hell of a long time ago. As a matter of fact it was my wife who introduced Dicky to Smarties. You remember that afternoon, Dicky? We'd had a pretty gloomy lunch, because we sort of knew we were breaking up the old home. Then she said, 'Smarties,' just like that, 'Smarties' . . . I don't know why. I suppose she thought we had to talk about something. She was a great one for appearances."

"I can't say I do remember, Willie. Smarties seem to me to date back a long time in my life. Thought I'd discovered them for myself. Give the Colonel another dry, Joe."

"No, if you don't mind . . . I've really got to get home."

"It's my turn," the man called Dicky said. "Top up his glass, Joe. He's come from a funeral. He needs cheering up."

"I got used to funerals very early," Daintry said to his own surprise after he had taken a swig of the third dry martini. He realized he was talking more freely than he usually did with strangers and most of the world to him were strangers. He would have liked to pay for a round himself, but of course it was their club. He felt very friendly toward them, but he remained—he was sure of it—in their eyes a stranger still. He wanted to interest them, but so many subjects were barred to him.

"Why? Were there a lot of deaths in your family?" Dicky asked with alcoholic curiosity.

"No, it wasn't exactly that," Daintry said, his shyness drowning in the third martini. For some reason he remembered a country railway station where he had arrived with his platoon more than thirty years ago—the signs naming the place had all been removed after Dunkirk against a possible German invasion. It was as though once again he were delivering himself of a heavy pack, which he let drop resoundingly on the floor of White's. "You see," he said, "my father was a clergyman, so I went to a lot of funerals when I was a child."

"I would never have guessed it," Buffy said. "Thought you'd come from a military family—son of a general, the old regiment, and all that cock. Joe, my glass is crying to be refilled. But, of course, when you come to think of it, your father being a clergyman does explain quite a lot."

"What does it explain?" Dicky asked. For some reason he seemed to be annoyed and in the mood to question everything. "The Maltesers?"

"No, no, the Maltesers are a different story. I can't tell you about them now. It would take too long. What I meant was the Colonel belongs to the hush-hush boys, and so in a way does a clergyman, when you come to think of it . . . You know, the secrets of the confessional and all that, they are in the hush-hush business too."

"My father wasn't a Roman Catholic. He wasn't even High Church. He was a naval chaplain. In the first war."

"The first war," said the morose man called Willie who had once been married, "was the one between Cain and Abel." He made his statement flatly as though he wanted to close an unnecessary conversation.

"Willie's father was a clergyman too," Buffy explained. "A big shot. A bishop against a naval chaplain. Trumps."

"My father was in the Battle of Jutland," Daintry told them. He didn't mean to challenge anyone, to set up Jutland against a bishopric. It was just another memory which had returned.

"As a non-combatant, though. That hardly counts, does it?" Buffy said. "Not against Cain and Abel."

"You don't look all that old," Dicky said. He spoke with an air of suspicion, sucking at his glass.

"My father wasn't married then. He married my mother after the war. In the twenties." Daintry realized the conversation was becoming absurd. The gin was acting like a truth drug. He knew he was talking too much.

"He married your mother?" Dicky asked sharply like an interrogator.

"Of course he married her. In the twenties."

"She's still alive?"

"They've both been dead a long time. I really must be getting home. My meal will be spoiled," Daintry added, thinking of the sardines drying on a plate. The sense of being among friendly strangers left him. The conversation threatened to turn ugly.

"And what has all this to do with a funeral? What funeral?"

"Don't mind Dicky," Buffy said. "He likes interrogating. He was in MI5 during the war. More gins, Joe. He's already told us, Dicky. It was some poor bugger in the office."

"Did you see him properly into the ground?"

"No, no. I just went to the service. In Hanover Square."

"That would be St. George's," said the son of the bishop. He held his glass out to Joe as though it were a communion cup.

It took quite a time for Daintry to detach himself from the bar at White's. Buffy even conducted him as far as the steps. A taxi passed. "You see what I mean," Buffy said. "Buses in St. James's. No one was safe." Daintry had no idea what he meant. As he walked down the street toward the palace he was aware that he had drunk more than he had drunk for years at this hour of the day. They were nice fellows, but one had to be careful. He had spoken far too much. About his father, his mother. He walked past Lock's hat shop; past Overton's Restaurant; he halted on the pavement at the corner of Pall Mall. He had overshot the mark—he realized that in time. He turned on his heel and retraced his steps to the door of the flat where his lunch awaited him.

The cheese was there all right and the bread, and the tin of sardines which after all he had not yet decanted. He was not very clever with his fingers, and the small leaf of the tin broke before the tin was a third open. All the same he managed to fork out half the sardines in bits and pieces. He wasn't hungry—that was enough. He hesitated whether he should drink any more after the dry martinis and then chose a bottle of Tuborg.

His lunch lasted for less than four minutes, but it seemed to him quite a long time because of his thoughts. His thoughts wobbled like a drunken man's. He thought first of Doctor Percival and Sir John Hargreaves going off together down the street in front of him when the service was over, their heads bent like conspirators. He thought next of Davis. It wasn't that he had any personal liking for Davis, but his death worried him. He said aloud to the only witness, which happened to be a sardine tail balanced on his fork, "A jury would never convict on that evidence." Convict? He hadn't any proof that Davis had not died, as the postmortem showed, a natural death—cirrhosis was what one called a natural death. He tried to remember what Doctor Percival had said to him on the night of the shoot. He had drunk too much that night, as he had done this morning, because he was ill at ease with people whom he didn't understand, and Percival had come uninvited to his room and talked about an artist called Nicholson.

Daintry didn't touch the cheese; he carried it back with the oily plate to the kitchen—or kitchenette as it would be called nowadays —there was only room for one person at a time. He remembered the vast spaces of the basement kitchen in that obscure rectory in Suffolk where his father had been washed up after the Battle of Jutland, and he remembered Buffy's careless words about the confessional. His father had never approved of confession nor of the confessional box set up by a High Church celibate in the next parish. Confessions came to him, if they came at all, secondhand, for people did confess sometimes to his mother, who was much loved in the village, and he had heard her filter these confessions to his father, with any grossness, malice or cruelty removed. "I think you ought to know what Mrs. Baines told me yesterday."

Daintry spoke aloud—the habit was certainly growing on him—to the kitchen sink, "There was *no* real evidence against Davis." He felt guilty of failure—a man in late middle age near to retirement—retirement from what? He would exchange one loneliness for another. He wanted to be back in the Suffolk rectory. He wanted to walk up the long weedy path lined with laurels that never flowered and enter the front door. Even the hall was larger than his whole flat. A number of hats hung from a stand on the left and on the right a brass shell-case held the umbrellas. He crossed the hall and, very softly opening the door in front of him, he surprised his parents where they sat on the chintz sofa hand in hand because they thought they were alone. "Shall I resign," he asked them, "or wait for retirement?" He knew quite well that the answer would be "No" from both of them—from his father because the captain of his cruiser had shared in his eyes something of the divine right of kings —his son couldn't possibly know better than his commanding officer the right action to take—and from his mother—well, she would always tell a girl in the village who was in trouble with her employer, "Don't be hasty. It's not so easy to find another situation." His father, the ex-naval chaplain, who believed in his captain and his God, would have given him what he considered to be the Christian reply, and his mother would have given him the practical and worldly answer. What greater chance had he to find another job if he resigned now than a daily maid would have in the small village where they had lived?

Colonel Daintry went back into his sitting room, forgetting the oily fork he carried. For the first time in some years he possessed his daughter's telephone number—she had sent it to him after her marriage on a printed card. It was the only link he had with her day-to-day life. Perhaps it would be possible, he thought, to invite himself to dinner. He wouldn't actually suggest it, but if she made an offer . . .

He didn't recognize the voice which answered. He said, "Is that 6731075?"

"Yes. Who do you want?" It was a man speaking—a stranger.

He lost his nerve and his memory for names. He replied, "Mrs. Clutter."

"You've got the wrong number."

"I'm sorry." He rang off. Of course he should have said, "I meant Mrs. Clough," but it was too late now. The stranger, he supposed, was his son-in-law.

4

"You didn't mind," Sarah asked, "that I couldn't go?"

"No. Of course not. I couldn't go myself—I had a date with Muller."

"I was afraid of not being back here before Sam returned from school. He'd have asked me where I'd been."

"All the same, he has to know sometime."

"Yes, but there's still a lot of time. Were there many people there?"

"Not many, so Cynthia said. Watson, of course, as the head of the section. Doctor Percival. C. It was decent of C to go. It wasn't as though Davis was anyone important in the firm. And there was his cousin—Cynthia thought it was his cousin, because he wore a black band."

"What happened after the service?"

"I don't know."

"I meant—to the body."

"Oh, I think they took it out to Golders Green to be burned. That was up to the family."

"The cousin?"

"Yes."

"We used to have better funerals in Africa," said Sarah.

"Oh well . . . other countries, other manners."

"Yours is supposed to be an older civilization."

"Yes, but old civilizations are not always famous for feeling deeply about death. We are no worse than the Romans."

Castle finished his whisky. He said, "I'll go up and read to Sam for five minutes—otherwise he may think something's wrong."

"Swear that you won't say anything to him," Sarah said.

"Don't you trust me?"

"Of course I trust you, but . . ." The "but" pursued him up the stairs. He had lived a long time with "buts"—we trust you, but . . . Daintry looking in his briefcase, the stranger at Watford, whose duty it was to make sure he had come alone to the rendezvous with Boris. Even Boris. He thought: Is it possible that one day life will be as simple as childhood, that I shall have finished with buts, that I will be trusted naturally by everyone, as Sarah trusts me—and Sam?

Sam was waiting for him, his face black against the clean pillow-case. The sheets must have been changed that day, which made the contrast stronger like an advertisement for Black and White whisky. "How are things?" he asked because he could think of nothing else to say, but Sam didn't reply—he had his secrets too.

"How did school go?"

"It was all right."

"What lessons today?"

"Arithmetic."

"How did that go?"

"All right."

"What else?"

"English compo—"

"Composition. How was that?"

"All right."

Castle knew that the time had almost come when he would lose the child forever. Each "all right" fell on the ear like the sound of distant explosions that were destroying the bridges between them. If he asked Sam, "Don't you trust me?" perhaps he would answer, "Yes, but . . ."

"Shall I read to you?"

"Yes, please."

"What would you like?"

"That book about a garden."

Castle for a moment was at a loss. He looked along the single shelf of battered volumes which were held in place by two china dogs that bore a likeness to Buller. Some of the books belonged to his own nursery days: the others had nearly all been chosen by himself, for Sarah had come late to books and her books were all adult ones. He took down a volume of verse which was one he had guarded from his childhood. There was no tie of blood between Sam and himself, no guarantee that they would have any taste in common, but he always hoped—even a book could be a bridge. He opened the book at random, or so he believed, but a book is like a sandy path which keeps the indent of footsteps. He had read in this one to Sam several times during the last two years, but the foot-prints of his own childhood had dug deeper and the book opened on a poem he had never read aloud before. After a line or two he realized that he knew it almost by heart. There are verses in child-hood, he thought, which shape one's life more than any of the scrip-tures.

> "*Over the borders a sin without pardon,*
>   *Breaking the branches and crawling below,*
>   *Out through the breach in the wall of the garden,*
>   *Down by the banks of the river, we go.*"

"What are borders?"

"It's where one country ends and another begins." It seemed, as soon as he spoke, a difficult definition, but Sam accepted it.

"What's a sin without pardon? Are they spies?"

"No, no, not spies. The boy in the story has been told not to go out of the garden, and . . ."

"Who told him?"

"His father, I suppose, or his mother."

"And that's a sin?"

"This was written a long time ago. People were more strict then, and anyway it's not meant seriously."

"I thought murder was a sin."

"Yes, well, murder's wrong."

"Like going out of the garden?"

Castle began to regret he had chanced on that poem, that he had trodden in that one particular footprint of his own long walk. "Don't you want me to go on reading?" He skimmed through the lines ahead—they seemed innocuous enough.

"Not that one. I don't understand that one."

"Well, which one then?"

"There's one about a man . . ."

"The lamplighter?"

"No, it's not that one."

"What does the man do?"

"I don't know. He's in the dark."

"That's not much to go by." Castle turned back the pages, looking for a man in the dark.

"He's riding a horse."

"Is it this one?"

Castle read,

> "*Whenever the moon and stars are set,*
>   *Whenever the wind is high,*
>   *All night long in the dark and wet . . .*"

"Yes, yes, that's the one."

> *"A man goes riding by.*
> *Late in the night when the fires are out,*
> *Why does he gallop and gallop about?"*

"Go on. Why do you stop?"

> *"Whenever the trees are crying aloud,*
> *And ships are tossed at sea,*
> *By, on the highway, low and loud,*
> *By at the gallop goes he.*
> *By at the gallop he goes, and then*
> *By he comes back at the gallop again."*

"That's the one. That's the one I like best."

"It's a bit frightening," Castle said.

"That's why I like it. Does he wear a stocking mask?"

"It doesn't say he's a robber, Sam."

"Then why does he go up and down outside the house? Has he a white face like you and Mr. Muller?"

"It doesn't say."

"I think he's black, black as my hat, black as my cat."

"Why?"

"I think all the white people are afraid of him and lock their house in case he comes in with a carving knife and cuts their throats. Slowly," he added with relish.

Sam had never looked more black, Castle thought. He put his arm round him with a gesture of protection, but he couldn't protect him from the violence and vengeance which were beginning to work in the child's heart.

He went into his study, unlocked a drawer and took out Muller's notes. There was a heading: "A Final Solution." Muller apparently had felt no hesitation at all in speaking that phrase into a German ear, and the solution, it was obvious, had not been rejected—it was still open for discussion. The same image recurred like an obsession —of the dying child and the vulture.

He sat down and made a careful copy of Muller's notes. He didn't even bother to type them. The anonymity of a typewriter, as the Hiss case indicated, was very partial and anyway he had no desire to take trivial precautions. As for the book code, he had abandoned that with his last message which ended in "goodbye." Now as he wrote "Final Solution" and copied the words which fol- lowed with exactitude he identified himself truly for the first time with Carson. Carson at this point would have taken the ultimate risk. He was, as Sarah had once put it, "going too far."

5

At two o'clock in the morning Castle was still awake when he was startled by a cry from Sarah. "No!" she cried. "No!"

"What is it?"

There was no reply, but when he turned on the light, he could see that her eyes were wide with fear.

"You've had another nightmare. It's only a nightmare."

She said, "It was terrible."

"Tell me. A dream never comes back if you tell it quickly before you forget."

He could feel how she trembled against his side. He began to catch her fear. "It's only a dream, Sarah, just tell me. Get rid of it."

She said, "I was in a railway train. It was moving off. You were left on the platform. I was alone. You had the tickets. Sam was with you. He didn't seem to care. I didn't even know where we were supposed to be going. And I could hear the ticket collector in the next compartment. I knew I was in the wrong coach, reserved for whites."

"Now you've told it the dream won't come back."

"I knew he'd say, Get out of there. You've no business there. This is a white coach."

"It's only a dream, Sarah."

"Yes. I know. I'm sorry I woke you. You need your sleep."

"It was a bit like the dreams Sam had. Remember?"

"Sam and I are color conscious, aren't we? It haunts us both in sleep. Sometimes I wonder whether you love me only because of my color. If you were black you wouldn't love a white woman only because she was white, would you?"

"No. I'm not a South African off on a weekend in Swaziland. I knew you for nearly a year before I fell in love. It came slowly. All those months when we worked secretly together. I was a so-called diplomat, safe as houses. You ran all the risks. I didn't have nightmares, but I used to lie awake, wondering whether you'd come to our next rendezvous or whether you'd disappear and I'd never know what happened to you. Just a message perhaps from one of the others saying that the line was closed."

"So you worried about the line."

"No. I worried about what would happen to you. I'd loved you for months. I knew I couldn't go on living if you disappeared. Now we are safe."

"Are you sure?"

"Of course I'm sure. Haven't I proved it over seven years?"

"I don't mean that you love me. I mean are you sure we are safe?"

To that question there was no easy answer. The last encoded report with the final word "goodbye" had been premature and the passage he had chosen, "I have lifted my hand and let it fall," was no mark of freedom in the world of Uncle Remus.

Part Five

Chapter I

1

Darkness had fallen early with the mist and the drizzle of November, when he left the telephone box. There had been no reply to any of his signals. In Old Compton Street the blurred red light of the sign "Books," marking where Halliday Junior carried on his dubious trade, shone down the pavement with less than its normal effrontery; Halliday Senior in the shop across the way stooped as usual under a single globe, economizing fuel. When Castle came into the shop the old man touched a switch without raising his head so as to light up on either side the shelves of outmoded classics.

"You don't waste your electricity," Castle said.

"Ah! It's you, sir. Yes, I do my little bit to help the Government, and anyway I don't get many real customers after five. A few shy sellers, but their books are seldom in good enough condition, and I have to send them away disappointed—they think there's value in any book that's a hundred years old. I'm sorry, sir, about the delay over the Trollope if that's what you are seeking. There's been difficulty about the second copy—it was on television once, that's the trouble—even the Penguins are sold out."

"There's no hurry now. One copy will do. I came in to tell you that. My friend has gone to live abroad."

"Ah, you'll miss your literary evenings, sir. I was saying to my son only the other day . . ."

"It's odd, Mr. Halliday, but I've never met your son. Is he in? I thought I might discuss with him some books I can spare. I've rather grown out of my taste for *curiosa*. Age, I suppose. Would I find him in?"

"You won't, sir, not now. To tell you the truth he's got himself into a bit of trouble. From doing too well. He opened another shop last month in Newington Butts and the police there are far less understanding than those here—or more expensive if you care to be cynical. He had to attend the magistrate's court all the afternoon about some of those silly magazines of his and he's not back yet."

"I hope his difficulties don't make trouble for you, Mr. Halliday."

"Oh dear me, no. The police are very sympathetic. I really think they're sorry for me having a son in that way of business. I tell them, if I was young, I might be doing the same thing, and they laugh."

It had always seemed strange to Castle that "they" had chosen so dubious an intermediary as young Halliday, whose shop might be searched at any time by the police. Perhaps, he thought, it was a kind of double bluff. The Vice Squad would hardly be trained in the niceties of intelligence. It was even possible that Halliday Junior was as unaware as his father of the use to which he was being put. That was what he wanted very much to know, for he was going to entrust him with what amounted to his life.

He stared across the road at the scarlet sign and the girlie magazines in the window and wondered at the strange emotion that was driving him to take so open a risk. Boris would not have approved, but now he had sent "them" his last report and resignation he felt an irresistible desire to communicate directly by word of mouth, without the intervention of safe drops and book codes and elaborate signals on public telephones.

"You've no idea when he'll return?" he asked Mr. Halliday.

"No idea, sir. Couldn't I perhaps help you myself?"

"No, no. I won't bother you." He had no code of telephone rings to attract the attention of Halliday Junior. They had been kept so scrupulously apart he sometimes wondered whether their only meeting might be scheduled for the final emergency.

He asked, "Has your son by any chance a scarlet Toyota?"

"No, but he sometimes uses mine in the country—for sales, sir. He helps me there now and then, for I can't get about as much as I used to do. Why did you ask?"

"I thought I saw one outside the shop once."

"That wouldn't be ours. Not in town it wouldn't. With all the traffic jams it wouldn't be economic. We have to do our best to economize when the Government asks."

"Well, I hope the magistrate has not been too severe with him."

"It's a kind thought, sir. I'll tell him you called."

"As it happens I brought a note with me you might let him have. It's confidential, mind. I wouldn't want people to know the kind of books I collected when I was young."

"You can trust me, sir. I've never failed you yet. And the Trollope?"

"Oh, forget the Trollope."

At Euston Castle took a ticket to Watford—he didn't want to show his season to and from Berkhamsted. Ticket collectors have a memory for seasons. In the train he read, to keep his mind occupied, a morning paper which had been left behind on the next seat. It contained an interview with a film star whom he had never seen (the cinema at Berkhamsted had been turned into a Bingo hall). Apparently the actor had married for a second time. Or was it a third? He had told the reporter during an interview several years before that he was finished with marriage. "So you've changed your mind?" the gossip writer impudently asked.

Castle read the interview to the last word. Here was a man who could talk to a reporter about the most private things in his life: "I was very poor when I married my first wife. She didn't understand . . . our sex life went all wrong. It's different with Naomi. Naomi knows that when I come back exhausted from the studio . . . whenever we can we take a week's holiday all alone in some quiet spot like St. Tropez and work it all off." I'm hypocritical to blame him, Castle thought: I am going to talk if I can to Boris: a moment arrives when one has to talk.

At Watford he went carefully through his previous routine, hesitating at the bus stop, finally walking on, waiting round the next corner for any followers. He reached the coffee shop, but he didn't go in but walked straight on. Last time he had been guided by the man with the loose shoelace, but now he had no guide. Did he turn left or right at the corner? All the streets in this part of Watford looked alike—rows of identical gabled houses with small front gardens planted with rose trees that dripped with moisture—one house joined to another by a garage for one car.

He took another cast at random, and another, but he found always the same houses, sometimes in streets, sometimes in crescents, and he felt himself mocked by the similarity of the names—Laurel Drive, Oaklands, The Shrubbery—to the name he was seeking, Elm View. Once a policeman seeing him at a loss asked whether he could be of help. Muller's original notes seemed to weigh like a revolver in his pocket and he said no, that he was only looking for a To Let notice in the area. The policeman told him that there were two of these some three or four turns to the left, and by a coincidence the third brought him into Elm View. He hadn't remembered the number, but a lamp in the street shone on to the stained glass of a door and he recognized that. There was no light in any window, and it was without much hope that, peering closely, he made out the mutilated card "ition Limited" and rang the bell. It was unlikely Boris would be here at this hour: indeed, he might not be in England at all. He had severed his connection with them, so why should they preserve a dangerous channel open? He tried the bell a second time, but there was no reply. He would have welcomed at that moment even Ivan who had tried to blackmail him. There was no one—literally no one—left to whom he could speak.

He had passed a telephone box on his way and now he returned to it. At a house across the road he could see through the uncurtained window a family sitting down to a high tea or an early dinner: a father and two teenage children, a boy and a girl, took their seats, the mother entered carrying a dish, and the father seemed to be saying grace, for the children bowed their heads. He remembered that custom in his childhood but thought it had died out a long time ago—perhaps they were Roman Catholics, customs seemed to survive much longer with them. He began to dial the only number left for him to try, a number to be used only in the final emergency, replacing the receiver at intervals which he timed on his watch. After he had dialed five times with no response he left the box. It was as though he had cried aloud five times in the empty street for help—and he had no idea whether he had been heard. Perhaps after his final report all lines of communication had been cut forever.

He looked across the road. The father made a joke and the mother smiled her approval and the girl winked at the boy, as much as to say "The old boy's at it again." Castle went on down the road toward the station—nobody followed him, no one looked at him through a window as he went by, nobody passed him. He felt invisible, set down in a strange world where there were no other human beings to recognize him as one of themselves.

He stopped at the end of the street which was called The Shrubbery beside a hideous church so new it might have been constructed overnight with the glittering bricks of a build-it-yourself kit. The lights were on inside and the same emotion of loneliness which had driven him to Halliday's drove him to the building. He recognized from the gaudy bedizened altar and the sentimental statues that it was a Roman Catholic church. There was no sturdy band of bourgeois faithful standing shoulder to shoulder singing of a green hill far away. One old man slumbered over his umbrella knob not far from the altar, and two women who might have been sisters in their similar subfusc clothing waited by what he guessed was a confessional box. A woman in a macintosh came out from behind a curtain and a woman without one went in. It was like a weather house indicating rain. Castle sat down not far away. He felt tired—the hour had struck long past for his triple J & B; Sarah would be growing anxious, and as he listened to the low hum of conversation in the box the desire to talk openly, without reserve, after seven years of silence grew in him. Boris had been totally withdrawn, he thought, I shall never be able to speak again—unless, of course, I end up in the dock. I could make what they call a "confession" there—*in camera*, of course, the trial would be *in camera*.

The second woman emerged, and the third went in. The other two had got rid briskly enough of their secrets—*in camera*. They were kneeling separately down before their respective altars with looks of smug satisfaction at a duty well performed. When the third woman emerged there was no one left waiting but himself. The old man had woken and accompanied one of the women out. Between a crack in the priest's curtain he caught a glimpse of a long white face; he heard a throat being cleared of the November damp. Castle thought: I want to talk; why don't I talk? A priest like that has to keep my secret. Boris had said to him, "Come to me whenever you feel you have to talk: it's a smaller risk," but he was convinced Boris had gone forever. To talk was a therapeutic act—he moved slowly toward the box like a patient who is visiting a psychiatrist for the first time with trepidation.

A patient who didn't know the ropes. He drew the curtain to behind him and stood hesitating in the little cramped space which was left. How to begin? The faint smell of eau-de-cologne must have been left by one of the women. A shutter clattered open and he could see a sharp profile like a stage detective's. The profile coughed, and muttered something.

Castle said, "I want to talk to you."

"What are you standing there for like that?" the profile said. "Have you lost the use of your knees?"

"I only want to talk to you," Castle said.

"You aren't here to talk to me," the profile said. There was a chink–chink–chink. The man had a rosary in his lap and seemed to be using it like a chain of worry beads. "You are here to talk to God."

"No, I'm not. I'm just here to talk."

The priest looked reluctantly round. His eyes were bloodshot. Castle had an impression that he had fallen by a grim coincidence on another victim of loneliness and silence like himself.

"Kneel down, man, what sort of a Catholic do you think you are?"

"I'm not a Catholic."

"Then what business have you here?"

"I want to talk, that's all."

"If you want instruction you can leave your name and address at the presbytery."

"I don't want instruction."

"You are wasting my time," the priest said.

"Don't the secrets of the confessional apply to non-Catholics?"

"You should go to a priest of your own Church."

"I haven't got a Church."

"Then I think what you need is a doctor," the priest said. He slammed the shutter to, and Castle left the box. It was an absurd end, he thought, to an absurd action. How could he have expected the man to understand him even if he had been allowed to talk? He had far too long a history to tell, begun so many years ago in a strange country.

2

Sarah came out to greet him as he was hanging his coat in the hall. She asked, "Has something happened?"

"No."

"You've never been as late as this without telephoning."

"Oh, I've been going here and there, trying to see people. I couldn't find any of them in. I suppose they are all taking long weekends."

"Will you have your whisky? Or do you want dinner straight away?"

"Whisky. Make it a large one."

"Larger than usual?"

"Yes, and no soda."

"Something *has* happened."

"Nothing important. But it's cold and wet almost like winter. Is Sam asleep?"

"Yes."

"Where's Buller?"

"Looking for cats in the garden."

He sat down in the usual chair and the usual silence fell between them. Normally he felt the silence like a comforting shawl thrown round his shoulders. Silence was relaxation, silence meant that words were unnecessary between the two of them—their love was too established to need assurance; they had taken out a life policy in their love. But this night, with the original of Muller's notes in his pocket and his copy of it by this time in the hands of young Halliday, silence was like a vacuum in which he couldn't breathe: silence was a lack of everything, even trust, it was a foretaste of the tomb.

"Another whisky, Sarah."

"You *are* drinking too much. Remember poor Davis."

"He didn't die of drink."

"But I thought . . ."

"You thought like all the others did. And you're wrong. If it's too much trouble to give me another whisky, say so and I'll help myself."

"I only said remember Davis . . ."

"I don't want to be looked after, Sarah. You are Sam's mother, not mine."

"Yes, I *am* his mother and you aren't even his father."

They looked at each other with astonishment and dismay. Sarah said, "I didn't mean . . ."

"It's not your fault."

"I'm sorry."

He said, "This is what the future will be like if we can't talk. You asked me what I'd been doing. I've been looking for someone to talk to all this evening, but no one was there."

"Talk about what?"

The question silenced him.

"Why can't you talk to *me?* Because They forbid it, I suppose. The Official Secrets Act—all that stupidity."

"It's not them."

"Then who?"

"When we came to England, Sarah, Carson sent someone to see me. He had saved you and Sam. All he asked in return was a little help. I was grateful and I agreed."

"What's wrong with that?"

"My mother told me that when I was a child I always gave away too much in a swap, but it wasn't too much for the man who had saved you from BOSS. So there it is—I became what they call a double agent, Sarah. I rate a lifetime in jail."

He had always known that one day this scene would have to be played out between them, but he had never been able to imagine the kind of words they would say to each other. She said, "Give me your whisky." He handed her his glass and she drank a finger from it. "Are you in danger?" she asked. "I mean now. Tonight."

"I've been in danger all our life together."

"But is it worse now?"

"Yes. I think they've discovered there's a leak and I think they thought it was Davis. I don't believe Davis died a natural death. Something Doctor Percival said . . ."

"You think they killed him?"

"Yes."

"So it might have been you?"

"Yes."

"Are you still going on with it?"

"I wrote what I thought was my last report. I said goodbye to the whole business. But then—something else happened. With Muller. I had to let them know. I hope I have. I don't know."

"How did the office discover the leak?"

"I suppose they have a defector somewhere—probably in place— who had access to my reports and passed them back to London."

"But if he passes back this one?"

"Oh, I know what you are going to say. Davis is dead. I'm the only man at the office who deals with Muller."

"Why have you gone on, Maurice? It's suicide."

"It may save a lot of lives—lives of your people."

"Don't talk to me of my people. I have no people any longer. You are 'my people.' " He thought, Surely that's something out of the Bible. I've heard that before. Well, she'd been to a Methodist school.

She put her arm round him and held the glass of whisky to his mouth. "I wish you hadn't waited all these years to tell me."

"I was afraid to—Sarah." The Old Testament name came back to him with hers. It had been a woman called Ruth who had said what she had said—or something very like it.

"Afraid of me and not of Them?"

"Afraid for you. You can't know how long it seemed, waiting for you in the Hotel Polana. I thought you'd never come. While it was daylight I used to watch car numbers through a pair of binoculars. Even numbers meant Muller had got you. Odd numbers that you were on the way. This time there'll be no Hotel Polana and no Carson. It doesn't happen twice the same way."

"What do you want me to do?"

"The best thing would be for you to take Sam and go to my mother's. Separate yourself from me. Pretend there's been a bad quarrel and you are getting a divorce. If nothing happens I'll stay here and we can come together again."

"What should I do all that time? Watch car numbers? Tell me the next best thing."

"If they are still looking after me—I don't know whether they are —they promised me a safe escape route, but I'll have to go alone. So that way too you must go to my mother with Sam. The only difference is we won't be able to communicate. You won't know what has happened—perhaps for a long time. I think I'd prefer the police to come—at least that way we'd see each other again in court."

"But Davis never reached a court, did he? No, if they are looking after you, go, Maurice. Then at least I'll know you are safe."

"You haven't said a word of blame, Sarah."

"What sort of word?"

"Well, I'm what's generally called a traitor."

"Who cares?" she said. She put her hand in his: it was an act more intimate than a kiss—one can kiss a stranger. She said, "We have our own country. You and I and Sam. You've never betrayed that country, Maurice."

He said, "It's no good worrying any more tonight. We've still time and we've got to sleep."

But when they were in bed, they made love at once without thinking, without speaking, as though it had been something they had agreed together an hour ago and all their discussion had only been a postponement of it. It had been months since they had come together in this way. Now that his secret was spoken love was released, and he fell asleep almost as soon as he withdrew. His last thought was: There is still time—it will be days, perhaps weeks, before any leak can be reported back. Tomorrow is Saturday. We have a whole weekend before us in which to decide.

Chapter II

Sir John Hargreaves sat in his study in the country reading Trollope. It should have been a period of almost perfect peace—the weekend calm, which only a duty officer was allowed to break with an urgent message, and urgent messages were of extreme rarity in the Secret Service—the hour of tea when his wife respected his absence, as she knew that Earl Grey in the afternoons spoiled for him the Cutty Sark at six. During his service in West Africa he had grown to appreciate the novels of Trollope, though he was not a novel reader. At moments of irritation, he had found *The Warden* and *Barchester Towers* reassuring books, they reinforced the patience which Africa required. Mr. Slope would remind him of an importunate and self-righteous District Commissioner, and Mrs. Proudie of the Governor's wife. Now he found himself disturbed by a piece of fiction which should have soothed him in England as he had been soothed in Africa. The novel was called *The Way We Live Now*—somebody, he couldn't remember who it was, had told him the novel had been turned into a good television series. He didn't like television, yet he had been sure he would like the Trollope.

So all that afternoon he felt for a while the same smooth pleasure he always received from Trollope—the sense of a calm Victorian world, where good was good and bad was bad and one could distinguish easily between them. He had no children who might have taught him differently—he had never wanted a child nor had his wife; they were at one in that, though perhaps for different reasons. He hadn't wanted to add to his public responsibilities private responsibilities (children would have been a constant anxiety in Africa), and his wife—well—he would think with affection—she wished to guard her figure and her independence. Their mutual indifference to children reinforced their love for each other. While he read Trollope with a whisky at his elbow, she drank tea in her room with equal content. It was a weekend of peace for both of them—no shoot, no guests, darkness falling early in November over the park—he could even imagine himself in Africa, at some rest-house in the bush, on one of the long treks which he always enjoyed, far from headquarters. The cook would now be plucking a chicken behind the resthouse and the pie-dogs would be gathering in the hope of scraps . . . The lights in the distance where the motorway ran might well have been the lights of the village where the girls would be picking the lice out of each other's hair.

He was reading of old Melmotte—the swindler as his fellow members judged him. Melmotte took his place in the restaurant of the House of Commons—"It was impossible to expel him—almost as impossible to sit next him. Even the waiters were unwilling to serve him; but with patience and endurance he did at last get his dinner."

Hargreaves, unwillingly, felt drawn to Melmotte in his isolation, and he remembered with regret what he had said to Doctor Percival when Percival expressed a liking for Davis. He had used the word "traitor" as Melmotte's colleagues used the word "swindler." He read on, "They who watched him declared among themselves that he was happy in his own audacity;—but in truth he was probably at that moment the most utterly wretched man in London." He had never known Davis—he wouldn't have recognized him if he had met him in a corridor of the office. He thought: Perhaps I spoke hastily—I reacted stupidly—but it was Percival who eliminated him—I shouldn't have left Percival in charge of the case . . . He went on reading: "But even he, with all the world now gone from him, with nothing before him but the extremest misery which the indignation of offended laws could inflict, was able to spend the last moments of his freedom in making a reputation at any rate for audacity." Poor devil, he thought, one has to grant him courage. Did Davis guess what potion Doctor Percival might be dropping into his whisky when he left the room for a moment?

It was then the telephone rang. He heard it intercepted by his wife in her room. She was trying to protect his peace better than Trollope had done, but all the same, owing to some urgency at the other end, she was forced to transfer the call. Unwillingly he lifted the receiver. A voice he didn't recognize said, "Muller speaking."

He was still in the world of Melmotte. He said, "Muller?"

"Cornelius Muller."

There was an uneasy pause and then the voice explained, "From Pretoria."

For a moment Sir John Hargreaves thought the stranger must be calling from the remote city, and then he remembered. "Yes. Yes. Of course. Can I be of any help?" He added, "I hope Castle . . ."

"I would like to talk to you, Sir John, *about* Castle."

"I'll be in the office on Monday. If you'd ring my secretary . . ." He looked at his watch. "She will still be at the office."

"You won't be there tomorrow?"

"No. I'm taking this weekend at home."

"Could I come and see you, Sir John?"

"Is it so very urgent?"

"I think it is. I have a strong feeling I've made a most serious mistake. I do want badly to talk to you, Sir John."

There goes Trollope, Hargreaves thought, and poor Mary—I try to keep the office away from us when we are here and yet it's always intruding. He remembered the evening of the shoot when Daintry had been so difficult . . . He asked, "Have you a car?"

"Yes. Of course."

He thought, I can still have Saturday free if I'm reasonably hospitable tonight. He said, "It's less than two hours' drive if you'd care to come to dinner."

"Of course. It's very kind of you, Sir John. I wouldn't have disturbed you if I hadn't thought it important. I . . ."

"We may not be able to rustle up more than an omelet, Muller. Pot luck," he added.

He put down the receiver, remembering the apocryphal story he knew they told about him and the cannibals. He went to the window and looked out. Africa receded. The lights were the lights of the motorway leading to London and the office. He felt the approaching suicide of Melmotte—there was no other solution. He went to the drawing room: Mary was pouring out a cup of Earl Grey from the silver teapot which she had bought at a Christie sale. He said, "I'm sorry, Mary. We've got a guest for dinner."

"I was afraid of that. When he insisted on speaking to you . . . Who is it?"

"The man BOSS has sent over from Pretoria."

"Couldn't he wait till Monday?"

"He said it was too urgent."

"I don't like those apartheid buggers." Common English obscenities always sounded strange in her American accent.

"Nor do I, but we have to work with them. I suppose we can rustle up something to eat."

"There's some cold beef."

"That's better than the omelet I promised him."

It was a stiff meal because no business could be talked, though Lady Hargreaves did her best, with the help of the Beaujolais, to find a possible subject. She confessed herself completely ignorant of Afrikaaner art and literature, but it was an ignorance which Muller appeared to share. He admitted there were some poets and novelists around—and he mentioned the Hertzog Prize, but he added that he had read none of them. "They are unreliable," he said, "most of them."

"Unreliable?"

"They get mixed up in politics. There's a poet in prison now for helping terrorists." Hargreaves tried to change the subject, but he could think of nothing in connection with South Africa but gold and diamonds—they were mixed up with politics too, just as much as the writers. The word diamonds suggested Namibia and he remembered that Oppenheimer, the millionaire, supported the progressive party. His Africa had been the impoverished Africa of the bush, but politics lay like the detritus of a mine over the south. He was glad when they could be alone with a bottle of whisky and two easy chairs—it was easier to talk of hard things in an easy chair—it was difficult, he had always found, to get angry in an easy chair.

"You must forgive me," Hargreaves said, "for not having been in London to greet you. I had to go to Washington. One of those routine visits that one can't avoid. I hope my people have been looking after you properly."

"I had to go off too," Muller said, "to Bonn."

"But not exactly a routine visit there, I imagine? The Concorde has brought London so damnably close to Washington—they almost expect you to drop over for lunch. I hope all went satisfactorily in Bonn—within reason, of course. But I suppose you've been discussing all that with our friend Castle."

"Your friend, I think, more than mine."

"Yes, yes. I know there was a little trouble between you years ago. But that's ancient history surely."

"Is there such a thing, sir, as ancient history? The Irish don't think so, and what you call the Boer War is still very much our war, but we call it the war of independence. I'm worried about Castle. That's why I'm bothering you tonight. I've been indiscreet. I let him have some notes I made about the Bonn visit. Nothing very secret, of course, but all the same someone reading between the lines . . ."

"My dear fellow, you can trust Castle. I wouldn't have asked him to brief you if he wasn't the best man . . ."

"I went to have dinner with him at his home. I was surprised to find he was married to a black girl, the one who was the cause of what you call a little trouble. He even seems to have a child by her."

"We have no color bar here, Muller, and she was very thoroughly vetted, I can assure you."

"All the same, it was the Communists who organized her escape. Castle was a great friend of Carson. I suppose you know that."

"We know all about Carson—and the escape. It was Castle's job to have Communist contacts. Is Carson still a trouble to you?"

"No. Carson died in prison—from pneumonia. I could see how upset Castle was when I told him."

"Why not? If they were friends." Hargreaves looked with regret at his Trollope where it lay beyond the bottle of Cutty Sark. Muller got abruptly to his feet and walked across the room. He halted before the photograph of a black man wearing a soft black hat of the kind missionaries used to wear. One side of his face was disfigured by lupus and he smiled at whoever held the camera with one side of his mouth only.

"Poor fellow," Hargreaves said, "he was dying when I took that photograph. He knew it. He was a brave man like all the Krus. I wanted something to remember him by."

Muller said, "I haven't made a full confession, sir. I gave Castle the wrong notes by accident. I'd made one lot to show him and one to draw on for my reports and I confused them. It's true there's nothing very secret—I wouldn't have put anything very secret on paper over here—but there were some indiscreet phrases . . ."

"Really, you don't have to worry, Muller."

"I can't help worrying, sir. In this country you live in such a different atmosphere. You have so little to fear compared with us. That black in the photograph—you liked him?"

"He was a friend—a friend I loved."

"I can't say that of a single black," Muller replied. He turned. On the opposite side of the room, on the wall, hung an African mask.

"I don't trust Castle." He said, "I can't prove anything, but I have an intuition . . . I wish you had appointed someone else to brief me."

"There were only two men dealing with your material. Davis and Castle."

"Davis is the one who died?"

"Yes."

"You take things so lightly over here. I sometimes envy you. Things like a black child. You know, sir, in our experience there is no one more vulnerable than an officer in secret intelligence. We had a leak a few years back from BOSS—in the section which deals with the Communists. One of our most intelligent men. He too cultivated friendships—and the friendships took over. Carson was concerned in that case too. And there was another case—one of our officers was a brilliant chess player. Intelligence became to him just another game of chess. He was interested only when he was pitted against a really first-class player. In the end he grew dissatisfied. The games were too easy—so he took on his own side. I think he was very happy as long as the game lasted."

"What happened to him?"

"He's dead now."

Hargreaves thought again of Melmotte. People talked of courage as a primary virtue. What of the courage of a known swindler and bankrupt taking his place in the dining room of the House of Commons? Is courage a justification? Is courage in whatever cause a virtue? He said, "We are satisfied that Davis was the leak we had to close."

"A fortunate death?"

"Cirrhosis of the liver."

"I told you Carson died of pneumonia."

"Castle, I happen to know, doesn't play chess."

"There are other motives too. Love of money."

"That certainly doesn't apply to Castle."

"He loves his wife," Muller said, "and his child."

"What of that?"

"They are both black," Muller replied with simplicity, looking across the room at the photograph of the Kru chief upon the wall as though, thought Hargreaves, even I am not beyond his suspicion, which, like some searchlight on the Cape, swept the unfriendly seas beyond in search of enemy vessels.

Muller said, "I hope to God you are right and the leak really was Davis. I don't believe it was."

Hargreaves watched Muller drive away through the park in his black Mercedes. The lights slowed down and became stationary; he must have reached the lodge, where since the Irish bombings began, a man from the Special Branch had been stationed. The park seemed no longer to be an extension of the African bush—it was a small parcel of the Home Counties which had never been home to Hargreaves. It was nearly midnight. He went upstairs to his dressing room, but he didn't take off his clothes further than his shirt. He wrapped a towel round his neck and began to shave. He had shaved before dinner and it wasn't a necessary act, but he could always think more clearly when he shaved. He tried to recall exactly the reasons Muller had given for suspecting Castle—his relations with Carson—those meant nothing. A black wife and child—Hargreaves remembered with sadness and a sense of loss the black mistress whom he had known many years ago before his marriage. She had died of blackwater fever and when she died he had felt as though a great part of his love for Africa had gone to the grave with her. Muller had spoken of intuition—"I can't prove anything, but I have an intuition . . ." Hargreaves was the last man to laugh at intuition. In Africa he had lived with intuition, he was accustomed to choose his boys by intuition—not by the tattered notebooks they carried with illegible references. Once his life had been saved by an intuition.

He dried his face, and he thought: I'll ring up Emmanuel. Doctor Percival was the only real friend he had in the whole firm. He opened the bedroom door and looked in. The room was in darkness and he thought his wife was asleep until she spoke. "What's keeping you, dear?"

"I won't be long. I just want to ring up Emmanuel."

"Has that man Muller gone?"

"Yes."

"I don't like him."

"Nor do I."

Chapter III

1

Castle woke and looked at his watch, though he believed that he carried time in his head—he knew it would be a few minutes to eight, giving him just long enough to go to his study and turn on the news without waking Sarah. He was surprised to see that his watch marked eight five—the inner clock had never failed him before, and he doubted his watch, but by the time he reached his room the important news was over—there were only the little scraps of parochial interest which the reader used to fill the slot: a bad accident on the M4, a brief interview with Mrs. Whitehouse welcoming some new campaign against pornographic books, and perhaps as an illustration of her talk, a trivial fact, that an obscure bookseller called Holliday—"I'm sorry, *Halliday*"—had appeared before a magistrate in Newington Butts for selling a pornographic film to a boy of fourteen. He had been remanded for trial at the Central Criminal Court, and his bail had been set at two hundred pounds.

So he was at liberty, Castle thought, with the copy of Muller's notes in his pocket, presumably watched by the police. He might be afraid to pass them on at whatever drop they had given him, he might be afraid even to destroy them; what seemed his most likely choice was to keep them as a bargaining asset with the police. "I'm a more important man than you think: if this little affair can be arranged, I can show you things . . . let me talk to someone from the Special Branch." Castle could well imagine the kind of conversation which might be going on at that moment: the skeptical local police, Halliday exposing the first page of Muller's notes as an inducement.

Castle opened the door of the bedroom: Sarah was still asleep. He told himself that now the moment had arrived which he had always expected, when he must think clearly and act decisively. Hope was out of place just as much as despair. They were emotions which would confuse thought. He must assume Boris had gone, that the line was cut, and that he must act on his own.

He went down to the sitting room where Sarah wouldn't hear

him dial and rang a second time the number he had been given to use only for a final emergency. He had no idea in what room it was ringing—the exchange was somewhere in Kensington: he dialed three times with an interval of ten seconds between and he had the impression that his SOS was ringing out to an empty room, but he couldn't tell. . . . There was no other appeal for help which he could make, nothing left for him to do but clear the home ground. He sat by the telephone and made his plans, or rather went over them and confirmed them, for he had made them long ago. There was nothing important left to be destroyed, he was almost sure of that, no books he had once used for coding . . . he was convinced there were no papers waiting to be burned . . . he could leave the house safely, locked and empty . . . you couldn't, of course, burn a dog . . . what was he to do with Buller? How absurd at this moment to be bothered by a dog, a dog he had never even liked, but his mother would never allow Sarah to introduce Buller into the Sussex house as a permanent lodger. He could leave him, he supposed, at a kennels, but he had no idea where . . . This was the one problem he had never worked out. He told himself that it was not an important one, as he went upstairs to wake Sarah.

Why this morning was she so deeply asleep? He remembered, as he looked at her, with the tenderness one can feel even for an enemy who sleeps, how after making love he had fallen into the deepest nullity he had known for months, simply because they had talked frankly, because they had ceased to have secrets. He kissed her and she opened her eyes and he could tell she knew at once there was no time to be lost; she couldn't, in her usual fashion, wake slowly, and stretch her arms and say, "I was dreaming . . ."

He told her, "You must ring my mother now. It will seem more natural for *you* to do it if we've had a quarrel. Ask if you can stay a few days with Sam. You can lie a little. All the better if she thinks you are lying. It will make it easier, when you are there, to let the story out slowly. You can say that I've done something unforgivable . . . We talked about it all last night."

"But you said we had time . . ."

"I was wrong."

"Something's happened?"

"Yes. You've got to get away with Sam right away."

"And you are staying here?"

"Either they'll help me to get out or the police will come for me. You mustn't be here if that happens."

"Then it's the end for us?"

"Of course it's not the end. As long as we are alive we'll come together again. Somehow. Somewhere."

They hardly spoke to each other, dressing rapidly, like strangers on a journey who have been forced to share the same *wagon lit*. Only as she turned at the door on her way to wake up Sam she asked, "What about the school? I don't suppose anyone will bother . . ."

"Don't worry now. Telephone on Monday and say he's ill. I want you both out of the house as quickly as possible. In case the police come."

She returned five minutes later and said, "I spoke to your mother. She wasn't exactly welcoming. She has someone for lunch. What about Buller?"

"I'll think of something."

At ten to nine she was ready to leave with Sam. A taxi was at the door. Castle felt a terrible sense of unreality. He said, "If nothing happens you can come back. We shall have made up our quarrel." Sam at least was happy. Castle watched him as he laughed with the driver.

"If . . ."

"You came to the Polana."

"Yes, but you said once things never happened twice the same way."

At the taxi they even forgot to kiss and then they clumsily remembered—a kiss which was meaningless, empty of everything except the sense that his going away couldn't be true—it was something they were dreaming. They had always exchanged dreams—those private codes more unbreakable than Enigma.

"Can I telephone?"

"Better not. If all's well, I'll telephone you in a few days from a call box."

When the taxi drove away, he couldn't even see the last of her because of the tinted glass in the rear window. He went indoors and began to pack a small bag, suitable for a prison or an escape. Pajamas, washing things, a small towel—after hesitation he added his passport. Then he sat down and began to wait. He heard one neighbor drive away and then the silence of Saturday descended. He felt as though he were the only person left alive in King's Road, except for the police at the corner. The door was pushed open and Buller came waddling in. He settled on his haunches and fixed Castle with bulging and hypnotic eyes. "Buller," Castle whispered, "Buller, what a bloody nuisance you've always been, Buller." Buller went on staring—it was the way to get a walk.

Buller was still watching him a quarter of an hour later when the telephone rang. Castle let it ring. It rang over and over, like a child crying. This could not be the signal he hoped for—no control would have remained on the line so long—it was probably some friend of Sarah's, Castle thought. It would not, in any case, be for him. He had no friends.

2

Doctor Percival sat waiting in the hall of the Reform, near the great wide staircase, which looked as though it had been built to stand the heavy weight of old Liberal statesmen, those bearded or whiskered men of perpetual integrity. Only one other member was visible when Hargreaves came in and he was small and insignificant and short-sighted—he was having difficulty in reading the ticker tape. Hargreaves said, "I know it's my turn, Emmanuel, but the Travellers is closed. I hope you don't mind my asking Daintry to join us here."

"Well, he's not the gayest of companions," Doctor Percival said. "Security trouble?"

"Yes."

"I hoped you would have a little peace after Washington."

"One doesn't expect peace for long in this job. I don't suppose I'd enjoy it anyway, or why is it that I don't retire?"

"Don't talk of retirement, John. God knows what Foreign Office type they might foist on us. What's troubling you?"

"Let me have a drink first." They moved up the staircase and took their seats at a table on the landing outside the restaurant. Hargreaves drank his Cutty Sark neat. He said, "Suppose you killed the wrong man, Emmanuel?"

Doctor Percival's eyes showed no surprise. He examined carefully the color of his dry martini, smelled it, removed with a nail the nick of lemon peel as though he were making up his own prescription.

"I'm confident I didn't," he said.

"Muller doesn't share your confidence."

"Oh, Muller! What does Muller know about it?"

"He knows nothing. But he has an intuition."

"If that's all . . ."

"You've never been in Africa, Emmanuel. You get to trust an intuition in Africa."

"Daintry will expect a great deal more than intuition. He wasn't even satisfied with the facts about Davis."

"Facts?"

"That business of the Zoo and the dentist—to take only one example. And Porton. Porton was decisive. What are you going to tell Daintry?"

"My secretary tried to get Castle on the phone first thing this morning. There was no reply at all."

"He's probably gone away with his family for the weekend."

"Yes. But I've had his safe opened—Muller's notes aren't there. I know what you'll say. Anyone can be careless. But I thought if Daintry went down to Berkhamsted—well, if he found nobody there, it would be an opportunity to have the house looked over discreetly, and if he's in . . . he'll be surprised to see Daintry, and if he's guilty . . . he'd be a bit on edge . . ."

"Have you told 5?"

"Yes, I've spoken to Philips. He's having Castle's phone monitored again. I hope to God nothing comes of all this. It would mean Davis was innocent."

"You shouldn't worry so much about Davis. He's no loss to the firm, John. He should never have been recruited. He was inefficient and careless and drank too much. He'd have been a problem sooner or later anyway. But if Muller should be right, Castle will be a serious headache. Aflatoxin can't be used. Everyone knows he's not a heavy drinker. It will have to be the law courts, John, unless we can think of something else. Counsel for the defense. Evidence *in camera*. How the journalists hate that. Sensational headlines. I suppose Daintry will be satisfied if no one else is. He's a great stickler for doing things the legal way."

"And here he comes at last," Sir John Hargreaves said.

Daintry came up the great staircase toward them, slowly. Perhaps he wished to test every tread in turn as though it were a circumstantial piece of evidence.

"I wish I knew how to begin."

"Why not as you did with me—a little brutally?"

"Ah, but he hasn't your thick skin, Emmanuel."

3

The hours seemed very long. Castle tried to read, but no book could relieve the tension. Between one paragraph and another he would be haunted by the thought that somewhere he had left in the house something which would incriminate him. He had looked at every book on every shelf—there was not one he had ever used for coding: *War and Peace* was safely destroyed. From his study he had taken every sheet of used carbon paper—however innocent—and burned them: the list of telephone numbers on his desk contained nothing more secret than the butcher's and the doctor's, and yet he felt certain somewhere there must be a clue he had forgotten. He remembered the two men from Special Branch searching Davis's flat; he remembered the lines which Davis had marked with a "c" in his father's Browning. There would be no traces of love in this house. He and Sarah had never exchanged love letters—love letters in South Africa would have been the proof of a crime.

He had never spent so long and solitary a day. He wasn't hungry, though only Sam had eaten any breakfast, but he told himself one could not tell what might happen before night or where he would eat his next meal. He sat down in the kitchen before a plate of cold ham, but he had only eaten one piece before he realized it was time to listen to the one o'clock news. He listened to the end—even to the last item of football news because one could never be sure—there might be an urgent postscript.

But, of course, there was nothing which in the least concerned him. Not even a reference to young Halliday. It was unlikely there would be; his life from now on was totally *in camera*. For a man who had dealt for many years with what was called secret information he felt oddly out of touch. He was tempted to make again his urgent SOS, but it had been imprudent to make it even the second time from home. He had no idea where his signal rang, but those who monitored his telephone might well be able to trace the calls. The conviction he had felt the evening before that the line had been cut, that he was abandoned, grew with every hour.

He gave what was left of the ham to Buller, who rewarded him with a string of spittle on his trousers. He should long before this have taken him out, but he was unwilling to leave the four walls of the house, even to go into the garden. If the police came he wanted to be arrested in his home, and not in the open air with the neighbors' wives peering through their windows. He had a revolver upstairs in a drawer beside his bed, a revolver which he had never admitted to Davis he possessed, a quite legal revolver dating from his days in South Africa. Nearly every white man there possessed a gun. At the time he bought it he had loaded one chamber, the second chamber to prevent a rash shot, and the charge had remained undisturbed for seven years. He thought: I could use it on myself if the police broke in, but he knew very well that suicide for him was out of the question. He had promised Sarah that one day they would be together again.

He read, he put on the television, he read again. A crazy notion struck him—to catch a train to London and go to Halliday's father and ask for news. But perhaps already they were watching his house and the station. At half-past four, between the dog and the wolf, as the gray evening gathered, the telephone rang a second time and this time illogically he answered the call. He half hoped to hear Boris's voice, though he knew well enough that Boris would never take the risk of calling him at home.

The stern voice of his mother came out at him as though she were in the same room. "Is that Maurice?"

"Yes."

"I'm glad you're there. Sarah seemed to think you might have gone away."

"No, I'm still here."

"What's all this nonsense between you?"

"It's not nonsense, Mother."

"I told her she ought to leave Sam with me and go straight back."

"She's not coming, is she?" he asked with fear. A second parting seemed an impossible thing to bear.

"She refuses to go. She says you wouldn't let her in. That's absurd, of course."

"It's not absurd at all. If she came I should leave."

"What on earth has happened between you?"

"You'll know one day."

"Are you thinking of a divorce? It would be very bad for Sam."

"At present it's only a question of a separation. Just let things rest for a while, Mother."

"I don't understand. I hate things I don't understand. Sam wants to know whether you've fed Buller."

"Tell him I have."

She rang off. He wondered whether a recorder somewhere was playing over their conversation. He needed a whisky, but the bottle was empty. He went down to what had once been a coal cellar where he kept his wine and spirits. The chute for the delivery of coal had been turned into a sort of slanting window. He looked up and saw on the pavement the reflected light of a street lamp and the legs of someone who must be standing below it.

The legs were not in uniform, but of course they might belong to a plain clothes officer from Special Branch. Whoever it was had placed himself rather crudely opposite the door, but of course the object of the watcher might be to frighten him into some imprudent action. Buller had followed him down the stairs; he too noticed the legs above and began to bark. He looked dangerous, sitting back on his haunches with his muzzle raised, but if the legs had been near enough, he would not have bitten them, he would have dribbled on them. As the two of them watched, the legs moved out of sight, and Buller grunted with disappointment—he had lost an opportunity of making a new friend. Castle found a bottle of J & B (it occurred to him that the color of the whisky no longer had any importance) and went upstairs with it. He thought: If I hadn't got rid of *War and Peace* I might now have the time to read some chapters for pleasure.

Again restlessness drove him to the bedroom to rummage among Sarah's things for old letters, though he couldn't imagine how any letters he had ever written her could be incriminating, but then in the hands of Special Branch perhaps the most innocent reference could be twisted to prove her guilty knowledge. He didn't trust them not to want that—there is always in such cases the ugly desire for revenge. He found nothing—when you love and you are together old letters are apt to lose their value. Someone rang the front door bell. He stood and listened and heard it ring again and then a third time. He told himself that his visitor was not to be put off by silence and it was foolish not to open the door. If the line after all hadn't been cut there might be a message, an instruction . . . Without thinking why, he drew out of the drawer by his bed the revolver and put it with its single charge in his pocket.

In the hall he still hesitated. The stained glass above the door cast lozenges of yellow, green and blue upon the floor. It occurred to him that if he carried the revolver in his hand when he opened the door the police would have the right to shoot him down in self-defense—it would be an easy solution; nothing would ever be publicly proved against a dead man. Then he reproached himself with the thought that none of his actions must be dictated by despair any more than by hope. He left the gun in his pocket and opened the door.

"Daintry," he exclaimed. He hadn't expected a face he knew.

"Can I come in?" Daintry asked in a tone of shyness.

"Of course."

Buller suddenly emerged from his retirement. "He's not dangerous," Castle said as Daintry stepped back. He caught Buller by the collar, and Buller dropped his spittle between them like a fumbling bridegroom might drop the wedding ring. "What are you doing here, Daintry?"

"I happened to be driving through and I thought I'd look you

up." The excuse was so palpably untrue that Castle felt sorry for
Daintry. He wasn't like one of those smooth, friendly and fatal in-
terrogators who were bred by MI5. He was a mere security officer
who could be trusted to see that rules were not broken and to
check briefcases.

"Will you have a drink?"

"I'd like one." Daintry's voice was hoarse. He said—it was as
though he had to find an excuse for everything—"It's a cold wet
night."

"I haven't been out all day."

"You haven't?"

Castle thought: That's a bad slip if the telephone call this morning was from the office. He added, "Except to take the dog into the
garden."

Daintry took the glass of whisky and looked long at it and then
round the sitting room, little quick snapshots like a press photographer. You could almost hear the eyelids click. He said, "I do
hope I'm not disturbing you. Your wife . . ."

"She's not here. I'm quite alone. Except of course for Buller."

"Buller?"

"The dog."

The deep silence of the house was emphasized by the two voices.
They broke it alternately, uttering unimportant phrases.

"I hope I haven't drowned your whisky," Castle said. Daintry
still hadn't drunk. "I wasn't thinking . . ."

"No, no. It's just as I like it." Silence dropped again like the
heavy safety curtain in a theater.

Castle began with a confidence, "As a matter of fact I'm in a bit
of trouble." It seemed a useful moment to establish Sarah's innocence.

"Trouble?"

"My wife has left me. With my son. She's gone to my mother's."

"You mean you've quarreled?"

"Yes."

"I'm very sorry," Daintry said. "It's awful when these things happen." He seemed to be describing a situation which was as inevitable as death. He added, "Do you know the last time we met—at my
daughter's wedding? It was very kind of you to come with me to
my wife's afterward. I was very glad to have you with me. But
then I broke one of her owls."

"Yes. I remember."

"I don't think I even thanked you properly for coming. It was a

Saturday too. Like today. She was terribly angry. My wife, I mean, about the owl."

"We had to leave suddenly because of Davis."

"Yes, poor devil." Again the safety curtain dropped as though after an old-fashioned curtain line. The last act would soon begin. It was time to go to the bar. They both drank simultaneously.

"What do you think about his death?" Castle asked.

"I don't know what to think. To tell you the truth I try not to think."

"They believe he was guilty of a leak in my section, don't they?"

"They don't confide much in a security officer. What makes you think that?"

"It's not a normal routine to have Special Branch men in to search when one of us dies."

"No, I suppose not."

"You found the death odd too?"

"Why do you say that?"

Have we reversed our roles, Castle thought, am *I* interrogating *him?*

"You said just now you tried not to think about his death."

"Did I? I don't know what I meant. Perhaps it's your whisky. You didn't exactly drown it, you know."

"Davis never leaked anything to anyone," Castle said. He had the impression Daintry was looking at his pocket where it sagged on the cushion of the chair with the weight of the gun.

"You believe that?"

"I know it."

He couldn't have said anything which damned himself more completely. Perhaps after all Daintry was not so bad an interrogator; and the shyness and confusion and self-revelations he had been displaying might really be part of a new method which would put his training as a technician in a higher class than MI5's.

"You know it?"

"Yes."

He wondered what Daintry would do now. He hadn't the power of arrest. He would have to find a telephone and consult the office. The nearest telephone was at the police station at the bottom of King's Road—he would surely not have the nerve to ask if he might use Castle's? And had he identified the weight in the pocket? Was he afraid? I would have time after he leaves to make a run for it, Castle thought, if there was anywhere to run to; but to run without a destination, simply to delay the moment of capture, was an act of panic. He preferred to wait where he was—that would have at least a certain dignity.

"I've always doubted it," Daintry said, "to tell the truth."

"So they did confide in you?"

"Only for the security checks. I had to arrange those."

"It was a bad day for you, wasn't it, first to break that owl and then to see Davis dead on his bed?"

"I didn't like what Doctor Percival said."

"What was that?"

"He said, 'I hadn't expected this to happen.'"

"Yes. I remember now."

"It opened my eyes," Daintry said. "I saw what they'd been up to."

"They jumped too quickly to conclusions. They didn't properly investigate the alternatives."

"You mean yourself?"

Castle thought, I'm not going to make it that easy for them, I'm not going to confess in so many words, however effective this new technique of theirs may be. He said, "Or Watson."

"Oh yes, I'd forgotten Watson."

"Everything in our section passes through his hands. And then, of course, there's 69300 in L.M. They can't properly check his accounts. Who knows if he hasn't a bank deposit in Rhodesia or South Africa?"

"True enough," Daintry said.

"And our secretaries. It's not only our personal secretaries who may be involved. They all belong to a pool. Don't tell me that a girl doesn't go sometimes to the loo without locking up the cable she's been decoding or the report she's been typing?"

"I realize that. I checked the pool myself. There has always been a good deal of carelessness."

"Carelessness can begin at the top too. Davis's death may have been an example of criminal carelessness."

"If he wasn't guilty it was murder," Daintry said. "He had no chance to defend himself, to employ counsel. They were afraid of the effect a trial might have upon the Americans. Doctor Percival talked to me about boxes . . ."

"Oh yes," Castle said. "I know that *spiel*. I've heard it often myself. Well, Davis is in a box all right now."

Castle was aware that Daintry's eyes were on his pocket. Was Daintry pretending to agree with him so as to escape safely back to his car? Daintry said, "You and I are making the same mistake—

jumping to conclusions. Davis may have been guilty. What makes you so certain he wasn't?"

"You have to look for motives," Castle said. He had hesitated, he had evaded, but he had been strongly tempted to reply, "Because I am the leak." He felt sure by this time that the line was cut and he could expect no help, so what was the purpose of delaying? He liked Daintry, he had liked him ever since the day of his daughter's wedding. He had become suddenly human to him over the smashed owl, in the solitude of his smashed marriage. If anyone were to reap credit for his confession he would like it to be Daintry. Why therefore not give up and go quietly, as the police often put it? He wondered if he were prolonging the game only for the sake of company, to avoid the solitude of the house and the solitude of a cell.

"I suppose the motive for Davis would have been money," Daintry said.

"Davis didn't care much about money. All he needed was enough to bet a little on the horses and treat himself to a good port. You have to examine things a bit closer than that."

"What do you mean?"

"If our section was the one suspected the leaks could only have concerned Africa."

"Why?"

"There's plenty of other information that passes through my section—that we pass on—that must be of greater interest to the Russians, but if the leak was there, don't you see, the other sections would be suspect too? So the leak can only be about our particular share of Africa."

"Yes," Daintry agreed, "I see that."

"That seems to indicate—well, if not exactly an ideology—you don't need to look necessarily for a Communist—but a strong attachment to Africa—or to Africans. I doubt if Davis had ever known an African." He paused and then added with deliberation and a certain feeling of joy in the dangerous game, "Except, of course, my wife and my child." He was putting the dot on an i, but he wasn't going to cross the t's as well. He went on, "69300 has been a long time in L.M. No one knows what friendships he's made—he has his African agents, many of them Communist."

After so many years of concealment he was beginning to enjoy this snake-and-ladder game. "Just as I had in Pretoria," he continued. He smiled. "Even C, you know, has a certain love of Africa."

"Oh, there you are joking," Daintry said.

"Of course I'm joking. I only want to show how little they had against Davis compared with others, myself or 69300—and all those secretaries about whom we know nothing."

"They were all carefully vetted."

"Of course they were. We'll have the names of all their lovers on the files, lovers anyway of that particular year, but some girls change their lovers like they change their winter clothes."

Daintry said, "You've mentioned a lot of suspects, but you are so sure about Davis." He added, unhappily, "You're lucky not to be a security officer. I nearly resigned after Davis's funeral. I wish I had."

"Why didn't you?"

"What would I have done to pass the time?"

"You could have collected car numbers. I did that once."

"Why did you quarrel with your wife?" Daintry asked. "Forgive me. That's no business of mine."

"She disapproved of what I'm doing."

"You mean for the firm?"

"Not exactly."

Castle could tell the game was nearly over. Daintry had surreptitiously looked at his wrist watch. He wondered whether it was a real watch or a disguised microphone. Perhaps he thought he had come to the end of his tape. Would he ask to go to the lavatory so that he could change it?

"Have another whisky."

"No, I'd better not. I have to drive home."

Castle went with him to the hall, and Buller too. Buller was sorry to see a new friend leave.

"Thanks for the drink," Daintry said.

"Thank you for the chance to talk about a lot of things."

"Don't come out. It's a beastly night." But Castle followed him into the cold drizzle. He noticed the tail lights of a car fifty yards down the road opposite the police station.

"Is that your car?"

"No. Mine's a little way up the road. I had to walk down because I couldn't see the numbers in this rain."

"Goodnight then."

"Goodnight. I hope things go all right—I mean with your wife."

Castle stood in the slow cold rain long enough to wave to Daintry as he passed. His car didn't stop, he noticed, at the police station but turned right and took the London road. Of course he could always stop at the King's Arms or the Swan to use the telephone, but even in that case Castle doubted whether he would have a very clear report to make. They would probably want to hear his tape before making a decision—Castle felt sure now the watch was a microphone. Of course, the railway station might already be watched and the immigration officers warned at the airports. One fact had surely emerged from Daintry's visit. Young Halliday must have begun to talk or they would never have sent Daintry to see him.

At his door he looked up and down the road. There was no apparent watcher, but the lights of the car opposite the police station still shone through the rain. It didn't look like a police car. The police—he supposed even those of the Special Branch—had to put up with British makes, and this—he couldn't be sure but it looked like a Toyota. He remembered the Toyota on the road to Ashridge. He tried to make out the color, but the rain obscured it. Red and black were indistinguishable through the drizzle which was beginning to turn to sleet. He went indoors and for the first time he dared to hope.

He took the glasses to the kitchen and washed them carefully. It was as though he were removing the fingerprints of his despair. Then he laid two more glasses in the sitting room, and for the first time he encouraged hope to grow. It was a tender plant and it needed a great deal of encouragement, but he told himself that the car was certainly a Toyota. He wouldn't let himself think how many Toyotas there were in the region but waited in patience for the bell to ring. He wondered who it was who would come and stand in Daintry's place on the threshold. It wouldn't be Boris—he was sure of that—and neither would it be young Halliday, who was only out of custody on sufferance and was probably deeply engaged now with men from the Special Branch.

He went back to the kitchen and gave Buller a plate of biscuits—perhaps it would be a long time before he would be able to eat again. The clock in the kitchen had a noisy tick which seemed to make time go more slowly. If there was really a friend in the Toyota he was taking a long time to appear.

4

Colonel Daintry pulled into the yard of the King's Arms. There was only one car in the yard, and he sat for a while at the wheel, wondering whether to telephone now and what to say if he did. He had been shaken with a secret anger during his lunch at the Reform with C and Doctor Percival. There were moments when he had wanted to push his plate of smoked trout aside and say, "I resign. I don't want to have any more to do with your bloody firm." He was tired to death of secrecy and of errors which had to be covered up and not admitted. A man came across the yard from the outside lavatory whistling a tuneless tune, buttoning his fly in the security of the dark, and went on into the bar. Daintry thought: They killed my marriage with their secrets. During the war there had been a simple cause—much simpler than the one his father knew. The Kaiser had not been a Hitler, but in the cold war they were now fighting it was possible, as in the Kaiser's war, to argue right and wrong. There was nothing clear enough in the cause to justify murder by mistake. Again he found himself in the bleak house of his childhood, crossing the hall, entering the room where his father and his mother sat hand in hand. "God knows best," his father said, remembering Jutland and Admiral Jellicoe. His mother said, "My dear, at your age, it's difficult to find another job." He turned off his lights and moved through the slow heavy rainfall into the bar. He thought: My wife has enough money, my daughter is married, I could live—somehow—on my pension.

On this cold wet night there was only one man in the bar—he was drinking a pint of bitter. He said, "Good evening, sir," as though they were well acquainted.

"Good evening. A double whisky," Daintry ordered.

"If you can call it that," the man said as the barman turned away to hold a glass below a bottle of Johnnie Walker.

"Call what?"

"The evening, I meant, sir. Though this weather's only to be expected, I suppose, in November."

"Can I use your telephone?" Daintry asked the barman.

The barman pushed the whisky across with an air of rejection. He nodded in the direction of a box. He was clearly a man of few words: he was here to listen to what customers chose to say but not to communicate himself more than was strictly necessary, until—no doubt with pleasure—he would pronounce the phrase, "Time, Gentlemen."

Daintry dialed Doctor Percival's number and while he listened to the engaged tone, he tried to rehearse the words he wished to use. "I've seen Castle . . . He's alone in the house . . . He's had a quarrel with his wife . . . There's nothing more to report . . ." He would slam down the receiver as he slammed it down now—then he went back to the bar and his whisky and the man who insisted on talking.

"Uh," the barman said, "uh" and once, "That's right."

The customer turned to Daintry and included him in his conversation. "They don't even teach simple arithmetic these days. I said to my nephew—he's nine—what's four times seven, and do you think he could tell me?"

Daintry drank his whisky with his eye on the telephone box, still trying to make up his mind what words to use.

"I can see you agree with me," the man said to Daintry. "And you?" he asked the barman. "Your business would go to pot, wouldn't it, if you couldn't say what four times seven was?"

The barman wiped some spilled beer off the bar and said, "Uh."

"Now you, sir, I can guess very easily what profession you follow. Don't ask me how. It's a hunch I have. Comes from studying faces, I suppose, and human nature. That's how I came to be talking about arithmetic while you were on the telephone. That's a subject, I said to Mr. Barker here, about which the gentleman will have strong opinions. Weren't those my very words?"

"Uh," Mr. Barker said.

"I'll have another pint if you don't mind."

Mr. Barker filled his glass.

"My friends sometimes ask me for an exhibition. They even have a little bet on it now and then. He's a schoolmaster, I say, about someone in the tube, or he's a chemist, and then I inquire politely—they don't take offense when I explain to them—and nine times out of ten, I'm right. Mr. Barker has seen me at it in here, haven't you, Mr. Barker?"

"Uh."

"Now you, sir, if you'll excuse me playing my little game just to amuse Mr. Barker here on a cold wet evening—you are in Government service. Am I right, sir?"

"Yes," Daintry said. He finished his whisky and put down his glass. It was time to try the telephone again.

"So we're getting warm, eh?" The customer fixed him with beady eyes. "A sort of confidential position. You know a lot more about things than the rest of us."

"I have to telephone," Daintry said.

"Just a moment, sir. I just want to show Mr. Barker . . ." He wiped a little beer from his mouth with a handkerchief and thrust his face close to Daintry's. "You deal in figures," he said. "You are in the Inland Revenue."

Daintry moved to the telephone box.

"You see," the customer said, "touchy fellow. They don't like to be recognized. An inspector probably."

This time Daintry got the ringing tone and soon he heard Doctor Percival's voice, bland and reassuring as though he had kept his bedside manner long after he had abandoned bedsides. "Yes? Doctor Percival here. Who is that?"

"Daintry."

"Good evening, my dear fellow. Any news? Where are you?"

"I'm at Berkhamsted. I've seen Castle."

"Yes. What's your impression?"

Anger took the words he meant to speak and tore them in pieces like a letter one decides not to send. "My impression is that you've murdered the wrong man."

"Not murdered," Doctor Percival said gently, "an error in the prescription. The stuff hadn't been tried before on a human being. But what makes you think that Castle . . . ?"

"Because he's certain that Davis was innocent."

"He said that—in so many words?"

"Yes."

"What's he up to?"

"He's waiting."

"Waiting for what?"

"Something to happen. His wife's left him, taking the child. He says they've quarreled."

"We've already circulated a warning," Doctor Percival said, "to the airports—and the sea ports too of course. If he makes a run for it, we'll have *prima facie* evidence—but we'll still need the hard stuff."

"You didn't wait for the hard stuff with Davis."

"C insists on it this time. What are you doing now?"

"Going home."

"You asked him about Muller's notes?"

"No."

"Why?"

"It wasn't necessary."

"You've done an excellent job, Daintry. But why do you suppose he came clean like that to you?"

Daintry put the receiver down without answering and left the box. The customer said, "I was right, wasn't I? You are an inspector of the Inland Revenue."

"Yes."

"You see, Mr. Barker. I've scored again."

Colonel Daintry went slowly out to his car. For a while he sat in it with the engine running and watched the drops of rain pursue each other down the windscreen. Then he drove out of the yard and turned in the direction of Boxmoor and London and the flat in St. James's Street where yesterday's Camembert was awaiting him. He drove slowly. The November drizzle had turned into real rain and there was a hint of hail. He thought: Well, I did what they would call my duty, but though he was on the road toward home and the table where he would sit beside the Camembert to write his letter, he was in no hurry to arrive. In his mind the act of resignation had already been accomplished. He told himself he was a free man, that he had no duties any longer and no obligations, but he had never felt such an extreme solitude as he felt now.

5

The bell rang. Castle had been waiting for it a long time and yet he hesitated to go to the door; it seemed to him now that he had been absurdly optimistic. By this time young Halliday would surely have talked, the Toyota was one of a thousand Toyotas, the Special Branch had probably been waiting for him to be alone, and he knew how absurdly indiscreet he had been with Daintry. A second time the bell rang and then a third; there was nothing he could do but open. He went to the door with his hand on the revolver in his pocket, but it was of no more value than a rabbit's foot. He couldn't shoot his way out of an island. Buller gave him a spurious support, growling heavily, but he knew, when the door opened, Buller would fawn on whoever was there. He couldn't see through the stained glass which ran with the rain. Even when he opened the door he saw nothing distinctly—only a hunched figure.

"It's a shocking night," a voice he recognized complained to him out of the dark.

"Mr. Halliday—I wasn't expecting you."

Castle thought: He's come to ask me to help his son, but what can I do?

"Good boy. Good boy," the almost invisible Mr. Halliday said nervously to Buller.

"Come in," Castle assured him. "He's quite harmless."

"I can see he's a very fine dog."

Mr. Halliday entered cautiously, hugging the wall, and Buller wagged what he had of a tail and dribbled.

"You can see, Mr. Halliday, he's a friend of all the world. Take off your coat. Come and have a whisky."

"I'm not much of a drinking man, but I won't say No."

"I was sorry to hear on the radio about your son. You must be very anxious."

Mr. Halliday followed Castle into the living room. He said, "He had it coming to him, sir, perhaps it will teach him a lesson. The police have been carting a lot of stuff out of his shop. The inspector showed me one or two of the things and really disgusting they were. But as I said to the inspector I don't suppose he read the stuff himself."

"I hope the police have not been bothering you?"

"Oh no. As I told you, sir, I think they feel quite sorry for me. They know I keep a very different kind of shop."

"Did you have a chance to give him my letter?"

"Ah, there, sir, I thought it wiser not. Under the circumstances. But don't you worry. I passed the message on where it truly belongs."

He raised a book which Castle had been trying to read and looked at the title.

"What on earth do you mean?"

"Well, sir, you've always been, I think, under a bit of a misunderstanding. My son never concerned himself with things in your way of business. But *they* thought it just as well—in case of trouble —that *you* believed . . ." He bent and warmed his hands in front of the gas fire, and his eyes looked up with a sly amusement. "Well, sir, things being as they are, we've got to get you out of here pretty quick."

It came as a shock to Castle to realize how little he had been trusted even by those who had the most reason to trust.

"If you'll forgive my asking, sir, where exactly are your wife and your boy? I've orders . . ."

"This morning, when I heard the news about your son, I sent them away. To my mother. She believes we've had a quarrel."

"Ah, that's one difficulty out of the way."

Old Mr. Halliday, after warming his hands sufficiently, began to move around the room: he cast his eye over the bookshelves. He said, "I'll give as good a price for those as any other bookseller. Twenty-five pounds down—it's all you are allowed to take out of the country. I've got the notes on me. They fit my stock. All these World's Classics and Everyman's. They are not reprinted as they should be, and when they do reprint, what a price!"

"I thought," Castle said, "we were in a bit of a hurry."

"There's one thing I've learned," Mr. Halliday said, "in the last fifty years is to take things easy. Once start being hurried and you are sure to make mistakes. If you've got half an hour to spare always pretend to yourself you've got three hours. You did say something, sir, about a whisky?"

"If we can spare the time . . ." Castle poured out two glasses.

"We've got the time. I expect you have a bag packed with all the needful?"

"Yes."

"What are you going to do about the dog?"

"Leave him behind, I suppose. I hadn't thought . . . Perhaps you could take him to a vet."

"Not wise, sir. A connection between you and me—it wouldn't do —if they went searching for him. All the same we've got to keep him quiet for the next few hours. Is he a barker when he's left alone?"

"I don't know. He's not used to being alone."

"What I have in mind is the neighbors complaining. One of them could easily ring the police, and we don't want them finding an empty house."

"They'll find one soon enough anyway."

"It won't matter when you're safe abroad. It's a pity your wife didn't take the dog with her."

"She couldn't. My mother has a cat. Buller kills cats at sight."

"Yes, they're naughty ones, those boxers, where cats are concerned. I have a cat myself." Mr. Halliday pulled at Buller's ears and Buller fawned on him. "It's what I said. If you are in a hurry you forget things. Like the dog. Have you a cellar?"

"Not a soundproof one. If you mean to shut him up there."

"I notice, sir, that in your right pocket you seem to have a gun— or am I mistaken?"

"I thought if the police came . . . There's only one charge in it."

"The counsel of despair, sir?"

"I hadn't made up my mind to use it."

"I would rather you let me have it, sir. If we were stopped, at least I have a license, with all this shoplifting we have nowadays. What's his name, sir? I mean the dog."

"Buller."

"Come here, Buller, come here. There's a good dog." Buller laid his muzzle on Mr. Halliday's knee. "Good dog, Buller. Good dog. You don't want to cause any trouble, do you, not to a good master like you have." Buller wagged his stump. "They think they know when you like them," Mr. Halliday said. He scratched Buller behind the ears and Buller showed his appreciation. "Now, sir, if you wouldn't mind giving me the gun . . . Ah, you kill cats, eh . . . Ah, the wicked one."

"They'll hear the shot," Castle said.

"We'll take a little walk down to the cellar. One shot—nobody pays any attention. They think it's a backfire."

"He won't go with you."

"Let's see. Come on, Buller, my lad. Come for a walk. A walk, Buller."

"You see. He won't go."

"It's time to be off, sir. You'd better come down with me. I wanted to spare you."

"I don't want to be spared."

Castle led the way down the stairs to the cellar. Buller followed him and Mr. Halliday tailed Buller.

"I wouldn't put on the light, sir, a shot and a light going out. *That* might arouse curiosity."

Castle closed what had once been the coal chute.

"Now, sir, if you'll give me the gun . . ."

"No, I'll do this." He held the gun out, pointing it at Buller, and Buller, ready for a game and probably taking the muzzle for a rubber bone, fastened his jaws around it and pulled. Castle pressed the trigger twice because of the empty chamber. He felt nausea.

"I'll have another whisky," he said, "before we go."

"You deserve one, sir. It's odd how fond one can get of a dumb animal. My cat . . ."

"I disliked Buller intensely. It's only . . . well, I've never killed anything before."

6

"It's hard driving in this rain," Mr. Halliday said, breaking a very long silence. The death of Buller had clogged their tongues.

"Where are we going? Heathrow? The immigration officers will be on the look-out by this time."

"I'm taking you to a hotel. If you open the glove compartment, sir, you'll find a key. Room 423. All you have to do is take the lift straight up. Don't go to the desk. Wait in the room until someone comes for you."

"Suppose a maid . . ."

"Hang a Don't Disturb notice on the door."

"And after that . . ."

"I wouldn't know, sir. Those were all the instructions I have."

Castle wondered how the news of Buller's death would reach Sam. He knew that he would never be forgiven. He asked, "How did you get mixed up in this?"

"Not mixed up, sir. I've been a member of the Party, on the quiet as you might say, since I was a boy. I was in the army at seventeen —volunteered. Gave my age wrong. Thought I was going to France, but it was Archangel they sent me to. I was a prisoner for four years. I saw a lot and learned a lot in those four years."

"How did they treat you?"

"It was hard, but a boy can stand a lot, and there was always someone who was friendly. I learned a bit of Russian, enough to interpret for them, and they gave me books to read when they couldn't give me food."

"Communist books?"

"Of course, sir. A missionary hands out the Bible, doesn't he?"

"So you are one of the faithful."

"It's been a lonely life, I have to admit that. You see, I could never go to meetings or walk in marches. Even my boy doesn't know. They use me when they can in little ways—like in your case, sir. I've picked up from your drop many a time. Oh, it was a happy day for me when you walked into my shop. I felt less alone."

"Have you never wavered a bit, Halliday? I mean—Stalin, Hungary, Czechoslovakia?"

"I saw enough in Russia when I was a boy—and in England too with the Depression when I came home—to inoculate me against little things like that."

"Little?"

"If you will forgive me saying so, sir, your conscience is rather selective. I could say to you—Hamburg, Dresden, Hiroshima. Didn't they shake your faith a bit in what you call democracy? Perhaps they did or you wouldn't be with me now."

"That was war."

"My people have been at war since 1917."

Castle peered into the wet night between the sweeps of the wipers. "You *are* taking me to Heathrow."

"Not exactly." Mr. Halliday laid a hand light as an autumn Ashridge leaf on Castle's knee. "Don't you worry, sir. *They* are looking after you. I envy you. You'll be seeing Moscow I shouldn't wonder."

"Have you never been there?"

"Never. The nearest I ever came to it was the prison camp near Archangel. Did you ever see *The Three Sisters?* I saw it only once, but I always remember what one of them said and I say it to myself when I can't sleep at night—'To sell the house, to make an end of everything here, and off to Moscow . . .'"

"You'd find a rather different Moscow to Chekhov's."

"There's another thing one of those sisters said, 'Happy people don't notice if it's winter or summer. If I lived in Moscow I wouldn't mind what the weather was like.' Oh well, I tell myself when I'm feeling low, Marx never knew Moscow either, and I look across Old Compton Street and I think, London is still Marx's London. Soho's Marx's Soho. This was where the *Communist Manifesto* was first printed." A lorry came suddenly out of the rain and swerved and nearly hit them and went on indifferently into the night. "Shocking drivers there are," Mr. Halliday said, "they know nothing's going to hurt *them* in those juggernauts. We ought to have bigger penalties for dangerous driving. You know, sir, that's what was really wrong in Hungary and Czechoslovakia—dangerous driving. Dubcek was a dangerous driver—it's as simple as that."

"Not to me it isn't. I've never wanted to end up in Moscow."

"I suppose it will seem a bit strange—you not being one of us, but you shouldn't worry. I don't know what you've done for us, but it must be important, and they'll look after you, you can be sure of that. Why, I wouldn't be surprised if they didn't give you the Order of Lenin or put you on a postage stamp like Sorge."

"Sorge was a Communist."

"And it makes me proud to think you are on the road to Moscow in this old car of mine."

"If we drove for a century, Halliday, you wouldn't convert me."

"I wonder. After all, you've done a lot to help us."

"I've helped you over Africa, that's all."

"Exactly, sir. You are on the road. Africa's the thesis, Hegel would say. You belong to the antithesis—but you are an active part of the antithesis—you are one of those who will belong to the synthesis yet."

"That's all jargon to me. I'm no philosopher."

"A militant doesn't have to be, and you are a militant."

"Not for Communism. I'm only a casualty now."

"They'll cure you in Moscow."

"In a psychiatric ward?"

That phrase silenced Mr. Halliday. Had he found a small crack in the dialectic of Hegel, or was it the silence of pain and doubt? He would never know, for the hotel was ahead of them, the lights smudging through the rain. "Get out here," Mr. Halliday said. "I'd better not be seen." Cars passed them when they halted, in a long illuminated chain, the headlamps of one car lighting the rear lamps of another. A Boeing 707 slanted noisily down on London Airport. Mr. Halliday scrabbled in the back of the car. "There's something I've forgotten." He pulled out a plastic bag which might once have contained duty free goods. He said, "Put the things out of your case into this. They might notice you at the desk if you go to the lift carrying a suitcase."

"There's not enough room in it."

"Then leave what you can't get in."

Castle obeyed. Even after all those years of secrecy he realized that in an emergency the young recruit of Archangel was the real expert. He abandoned with reluctance his pajamas—thinking, a prison will provide them—his sweater. If I get so far, they will have to give me something warm.

Mr. Halliday said, "I have a little present. A copy of that Trollope you asked for. You won't need a second copy now. It's a long book, but there'll be a lot of waiting. There always is in war. It's called *The Way We Live Now*."

"The book recommended by your son?"

"Oh, I deceived you a little there. It's me that reads Trollope, not him. His favorite author is a man called Robbins. You must forgive me my little deception—I wanted you to think a bit better of him in spite of that shop. He's not a bad boy."

Castle shook Mr. Halliday's hand. "I'm sure he's not. I hope all goes well with him."

"Remember. Go straight to room 423, and wait."

Castle walked away toward the light of the hotel carrying the plastic bag. He felt as though he had already lost contact with everything he had known in England—Sarah and Sam were out of reach in the house of his mother which had never been his home. He thought: I was more at home in Pretoria. I had work to do there. But now there's no work left for me to do. A voice called after him through the rain, "Good luck, sir. The best of luck," and he heard the car drive away.

7

He was bewildered—when he walked through the door of the hotel he walked straight into the Caribbean. There was no rain. There were palm trees around a pool, and the sky shone with innumerable pinpoint stars; he smelled the warm stuffy wet air which he remembered from a distant holiday he had taken soon after the war: he was surrounded—that was inevitable in the Caribbean—by American voices. There was no danger of his being remarked by anyone at the long desk—they were far too busy with an influx of American passengers, just deposited from what airport, Kingston? Bridgetown? A black waiter went by carrying two rum punches toward a young couple sitting by the pool. The lift was there, beside him, waiting with open doors, and yet he hung back amazed . . . The young couple began to drink their punch through straws under the stars. He put out a hand to convince himself that there was no rain and someone close behind him said, "Why, if it isn't Maurice? What are you doing in this joint?" He stopped his hand halfway to his pocket and looked round. He was glad he no longer had his revolver.

The speaker was someone called Blit who had been his contact a few years back in the American Embassy until Blit was transferred to Mexico—perhaps because he could speak no Spanish. "Blit!" he exclaimed with false enthusiasm. It had always been that way. Blit had called him Maurice from their first meeting, but he had never got further than "Blit."

"Where are you off to?" Blit asked, but didn't wait for an answer. He had always preferred to talk about himself. "Off to New York," Blit said. "Non-arrival of incoming plane. Spending the night here. Smart idea, this joint. Just like the Virgin Islands. I'd put on my Bermuda shorts if I had them."

"I thought you were in Mexico."

"That's old history. I'm on the European desk again now. You still on darkest Africa?"

"Yes."

"You delayed here too?"

"I've got to wait around," Castle said, hoping his ambiguity would not be questioned.

"What about a Planter's Punch? They do them OK here, so I'm told."

"I'll meet you in half an hour," Castle said.

"OK. OK. By the pool then."

"By the pool."

Castle got into the lift and Blit followed him. "Going up? So am I. Which floor?"

"Fourth."

"Me too. I'll give you a free ride."

Was it possible that the Americans too might be watching him?

In these circumstances it seemed unsafe to put down anything to coincidence.

"Eating here?" Blit asked.

"I'm not sure. You see, it depends . . ."

"You sure are security minded," Blit said. "Good old Maurice." They walked together down the corridor. Room 423 came first, and Castle fumbled with his key long enough to see that Blit went on without a pause to 427—no, 429. Castle felt safer when his door was locked and the Don't Disturb notice was hanging outside.

The dial of the central heating stood at 75°. It was hot enough for the Caribbean. He went to the window and looked out. Below was the round bar and above the artificial sky. A stout woman with blue hair weaved her way along the edge of the pool: she must have had too many rum punches. He examined the room carefully in case it contained some hint of the future, as he had examined his own house for any hint of the past. Two double beds, an armchair, a wardrobe, a chest of drawers, a desk which was bare except for a blotting pad, a television set, a door that led to the bathroom. The lavatory seat had a strip of paper pasted across it assuring him that it was hygienic: the toothglasses were swathed in plastic. He went back into the bedroom and opened the blotting pad and learned from the printed notepaper that he was in the Starflight Hotel. A card listed the restaurants and the bars—in one restaurant there was music and dancing—it was called the Pizarro. The grill room by contrast was called the Dickens, and there was a third, self-service, which was called the Oliver Twist. "You help yourself to more." Another card informed him that there were buses every half-hour to Heathrow airport.

He discovered under the television set a refrigerator containing miniature bottles of whisky and gin and brandy, tonic water and soda, two kinds of beer and quarter bottles of champagne. He chose a J & B from habit and sat down to wait. "There'll be a lot of waiting," Mr. Halliday had said, when he gave him the Trollope, and he began to read for want of anything else to do: "Let the reader be introduced to Lady Carbury, upon whose character and doings much will depend of whatever interest these pages may have, as she sits at her writing table in her own room in her own house in Welbeck Street." He found it was not a book which could distract him from the way he lived now.

He went to the window. The black waiter passed below him, and then he saw Blit come out and gaze around. Surely half an hour couldn't possibly have gone by: he reassured himself—ten minutes.

Blit would not have really missed him yet. He turned the lights out in his room, so that Blit, if he looked up, would not see him. Blit sat himself down by the circular bar: he gave his order. Yes, it was a Planter's Punch. The waiter was putting in the slice of orange and the cherry. Blit had taken off his jacket and he was wearing a shirt with short sleeves, which added to the illusion of the palm trees and the pool and the starry night. Castle watched him use the telephone in the bar and he rang a number. Was it only in Castle's imagination that Blit seemed to raise his eyes toward the window of room 423 while he talked? Reporting what? To whom?

He heard the door open behind him and the lights went on. Turning quickly, he saw an image flash across the looking-glass of the wardrobe door like someone who didn't want to be seen—the image of a small man with a black moustache wearing a dark suit and carrying a black attaché case. "I was delayed by the circulation," the man said in precise but rather incorrect English.

"You've come for me?"

"Time is a little lacking for us. There is a necessity for you to catch the next autobus to the airport." He began to unpack the attaché case on the desk: first an air ticket, then a passport, a bottle which looked as if it might contain gum, a bulging plastic bag, a hairbrush and comb, a razor.

"I have with me everything I need," Castle said, catching the precise tone.

The man ignored him. He said, "You will find your ticket is to Paris only. That is something I will explain to you."

"Surely they'll be watching all the planes wherever they go."

"They will be watching in particular the one to Prague which is due to leave at the same time as the one to Moscow which has been delayed due to trouble with the engines. An unusual occurrence. Perhaps Aeroflot await an important passenger. The police will be very attentive to Prague and Moscow."

"The watch will be set earlier—at the immigration desks. They won't wait at the gates."

"That will be taken care of. You must approach the desks—let me see your watch—in about fifty minutes. The bus will leave in thirty minutes. This is your passport."

"What do I do in Paris if I get that far?"

"You will be met as you leave the airport, and you will be given another ticket. You will have just time to catch another plane."

"Where to?"

"I have no idea. You will learn all that in Paris."

"Interpol will have warned the police there by this time."

"No. Interpol never act in a political case. It is against the rules."

Castle opened the passport. "Partridge," he said. "You've chosen a good name. The shooting season isn't over." Then he looked at the photograph. "But this photo will never do. It's not like me."

"That is true. But now we shall make you more like the photograph."

He carried the tools of his trade into the bathroom. Between the toothglasses he propped an enlarged photograph of the one in the passport.

"Sit on this chair, please." He began to trim Castle's eyebrows and then began on his hair—the man of the passport had a crewcut. Castle watched the scissors move in the mirror—he was surprised to see how a crewcut changed the whole face, enlarging the forehead; it seemed to change even the expression of the eyes. "You've taken ten years off my age," Castle said.

"Sit still, please."

The man then began to attach the hairs of a thin moustache—the moustache of a timid man who lacked confidence. He said, "A beard or a heavy moustache is always an object of suspicion." It was a stranger who looked back at Castle from the mirror. "There. Finished. I think it is good enough." He went to his briefcase and took from it a white rod which he telescoped into a walking stick. He said, "You are blind. An object of sympathy, Mr. Partridge. An Air France hostess has been asked to meet the autobus from the hotel and she will lead you through immigration to your plane. In Paris at Rossy when you depart from the airport you will be driven to Orly—another plane there with engine trouble. Perhaps you will no longer be Mr. Partridge, another make-up in the car, another passport. The human visage is infinitely adaptable. That is a good argument against the importance of heredity. We are born with much the same face—think of a baby—but environment changes it."

"It seems easy," Castle said, "but will it work?"

"We think it will work," the little man said as he packed his case. "Go out now, and remember to use your stick. Please do not move your eyes, move your whole head if someone speaks to you. Try to keep the eyes blank."

Without thinking Castle picked up *The Way We Live Now*.

"No, no, Mr. Partridge. A blind man is not likely to possess a book. And you must leave that sack behind."

"It only holds a spare shirt, a razor . . ."

"A spare shirt has the mark of a laundry."

"Won't it seem odd if I have no luggage?"

"That is not known to the immigration officer unless he asks to see your ticket."

"He probably will."

"Never mind, you are only going home. You live in Paris. The address is in your passport."

"What profession am I?"

"Retired."

"That at least is true," Castle said.

He came out of the lift and began to tap his way toward the entrance where the bus waited. As he passed the doors which led to the bar and the pool he saw Blit. Blit was looking at his watch with an air of impatience. An elderly woman took Castle's arm and said, "Are you catching the bus?"

"Yes."

"I am too. Let me help you."

He heard a voice calling after him. "Maurice!" He had to walk slowly because the woman walked slowly. "Hi! Maurice."

"I think someone's calling you," the woman said.

"A mistake."

He heard footsteps behind them. He took his arm away from the woman and turned his head as he had been instructed to do and stared blankly a little to the side of Blit. Blit looked at him with surprise. He said, "I'm sorry. I thought . . ."

The woman said, "The driver's signaling to us. We must hurry."

When they were seated together in the bus she looked through the window. She said, "You sure must be very like his friend. He's still standing there staring."

"Everybody in the world, so they say, has a double," Castle replied.

Part Six

Chapter I

She had turned to look back through the window of the taxi and seen nothing through the smoke-gray glass: it was as though Maurice had deliberately drowned himself, without so much as a cry, in the waters of a steely lake. She was robbed, without hope of recovery, of the only sight and sound she wanted, and she resented all that was charitably thrust on her like the poor substitute a butcher offers for the good cut which he has kept for a better customer.

Lunch in the house among the laurels was an ordeal. Her mother-in-law had a guest she couldn't cancel—a clergyman with the unattractive name of Bottomley—she called him Ezra—who had come home from a mission field in Africa. Sarah felt like an exhibit at one of the lantern lectures he probably gave. Mrs. Castle didn't introduce her. She simply said, "This is Sarah," as though she had come out of an orphanage, as indeed she had. Mr. Bottomley was unbearably kind to Sam and treated her like a member of his colored congregation with calculated interest. Tinker Bell, who had fled at the first sight of them, fearing Buller, was now too friendly and scratched at her skirts.

"Tell me what it's really like in a place like Soweto," Mr. Bottomley said. "My field, you know, was Rhodesia. The English papers exaggerated there too. We are not as black as we are painted," he added and then blushed at his mistake. Mrs. Castle poured him another glass of water. "I mean," he said, "can you bring up a little fellow properly there?" and his bright gaze picked Sam out like a spotlight in a night club.

"How would Sarah know, Ezra?" Mrs. Castle said. She explained with reluctance, "Sarah is my daughter-in-law."

Mr. Bottomley's blush increased. "Ah, then you are over here on a visit?" he asked.

"Sarah is living with me," Mrs. Castle said. "For the time being. My son has never lived in Soweto. He was in the Embassy."

"It must be nice for the boy," Mr. Bottomley said, "to come and see Granny."

Sarah thought: Is this what life is to be from now on?

After Mr. Bottomley had departed Mrs. Castle told her that they must have a serious conversation. "I rang up Maurice," she said, "he was in a most unreasonable mood." She turned to Sam. "Go into the garden, dear, and have a game."

"It's raining," Sam said.

"I'd forgotten, dear. Go upstairs and play with Tinker Bell."

"I'll go upstairs," Sam said, "but I won't play with your cat. Buller is my friend. He knows what to do with cats."

When they were alone Mrs. Castle said, "Maurice told me if you returned home he would leave the house. What *have* you done, Sarah?"

"I'd rather not talk about it. Maurice told me to come here, so I've come."

"Which of you is—well, what they call the guilty party?"

"Does there always have to be a guilty party?"

"I'm going to ring him again."

"I can't stop you, but it won't be any use."

Mrs. Castle dialed the number, and Sarah prayed to God whom she didn't believe in that she might at least hear Maurice's voice, but "There's no reply," Mrs. Castle said.

"He's probably at the office."

"On a Saturday afternoon?"

"Times are irregular in his job."

"I thought the Foreign Office was better organized."

Sarah waited until the evening, after she had put Sam to bed, then walked down into the town. She went to the Crown and gave herself a J & B. She made it a double in memory of Maurice and then went to the telephone box. She knew Maurice had told her not to contact him. If he were still at home, and his telephone was tapped, he would have to pretend anger, continue a quarrel which didn't exist, but at least she would know he was there in the house and not in a police cell or on his way across a Europe she had never seen. She let the telephone ring a long time before she put down the receiver—she was aware she was making it easy for Them to trace the call, but she didn't care. If They came to see her at least she would have news of him. She left the box and drank her J & B at the bar and walked back to Mrs. Castle's house. Mrs. Castle said, "Sam's been calling for you." She went upstairs.

"What is it, Sam?"

"Do you think Buller's all right?"

"Of course he's all right. What could be wrong?"

"I had a dream."

"What did you dream?"

"I don't remember. Buller will miss me. I wish we could have him here."

"We can't. You know that. Sooner or later he'd be sure to kill Tinker Bell."

"I wouldn't mind that."

She went reluctantly downstairs. Mrs. Castle was watching television.

"Anything interesting on the news?" Sarah asked.

"I seldom listen to the news," Mrs. Castle said. "I like to read the news in *The Times*." But next morning there was no news which could possibly interest her in the Sunday papers. Sunday—he never had to work on Sunday. At midday she went back to the Crown and rang the house again, and again she held on for a long while— he might be in the garden with Buller, but at last she had to give up even that hope. She comforted herself with the thought that he *had* escaped, but then she reminded herself that They had the power to hold him—wasn't it for three days?—without a charge.

Mrs. Castle had lunch—a joint of roast beef—served very punctually at one. "Shall we listen to the news?" Sarah asked.

"Don't play with your napkin ring, Sam dear," Mrs. Castle said. "Just take out your napkin and put the ring down by your plate." Sarah found Radio 3. Mrs. Castle said, "There's never news worth listening to on Sundays," and she was right, of course.

Never had a Sunday passed more slowly. The rain stopped and the feeble sun tried to find a gap through the clouds. Sarah took Sam for a walk across what was called—she didn't know why—a forest. There were no trees—only low bushes and scrub (one area had been cleared for a golf course). Sam said, "I like Ashridge better," and a little later, "A walk's not a walk without Buller." Sarah wondered: How long will life be like this? They cut across a corner of the golf course to get home and a golfer who had obviously had too good a lunch shouted to them to get off the fairway. When Sarah didn't respond quickly enough he called, "Hi! You! I'm talking to you, Topsy!" Sarah seemed to remember that Topsy had been a black girl in some book the Methodists had given her to read when she was a child.

That night Mrs. Castle said, "It's time we had a serious talk, dear."

"What about?"

"You ask me what about? Really, Sarah! About you and my grandson of course—and Maurice. Neither of you will tell me what this quarrel is all about. Have you or has Maurice grounds for a divorce?"

"Perhaps. Desertion counts, doesn't it?"

"Who has deserted whom? To come to your mother-in-law's house is hardly desertion. And Maurice—he hasn't deserted you if he's still at home."

"He isn't."

"Then where is he?"

"I don't know, I don't know, Mrs. Castle. Can't you just wait awhile and not talk?"

"This is *my* home, Sarah. It would be convenient to know just how long you plan to stay. Sam should be at school. There's a law about that."

"I promise if you'll just let us stay for a week . . ."

"I'm not driving you away, dear, I'm trying to get you to behave like an adult person. I think you should see a lawyer and talk to him if you won't talk to me. I can telephone Mr. Bury tomorrow. He looks after my will."

"Just give me a week, Mrs. Castle." (There had been a time when Mrs. Castle had suggested Sarah should call her "mother," but she had been obviously relieved when Sarah continued to call her Mrs. Castle.)

On Monday morning she took Sam into the town and left him in a toyshop while she went to the Crown. There she telephoned to the office—it was a senseless thing to do, for if Maurice were still in London at liberty he would surely have telephoned her. In South Africa, long ago when she had worked for him, she would never have been so imprudent, but in this peaceful country town which had never known a racial riot or a midnight knock at the door the thought of danger seemed too fantastic to be true. She asked to speak to Mr. Castle's secretary, and, when a woman's voice answered, she said, "Is that Cynthia?" (She knew her by that name, though they had never met or talked to each other). There was a long pause—a pause long enough for someone to be asked to listen in—but she wouldn't believe it in this small place of retired people as she watched two lorry drivers finish their bitter. Then the dry thin voice said, "Cynthia isn't in today."

"When will she be in?"

"I'm afraid I can't say."

"Mr. Castle then?"

"Who is that speaking, please?"

She thought: I was nearly betraying Maurice and she put down the receiver. She felt she had betrayed her own past too—the secret meetings, the coded messages, the care which Maurice had taken in Johannesburg to instruct her and to keep them both out of the reach of BOSS. And, after all that, Muller was here in England—he had sat at table with her.

When she got back to the house she noticed a strange car in the laurel drive, and Mrs. Castle met her in the hall. She said, "There's someone to see you, Sarah. I've put him in the study."

"Who is it?"

Mrs. Castle lowered her voice and said in a tone of distaste, "I think it's a policeman."

The man had a large fair moustache which he stroked nervously. He was definitely not the kind of policeman that Sarah had known in her youth and she wondered how Mrs. Castle had detected his profession—she would have taken him for a small tradesman who had dealt with local families over the years. He looked just as snug and friendly as Doctor Castle's study, which had been left unchanged after the doctor's death: the pipe rack still over the desk, the Chinese bowl for ashes, the swivel armchair in which the stranger had been too ill at ease to seat himself. He stood by the bookcase partly blocking from view with his burly form the scarlet volumes of the Loeb classics and the green leather *Encyclopaedia Britannica*, 11th edition. He asked, "Mrs. Castle?" and she nearly answered, "No. That's my mother-in-law," so much a stranger did she feel in this house.

"Yes," she said. "Why?"

"I'm Inspector Butler."

"Yes?"

"I've had a telephone call from London. They asked me to come and have a word with you—that is, if you were here."

"Why?"

"They thought perhaps you could tell us how to get in touch with your husband."

She felt an immense relief—he wasn't after all in prison—till the thought came to her that this might be a trap—even the kindness and shyness and patent honesty of Inspector Butler might be a trap, the kind of trap BOSS were likely to lay. But this wasn't the country of BOSS. She said, "No. I can't. I don't know. Why?"

"Well, Mrs. Castle, it's partly to do with a dog."

"Buller?" she exclaimed.

"Well . . . if that's his name."

"It is his name. Please tell me what this is all about."

"You have a house in King's Road, Berkhamsted. That's right, isn't it?"

"Yes." She gave a laugh of relief. "Has Buller been killing a cat again? But I'm here. I'm innocent. You must see my husband, not me."

"We've tried to, Mrs. Castle, but we can't reach him. His office says he's not been in. He seems to have gone away and left the dog, although . . ."

"Was it a very valuable cat?"

"It's not a cat we are concerned about, Mrs. Castle. The neighbors complained about the noise—a sort of whining—and someone telephoned the police station. You see, there've been burglars recently at Boxmoor. Well, the police sent a man to see—and he found a scullery window open—he didn't have to break any glass . . . and the dog . . ."

"He wasn't bitten? I've never known Buller to bite a *person*."

"The poor dog couldn't do any biting: not in the state he was in. He'd been shot. Whoever had done it made a messy job. I'm afraid, Mrs. Castle, they had to finish your dog off."

"Oh God, what will Sam say?"

"Sam?"

"My son. He loved Buller."

"I'm fond of animals myself." The two-minute silence that followed seemed very long, like the two-minute tribute to the dead on Armistice Day. "I'm sorry to bring bad news," Inspector Butler said at last and the wheeled and pedestrian traffic of life started up again.

"I'm wondering what I'll say to Sam."

"Tell him the dog was run over and killed right away."

"Yes. I suppose that's best. I don't like lying to a child."

"There are white lies and black lies," Inspector Butler said. She wondered whether the lies he would force her to tell were black or white. She looked at the thick fair moustache and into the kindly eyes and wondered what on earth had made him into a policeman. It would be a little like lying to a child.

"Won't you sit down, Inspector?"

"You sit down, Mrs. Castle, if you'll excuse me. I've been sitting down all the morning." He looked at the row of pipes in the pipe rack with concentration: it might have been a valuable picture of which, as a connoisseur, he could appreciate the value.

"Thank you for coming yourself and not just telling me over the telephone."

"Well, Mrs. Castle, I had to come because there are some other questions. The police at Berkhamsted think there may have been a robbery. There was a scullery window open and the burglar may have shot the dog. Nothing seems to have been disturbed, but only you or your husband can tell, and they don't seem able to get in touch with your husband. Did he have any enemies? There's no sign of a struggle, but then there wouldn't be if the other man had a gun."

"I don't know of any enemies."

"A neighbor said he had an idea he worked in the Foreign Office. This morning they had quite a difficulty trying to find the right department and then it seemed they hadn't seen him since Friday. He should have been in, they said. When did you last see him, Mrs. Castle?"

"Saturday morning."

"You came here Saturday?"

"Yes."

"He stayed behind?"

"Yes. You see, we had decided to separate. For good."

"A quarrel?"

"A decision, Inspector. We've been married for seven years. You don't flare up after seven years."

"Did he own a revolver, Mrs. Castle?"

"Not that I know of. It's possible."

"Was he very upset—by the decision?"

"We were neither of us happy if that's what you mean."

"Would you be willing to go to Berkhamsted and look at the house?"

"I don't want to, but I suppose they could make me, couldn't they?"

"There's no question of making you. But, you see, they can't rule out a robbery . . . There might have been something valuable which they couldn't tell was missing. A piece of jewelry?"

"I've never gone in for jewelry. We weren't rich people, Inspector."

"Or a picture?"

"No."

"Then it makes us wonder if he might have done something

foolish or rash. If he was unhappy and it was his gun." He picked
up the Chinese bowl and examined the pattern, then turned to examine her in turn. She realized those kindly eyes were not after all
the eyes of a child. "You don't seem worried about *that* possibility,
Mrs. Castle."

"I'm not. It isn't the kind of thing he'd do."

"Yes, yes. Of course you know him better than anyone else and
I'm sure you're right. So you'll let us know at once, won't you, if he
gets in touch with you, I mean?"

"Of course."

"Under strain people sometimes do odd things. Even lose their
memory." He took a last long look at the pipe rack as if he were unwilling to part from it. "I'll ring up Berkhamsted, Mrs. Castle. I
hope you won't have to be troubled. And I'll let you know if I get
any news."

When they were at the door she asked him, "How did you know
I was here?"

"Neighbors with children get to know more than you'd allow for,
Mrs. Castle."

She watched him until he was safely in his car and then she went
back into the house. She thought: I shan't tell Sam yet. Let him get
used to life without Buller first. The other Mrs. Castle, the true
Mrs. Castle, met her outside the sitting room. She said, "Lunch is
getting cold. It *was* a policeman, wasn't it?"

"Yes."

"What did he want?"

"Maurice's address."

"Why?"

"How would I know?"

"Did you give it to him?"

"He's not at home. How should I know where he is?"

"I hope that man won't come back."

"I wouldn't be surprised if he does."

<h2 style="text-align:center">2</h2>

But the days passed without Inspector Butler and without news.
She made no further telephone calls to London. There was no point
to it now. Once when she telephoned to the butcher on her mother-
in-law's behalf to order some lamb cutlets she had an impression
the line was tapped. It was probably imagination. Monitoring had
become too fine an art for an amateur to detect. Under pressure
from Mrs. Castle she had an interview at the local school and she

arranged for Sam to attend it; from this meeting she returned in deep depression—it was as though she had just finalized the new life, stamped it like a document with a wax seal, nothing would ever change it now. On her way home she called at the greengrocer's, at the library, at the druggist's—Mrs. Castle had provided her with a list: a tin of green peas, a novel of Georgette Heyer's, a bottle of aspirin for the headaches of which Sarah felt sure that she and Sam were the cause. For no reason she could put a name to she thought of the great gray-green pyramids of earth which surrounded Johannesburg—even Muller had spoken of their color in the evening, and she felt closer to Muller, the enemy, the racialist, than to Mrs. Castle. She would have exchanged this Sussex town with its liberal inhabitants who treated her with such kindly courtesy even for Soweto. Courtesy could be a barrier more than a blow. It wasn't courtesy one wanted to live with—it was love. She loved Maurice, she loved the smell of the dust and degradation of her country—now she was without Maurice and without a country. Perhaps that was why she welcomed even the voice of an enemy on the telephone. She knew at once it was an enemy's voice although it introduced itself as "a friend and colleague of your husband."

"I hope I'm not ringing you up at a bad time, Mrs. Castle."

"No, but I didn't hear your name."

"Doctor Percival."

It was vaguely familiar. "Yes. I think Maurice has spoken of you."

"We had a memorable night out once in London."

"Oh yes, I remember now. With Davis."

"Yes. Poor Davis." There was a pause. "I was wondering, Mrs. Castle, if we could have a talk."

"We are having one now, aren't we?"

"Well, a rather closer talk than a telephone provides."

"I'm a long way from London."

"We could send a car for you if it would help."

"We," she thought, "we." It was a mistake on his part to speak like an organization. "We" and "they" were uncomfortable terms. They were a warning, they put you on your guard.

The voice said, "I thought if you were free for lunch one day this week . . ."

"I don't know if I can manage."

"I wanted to talk to you about your husband."

"Yes. I guessed that."

"We are all rather anxious about Maurice." She felt a quick elation. "We" hadn't got him in some secret spot unknown to Inspector Butler. He was well away—all Europe was between them. It was as though she too, as well as Maurice, had escaped—she was already on her way home, that home which was where Maurice was. She had to be very careful just the same, as in the old days in Johannesburg. She said, "Maurice doesn't concern me any more. We've separated."

"All the same, I expect, you'd like some news of him?"

So they *had* news. It was as when Carson told her, "He's safe in L.M. waiting for you. Now we've only got to get you there." If he were free, they would soon be together. She realized she was smiling at the telephone—thank God, they hadn't yet invented a visual telephone, but all the same she wiped the smile off her face. She said, "I'm afraid I don't much care where he is. Couldn't you write? I have a child to look after."

"Well no, Mrs. Castle, there are things one can't write. If we could send a car for you tomorrow . . ."

"Tomorrow's impossible."

"Thursday then."

She hesitated as long as she dared. "Well . . ."

"We could send a car for you at eleven."

"But I don't need a car. There's a good train at 11:15."

"Well then, if you could meet me at a restaurant, Brummell's—close to Victoria."

"What street?"

"There you have me. Walton—Wilton—never mind, any taxi driver will know Brummell's. It's very quiet there," he added soothingly as though he were recommending with professional knowledge a good nursing home, and Sarah had a quick mental picture of the speaker—a very self-assured Wimpole Street type, with a dangling eyeglass which he would only use when it came to writing out the prescription, the signal, like royalty rising, that it was time for the patient to depart.

"Until Thursday," he said. She didn't even reply. She put down the receiver and went to find Mrs. Castle—she was late again for lunch and she didn't care. She was humming a tune of praise the Methodist missionaries had taught her, and Mrs. Castle looked at her in astonishment. "What's the matter? Is something wrong? Was it that policeman again?"

"No. It was only a doctor. A friend of Maurice. Nothing's wrong. Would you mind just for once if I went up to town on Thursday?"

I'll take Sam to school in the morning and he can find his own way back."

"I don't *mind*, of course, but I was thinking of having Mr. Bottomley for lunch again."

"Oh, Sam and Mr. Bottomley will get on very well together."

"Will you go and see a solicitor when you are in town?"

"I might." A half-lie was a small price to pay in return for her new happiness.

"Where will you have lunch?"

"Oh, I expect I'll pick up a sandwich somewhere."

"It's such a pity you've chosen Thursday. I've ordered a joint. However"—Mrs. Castle sought for a silver lining—"if you had lunch at Harrods there are one or two things you could bring me back."

She lay in bed that night unable to sleep. It was as if she had procured a calendar and could now begin to mark off the days of term. The man she had spoken to was an enemy—she was convinced of that—but he wasn't the Security Police, he wasn't BOSS, she wouldn't lose her teeth or the sight of an eye in Brummell's: she had no reason to fear.

3

Nonetheless she felt a little let down when she identified him where he waited for her at the end of a long glassy glittering room at Brummell's. He wasn't, after all, a Wimpole Street specialist: he was more like an old-fashioned family doctor with his silver-rimmed spectacles and a small rounded paunch which seemed to prop itself on the edge of the table when he rose to greet her. He was holding an outsize menu in his hand in place of a prescription. He said, "I'm so glad you had the courage to come here."

"Why courage?"

"Well, this is one of the places the Irish like to bomb. They've thrown a small one already, but unlike the blitz their bombs are quite liable to hit the same place twice." He gave her a menu to read: a whole page was given up she saw to what were called Starters. The whole menu, which bore the title Bill of Fare above a portrait, seemed almost as long as Mrs. Castle's local telephone directory. Doctor Percival said helpfully, "I'd advise you against the smoked trout—it's always a bit dry here."

"I haven't got much appetite."

"Let's wake it up, then, while we consider matters. A glass of sherry?"

"I'd rather have a whisky if you don't mind." When asked to choose, she said, "J & B."

"You order for me," she implored Doctor Percival. The sooner all these preliminaries were over, the sooner she would have the news she waited for with a hunger she hadn't got for food. While he made his decision she looked around her. There was a dubious and glossy portrait on the wall labeled George Bryan Brummell—it was the same portrait as on the menu—and the furnishing was in impeccable and tiring good taste—you felt no possible expense had been spared and no criticism would be sanctioned: the few customers were all men and they all looked alike as though they had come out of the chorus of an old-fashioned musical comedy: black hair, neither too long nor too short, dark suits and waistcoats. Their tables were set discreetly apart and the two tables nearest to Doctor Percival's were empty—she wondered whether this was by design or chance. She noticed for the first time how all the windows were wired.

"In a place like this," Doctor Percival said, "it's best to go English and I would suggest the Lancashire hot pot."

"Anything you say." But for a long time he said nothing except some words to the waiter about the wine. At last he turned his attention and his silver-rimmed glasses toward her with a long sigh. "Well, the hard work's done. It's up to them now," and he took a sip of his sherry. "You must have been having a very anxious time, Mrs. Castle." He put out a hand and touched her arm as though he really were her family doctor.

"Anxious?"

"Not knowing from day to day . . ."

"If you mean Maurice . . ."

"We were all very fond of Maurice."

"You speak as though he were dead. In the past tense."

"I didn't mean to. Of course we are still fond of him—but he's taken a different road and I'm afraid a very dangerous one. We all hope you won't get involved."

"How can I? We're separated."

"Oh yes, yes. It was the obvious thing to do. It would have been a little conspicuous to have gone away together. I don't think Immigration would have been quite so foolish as all that. You are a very attractive woman and then your color . . ." He said, "Of course we know he hasn't telephoned you at home, but there are so many ways of sending messages—a public telephone box, an intermediary —we couldn't monitor all his friends, even if we knew them all." He pushed aside his sherry and made room for the hot pot. She began to feel more at ease now that the subject was laid plainly there on the table before them—like the hot pot. She said, "You think I'm a traitor too?"

"Oh, in the firm, you know, we don't use a word like traitor. That's for the newspapers. You are African—I don't say *South* African—and so is your child. Maurice must have been a good deal influenced by that. Let's say—he chose a different loyalty." He took a taste of the hot pot. "Be careful."

"Careful?"

"I mean the carrots are very hot." If this was really an interrogation it was a very different method to that practiced by the Security Police in Johannesburg or Pretoria. "My dear," he said, "what do you intend to do—when he *does* communicate?"

She gave up caution. As long as she was cautious she would learn nothing. She said, "I shall do what he tells me to do."

Doctor Percival said, "I'm so glad you've said that. It means we can be frank with each other. Of course we know, and I expect you know, that he's arrived safely in Moscow."

"Thank God."

"Well, I'm not sure about God, but you can certainly thank the KGB. (One mustn't be dogmatic—they may be on the same side, of course.) I imagine that sooner or later he'll ask you to join him there."

"And I'll go."

"With your child?"

"Of course."

Doctor Percival plunged again into his hot pot. He was obviously a man who enjoyed his food. She became more reckless in her relief at knowing that Maurice was safe. She said, "You can't stop me going."

"Oh, don't be so sure of that. You know, at the office we have quite a file on you. You were very friendly in South Africa with a man called Carson. A Communist agent."

"Of course I was. I was helping Maurice—for your service, though I didn't know it then. He told me it was for a book on apartheid he was writing."

"And Maurice perhaps was even then helping Carson. And Maurice is now in Moscow. It's not strictly speaking our business, of course, but MI5 might well feel you ought to be investigated—in depth. If you'll let an old man advise you—an old man who was a friend of Maurice . . ."

A memory flashed into her mind of a shambling figure in a teddy-bear coat playing hide-and-seek with Sam among the wintry trees. "And of Davis," she said, "you were a friend of Davis too, weren't you?"

A spoonful of gravy was stopped on the way to Doctor Percival's mouth.

"Yes. Poor Davis. It was a sad death for a man still young."

"I don't drink port," Sarah said.

"My dear girl, how irrelevant can you be? Let's wait to decide about port until we get to the cheese—they have excellent Wensley-dale. All I was going to say was do be reasonable. Stay quietly in the country with your mother-in-law and your child . . ."

"Maurice's child."

"Perhaps."

"What do you mean, perhaps?"

"You've met this man Cornelius Muller, a rather unsympathetic type from BOSS. And what a name! He's under the impression that the real father—my dear, you must forgive a little plain speaking—I don't want you to make the sort of mistake Maurice has made—"

"You aren't being very plain."

"Muller believes that the father was one of your own people."

"Oh, I know the one he means—even if it was true he's dead."

"He isn't dead."

"Of course he's dead. He was killed in a riot."

"Did you see his body?"

"No, but . . ."

"Muller says he's safely under lock and key. He's a lifer—so Muller says."

"I don't believe it."

"Muller says this fellow is prepared to claim paternity."

"Muller's lying."

"Yes, yes. That's quite possible. The man may well be a stooge. I haven't been into the legal aspects yet myself, but I doubt if he could prove anything in our courts. Is the child on your passport?"

"No."

"Has he a passport?"

"No."

"Then you'd have to apply for a passport to take him out of this country. That means a lot of bureaucratic rigmarole. The passport people can sometimes be very, very slow."

"What bastards you are. You killed Carson. You killed Davis. And now . . ."

"Carson died of pneumonia. Poor Davis—that was cirrhosis."

"Muller says it was pneumonia. You say it was cirrhosis, and now you are threatening me and Sam."

"Not threatening, my dear, advising."

"Your advice . . ."

She had to break off. The waiter had come to clear their plates. Doctor Percival's was clean enough, but most of her portion had remained uneaten.

"What about an old English apple pie with cloves and a bit of cheese?" Doctor Percival asked, leaning seductively forward and speaking in a low voice as though he were naming the price he was prepared to pay for certain favors.

"No. Nothing. I don't want any more."

"Oh dear, the bill then," Doctor Percival told the waiter with disappointment, and when the waiter had gone he reproached her. "Mrs. Castle, you mustn't get angry. There's nothing personal in all this. If you get angry you are sure to make the wrong decision. It's just an affair of boxes," he began to elaborate, and then broke off as though for once he was finding that metaphor inapplicable.

"Sam is *my* child and I shall take him wherever I want. To Moscow, to Timbuctoo, to . . ."

"You can't take Sam until he has a passport, and I'm anxious to keep MI5 from taking any preventive action against you. If they learned you were applying for a passport . . . and they would learn . . ."

She walked out, she walked out on everything, leaving Doctor Percival to wait behind for the bill. If she had stayed a moment longer she wasn't sure that she could have trusted herself with the knife which remained by her plate for the cheese. She had once seen a white man just as well fed as Doctor Percival stabbed in a public garden in Johannesburg. It had looked such a very easy thing to do. From the door she looked back at him. The wire grill over the window behind made him appear to be sitting at a desk in a police station. Obviously he had followed her with his eyes, and now he raised an index finger and shook it gently to and fro in her direction. It could be taken for an admonition or a warning. She didn't care which.

Chapter II

From the window on the twelfth floor of the great gray building Castle could see the red star over the University. There was a certain beauty in the view as there is in all cities at night. Only the daylight was drab. They had made it clear to him, particularly Ivan, who had met his plane in Prague and accompanied him to a debriefing in some place near Irkutsk with an unpronounceable name, that he was extraordinarily lucky in his apartment. It had belonged, both rooms of it with a kitchen and a private shower, to a comrade recently dead who had nearly succeeded before his death in furnishing it completely. An empty apartment as a rule contained only a stove—everything else even to the toilet had to be bought. That was not easy and wasted a great deal of time and energy. Castle wondered sometimes if that was why the comrade had died, worn out by his long hunt for the green wicker armchair, the brown sofa hard as a board, without cushions, the table which looked as though it had been stained a nearly even color by the application of gravy. The television set, the latest black and white model, was a gift of the government. Ivan had carefully explained that when they first visited the apartment. In his manner he hinted his personal doubt whether it had been truly earned. Ivan seemed to Castle no more likable here than he had been in London. Perhaps he resented his recall and blamed it on Castle.

The most valuable object in the apartment seemed to be the telephone. It was covered with dust and disconnected, but all the same it had a symbolic value. One day, perhaps soon, it could be put to use. He would speak through it to Sarah—to hear her voice meant everything to him, whatever comedy they would have to play for the listeners, and there certainly would be listeners. To hear her would make the long wait bearable. Once he broached the matter to Ivan. He had noticed Ivan preferred to talk out of doors even on the coldest day, and as it was Ivan's job to show him around the city he took an opportunity outside the great GUM department store (a place where he felt almost at home because it reminded him of photographs he had seen of the Crystal Palace). He asked, "Is it possible, do you think, to have my telephone connected?" They had gone to GUM to find Castle a fur-lined overcoat—the temperature was twenty-three degrees.

"I'll ask," Ivan said, "but for the moment I suppose they want to keep you under wrappers."

"Is that a long process?"

"It was in the case of Bellamy, but you're not such an important case. We can't get much publicity out of you."

"Who's Bellamy?"

"You must remember Bellamy. A most important man in your British Council. In West Berlin. That was always a cover, wasn't it, like the Peace Corps?"

Castle didn't bother to deny it—it was none of his business.

"Oh yes, I think I remember now." It had happened at the time of his greatest anxiety, while he waited for news of Sarah in Lourenço Marques, and he couldn't recall the details of Bellamy's defection. Why did one defect from the British Council and what value or harm would such a defection have to anyone? He asked, "Is he still alive?" It all seemed such a long time ago.

"Why not?"

"What does he do?"

"He lives on our gratitude." Ivan added, "As you do. Oh, we invented a job for him. He advises our publications division. He has a *dacha* in the country. It's a better life than he would have had at home with a pension. I suppose they will do the same for you."

"Reading books in a *dacha* in the country?"

"Yes."

"Are there many of us—I mean living like that on your gratitude?"

"I know at least six. There was Cruickshank and Bates—you'll remember them—they were from your service. You'll run into them I expect in the Aragvi, our Georgian restaurant—they say the wine's good there—I can't afford it—and you will see them at the Bolshoi, when they take the wrappers off."

They passed the Lenin Library—"You'll find them there too." He added with venom, "Reading the English papers."

Ivan had found him a large stout middle-aged woman as a daily who would also help him to learn a little Russian. She gave a Russian name to everything in the flat, pointing a blunt finger at everything in turn, and she was very fussy about pronunciation. Al-

though she was several years younger than Castle she treated him
as though he were a child, with an admonitory sternness which
slowly melted into a sort of maternal affection as he became more
house-trained. When Ivan was otherwise occupied she would en-
large the scope of her lessons, taking him with her in search of food
at the Central Market and down into the Metro. (She wrote figures
on a scrap of paper to explain the prices and the fares.) After a
while she began to show him photographs of her family—her husband a young man in uniform, taken somewhere in a public park
with a cardboard outline of the Kremlin behind his head. He wore
his uniform in an untidy way (you could see he wasn't used to it),
and he smiled at the camera with a look of great tenderness—
perhaps she had been standing behind the photographer. He had
been killed, she conveyed to him, at Stalingrad. In return he produced for her a snapshot of Sarah and Sam which he hadn't confessed to Mr. Halliday that he had secreted in his shoe. She showed
surprise that they were black, and for a little while afterward her
manner to him seemed more distant—she was not so much shocked
as lost, he had broken her sense of order. In that she resembled his
mother. After a few days all was well again, but during those few
days he felt an exile inside his exile and his longing for Sarah was
intensified.

He had been in Moscow now for two weeks, and he had bought
with the money Ivan had given him a few extras for the flat. He
had even found school editions in English of Shakespeare's plays,
two novels of Dickens, *Oliver Twist* and *Hard Times, Tom Jones*
and *Robinson Crusoe*. The snow was ankle deep in the side streets
and he had less and less inclination to go sightseeing with Ivan or
even on an educational tour with Anna—she was called Anna. In
the evening he would warm some soup and sit huddled near the
stove, with the dusty disconnected telephone at his elbow, and read
Robinson Crusoe. Sometimes he could hear Crusoe speaking, as
though on a tape recorder, with his own voice: "I drew up the state
of my affairs in writing; not so much to leave them to any that were
to come after me, for I was like to have but few heirs, as to deliver
my thoughts from daily poring upon them, and afflicting my mind."
Crusoe divided the comforts and miseries of his situation into
Good and Evil and under the heading Evil he wrote: "I have no
soul to speak to, or relieve me." Under the opposing Good he
counted "so many necessary things" which he had obtained from
the wreck "as will either supply my wants, or enable me to supply
myself even as long as I live." Well, he had the green wicker arm-

chair, the gravy-stained table, the uncomfortable sofa, and the stove which warmed him now. They would have been sufficient if Sarah had been there—she was used to far worse conditions and he remembered some of the grim rooms in which they had been forced to meet and make love in dubious hotels without a color bar in the poorer quarters of Johannesburg. He remembered one room in particular without furniture of any kind where they had been happy enough on the floor. Next day when Ivan made his snide references to "gratitude" he broke furiously out: "You call this gratitude."

"Not so many people who live alone possess a kitchen and shower all to themselves . . . and two rooms."

"I'm not complaining of that. But they promised me I wouldn't be alone. They promised me that my wife and child would follow."

The intensity of his anger disquieted Ivan. Ivan said, "It takes time."

"I don't even have any work. I'm a man on the dole. Is that your bloody socialism?"

"Quiet, quiet," Ivan said. "Wait awhile. When they take the wrappers off . . ."

Castle nearly struck Ivan and he saw that Ivan knew it. Ivan mumbled something and backed away down the cement stairs.

2

Was it perhaps a microphone that conveyed this scene to a higher authority or had Ivan reported it? Castle would never know, but all the same his anger had worked the trick. It had swept away the wrappers, swept away, as he realized later, even Ivan. Just as when Ivan was removed from London because they must have decided he had the wrong temperament to be the right control for Castle, so now he put in only one more appearance—a rather subdued appearance—and then disappeared forever. Perhaps they had a pool of controls, just as in London there had been a pool of secretaries, and Ivan had sunk back into the pool. No one in this sort of service was ever likely to be sacked, for fear of revelations.

Ivan made his swan song as an interpreter in a building not far from the Lubianka prison, which he had pointed proudly out to Castle on one of their walks. Castle asked him that morning where they were going and he answered evasively, "They have decided on your work."

The room where they waited was lined with books in ugly economy bindings. Castle read the names of Stalin, Lenin, Marx in Russian script—it pleased him to think he was beginning to make out the script. There was a big desk with a luxurious leather blotting pad and a nineteenth-century bronze of a man on horseback too large and heavy to use as a paperweight—it could only be there for decorative purposes. From a doorway behind the desk emerged a stout elderly man with a shock of gray hair and an old-fashioned moustache yellowed by cigarette smoke. He was followed by a young man dressed very correctly who carried a file. He was like an acolyte attending a priest of his faith, and in spite of the heavy moustache there *was* something priestly about the old man, about his kindly smile and the hand he extended like a blessing. A lot of conversation—questions and answers—went on among the three of them, and then Ivan took the floor as translator. He said, "The comrade wants you to know how highly your work has been appreciated. He wants you to understand that the very importance of your work has presented us with problems which had to be solved at a high level. That is why you have been kept apart during these two weeks. The comrade is anxious that you should not think it was through any lack of trust. It was hoped that your presence here would only become known to the Western Press at the right moment."

Castle said, "They must know I am here by now. Where else would I be?" Ivan translated and the old man replied, and the young acolyte smiled at the reply with his eyes cast down.

"The comrade says, 'Knowing is not the same as publishing.' The Press can only publish when you are officially here. The censorship would see to that. A press conference is going to be arranged very soon and then we will let you know what you should say to the journalists. Perhaps we will rehearse it all a little first."

"Tell the comrade," Castle said, "that I want to earn my keep here."

"The comrade says you have earned it many times over already."

"In that case I expect him to keep the promise they made me in London."

"What was that?"

"I was told my wife and son would follow me here. Tell him, Ivan, that I'm damned lonely. Tell him I want the use of my telephone. I want to telephone my wife, that's all, not the British Embassy or a journalist. If the wrappers are off, then let me speak to her."

The translation took a lot of time. A translation, he knew, always turned out longer than the original text, but this was inordinately longer. Even the acolyte seemed to be adding more than a sentence or two. The important comrade hardly bothered to speak—he continued to look as benign as a bishop.

Ivan turned back to Castle at last. He had a sour expression which the others couldn't see. He said, "They are very anxious to have your cooperation in the publishing section which deals with Africa." He nodded in the direction of the acolyte, who permitted himself an encouraging smile which might have been a plaster cast of his superior's. "The comrade says he would like you to act as their chief adviser on African literature. He says there are a great number of African novelists and they would like to choose the most valuable for translation, and of course the best of the novelists (selected by you) would be invited to pay us a visit by the Writer's Union. This is a very important position and they are happy to offer it to you."

The old man made a gesture with his hand toward the bookshelves as though he were inviting Stalin, Lenin and Marx—yes, and there was Engels too—to welcome the novelists whom he would pick for them.

Castle said, "They haven't answered me. I want my wife and son here with me. They promised that. Boris promised it."

Ivan said, "I do not want to translate what you are saying. All that business concerns quite a different department. It would be a big mistake to confuse matters. They are offering you . . ."

"Tell him I won't discuss anything until I've spoken to my wife."

Ivan shrugged his shoulders and spoke. This time the translation was no longer than the text—an abrupt angry sentence. It was the commentary by the old comrade which took up all the space, like the footnotes of an over-edited book. To show the finality of his decision Castle turned away and looked out of the window into a narrow ditch of a street between walls of concrete of which he couldn't see the top through the snow which poured down into the ditch as though from some huge inexhaustible bucket up above. This was not the snow he remembered from childhood and associated with snowballs and fairy stories and games with toboggans. This was a merciless, interminable, annihilating snow, a snow in which one could expect the world to end.

Ivan said angrily, "We will go away now."

"What do they say?"

"I do not understand the way they are treating you. I know from London the sort of rubbish you sent us. Come away." The old comrade held out a courteous hand: the young one looked a bit perturbed. Outside the silence of the snow-drowned street was so extreme that Castle hesitated to break it. The two of them walked rapidly like secret enemies who are seeking the right spot to settle their differences in a final fashion. At last, when he could bear the uncertainty no longer, Castle said, "Well, what was the result of all that talk?"

Ivan said, "They told me that I was handling you wrongly. Just the same as they told me when they brought me back from London. 'More psychology is needed, comrade, more psychology.' I would be much better off if I was a traitor like you." Luck brought them a taxi and in it he leaped into a wounded silence. (Castle had already noticed that one never talked in a taxi.) In the doorway of the apartment block Ivan gave grudgingly the information Castle demanded.

"Oh, the job will wait for you. You have nothing to fear. The comrade is very sympathetic. He will speak to others about your telephone and your wife. He begs you—begs, that was the word he used himself—to be patient a little longer. You will have news, he says, very soon. He understands—understands, mark you—your anxiety. I do not understand a thing. My psychology is obviously bad."

He left Castle standing in the entry and strode away into the snow and was lost to Castle's eyes forever.

3

The next night, while Castle was reading *Robinson Crusoe* by the stove, someone knocked at his door (the bell was out of order). A sense of distrust had grown in him through so many years that he called out automatically before he opened, "Who is it?"

"The name is Bellamy," a high-pitched voice answered, and Castle unlocked the door. A small gray man in a gray fur coat and a gray astrakhan hat entered with an air of shyness and timidity. He was like a comedian playing a mouse in a pantomime and expecting the applause of little hands. He said, "I live so near here, so I thought I'd take up my courage and call." He looked at the book in Castle's hand. "Oh dear, I've interrupted your reading."

"Only *Robinson Crusoe*. I've plenty of time for that."

"Ah ha, the great Daniel. He was one of us."

"One of us?"

"Well, Defoe perhaps was more an MI5 type." He peeled off gray fur gloves and warmed himself at the stove and looked around. He said, "I can see you're still at the bare stage. We've all passed through it. I never knew where to find things myself till

Cruickshank showed me. And then later, well, I showed Bates. You haven't met them yet?"

"No."

"I wonder they haven't called. You've been unwrapped, and I hear you're having a press conference any day now."

"How do you know?"

"From a Russian friend," Bellamy said with a little nervous giggle. He produced a half bottle of whisky from the depths of his fur coat. "A little *cadeau*," he said, "for the new member."

"It's very kind of you. Do sit down. The chair is more comfortable than the sofa."

"I'll unwrap myself first if I may. Unwrap—it's a good expression." The unwrapping took some time—there were a lot of buttons. When he was settled in the green wicker chair he giggled again. "How is *your* Russian friend?"

"Not very friendly."

"Get rid of him then. Have no nonsense. They *want* us to be happy."

"How do I get rid of him?"

"You just show them that he's not your type. An indiscreet word to be caught by one of those little gadgets we are probably talking into now. Do you know, when I came here first, they entrusted me to—you'll never guess—to a middle-aged lady from the Union of Writers? That was because I had been British Council, I suppose. Well, I soon learned how to deal with *that* situation. Whenever Cruickshank and I were together I used to refer to her scornfully as 'my governess' and she didn't last very long. She was gone before Bates arrived and—it's very wrong of me to laugh—Bates married her."

"I don't understand how it was—I mean why it was they wanted you here. I was out of England when it all happened. I didn't see the newspaper reports."

"My dear, the newspapers—they were quite awful. They *grilled* me. I read them in the Lenin Library afterward. You would really have thought I was a sort of Mata Hari."

"But what value were you to them—in the British Council?"

"Well, you see, I had a German friend and it seems he was running a lot of agents in the East. It never occurred to him that little me was watching him and making my notes—then the silly boy went and got seduced by a quite awful woman. He deserved to be punished. He was safe enough, I would never have done anything to endanger *him*, but his agents . . . of course he guessed who had given him away. Well, I admit I didn't make it difficult for him to guess. But I had to get away very quickly because he went to the Embassy about me. How glad I was when I put Checkpoint Charlie behind me."

"And you are happy here?"

"Yes, I am. Happiness always seems to me a matter of persons not of places, and I have a very nice friend. It's against the law, of course, but they do make exceptions in the service, and he's an officer in the KGB. Of course, poor boy, he has to be unfaithful sometimes in the course of duty, but that's quite different from my German friend—it isn't *love*. We even have a little laugh about it sometimes. If you're lonely, he knows a lot of girls . . ."

"I'm not lonely. As long as my books last."

"I'll show you a little place where you can pick up English language paperbacks under the counter."

It was midnight before they had finished the half bottle of whisky and then Bellamy took his leave. He spent a long time getting back into his furs, and he chattered all the while. "You must meet Cruickshank one day—I'll tell him I've seen you—and Bates too, of course, but that means meeting Mrs. Union-of-Writers Bates." He warmed his hands well before pulling on his gloves. He had an air of being quite at home, although "I was a bit unhappy at first," he admitted. "I felt rather lost until I had my friend—like in that chorus of Swinburne's, 'the foreign faces, the tongueless vigil and'—how does it go?—'all the pain.' I used to lecture on Swinburne —an underrated poet." At the door he said, "You must come out and see my *dacha* when the spring comes . . ."

4

Castle found that after a few days he even missed Ivan. He missed having someone to dislike—he couldn't in justice dislike Anna, who seemed to realize that now he was more alone than ever. She stayed a little longer in the morning and pressed even more Russian names on his attention with her pointing finger. She became even more exigent too over his pronunciation: she began to add verbs to his vocabulary, beginning with the word for "run," when she made motions of running, raising her elbows and each knee. She must have been receiving wages from some source for he paid her none; indeed the little store of rubles Ivan had given him on his arrival had been much diminished.

It was a painful part of his isolation that he earned nothing. He began even to long for a desk at which he could sit and study lists of African writers—they might take his mind for a little from what had happened to Sarah. Why hadn't she followed him with Sam? What were they doing to fulfill their promise?

At nine thirty-two one evening he came to the end of Robinson Crusoe's ordeal—in noting the time he was behaving a little like Crusoe. "And thus I left the island, the nineteenth of December, and I found by the ship's account, in the year 1686, after I had been upon it eight and twenty years, two months and nineteen days . . ." He went to the window: the snow for the moment was not falling and he could see clearly the red star over the University. Even at that hour women were at work sweeping the snow: from above they looked like enormous turtles. Somebody was ringing at the door—let him, he wouldn't open, it was probably only Bellamy or perhaps someone even more unwelcome, the unknown Cruickshank or the unknown Bates—but surely, he remembered, the bell was out of order. He turned and stared at the telephone with amazement. It was the telephone which was ringing.

He lifted the receiver and a voice spoke to him in Russian. He couldn't understand a word. There was nothing more—only the high-pitched dialing sound—but he kept the receiver to his ear, stupidly waiting. Perhaps the operator had told him to hold on. Or had he told him—"Replace the receiver. We will ring you back"? Perhaps a call was coming from England. Unwillingly he put the receiver back and sat on beside the telephone waiting for it to ring again. He had been "unwrapped" and now it seemed he had been "connected." He would have been "in touch" if only he had been able to learn the right phrases from Anna—he didn't even know how to ring the operator. There was no telephone book in the flat— he had checked that two weeks ago.

But the operator must have been telling him something. At any moment he was sure the telephone would call to him. He fell asleep beside it and dreamt, as he had not dreamt for a dozen years, of his first wife. In his dream they quarreled as they had never done in life.

Anna found him in the morning asleep in the green wicker chair. When she woke him he said to her, "Anna, the telephone's connected," and because she didn't understand, he waved toward it and said "Ting-a-ling-a-ling," and they both laughed with pleasure at the absurdity of such a childish sound in the mouth of an elderly man. He took out the photograph of Sarah and pointed at the telephone and she nodded her head and smiled to encourage him, and he thought: She'll get on with Sarah, she will show her where to shop, she will teach her Russian words, she will like Sam.

5

When later that day the telephone rang he felt certain it would be Sarah—someone in London must have conveyed the number to her, perhaps Boris. His mouth was dry when he answered and he could hardly bring out the words "Who is that?"

"Boris."

"Where are you?"

"Here in Moscow."

"Have you seen Sarah?"

"I have talked to her."

"Is she all right?"

"Yes, yes, she is all right."

"And Sam?"

"He is all right too."

"When will they be here?"

"That is what I want to speak to you about. Stay in, please. Do not go out. I am coming to the apartment now."

"But when will I see them?"

"That is something we have to discuss. There are difficulties."

"What difficulties?"

"Wait till I see you."

He couldn't stay still: he picked up a book and put it down; he went into the kitchen, where Anna was making soup. She said, "Ting-a-ling-a-ling," but it wasn't funny any more. He walked back to the window—snow again. When the knock came on the door he felt that hours had passed.

Boris held out a duty free plastic sack. He said, "Sarah told me to get you J & B. One bottle from her and one from Sam."

Castle said, "What are the difficulties?"

"Give me time to get my coat off."

"Did you really see her?"

"I spoke to her on the telephone. At a call box. She's in the country with your mother."

"I know."

"I would have looked a little conspicuous visiting her there."

"Then how do you know she's well?"

"She told me so."

"Did she sound well?"

"Yes, yes, Maurice. I am sure . . ."

"What are the difficulties? You got *me* out."

"That was a very simple affair. A false passport, the blind man dodge, and that little trouble we arranged at the immigration while you were led through by the Air France hostess. A man rather like you. Bound for Prague. His passport wasn't quite in order . . ."

"You haven't told me what difficulties."

"We always assumed, when you were safely here, they couldn't stop Sarah joining you."

"They can't."

"Sam has no passport. You should have put him on his mother's. Apparently it *can* take a lot of time to arrange. And another thing—your people have hinted that if Sarah tries to leave she can be arrested for complicity. She was a friend of Carson, she was your agent in Johannesburg . . . My dear Maurice, things are not simple at all, I'm afraid."

"You promised."

"I know we promised. In good faith. It might still be possible to smuggle her out if she left the child behind, but she says she won't do that. He's not happy at school. He's not happy with your mother."

The duty free plastic bag waited on the table. There was always whisky—the medicine against despair. Castle said, "Why did you fetch me out? I wasn't in immediate danger. I thought I was, but you must have known . . ."

"You sent the emergency signal. We answered it."

Castle tore the plastic, opened the whisky, the lable J & B hurt him like a sad memory. He poured out two large measures. "I have no soda."

"Never mind."

Castle said, "Take the chair. The sofa's as hard as a school bench." He took a drink. Even the flavor of J & B hurt him. If only Boris had brought him a different whisky—Haig, White Horse, Vat 69, Grant's—he recited to himself the names of the whiskies which meant nothing to him, to keep his mind blank and his despair at bay until the J & B began to work—Johnnie Walker, Queen Anne, Teacher's. Boris misunderstood his silence. He said, "You do not have to worry about microphones. Here in Moscow, you might say we are safe at the center of the cyclone." He added, "It was very important for us to get you out."

"Why? Muller's notes were safe with old Halliday."

"You have never been given the real picture, have you? Those bits of economic information you sent us had no value in themselves at all."

"Then why . . . ?"

"I know I am not very clear. I am not used to whisky. Let me try to explain. Your people imagined they had an agent in place, here in Moscow. But it was we who had planted him on them. What you gave us he passed back to them. Your reports authenticated him in the eyes of your service, they could check them, and all the time he was passing them other information which we wanted them to believe. That was the real value of your reports. A nice piece of deception. But then came the Muller affair and Uncle Remus. We decided the best way to counter Uncle Remus was publicity—we couldn't do that and leave you in London. You had to be our source —you brought Muller's notes with you."

"They'll know I brought news of the leak too."

"Exactly. We couldn't carry on a game like that much longer. Their agent in Moscow will disappear into a great silence. Perhaps in a few months rumors will come to your people of a secret trial. It will make them all the more certain that all the information he gave them was true."

"I thought I was only helping Sarah's people."

"You were doing much more than that. And tomorrow you meet the Press."

"Suppose I refuse to talk unless you bring Sarah . . ."

"We'll do without you, but you couldn't expect us then to solve the Sarah problem. We are grateful to you, Maurice, but gratitude like love needs to be renewed daily or it's liable to die away."

"You are talking as Ivan used to talk."

"No, not like Ivan. I am your friend. I want to stay your friend. One needs a friend badly to make a new life in a new country."

Now the offer of friendship had the sound of a menace or a warning. The night in Watford came back to him when he searched in vain for the shabby tutorial flat with the Berlitz picture on the wall. It seemed to him that all his life after he joined the service in his twenties he had been unable to speak. Like a Trappist he had chosen the profession of silence, and now he recognized too late that it had been a mistaken vocation.

"Take another drink, Maurice. Things are not so bad. You just have to be patient, that's all."

Castle took the drink.

Chapter III

The doctor confirmed Sarah's fears for Sam, but it was Mrs. Castle who had been the first to recognize the nature of his cough. The old don't need medical training—they seem to accumulate diagnoses through a lifetime of experience instead of through six years of intensive training. The doctor was no more than a kind of legal requirement—to put his signature at the end of *her* prescription. He was a young man who treated Mrs. Castle with great respect as though she were an eminent specialist from whom he could learn a lot. He asked Sarah, "Do you have much whooping cough—I mean at home?" By home he obviously meant to indicate Africa.

"I don't know. Is it dangerous?" she asked.

"Not dangerous." He added, "But a rather long quarantine"—a sentence which was not reassuring. Without Maurice it proved more difficult to disguise her anxiety because it wasn't shared. Mrs. Castle was quite calm—if a little irritated at the break in routine. If there had not been that stupid quarrel, she obviously thought, Sam could have had his sickness well away in Berkhamsted, and she could have conveyed the necessary advice over the telephone. She left the two of them, throwing a kiss in Sam's direction with an old leaflike hand, and went downstairs to watch the television.

"Can't I be ill at home?" Sam asked.

"No. You must stay in."

"I wish Buller were here to talk to." He missed Buller more than Maurice.

"Shall I read to you?"

"Yes, please."

"Then you must go to sleep."

She had packed a few books at random in the hurry of departure, among them what Sam always called the Garden book. He liked it a great deal better than she did—her memories of childhood contained no garden: the hard light had struck off roofs of corrugated iron onto a playground of baked clay. Even with the Methodists there had been no grass. She opened the book. The television voice muttered on below in the sitting room. It couldn't be mistaken even at a distance for a living voice—it was a voice like a tin of sardines. Packaged.

Before she even opened the book Sam was already asleep with one arm flung out of the bed, as his habit was, for Buller to lick. She thought: Oh yes, I love him, of course I love him, but he's like the handcuffs of the Security Police around my wrists. It would be weeks before she was released, and even then . . . She was back at Brummell's staring down the glittering restaurant papered with expense accounts to where Doctor Percival raised his warning finger. She thought: Could they even have arranged this?

She closed the door softly and went downstairs. The tinned voice had been cut off and Mrs. Castle stood waiting for her at the bottom of the stairs.

"I missed the news," Sarah said. "He wanted me to read to him, but he's asleep now." Mrs. Castle glared past her as though at a horror only she could see.

"Maurice is in Moscow," Mrs. Castle said.

"Yes. I know."

"There he was on the screen with a lot of journalists. Justifying himself. He had the nerve, the effrontery . . . Was that why you quarreled with him? Oh, you did right to leave him."

"That wasn't the reason," Sarah said. "We only pretended to quarrel. He didn't want me involved."

"Were you involved?"

"No."

"Thank God for that. I wouldn't want to turn you out of the house with the child ill."

"Would you have turned Maurice out if you had known?"

"No. I'd have kept him just long enough to call the police." She turned and walked back into the sitting room—she walked all the way across it until she stumbled against the television set like a blind woman. She was as good as blind, Sarah saw—her eyes were closed. She put a hand on Mrs. Castle's arm.

"Sit down. It's been a shock."

Mrs. Castle opened her eyes. Sarah had expected to see them wet with tears, but they were dry, dry and merciless. "Maurice is a traitor," Mrs. Castle said.

"Try to understand, Mrs. Castle. It's my fault. Not Maurice's."

"You said you were not involved."

"He was trying to help my people. If he hadn't loved me and

Sam . . . It was the price he paid to save us. You can't imagine here in England the kind of horrors he saved us from."

"A traitor!"

She lost control at the reiteration. "All right—a traitor then. A traitor to whom? To Muller and his friends? To the Security Police?"

"I have no idea who Muller is. He's a traitor to his country."

"Oh, his country," she said in despair at all the easy clichés which go to form a judgment. "He said once I was his country—and Sam."

"I'm glad his father's dead."

It was yet another cliché. In a crisis perhaps it is old clichés one clings to, like a child to a parent.

"Perhaps his father would have understood better than you."

It was a senseless quarrel like the one she had that last evening with Maurice. She said, "I'm sorry. I didn't mean to say that." She was ready to surrender anything for a little peace. "I'll leave as soon as Sam is better."

"Where to?"

"To Moscow. If they'll let me."

"You won't take Sam. Sam is my grandson. I'm his guardian," Mrs. Castle said.

"Only if Maurice and I are dead."

"Sam is a British subject. I'll have him made a Ward in Chancery. I'll see my lawyer tomorrow."

Sarah hadn't the faintest notion what a Ward in Chancery was. It was, she supposed, one more obstacle which even the voice that had spoken to her over the telephone of a public call box had not taken into account. The voice had apologized: the voice claimed, just as Doctor Percival had done, to be a friend of Maurice, but she trusted it more, even with its caution and its ambiguity and its trace of something foreign in the tone.

The voice apologized for the fact that she was not already on the way to join her husband. It could be arranged almost at once if she would go alone—the child made it almost impossible for her to pass unscrutinized, however effective any passport they arranged might seem to be.

She had told him in the flat voice of despair, "I can't leave Sam alone," and the voice assured her that "in time," a way would be found for Sam. If she would trust him . . . The man began to give guarded indications of how and when they could meet, just some hand-luggage—a warm coat—everything she lacked could be bought at the other end—but "No," she said. "No. I can't go without Sam" and she dropped the receiver. Now there was his sickness and there was the mysterious phrase which haunted her all the way to the bedroom, "a Ward in Chancery." It sounded like a room in a hospital. Could a child be forced into a hospital as he could be forced into a school?

2

There was nobody to ask. In all England she knew no one except Mrs. Castle, the butcher, the greengrocer, the librarian, the schoolmistress—and of course Mr. Bottomley, who had been constantly cropping up, on the doorstep, in the High Street, even on the telephone. He had lived so long on his African mission that perhaps he felt really at home only with her. He was very kind and very inquisitive and he dropped little pious platitudes. She wondered what he would say if she asked him for help to escape from England.

On the morning after the press conference Doctor Percival telephoned for what seemed an odd reason. Apparently some money was due to Maurice and they wanted the number of his bank account so that they might pay it in: they seemed to be scrupulously honest in small things, though she wondered afterward if they were afraid that money difficulties might drive her to some desperate course. It might be a sort of bribe to keep her in place. Doctor Percival said to her, still in the family doctor voice, "I'm so glad you are being sensible, my dear. Go on being sensible," rather as he might have advised "Go on with the antibiotics."

And then at seven in the evening when Sam was asleep and Mrs. Castle was in her room, "tidying" as she called it, for dinner, the telephone rang. It was a likely hour for Mr. Bottomley, but it was Maurice. The line was so clear that he might have been speaking from the next room. She said with astonishment, "Maurice, where are you?"

"You know where I am. I love you, Sarah."

"I love you, Maurice."

He explained, "We must talk quickly, one never knows when they may cut the line. How's Sam?"

"Not well. Nothing serious."

"Boris said he was well."

"I didn't tell him. It was only one more difficulty. There are an awful lot of difficulties."

"Yes. I know. Give Sam my love."

"Of course I will."

"We needn't go on pretending any more. They'll always be listening."

There was a pause. She thought he had gone away or that the line had been cut. Then he said, "I miss you terribly, Sarah."

"Oh, so do I. So do I, but I can't leave Sam behind."

"Of course you can't. I can understand that."

She said on an impulse she immediately regretted, "When he's a little older . . ." It sounded like the promise of a distant future when they would both be old. "Be patient."

"Yes—Boris says the same. I'll be patient. How's Mother?"

"I'd rather not talk about *her*. Talk about us. Tell me how you are."

"Oh, everyone is very kind. They have given me a sort of job. They are grateful to me. For a lot more than I ever intended to do." He said something she didn't understand because of a crackle on the line—something about a fountain pen and a bun which had a bar of chocolate in it. "My mother wasn't far wrong."

She asked, "Have you friends?"

"Oh yes, I'm not alone, don't worry, Sarah. There's an Englishman who used to be in the British Council. He's invited me to his *dacha* in the country when the spring comes. When the spring comes," he repeated in a voice which she hardly recognized—it was the voice of an old man who couldn't count with certainty on any spring to come.

She said, "Maurice, Maurice, please go on hoping," but in the long unbroken silence which followed she realized that the line to Moscow was dead.

007508295

Greene   c. 15
    The human factor.

SUTHERLAND SPRINGS

SUTHERLAND SPRINGS

GOD, GUNS, AND HOPE IN A TEXAS TOWN

JOE HOLLEY

NEW YORK

Hachette Books
Hachette Book Group
1290 Avenue of the Americas
New York, NY 10104
HachetteBooks.com
Twitter.com/HachetteBooks
Instagram.com/HachetteBooks

First Edition: March 2020

Published by Hachette Books, an imprint of Perseus Books, LLC, a subsidiary of Hachette Book Group, Inc. The Hachette Books name and logo is a trademark of the Hachette Book Group.

The Hachette Speakers Bureau provides a wide range of authors for speaking events. To find out more, go to www.hachettespeakersbureau.com or call (866) 376-6591.

The publisher is not responsible for websites (or their content) that are not owned by the publisher.

Print book interior design by Sean Ford

Library of Congress Cataloging-in-Publication Data has been applied for.

ISBNs: 978-0-316-45115-4 (hardcover), 978-0-316-45111-6 (ebook)

Printed in the United States of America

LSC-C

10 9 8 7 6 5 4 3 2 1

For the people of Sutherland Springs

When peace like a river attendeth my way,
When sorrows like sea billows roll;
Whatever my lot, thou hast taught me to say,
"It is well, it is well with my soul."
—Hymn written by Horatio Spafford (1873)

However it happens, sometimes hearts *do* heal,
through what I can only call grace.
—Elaine Pagels, *Why Religion?*

It's not just our story. It's America's story.
—Holly Hannum, whose brother was killed at the
First Baptist Church of Sutherland Springs

SUTHERLAND SPRINGS

Prologue

On a fall afternoon in Austin, a Sunday, I was sitting at a table in a large, crowded tent at the Texas Book Festival signing copies of a book I'd written called *Hometown Texas*. The book was a collection of my columns about small-town Texas that appear weekly in the *Houston Chronicle*. From near the tail end of the line, my daughter Kate walked up.

"Did you hear about the shooting?" she asked.

I had not. I wasn't sure what she was talking about, because what we have come to call mass shootings have become so depressingly familiar in this country, it's hard to keep up with the most recent. This one had happened just a few hours earlier, Kate said. In Texas. She hadn't caught exactly where, although she thought it was a small town near San Antonio.

After my signing chores, I walked to my car and headed eastward toward Houston, tuning in CNN on satellite radio for the three-hour drive home. A small Texas town, I heard. A Baptist church. Multiple deaths. Sutherland Springs. It was November 5, 2017.

Despite decades of writing about Texas, including about many unlikely and overlooked people and places in my native state, I had never written about Sutherland Springs. I had written about the small Central Texas town of Hillsboro, where in the early 1930s, my Uncle Joe—I'm his namesake—had ended up in a jail cell with Raymond Hamilton, one of Bonnie and Clyde's drivers. That Joe Holley had been incarcerated for stealing chickens to feed his family; Hamilton had robbed a jewelry store and killed the owner.

I had written about the venerable opera house in Nacogdoches, where

in 1907 a musical quartet of young vaudeville performers calling themselves the Four Nightingales were upstaged by a runaway mule; that
bizarre incident prompted the Nightingales (actually the Marx brothers)
to realize they were comedians, not musicians.

I had written about cowboy poets in Alpine, buffalo soldiers in Fort
Davis, the author of the longest novel in the English language in Waco,
and a tinkerer in the picturesque German community of Fredericksburg
who may have invented the airplane in the mid-1800s.

I had written about the rascally old Indian fighter/Texas Ranger
Bigfoot Wallace—who called his trusty rifle "Sweet Lips"—and the tiny
South Texas town named in his honor. Not Wallace. Bigfoot. My mother
was the Bigfoot High School valedictorian, class of 1932. Most small
Texas towns were replete with the three Ps—place, people, and a colorful
past—and I was familiar with dozens of them. Sutherland Springs was
only about sixty-five miles northeast of Bigfoot, but not only had I never
written about the place, I had never heard of it, had never noticed it on a
map. As I would come to find out, it was easy to miss.

As I listened to increasingly grim and distressing reports as I drove,
an old reporter's instinct kicked in. I had to go find out. I took the I-35
toward San Antonio, eighty miles southward.

A little more than an hour later, I looped around San Antonio's suburban
fringe, a network of subdivisions and strip centers, and turned southeast
along a two-lane blacktop through gently rolling pastureland dotted with
mesquite and mottes of live oak. I passed cattle grazing, occasionally
horses, fields of baled hay. Brick or stone ranch-style houses set away from
the road behind wire fencing were attractive and well kept. *Giant* they
were not. They appeared to be country getaways or maybe ranchettes,
small cattle operations that retirees or refugees from the city operated. It
was rural South Texas, pleasant enough but nothing spectacular, nothing
out of the ordinary.

Sutherland Springs is not really a town but an unincorporated community bisected by a busy highway. Traffic ignores the blinking yellow
light. Sutherland Springs has no downtown business district, no school,

no noticeable landmark. (It does have a colorful history, but I didn't know that at the time.)

The sun set as I drove. Crossing narrow, tree-lined Cibolo Creek and heading up a slight incline, I passed a Sutherland Springs city limits sign. I slowed to a crawl as knots of people loomed out of the darkness. Huge satellite trucks and police vehicles, red lights flashing, crowded the highway. Rubberneckers spilled into the blinking-light intersection of state Highway 87 and Farm Road 539. A sheriff's deputy in a western hat and reflective vest directed motorists unaccustomed to slowing down.

I parked along a street of modest frame houses and ramshackle mobile homes a couple of blocks from the First Baptist Church of Sutherland Springs, the site a few hours earlier of the worst mass shooting in modern Texas history. The small, boxy building, its exterior walls clad in weathered white siding, its wooden front door positioned under a squat steeple, was bathed in harsh light brighter than a summer day's. Yellow crime scene tape kept the curious out of the front yard.

In the post office parking lot across the highway from the church, a middle-aged Hispanic man wearing all black was conducting a candlelight prayer vigil. "I propose that we make a pact that in this small town that evil will not prevail," he was saying as I walked up. Recorded gospel music played from a speaker on the ground nearby.

Mike Gonzales, the man conducting the service (a retired Army warrant officer with two tours of duty in Iraq, he would tell me later), was surrounded by dozens of men, women, and children holding candles, clutching each other and sobbing. Surrounding the inner circle was a ring of reporters with notebooks and iPhones, photographers jostling for shots, and cameramen maneuvering bulky equipment.

"I mean, you hear about Vegas," a middle-aged man said in a quiet voice, speaking to himself as much as to me, "but when it's a stone's throw from your house…" He looked down at the ground and shook his head. "It's so quiet here. It doesn't happen here." (Just a few weeks earlier in Las Vegas, more than fifty people had been killed and more than five hundred injured when a gunman in a high-rise hotel room opened fire on an outdoor concert below.)

As the impromptu service continued, I was careful not to step in front of a slender gray-haired man in a blue polo shirt and khakis who sat in a wheelchair beside me. He was holding high a candle in a plastic cup. It took me a second to realize I was standing beside Texas governor Greg Abbott, who seemed to be alone in the crowd. Years earlier, a tree limb had fallen on him as he jogged along a residential street in Houston. He has been a paraplegic ever since.

As Gonzales continued to speak, I glanced across the road at the little church, now surrounded by portable fencing. Bright lights illuminated police officers and investigators going about their business. I tried to take in the horror of what had happened inside the white frame building that morning. I tried to imagine swarms of bullets from a military-style assault rifle burrowing into bodies of helpless men, women, and children as they prayed and sang hymns of praise. What had happened was beyond imagining. In time I would come to know the details.

That evening I didn't know Ryland Ward, a five-year-old boy who miraculously survived being shot numerous times at point-blank range. I didn't know Kris Workman, the church's young praise team director, shot in the back and instantly paralyzed from the waist down. Both were in the hospital that Sunday evening—the little boy fighting to stay alive; the active young man, a former college tennis player and dirt-track race car driver, undergoing surgery and contemplating life with useless legs. I didn't know that at that very moment numerous family members were still waiting at a church a couple of miles up the road—waiting to hear from authorities whether their loved ones were alive or dead.

I didn't know Sherri Pomeroy, the pastor's soft-spoken wife, who, with her husband Frank, had lost beloved Annabelle, their dark-haired, dark-eyed fourteen-year-old. Friends would recall that the teenager was always smiling. I didn't know Sarah Slavin, a young woman with dyed-purple hair who lost nine members of her family, or her sister-in-law Jennifer Holcombe, whose infant daughter was shot and killed as she held the little girl. I didn't know David Colbath, who lay on the floor as the shooter buried the muzzle of his assault rifle into his back and pulled the trigger.

I knew none of the people I would come to appreciate and respect in the ensuing weeks and months.

Journalists by the nature of our work parachute in to the site of a tragedy or a natural disaster; we stay for a day or so, notebooks, cameras, and tape recorders at the ready; and then take off for the next big story. We briefly meet people like Sarah Slavin and Sherri Pomeroy, and then we move on. But they do not move on. Their heartache does not heal in a day or a week or a month. Neither do their physical wounds. As in Newtown and Charleston and Las Vegas and Orlando and Santa Fe and Pittsburgh and El Paso—and other sites from an ever-lengthening list—in Sutherland Springs lives were forever changed that November morning.

Glancing back at the governor on that warm evening, I remembered a Facebook ad he had posted in 2013, shortly before he announced his running for the state's highest office. Abbott was the Texas attorney general at the time. The ad, designed to assuage any doubts the state's hard-right Republican base might harbor about him, was anything but subtle. It featured a semiautomatic pistol lying next to a well-thumbed Bible.

"Two things every American should know how to use," the ad proclaimed in block letters beneath the gun and Bible. "Neither of which are taught in schools."

I know the governor. He is a congenial man in person. I admired him for showing up unannounced that evening in Sutherland Springs and not claiming the spotlight. I had been less than admiring in a series of *Houston Chronicle* editorials I had written throughout the year about guns and the Texas gun culture, work that had been honored a few months earlier with a Pulitzer Prize nomination. The editorials usually explored policy; in the little church across the road, policy was secondary. People had suffered and died in that invaded sanctuary.

In the editorials, I had chided the governor about the Facebook ad and about the relentless crusade he and his allies had launched in the Texas legislature to make firearms ubiquitous and unregulated. In my reporting and research, nonetheless, I sought to understand a belief among many of my fellow Texans that was almost religious in its depth and intensity, a belief in the sanctity of a sophisticated machine crafted to kill, a belief that Abbott proudly shared. "Gundamentalism" is the word that retired Presbyterian minister James Atwood coined to describe the almost mystical hold that grips Second Amendment absolutists.

In Sutherland Springs, faith in guns had collided with faith in God. Defenseless Christians, many of them ardent gun owners themselves, had become collateral damage in a holy war.

Twenty-six people died that morning less than a hundred yards from where I stood next to the governor. Twenty more were wounded. Paradoxically, we would soon learn that a gun-wielding "hero" may have saved many of the survivors from being slaughtered. Months later, that same hero, a soft-spoken plumber and certified National Rifle Association instructor, used his vast personal gun collection to give me a gun tutorial in the living room of his home across the road from the church. "All I ask is that you don't make me look bad," he requested.

I assured him that I wouldn't—and I won't. But I would try to understand him and others like him, men and women devoted to their guns, despite the mortal peril the misuse of guns has unleashed in this country.

As the prayers and hymns continued that autumn evening, someone tapped me on the shoulder. I instinctively stepped aside, thinking it was a cameraman angling for a better view of the governor. It turned out to be my son Pete, a reporter for the *Washington Post*. Back home in Texas for the weekend to attend a family reunion, he had been at the gathering for all of ten minutes when he got the call from the *Post* news desk to head to a place he, too, had never heard of.

Despite the fact that he wore a *Washington Post* "Democracy Dies in Darkness" T-shirt on his foray into fervid-red Texas, I was proud to watch him work. It's not often that father and son cover a story together.

I realized I was fortunate. I had seen two of my kids that day, both grown and on their own. Thinking as a father helped me feel, viscerally, the depth of loss the people of Sutherland Springs were trying to comprehend. Pete and I, along with hundreds of journalists from around the world, now presumed to tell their story. We had descended on an unassuming little town at a time when residents and church members were trying to cope with almost unimaginable horror. I'd been in similar situations—covering a rarely remembered mass shooting in a Fort Worth church twenty years earlier, reporting on the little town of West, Texas, after a 2013 fertilizer plant explosion—but to intrude on people's grief and sorrow never gets easy.

In an article that ran a couple of weeks after the shooting, reporter Lauren McGaughy of the *Dallas Morning News* described knocking on the door of a home near the church. She introduced herself to members of the Ward family, just returned from the hospital and awaiting news about four relatives—three kids (including Ryland, the five-year-old) and their mother. They invited her in.

"Maybe they opened up because they trusted me, or it was a welcome distraction," Lauren recalled. "Maybe it was just luck and timing. Whatever the reason, I wrote their story sitting at their kitchen table....I decided to choose my interactions carefully. But I was still there, a stranger, an outsider, my presence an intrusion." (Two of the youngsters died, as did their mother.)

Most reporters feel a similar unease in such situations—I know I do—and yet driving home through the dark countryside that night, I decided I would stay a while. I banked on getting to know the people I would write about and allowing them to get to know me. I realized it would take more than a quick interview at the local Dairy Queen (if Sutherland Springs had a Dairy Queen) to reach the heart of the story.

I suspected that Sutherland Springs had something to tell us all about the epidemic of mass shootings in this country and the culture of fear those shootings engender. Maybe what happened in that little church on a Sunday morning—the Lord's Day, Pastor Frank Pomeroy often reminds his parishioners—would reveal something about this nation's trust in guns, about the tenets of fundamentalist Christianity that tolerate such trust, and about everyday life in twenty-first-century rural America at a time when urban and rural, red and blue, old and young seem irrevocably estranged. Sutherland Springs could have been any one of dozens of American communities that have suffered through a mass shooting. I hoped it would be possible to connect this unprepossessing little place, its concreteness and specificity, to larger discussions and debate and perhaps mutual understanding.

Adam Winkler, a University of California, Los Angeles (UCLA), law professor who writes about America's gun culture (*Gunfight: The Battle over the Right to Bear Arms in America*), has suggested that Texas might be the prototype for an armed America, with no controls, no limits on our Second Amendment freedoms. Winkler posited that the nation, with a newly installed conservative majority on the US Supreme Court, might be only a ruling away from that National Rifle Association (NRA) ideal. I wondered whether a tiny community no one had ever heard of was the American future in microcosm.

Although I knew nothing about Sutherland Springs, I knew its people in a way. I am, in fact, a native Texan who grew up in a small, working-class community near Waco (where folks might have owned a shotgun or a .22 for dove hunting, but not an assault rifle, or rifles). Like the residents whose lives revolve around their faith, I was deeply involved as a youngster with my extended family's fundamentalist church. We, too, believed in the Bible, literally.

I would come to learn, from that first evening, that the people of Sutherland Springs are people of deep, even desperate, faith. Would their faith sustain them in the face of grievous loss? Despite my own early immersion in fundamentalist Christianity, I was confounded initially by what seemed to be their unquestioning trust and acceptance. I simply couldn't believe what they were telling me. Surely, they were deluding themselves. Surely, rage, however impotent, would have been a more appropriate response.

When I expressed my skepticism and befuddlement to my old friend Robert Abzug, a historian who heads the Schusterman Center for Jewish Studies at the University of Texas at Austin, he reminded me that many Holocaust survivors rejected their faith once they set about rebuilding their shattered lives. Dismayed and disillusioned, they could not imagine paying homage to a God who would allow such horror to happen.

Wouldn't a similar disillusion set in among the people of Sutherland Springs? They professed to accept with equanimity, with all-embracing faith, what had happened to them. How could that be, I wondered.

For more than a year—from the night of the shooting until the first anniversary—I attended Sunday morning services and Thursday evening Bible classes, visited in homes, shared meals at Baldy's Diner and elsewhere. I asked impertinent questions, probed for deep and honest responses, gently urged men and women who didn't really know the guy with the reporter's notebook to revisit—indeed, to re-create for me—the most painful experience of their lives. I'm grateful that most were willing to help, and I deeply appreciate their trust. I also understand that some I asked simply could not. I do understand.

Three hundred or so miles northeast of Sutherland Springs is a little Piney Woods town near the Louisiana line called New London. About the same size as Sutherland Springs, it's known—if it's known at all these days—for one thing: On a March afternoon in 1937, a gas explosion destroyed the New London public school. Walls collapsed and the roof fell in, burying victims in a mass of brick, steel, and concrete debris. Of the 500 students and 40 teachers in the building that afternoon, nearly 300 died. Only about 130 youngsters escaped serious injury. To this day, the town commemorates its loss.

Chances are, the little town of Sutherland Springs will be remembered eight decades from now, a century from now—if it's remembered at all—for what happened on a Sunday morning in the fall of 2017. Travelers in their self-driving cars on Highway 87 will repeat the story as they pass by. Reporters now and then will offer up anniversary retellings.

Pastor Frank insisted otherwise. The First Baptist Church of Sutherland Springs will be a city set on a hill, he proclaimed from the pulpit on a Sunday morning not long after the tragedy. It will be known for turning evil into good, known for good works among the community. As he spoke—prophesying, if you will—his people said amen. On that Sunday morning, as on every Sunday morning, the prophet wore a pistol on his hip.

Chapter One

"Shattered"

SARAH HOLCOMBE SLAVIN WAS running late for church. The fact that she and her husband, Rocky, lived fifteen miles out in the country and that their daughter, Elene, was two years old had something to do with her tardiness. So also did a certain spiritual malaise she had been feeling for, who knows, maybe a couple of years. On this November morning, however, her dad was the fill-in preacher, and her mom would be giving the announcements. She couldn't miss that.

Sarah was thirty-three, although with her dyed-purple hair, her small stature, and her penchant for faded jeans and T-shirts, many assumed she was a teenager. A country girl, she had grown up in a large extended family outside Floresville, a little ranching town with a frontier square, a venerable stone courthouse, and a large concrete peanut on the courthouse lawn (commemorating what used to be the area's cash crop). Like most small-town kids, she had cheered for the Mighty Tigers football team on Friday nights and hung out with friends at the local Sonic Drive-In. She had worked at Dairy Queen, where she was known for her smile and her courtesy. She and Rocky, a computer geek, married early.

She was a math major in college and had taught high school math after graduating, but a year in the classroom was enough to convince her that teaching wasn't for her. She quit to work with her dad, Bryan Holcombe, who made custom canvas covers for cattle trailers in an old, Army surplus building in the country. Amid the whir of industrial-sized sewing machines, surrounded by giant rolls of tarp, she got to know her dad not only as a parent but also as a friend and mentor. While Sarah worked, little Elene contented herself in the "baby jail," a penned-off area against one wall with toys, a TV, and colored chalk for scribbling on the blackboard on the wall beside the "jail." Some days, Sarah's sister-in-law, Jenni Holcombe, came out to the shop. Her baby girl Noah Grace sat and played in the baby jail with Elene while their mothers visited.

Like Paul the apostle, Bryan was a tentmaker of sorts, when he wasn't preaching or playing his ukulele and sharing his faith with inmates in the Wilson County Jail. His American Canvas Works customers were local farmers and ranchers, truck drivers, small-business people in places like Floresville and Stockdale and Karnes City. They were small-town, hardworking people. A native of Victoria, Texas, near the Gulf Coast, Bryan was one of them.

As a child, Sarah detested church, but her parents made her go. "I would fight, because they made me wear a dress, and I thought I already knew all the Sunday school lessons anyway," she recalled. "Sometime in my early teenage years, I started actually enjoying going to church. I started reading the Bible for myself instead of just learning what I was taught. I got really into it and became a bit pushy and arrogant about it all. What I believed was right, and anybody who disagreed was wrong."

Maturity, she said, brought a bit of humility and an acknowledgment that she didn't know everything. For her own life, she settled on a kind of divine wager worthy of Pascal's. "If you gain, you gain all; if you lose, you lose nothing," the French philosopher had written. Sarah agreed.

Her parents' deep devotion made her a bit uncomfortable at times, and yet she saw how their faith affected people around them. Her mother, Karla Holcombe, was in charge of Vacation Bible School at church. She fed the homeless and made weekly bread runs for the church's food pantry. Bryan had his jail ministry. As a young wife and mother, as a member of a close extended family, Sarah wanted her own life to be as purposeful and as contented as her parents' lives seemed to be.

She made a conscious decision in the tradition of William James, the agile and profound American thinker who devoted much of his life to pondering "the reality of the unseen." She would nurture a will to believe.

In Sarah's words, "I decided that I wasn't sure whether Christianity was true, but that it could be true and that it was beneficial to believe it was true, whether it was really true or not."

Doubt assailed her Christian pragmatism during her late twenties. Was there really a God, and was he truly the God she read about in the New Testament? Why would he allow terrible things to happen? Although she laughs about her musings now, she went so far as to think that maybe God was some kind of alien life-form.

"So, anyway," she recalled, "my prayers became more along the lines of 'God, I don't mean to be disrespectful, but I really would like to know if you are real and if you really love us and know us each personally, and why some things in the Bible are so crazy, and I would like you to speak to me somehow to let me know, without scaring the crap out of me if possible, because in the Bible whenever someone hears from God or an angel they are always scared to death.'"

She was waiting for answers, but other concerns kept her occupied—her beautiful, little dark-haired daughter; her marriage; her daily work with her dad; her extended family. Three generations of Holcombes all lived near each other on a wooded three-hundred-acre tract of land fifteen miles outside Floresville. They called it "the farm." Sarah and Rocky and the other younger Holcombes lived in double-wide mobile homes. The grandparents, in their mid-eighties at the time of the shooting, lived in a spacious log cabin on the property.

On that Sunday morning, Sarah got Elene buckled into her car seat and headed to Sutherland Springs, twenty minutes away. (Rocky usually didn't attend church.) "I wasn't really worried about being late because, honestly, I just really didn't care that much," she recalled months later. She also knew that starting times at the First Baptist Church of Sutherland Springs could be a bit flexible.

But then, something happened, something strange. As she drove along the winding country road, cows grazing in pastures, trees turning to fall colors, she felt what she could only describe as "a really strong presence in the car with me." It was so strong, she glanced over at the passenger seat. As strange as it was, the presence wasn't frightening. It was somehow reassuring. "I heard God tell me—not audibly but just somehow heard on some other level—'I am here, and I love you,'" she recalled. "I don't have words to describe that moment, other than pure peace and comfort and joy."

She was so struck by the sensation, she almost stopped at her grandparents' house to tell them about it. "It was like an awakening inside me or something," she said.

She chose instead to keep driving and found a place to park directly in front of the small church. Then, before she could take the keys out of the ignition, a man—a neighbor who lived across the street—frantically rapped on her car window. "Leave!" he shouted. "Leave! There's been a shooting."

She didn't ask questions. She backed out, tires spinning on the gravel as she accelerated, and drove to a house near the church where the mother of a friend lived. Yes, the woman told her, there had been a shooting. No, she didn't have details.

Sarah realized later that she had pulled up to the church building during the few minutes between the time the shooter had fled and when the police and first responders began arriving. That mystical experience she had felt while driving had occurred at about the time the shooter had opened fire on the helpless worshippers inside the building.

"My main feeling at that point was confusion and uncertainty," she said, "but I remember feeling and hearing my pulse in my ears and body, so I know I was already going into shock. My main thought was, 'Keep Elene safe.'"

With ambulance and police sirens screaming, with helicopters already circling the normally quiet little community, and with little Elene crying in her car seat in back, she then drove to the Community Building a few blocks away. Frantic family members who had begun converging on the church were being instructed to gather at the building, both to get them away from the desperate scene and to allow Texas Rangers to find them more easily if they needed help identifying victims.

The small frame building began to fill with volunteers eager to help. First responders came in, their faces grim, often with tears in their eyes.

Neighbors dropped by with food. Texas Rangers, sheriff's deputies, and state troopers called people out for interviews. FBI agents showed up. It was crowded, chaotic. Among the gathering crowd were people like Sarah, people waiting. In midafternoon she looked into the eyes of a friend and heard the news she'd been dreading:

"Mom?"

"Gone."

"Dad?"

"Gone."

"Noah?"

"Gone."

Eight times she heard the same unequivocal answer, the same dreaded response. Her parents. Her brother Danny. Her sister-in-law Crystal and Crystal's unborn child. Four youngsters—Emily, Megan, Noah Grace, Greg. Three generations of her family were gone.

Sarah's older brother, John Holcombe, Crystal's husband, was wounded but survived, as did John's seven-year-old stepdaughter, Evelyn. Her sister-in-law, Jennifer Holcombe, Danny's wife and mother to seventeen-month-old Noah Grace, also survived. But the family's loss was staggering.

"When I found out they had all been killed, I was shattered," Sarah told us at church one Sunday morning months later. Barely tall enough to peer over the lectern, she was surrounded on the rostrum by several churchwomen who had returned from a weekend retreat. They wore purple T-shirts with the word "UNSHAKEABLE" printed in sparkly silver letters across the back.

"I was shattered into a million pieces," she continued in a soft voice. "I was just broken. I can't put into words how broken I was. I didn't like feeling broken, so I began to try to put myself back together. I worked really hard to pull myself back together, but I could not put myself back together."

Despite the lingering pain, despite the profound sadness, she did not go away. Unlike a few survivors who couldn't bear to be in a place where they had lost so much, she did not go to another church. Or no church. "I have thought about going to a different church, but at least for right now, I need to be here," she told me via email.

Her parents were so involved in the church, it was their extended family. She felt an obligation to stay—and a sense of comfort. "Every Sunday whenever I pull up—late as usual—to a full parking lot, it brings tears to my eyes," she said. "Before November, I can't remember the parking lot ever being full. My family would have been so happy how many souls have come into a relationship with Christ through our tragedy."

I heard echoes of Sarah's story in many other accounts of that day. All who might have been at church that morning had mixed feelings. They felt a form of survivor's guilt, as did the actual survivors. They felt grateful to God. They felt they were spared for some divine reason, some mission that they prayed would be revealed to them.

Ted Montgomery, a church deacon and Vietnam veteran, got up and got ready that morning, but his wife, Ann, wasn't feeling well. Sitting on the front porch drinking coffee with Ted's sister Helen Fidler, also a church member, they decided to stay home. "Something came over me," Ann recalled, "and we just decided not to go that morning." Everybody sitting in the pew where the Montgomerys and their extended family usually sat was killed.

Rod Green, also a Vietnam vet, hopped on his Harley for the short ride to church that morning but decided on the spur of the moment to drop by a yard sale that had "hog badges" for sale. He pulled into the churchyard shortly after the shooting. Green, a former deputy sheriff in Montana, always carried a pistol, even at church, and he felt guilty that he wasn't there that morning to confront the shooter. He conceded he might not have been able to stop a man shooting through walls with an AR-15.

Windy Choate, who became the church secretary a few weeks after the shooting, had been sick all week, and her husband, Stormy, was at work. The Choates—yes, Windy and Stormy—had been church members for eight years. She had turned her phone off so she could sleep and didn't turn it back on until one p.m. Among the first of many messages was one from a friend: "I can't even tell you; turn the news on."

"It was probably fortunate for me that I didn't need to be up here [at the church] and in the way," Windy said. "I watched a lot of those kids grow up."

The men, women, and children who did walk into their church's little sanctuary that morning, as they had done countless times before, found themselves in a hell beyond imagining. David Colbath, an irrepressible fellow who liked to talk and to preach—regardless of whether he was in the pulpit, church members said with a smile—recalled that he taught Sunday school that morning. "And I taught on James 1, and it was so ironic," he told me. "I taught on James 1 that God cannot be tempted, that God is incapable of doing evil. And it was a good Sunday school lesson. We talked and, like I said, it's one of my favorite books in the Bible, and I knew the Word pretty well.

"And that Sunday morning I can remember going and sitting down, shaking people's hands, and we sang our first song. And after the first song, we get up and go shake people's hands and talk and meet everybody and then go back and sit down and wait for the messages coming on."

When Colbath got back to the pew where he'd been sitting, he found that a little girl named Evelyn Hill—Sarah Slavin's niece—had joined him. Seven years old, blonde-haired Evelyn and Colbath's daughter were best friends. "Farida Brown had been sitting next to me," he said, "and Evelyn decided to sit between the two of us, and I said, 'Evelyn, what are you doing sitting here right now?' And she says, 'I just wanted to sit next to you.' And that's never happened before."

As Colbath was sitting down, Karla Holcombe, Evelyn's grandmother and Sarah's mother, got up from a front pew and walked to the pulpit to read the announcements for the week—coming church events, who was sick, who had requested prayers. Colbath heard what sounded like firecrackers at the front door of the church. Colbath, also a gun enthusiast, was shot multiple times and almost bled to death on the floor of the church. During sleepless nights in the weeks and months to come, nights interrupted by anxious bouts of post-traumatic stress disorder (PTSD), he would fantasize about what he might have done had he been carrying a gun.

"I've been through the guilt that I couldn't do anything that morning," he told me one morning after church. "But there was nothing we could do. Now I know that God saved me for a higher purpose."

Ben and Michelle Shields, the shooter's in-laws—and likely targets—had stayed up late the night before, attending a stock car race where they watched their friend Kris Workman compete. They were getting ready for church the next morning, even though Ben's back was hurting.

"I knew he was in pain," Michelle recalled. "At the last minute, the Lord spoke to me. I heard the Lord tell me to stay home."

Michelle's mother, Lula White, perhaps a target, as well, was among the victims.

Months after the shooting, Michelle was still barely sleeping. As she explained to *San Antonio Express-News* reporter Silvia Foster-Frau, her head would hit the pillow and her mind would start racing. She would see her church family huddled under pews, terrified. She would see her son-in-law coming toward her, finger on the trigger of his AR-15. The screams of friends and family members echoed inside her head.

"I still feel responsible," she told Foster-Frau, her voice and body shaking with grief. "I feel responsible for trying to reach out and trying to bring [her son-in-law] closer to the Lord. Because I feel like all I did was bring the devil closer to our church."

Chapter Two

"A glow after bathing"

IN 1877, A WRITER for the *San Antonio Express-News* observed that the town called Sutherland Springs was "uninviting in appearance." Nearly a century and a half later, *uninviting* is too strong a word, although the little community, population about four hundred, is certainly nondescript. Until the mass shooting, it had gone unnoticed for decades.

As the name suggests, the community owed its origin to water—"healing waters," Native American tribes and early Anglo settlers believed. The waters originate in the Texas Hill Country forty miles northwest of San Antonio, where springs bubble up through the porous limestone of the Edwards Plateau to feed a hundred-mile-long stream that eventually flows into the San Antonio River. The Coahuiltecan Indians called the stream Xoloton; to the Tonkawas, it was Bata Coniquiyoqui. Near the site that became Sutherland Springs, a subterranean fault pushes the underground water to the surface. As the water percolates upward, it collects a variety of minerals—alum, iron, manganese, and several varieties of sulfur.

The minerals give the water a reddish color and a distinctive odor. The smell still pervades Sutherland Springs kitchens and bathrooms. Longtime residents insist that the odiferous water combats cancer—and mosquitoes. The stream first appeared in historical records when Spanish authorities rode into Texas to counter the French intrusion from the east during the late seventeenth century. In 1721, the Marqués de San Miguel de Aguayo, who initiated an ambitious effort to build missions and presidios in Texas, christened the waterway the Rio Cibolo. He probably named it for the bison that still grazed along its banks, although historian Richard McCaslin, author of a definitive history of Sutherland Springs, notes the similarity to *Cibola*, the name of the fabled city of gold that mesmerized Spanish explorers.

The Spanish did not establish permanent settlements on the Cibolo, although several missions located in San Antonio—including the Alamo—pastured livestock on ranches near the springs. The young Native Americans who herded the mission cattle, sheep, and goats could be considered the first Texas cowboys.

Anglos began moving into the area in the mid-1830s, among them a New Yorker named Joseph H. Polley, who arrived in 1847 and built a magnificent sandstone mansion that still stands three miles north of today's Sutherland Springs. He called it Whitehall, after the town where he lived in Upstate New York.

Polley was born in Whitehall in 1795 and served as a fifteen-year-old teamster in the War of 1812. He was one of the first twenty-two immigrants to follow colonizer Stephen F. Austin to Texas in 1821. Texas at the time was a part of Mexico.

Polley also was the first sheriff of Austin's colony, and during the Texas Revolution in the spring of 1836 he was assigned to watch over women and children fleeing Mexican general Santa Anna's army in what Texans call the Runaway Scrape. Their menfolk had gone off to fight.

In 1847, two years after the United States annexed Texas, Polley and his wife, Mary Augusta Bailey Polley, moved from their home near the Texas Gulf Coast to a site on a knoll overlooking the Cibolo Valley, about two miles north of today's Sutherland Springs. They were the first settlers in an area still raided by Indians.

While the Polleys lived in a temporary "stake house" on the property, a team of twenty slaves quarried hardened sandstone from the banks of nearby Elm Creek for the walls of the new house and crushed mussel shells from the creek for lime to mix mortar.

Joseph Polley's brother John Polley drew up the blueprints for the house, using the family home in Whitehall as inspiration. He also purchased doors, sashes, cabinetry, window panes, and furnishings in New York for his brother's new home and had them shipped to Indianola, a port on the Texas Gulf Coast. Oxcarts hauled the materials to the frontier site.

The eight-room, two-story house was completed by 1854, and the large Polley family (eleven children in all) moved in. By that time, Joseph Polley was in the process of accumulating vast holdings of land and cattle. Shortly before the war he owned 150,000 head, more than any rancher in Texas with the exception of the fabled King Ranch. Mary Polley managed the large household.

Despite being a slaveholder, Joseph Polley was a reluctant supporter of the Confederacy. His son, Joseph Benjamin Polley, became a corporal in Company F of the 4th Texas Infantry, which fought under Col. John Bell Hood and Gen. Robert E. Lee. The younger Polley saw action at Gaines Mill, Second Manassas, Antietam, and Gettysburg and had to have a wounded foot amputated in 1864. He would go on to write *A Soldier's Letters to Charming Nellie,* published in 1908, and *Hood's Texas Brigade,* 1910, considered a classic Civil War memoir. Polley died in Floresville in 1918.

The war wrought financial ruin on the Polleys. Joseph Polley received a pardon from President Andrew Johnson but was unable to rebuild the family's fortunes before his death in 1869. Mary Polley turned Whitehall into a boardinghouse after her husband's death, catering to the many visitors who came to nearby Sutherland Springs to take the cure in the sulfur waters of Cibolo Creek. She lived until 1888.

The mansion stayed in the Polley family until 1907, when it was sold to a county commissioner. Pattillo Higgins, the legendary driller who discovered oil at Spindletop, showed up in the area in 1923; oil was discovered on the Sutherland Springs property in 1955, but the find didn't amount to much.

One of the comfortable rocking chairs on the expansive Whitehall front porch—a chair that occasionally rocks on its own, for some reason— would offer an eye-witness view of the cavalcade of Texas history: the mansion built by slave labor; Col. Robert E. Lee spending the night in an upstairs bedroom; Confederate volunteers from the area marching off to war; bloody battles with the Comanches; oil discoveries; visitors from up north arriving to "take the waters"; and bootleggers plying their wares during Prohibition.

*　　*　　*

A doctor named John T. Sutherland Jr. brought his wife and nine children to the Cibolo Creek area shortly after Polley built his mansion. Sutherland had been in Texas since the fall of 1835, when he arrived from his home in Alabama to visit his older brother George, who had emigrated a few years earlier.

John Sutherland, forty-two at the time, discovered that his brother had become a leader among restive settlers seeking to break away from Mexico. George, in fact, was one of the armed rebels who had recently stormed into the largest city in Texas, San Antonio de Béxar, in December 1835, seeking to drive the Mexican Army out of Texas.

Known as "War Dogs" or "craze-orians" among settlers reluctant to break with Mexico, the Anglo-American rebels expected to establish a new republic or seek annexation to the United States as a slaveholding state. Many of the newcomers had arrived from the American South and anticipated establishing a new Cotton Kingdom in the fertile soil of Texas. It rankled them that Mexico had outlawed slavery.

John Sutherland, who had studied medicine in Alabama, decided to stay in Texas, where, for a brief time, he would associate with men whose names in years to come would grace Texas cities, thoroughfares, history books, and myth. Like his brother, he embraced the Texan cause and joined Capt. William H. Patton's company when it moved into San Antonio in preparation for confronting the Mexican Army, then making its slow way northward into the heart of Texas. Patton's company also included William D. Sutherland, George's teenaged son and John's nephew.

Patton turned his men over to the commander of Texan forces in San Antonio, a young lawyer and prominent rabble-rouser named William Barret Travis, also from Alabama. Col. Travis was happy to have a man with medical experience in their midst. Among Sutherland's patients was Travis's co-commander, Col. James Bowie, the larger-than-life adventurer and slave trader known far and wide for his namesake knife. Bowie was seriously ill with a malady Sutherland described "as being of a peculiar nature," perhaps malaria.

At the time, worrisome rumors were circulating that Gen. Antonio Lopez de Santa Anna and his massive army were within a few miles of the city. Dr. Sutherland approached Travis with an idea. He told the young commander he was a relative newcomer to the area, but "if any one who knew the country would accompany me, I would go out and ascertain to a certainty the truth or falsity of the whole."

John W. Smith, known as El Colorado (Redhead), volunteered. As Dr. Sutherland climbed into the saddle, he told Travis that if his men saw the two of them "returning in any other gait than a slow pace, he might be sure we had seen the enemy."

The trails were slick from recent rains, so Sutherland and Smith rode westward at a moderate pace. Topping a gentle rise about a mile and a half from town, they were shocked at what they saw arrayed below them. Sutherland wrote that they were "within one hundred and fifty yards of fifteen hundred men, well mounted and equipped, their polished armor glistening in the rays of the sun."

Worried they had been spotted, the two scouts wheeled their horses and galloped back toward town. Sutherland's smooth-shod horse slipped in the mud and somersaulted, tossing its rider over its head before rolling onto Sutherland's legs. Sutherland's rifle snapped at the breech; his legs were seriously injured. Smith galloped back to help his companion remount.

Although the Mexicans had not seen them, the two men raced back into San Antonio, the bells inside the squat, octagonal belfry of San Fernando Cathedral peeling frantically as they galloped into Main Plaza. There they met David Crockett astride his own horse. The recently arrived Tennessean advised them that Travis had assembled his men—fewer than two hundred in all—inside the three-acre compound of the mission-fortress across the river known as the Alamo.

Their situation was desperate. Unless reinforcements arrived, they soon would be overwhelmed by Santa Anna's minions. Nevertheless, Sutherland and Smith joined the Texans behind the crumbling walls of the old mission, although as Sutherland dismounted outside Travis's headquarters, one of his injured legs gave way and he collapsed in a heap. Leaning on Crockett's shoulder, he limped into Travis's room, where the young colonel was sitting at a wooden table writing out a call for help.

It was obvious that Sutherland was unable to stand and fight, but he could still ride. Travis handed him a note to deliver to the people of Gonzales, a town seventy-five miles to the northeast. "The enemy in large force is in sight," the desperate young commander had written. "We want men and provisions. Send them to us. We have 150 men and are determined to defend the Alamo to the last. Give us assistance."

Sutherland and Smith, who would later become mayor of San Antonio, left the Alamo on February 23, 1836. In Gonzales they found volunteers eager to come to the aid of their besieged fellow Texans, but by the time they returned to San Antonio, they were too late. As they warily approached the town, the men realized they weren't hearing the eighteen-pound signal gun that, before the siege, was fired three times daily from inside the Alamo. Coming closer, they saw smoke from funeral pyres rising into the Texas sky. The Alamo had fallen. Every Texan was dead, as were more than five hundred Mexican infantry, with many wounded. The bodies of the Alamo defenders were piled together and burned. Among them was Dr. Sutherland's seventeen-year-old nephew, William.

After the fall of the Alamo, Gen. Sam Houston led his ragtag army in retreat, the ill-trained men shuffling through spring rains and mud toward the border between Texas and Louisiana, where Houston expected assistance from American troops. With his sullen and angry men near mutiny, Houston caught Santa Anna by surprise on marshland near the San Jacinto River and in a battle lasting less than twenty minutes routed the Mexican Army. The unlikely San Jacinto victory in April 1836 prompted Texas to proclaim its independence.

After San Jacinto, Sutherland returned briefly to Alabama and then settled with his family on the Colorado River near the community of Egypt, Texas, east of the new town called Houston. When his second wife died in 1841, he married again, and the union produced three children, as had Sutherland's previous two marriages. Working hard to support his large family, he operated a ferry on the Colorado (as his father had done on the Clinch River in Tennessee) and established a stage line from Houston to Victoria, Texas, by way of Egypt. He traded in livestock and tried to grow cotton but wrote to a daughter in 1842 that his crop was "almost an entire failure" after a long drought ended with fifty days of rain and an infestation of pests.

More than a dozen years after the fall of the Alamo, Sutherland's wife, Ann, complained about her husband's frequent absences from home tending to various business enterprises. John Sutherland also was involved in a business dispute with his brother George, one perhaps fueled by lingering accusations that John had abandoned his nephew William in the Alamo.

After George's death in 1853, his widow and children agreed to pay John $2,000 "for the purposes of peace and quiet" and ceded their rights to a parcel of land they owned in Bexar County (San Antonio). That same year, John Sutherland and his family began a new life on the banks of Cibolo Creek, twenty miles northeast of Alamo City.

Sutherland, a self-taught physician, was a follower of Samuel Thomson, who was considered the father of the American herbal movement. Born in New Hampshire in 1769, Thomson began exploring the medicinal properties of herbs and roots as a teenager. At nineteen, he watched his mother die of measles while being treated by a succession of doctors whose methods likely were more lethal than the disease. When the red spots erupted on his own body, he treated the illness with herbs and survived.

Thomson's reputation grew, and neighbors began knocking on his door. By the time he was in his early thirties, the self-taught healer had refined a basic set of medicines and steam treatment that he maintained would cure most ailments. By the 1820s, Thomson's fame and the use of his plant-based medicines had spread across New England. Promoting his system through a series of books and magazines, he soon gained a reputation as an enemy of "modern medicine." Physicians sued him several times during the course of his career, but by the time of his death in 1843, Thomsonian medicine had adherents throughout the United States and around the world.

How Sutherland came to be a Thomsonian is lost to history. He might have read about Thomson in books or magazines or even attended a traveling medicine show. However it happened, his new home on the Cibolo was an ideal spot for a doctor who practiced natural medicine. In an 1849 letter to his daughter, Sutherland described the home site as "handsome," "healthy," and a "place of great resort." He also noted that "we have quite a variety of waters close at hand to wit—white & black sulphur, calibrate, magnesia & alum springs within one hundred yards of my dwelling."

The mineral-rich creek's reputation as a fount of healing waters was already well established by the time Sutherland arrived in 1855. Juan Almonte, a Mexican army officer who toured Texas in 1834 and wrote a report for President Santa Anna, described the Cibolo's water as "thermal springs held in great regard for rheumatism and other ailments of this nature." Gideon Lee Jr., who came to Texas from Putnam County, New York, in 1846 to fight against the Mexicans, reportedly planned to construct a resort on the creek. When a cholera epidemic ravaged San Antonio in 1849, he built cabins near the springs to board patients. An 1878 travelers' guide claimed the water could help anyone who suffered from "dropsy, liver complaint, dyspepsia, consumption and all diseases of the kidneys."

Sutherland, like Lee, also boarded patients who came to "take the waters" and gained a reputation for curing various maladies with his Thomsonian regimen of plants, herbs, and steam. Cholera, a disease that regularly swept through Texas settlements, leaving widespread death in its wake, was his specialty. In 1849, an epidemic ravaged Galveston and settlements along the Rio Grande and the Brazos before moving into San Antonio, claiming more than five hundred victims. "The dead and the dying were packed up in the open air unattended," an observer wrote.

Each time the malady struck, people fled to the Cibolo, boarding with Sutherland or in the "comfortable houses" erected by a man named Joseph F. Johnson near the springs on Gideon Lee's property. As historian McCaslin notes, stories of cures on the Cibolo were widespread, despite skeptics such as Mary Maverick, a Texas pioneer and inveterate diarist whose husband, Sam, participated in the Texas Revolution before becoming a prominent rancher. (The family name became part of the American vernacular as a result of Maverick's penchant for claiming unbranded cattle as his own.) Although she insisted the springs did little good, Maverick returned each year with friends and relatives to sit in or drink the waters.

Ever the energetic entrepreneur, Sutherland established a stage line at the intersection of two important roads near the Cibolo—the Chihuahua Road from the Texas port city of Indianola to Chihuahua, Mexico, and the Goliad Road that ran east along the San Antonio River and then north to intersect the Chihuahua Road at Victoria, Texas. He also sold supplies to the Army and in 1851 opened a post office inside his stage stop.

The sparse settlement on the creek went by several names, including Cibolo Springs, Mineral Springs, and Sulphur Springs, until Sutherland renamed it for himself. He served as the local postmaster intermittently until 1866.

By the time Sutherland died in 1867, his little settlement was prospering. Sutherland Springs boasted "half a dozen residences, one hotel, and two or three stores," the son of Joseph and Mary Polley recalled. The new community also supported a school and a church and in 1860 became the temporary county seat of the newly established Wilson County. With its stage stop, several saloons, and a horse-racing track, it was a typical little frontier town, except for the springs. Few towns could boast well-known medicinal waters like those that flowed from Cibolo Creek.

The Civil War was hard on Sutherland Springs. Many of its young men went off to fight for the Confederacy and never returned. The war—and a prolonged drought—ruined local farms and ranches, as well as businesses that relied on agriculture. In wartime, visitors to the springs dried up, as well. Still, as McCaslin notes, "the springs continued to flow along the Cibolo, and so dreams of a better future persisted."

The same writer who disparaged Sutherland Springs as "uninviting" in 1877 conceded that it was, nonetheless, an "important place," because of the water still bubbling up from more than a hundred springs within two miles of the town center. McCaslin points out that "warm and cold chalybeate (or iron) springs were good for drinking, as were seltzer and soda waters. The most popular for bathing were the black and white sulfur springs on the far side of the Cibolo from Sutherland Springs."

McCaslin quotes a Galveston writer who reported that "on crossing the Cibolo, upon whose banks the town is built, the olfactories [sic] are assailed by a savory smell from an immense black sulphur spring, ten feet in diameter, boiling up with gas, like a huge cauldron; and, to add to his surprise, he finds, upon jumping into this tempting bath, that the human body floats around, and is tossed about like a cork, and the astonishment is still more increased when he finds that to sink beneath the water is an impossibility."

One visitor reported that a dip in the pool, open to both genders, left "a glow after bathing." Another wrote that the stench of the black sulfur water "forcibly reminds one of all the defunct embryo chicks in the infernal regions." Yet another insisted that "a bath in the pure white sulphur, and alternated by a dip in the black sulphur, interluded by a reading from Emerson and a draught from the chalybeate waters, is a pleasure to be envied, even by Oscar Wilde."

By the turn of the twentieth century, landowners and investors were more interested in oil than water, especially after the legendary Pattillo Higgins showed up. In 1900, the eccentric, self-taught geologist had pinpointed a salt dome near Beaumont, Texas, as a bounteous source of oil, and when Spindletop erupted the next year at the very spot he predicted, a hundred thousand barrels a day began gushing out of the ground. Soon, Texas was the nation's leading oil producer, thanks to Spindletop's "black gold."

Investors combed Texas looking for the next oil bonanza. They found them—in East Texas, West Texas, and South Texas—but not around Sutherland Springs. When they drilled nothing but dry holes in the area, they turned to water. Platting another town across the creek and naming it New Sutherland Springs, investors from San Antonio and elsewhere envisioned a "Saratoga of the South."

In 1910, the fifty-two-room luxury Hotel Sutherland opened, along with a sanitarium, a movie theater, a boardinghouse, a spacious pool and pavilion, and a hundred-acre park shaded by venerable live oaks. Wealthy tourists from Chicago and other points north and east took the train to San Antonio, switched to a Sutherland Springs trunk line, and luxuriated in the healing waters.

A 1909 newspaper advertisement produced by the Sutherland Springs Development Company boasted that visitors "can fish in the Cibolo river, enjoy a swim in the largest concrete pool in the world, go to the theater, eat in a hotel that cannot be beaten for cuisine anywhere, and hobnob with the best of people from all over the world." Sunday rail excursions from San Antonio cost fifty cents round trip.

Unfortunately, the resort's heyday was brief. A 1913 flood destroyed the pool and bathing pavilions, and the Hotel Sutherland closed in 1923, the sanitarium in the 1940s. Sutherland Springs native Fred Anderson, a retired 7-Eleven executive, recalled his grandfather's grocery store and a handful of other New Town businesses still open in the 1950s, including a bank and the movie theater. It was a lively place, even after the spa's demise, Anderson recalled.

Alice Garcia, who lives with her husband, Oscar, a block and a half from the First Baptist Church, grew up in Sutherland Springs a couple of decades beyond Fred Anderson. She remembered "a little sleepy community" where she and her pals would play basketball at the Community Building or ride their bikes all over town, since there was little traffic. Kids attended Vacation Bible School at the Baptist church every summer, regardless of their family's denominational preference. It was something to do. "People still hung clothes on clothes lines," she recalled.

"Everybody in the community cared about each other," said Barbara Wood, a fourth-generation resident whose parents raised peanuts and watermelons on a farm outside town. "Somebody got sick, got down, and people would bring in food or do the laundry. It was like a family.

"It's not like that anymore," Wood added. "Times are just different."

Little remains of Sutherland Springs's brief period as the "Saratoga of the South." The once-magnificent pool is a grassy depression in a post-oak thicket, just off Farm Road 539. The railroad depot was dismantled and removed in the 1930s, the tracks taken up in 1971. The few businesses eventually migrated back across the creek to Old Town, where the church, two gas stations, and the Dollar General are located. New Town is now a ghost town. All that's left are scattered residences and the dilapidated shells of commercial buildings, partially hidden by weeds and tall grass. Shoots of spindly trees stretch upward through collapsed roofs.

Old Sutherland Springs has the church and two gas stations, but no traditional business district. Because the community never incorporated as an official town, it has no city government, no police department, no municipal buildings.

Sutherland Springs is struggling, like small towns across Texas—indeed, across the nation—unless they happen to be a bedroom community like nearby La Vernia or a tourist destination like the charming German towns in the Texas Hill Country. All over the state once-prosperous railroad towns, market towns for nearby farms and ranches, and county seats are now boarded-up brick buildings around a once-lively town square. Houses where for decades families lived and kids grew up are now abandoned or neglected. Schools are shuttered, kids bused to a nearby town. And so it is in Sutherland Springs.

Churches in small towns also have withered. "Churches and the religious life are strained by the realities of this modern age—job losses, geographic mobility, and the breakup of extended families," historian Rob Hines of San Antonio told *USA Today* shortly after the shooting. "When a small town loses its schools and churches, it's the beginning of the end."

The Sutherland Springs school burned in 1947 and was never rebuilt. Memories treasured by folks of a certain age and a couple of faded green-and-white SS letter sweaters exhibited at the local museum are about all that's left of good ol' Sutherland Springs High, home of the Fightin' Frogs.

First Baptist, the only church in town, hung on as the heart of a community experiencing for decades what sociologists call "adverse selection." The term is borrowed from the insurance industry to describe a double-helix spiral downward of population and opportunity. People who can, go. But when small-town folks abandon their little towns for opportunities elsewhere, they leave behind a concentration of people who sometimes struggle. Not all, of course, but enough that community leaders like Terrie Smith and museum director Tambria Read have to work extra hard to keep the community alive and engaged. The church continued to thrive, in part, because it didn't rely exclusively on the local community.

A few blocks from the church is a volunteer fire department

and the small, live oak–shaded Community Building, where residents hold quinceañeras, reunions, and wedding receptions, and where family members gathered after the shooting. Except for the buzz of highway traffic, the town is as quiet as it was when Alice Garcia and her friends were playing in the street as kids.

One other building in town that was open to the public (at least when someone was around to unlock the front door) used to be an auto garage. Not far from the Community Building, it had become home to the Sutherland Springs Historical Museum. The museum was a labor of love staffed and administered entirely by volunteers. Tambria Read, its volunteer director, was a longtime visual fine arts teacher at Floresville High School and the school sponsor of the Junior Historians' Club. Read, whose great-grandfather was Pattillo Higgins, grew up in Sutherland Springs, where her grandfather invented a popular strain of pasture grass called Buffel grass. A stand of the tall green grass grew in a field just north of town, a field where Robert Redford flew a biplane for director George Roy Hill's 1975 film, *The Great Waldo Pepper*.

Read was usually at the museum on weekends, either painting, shelving, sawing, or helping fellow volunteers install new exhibits that reflect the town's 150-year history. Several months after the November tragedy, she began organizing the thousands of stuffed animals, toys, notes of condolence, and other items left along the fence at the church.

The busiest spot in town was the Valero gas station and convenience store. It was the morning gathering place, both for Sutherland Springs residents and for motorists who regularly drive through town on state Highway 87. Oil field workers, construction crews, truck drivers, delivery people—they gassed up in the mornings on their way to work and grabbed a cup of coffee and a couple of Terrie Smith's breakfast tacos— bacon con huevo, chorizo con huevo, papas con huevo, migas con huevo, barbacoa, and more—and then maybe a couple to go for lunch.

Smith was very busy. The short, friendly woman, always in motion, ran not only the gas station but also Theresa's Kitchen, Lady Bug Designs, the Cookie Lady, and a catering service called Theresa's Special Occasions. She was president of the Sutherland Springs Civic Association and supervised the remodeling of the Community Building. Her companion, Lorenzo Flores Jr., was a welder by trade. He had his own side business, BBQ Express. They knew everybody in town.

Across the highway from the station was the church, and bordering the church property was a junkyard crammed with gaunt and motionless oil field equipment—an ancient derrick and numerous decrepit old trucks, rusting pipes and valves, an old white school bus. Twenty-six white wooden crosses, like the makeshift memorials along highway crash sites across America, lined the chain-link fence beside the highway. Trucks roared through the intersection despite the blinking light—or the commemorative crosses.

Off the highway, the dwellings along leafy streets near the church were modest, either dingy and rusting mobile homes, modular ranch-style dwellings, or sagging farmhouses succumbing to decades of neglect and disrepair. Dogs too content in their lethargy to chase the occasional passing car lounged in the quiet streets. The most notable feature of residences belonging to several church members were newly constructed ramps to the front doors, the raw wood still an unweathered yellow. Eight homes had been remodeled to make them wheelchair accessible.

Sutherland Springs is poor. The median annual income for Wilson County is $40,000. For Sutherland Springs, it's lower. Many of its residents are retirees or exiles from the city drawn by the low cost of living and the absence of property taxes. Some work on nearby farms and ranches or in the oil fields to the south, where fracking has sparked a boom. Others make the fifty-mile round trip into San Antonio to work, or they hold jobs in nearby Floresville, Seguin, or Stockdale. A number are on governmental assistance; the church's weekly food pantry is a lifesaver. Nearly half the residents are Hispanic; most of the others are white.

A quarter mile north of the church, the coffee-colored waters of the Cibolo still flow through their tree-lined channel, but the life-giving springs have been vastly depleted over the years, the water claimed by fast-growing San Antonio suburbs before it ever gets to Sutherland Springs. A 2005 study found only nine identifiable springs. None of them produced more than a trickle.

Chapter Three

"I chose not to be that person."

On a crisp fall morning, Pastor Frank and I were sitting in his cramped church office talking about guns. On a table near his desk sat two books, *Theology Made Practical* and *Of Moose and Men: Lost and Found in Alaska*, the latter of which he purchased in anticipation of the first vacation he and his wife, Sherri, had taken since the shooting. On the wall were various certificates: one for designation as a fire control technician awarded to Donnell Frank Pomeroy by the US Navy in 1989 and a diploma, a bachelor of arts in biological anthropology from Texas State University in 2016. His minor was in medieval and Renaissance studies.

Perhaps his atypical background explained why Pastor Frank, fifty-two at the time of the shooting, resembled a bouncer more than the stereotypical minister. Tattooed, of medium height, thick-necked, and barrel chested, the Navy veteran wore rimless glasses and a Fu Manchu mustache, the dangling ends turning white. He kept his florid head billiard-ball slick. Occasionally, he wore a navy-blue suit, maybe with a garish Donald Duck tie, but more often he wore jeans or slacks and a short-sleeved sport shirt, usually with a tie. He carried a small pistol in a holster on his right hip or in his right-front pants pocket.

Like many native Texans, Pastor Frank had been around guns his whole life. As a teenager, he always had a gun on a rack in the back window of his pickup, either a shotgun or a rifle, usually a .22 or a 12 gauge, or both. Having a firearm of some sort, including during his time in the military, seemed natural. He had acquired his concealed carry permit years earlier.

"I've always believed in the fact that in American culture we own firearms, and I was taught at an early age how to utilize firearms," he said as we sat in his office nearly a year after the shooting. As usual, he was forthright about guns and about the most terrible day in his life. In the outer office, church secretary Windy Choate was trying to get the Sunday bulletin typed up on her computer while tending to Zacchaeus, a rambunctious miniature Australian shepherd puppy confined to a makeshift pen behind her desk. The pup was named after the "wee, little man" who climbed up a sycamore tree to catch a glimpse of Jesus as he walked by.

"I've always believed that we should train up our children early with firearms to take away the wow factor," Frank said. "All my kids, the girls specifically, I took 'em out very early—let 'em shoot if they could, or at least watch what happens. You hit that watermelon, it explodes. It doesn't re-impose itself like it does on video. It's gone. Let 'em see that there's causes. Let 'em see that there's consequences. Let 'em see the safety aspects to that firearm. Let 'em hear how loud it is, when they're old enough to feel the kick of that firearm."

Frank is a hunter: deer in Texas and elk in Montana. His study at home featured a stuffed bear worthy of mountain man Jeremiah Johnson's abode. He likes shooting old-time flintlock, black-powder rifles—and using a bow, too.

"I prefer primitive weaponry and archery. To me, it's more of a fair chase. You have to get closer," he said. "Any monkey can put a shell in a gun and fire it. For black powder, you've gotta think, you've gotta load, you've gotta compensate. You're throwing a .54-caliber slug of lead out there. You've got to calculate how many inches."

"You know, Frank, you were born in the wrong century," I told him. He laughed and agreed.

Guns are not Pastor Frank's only connections to a frontier past. His personal Texas was rough country, a working-class environment marked by violence, chaos, and instability. He grew up in a blue-collar suburb near the Houston Ship Channel, the forty-mile-long man-made conduit for oceangoing vessels between Houston-area terminals and the Gulf of

Mexico. Lining the busy channel is the largest conglomeration of refineries and petrochemical plants in the world. Communities near the heavily industrialized water worry about clean air and clean water, suspicious cancer clusters, and other serious health issues. It's Houston's backyard, an area that tourists and residents of the more affluent neighborhoods on the city's west side are only vaguely aware of.

Pastor Frank knew it well, too well. He felt no affection for big cities, particularly the sprawling megalopolis on Buffalo Bayou. "I know it's in my head, but I think I smell Houston about an hour before I get there," he said.

He grew up in Cloverleaf, a densely populated community known for drugs, gangs, and prostitution. Its reputation has changed little over the years, with residents complaining about abandoned homes, trash-filled empty lots, and assault rates triple those of unincorporated Harris County. Burglary and theft rates are almost double.

In 2010, a newcomer to Houston asked subscribers to an online forum called "Houston Parents" about living in Cloverleaf. A respondent, relying on the experience of a relative who was a paramedic, advised her to "wear body armor and pack iron" if she made that unwise choice. "On the positive side of things, there's a good barbecue place there called Brothers-in-Law," she wrote.

Pomeroy's parents divorced when he and his brother, Scott, were young. The boys' homelife was unstable, if not dangerous. Their mother worked as a bartender. She remarried, and the two boys lived with their father until the day Child Protective Services intervened and sent the two boys to live with their mother in another ship-channel community nearby. Frank was fourteen, his brother seven years younger. Their mother had her own problems, but she and her husband at least took care of her sons. Both eventually became preachers.

"For a long time I had trouble forgiving child abuse," Pastor Frank told his congregation one morning. "I'd just as soon they rot in Hell. I had to remind myself that God loves them too."

Once Frank and Scott left their dad's home, the boys no longer had reason to fear for their lives, but Frank ran with a rough crowd. For a while, he rode with a motorcycle club, The Bandidos. Founded by Don Chambers, a Houstonian convicted of murdering two drug dealers in 1972, the club took as its motto "We are the people our parents warned us about."

The summer he was seventeen, as Frank tells the story, he was hanging out with friends on the beach at Galveston. Glancing up at his pickup truck parked on the boulevard that runs atop the seawall, he happened to see a young man "key his truck." As Frank raced up the stone steps toward the street, he could see the long, ugly gash the kid had left along the passenger door. Enraged, he grabbed the teenager before he could run and "almost beat the kid half to death."

Leaving the teenager lying on the hot sidewalk, bloodied and whimpering, Frank climbed into his truck, drove home, and waited for the cops to arrive. They came that night and arrested him for assault and battery. The kid he beat up was sixteen, a juvenile. Instead of finishing his senior year of high school, Frank spent six months in county jail. Inmate fights were an everyday rite of passage.

"Frank fought with everybody he met," wife Sherri recalls. "He either picked a fight or he finished a fight."

In a sermon years later about overcoming addiction, Frank talked about anger—his own anger growing up and that of his biological father, "a very harsh abuser." After becoming a Christian and a minister, Frank, probably in his late thirties by then, went to see his father, who told him, "My daddy did it to me; therefore, I did it to y'all." Frank says he told his father he was forgiven. "I chose not to be that person," he told his congregation.

After the teenaged Frank got out of jail, he seemed to find a direction for his life. He enlisted in the Marines, got his general equivalency diploma (GED), and was accepted for Navy SEALs training. He survived the brutal physical regimen that drums out 75 percent of each class but was told by instructors that his performance had fallen just short. The Navy transferred him to electrical engineering training in Connecticut and then to submarine duty.

Frank credits the military with saving his life. He learned discipline, a sense of responsibility, a marketable skill. Before enlisting, he had met a petite girl with straight, light-brown hair, an oval face, and an engaging smile. From a neighboring suburb and another high school—both more upscale than Frank's—Sherri Newman was the daughter of a railroad engineer and the granddaughter of a preacher who had founded his own church. She was going with a friend of Frank's named Billy when he met her.

Frank often warned her about Billy. "You're a good girl," he told her. "Billy's not a good guy."

After a while, Sherri started coming over and cleaning Frank's apartment while he was at work. Eventually, she broke up with Billy and in 1986 married Frank. He was nineteen; she was seventeen. Their son Kaleb was born in 1988, daughter Kandi in 1990, son Kameron in 1992, and son Korey in 1993. For the first few years of their marriage, she drove an hour one way every Sunday to attend her grandfather's church. Frank did not.

Sherri's father, a railroad engineer who worked his whole life for Southern Pacific, never accepted the volatile young man from notorious Cloverleaf. He always called him "a long-haired hippie freak." Shortly after his daughter married Frank, a car tried to outrun Engineer Newman's train at a crossing, and he couldn't come to a stop before he hit the car, killing all its occupants. He never got over it, Frank said. He also never got over a bruise on his hip from the collision. Two months later, he went to a doctor and was found to have a hole the size of an orange in his pelvic bone. Cancer. Even on his deathbed, he couldn't accept his young son-in-law.

Frank got special leave to come home. He remembered feeling awkward, unsure of what to say as he stepped into the room where Sherri's father lay dying. All that came to mind was, "Mr. Newman, how do you like my hair now?" He ran his hand over his bristly boot-camp haircut. "It's still too damn long," the old man growled.

After Frank's military service, the Pomeroys and their growing family came home to the Houston area. They lived in Pasadena, another gritty, blue-collar community that tolerated the smells and smog of refineries and petrochemical plants ("the smell of money," politicians and business tycoons have been known to say). Using his Navy electrical engineering training, Frank worked for a crane company on the ship channel, in motor controls for MMM Square D Company, and later for Manning, Maxwell and Moore, a railroad equipment supply manufacturing company. Later he worked as a steel mill manager and as manager of a paper mill for Kimberly-Clark.

They were good jobs, but Frank in those days was not a good man, as both Pomeroys acknowledge. He drank too much, smoked too much—two and a half packs of Pall Malls a day, he recalled—and spent far too many evenings after work in the boisterous blue-collar bars on Houston's east side, bars equipped with jukeboxes, shuffleboards, gregarious drunks like Frank, and—as the writer Larry McMurtry once observed—"where from 3 p.m. on girls gyrate at one's elbow with varying degrees of grace."

Fights, if not killings, were regular occurrences, which meant that Frank Pomeroy fit right in. Back home, Sherri and the kids never knew what time of the night or early morning he'd come staggering in.

Baptists relish good redemption stories, the more dramatic the better. Pastor Frank has one of those stories, even though the experience he recounts wasn't Saul-struck-blind dramatic. He was driving home after the bars closed, driving the way someone who's had too much to drink often drives—too slowly, too deliberately, trying not to attract the attention of cops. He didn't hit anybody that night, didn't wreck his car, but as he drove, the thirty-five-year-old father of three youngsters, with another on the way, simply resolved to change his life.

Pulling into the driveway, he expected he would have to sleep in the car. A disgusted Sherri probably had locked the doors. He was surprised when the door knob turned in his hand. As he stepped into the dark front room, he glimpsed his wife in the hallway. He saw the look on her face.

"I'm going to change," he said. "I'm not going to drink anymore."

"Whatever," she said, and went back to bed.

She had heard it before. She didn't want to be disappointed yet again. But then came the next weekend and he didn't go out, and then the next weekend. She began to believe that maybe something really was happening. Maybe he really had stopped drinking, just as he had stopped smoking a few months earlier. She had to give him credit. With the cigarettes, he had quit one day and never bought another pack. ("The Lord made me die for a year," Frank recalled ruefully, years later.)

"After months I believed him," she said.

"I was pretty wild; I don't hide that," Frank told his congregation one morning, "but once I came to know Christ, it was amazing to me how many people said they had been praying for me. I didn't even know it! But their prayers and their actions, when I started thinking back, it was like, 'Wow! They were nice to me here. Or they helped me there. Or they were praying for me here.'

"I'll never forget, it was years later, I went back to see my mother's best friend—I happened to be doing a job where she lived—and I showed up on her doorstep. I knocked and Billie answered the door, and she kind of stepped back in shock, and she said, 'I just assumed you drank yourself to death by now.' But then she said, 'But I prayed for you every day.'"

He went to church with Sherri for the first time on July 4, 1993.

The Pomeroys moved to Magnolia, a little town on the edge of the Piney Woods, forty-five miles northwest of Houston. "That's where the good part of our marriage began," Sherri recalled, "when Frank met Pastor Jesse Leonard."

Leonard, minister at the Silver Springs Baptist Church in Magnolia, had been a baseball player before World War II, a Marine during the war, and a former bodyguard for President Harry Truman. Like the muscular Christianity decades earlier of his mentor Billy Sunday, the professional baseball player turned loud and lively preacher, Leonard showed his flock, and Frank, that a man of God could be as strong and manly as anyone else.

"It took a man's man living out his faith to show me it was okay to be calloused in life and still be used by God," Frank said. "He showed me that real faith does not mean an overly spiritual upbringing and then living an overly spiritual life. It meant allowing God to use the testimonies of your past to witness to those today. He was the example of someone being real and not holier-than-thou in his ministry like so many that I had come into contact with."

After the young couple had been members of his church for a few months, Leonard asked Frank to help with the young people in the community. Frank said yes, and after a while realized that he had a gift, particularly for reaching problem kids—kids like the young Frank Pomeroy.

Enjoying the church work, Frank continued helping out with young people and preaching part-time when he and the family moved to La Vernia. In 2002, he applied for a position as assistant minister at the little country church down the road, the First Baptist Church of Sutherland Springs. He was tired of being out of town and overseas for his job. He wanted to spend more time with family.

By the time Frank applied for the assistant minister's job, the congregation had gone through a bitter split. Membership was down to about twenty people, not including the six-member Pomeroy family. Some members had started a new congregation a few miles out of town, because they wanted a church north of Cibolo Creek. Others joined the cowboy church on the highway between Sutherland Springs and La Vernia.

Church elder Ted Montgomery and his wife, Ann, the Sunday school director, have been Sutherland Springs members longer than anybody. They joined in 1982 and recalled that the church had dwindled by the early 2000s. Members were satisfied with the number they had and, unlike most Baptists, felt no call to evangelize.

One Sunday after church I joined the Montgomerys for lunch at Baldy's American Diner, a down-home eatery beside the highway a few miles east of Sutherland Springs. Baldy's, the type of place where the waitress calls you "Sweetie," is open for breakfast, lunch, and dinner and is known for its juicy, old-fashioned burgers and chicken-fried steaks slathered in white gravy. It's the place where the church crowd gathers if there's nothing for lunch at home and they don't want to drive into La Vernia for Mexican food or McDonald's or on into San Antonio. On Sundays so many church members are usually dining at Baldy's that Pastor Frank could conduct a second service.

The Montgomerys laughed that Sunday as they recalled the church before Frank arrived. An elderly woman had the whole congregation under her thumb, particularly the preacher. She sat in the middle pew near the front, and if the sermon went beyond noon, she'd start jingling her keys. If the preacher still hadn't wrapped up, she would get up and walk out. After a while, she had the elders install a clock on the back wall so the man delivering the message would always know when he was approaching high noon.

Ted recalled that Frank's application for the position included a two-paragraph résumé, handwritten. "I kept it in my Bible for six months," he said. "I called Ann. I told her, 'I think we've found ourselves a preacher.' There was just something about him."

The little church realized almost immediately what Ted Montgomery had sensed: Their new preacher was different. He could be a bit rough around the edges—he laughed along with the congregation about his "Frankisms," words he seems to make up on the fly—but his godliness was seasoned with knowledge about the real world, knowledge and awareness that made folks feel he was one of them. Plus, members could tell he relished country living. The church began to grow, both in numbers and enthusiasm.

A number of new members, hearing about the new preacher, drove in from nearby communities—Seguin, La Vernia, Floresville, Stockdale. In fact, more members then and now live outside Sutherland Springs, the Pomeroys among them. The Pomeroys had school-age kids, one reason they lived first in La Vernia and then in Seguin. Nevertheless, they were deeply involved in the church community, teaching Sunday school classes and Vacation Bible School, cooking for various church gatherings, and getting to know the needs of the congregation. Frank's pickup truck or his Harley was almost always parked out front.

The Pomeroys learned, for example, that for many years the Montgomerys had been foster parents. Ann Montgomery told Sherri Pomeroy that as they got older she and Ted felt they could no longer endure the emotional turmoil and the separation anxiety each time a child left their home—particularly after a little girl named Diamond, two years old, was beaten to death after being returned to her biological mother. "We can't go through that again," they told each other.

In the summer of 2004, the year Frank became the church's full-time minister, the Montgomerys were providing respite care for other foster parents. That summer they enrolled the two little girls in their keeping in the church's Vacation Bible School.

One of the children, seven-year-old Marina, started bawling one morning, and her teacher couldn't get her to say what was wrong, couldn't get her to stop crying. Frank walked in to see if he could help.

"I sat down beside her on the pew and got her quieted down," he recalled. "She told me, 'My mother signed away her rights to me today. She says she loves me, but I get in the way of her partying.' She looked up at me with those eyes, and she just melted my heart."

Sherri was helping with the younger children that morning. Frank stepped out to the breezeway beside the classrooms, and there was Sherri holding a dark-haired, brown-eyed baby in her arms. Her name was Annabelle.

He started telling Sherri about Marina, about what the crying little girl had told him. "That's weird," Sherri said. "This is her sister."

They fell in love with the little girls, Marina and Annabelle, from a little South Texas town called Cuero. They decided that very day to give them a home. "For us to meet in the breezeway like that was nothing short of a miracle," Frank said.

Now there were six kids in a family living on a country preacher's modest salary. With Marina in particular, it wasn't easy. She would start screaming and yelling, at home or wherever she happened to be, for no apparent reason.

During one of the screaming episodes one evening, Frank knelt down beside her, gently held her by her thin shoulders, and looked into her red, tearful eyes. "I'm not throwing you away," he told her. "I'm not throwing you away. I'll be here the rest of your life."

He had told her that many times, but this time the little girl looked back at him as if she finally understood. She stopped crying. "You mean it?" she said, her voice quivering.

"I mean it," he said.

Marina, nineteen on the day of the shooting, wasn't in church that day. Her fourteen-year-old sister was.

Chapter Four

"I am not so anxious to wear
a martyr's crown"

ON A SHELF IN Frank Pomeroy's church office is a small book called *Pistol Packin' Preachers*, a collection of brief biographies about circuit riders who carried the gospel to isolated settlements across frontier Texas. One preacher in particular, a Methodist named Andrew Jackson Potter, is Pomeroy's hero. In the weeks and months since the shooting, he came to identify with the frontier preacher's tribulations.

Religion had to run to get ahead of the godless ways that prevailed in Potter's Texas. When American colonists began streaming into Texas in 1825 as part of Stephen F. Austin's colony, Catholicism was the official religion under Mexican rule, although few of the newcomers had any church affiliation, much less Catholic. A minister named William DeWeese wrote in 1831, "There is no such thing as attending church....Indeed, I have not heard a sermon since I left Kentucky, except at a camp meeting in Arkansas."

Potter told of being asked to say grace over a meal while visiting a frontier family. As he bowed his head and humbly asked a blessing over the food and those about to partake, a ten-year-old nephew of the host sat staring at the man and his strange ritual. The youngster was so bewildered that when he encountered the preacher on the street the next day, he asked him, "Are you the preacher that talks to the plate?"

In June 1839, two years after Houston became the capital of Texas, a local newspaper lamented that "while we have a theatre, a courthouse, a jail, and even a capitol in Houston, we have not a single church."

The godless frontier was "Fightin' Jack" Potter's home. He was born in Missouri in 1830 and orphaned at age ten. For the next six years he survived as a jockey on the horse-racing circuit. As an early biographer notes, during those six years the unschooled, unlettered teenager got an education in "horse-swapping, gambling, racing, and drinking."

When Potter surpassed a typical jockey's weight around age sixteen or so, he became a soldier in the Mexican War, then an Army nurse in Santa Fe and at Fort Leavenworth, a teamster along the Santa Fe Trail, an Indian fighter and cowboy in West Texas, a gambler in the cowtowns of Kansas, a prospector in California, and, after he found Jesus, a Confederate Army chaplain.

His biographer, Methodist minister H. A. Graves, wrote with ornate Victorian fervor in 1881: "Andrew's first decade on the earth having been passed amid the rude scenes of border-life, where men were daily armed with the deadly implements of predatory warfare, where and when schools and churches were little thought of, and having a natural inclination to combativeness toward an enemy, the disposition to fight early displayed itself in his youthful activities."

Jesus entered Potter's life one Saturday evening in 1856, when he and some of his fellow cowpunchers attended a camp meeting near the small Central Texas town of Bastrop. "The community was one of the worst I ever saw," Potter himself recalled years later. "Perhaps I was the ring-leader in sin. On the Sabbath-day, large crowds under my leading would assemble at the grocery, and drink, get drunk, blaspheme, fight, gamble, and horse-race."

Potter and his booze-addled posse staggered over to the church service to hurraw the minister. As planned, they began their heckling at the zenith of the preacher's shouting, arm-waving, spirit-filled message. As his pals disrupted the service, something strange happened to Potter. Instead of joining in, the tall, young cowboy stood up and moved toward the front, as if in a trance. He turned toward his friends. "You better quieten down," he warned, "or you'll answer to me."

Potter became a Christian that night, and for the next forty years, the rough, barely literate frontiersman traveled the backwoods spreading the Word. He preached in brush arbors, country churches, Army forts, cattle camps, and saloons. He traveled untold miles across frontier Texas, endured danger and disease, and slept many nights on the hard, cold ground. Back home, wherever home happened to be for the restless man of God, wife Emily managed the household and looked after their fifteen children.

Potter's biographer—actually, hagiographer—compared the West Texas preacher to Saul, who became the apostle Paul. "Saul of Tarsus was a learned, proud Pharisee—a Jewish moralist; Mr. Potter was an unlearned, wicked sinner, denizened with the slum and garbage of the world. Saul was a bigoted zealot, persecuting the Church of God—in Scripture phrase, 'he breathed out threatenings and slaughter, and made havoc of its members.' Mr. Potter had no religious creed, but drank, gambled, blasphemed, and fought anyone who might enrage his ire, whether good or bad....Saul was converted in a little room on the street which is called Straight, in the historic city of Damascus; Mr. Potter was converted in camp meeting....Paul planted Christianity in the domains of the pagan world; Mr. Potter planted it on the empired frontier of west Texas."

The camp-meeting conversion didn't result in a total transformation. Potter was still "Fightin' Jack," just as zealous and indefatigable Saul remained a part of Paul. Potter, for the rest of his life, was always armed with God's Word—and with a weapon. If not spoiling for a scrape, he was not a person to avoid one either.

On one occasion, he rode into San Angelo, a rowdy West Texas ranching town across the Concho River from a dusty Army outpost called Fort Concho. The only structure big enough for a church service was a saloon. His pews were fashioned out of two-by-twelve planks supported by empty beer kegs. A big box served as a pulpit. Kerosene lamps cast a dim glow over the impromptu church.

Locals began to wander in at the appointed time, in part because they expected young rowdies to torment the preacher the same way Potter and his cowboy buddies had years earlier. To the surprise of those assembled at the appointed time, Fightin' Jack walked into the saloon carrying his Winchester. The crowd quieted as the tall man with rugged features leaned the rifle against the makeshift pulpit and pulled his .45 "pet maker" revolver out from under his long black coat. He laid the gun atop his well-thumbed Bible and slowly scanned the congregation, mostly men, seated on the rude benches before him.

"According to rumor," he said, "some unregenerative sinners have bragged around town that they were going to break up this meeting. Maybe they will, but I'll guarantee one thing: They will be a bunch of mighty sick roosters before they get it done."

There were no disruptions in San Angelo that night.

One day in 1878, Potter was traversing the circuit along the Rio Grande in far West Texas, traveling through rugged hills in a wagon pulled by two Spanish mules.

"His road led him from Frio to Sabinal Canyon, through narrow defiles, steep ravines, interspersed with dense thickets and spaces of prairie glades," Potter's florid biographer recounts. "In one of those wild, lonely defiles, hemmed in by vast ranges of mountain solitudes, Mr. Potter met a squad of four savage Indians."

As Graves told the tale, two of Potter's assailants opened fire, bullets skittering into the dust near his right arm. Potter returned fire, wounding one of the Indians. The man's companions got their injured comrade on his feet, and the four retreated down the ravine. Potter might have shot all four, his biographer writes, but his rifle had gotten wet and he was afraid it would misfire if he pulled the trigger a second time. Potter's assailants "retreated away into the invisible domain of the unpeopled mountain world, to meet their antagonist no more till the last trump shall summon the tribes of all ages and nations to meet at the great judgment, to give an account of the deeds done in the body."

It's easy to see why Frank Pomeroy admires Fightin' Jack Potter. The old preacher was tough, he was unconventional, and he had no compunction about guns. Potter had numerous encounters with Indians, bandits, enemy soldiers, and assorted desperadoes during his long life on the frontier. Sometimes he tried to talk his way out of danger or retreat; sometimes he used his trusty Winchester or his pistol or his Bowie knife. On those long, lonely journeys across frontier Texas, he seems to have thought deeply about how he, when his time came, would "give an account of the deeds done in the body."

Biographer Graves puts it this way: "In the pious minds of those who have attained high plateau in Christian virtues under the peaceful shades of civilized life, in the olden States, far removed from the blood-stained path of the savage, there is a seeming paradox in the fellowship of the Bible and the sword—the preacher and his rifle on the frontier borders of western Texas, where Indian barbarism and quasi-civilization meet and interlap."

Graves concedes that Jesus taught his disciples not to defend their religion with the sword, "telling them that when they were persecuted in one city to flee into another; saying, also, that whosoever might lose his life for his sake should find it in the world to come."

With the often violent life of his deeply admired subject in mind, Graves worked to unravel the paradox: "But there must be a limit to the moral duty of non-resisting submission, where life is imperiled, even with civilized contestants, where the cause of contest is not religion, but if it is a religious persecution, Christians must not unsheath the sword in defense of the cross, but submit, even to martyrdom, for Jesus's sake, as he did for us. But where a man is attacked by a band of lawless savages, or a reckless desperado, who is little if any better than a savage, does moral duty bind him to stand still and quietly yield up his life to their barbarous rage?"

Of course, the Christian should make every effort to avoid taking a life, Graves acknowledges. But there has to be a limit to "non-resistance of evil-doing among men, as there is a bound to oceans' maddening waves, where they rebound in foaming fury to their sky-pent home."

Such was Potter's view, Graves assures his readers—and appends a letter from the minister to a friend in Georgia wrestling with similar issues. Potter wrote,

> When God calls me to travel in a region of country infested with lurking savages, my Winchester gun and a full belt of cartridges shall ever prevent distressing alarms about my safety when meeting a savage foe, feeling that in the fearful struggle

for life I have some safe means to preserve my God-given manhood. Had it not been for my faithful "Winchester," my bloody scalp would have long since graced the warrior's victory, and heightened the wild glee of the merry dance in some distant mountain-gorge.

I am not so anxious to wear a martyr's crown as to sacrifice my life when God requires me to use means to preserve it. It is no evidence of a preacher's want of trust in God when he carries a gun to shield his life in the time of peril. It would be the most sinful presumption not to do so. Indeed, I do not carry a gun because I am afraid to die, but because it is a duty to use means to preserve life. It is not a sin to resort to the doctor's skill and the virtue of medicine to prevent or cure diseases; nor do lightning-rods on homes and churches argue a distrust in Providence, but are means of security. A little experience along this perilous border may greatly alter the views of tender-conscienced men who only see such scenes at a vast distance from their peaceful home-retreats.

Fightin' Jack Potter died preaching, not brawling. On a Sunday morning in the fall of 1895, he was delivering a sermon in a little country church south of Austin when he fell over dead in the pulpit. He was sixty-five.

By the time of Potter's death, Texas was pretty much tamed, in no small measure because of the civilizing effects of itinerant frontier preachers, Protestant missionaries, Catholic priests, and settlers who brought to their new home long traditions of churchgoing. According to Robert Wuthnow, a Princeton sociologist and author of *Rough Country: How Texas Became America's Most Powerful Bible-Belt State,* religion was preeminent in affirming the social order and combating evil.

Texas became a Baptist stronghold and, as one Roman Catholic said, the place also seemed to be "crawling with Methodists and ants." Wuthnow writes that heavily Baptist and Methodist versions of Christianity provided a language to express worries and fears, gave strength and solace in the face of enormous difficulties, and, in the "rough country" where they sought to build a new life, offered hope for a better future, both in this life and the life to come.

"For generations of Americans who came as immigrants and carved a new life in small towns and on the open frontier," Wuthnow writes, "the idea of a rough country was a way of describing the exigencies of life. Rough country was terrain difficult to traverse, farmland yet to be improved, thickets needed to be cleared, and roads impassable from rain and mud. It was dangerous territory inhabited by villains and scoundrels."

Religion was an afterthought on the frontier throughout most of American history—from the arrival of immigrants on the *Mayflower* through at least the Civil War—but Wuthnow contends that religion-less Texas was rougher than most regions on the margins of civilization. It's an arguable thesis, but he points to extreme distances and extreme terrain, whether the dry and treeless expanse of West Texas or the impenetrable thickets of parts of East Texas. To travel through Texas, much less tame it, was an immensely difficult task. It would take decades.

Weather also was extreme, whether hurricanes and floods along the Gulf Coast, tornadoes in North and Central Texas, and drought in the West. The great Galveston flood of 1900, with more than eight thousand casualties, was the most devastating natural disaster in American history, but as Wuthnow notes, it was only the worst in a succession of devastating storms along the Gulf. Galveston, always prey to storms, lacked drainage and fresh water, noted a visitor in the 1840s, who also observed pigs hunting snakes and cleaning the garbage off the streets. It was a "hard-swearing, rough society," he observed, "where women were so scarce they had to marry in self-defense."

The port city of Galveston, on an island two miles offshore in the Gulf of Mexico, was founded in 1838 and was for many years the largest and most important city in Texas. Urban it may have been, but frontier lawlessness still prevailed. "Nobody who cares for his life ventures out after dark," a visitor observed. Men "shoot and cut up each other on the least provocation" and "bowie knives and pistols are conspicuous ornaments."

Galveston was hardly an exception. Wuthnow mentions Abbe Emmanuel Domenech, a French-born Catholic priest who arrived in Texas in 1848 at age twenty-two and served in the Brownsville area for six years. His engaging account of his Texas adventures prompted an English reader to write, "We can scarcely conceive how it is possible to live and be happy in a country where every man's hand seems to be raised against his neighbor; where the law is disregarded from the inefficiency of the central government to enforce its execution, where each member is the sentinel of his own safety, and where the shedding of blood, and even of life, is held to be a mere bagatelle." And if the chaos and casual violence weren't enough, "The ceaseless presence of mosquitoes, flies, scorpions, heat, and drought must naturally drive us away from such inhospitable regions."

So would disease. In the 1850s and 1860s, thousands of Texans fell victim to cholera and such related illnesses as fever, pneumonia, consumption, diarrhea, scarlet fever, congestive fever, and bilious fever. Women died in childbirth. Others died of worms. According to data compiled by historians Robert W. Fogel and Stanley L. Engerman, a hundred thousand deaths occurred in seven states in 1850, and the median age of death for females in Texas was seven years, for males, eleven. Those figures compared to sixteen years for females and twenty-one years for males in neighboring Louisiana. The median age of death for African Americans in Texas was six. In Louisiana, it was twenty.

In 1868, the US Congress ordered a special investigation of lawlessness and violence in Texas. As Wuthnow notes, the report concluded that 939 people had been killed in the state between 1865 and 1868, including 429 African Americans, and that only 5 of the perpetrators had been convicted.

At the same time, Texans feared slave insurrections, feared Mexico, with its threatening Catholic religion. Slaves endured abominable treatment, and Texans of Mexican descent were mistreated, as well. With so much "evil" out there, efforts at resisting it, restraining it, changing it, and even destroying it were paramount.

Gradually, religion began to exert an influence over the state, began to smooth away the rough edges. Religious commitment, Wuthnow notes, traditionally contributes to institution building—hospitals, orphanages, schools, and colleges. In Texas, he suggests, the process took approximately a century and a half. Some would say it's still a work in progress.

Progress or not, the image of the gun-toting preacher still enjoys wide appeal, in Texas and elsewhere. Steve Pinkerton, author of a study called "Outlaw Preachers and Profane Prophets," notes that well-armed American preachers, both real and fictional, seem to embody distinctive national attitudes toward guns and religion, violence and justice. Pinkerton mentions a real-life Pentecostal preacher named James McAbee, who's known for offering firearms training in his church. McAbee is a Texan, of course, from the East Texas city of Beaumont. He also mentions Jesse Custer, the protagonist of the popular AMC TV series *Preacher*. Jesse may wear a preacher's collar, but he's not averse to protecting his little Texas church with a semiautomatic rifle.

They're tolerated, even celebrated, he says, because of two notable features of US culture (particularly Texas culture). First, this remains a remarkably Christian country, with some 70 to 83 percent of Americans identifying as Christian. And second, the United States has a uniquely robust gun culture, as well as the world's highest rate of gun ownership and extraordinary levels of gun violence.

"Put these national characteristics together—the religion and the guns—and it's not hard to see the appeal of figures, both real and fictional, that combine the two," Pinkerton writes.

The gun-toting preacher also plays into another archetype: the holy avenger. Think of Clint Eastwood's gun-wielding preacher in the 1985 Western *Pale Rider*. Riding into a small town from parts unknown, the lone avenger rescues a rural community from the malevolent forces that threaten it.

"Where other vigilantes might appeal to their own, individual codes of justice, the preacher figure carries the authority to discharge God's justice. His vengeance carries always the suggestion that it's divinely inspired," Pinkerton writes. "The idea of the gun-toting preacher thus showcases the power of individual self-assertion, while also often emphasizing the importance of protecting and preserving a wider community."

Pastor Frank's Texas (and mine) is more urban, more interdependent—more civilized, so to speak—than Fightin' Jack Potter could have imagined. And yet many of our fellow Texans still prefer to think of our state as the rugged frontier, even though 80 percent of the populace lives in one of the major metropolitan areas. (Four of the nation's eleven largest cities are in Texas.) Texas politicians wear cowboy boots under their pinstripe business suits. Bankers drive pickups, even though a bale of hay or a sack of cattle feed has never tarnished the truck's bed. And gun laws reflect Fightin' Jack's Texas, where danger potentially lurked behind every bend in the trail, where Marshall Dillon was far away, and where a trusty Winchester was the only protection a law-abiding, God-fearing citizen had against death and destruction.

The church history of Sutherland Springs traces back to the frontier, as well. Dr. John Sutherland and early settler Joseph Polley established a Methodist Episcopal Church in 1863, but it was abolished in 1876. Methodist parishioners in the area then relied on a circuit-riding pastor who came twice a month to hold services. He usually got paid in fresh milk and butter, vegetables, and freshly laid eggs. Traveling pastors from the Episcopal and Presbyterian churches also visited the community. More recently, Hispanic families were members of a holiness church in town.

The present-day Baptist church was founded in 1926 as the Sutherland Springs Central Baptist Church. The first baptisms were held in Cibolo Creek. The first building was an old grocery store the church paid for by selling chickens, pigs, and hand-cranked ice cream to supplement monetary donations.

Perhaps because of the congregation's small size, details of the church's middle years are sketchy. A church history compiled in 1996 by Barbara J. Wood, a fourth-generation Sutherland Springs native, noted that the church had a parsonage from 1964 until it was sold in 1986. In 1993, the church bought a 1985 Fleetwood double-wide mobile home to house its preacher and his family. The congregation constructed the sanctuary where the shooting took place in 1949. Members bought a surplus Army barracks to serve as the fellowship hall some years afterward.

Reaching back "into the hinterland of my memory," a member named Joe Faye Hudson, born in 1921, told Wood that the only "air conditioning" the church had were little pasteboard fans a funeral home had donated. "Every time we met during the abysmally hot summers, the little white fans would be fanning furiously," she recalled.

Hudson's sister Vada remembered that a member would bring the preacher a large pitcher of ice water and a glass when he launched into his sermon, and the rest of the congregation would sit and "salivate." She said he would "rear back and hold our feet to the fire, then stop and pour a glass of water and drink it while the message sunk in."

Hudson, known as "Babe," was "a hoot," Wood recalled. When she was thirteen, she committed her life to Jesus at an outdoor summer revival. She was terrified of walking down the aisle, so her friend Esther went with her as "my morale support." Sister Vada followed.

"Phew! What a relief it was to know I would not be going to that place 'where the worm dieth not' and you burn forever and ever and ever eternally," she recalled. "I was almost drowned in the Cibolo when I was baptized. To this day it's a terrifying thought. As we were baptized, the preacher would say, 'buried to sin and raised to walk in the newness of life.' Only when I was raised to walk in newness of life I came up strangling and coughing with water in my nose and lungs, and I thought I was about to die. And I was embarrassed as I went flappety, flop up the hill with my wet clothes clinging to me. I'm sure I looked like a drowned cat."

Hudson recalled church domino parties, ice cream suppers, and the occasional "dinner on the ground" during the summer. Playing dominoes, she noted, was not considered a sin in those days, the 1920s and 1930s.

"At these feasts," she recalled, "there would always be several women with large fans made out of newspaper cut in strips and attached to sticks. They stood fanning the flies from the food. It was a losing battle, and someone always brought a banana cake, which was especially relished by the flies. This was during the Depression, and there was no money to be spent on worldly attractions, had there been any. So we just sang and ate to our heart's content, as gluttony was not a sin either."

A charter member named Virginia Baker remembered the original building: "The building did not have sub-flooring. It was just one thing with the cracks in it…. The walls were never finished. They never had sheetrock on them or anything like that…. The pews were possibly donated from a San Antonio church. They were kidney-shaped, not just straight. No cushions were on them. You had to be careful getting up, as those boards would spread apart and sometimes pinch."

The windows had no screens, Baker recalled, and the only air conditioning was the breeze coming in from outside. Sticks held up the windows.

"Back in those days," Baker told Wood, "very few people had radios much less televisions. So, most of the time, there was as about as big a congregation on the outside as there was on the inside. Men that would never think about darkening a church's door would stand out there and listen to the preaching and the singing. So it was not an ill-wind that blew nobody good."

Those recollections are of a time long past, and yet the humble, unassuming personality of the current church today was not all that different. The small sanctuary, the fellowship hall that once was an Army barracks, the church as social center—they were all reminders that the people who belonged to the First Baptist Church of Sutherland Springs were country folks, or at least people who favored rural ways.

That's what Wood, the church historian, liked about it when she and her husband and their children were members through the 1980s. "It was the sweetest church," she said. "It was like a little family reunion on Sundays, even though we might have seen each other several times during the week. When church let out, we'd talk for a good hour, just standing around outside the church."

Despite the spirit of rural fellowship that lingered, the rectitudinous lady who kept the preacher on the clock would have been shocked at what had become of First Baptist in the years since members found their current preacher, a determinedly informal fellow who wears jeans and an open-necked sport shirt in the pulpit and who calls his parishioners "guys."

She might have fainted had she walked in on Pirate Day, not long before Halloween. She would have been greeted by jaunty members wearing eye patches, nose rings, gold chains, earrings. For no particular reason. I talked to one former member who disapproved of women in shorts on a Sunday morning, of kids dancing and caterwauling up and down the aisles during services, of "foolishness" like Pirate Day. She and her husband chose to leave, as did a few others once the stamp of Frank's personality began to assert itself on the congregation. The discontented were in the minority, though.

"We used to joke with Karla [Holcombe] that we have a real motley crew in Sutherland Springs, and we still say to this day it's 'Sutherland Sprung,' if something's broke," Sherri Pomeroy told the *San Antonio Express-News*. "We do have an unconventional pastor, building, congregation—none of that is typical of a church. It's really quite the opposite. Everything you would think you'd see at a church is what you're not gonna see at our church."

"If you think about all the different personalities, we should not work," Unitia "Nish" Harris told the *Express-News*. "This place goes against all reason. I was raised a military brat, I've seen a lot of people. You'd think this would be a boring, small-town church," Harris said. "But it's not. I hate to say we're a bunch of oddballs, but we are."

Harris was not in church that morning, but her twenty-year-old daughter Morgan and two sons-in-law were. All three survived.

Chapter Five

*"I don't know how He got a bush to burn
without being consumed."*

MOST MEMBERS OF First Baptist Church of Sutherland Springs have at least a passing acquaintance with Cibolo Creek and the community's venerable healing-springs tradition. They themselves are devoted to healing. At every church gathering—and there are many—they pray that God will heal the sick in their church community. They're not faith healers like the old-time tent preachers; they don't smack the halt and lame on the forehead and command them to walk again or expect cancers to wither instantaneously in response to fervent prayer. They do pray, fervently, and they believe in medical miracles in response to responsible medical treatment. (As far as I know, no one prescribes a hearty draft of foul-smelling sulfur water from the Cibolo.)

The prayers are for relief from physical illness, but the primary focus for First Baptist members is spiritual healing. Getting themselves right with God and staying that way require a regimen as intense as an Olympic swimmer might follow. Healing of the spiritual sort is the underlying theme for their every get-together. Sociologist Arlie Russell Hochschild found something similar among fundamentalists in southern Louisiana while doing research for her book *Strangers in Their Own Land* (2016). The focus on healing, she observed, seems to fill a need the way psychotherapy and meditation fill a need for those in less religious cultures.

Like the community itself, First Baptist members are blue-collar people, working-class people. They are welders, plumbers, pipe fitters, electricians. They drive trucks or lay pipe in the oil fields, work as ranch hands and feedlot wranglers. Shake a man's hand during the Sunday walk-around before the sermon, and the firm grips and the calloused palms convey the fact that many do hard manual labor. They work construction, do maintenance work for nearby municipalities, repair cars and trucks. Women members who work outside the home are waitresses, clerks, caretakers for children or elderly persons. One is a nurse.

Some members hold jobs in San Antonio and drive in every day. Some are retired military who likely were stationed at one of the eight large bases around San Antonio; they hunt and fish and spoil the grandkids. One is a chemical engineer. Another is an attorney, but he's giving up his practice to go into the ministry.

Julie Workman, the nurse, was, in many ways, a typical devoted member. Fifty-four at the time of the shooting, she grew up in Kirby, a San Antonio suburb, but got to know Sutherland Springs when she visited friends living in the country as a teenager on weekends and during the summer. After she and husband Kip married in 1986, he started a welding business, and they moved to the small town of La Vernia to raise their family. Kip also became La Vernia's fire chief. They homeschooled their two sons, Kris and Kyle, now grown and married; the young couples also are members of the church.

The Workmans liked the country atmosphere, the slower pace, the lack of pretense. "You didn't have to put on any facade out here," Julie says. "Everyone was down to earth and real."

She's been a nurse since 1985—these days a circulating nurse in the operating room at Christus Santa Rosa Hospital in San Antonio. She goes on regular medical mission trips to Central America with a Houston-based group called Faith in Practice. On a Sunday morning in June 2018, she reported to the church congregation about her trip to Guatemala, where her group had seen 102 patients while volcano Fuego erupted not far away. Nearly two hundred people died from earthquake destruction while Julie was in the country.

"After everything we've been through here, we don't make our decisions out of fear," she told the congregation. "We use experience and intelligence. These people were watching what these people who called themselves Christians were going to do. We stayed. We were God's hands and feet."

Almost every Sunday, Julie, usually wearing a stylish dress and high heels, was at the front of the church singing with the praise team and "signing" the lyrics with her own spontaneous hand gestures. Her voice and gestures were part of the church's message of hope. Son Kris, a manager with a San Antonio–based cloud computing company and, before the shooting, a stock car racer, was the guitarist and praise team leader. Julie had also started a children's program more than a decade earlier and taught a children's class on Thursday evenings. She was at the church almost every time the doors opened. It was her refuge, her space of calm and acceptance.

"What I like is the love of the people here," she said. "If that wasn't here, I wouldn't be here."

Not all the church members lived in or around the little town with the healing waters. Several drove in from Seguin, a college town and county seat twenty miles to the north that's named after Juan Seguin, a Tejano military and political figure of the Texas Revolution. Others lived in Floresville, the little town fifteen miles to the south, also a county seat, that's best known as the hometown of the late John Connally, a Texas governor, Treasury secretary during the Nixon administration, and presidential hopeful. (Floresville calls itself the peanut capital of Texas, Seguin the pecan capital.) Still others, drawn by the small country church atmosphere, drove out from San Antonio. They passed other Baptist churches to get to Sutherland Springs.

On a typical Sunday morning, cars, pickup trucks, SUVs, and a few Harleys began pulling into the grassy parking lot next to the church as early as 8:30. Like Sarah Slavin—and unlike Julie Workman—most church members strolling into the temporary fellowship hall near the sanctuary wore casual shirts and jeans or well-worn work clothes; the minister's wife occasionally showed up in shorts and flip-flops. Tattoos were popular, particularly among the biker enthusiasts, most of them middle-aged and beyond.

Sunday early birds gathered for a bountiful country-style breakfast. For fifteen years, Sherri Pomeroy prepared the meals every Sunday, but when she took a job with the Federal Emergency Management Agency (FEMA) in 2017, a rotating team of volunteers took over. The menu varied—eggs, pancakes, bacon and sausage, donuts and cereal, an egg casserole—depending on the whims and culinary specialties of the team that week. Members sat at school cafeteria–style tables, each decorated with a brightly colored plastic tablecloth, and shared the latest news and gossip as they ate. On the wall were architectural drawings of the new church building under construction behind the original sanctuary.

They also shared a meal on Thursday evenings before Bible class, and the offerings were even heartier—turkey and dressing, roast beef, meat-loaf, and always dessert. Every year the Pomeroys cook Thanksgiving dinner for the congregation and the wider community. An aproned Pastor Frank barbecues on a pit just outside the hall for Vacation Bible School and other special occasions. "We may be the eatin'-est congregation you ever saw," he says.

The shared meals are a reminder that First Baptist is an extended family—in some cases, literally; interfamily marriage entanglements make it hard for newcomers to figure out who's related to whom. They worship and study the Bible together several times a week, they eat together, they vacation together, go on hunting trips together, watch the Super Bowl together. Sunday after Sunday, month after month, year after year, their lives layer with familiarity, interdependence, and affection.

In a difficult and unpredictable world, their small, tightly knit congre-gation provides solace, mutual respect, and social solidarity. As I listened to sermons and lessons week after week, I realized that the church offered clarity in a muddled and morally chaotic world, direction in the on-going quest to avoid evil and wrongdoing—in the workplace, at home, in relationships. Church members longed to go to heaven when they died, a longing made even more urgent by what happened in their midst. They spent a great deal of time together seeking to tease out the subtleties of God's Word and its application to their everyday lives. Prayer for First Baptist members was a way both to communicate with God and to focus on their relationship with God and with each other. They prayed regularly that God would forgive them of their shortcomings. Faith saturated every element of their life.

Except for the congregation's food pantry, outreach to the broader community seemed to be an afterthought. Members' spiritual well-being was the focus.

After the Sunday morning breakfast, they spent an hour in Bible classes for various age groups. Pastor Frank taught the adult class. The lesson was usually a close reading of a passage of Scripture from either the Old or New Testament—hermeneutics, in other words, although that's not a word Pomeroy would use—interspersed with comments, questions, and observations from class members. Members held their pastor in high esteem, but they were not reluctant to question or debate with him over a particular passage of Scripture. They teased him about "Frankisms," but they trusted his good sense and his biblical acumen. They stood by him.

The pastor and his flock are Southern Baptists, members of the largest denomination in Texas and in the nation. With around fifteen million members, the Southern Baptist Convention is the world's largest group of Southern Baptists, who—despite the name—are not confined to the American South. Twice as many Southern Baptists live in Texas as in any other state. Southern Baptist congregations, more than forty-seven thousand in all, are independent and self-governing.

It's not surprising that the one church in Sutherland Springs is Baptist. Since the earliest days of statehood, Baptists have exerted an outsized influence in Texas communities large and small. They have built not only churches but also schools, colleges, hospitals, and homes for orphan children. Baptist-affiliated Baylor University is the second-oldest institution of higher learning in the state, its medical school is one of the most prestigious in the country, and its football team has long aspired to be a Southern Baptist Notre Dame.

Although notorious Waco newspaper editor William Cowper Brann, writing in his widely known newspaper *The Iconoclast* in the 1890s, regularly excoriated his Baptist neighbors for their pseudo-piety and hypocrisy—and ended up getting shot in the back and then arrested for his trouble—the denomination over the years has set the tone for the state's conservative cast, politically and culturally. In the early days, the issues that the Baptists cared about were slavery and secession (the Baptists supported both), later Prohibition and opposition to evolution and communism. More recently, abortion has been the paramount political issue.

Baptist preachers have long exerted influence, locally and beyond. In Fort Worth in the 1920s, J. Frank Norris was the most influential fundamentalist preacher in the South. His First Baptist Church boasted twelve thousand members and regularly featured high-profile fundamentalists in the pulpit, including William Jennings Bryan in 1924 and 1925.

Norris became a national figure—rivaling Aimee Semple McPherson and Billy Sunday—when he went on trial for murder in 1926. A well-known Fort Worth businessman, D. E. Chipps, had threatened the preacher for his attacks against the city's mayor. According to Norris, Chipps, probably drunk, told Norris repeatedly, "I'm going to kill you for what you said in your sermons, damn you."

When Chipps came to the church and followed Norris to his office, still spewing threats, the preacher slid open his desk drawer, pulled out the night watchman's revolver, and, as historian Barry Hankins cheekily puts it, "said 'goodbye Mr. Chips.'" Norris then calmly phoned his wife. "I've just killed me a man," he reported. He then called the police.

After a trial that lasted sixteen days, jurors took less than two hours and only two ballots to acquit Norris of murder. The unrepentant evangelist went back to preaching the very night of his acquittal, before a packed house. A couple of years later, he played a major role in the presidential election of 1928, fighting to maintain Prohibition and to prevent a Catholic from becoming president. His already-large church doubled in size.

Thirty miles to the east of Fort Worth, Pastor W. A. Criswell presided for more than half a century over the largest Southern Baptist congregation in America, the First Baptist Church in Dallas. Officially, the congregation in 1980 had 21,793 members on its rolls, including the famed evangelist Billy Graham, popular radio commentator Paul Harvey, and acclaimed motivational speaker Zig Ziglar. Not everyone faithfully attended, and yet First Baptist's thirty-five hundred seats were generally filled to capacity at least twice on Sunday mornings. As many as fifty thousand tuned in to the church's radio and TV broadcasts.

Criswell, whose tenure at First Baptist began in 1944, exerted a profound influence over Dallas and the Southern Baptist denomination. As sociologist Robert Wuthnow points out in *Rough Country,* "He had consolidated power within the congregation by surrounding himself with loyalists who were themselves influential in banking, oil, and real estate, as well as with staff and associate pastors who commanded authority in the denomination. In a state that took pride in being big and in a city that liked to call itself 'Big D,' being the president of the nation's largest Protestant denomination—as Criswell was from 1968 to 1970—and being able to speak as head of the denomination's largest congregation mattered."

Author of fifty-three books, including one entitled *Why I Preach That the Bible Is Literally True,* Criswell vociferously opposed big government and was a staunch anti-communist during the Cold War. He railed against campus unrest and sexual permissiveness during the 1960s.

Criswell once told the South Carolina Legislature that integration was "idiocy," but he announced after his election to the convention presidency in 1968 that he was renouncing segregation, a practice still common in Southern Baptist congregations at the time, including in Criswell's own.

Although the Dallas pastor's positions on the issues of the day were no secret, he mostly eschewed partisan politics in the pulpit. But in 1976, with President Gerald Ford seated in the sanctuary, Criswell endorsed him for reelection over his Democratic opponent, a Southern Baptist Sunday school teacher and born-again Christian named Jimmy Carter.

Criswell's successor decades later, Robert Jeffress Jr., was one of the nation's most outspoken apologists for President Donald Trump. From his influential pulpit in Dallas, he regularly hurled apocalyptic warnings about the dangers of opposing the president.

In the little country church he pastors in Sutherland Springs, Pomeroy played down denominational differences and, for the most part, avoided controversial political and social issues from the pulpit. Occasionally, he would mention abortion or support for Israel, core tenets of the fundamentalist faith, but he didn't tie those positions to endorsement for a particular candidate or party (perhaps because he knew there was no need to debate; everybody agreed).

He adheres to basic Baptist tenets. I asked him one morning, sitting in his tiny church office where the walls are painted robin's egg blue, what it meant to be a Baptist. He handed me a small booklet entitled "The Baptist Faith & Message: A Statement Adopted by the Southern Baptist Convention in 2000." Baptist beliefs, I read, include the following:

1. "The Bible was written by divinely inspired men and is God's revelation of Himself to men."
2. "There is one and only one living and true God."
3. "God as Father reigns with providential care over His universe, His creatures, and the flow of the stream of human history according to the purposes of His grace."
4. "Christ is the eternal Son of God."
5. "The Holy Spirit is the Spirit of God, fully divine."
6. "Man is the special creation of God, made in His own image. He created them male and female as the crowning work of His creation. The gift of gender is thus part of the goodness of God's creation."
7. "Salvation involves the redemption of the whole man, and is offered freely to all who accept Jesus Christ as Lord and Saviour, who by His own blood obtained eternal redemption for the believer."
8. "Election is the gracious purpose of God, according to which He regenerates, justifies, sanctifies, and glorifies sinners. It is consistent with the free agency of man."
9. "A New Testament church of the Lord Jesus Christ is an autonomous local congregation of baptized believers, associated by covenant in the faith and fellowship of the gospel."
10. "Christian baptism is the immersion of a believer in water in the name of the Father, the Son, and the Holy Spirit."

11. "God, in His own time and in His own way, will bring the world to its appropriate end. According to His promise, Jesus Christ will return personally and visibly in glory to the earth; the dead will be raised; and Christ will judge all men in righteousness. The unrighteous will be consigned to Hell, the place of everlasting punishment. The righteous in their resurrection and glorified bodies will receive their reward and will dwell forever in Heaven with the Lord."

Pomeroy and his Sutherland Springs flock not only are Southern Baptists; they are fundamentalist Southern Baptists. (Some Baptists are not fundamentalists.) Like pastors Norris and Criswell before them, they wear the label with pride. It's an identifying mark open to interpretation, in part because it connotes a way of life with subtle variations as much as it does a set of prescribed beliefs. Although they may be reluctant to admit it, First Baptist members, like most conservative Christians who identify as fundamentalist, are conservative first—socially, culturally, and politically. Their fundamentalist religious beliefs buttress their intrinsically conservative outlook. Scholars of fundamentalism call it "cultural Christianity."

At First Baptist, the most obvious expression of fundamentalism is a belief that Scripture must be taken literally, not as myth, metaphor, or poetry but as error-free divine revelation. "It's a Bible-based church," said Judy Green, who, with her husband Rod, oversees the church's food pantry for the needy. "We study strictly out of the Bible."

The Greens and their fellow members believe that the world was created in six days. They believe that every story they read and study in the Old Testament—Adam and Eve, Noah and the flood, young David's slingshot triumph over Goliath, Jonah and the giant fish, Moses and the Ten Commandments—happened as written.

"I can't explain to you how He got a jenny [an ass] to talk to Balaam, but He did," Pomeroy told the congregation in his Sunday sermon the week before the shooting. "I don't know how He got a bush to burn without being consumed. I don't know how He got a fish to swallow Jonah and be in the belly for three days and spit him back out to be whole and ready to go and share with Nineveh. I can't tell you how God can do these things, but what I can tell you is, He did. And He can. And He will work miracles in your life, as well."

For Pastor Frank's flock, every gospel account of Jesus's life is a God-authorized biography. Every account of the early church in the gospels and in Paul's letters is historical. Every arcane prophecy in Revelation is a glimpse into a God-ordained future. They also believe in a literal Hell, where those who ignore Jesus's invitation to accept him as their savior will suffer for time never-ending. Satan—Hell's landlord—is real. Hell, in fact, as the writer Meghan O'Gieblyn puts it, is "humanity's default destination."

Believing that God is at work in the world today, fundamentalists are ever alert to signs and wonders, to divine coincidence, if you will. Maybe it's an aching back that kept a person home from church on the Sunday of the shooting or a chance meeting with a future boss or spouse or friend. It's God moving in His mysterious way.

Here's an example: One evening months after the shooting, I asked Julie Workman about her son Kris, whether he would ever get back to dirt-track stock car racing; he had been a driver before he was shot and paralyzed. At the moment, she said, he was into sled hockey, a popular Paralympic sport played on ice, but he was hoping to eventually outfit a car with hand controls and start racing again.

Two weeks before the shooting, she said, she was at the track one night to watch her son. He told her to keep her eye on a car being driven by a paraplegic driver he had just met. Although he was paralyzed from the waist down, he had learned how to hoist himself into the car through the window, had mastered hand controls, and was a competitor just like everybody else on the track.

"I never thought about somebody being paralyzed driving a race car," she said. "I remember thinking, 'What does that have to do with us?' In retrospect, it was a hint to us that we were going to be okay."

Occasionally, First Baptist members alluded to their belief in a so-called dispensational view of the Bible. In other words, they have a particular understanding of sacred time, where the activity of God and history is divided up into particular eras. Different things happen in the different eras, or dispensations. They also believe that in the present dispensation, just as in previous ones, that God moves in their own lives—and in the world—in mysterious ways. Fundamentalists believe the world is at either the end of the sixth dispensation or the beginning of the seventh. These dispensations are leading to "the End Times," the return of Jesus to Earth and the end of human history as we know it.

Colbath, who served as the church's unofficial assistant minister, put it this way during a Thursday night Bible class: "It's 2018 right now, and politics is crazy, the world is crazy. I tell people in my testimony—this has nothing to do with the shooting—but in my heart, my whole heart, I believe time is short. Why is time short? Because I believe we're truly closer and closer to Christ and his Second Coming. I'm no theologian, and I don't have all the perspectives and all the reasonings to give you, but I know that Christ said that in the End Days, good'll be bad, bad'll be good, up'll be down, down'll be up. People will be lovers of all kinds of stuff and lovers of themselves, but not lovers of God. The whole people in this world—what about me? Debauchery. Sensualism. Anything and everything of what I want and what I need and not necessarily of how God wants it done."

In the fall of 2017, when hurricanes and floods were ravaging Texas, Puerto Rico, and other parts of the country, Pastor Frank felt the need to temper some of those concerns.

"There's a lot of folks panicking, saying that with all these new storms that have hit America this is the End Times," he noted from the pulpit on a Sunday morning. "Let me say this: I'm not saying it's not—no man knows—but I think it's somewhat self-centered when we think of all the storms hitting America and it's not hitting the rest of the world....I know there's earthquakes and storms, but don't just jump the boat because we had four hurricanes and say it's the end of the world, guys. Be real careful....When God comes, it's the entire world that will hear. When he blows that horn and sets the eastern sky, it's not just the United States that's going to hear that. And if you know Jesus Christ as your Lord and Savior, don't panic. If not? Then panic."

On a hot and hazy Sunday morning in June, Frank himself explored the End Times with a disquisition on Israel. Frank, like many fundamentalists, is a Christian Zionist. He believes that Israel plays a central role in End Time prophecy.

"God has not finished with Israel," he proclaimed. "Yeshua's return to take up His thousand-year reign is dependent on Israel's salvation. You will be blessed if you bless the Jewish people. It is your duty to help the Jewish people. The Word of God commands us to pray for the peace of Jerusalem.

"I'm not going into a lot of eschatology this morning, but when you examine the Scriptures you'll see that the Jewish people play a very active role in the End Times. The Jewish people are still God's chosen people, just as we also are God's people, a royal priesthood. Understand that you have chosen to follow a Jewish carpenter who chose to follow His Father to the cross, a Jewish man from the Middle East with nonwhite skin, whose eyes were likely not blue, whose hair was not blond."

These relatively abstruse notions rarely came up. Colbath might entertain such ideas on a Thursday evening, but Sunday morning was usually devoted to worship, prayer, and daily-living admonition. The service officially started at 11, although members joked that they usually were on Sutherland Springs time, maybe 11:10 or 11:15. They liked to visit under a row of hackberry trees near the old sanctuary or outside the fellowship hall before they strolled in and took a seat.

A couple of weeks after the shooting, the congregation began meeting in a prefab building donated by the Southern Baptists of Texas Convention and erected on the property near the old sanctuary. With theater seats, not pews, it was light and airy inside and twice as large as the old building. Wooden ramps accommodated those injured that Sunday morning.

The old sanctuary, windows and walls repaired, became a memorial, never to be used for church services again. In a flower bed next to the building were twenty-six flat stones, the name of a victim etched on each one.

Before the shooting, fifty or so would be a good Sunday morning turnout; even though the building was small, a number of pews would be empty. Afterward, the Sunday service began attracting a hundred or more. Some came during the first few weeks after the shooting to show their solidarity with the grieving congregation; a number decided to stay. Others found the unpretentious, informal atmosphere appealing.

The order of worship and the tone were the same as they were before the shooting—only more so. Before November, the so-called praise team consisted of Julie Workman singing and Kris Workman and Bob Corrigan playing guitars and joining in, their earnest, reedy voices leading the tiny congregation in simple unison. Corrigan, a retired Air Force officer, wrote many of the songs. After the shooting, the team mushroomed into a full-fledged band—two or three guitars, drums and keyboard, occasionally a flute—plus a group of eight or so members, including Julie, who stood up front and functioned as an arm-waving, impromptu choir.

Barry Mason, a congenial man in his late forties, was the most demonstrative choir member. With a beatific smile on his face, he waved heavily tattooed arms toward heaven through every song. A backhoe operator for the city of Seguin, he told me one morning he sang all the time, even at work. He and his wife, Dawn, moved to the area a few years earlier from Colorado. He missed the cold weather and snowboarding, he said, but he would never give up the joy he had found at church.

The music tended toward plaintive Christian rock tunes resembling love songs to Jesus—"His love is strong / it is furious / His love is sweet / it is wild"—with more traditional gospel standards mixed in. Lyrics appeared on two video screens on each side of the pulpit.

The worship service was louder than it used to be, more spirited, and slightly more professional, even as the simple, sentimental love songs continued to dominate God's hit parade. ("This is the air I breathe / This is the air I breathe / And I, I'm desperate for you / And I, I'm lost without you.") Members swayed to the music, lifted their arms toward heaven, and applauded at the end of each song.

"Praise the Lord!" Pastor Frank often exclaimed from the front pew before ascending to the pulpit. Members echoed his exultation.

"We're Bapti-costals," the pastor liked to say, meaning their churchly demeanor was a combination of Baptist reserve and Pentecostal exuberance.

They didn't speak in unknown tongues, cavort with poisonous snakes, or fall out on the floor in spiritual ecstasy, but they would shout hallelujah or encourage the preacher with a hearty "Tell it, brother!" They frequently applauded a sermon, a song, a baptism. They laughed and joked a lot.

After a couple of songs from the praise team, with the congregation joining in, after announcements and a prayer, Pastor Frank stepped up to the pulpit and encouraged the congregants to greet those sitting next to them. Most strolled around the sanctuary, greeting friends and welcoming strangers, offering hugs and embraces to members still struggling with what happened that November day. Gleeful children ran through the sanctuary, dodging grown-ups like they were trees in a forest. They'd join hands in a spontaneous ring-around-the-rosie circle; they jumped up and down; they danced. Like the kids, the members enjoyed the impromptu socializing so much that the pastor sometimes had trouble getting his flock to settle down again.

Pastor Frank is a commanding speaker, but never histrionic. He doesn't shout and wave his arms like a modern-day Billy Sunday. His voice doesn't break or tremble like an emotion-addled Jimmy Swaggart or rain down rhetorical fire and brimstone like John Hagee, the San Antonio–based megachurch minister with a worldwide media following. His informal preaching style is casual, conversational, closer to Houston televangelist Joel Osteen, although Frank (except for his shaved head) is not as slick as Osteen. More teacher than preacher in the pulpit, he is determinedly casual, bordering—as he will admit—on the irreverent.

"We have been called to a higher countenance," he reminded his flock one morning. "We cannot lower ourselves to the ways of Satan. We were under attack by Satan before the event, and I think he thought the event was the final blow. We must be doing some real bottom-kicking; otherwise, he would have passed us by."

On a spring morning nearly six months after the shooting ("the event"), he opened his sermon with a video clip on screens behind the pulpit of a scene from the 1976 Clint Eastwood movie *The Outlaw Josey Wales*.

In the movie, Eastwood is Josey Wales, a peaceable Missouri farmer who seeks revenge after a band of renegade Union marauders murders his wife and son and burns out his farm. After grieving and burying his family, Wales joins a group of Confederate guerillas and seeks revenge throughout the war. At the end of the war most of his unit is massacred while surrendering. Vowing revenge against the men responsible for both tragedies, he becomes an outlaw, hunted by both Union militia and bounty hunters eager to claim the $5,000 reward.

Eastwood has described *The Outlaw Josey Wales* as an "anti-war film." For Frank, the movie prompted the question, "Why should we forgive those people who've done us wrong, particularly those among us who've lost so much?"

The clip Frank chose showed the iconic dialogue between Wales and the Comanche chieftain Ten Bears, played by Will Sampson.

Josey Wales: I'm just giving you life and you're giving me life. And I'm saying that men can live together without butchering one another.

Ten Bears: It's sad that governments are chiefed by the double tongues. There is iron in your words of death for all Comanche to see, and so there is iron in your words of life. No signed paper can hold the iron. It must come from men. The words of Ten Bears carry the same iron of life and death. It is good that warriors such as we meet in the struggle of life…or death. It shall be life.

"There shall be life," Pastor Frank echoed, pacing back and forth across the dais, a Bible in his hand and a pistol on his hip. "I'm not saying it's simple. I'm not saying it's easy. But I'm saying that God has given us the ability to do so."

He never mentioned the shooting explicitly on that Sunday movie morning; his illustrations came from personal and family interactions, church families, and communities. And yet the idea of forgiving the man who had done such damage to the church surely must have been on the mind of Frank's listeners.

"I choose life. I choose peace. I choose forgiveness," he said.

And the congregation said amen. Numerous times.

Pastor Frank concludes every sermon with "the invitation." Having grown up in a fundamentalist church myself—not Baptist—I was accustomed to Holy Communion being the apex of worship—small uneven crackers on a silver plate symbolizing the body of Christ, grape juice in small glass cups slotted into a silver tray symbolizing the blood. In our small church, ushers passed the Lord's Supper, "unleavened bread and wine," from row to row, and, because they were still up, they usually concluded the ceremony by passing the collection plate, as well. (As a six-year-old one Sunday, I got so excited about contributing my dime, I dropped it into a little grape juice cup as the tray passed by above my head instead of in the collection plate.)

At Sutherland Springs, Communion was a rare event. Pastor Frank told me he didn't want it to become ritualized; I got the feeling it rarely crossed his mind.

The invitation, though, is the high point of every worship service at First Baptist. It's the opportunity for those convicted of their sins and their nagging need to get right with God to make that conviction public. Pomeroy is "inviting" them to dedicate, or rededicate, their lives to God.

Here are portions of a random invitation from a Sunday morning in February 2019, as Pastor Frank concluded a sermon about Christians' obligation to act in the world to demonstrate their faith by doing good and to counter false stereotypes prevalent in the media: "If you're here this morning, and you may be saying, 'I don't have an amazing, extraordinary life.' I'm not talking about getting to fly around the world and do all these great things. The very fact that when you know Jesus—and I'm speaking for myself, I guess—and you get up in the morning, and if you're like me you creak and pop and moan, but you still take that breath and say, 'Man! Isn't this extraordinary? God's gonna use me again today to do something for Him.' And you're gonna have peace, because in the midst of circumstances your life isn't about yourself anymore. It's about something greater than yourself....

"I'm asking you this morning: Do you know Jesus Christ as your Lord and Savior? Because, if not, Jesus is saying, 'Come unto Me, and you will see.' You may be here this morning, and you may have been in church your whole life and you realize, 'I don't have that extraordinary life. I don't know when I was saved. I don't know that I really have something to believe in. Yeah, I walked an aisle one time. Yeah, a Sunday school teacher led me in a prayer one time, but, you know, I don't really know if I know Him as my Lord and Savior.' You can't really leave out of here today and say that God did not call out to you. You're here this morning, and my God is reaching to you, and He's saying, 'What do you want?' And all you have to say is, 'I want something to believe in.' And He'll say, 'Come and follow me....' Where are you today?"

Invariably, two or three or four people responded to the invitation by "coming forward," walking resolutely up the aisle to the front pew and asking Frank or David Colbath to pray with them. Either they were asking for help with a particular sin or they were asking for help to "get right with God" or they were re-dedicating themselves to God. Often they were in tears, in part because responding to the invitation in public is an intrinsically humbling act. The ministers draped their arms over the shoulders of the person seeking prayer, and the two prayed privately, heads bowed, as the congregation looked on. Often there were tears on the part of friends or family members who might have known something about the burden the person who came forward was bearing. After the prayer, the person returned to the place where they were sitting, usually with tears moistening the furrows of a smile.

Occasionally, a young person came forward to be baptized. Baptism is a joyful moment in the congregation's life, invariably greeted with a chorus of "Amen!" and "Praise the Lord!" Since this is a Baptist congregation, full immersion is required—something of a challenge in the temporary building. Unlike the old sanctuary, it lacked a baptistery, and a trek to the nearby creek, where baptisms were held in the old days, would have been impractical.

A rounded metal horse trough, about two feet high, was the church's temporary solution. The person being immersed donned a brown robe with cream-colored trim and sat feet forward in the trough. Frank rolled up his shirt sleeves and knelt beside them. He offered up a brief prayer, and, just before lowering the person underwater, assured them he would let them up when the bubbles stopped. "Out with the old, in with the new," he proclaimed and leaned them back into the water. As he helped the dripping new believer out of the trough, a bewildered look on his or her face, the congregation cheered and clapped. They had witnessed a new Christian, rising from a watery grave and born again into "newness of life."

A smaller group returned on Sunday evening for prayer and another Bible lesson, and women gathered on Tuesday morning for Ladies' Bible Class. On Thursday evenings members returned to the fellowship hall for supper and, when the dishes were put away, another Bible lesson.

On a rainy Sunday morning in September, nearly a year after the shooting, Pastor Frank reminded the congregation that the annual fall festival was only a month away and was sure to attract media attention. The congregation in the months after the shooting had become media-savvy. They had their favorites among those who had covered them; they also had their blacklist—journalists national and otherwise who had been rude, who got the story wrong, who misquoted them. *People* magazine and Telemundo were among those on the blacklist, for whatever reason.

"Guys, we should be praying that we witness the way God has called us to be," he said. "Everything we've been doing since that tragic day has been to praise the Lord."

He took as his text that morning Matthew 8, the story of Jesus healing a leper. "People used to ostracize divorced people, alcoholics, the severely depressed, those trapped in an alternative lifestyle," he said, strolling back and forth across the podium, speaking without notes in a strong baritone voice seasoned with a hint of East Texas twang.

"Oftentimes, these people want help, but they retreat," he said. "They don't want to experience the rejection. They never get to hear what God wants to reveal to them."

Frank told me afterward that an incident at the church a few days earlier had prompted the sermon. Apparently, a couple of teenagers had taunted a young unwed mother, and she had fled in tears.

"Maybe it's that guy or girl in school who's not as pretty as everyone else, who's not as handsome as everyone else," he continued. "Maybe they're covered in tattoos or have piercings all over them; they look like they fell face-first in a tackle box. That's what a twenty-first-century leper looks like."

For a denomination that has squabbled like Moses's contentious Israelites about homosexuality and women's role in the church, a denomination that felt compelled to officially apologize in recent years for its mistreatment of African Americans, Frank's open-arms approach was surprising (to me, at least). He reminded his listeners that Jesus reached out and touched the leper, the outcast. "If Christ accepted the leper then, he'd accept the twenty-first-century leper today," he said. "If God allowed me to come before you and preach the gospel, with all my mistakes, all my shortcomings, all my sins…"

He told the congregation that he had been urging "a homosexual couple" to come to church. "Some have dressed me up one side and down the other," he said, "but I'm telling you that if that couple walks through the doors, they're as welcome as anyone else.

"Guys, what would Jesus do? What would Jesus have me do? The color of somebody's skin, their economic condition, their educational level— it's not for us to choose. It's Christ's."

James M. Ault Jr., a sociologist and documentary filmmaker who spent several years embedded in a fundamentalist Baptist church in Massachusetts, could have told me I should not have been surprised by Pastor Frank's openness and acceptance of difference. Fundamentalists champion moral absolutes, he discovered while researching the small congregation in the 1980s, but in the particularities of their daily lives they practice flexibility, tolerance, and fairness. They are pragmatists.

"Liberals accuse fundamentalists of being rigid, uncompromising, intolerant of ambiguity, hopelessly out of date and unable to accommodate change," Ault writes in his classic *Spirit and Flesh: Life in a Fundamentalist Baptist Church*. "Yet if all this were true of fundamentalist practice, it would be hard to imagine how it could attract to itself, as it has generation after generation, masses of Americans who find in it, above all, practical help in dealing with the tough and messy problems of life, such as marriage."

I witnessed that flexibility in action during a Thursday evening Bible class. Colbath, the teacher for the dozen or so sitting at tables, supper plates cleared away, took as his text Saul's conversion on the road to Damascus.

"I don't want to make light of anybody's hardship. We've all had them," David said, sitting on a high stool and leaning on the lectern where he had his big Bible opened. "We've all grieved, and we continue to grieve here, but I'm saying Christ does care. Christ wants us to get up. Christ wants us to talk to people about Him. Every person has a special, unique purpose in the world. Jesus said to Paul, 'Your purpose is to spread the Gospel to the Gentiles.'"

A young woman at a back table interrupted David. "It's confusing as the mother of four children," she said. The expression on David's face suggested he wasn't sure what she was getting at, so she started over.

"Raising children, it becomes hard to explain to them that God does everything for a reason," she said. "A woman having an abortion for a medical reason, for example."

David responded. "All a woman is in a pregnancy is an incubator," he said. "The baby in a womb is already a person. I put it this way: Killing a person is wrong. It's that simple, without justification."

No one raised objections to David's demeaning metaphor. For an outsider listening in, it represented the fundamentalist moral absolute. Pastor Frank, wearing shorts, a T-shirt, and running shoes, had dropped by for dinner and stayed for the lesson. He offered the practical application that Ault had discovered in the Massachusetts church.

"God knows my heart and knew my heart, and I have to make a decision," the preacher said. "When we talk about murder, we're talking about taking innocent life. We try to put so many things in a black-and-white closet. There's a lot of things that don't fit in those categories."

David interjected: "As a whole, killing unborn babies is wrong."

"And you can sit and pray for them as they go through this difficult decision," Frank said, referring to an abortion for medical reasons.

The woman in the back, Mary, got more explicit. "The doctor said, 'One of them we can save, but we may not can save both.' The husband doubted he could raise a baby by himself, so he said, 'I choose my wife.'"

And then she added, "Apparently, God had plans for my daughter, because we both came through it."

A voice from the kitchen at the rear of the hall spoke up. "We have to be careful not being judgmental when we encourage people to share their lives and past sins," Sherri Pomeroy said, looking up from the dinner dishes she was washing. "The bottom line is, our sins are forgiven by Jesus."

Colbath, the regular Thursday evening teacher, had been a member off and on for twenty-five years. A heavy-set auto mechanic, construction worker, and business owner in his mid-fifties, he was usually wearing workout shorts, running shoes, and a T-shirt. Boisterous, irreverent, and unpolished, Colbath is a self-taught Bible scholar who has strong opinions about many things, including which translation of the Bible that God prefers.

Colbath was shot eight times—in the arm, the buttocks, and the chest. A bullet remains lodged near his heart. His right inner forearm is gouged; a jagged, pink scar runs from wrist to elbow. He has trouble using a pen or making a grip. He complains that, because of his lingering injuries, he can't exercise the way he used to, which means he's gaining weight. He can't stand on his feet or on the rungs of a ladder for long periods of time, which makes it hard to do the kind of physical labor he's done all his life.

His fellow members like him, although they make sure he understands that he's one of them. Just because he's sitting before them on a high stool behind a lectern on Thursday evenings, his Bible flopped open before him as he interprets the Word of God, doesn't mean he's special. They'll call him out when he says "uhh" too often. They like to tease him, to distract him. He's good-natured about it.

"Thank you, God, for sending Donald Trump," Colbath prayed one evening, "but put a strap across his mouth. Make him a more wholesome man."

"Amen! Amen!" the class responded.

On another Thursday evening, Colbath, dressed in his usual gray running shorts and T-shirt, directed the class to 2 Samuel and the story of David and Bathsheba. He explored the king of Israel's betrayal of "a man of noble character," Bathsheba's husband, Uriah. (I thought he might mention Trump's sexual transgressions, but he didn't.)

"I was told not to use the word *crap* again in church," Colbath said, "but what David did was pretty crappy. We're talking about murder, illicit sex, and someone with no conscience."

Colbath seems to have a penchant for flawed human beings, particularly flawed human beings he reads about in the Old Testament. He identifies.

On a soft April evening he reminded his listeners that Moses was a murderer. "None of y'all in here are Moses, cuz none of y'all have killed somebody, praise God," he said. "But God used a murderer."

He thought of the apostle Peter, an unlettered fisherman, a country person. "Most country people are a little tough. We have to be, because we live in the country," he said. "Like Peter. If he'd had a gun in his hand the night Jesus was taken, he would probably have killed a few people. He was a little impetuous. But here's a man who stands boldly and brings three thousand people to Jesus. He was just like us."

Colbath mentioned Paul, who, as Saul before his conversion on the road to Damascus, had given permission for his followers to stone and kill Stephen, who Christians believe was the first martyr. "'He will be my instrument and must suffer for my name,'" Colbath read to the class.

"Peter was crucified; Paul had his head cut off," he reminded the class. "Our lives are going to have these tremendous highs; those highs and lows are our testament. Hurt is coming our way sooner or later. Abiding by Christ's principles doesn't mean those hurts won't hurt, but maybe they'll be lessened."

No one had to ask who or what he was talking about.

One rainy evening David talked about anger. "I took a twenty-five-year money-making business and walked out the door," he told us. "I was mad at God. I needed forgiveness, but I didn't want to ask God for forgiveness. That's what was happening to David" (the other David).

Sherri Pomeroy had a question: "What would your attitude now be if you were in that dark place on November 5?"

"When the events started, I was thrown to the ground," David reminded us. "I crawled to the front. I don't know how long it took. The old David would have said, 'What in the blankety-blank is happening?' My eyes were closed, and I was saying, 'I love you, Jesus. I love you, Morgan....' How can you worship God with hate in your heart?"

Elizabeth Briggs asked, "Should we include the forgiveness of that man who to me was demon-possessed? Should we have a cross up there for him?" She began to cry.

"Absolutely!" David said. "Thank you, God, for him being dead. That makes it easier to forgive him."

"I forgave him that day," Elizabeth said.

Elizabeth's question reminded Sherri of a story about her friend Karla Holcombe. As the congregation's youth leader, her Thursday evening lesson a couple of weeks before the shooting that took her life had been on forgiveness.

Sherri told the story: "One of our young men—he was about twelve—just kind of mouthing off; he was one of our bold little guys—he said, 'So, Miss Karla, you say we're supposed to forgive somebody. What if somebody comes in here and shoots up our whole church? Are we supposed to forgive him?' And Karla said, in true Karla form, 'Absolutely! We are to forgive him!' And that was her heart. And that was the heart of our church."

At the conclusion of each Thursday night lesson, a teenager walked among the dining tables handing out typed copies of the congregation's prayer list. It was invariably long—survivors and families of the deceased from the tragedy, church members in the hospital with various ailments, those who have requested prayers for whatever reason. The list included a special category for those battling cancer, either church members, family members, or friends. The cancer list was invariably long, as well. Good health, in fact, would seem to be a luxury for this congregation (as it would seem to be for working-class Americans everywhere).

On a random Thursday evening, August 30, 2018, the list included:

- Pray for the families of our victims.
- Pray for Santa Fe (Santa Fe is the Houston bedroom community where, on May 18, a high school student shot and killed 10 people—8 students and 2 teachers—and wounded 13 others. It was the second-deadliest school shooting in the United States in 2018, after the Stoneman Douglas High School shooting in February, which resulted in 17 deaths and 17 injuries).
- Pray for our first responders.
- Pray for our survivors & their families (23 names are listed).
- Pray for our family, friends, and community.
- Cancer: 15 names are on the list.
- Eighteen members are requesting "spiritual guidance."
- Twenty-six members are requesting health-related prayers for conditions that include kidney issues, an ATV accident, a second surgery for a finger infection, water on the brain, a heart attack, breathing problems, a broken elbow, gallbladder issues, and a Sutherland Springs relative's recovery from wounds incurred in the Santa Fe shooting.

Colbath and the others mentioned members and their ailments by name. Pam, for example, was suffering diabetes complications that week. "I know Pam," David said. "She struggles with her eyes. Course, when she's in Glory, she'll have a new set of eyes. Amen!"

On this August evening Colbath reminded the group to pray for "a new set of victims that had happened this weekend in Jacksonville, Fla." He was referring to a mass shooting at a video game tournament, where a lone gunman killed two people and injured another ten before committing suicide. "I want you to think about what we've been through, how many families have been broken, how many are hurting," Colbath said.

The members who showed up on Thursday nights represented the congregation's core group. Most were in church the Sunday before the shooting when Pastor Frank wheeled into the sanctuary his gleaming green-and-cream-colored Harley-Davidson, a 1993 Ultra Classic Electra Glide. The motorcycle was propped before the lectern as he began his sermon. "No, I'm not raffling it off," he said, laughing, "but we're going to have motorcycle lessons this morning."

The message came to him, he said, when daughter Annabelle was riding with him, and he noticed how she clinched her arms tighter around his waist when he leaned into a curve. "And I thought how incredibly natural that is," he said. "You see, folks, when you're riding, it is unnatural for us as human beings to lean into that road that's coming up so closely."

He showed a two-minute video that featured racing cycles roaring around a track at speeds of more than two hundred miles per hour, riders leaning so low into the turns that their knees almost scraped the asphalt. "It kind of boggles the imagination somewhat to be able to lean that hard on that bike going at that speed," he said.

He found a biblical parallel in Proverbs 3:5: "Trust in the Lord with all your heart and do not lean on your own understanding. Think about Him in all your ways, and He will guide you in the right path."

"Do not lean on your own understanding," Frank repeated. "Do not rely upon your own understanding. Even if it doesn't make sense to you, whatever may be going on at the time, when you start to lean on your understanding of a situation, that's when we tend to have issues. God's understanding is far greater. There may be things that are taking place that you don't understand, but you still need to do what God's calling you to do."

Toward the end of the sermon, Frank returned to daughter Annabelle— Belle, he called her—who was fourteen at the time. A special-needs child, she was thriving and had just won a part in a school play. She had ridden to church with him that morning on the bike.

"I have to put in a plug for her this morning," he said. "One of the gauges on the bike was showing thirty-four degrees this morning, and she was a trooper. She did not complain. She just sat behind me and rode. Now, once we got here, she did. She told me she couldn't feel her feet. I didn't notice she wore house shoes for boots this morning."

Frank preached for a long time that morning, longer than usual. He teased out additional metaphorical parallels between riding a bike and living a life of faith. He mentioned C. S. Lewis and how the renowned

Oxford don, author of the Narnia tales and other Christian classics, found God while riding in a motorcycle sidecar. Lewis, he said, was struck by the glory of God, more accessible from a motorcycle than through the windows of a car. "You see God's creation all around you," the pastor said.

Attendance was light that morning; front-row pews were empty. Pastor Frank's motorcycle lesson was unusual, but the message was basically the same one his congregation had been hearing from him for sixteen years: Christians have to get right, and stay right, with God.

Of course, neither the pastor nor his flock could know that he was preaching the last sermon several would ever hear. A week later, Bryan Holcombe, with his ever-present smile and his trademark Hawaiian shirts, would be gone. So would Karla, Bryan's wife of forty years, a woman who loved children. Gone would be Bob Corrigan, who played his guitar and led the congregation in song every Sunday, as well as his wife, Shani. Gone would be Joann Ward, who died trying to cover her four young children with her body. Gone, too, would be a dark-haired teenaged girl who trusted her dad on the bike when they leaned into a curve.

Chapter Six

"People who understand our struggle"

ONE SUNDAY MORNING after church, Ted Montgomery and I were sitting at a picnic table outside the fellowship hall. Burly and slow moving, with gray hair and a closely trimmed beard, Ted reminded me of a kindly bear. (Gentle Ben I'd call him, if his name wasn't Ted.) He grew up Catholic in Indiana, his wife, Ann, in a Pentecostal family in Northern California. They've cared for children their whole married life, foster children and their own.

As a way of explaining how troubling experiences bound church members together, he was telling me about his Vietnam. He spoke so softly I had to concentrate to hear what he was telling me.

It was 1970, and his Army unit was on patrol in the highlands. "We were in the jungle for eighty-five straight days with one change of clothes and no soap," he said. "It would be close to a hundred and twenty degrees in the daytime, and when it fell to eighty at night you'd feel like you were freezing."

His story jumped ahead to Sutherland Springs nearly four decades later. He is sitting in the living room of the Montgomery home reading a newspaper, while the two Montgomery boys, J.J. and Ted III, are roughhousing and playing war. On TV is *Major Payne,* the 1995 comedy about a career Marine (Damon Wayans) who's assigned to whip a bunch of ragtag ROTC kids into shape.

Montgomery glances up from his paper in time to see J.J. jab at his brother with the butt of his toy rifle. He's imitating something he saw on the screen.

The boys were just playing, of course, and nobody was hurt, but for Ted, suddenly, it's 1970 again, and his company is being overrun by Viet Cong. One of his buddies rises up out of a foxhole and is blasted apart; Ted watches his upper body simply disappear. He watches another pal, TC (Top Cat), take rounds in both legs as he clambers out of his foxhole and tries to retrieve more ammunition. Legs shredded and useless, in unbearable pain, TC uses his elbows to slowly drag himself along the ground back to the foxhole. He's pushing the heavy ammunition box ahead of him.

And then it happens. A boy, maybe eleven or twelve, maybe fifteen— "You couldn't always tell how old they were"—leaps over the rim of Ted's foxhole. He is armed with a machete; Ted is still trying to reload his weapon. As the boy slashes down at him with his deadly blade, Ted swings his rifle around and smashes it butt-first into the boy's face. The youthful visage caves in on itself. The boy crumples and dies at Ted's feet in the foxhole.

Five times that day choppers try to swoop in and rescue Ted's unit, but withering fire drives them away. There will not be a sixth, Ted and his men are informed.

Over the hellish din of weapons fire, exploding grenades, and the screams of wounded and dying men, TC shouts, "Monty, go! I've got your back." Ted scrambles out of the foxhole, reluctantly. As he retreats down the hill, he hears the blast. His buddy has ignited the box of ammunition he has retrieved, blowing himself up along with his unit's attackers.

"I buried that many years ago," Ted murmured as we sat at the picnic table. The trivial incident with his kids in the living room "opened a can of worms."

After that innocuous afternoon, he would be driving down the highway and suddenly he would be back in the jungle, not on a Texas road. He couldn't shake the panic, couldn't block out the images. They were classic symptoms of PTSD.

Family members knew he was depressed. They were concerned about him, but they couldn't reach him. They complained to him, about him, about how he couldn't connect with people. They implored him to get help. Ted didn't need anybody telling him; he knew it. For years he lived with it before finally agreeing to make an appointment with a Veterans Administration (VA) therapist.

"Death doesn't bother me," he said, staring down at his folded hands. "My mom and dad's death didn't bother me. I worry that I can't feel." There were tears in his eyes as he uttered those words—and in mine. He was thinking not only about Vietnam long ago but also about his little church a few months earlier.

Nothing could have prepared the Pomeroys or the Montgomerys or Sarah Holcombe Slavin or any of the other First Baptist members for what happened on that horrific Sunday morning. Granted, mass shootings in America have become, if not commonplace, distressingly frequent enough to be less than surprising when they occur, but no one goes to work or school or church or to a nightclub expecting someone to burst through the doors and start slaughtering people with a military-style weapon. Particularly in a country church in the middle of nowhere (a description I heard frequently from Sutherland Springs survivors).

There were portents. On the evening of June 17, 2015, a young white man walked into a classroom at the historically black Emanuel African Methodist Episcopal Church in Charleston, South Carolina, and sat down at a table among twelve members taking part in weekly Bible study. He remained quiet throughout the hour-long lesson and discussion, but when the twelve stood for closing prayer, Dylann Roof pulled out a pistol and began firing. Within a matter of minutes he killed nine people, including the church's senior pastor Clementa Pinckney (who was sitting next to Roof); eighty-seven-year-old Susie Jackson, a lifelong member; and Jackson's nephew, twenty-six-year-old Tywanza Sanders.

"Good people. Decent people. God-fearing people. People so full of life and so full of kindness. People who ran the race, who persevered. People of great faith," President Barack Obama eulogized the nine at Reverend Pinckney's funeral—before pausing briefly and then beginning to sing the opening verse of "Amazing Grace."

The shooting was on a Wednesday. Two days later, relatives of the dead stood at Roof's hearing and uttered profoundly simple words that reverberated across a nation battered by senseless killing: "I forgive you."

Two days after that, Father's Day, Pastor Frank's sermon was about fatherhood. "The requirements of a good dad, the task of every father," he told the congregation, "is to be the image of God to the best of our ability."

In videotaped remarks of his sermon, Frank does not mention Mother Emanuel (as Emanuel African Methodist Episcopal Church was commonly called)—neither the horror of what had happened nor the incredible response of church members. I was surprised. Current events rarely make it into Frank's sermons or the congregation's prayers—they're more focused on the requirements of personal salvation—but I was surprised that he didn't mention something about an outrage so hurtful to the broader Christian community. I knew that Frank wasn't avoiding the incident because the victims were black; as best I can tell, he doesn't see color. Perhaps the congregation prayed for their Charleston brethren before Frank stepped into the pulpit that morning, before John Holcombe began taping, but most likely, members simply didn't think about yet another mass shooting in another part of the country, even one in a church.

No one could have predicted, and yet a couple of years later another unsettling shooting event was on the mind of at least one member, a few weeks before November 5, 2017. On Sunday evening, October 1, in Las Vegas, a sixty-four-year-old retiree named Stephen Paddock rained down assault-rifle bullets on a crowd at a country music festival. Firing from his thirty-second-floor suite at the Mandalay Bay Resort and Casino, he killed fifty-eight people and injured hundreds more before killing himself. It was the deadliest mass shooting in modern American history.

In Sutherland Springs that same evening, the Steel Magnolias, a women's gospel singing group from the nearby town of San Marcos, sang for the Sunday evening service. Pastor Frank had forgotten to publicize their appearance on that morning, so the audience was slim.

Bryan Holcombe (John Holcombe and Sarah Slavin's father) was in the pew that evening. The next Sunday, October 8, he was assigned to read the morning Scripture. Wearing his trademark Hawaiian shirt—this one a relatively subdued light green—he talked about the spirit-filled concert the women had provided and then, "Monday morning you wake up and hear the news. About Las Vegas. It kind of worked on me, the way God works everything together in one place, and another place it seems like man gets involved and our wicked nature takes over."

Holcombe read a passage from Genesis. "It's nothing new," he continued. "This is God talking to Noah early on. Man had already gone south. Genesis 6:5 says that when the Lord saw that man's wickedness was widespread on the earth and that every scheme in his mind was nothing but evil all the time, the Lord regretted that He had made man, and He was grieved in His heart over this, because man had gone to evil."

The lay preacher reminded his listeners that we all have similar tendencies. "We might judge people," he suggested in his soft-voiced twang. "We might tend to say a lie to get ahead, either to put someone down or put ourselves up.... We might gossip about somebody. We might use diesel in fertilizer and blow up a building. Or we might take a gun to a crowd. In any case, it's not a problem of the item. It's a problem of our heart, of man's heart. So that's what we need to address, right?"

The service continued. No one else mentioned Las Vegas on that Sunday morning, less than a month before men, women, and children were massacred in a little church—a little church in the middle of nowhere.

No one could have expected. No one could have predicted. And yet more First Baptist members than I would have imagined have had experiences over the years with radical disruption in their lives, with dysfunction, with violence. Like Frank and his brother when they were kids. Like Ted, one of several Vietnam vets in the congregation who cope with PTSD decades after the war. Like members who have endured suicides in their families.

According to recent disturbing national studies, they're not out of the ordinary. Members of the white working class—whether in West Virginia coal-mining country, the industrial Midwest, or rural Texas— are struggling. They live with social isolation, economic precariousness, various addictions, class barriers, health issues (including insurance coverage). They've known domestic strife, depression, even so-called deaths of despair.

Most of the men and women who are in the pews at First Baptist every Sunday morning and Thursday night are white working-class Americans. They did not call down horror on themselves on a November Sunday morning—by thought, word, or deed. Nevertheless, they are not unfamiliar with havoc in their lives.

What distinguished them from their working-class counterparts around the country was their desperate faith, their belief that God will resolve whatever trouble and turmoil have come into their lives. And if He doesn't resolve it the way they would have hoped, He will at least give them strength to bear it. They don't expect the government to solve their problems. They don't expect their neighbors to come to their rescue. They rely on Jesus.

The church community was acquainted with Ted's PTSD. They knew about the combat stress that bedeviled his friend Rod Green. Green was another Vietnam vet who, unlike Ted, refused to talk to therapists at the VA hospital in San Antonio. "I told 'em. There's no way you could understand what I went through over there," he told me one afternoon.

Rod, a handsome man with a full head of gray hair and a neatly trimmed gray beard, didn't share his combat experiences with an intrusive reporter either, although he did share a bit of the turmoil he's had to cope with over the years. Seventy-one at the time of the shooting, he grew up on a ranch in Montana and has had a number of jobs over the years, "some where I made a lot of money, some where I didn't." One where he did almost killed him.

He was working with a company that had invented an innovative piece of dredging equipment and was in Tahiti overseeing its installation in a harbor. Something went wrong, and he found himself jammed against a pipe in the water, his leg almost torn apart at the knee. Coworkers managed to rescue him, and he made it back to the States several days later. It took him a year to recover.

He also served as a deputy sheriff in Montana and as a rider in the Kevin Costner movie *The Postman*. He got to Texas working on the crew of *Two for Texas*, the 1998 TV movie starring Kris Kristofferson and based on the novel of the same name by James Lee Burke. Set during the time of the Texas Revolution against Mexico, the movie was filmed near San Antonio. Rod was a featured extra, cast as a rider accompanying Kristofferson.

While he was in Texas, he found out that his wife of thirty years back in Montana had filed for divorce and sold off their ranch. Nothing was left for him back home in Montana, he realized, so he stayed around San Antonio.

A few years later he met Judy, who loved horses as much as he did. He fell in love with the slender, blonde-haired woman who, in Rod's admiring words, "knew how to sit a horse." They moved into a house on family property she owned near Sutherland Springs, and married at First Baptist in 2006. At the time of the shooting Rod was chairman of the church's board of trustees. For years he and Judy have both run In His Grace, the church's food pantry for needy members of the community. They've been happy together, happy to be part of a congregation of people who care for each other.

Despite the misfortune that Rod has experienced over the years—traumatic experiences in Vietnam, nearly losing a leg in Tahiti, and, yes, the shooting—he accepted the misfortune as part of God's will, even when he didn't understand it.

He even found it within himself to forgive the shooter. "He was a person that was deranged," he said, "and he was taken over by evil."

It was all part of God's plan. It would all work out in the end. From Rod's perspective the end would be the beginning, the beginning of his life with God after death.

For Ted and Rod and their fellow members, the church is a haven, a refuge from a world that has not always treated them well. Whether it's combat PTSD or alcoholism or childhood abuse—as with Pastor Frank and his brother—they feel a comforting camaraderie among men and women who also have experienced hardship. They're willing to share, perhaps because their pastor has shown them how.

David Colbath considered Frank Pomeroy a brother, in part because David was well aware they both survived difficult childhoods and found hope and purpose in their faith. Growing up in working-class San Antonio with two sisters and a stepsister, he endured his stepmother's neglect and his father's physical abuse.

"He had a horrible temper," Colbath recalled. "He mistreated his three kids—Margaret, Cyndi, and myself. It seemed like Margaret and I took the brunt of a lot. I was the youngest, and she was the oldest. Something would set him off, and he'd beat on us with rubber hoses, boards, hand, belts, sticks, switches. And he didn't have a preference of where he hit you, head to toe."

Grandparents on their dad's side were the children's saviors. Little David and his sisters spent most weekends at the grandparents' thirty-five-acre farm near the small town of Lytle, south of San Antonio. Colbath recalled how his grandmother would cook three meals a day for them, how he'd hang out with his granddad at the cattle auction or sneak off with him for a bottle of beer at Joe's Drive-Thru. (Young David waited in the truck.)

"We were loved so much," he said. "They were poor like we were, but they gave everything they could to us. We didn't want for nuthin'. We had bicycles, the girls had dolls, and I had toys. It was like a real family when we were there. No violence, no hollering, no whippings. Just no problems. It was like a heaven for us to go to on weekends."

David learned from an early age how to work—first as an eight-year-old helping his dad on a Canada Dry soft drink route, then mowing lawns, throwing newspapers, and repairing bicycles, among other youthful enterprises. When his stepmother complained about the bike parts strewn around the yard, he hauled them up to the flat roof of a backyard shed; the roof became his bike shop. As a freshman in high school, he taught himself to weld and got a job at a company that built trailers, Pull-Rite Trailers. From there he moved to Power Boat and Trailers by Sonny, until Sonny's checks started bouncing.

"I liked working and I liked working hard," he said. "It didn't bother me a bit. I liked making money."

He taught himself to be a mechanic and worked for a succession of auto dealers around San Antonio. He learned that he had "a really bad temper." Something would go wrong at work and he'd quit. Fortunately for Colbath, auto mechanics are always in demand, particularly those who know how to repair transmissions.

"I was pretty argumentative, pretty bull-headed," he said. "That's what it takes to survive sometimes, survive in a pretty rough world."

He borrowed money from his mother-in-law and started an auto repair business, the first of a succession of businesses he's had over the years— auto repair, construction, fence building, horse breeding. Some have been successful, some haven't.

His life was almost as tumultuous as his father's, without the violence and abuse directed at his children. He's had a succession of marriages, three in all, and tempestuous divorces. After the second divorce ended nine years of marriage, "I hitched a ride with the Devil for three years. Ran around, chased women, got drunk every night. It was a sad life."

His relationship with the church was on-again, off-again through the years—on-again beginning a couple of years before the shooting and on even more intensely since the shooting. He taught a men's Bible class on Monday mornings, a women's Bible class on Tuesday mornings, a church Bible class on Thursday evenings, and filled in for Frank in the pulpit occasionally. His near-death experience after being shot multiple times only reinforced his belief.

"God has given me an opportunity to talk about Him, to live for Him," he says. "I still have a hard time with a lot of issues, but I believe He's given us the tools to live in the spirit of the Lord. I want to make a difference somewhere."

One First Baptist member was caught up as a teenager in the 1980s in the devilish clutches of Mormon apostate Ervil LeBaron, the leader of a polygamous cult responsible for more than twenty murders. The nightmare still haunts her. Another is a registered sex offender. Yet another has spent time behind the bars of a women's prison on a drug charge, and still another has battled addiction to methamphetamines for several years. They have chased broken dreams, harbored past crimes and shameful desires; they have messed up. And yet like Colbath and the Pomeroys and the Workmans and the Holcombes, they found a community in Sutherland Springs. The church became their refuge, their strength when they were tempted by the world's destructive ways.

For all of Sutherland Springs' members, seasons changed and so did circumstance. Children were born, they grew up, they started their own families. Men and women lived and loved and worked, grew old and died. Through it all, their little church remained, unchanged.

"Subconsciously, we are drawn to people who understand our struggle," Kati Johnson Wall reminded me over barbecue sandwiches in Floresville one afternoon. "It's almost as if you feel that community between you without expressing it."

Wall, thirty-one at the time of the shooting, was not a member of First Baptist, but her grandparents were. Sara and Dennis Johnson were the oldest victims. As we talked, I noticed the tattoos on the arms of the young woman with curly goth-black hair: on her left arm, an image from Harry Potter; on her right, the axiom from Nietzsche, "That which does not kill me makes me stronger." She works as an instructor at a federal program for at-risk high school students who have had trouble in traditional schools. She and her husband, Jason, live in a mobile home next to her grandparents' house on seven acres outside the little town of Poth. She got married at sixteen and divorced at twenty, before marrying Jason at twenty-one.

The Johnsons had six kids, two adopted. Their daughter is Kati's biological mother, although Kati thought her grandparents were her parents until she was a teenager. Her immediate family, she said, includes a meth addict, an ex-con, and an alcoholic. Her mother is manic-depressive.

A few weeks before the shooting, Dennis Johnson offered his personal testimony to the congregation. A tall, white-haired man in a plaid, short-sleeved sport shirt, seventy-seven at the time, he stepped up to the pulpit, prayed briefly with Pastor Frank, and then, leaning into the microphone, began to speak in a slow Texas drawl.

"I used to drink a lot," he said. "I lived in a small town, and we'd go out on Friday and Saturday and Sunday and look for trouble. We were always in a fight somewhere. I don't know, I thank God that he let me live through all that, and I pray if there's anybody in here who has a drinking problem, they sure need to get shed of it, because it ain't no good.

"And I met Sara—well, I was married once before, and she died;

she went to sleep in a car and carbon monoxide killed her. That was Neil's mother. And then I met Sara, and she had two kids—Deanna and Jimmy—and I had one, so we had three, and shortly after we got married, it wasn't long before we had Michael. He's my youngest son.

"And I still drank a lot, but I give up the fightin'.... I would leave ever morning with no money, or with money, and I'd come back home drunk. And one night I come home, and the wife had the kids on the couch, and they were all sittin' there, and I walked in and she said, 'Listen, I've gotta talk to ya.' She said, 'You're gonna have to make a choice. Either your family or the drinkin'.'

"And I sure didn't want to lose my family, because I had a good family, and I told her, 'Well, I'll try to quit.' And I did purty good. I didn't drink anymore. And we moved to Pearson, a little, small town, and every Wednesday evening there'd be somebody come to the house and try to get us to go to church. And I talked with 'em, and I said, 'Well, they probably won't be back no more.' And next Wednesday, they were there again, a different man. And that went on for three Wednesdays. I told my wife, 'Honey, we might as well go on around there and get these people off our back, because they're gonna keep comin'.'"

Johnson continued testifying for another ten minutes or so, explaining how first the church in the little town of Pearson and later in Sutherland Springs had literally saved his life, set him on the right path, and provided a nurturing community during hard times.

Johnson didn't explain that morning how he and Sara ended up at First Baptist, but his granddaughter did. Eleven years before, she said, one of the Johnson children got involved with drugs and the pastor of the church they were attending told Dennis and Sara the youngster wasn't allowed to come to youth events. "Sara [her grandmother] got upset. The Holcombes invited them to church in Sutherland Springs. They loved Sutherland Springs, because it reminded them of their country church in Florida [where both Johnsons grew up]."

Like the Johnsons, Stephen Willeford has had crosses to bear, as well. He and his wife, Pamela, weren't members at the time of the shooting, but they live across the road from the church and knew most everybody. Stephen often drove the hayride tractor for the church's annual Fall Fest, and he rides his Harley with a motorcycle group from the church that delivers Christmas gifts to poor kids around Wilson County.

Born in 1962, Willeford is a fourth-generation resident of Sutherland Springs. When his daughter, Rachel Howe, had her first child, family roots extended to the sixth generation of Willefords. Short and stocky, with thinning white hair and a white beard, he carries what appears to be a substantial beer belly—except he hardly ever drinks. The Santa Claus lookalike is a retired plumber, on contract with University Hospital in San Antonio. He keeps a beeper on his belt so he can respond to any plumbing emergencies at the hospital.

"I squeezed more tits before I was eight than you will your whole life," Stephen told me. It's a standard Stephen joke, alluding to his childhood on the family dairy farm near Sutherland Springs.

Raised in a family of five, he started helping out at age eight. "I grew up milking cows," he told me over lunch at Baldy's one Sunday. "We'd get up at three, Mom would fix us breakfast, and we'd start milking at four. A hundred head of cattle. We'd finish by ten. We'd put hay out, eat lunch, take a little nap and start again about three."

In high school at nearby Stockdale, he was both a star athlete and what he calls a misfit. He suffered from low self-esteem, in large part because of severe dyslexia. He still sees the world through thick black-rimmed glasses. Even though he's learned how to control his dyslexia as he's gotten older, he refuses to bring a Bible to Bible study, in case someone asks him to read aloud.

During his junior year in high school, his left-handed dad fell off an open-top van and fractured his left elbow. The fall also jarred loose a steel plate in his forehead, causing seizures and making it impossible for him to drive. He required brain surgery. Stephen planned to go to college, but after his dad's accident he had to help run the farm. Between his junior and senior years in high school, he worked as an oil field roughneck, so he went back to that after high school.

"When he started truck-driving again, I was free to go," Stephen said.

He was twenty-two and moved to San Antonio. Six days later, somebody stole his motorcycle. "It was like, 'Welcome to the city, country boy.'"

Pamela Farmer moved to San Antonio from St. Louis, in part to escape the cold weather. The first time she saw the man she ended up marrying, daughter Rachel told me, he had a girl on each arm. Of course, they were at church, and the girls were just friends, Rachel assured me.

On Labor Day, 1993, the day before Stephen's thirty-first birthday, his parents were killed in a motorcycle accident. A drunk driver with four prior Driving While Intoxicated (DWI) convictions crossed the median and hit them head-on. "They went doing what they loved," Stephen said. "They went to sleep and woke up in the arms of God."

A week after his parents' deaths, an arsonist burned down their house. Their son never had a chance to go through their things and collect keepsakes, mementos. The day after their funeral, he and Pam learned she was pregnant, but during a second-trimester checkup six months later, there was no heartbeat. And not long after that, Stephen lost his job as a plumber. "I felt like Job," Stephen said, a wry grin on his face. "That year was one of the roughest of my life."

At the time, the Willefords were members of Oak Hills Church of Christ in San Antonio. As part of what the church called a shepherding group, they mentored eighteen singles; an older couple mentored them. Those fellow members restored the Willefords' faith in humanity, in God Himself.

"The day I turned the corner, I was at home and there was a knock on the door," Stephen recalled. "Here we were with two baby girls and just kinda wondering what we were going to do." The older couple, the husband and wife mentoring the Willefords, walked in, followed by eighteen single church members, all smiling. They explained to Stephen and Pamela that they would be babysitting their daughters that night, that reservations awaited them at a five-star French restaurant, the bill already paid with an open credit card.

"That was a powerful moment in my life," Stephen said. "It told me that God had never left me. I felt like Job, who had been through the devil's best test. The devil was pounding on us, but as God said to the devil, when the devil said he had not found one righteous man, 'Have you considered my man Job?' He was saying, 'Have you considered my man Stephen?' "

"We try very hard to welcome everybody, wherever they are in their life," Sherri Pomeroy told the *San Antonio Express-News* nearly a year after the shooting.

Jennifer Holcombe understood. "Danny and I were married nine years. Because of choices he made years before we met, he would not have been welcome in many churches," she wrote on Facebook nearly a year after the shooting. "We were blessed with a church family that looked past the labels, and welcomed him with open arms. What we saw in him (and what God sees in all of us) was his amazing heart, and the changes in his life when he allowed Christ to take control."

A Facebook friend of Jenni's recalled visiting the church for the first time. A woman sitting behind her tapped her on the back. "Nice tats!" she said, noticing the images on her shoulder. "I knew I was in the right place," Jenni's friend commented.

In that spirit, Sherri Pomeroy's best friend, Michelle Shields, and Michelle's husband, Ben, had tried to welcome their new son-in-law into the family and, they hoped, into the church. They tried, even though the moody young man was difficult—and was making life difficult for their daughter Danielle and for themselves. No one ever knew when he was going to be rude, hard to deal with. He refused to allow his wife to see her parents or to go to church with them. He became a recluse. Danielle couldn't go anywhere without asking his permission.

"We tried to make it work," Michelle said. "We told him we loved him. We tried to treat him like a son. We tried."

"We thought we were making progress," Ben Shields said.

Chapter Seven

"He was a dude on the edge."

"Let's let the world see that it's okay to have fun in God's house, even though Satan may think he can take a day that God created and can make it anything he so desires. When the Bible said, 'This is a day the Lord hath made, so I'll rejoice and be glad in it,' he did not go with another verse, 'except Halloween.' Every day is God's day! Amen?"

On a Sunday morning in late October 2017, Pastor Frank was talking up Fall Fest, an eagerly anticipated event at First Baptist every year. Held on the congregation's front yard beside the sanctuary, the festival attracts church members and townspeople alike on a weekday evening a few days before Halloween. Kids and adults show up in masks and costumes to enjoy carnival-style games and bid for door prizes. They binge on hot dogs, popcorn, and cotton candy, try their luck in a cake walk. Members of the Sutherland Springs Volunteer Fire Department ferry kids around town on a bright-red pumper, siren wailing every few blocks. A tractor-pulled wagon takes passengers on a slow hayride through the dark streets of the little town. Music blares.

On a warm Tuesday evening, scary dinosaurs and speedy Batmen jostled with miniature Cinderellas and Wonder Women as they scampered from one game to another, stuffing themselves with candy while adults manned game booths and concession stands. A heavy-set young man, round-faced with short brown hair, strolled into the yard, a dark-haired young woman at his side, an infant in her arms. The man wore all black. Tiny silver rings glinted in the woman's nose.

Rod and Judy Green noticed the young family. They knew Devin

Kelley, but not well, and they didn't know anything about his past. They had known Danielle, his wife, since she was a baby. The twenty-three-year-old was the adopted daughter of Michelle and Ben Shields, their longtime friends. They hadn't seen much of Danielle since her marriage.

Both Greens had a sense that something wasn't quite right that evening. Kelley, with laughing kids and happy adults all around him, "was completely distant and way out in thought," Judy recalled. "He didn't even blink—he just stared."

Judy's husband, Rod, always looks serious, but the expression on his face that night was more somber than usual once he spotted Kelley. He remembered a Christmas dinner at the church a year earlier. That night Kelley had been talking about guns, talking loudly. In his tough-guy, know-it-all voice, the young Air Force veteran had boasted about being armed.

"He was being an ass," Rod recalled. "He was bragging about the Glock he carried with him. He asked me what I carried."

"He thought he knew everything about guns," Ben Shields, Kelley's father-in-law, recalled months later. "We told him he couldn't bring them on the property. He'd hide them. He even had one in the baby's bag."

In the happy chaos and semidarkness at Fall Fest, Rod tried to see whether Kelley was carrying a weapon. A licensed carrier himself, he was prepared to escort the young man off church property if he saw a gun. Children darted like fireflies from one booth to another as Rod kept his quiet vigil.

Judy, also a licensed carrier, positioned herself to keep an eye on Kelley at all times. "There was something wrong with the picture," she said later. "I was thinking forward, and that was what was scaring me."

Julie Workman noticed Kelley, as well. A nurse in real life, she strolled around the yard in her costume, a hospital patient's gown that appeared to be open down the back. Later in the evening, her costume would win a trophy.

"I thought he had changed, letting grandma hold the baby," she recalled months later. "The other kid was asleep in the car. Of course, that raises other issues, but it was a cool day and there was no problem. We thought something had changed, maybe they went to counseling, maybe they were trying to mend their marriage."

Pastor Frank noticed him, too, but didn't pay much attention. His previous encounters with the belligerent young man had not been pleasant. "I tried to talk to him a few times, but he wouldn't listen or engage," he recalled. "He acted entitled and spoke often in a harsh and ugly way. He seemed like an angry person who had never been taught to treat people the right way."

He had seen Kelley in church once or twice a year during the previous three years. He always sat in a back pew, out of range of the camera that recorded the services for online viewing. Kelley made it clear that he "despised" the church, Pastor Frank said. He wanted everybody to know he was an atheist. "He would throw these snide remarks in there when I was talking to his wife."

Once Danielle married him, she rarely showed up at church either. "She was pretty much gone," Frank said.

Kelley had called his in-laws a few days earlier to ask if he could bring Danielle and the baby to Fall Fest. Michelle Shields was very happy to see her daughter and son-in-law, ecstatic to see her six-month-old granddaughter, Raeleigh—see her and hold her for the first time, even though the couple lived only thirty-five miles away.

Michelle, fifty-five, a longtime bank teller in nearby Floresville, tried not to dwell on the fact that Devin had kept Danielle and the baby away from her and other members of the family, including Michelle's mother, Lula White (Danielle's grandmother). She hoped their appearance at Fall Fest was a sign that things would be better, that he was trying to reestablish family connections. Danielle had told her he was taking medication for his mood swings. Michelle was relieved.

"We walked around and talked and enjoyed everything, and ate some food together," she recalled. "And he went walking around without us. Which I didn't think anything of. I thought he was just letting me and Danielle have time with the baby."

During the tears and sleepless nights to come, the petite woman with the trademark snow-white hair would wonder whether he had a more sinister motive that evening. Maybe he was reconnoitering, plotting his attack on the church in a few days. "I didn't know his problems were that deep, that he had that many problems," she said.

"I think he came to scope the place out, to kill Michelle," Ben Shields said. "I think he came for all of us. There would be no interference if he killed the whole church. We were told that if he didn't find us here [at the church], he was coming to the house."

When Frederick Law Olmsted, future designer of New York's Central Park, toured Texas with his brother in 1853—they were on assignment for the *New York Times*—he was heartily unimpressed with the recently annexed state—until he got to New Braunfels, thirty miles north of San Antonio. On the eastern edge of the isolated Texas Hill Country, the avid abolitionist found his ideal among the non-slaveholding German settlers. He loved their tidy, well-constructed houses, the carefully tended fields and pastures, and the civility of the people. In New Braunfels and environs, the brothers imagined they were in Bavaria, which they had admired on a walking tour a few years earlier.

New Braunfels these days is synonymous with Schlitterbahn, a giant water park on the Comal River, a green, cypress-lined stream that runs through the heart of town. It's still a handsome town. The sturdy stone cottages, traditional fachwerk architecture, and annual WurstFest commemorate the community's proud heritage, although the small-town quaintness is rapidly giving way to sprawling subdivisions and city-style traffic. New Braunfels is one of the fastest-growing cities in the nation.

For Devin Patrick Kelley, born in 1991, New Braunfels was home. When he was two, his parents, Rebecca and Michael Kelley, bought a sprawling ranch-style house on twenty-eight acres in the rolling limestone hills between New Braunfels and a large body of water called Canyon Lake, a Hill Country tourist mecca. The house, multiple outbuildings, and a pool were set back in the trees and separated from the nearest road by a winding lane. The property was valued at close to $1 million.

Michael Kelley was a computer programmer and accountant. He and his wife owned a billing service based in their home that incorporated in 1990 under the name Dilloware. On the company website, Michael Kelley writes that he graduated from Texas A&M University in 1979 with a bachelor's degree in economics and began working for his parents' flower shops and doing accounting work for a small bookkeeping firm.

"I had developed a true fascination with computers when taking the Introduction to Computers class required of all business majors in college in the late '70s," Kelley writes. "In fact, that was the last year computer classes actually used punch cards (if you know what those are, you just dated yourself)."

That fascination led to positions with the Burroughs Corporation in El Paso and Austin, and then for a Prudential health maintenance organization (HMO) start-up called Prucare in Austin and San Antonio, before the Kelleys started their own business and moved into their large house outside New Braunfels. Growing up in the country, their middle child loved the family's farm animals—cows, horses, guineas—and the dogs, cats, "and whatever strays that would show up," his father would recount to a military jury determining Devin's fate years later. "He always had a natural attraction to animals and loving and caring with them," Michael Kelley said.

The middle child of three and only son, Devin was a Boy Scout and was exposed to the military at an early age. His father, grandfather, and his two sisters had been members of the prestigious Corps of Cadets at Texas A&M University. His grandfather served in the Air Force during the Korean War, and young Devin loved playing with the contents of a duffel bag full of memorabilia his grandfather had brought home decades earlier.

"So, you know when he decided to go into the Air Force, it was a very meaningful thing to me," Michael Kelley told the jury. "Unfortunately, my dad didn't get to live to see it, but…" (According to the trial transcript, the judge called a momentary halt in the proceedings, so Kelley could compose himself.)

"It didn't start with a murder plot," Dave Cullen wrote of Eric Harris, mastermind of the Columbine duo. "The symptoms were stark in retro-spect, but subtle at the time—invisible to the untrained eye."

And so it was with young Devin Kelley. He was homeschooled before attending New Braunfels High School, where he was diagnosed with attention deficit hyperactivity disorder. There's nothing foreboding or out of the ordinary about a diagnosis of ADHD, of course, but for whatever reason, the All-American youngster his father reminisced about during the court proceedings began to take a dark turn during his high school years. Female classmates said he groped or harassed them. They described him as "creepy."

Ralph Martinez and Kelley grew up together in New Braunfels. Martinez was twelve, Kelley, eleven, when they met at a skateboard park. "We immediately hit it off as best friends," Martinez told the *Daily Mail*. "We both were into skateboarding and video games, mainly skateboarding video games and Halo."

Both boys attended the Tree of Life Church in New Braunfels with their families. Both were hyperactive and regularly took prescription medication for their ADHD. "He was like a brother to me at the time," Martinez recalled.

Martinez said he spent a great deal of time at the Kelley home—sleepovers, family dinners with Devin's parents and sisters, playing video games all night long. "Over the years his father added onto to their house and it ended up being really nice, with a pool and Jacuzzi, even having statues of lions and tigers out by the pool," he said.

As a youngster, his friend had a hair-trigger temper, Martinez recalled. "I saw him get into plenty of verbally aggressive arguments, but I never saw him get physical with anyone. He was all talk, no action."

The New Braunfels Police Department arrested young Kelley in 2006 for possession of marijuana, a class B misdemeanor, and he was sentenced to six months of probation and sixty hours of community service. The New Braunfels Juvenile Probation Office dismissed the matter in 2007.

He was expelled from New Braunfels High School from December 2006 until February 2007, although he was enrolled in an alternative school during that period. Even though his grades slipped with each passing year, he managed to graduate from New Braunfels High in 2009. He ranked 260 out of 393 students in his graduating class.

Unlike his sisters and other family members, he would not be going to Texas A&M. In addition to earning mostly Cs in high school, he was suspended at least seven times for insubordination, profanity, dishonesty, and drugs, according to school records.

When Devin was seventeen, he met thirteen-year-old Danielle Shields, one of several young teenage girls he apparently pursued. Others complained that he was a nuisance, that he made them uncomfortable, but Danielle was different. She enjoyed his attention. Hanging out with mutual friends, the two were pleased to discover they had the same birthday.

Moody, with olive skin and a bleached-blonde streak running through her dark-brown hair, the young teenager had slash marks on her wrists and legs. She had fallen into the habit of cutting herself and couldn't stop. Danielle was, as she put it, "the weird, awkward kid with issues."

Michelle Shields had adopted Danielle through Child Protective Services when she was four years old. Her biological mother and father had hit her, thrown her, scalded her with boiling water. Michelle had lost three children through complications of pregnancy, and an adoption had fallen through at the last minute. After that experience, she resolved to adopt a child who needed rescuing.

"I wanted someone who needed me as much as I needed them," she told the *Express-News*. She found that child in Danielle, although the Shields home may not have been the haven Michelle and second husband Ben were committed to providing. Danielle said a male relative had sexually abused her after she was adopted. She refused to give details, citing an ongoing court case.

"I built up a lot of stuff, and I had a lot of issues from it. To the point where I don't really like men," she told the *Express-News*. She said the abuse was the reason she overdosed on pills her senior year of high school. It was a desperate plea for help, if not to kill herself. "I just didn't want to deal with life. Tired of everything. Tired of the feelings," she said.

A high school teacher in Floresville remembered Danielle. "She was a magnet for bad boys," the teacher recalled. "She was intrigued with the fellows who were in trouble."

Danielle told only one other person about the sexual abuse: her best friend, Devin. They talked about everything. He told her about his own troubled past. They both felt victimized, and, despite the age gap, bonded over their shared sense of mistreatment. "We had no secrets," Danielle said. "He only ever kept one from me."

Danielle was well aware that her friend's high school experience—like her own—was not Friday night football, Saturday night bashes, and a memorable senior prom. He was not one to float down the cypress-shaded Comal with his buddies during the summer, legs and arms flopped across an inner tube, an ice chest in a tube bobbing along behind. He didn't spend hot days skimming down the water slide at Schlitterbahn. He found it difficult to fit in with his classmates, and they had trouble with him. They picked on him when they noticed him at all. They made him an outcast.

What others thought of him mattered little to Danielle. She thought the "older man" in her life was handsome and smart. She knew him, knew him better than almost anyone else. "People thought he was really weird, and this awful person, but I could never see that in him," she told the *Express-News*.

Like many aimless young people in many different cultures, Kelley joined the military. He was looking for a fresh start somewhere else, maybe an opportunity to live up to his family's proud military tradition. Filling out Air Force enlistment papers a month after graduating from high school, he completed the "USAF Drug and Alcohol Abuse Certificate," where he answered no to the question, "Have you ever experimented with, used, or possessed Marijuana?" He also checked "No" to the question, "Have you ever experimented with, used, or possessed any illegal drug or narcotics?"

Kelley entered active military service on January 5, 2010, took his two-month basic training at Lackland Air Force Base in nearby San Antonio, and, upon graduation, was assigned to Goodfellow Air Force Base in San Angelo, Texas.

Based on above-average aptitude test scores, he was picked to become a so-called fusion analyst, an intelligence specialist trained to interpret and communicate the latest information on enemy tactics. He would be taking classes for the demanding and selective specialty for six months. To graduate he would have to pass a polygraph test and a background check for a top-secret security clearance.

Despite his troubled past, the young man seemed to be on his way. Successfully completing the first of two blocs of instruction, his assessment read, "an Excellent Airman; he had no derogatory paperwork." His grandfather would have been proud.

He ran into trouble during the second bloc. He failed four tests, had several minor disciplinary infractions, and was bounced out of the program. Reassigned in January 2011 to less rigorous traffic management training, he was transferred to Holloman Air Force Base near Alamogordo, New Mexico, north of El Paso, Texas. As a traffic management apprentice, his job included arranging logistics for people and freight.

In either 2007 or 2008, Kelley had met a young woman named Tessa Loge when both lived in New Braunfels. They began dating in February 2011 and married in April, six days before he reported to Holloman. Twenty years old at the time of the marriage, he had been in the Air Force a little over a year. Tessa, nineteen, had an infant son from a previous relationship. The new family moved into base housing, and Kelley received increased pay because he had dependents.

Trouble followed him to Holloman. Between June 19, 2011, and March 20, 2012, he accumulated four Memorandums of Record, four Letters of Counseling, and five Letters of Reprimand. His misdeeds included using his personal cell phone while in the unit warehouse and texting during the Hazardous Materials course, a course he failed. He also missed a scheduled medical appointment, wore headphones while in uniform, failed to log off his computer, lied to his supervisor and called her a "disparaging word," lost his military ID card, and failed to report to his duty section after being ordered to do so. Each of the disciplinary notices included the phrase "You are hereby reprimanded!"

"He was a dude on the edge," said Jessika Edwards, a former Air Force staff sergeant who worked with Kelley at Holloman. In an interview with the *New York Times,* Edwards recalled that he would appear at informal squadron social functions wearing all black, including a black trench coat.

"This is not just in hindsight. He scared me at the time," Edwards told the *Times*. Even after he left the military, he contacted her on Facebook with disturbing posts about his obsession with Dylann Roof, the young man who murdered nine people at a historic African American church in Charleston, South Carolina.

Edwards said the military tried counseling and tough love with Kelley, but nothing seemed to work. Punished for poor performance, he would cry, scream, and shake with rage, vowing to kill his superiors, she recalled. She warned others in the squadron to be careful around him or he might come back and "shoot up the place."

Meanwhile, Devin kept in touch with Danielle through letters. She was someone he could confide in about problems in his marriage and at work.

During the brief marriage, Kelley became embroiled in issues more serious than the relatively minor infractions the Air Force had been documenting. On June 2, 2011, Tessa Kelley took her son, not yet a year old, to the Army hospital at Fort Bliss, near El Paso. A nursing note flagged the possibility of child abuse or neglect, and the little boy was transferred to El Paso's Providence Hospital for treatment in the children's intensive care unit, where he was diagnosed with a fractured skull, which had caused a severe hematoma.

When an Air Force pediatrician questioned Tessa about her son's injuries, she volunteered that her husband had "kicked her" in the leg. That's all she said. The hospital released the child on June 4; a June 6 follow-up report said he "was doing well."

On June 8, the Kelleys—both of them—took their son to a hospital emergency room in Alamogordo, because he was vomiting and "falling over." Emergency room personnel called the pediatrician at the Air Force base, who went to the hospital and examined the child. The pediatrician noted bruising on the left cheek that had not been there during the examination two days earlier. The bruising "appeared to be fresh and a little purple" and "appeared to be a hand print."

The next day, the Air Force opened a criminal investigation for assault on a child, listing Devin as a subject. He denied striking the little boy and denied having any knowledge of his wife striking him. He told investigators he didn't spend much time with his stepson and suggested that the child had injured himself when he fell on the floor while crawling or playing in the crib.

On June 24, the New Mexico Children, Youth and Families Department took the child into custody and placed him in foster care because of the unexplained injuries and the suspicions of child abuse.

On that same day Tessa reported that Devin—five feet ten inches tall and 240 pounds—had grabbed her by the throat, choked her, and thrown her against a wall. Military police investigated but "determined no crime had been committed and there was no evidence of any injuries to either party." Tessa later told investigators that the incident was the result of stress related to her son being removed from the home. She said she and her husband fought frequently but planned to get marital counseling. She said her main goal was "to get her son back."

The Kelley case lay dormant for a couple of months while the case agent deployed to Afghanistan. On September 7, Devin voluntarily went to the base's mental health clinic as a walk-in patient. He said he was unable to cope with stress at work and that Child Protective Services was removing his stepson because of alleged child abuse caused by his stress. He also said his supervisor was constantly "yelling at work." A staff psychologist wrote that Devin would be seen weekly and prescribed atomoxetine, ibuprofen, albuterol, fluticasone, and omeprazole.

Reporting on Devin's October 11 visit, a psychologist wrote that he had difficulty interacting with authority figures and that he perceived they were criticizing him. The psychologist indicated that Devin was not in "acute mental status" and that there was no safety concern.

On January 10, 2012, the psychologist noted that Devin was "able to attend to and focus on pertinent material at home and work" and that there were "no significant changes in [his] symptoms."

On February 17, Devin told an officer in his chain of command that his wife had left a note at their house and that he couldn't find her. Later that day, a guard at the base front gate reported that a woman matching Tessa's description had left through the gate, suitcase in hand. Still later, Tessa called the 49th Security Forces Squadron at Holloman to report that Devin had abused her, that she was staying in El Paso, and that she feared for her life.

The Air Force launched an investigation. A few days later Tessa returned to Holloman, where she told investigators that Devin had been physically abusing her since July 2011 and that he had often choked her. She said that on one occasion she told him she didn't want to visit his family and that he had pushed her against a wall and choked her. "You better pack your bags or I'll choke you to the ceiling and pass you out," he threatened.

Another incident she remembered: She wanted to take a walk one night; he said no, that it was dangerous to go alone. When she headed toward the front door anyway, he choked her, kicked her in the stomach, and then dragged her by the hair into the bathroom. "I'm going to water-board you," he told her. He turned on the shower full force, shoved her in, and wrenched her head directly into the stream.

She told investigators that Devin would threaten to choke her if she didn't do as he said. She said he slapped her, kicked her, ripped out clumps of her hair, dragged her through the house, and kept her under his control. He told her that if she "said anything to anybody he would bury her in the desert somewhere."

Why didn't she report him sooner? She told investigators she feared he would kill her, maybe kill her baby boy. On February 17, a judge issued a "no contact order."

Four days later, Devin stepped up to the front desk of the Holloman AFB Mental Health Clinic as a walk-in patient. He told the staff psychologist he was upset because his wife had left him and because he believed she told investigators that he assaulted her. The next day he told a social worker at the clinic "he would like to go to the psychiatric hospital for help because he did not believe he could help himself on an outpatient basis."

He became a hospital patient on February 23, 2012, and stayed until March 8. The staff diagnosed him as having "an adjustment disorder with depressed mood" and reported that he had threatened to kill himself with a gun when his wife informed him she was filing assault charges. He told hospital personnel he experienced frequent mood swings and severe anxiety.

After his discharge from the hospital, he appeared at the base mental health clinic seven times. On April 26, he told clinic personnel he was experiencing more difficulty than ever before, because the final hearing for the adoption of his stepson was one hearing away from resolution.

Apparently, the couple disregarded the "no contact" order. At home one day in mid-March 2012, Tessa watched, horrified, as her husband loaded a bullet into the chamber of a .38 Special revolver, pointed the gun at his head, and pulled the trigger three times. Having survived his impromptu Russian roulette, he pointed the gun at her. He did not pull the trigger a fourth time.

On April 23, the two were driving to El Paso when a state trooper pulled them over and issued Devin a speeding ticket. A few miles down the road, Devin pulled over again. He turned off the ignition, took a gun from his holster, and placed the muzzle against Tessa's temple. When she pushed the gun away and began to cry, Devin put the gun in his mouth.

Lowering the gun, he asked, "Why do you want to be with me?" He told her she was "fucking stupid" for staying with him and that she should know the reason why. He had been abusing her son, he confessed. He had slapped him on that day nearly a year earlier when they had taken him to the hospital. He hit the kid often, he said.

On April 27, Tessa persuaded Devin to make a "confession recording." In the video he admitted to hitting her son in frustration. He confessed to pushing him, striking him, slapping him, and on two occasions shaking him. He again confessed to the bruising on the child's face, on June 8, 2011.

Devin handed the recording to Tessa. Two days later she gave it to her husband's first sergeant. Devin was readmitted to the psychiatric hospital at Holloman.

Tessa told investigators that her husband had threatened to kill her if she ever reported the abuse to police or to anyone else. He also told her,

"If the cops show up at my door, I will shoot them," and "My work is so lucky I do not have a shotgun, because I would go in there and shoot everyone."

On June 7, 2012, Devin escaped from the Peak Behavioral Health Services facility in Santa Teresa, New Mexico, a private hospital with special programs for the care of active-duty service members. Xavier Alvarez, a Peak Behavioral employee at the time, reported Kelley missing. He told El Paso officers that Kelley "was a danger to himself and others as he had already been caught sneaking firearms onto Holloman." He "was attempting to carry out death threats" he had made against his military superiors, the El Paso police report noted.

Alvarez told NBC News that during Kelley's time at the facility he "verbalized that he wanted to get some kind of retribution to his chain of command." He said other patients had reported that Kelley seemed to be doing something suspicious on computers they were allowed to use for paying bills and other routine matters. When investigators examined the computers, they discovered that Kelley had been "ordering weapons and tactical gear and magazines from a P.O. box in San Antonio," Alvarez said.

Alvarez said he had a strong relationship with all the service members in the military wing at Peak Behavioral except Kelley. "This kid—he was hollow," Alvarez said. "I could never reach him."

He vividly remembered when Kelley "jumped a fence" in the middle of the night. Alvarez guessed where he was headed. He hopped into his truck and sped through the desert toward El Paso. Meanwhile, staff at the facility questioned other patients about Kelley's intentions.

"It turned out that several times he had mentioned he was practicing for a 12-mile run," Alvarez told NBC. "So I asked Siri, 'What is the distance to the Greyhound station?' And lo and behold, it was 12 miles."

Alvarez, joined by police, said he spotted Kelley in jean shorts and a hooded sweatshirt getting out of a cab at the Greyhound bus station in downtown El Paso. Alvarez said he quickly detained him.

"He put up no fight," Alvarez recalled. "He laid on the ground and police were there in seconds....He was very quiet, but he did mention that, given the opportunity, he would try to go for the [officers'] guns." Kelley also told police he was on his way back to New Braunfels to plan his suicide.

So, what was wrong with the young man? Was he manic-depressive? Or was it something worse, something more insidious? He exhibited certain psychopathic hallmarks: defiance of authority, persistent aggression, ferocious bouts of anger, no clear goals or objectives, prone to resentment and self-pity, animal abuse.

The Air Force made no determination. Apparently, no one else did either. The system failed. The people in Devin Kelley's troubled life failed.

On June 8, 2012, Kelley was charged with four violations of the Uniform Code of Military Justice: absence without leave, assault on a child, communication of a threat, and assault.

During the court-martial, Kelley submitted pictures of himself as a Boy Scout, handling pets on his family ranch, and rock climbing with his family. He described being bullied on the football team in junior high, hiding "behind alcohol and self-denial," and considering suicide before reconnecting with God.

He shared the confession video he had made for Tessa. Later in the trial, his father reminded the court that he shared it because he thought it was the right thing to do. "Devin is my only son," the elder Kelley said, "and I've been very proud of his accomplishments in life. Devin didn't have to make that video, and we wouldn't be here. Devin would be going on with his life. But, we are Aggies, and we live by the Aggie code, and Devin was raised with honor and integrity. And he could have skipped all that, but he didn't. I know my son better than anyone else in this world, and there is absolutely no question, no doubt in my mind whatsoever, that he understands there is no such thing as excuses, no matter how sick you are. No matter how strenuous or how much stress you are under, there is no excuse from crossing the line. And he understands his mistake."

Kelley admitted to pushing his stepson while the toddler crawled on the floor and slapping him across the face when he wouldn't stop crying. He cracked the child's skull and broke his clavicle. Tessa wrote an affidavit that described in graphic detail how Kelley repeatedly hit her, choked her, and twice pointed a gun at her.

She wrote that when she suggested they get a divorce during a drive, Kelley lost control of their car while grabbing her hair, causing them to strike a guard rail.

"Sir, this is the worst thing I've done in my life and I will never allow myself to hurt someone like this again," Kelley said.

Prior to his scheduled court-martial in November, Kelley and his attorney had accepted a pretrial agreement specifying that in return for pleading guilty to assaulting his wife and stepson, the firearm charge would be dismissed and his confinement would not exceed three years.

Air Force prosecutors wanted four years of prison time so that he might get his anger under control, according to the trial transcript.

"Who's next?" said Capt. Brett Johnson, the assistant trial counsel. "What are we going to do to ensure that this does not happen again? That the next time he lashes out in anger to strike a child, to choke a woman, let him think back to the four (years) he sat in confinement, then maybe he will think again."

On November 7, 2012, a court-martial panel sentenced Kelley to a reduction in rank to Airman Basic, confinement for twelve months, and a Bad Conduct Discharge (not the more severe Dishonorable Discharge). He was incarcerated at the Naval Consolidated Brig at Miramar Naval Air Station, San Diego, from December 18, 2012, until his release on March 31, 2013.

The Kelleys' divorce was finalized in October 2012. "He just had a lot of demons or hatred inside of him," Tessa told the television show *Inside Edition* five years later, after the whole world learned of his demons.

During Kelley's time in the brig, Tessa worked at Taco Bell in Alamogordo for $7.50 an hour. When she filed for divorce in New Mexico, she told the court she had $25 in savings and got $300 a month in child support from the father of her son, the little boy Kelley abused.

"It will take a lifetime of living up to the promises I've made to myself, God, and here to prove I have changed," Kelley wrote in an affidavit. "I know I can be better, I just need a chance to prove it."

*   *   *

Kelley drifted back to New Braunfels after his divorce and release from prison. One night he looked up his old friend Ralph Martinez. "I need help," Kelley told him.

He told Martinez about the bad conduct discharge, told him he was moving back to New Braunfels and needed a place to stay. Martinez let him stay in the garage for about a week before persuading him to move back in with his parents. Kelley took up residence in a barn apartment behind the thirty-seven-hundred-square-foot home in the country, where the family had lived for more than twenty years.

In June 2017, Kelley applied for registration as a noncommissioned security officer. He was seeking work as a night security guard at Schlitterbahn, the New Braunfels water park. His duties would include patrolling on foot and bicycle and manning a security post. He would be unarmed.

He passed a Texas Department of Public Safety criminal background check and wrote in response to questions about his personal history that he had not been discharged from the military. He got the job but was fired after a little more than five weeks, as the summer season was nearing its peak. He was "not a good fit," a Schlitterbahn spokeswoman said.

Kelley later got a job in the seafood department at an H-E-B supermarket in New Braunfels. He lasted two months. His final job was a position as an overnight security guard at Summit Vacation and RV Resort on the Guadalupe River in New Braunfels. His manager told reporters she never received any complaints about him during the six weeks he was one of three unarmed security guards at the business. She planned to fire him, though. On his last night at work, November 4, he failed to lock up and also kept the keys to the property.

Kelley had been getting into trouble ever since returning to New Braunfels. On June 17, 2013, a twenty-year-old woman told the Comal County Sheriff's Office that Kelley had sexually assaulted her that night and that he had raped her a few weeks earlier. Detectives investigated but lost track of the woman. The case was "inactivated" without Kelley being interviewed.

On February 1, 2014, sheriff's deputies were called to Kelley's New Braunfels apartment just after ten o'clock at night. A friend of Kelley's girlfriend told authorities she had received a text message from the girlfriend that indicated "her boyfriend was abusing her." A deputy went to Kelley's residence, where an unidentified witness characterized the incident as a "misunderstanding and teenage drama." The deputy took no action.

Two months later Kelley married the girlfriend, Danielle Shields. She was nineteen, he was twenty-three.

"That's where things started to get weird," former colleague Edwards told the *New York Times*. The two had reconnected when Kelley called asking for a job reference. They chatted occasionally on Facebook, she said, until his posts grew so disturbing she cut him off.

At first, Kelley shared family photos and small updates, she said. Then—as he had done during his first marriage—he started complaining about his new wife, and about how his family was trying to get him to take medication. He told Edwards he hated his wife but feared she would leave and take the two children. He started sending Edwards photos of weapons he had bought and descriptions of killing animals. She assumed he was just an enthusiastic hunter, not that different from other sportsmen in the Texas Hill Country—until Dylann Roof became an obsession.

"He was excited about it. He went on and on and on about it, saying 'Isn't it cool? Isn't it cool? Have you watched the videos?'" Edwards said. She said she told him he was not acting normal and needed help. He told her he would never have the nerve to kill people; he only killed animals.

For Edwards, the breaking point came when he told her he was buying dogs online and using them as target practice. "I told him this was not normal, and he needed the kind of help I could not give him," she told the *Times*. "Before I unfriended him, I gave him my number. I told him, 'If you ever are thinking about hurting yourself or someone else, just call.'" She never heard from him.

Devin and Danielle moved to Colorado later in 2014 and rented a mobile home near Colorado Springs in a gravel lot called the Fountain View RV Park. Court records in El Paso County (Colorado) indicate

Kelley was cited on August 1, 2014, for misdemeanor animal cruelty. According to an El Paso County deputy's report obtained by the *Denver Post*, a woman saw Kelley yelling and chasing a puppy, a brown and white Husky. She and others called police.

"The suspect then started beating on the dog with both fists, punching it in the head and chest," a deputy wrote in the incident report. "He could hear the suspect yelling at the dog and while he was striking it, the dog was yelping and whining. The suspect then picked up the dog by the neck into the air and threw it onto the ground and then drug him away to lot 60."

One of the trailer park residents who had called police approached Kelley after he witnessed him beating the dog. When the neighbor saw that he had a large knife on him, he backed off and waited for officers to arrive, according to *USA Today*.

When El Paso County sheriff's deputies arrived at the scene, Kelley remained holed up inside his mobile home. When he finally came out after a couple of hours, a sheriff's deputy placed him in his squad car and prepared to arrest him. But after consulting with two other deputies on the scene, he decided to release Kelley on the scene with a misdemeanor summons for animal cruelty, according to an incident report. A sheriff's sergeant said he found the dog malnourished. The dog was transferred to the Humane Society for a full medical evaluation.

Kelley maintained he had jumped on the animal to keep it from acting aggressively toward another dog but denied hitting the dog, throwing it to the ground, or carrying it by its neck. He was given a deferred probationary sentence and was ordered to pay $368 in restitution. The cruelty to animals charge was dismissed in March 2016 after Kelley completed his sentence. The *Denver Post* also reported that court records indicated someone was granted a protection order against Kelley on January 15, 2015, also in El Paso County.

The couple moved back to New Braunfels shortly after the dog incident was resolved. Kelley told his in-laws the dog story wasn't true. Ben and Michelle Shields didn't know what to believe—about the dog or about their daughter's relationship with her troubled husband.

"At the dinner table one night he said he couldn't wait for his parents to die so he could get all their stuff," an embittered Ben Shields recalled. "He never held a job for more than three weeks. He said he didn't want to work for nobody."

"We tried to treat him like a son," Michelle Shields said. "We tried to show him what family could be like. We tried to show him to the Lord. I remember he was trying to learn how to use a hoverboard. Mom teased him, tried to hug him when he got ready to leave. He pushed her away."

"We had a dog that was shot with a BB gun," Ben recalled. "We thought we knew who did it, but we let it go, took care of the dog."

The Shieldses were seeing less and less of the couple. Now and then Danielle would hint to her mother that Devin was physically and mentally abusing her, but then, she would pretend it had never happened.

"I think she was afraid of him," Michelle told the *San Antonio Express-News*. "That if he found out—he'd always say he's sorry the next minute, you know, so she was like 'Oh, OK, if he found out I said something he's going to get more upset so we're just going to keep it calm because he apologized.'"

As in his first marriage, Kelley sought to control every aspect of his wife's life. The couple had one car and one phone, which Kelley kept. Whenever his mother-in-law called, he demanded that Danielle turn on the speakerphone, so he could listen in. If he didn't like what was being said, he made her hang up. Sometimes, he refused to let them talk at all. "You had to walk on eggshells around him all the time because you're afraid of saying something to upset him," Michelle said.

The young couple gradually cut their ties to the church at Sutherland Springs, and when Danielle was able to persuade him to accompany her to other churches, he laughed and sneered as he sat and listened to the sermon. He told her he was an atheist.

When Danielle was pregnant with her second child, she often was sick. Michelle and her mother, Lu, went to see her in the hospital. Devin threw them out. "I wasn't going to disobey," Michelle said. "I didn't want to disrespect him, because I didn't know where the anger would have gone from there. If he would have forbidden us from seeing her permanently or where he would take my daughter. So, we just didn't go in."

When the child, Raeleigh, was born a few months later, Devin sent a series of threatening texts to his mother-in-law, telling her that if she entered the hospital room, "I will personally make it my mission to destroy your entire life. I suggest you don't test my resolve."

"We never realized that it was domestic violence, the way he treated us," Michelle said. "But after you go back and look, he was abusive, mentally, in the way he treated us."

When Michelle would argue with Devin, he would tell her that Danielle could make her own decisions. The more she tried to save her, Michelle told the *Express-News,* the further Danielle withdrew.

"I did pick him over her," Danielle said. "Because Devin was everything in my life."

Kelley's descent into madness seemed to accelerate in the last six months of his life. Abusing his antianxiety medication, abusing alcohol, he grew more depressed, more reclusive. Every disagreement with Danielle escalated into a fight.

His physical appearance changed alarmingly. Michelle Shields showed me a series of photos on her cell phone that documented how the boyish, clean-cut young man he had been at twenty-one bulked up, his face becoming round and bloated, his eyes cold, soulless. "Those chemicals can do a number on you," a Floresville judge told me.

"He was slowly becoming not the person that he was," Danielle said. "He was shutting down."

He also was buying guns, expensive guns. The purchases were possible because the Air Force had failed to report his domestic violence conviction to federal law enforcement.

He bought firearms on six different occasions, both during his military service and afterward, from stores that were Federal Firearms License dealers. Each time, he completed the ATF Form 4473, Firearms Transaction Record, and the FFL submitted the information to the National Instant Criminal Background Check System for any disqualifying information. Each time, the FFL was notified that the sale could proceed.

He bought his first gun, a European American Armory Windicator

.38 Special revolver, on February 12, 2012. The seller was the Holloman Air Force Base Exchange. Two months later he went back to the base exchange and bought a SIG Sauer P250, a 9-millimeter, semiautomatic handgun. In Colorado Springs on December 22, 2014, he purchased a Glock Model 19, a 9-millimeter, semiautomatic handgun, from Specialty Sports and Supply. On June 26, 2015, he bought a Ruger GP100, a .357 Magnum revolver handgun. On April 7, 2016, he purchased a Ruger AR-556, a 5.56-millimeter, semiautomatic rifle, from Academy Sports & Outdoors in San Antonio.

The cover photo on Kelley's Facebook page at the time appeared to show a Ruger 8515 rifle, equipped with additional aftermarket products, including a red-dot aiming sight for faster targeting and a two-stage trigger for greater accuracy. Such rifles have been legal for civilians to own in most of the United States since the federal assault weapons ban expired in 2004 and have become popular among many firearms owners. It's also the semiautomatic weapon, sometimes with modifications, that murderers often favor: Aurora, Colorado; Newtown, Connecticut; Orlando, Florida; San Bernardino, California; Las Vegas, Nevada. And a little place in Texas called Sutherland Springs.

Kelley seemed enamored with the weapon he bought. He posted a photograph with the caption "She's a bad bitch."

On October 18, 2017, he went to an Academy sporting goods store in the San Antonio suburb of Selma and purchased a Ruger SR22, a .22-caliber, semiautomatic handgun. He also accumulated more than a dozen magazines, each with a capacity of thirty bullets. Neighbors would report hearing incessant gunfire coming from the Kelley property, although they didn't think much about it. They were in the country. In Texas.

On the morning of November 5, 2017, Kelley asked his wife to make him a light breakfast. As Danielle told Silvia Foster-Frau of the *Express-News,* that wasn't like him. Usually, he had tacos and burritos. Lots of them. Danielle did as he asked. Minutes later, he vomited.

"Are you okay?" she asked.

"We only have an hour left," he said. Danielle assumed he meant he had to go to work at the RV park. After breakfast they sat quietly on the couch while *Alaska State Troopers* played on the National Geographic Channel. Danielle watched her husband closely. Something wasn't right. His mind seemed elsewhere.

Suddenly, Kelley stood up. He scooped up Michael, their two-year-old, and carried him to their bedroom. Raeleigh, their five-month-old daughter, was already in her crib. He came back to the living room, grabbed his wife, and dragged her toward the bedroom where Michael was. She was screaming, crying, struggling, trying to break free of his grasp. The little boy watched his father wrestle his mother onto the bed and tie her down with rope, handcuffs, and duct tape. The child wailed.

Strapped to the bed, duct tape over her mouth, Danielle watched her husband don black underwear and black socks. He pulled on a black shirt, black pants, a black utility belt, and then a black bulletproof vest. She watched him lace up black combat boots.

Kelley stood over Danielle and told her he loved her. He went to the crib and kissed Raeleigh. He looked down at the little boy, red-faced and crying. "I'll be right back," he told the child.

Gathering up his Ruger AR-556 and two handguns, he headed out the front door. Seconds later, Danielle heard the couple's Ford Explorer roar down the driveway. She lay helpless on the bed, terrified.

It was close to ten o'clock on a warm Sunday morning. A young man who had failed at almost everything he had tried, whose rage at the world was deep and inexplicable, had a plan. This time he would not fail.

Chapter Eight

"Jesus loves me, this I know..."

ON NOVEMBER 5, 2017, daylight savings time pushed the clock back an hour, and several people got to church too early that Sunday morning. The early arrivals drifted into the sanctuary, shaking their heads and smiling at their forgetfulness. They passed the time singing hymns. Others went back home. They weren't used to being early.

On the spur of the moment, Lensie Butler, with her two children, decided to drive to a Baptist church in Stockdale, ten miles to the east. During the service there an hour or so later, phones throughout the sanctuary began ringing incessantly. In the days to come, she couldn't help but think about what likely would have happened had she not been confused about the time.

Attendance would have been down anyway, even without the mix-up. Anytime Pastor Frank wasn't in the pulpit, the pews were a bit emptier. He had been in Oklahoma City all weekend, nearly four hundred miles away, getting himself qualified to teach black-powder rifle and pistol shooting to Royal Ambassadors, young summer campers from around the state. Shooting the old flintlock rifles is something he enjoys; he thought the youngsters would get a kick out of being Daniel Boone or Davy Crockett or Revolutionary War heroes.

Sherri Pomeroy was in Florida assessing hurricane damage as part of her new job as a contractor with FEMA. She never wanted to be simply "the pastor's wife" and was happy to be out in the world again.

Lula White, Michelle Shields's mother, was looking after Annabelle, the Pomeroys' fourteen-year-old special-needs seventh grader. As always when Frank was out of town, Bryan Holcombe, the tent maker and ukulele player, the sixty-year-old grandfather who loved kids and corny jokes, would deliver the sermon. Terrie Smith at the Valero station across the street would remember that Bryan had wandered into the store the day before with a taco song he'd written for the ukulele.

Julie Workman was singing with the praise team, so she sat near the front with her grown sons, Kris and Kyle. Kris had gotten to church early to rehearse music for the service with his fellow praise team member Bob Corrigan.

Julie almost didn't get to church at all. She just didn't feel like going and tried to convince herself that God could do without her. Three times that morning she heard God speaking to her. After the third time, she got up and got dressed.

Juan "Gunny" Macias was on time. The retired Marine sergeant had put in thirty-four years in uniform and had served in Iraq and Afghanistan, but it was his upbringing as much as his military discipline that guaranteed his presence in the pew that morning. His father, Bishop Juan Ignacio Macias of San Antonio, was a Church of God evangelist who for decades had traveled throughout South Texas and northern Mexico preaching for tent revivals. As a youngster, Juan had traveled with him. He helped erect the tent, set up the pulpit, and arrange the wooden pews.

"He really took to it," the elder Macias would tell me months after the shooting. "And he took to the Marines," he added, laughing, "because his mother had been his drill instructor when he was growing up."

The eleven a.m. service began at 11:11—"Sutherland Springs time"— with a song, and then the traditional mixing and mingling, meeting and greeting. For walking-around music, Kris and Bob had chosen to play the rousing gospel hymn "Are You Washed in the Blood of the Lamb?" ("Have you been to Jesus for the cleansing power? / Are you washed in the blood of the lamb? / Are you fully trusting in his grace this hour? / Are you washed in the blood of the lamb?")

Julie hugged five-year-old Brooke Ward and noticed Brooke's five-year-old half-brother, Ryland. No hugs for him; he had no time for hugs. As members strolled around the sanctuary, shaking hands and greeting each other, Ryland was sprinting around the periphery, veering past grown-ups like a race car driver on the track at Indianapolis. The sturdy little guy with the reddish-blond hair, always on the move, loved to pretend he was driving. A few months earlier he had managed to start up a truck when adults weren't looking.

As members began making their way back to their pews, Ryland flashed Julie an impish look, as if to say, "I know, I know, time to slow down." He took a seat beside his sisters and mother, Joann Ward.

When Julie heard the noise—POP! POP! POP!—her first thought was that a gaggle of fun-loving teenage boys had set off fireworks just outside the front door. "I'm gonna kill those guys," she said to herself.

She tried to remember who she had seen that morning. Greg? Philip? James? Had she seen them in a corner of the fellowship hall laughing together? Did they look like they were planning something, conspiring? Why they thought setting off fireworks out front during the service would be funny, she had no idea. When the service was over, she would tell them their little joke was highly inappropriate.

When Kris Workman heard the sounds, he initially thought the amplifiers he and Bob plugged in to their instruments were acting up, but after about the fourth loud pop in succession, he realized he was hearing something else. They didn't have that many amplifiers.

The light fixture above the second pew shattered, shards raining down on Julie and others sitting toward the front. No kids setting off fireworks, for sure. Julie had a passing thought it might be some kind of demonstration, a dramatic show-and-tell sermon Frank had arranged in his absence. Almost immediately, she heard a scream from the back of the sanctuary. A man shouted, "I'm hit!"

The man was David Colbath. He, too, thought he was hearing fireworks, until he realized that bullets were streaming through the paper-thin walls. Splintered wood flew through the air. He jumped up and turned toward the front door of the church, at the back of the sanctuary, realizing as he did that bullets were now coming from that direction.

He screamed, "Get on the floor! Get on the floor! Get on the floor!"

Arm outstretched as he turned, he staggered as a bullet blew a jagged hole in his right forearm. He could see straight through the wound to the crimson-colored carpet below. The force of the bullet floored him. Lying between the wooden pews, the sound of gunfire, of screams, echoing inside the small sanctuary, he glanced down and saw two bones jutting out of the bloody hole in his arm. He managed to get his phone out of his pocket and punch in 911 with his left hand. He couldn't get through.

Evelyn Hill, the blonde-haired seven-year-old who had chosen to sit beside him, was on the floor, too. She was crying, although she appeared to be uninjured. Farida Brown was trying to comfort her.

A big man, David couldn't hide under the pew where he had fallen, so he began crawling toward the front, using his elbows to move. As he crawled, he repeated a mantra out loud: "I love you, Jesus. I love you more than my son. I love you more than Olivia, my daughter. I love you, Jesus. I love you, Morgan. I love you, Olivia. I love you, Jesus. I love you, Morgan. I love you, Olivia."

As David crawled beneath four or five pews toward the front of the sanctuary, a man in black walked through the church's front door. Waves of bullets, like swarming angry hornets, streamed through walls and shattered windows seconds later. And then they were everywhere, it seemed. David heard the bullets thwack into bodies, heard the screams, heard children crying. He knew that if he stood up, he would die. He had known fear in his fifty-six years of life; he had never known fear like this.

He came to a halt beside Bryan Holcombe, who was lying on the floor against a wall, grievously wounded. He leaned in close to his old friend. "Bryan," he whispered. "Bryan. Let's get up and try to run over to that door."

"I can't," Bryan managed to respond. "I can't." His voice was part sob, part a strangled sound of the deepest sadness David had ever heard. The two men lay beside each other, bullets continuing to fly.

In the pulpit, Bryan's wife, Karla, still stood, head bowed down as if deep in prayer. Blood pooled over the announcement notes on the wooden lectern before her.

Like David, Gunny Macias had immediately jumped up when he heard the familiar sound of gunfire. That instinctive response probably saved the life of the fifty-four-year-old retired Marine gunnery sergeant. Standing, the bullets ripped through vital organs in the pelvic region instead of hitting him in the head or chest. He slumped to the floor, blood pulsing from multiple wounds.

Jennifer and Danny Holcombe were sitting in the back in their usual places with their seventeen-month-old, Noah Grace. The little girl—"the church's baby," is the way her mother described her—was one of the first to be hit. The bullets came through the walls, killing the little girl and her father.

Those who hadn't been shot huddled under pews, trying to make themselves as small as possible. Julie saw the shooter stride through the front door. She remembered her nurse's training and pointers she had picked up from her husband, Kip, the retired La Vernia fire chief. She tried to memorize details, to note specifics. Maybe the color of his eyes, tattoos, the color of his hair.

She could tell he was wearing military gear, all black, although from her vantage point on the floor, she couldn't see his face. Lying atop broken glass, she watched his boots as he strolled down the center aisle, spraying bullets left and right from his assault rifle. He seemed to target children, aiming at their heads. Precious little ones she thought of as her own were being pulverized before her eyes.

The man with the gun had to be the devil incarnate, she said to herself. She watched the black combat boots move up the aisle to the second pew. She watched them turn and stroll out. The acrid smell of gunfire, of blood, permeated the room.

She, too, punched in 911, several times, but couldn't get through. "Oh God, I'm not getting any help here," she was saying to herself. "You've got to take over."

Minutes later, the shooter was back. He had gone outside to get more ammo. "Oh, my God, here he comes again," she yelled.

He walked to where the Workmans had been sitting. He was standing next to Julie as she tried to hide under her pew. He was an arm's reach away, and she considered grabbing his foot. Maybe she could throw him off balance. Maybe she could pull his foot out from under him and he would hit his head on the stage and maybe that would knock him out. But if it didn't knock him out, she'd have a man on the floor beside her, eye level, with a gun. There were too many "ifs."

Kris and Kyle huddled under the pew next to their mother, Kris thankful that his wife, Colbey, and their daughter, Eevee, weren't in church that morning. Julie looked over at her son, her talented-musician son, her stock-car-racing son. She looked him in the eye. She saw the barrel of the gun pointed at his back. She heard the shot. She screamed as she watched Kris get lifted off the floor by the force of the bullet and then fall back down. She held his hand. He was still alive. The gunman shot him again, in the fleshy tissue of the hip.

"Are you okay?" she asked.

"I can't feel my legs," he said. The bullet had severed the L2 vertebra.

The shooter turned his attention to Julie, pointing the rifle toward her chest. "No!" she screamed to herself. "Just NO!" She was a breast cancer survivor and had undergone breast reconstruction surgery two weeks earlier. And now a stupid bullet was going to ruin that reconstruction. She was angry.

The shooter pulled the trigger. She looked down at her chest and noticed she wasn't bleeding. She told herself, "Oh God, if that's all that taking a bullet feels like, it's nothing bad."

Had the bullet glanced off? Did the shooter miss? She would never know, but afterward she would tell people, "I have wonder-boobs."

Kyle, her younger son, decided to take his chances. He leaped up and ran down the aisle between the far left side of the pews and the wall, his eyes on the front door. He stepped on David Colbath as he ran (and later apologized). As he approached the entrance, between the sound booth and the pews, he dropped to an army low crawl, then broke into a run toward the Valero station across the highway. A bullet had grazed his shoulder but left only a bruise.

When the shooter came back inside after reloading, he moved to the right side of the sanctuary and began firing single shots into people huddled beneath the pews. He was killing at point-blank range, targeting crying children clustered near the front of the sanctuary, adults trying to call on their cell phones. As he made his way around the room, he came back down the aisle where Bryan lay on the floor.

The tent maker, the jailhouse minister, the ukulele player, the man who loved the church, looked up at his executioner. David heard him moan, "Oh, God." The man in black shot Bryan Holcombe in the face.

He came back around to David, who was lying face down in an expanding pool of his own blood. He notched the gun in David's upper back, two or three inches below his neck, pretty much centered.

"Well, I guess this is it. I guess this is where I die," David was thinking as the gun barrel pressed into his back. "I guess it's over."

The shooter pulled the trigger. David felt the bullet burrow deeply into his body. He shuddered involuntarily. The feeling was that of being pushed forcefully down into the concrete floor. The bullet missed his spine. It missed the top of his heart by maybe a millimeter, ricocheted off a rib bone in front of the heart, and lodged close to his left armpit.

The man in black shot thirteen-year-old Greg Hill, a member of the Holcombe family, numerous times. The teenager had fallen across David, his head about halfway up David's back. After Kelley shot David in the back, he came back and fired at the teenager several more times, though he was already dead. A couple of those bullets passed through his body and into David's, lodging in his buttocks.

He could feel the rounds, but he didn't feel a tremendous amount of pain. He didn't make a sound. He could see that blood was pulsing out of the gaping forearm wound. Doctors would tell him later that he lost four quarts (out of five). At some point, he passed out.

Twenty-one-year-old Morgan Harris, Bob Braden, and John Holcombe, who videotapes each service and posts to YouTube, were trapped in a wooden box, the church's makeshift sound booth at the back of the sanctuary. Crouched below the window, they could hear the shots, but couldn't always see through the window. John's parents, his wife and stepchildren, his brother, and his brother's family were out there, at the shooter's mercy. So was Morgan's fiancé, Kyle Workman. They felt totally helpless.

Three times John punched in 911 but got no response, probably because the system was overwhelmed. As the information technology (IT) director for Wilson County, he knew the sheriff's direct number by heart but couldn't get through. The shooter heard him whispering and fired at the booth, wounding Morgan twice in the calf. Small pieces of shrapnel pierced John's back.

"It's hard to breathe in here," they heard the shooter sneer.

By then, three generations of the Holcombe family were gone— John's parents; his wife, Crystal, and their unborn child; his three step-children, Megan, Greg, and Emily; his brother Danny and Danny's infant daughter, Noah Grace. Danny's wife, Jennifer, survived; so did John's stepdaughter Emily.

A moment of silence, and the survivors who were huddled on the floor prayed that it was over. Joaquin Ramirez, fifty, and his wife Rosa Solis, fifty-two, thought the police had arrived when the shooter went outside. Everyone got quiet. But then they heard whispering: "Be quiet. It's him. It's him."

They heard the shooter yell, "Everybody die, motherfuckers!" He started firing again.

Joaquin saw the shooter fire at Annabelle, wounding her in the upper body. Whimpering, crying out for help, Annabelle made eye contact with him. Joaquin signaled with his finger across his lips for her to be quiet; the gunman homed in on anyone who made a sound. There was nothing else he could do for her.

Minutes later, she screamed out, in pain. The shooter, headed toward the door, heard the scream. He turned around, walked back to her pew, and shot her again.

"I asked God to save us, or take us if He wanted to," Joaquin said later, speaking to reporters in Spanish. Explaining how the shooter fired downward at children and adults lying on the floor, Joaquin held his bent right elbow high, at an angle above his shoulder, his trigger finger at about chest level.

The shooter killed seventy-one-year-old Lula White, his wife's grand-mother, a woman who loved to laugh. She died trying to shield Annabelle.

Lying a few pews away, all Rosa could see were the shooter's black boots as he stalked his prey. Next to her lay a young boy who had been shot and was crying out for his mother. Rosa didn't speak. With blood draining out of a gaping shoulder wound, she held her breath, hoping the man in the mask would think she was dead.

She turned to her husband. "Save your own life," she whispered. "Leave me here. I don't want us both to die." Joaquin waited until the shooter had his back turned. He crawled toward the front door. Rosa stayed under the pew. They both survived.

The siege lasted about eleven minutes. "Where are the cops? Where is the help?" David Colbath kept asking himself. "Where are the sirens? Where's the ambulance? Where's the first responders? Where is somebody? We need help."

Julie finally got through to 911 at 11:17. An operator called back at 11:28. Julie yelled, "First Baptist Church, Sutherland Springs, active shooter!" The operator asked her if the shooter was alone. She said yes. The call dropped.

The shooter strolled through the sanctuary targeting his victims. He killed Shani Corrigan and her husband, Bobby, the musician and retired master sergeant. They were high school sweethearts who had grown up together in Michigan. Less than a year earlier, the Corrigans had buried their son Fred, who at twenty-five had taken his own life.

He killed Sara and Dennis Johnson, Kati Wall's grandparents/parents. They were his oldest victims.

He killed Karen and Robert Scott Marshall, who were trying out a new church for the first time. The couple had recently moved back to their home in La Vernia after Karen had finished an Air National Guard assignment at Andrews Air Force Base. Scott had retired from the Air Force. On their way back to Texas, the couple stopped in Pennsylvania, where Scott's family threw him a fifty-eighth birthday party two Sundays before his death. "They thought they were just settling back into life together," a daughter, Holly Hannun, said.

He killed Therese and Richard Rodriguez, retirees who loved working in their yard. Like Julie, Therese had beaten breast cancer. Two weeks earlier, doctors had declared her cancer-free.

He killed Peggy Warden, who stepped in front of her grandson, seventeen-year-old Zachary Poston, when the shooter targeted the young man. She was shot in the back and died instantly. Zach, a tall, dark-haired farm boy, a football player for the La Vernia Bears, was shot eight times in the arms, legs, and torso. The last shot shattered a kneecap as he stretched out his leg to push a little girl under a pew. He survived and his action prevented the panicked child from crawling into the shooter's path.

He killed Haley Krueger, a sixteen-year-old who loved babies and wanted to become a nurse in a neonatal intensive care unit.

He killed Tara McNulty, who, at thirty-three, was raising two kids. Her childhood had been tumultuous, and the Holcombe family, Bryan and Karla, had taken her in. As a single mom, she struggled to make ends meet between a desk job and bartending.

A teenage girl lying on the floor, near death, locked eyes with Gunny, the retired Marine. She murmured, "Gunny, I'm scared." He told her they should sing.

"Jesus loves me, this I know, for the Bible tells me so. Little ones to him belong, they are weak, but he is strong."

Across the room from Gunny, Debbie Braden, shot three times, and her seven-year-old granddaughter Zoe, shot in the leg, also were softly singing "Jesus Loves Me." Debbie's husband, Keith, lay dead nearby. The Bradens had been married thirty-four years. An Army veteran, Keith had delivered death notices to the families of soldiers killed in combat.

The shooter moved toward Joann Ward, thirty, who was lying between pews atop three of her children, like a mother hen sheltering her chicks. He shot Joann and killed her, and then kept firing through her body to make sure he killed her children. Five-year-old Brooke died in her mother's arms. He shot Ryland, the little speedster, numerous times. Emily Garcia, Ryland's seven-year-old stepsister, was fatally wounded.

Before she died, Joann had shoved her nine-year-old daughter, Rihanna Tristan, into a corner, away from where the shooter was aiming at that moment. A woman shielded her, before that woman was cut down, as well. Rihanna saw everything. She survived when a bullet glanced off her glasses. Behind those glasses, the ghastly event was seared into her memory.

Farida Brown, the seventy-three-year-old woman young Evelyn Hill had chosen to sit beside, lay hiding under the back pew. She had moved to Houston a few years earlier to be closer to her son and his family, but in August Hurricane Harvey had flooded her out. She moved back to Sutherland Springs, had been back two weeks.

Four times bullets burned into her legs. Four shots hit the woman to her right. Farida held the woman's hand as the bullets slammed into her. She tried to comfort her, assuring her that soon it would be over, that soon she would be in heaven. The woman lay still, tears streaming down her face.

The shooter dropped his rifle where David Colbath had been sitting when the service began, back row in the middle, and wandered back outside. The sanctuary was eerily quiet. Survivors waited for him to return. Then they heard two shots. Outside. They heard the sound of tires spinning on gravel.

Lying on the floor bleeding to death, David was enraged. He was thinking, "That chicken-shit bastard's getting away."

Julie heard the spinning tires, too. She waited for the shooter to return and finish everyone off. When he didn't and with no one coming to help, she shifted into nurse mode. She hurried from one victim to another, starting with Karla Holcombe and checking for a pulse. The first seven people she approached were dead. She got to Brooke Ward; the five-year-old was beyond help. Julie began screaming.

From several pews away, Gunny rose up. He was drenched in blood. "Julie!" he ordered. "Do your duty!"

"Let me cry and scream over this baby," she said to herself, maybe to Gunny. "Then I'll do what I'm trained to do."

She went back to work. Twice more, anguish overwhelmed her. Twice more, Gunny rose up and ordered her back to work. "Julie! Do your duty!"

She remembered that she had brought hospital operating room towels to church and had stashed them in various places—in the kitchen, in the children's play area. "Julie's rags," Bryan Holcombe called them; they looked like blue hand towels.

She raced out of the sanctuary to where she thought she had left them, but now that she desperately needed towels for tourniquets, she couldn't find any. Suddenly, she remembered that she had a stash in her Ford Expedition, so she hurried outside to the parking lot and retrieved them. Back inside, she put her years of training to work on friends and loved ones near death—grinding her knee into the limb between the wound and the heart to pinch off the artery and stop the blood flow, taking the pressure off the limb long enough to knot the towel, moving on to the next dear soul.

She likely saved the life of Zach Poston, who was lying in a spreading pool of blood. "That strong boy was screaming," she told reporters. "He was hurt, he was bleeding and he was screaming."

She tied tourniquets for at least six of the wounded before first responders began rushing through the front door about four minutes after the shooter fled.

Among the first to arrive was her husband, Kip. He grabbed her; they held each other. She told him she thought Kyle had escaped and then led him to Kris, still lying on the floor. As they knelt beside their son, now paralyzed from the waist down, Kris told his mom that he was okay. "Go help others," he said.

Julie told her husband she had felt a presence in the church. A quiet calm. She told him that it had been her privilege to watch God's hands at work, God deciding, "This one, but not this one." She said she watched souls go home. She literally saw it happen, she said.

Kip listened. He gently told her that what she had seen had been gun smoke dissipating into the air. She didn't argue, but she knew what she had seen. Nothing would ever make her change her mind.

David Colbath had dozed off from lack of blood. When he came to, the first thing he saw was the muzzle of a gun coming out of a small closet. "Oh, God, here it goes again," he said to himself.

As he watched, he saw it was a man in uniform, a La Vernia police officer helping clear the building. The deputy didn't know whether the shooter had left the scene or whether there might be more than one. As he walked by, David spoke: "Sir, please, can you get this kid off my back? I can't breathe."

A game warden probably saved his life by tying a tourniquet around his arm. He told David weeks later that he had been to a seminar for first responders and was told to buy a box of multiple-sized tourniquets and keep them in his car.

"Apparently he was one of the only ones who listened," David said, "because he had those tourniquets, and he brought them in and saved my life that day, because I would have bled out shortly after that."

Ted Montgomery, the church deacon and Vietnam vet, hurried to the building from home four miles away, his son J.J. and grandson Jayden in the car with him. They pulled up to the church just as law enforcement and medical personnel were arriving. A Texas Ranger stopped him as he tried to enter the sanctuary. "You don't understand," Ted told him. "These are my people." The Ranger stepped aside.

What Ted saw was as bad as anything he'd seen in combat. "It was a slaughter," he said later that evening. He helped carry out seven or eight of the wounded on stretchers. He tried to comfort others wandering in the yard in a daze, drying blood covering their arms and legs. Victims were being loaded onto helicopters, blades turning, ready to lift off. Jayden, seventeen, saw one of his best friends, a young woman, in the throes of dying.

Going in and out of the sanctuary, Ted didn't realize that J.J., twenty-one, had followed him in. A grim-faced medic kneeling beside a bloodied man reached out to the young man. "Hey! Put your fingers in these holes!" he shouted, showing J.J. where to plug two bullet holes gushing blood in the man's thigh. Medics lifted the man, still conscious and in excruciating pain, onto a stretcher, J.J.'s fingers stanching the blood and helping save the life of Gunny Macias.

Michelle Shields got a call from her daughter, Danielle. Calling from her in-laws' house in New Braunfels, Danielle was hysterical. "Did you go to church? Did you go to church?" she kept asking, screaming the question really. Michelle heard a male voice in the background ordering her daughter to hang up. She assumed it was Devin. The phone went dead.

The Shieldses didn't know there had been a shooting. Hearing helicopters, they raced outside, climbed into their SUV, and drove toward the church. Seeing all the commotion, they realized something horrible had happened. Michelle kept asking everybody, "Have you seen Mom? Have you seen Annabelle?" Nobody would tell her.

Finally, a friend told her. "Lula and Annabelle went home." Standing by her car, Michelle felt a sense of relief rush over her—until she realized what the woman meant.

Rusty Duncan of the Stockdale Volunteer Fire Department also was among the first of the first responders. He parked his gleaming red truck near the front door of the weathered white chapel just off the highway. Sirens pierced the Sunday morning quiet. SUVs from the Wilson County Sheriff's Department and the Texas Department of Public Safety had just arrived, as well. He stepped inside the open front doors. It was quiet inside.

In the morning light from shattered windows, he tried to steel himself but wasn't prepared for what he saw—blood drenching the floor, splashed on splintered walls, on pews; pews turned on their sides, scattered like dominoes in disarray, blood-soaked victims lying under or between them. Some were dead, some dying, some in shock and unable to speak. Bodies lay atop bodies. Many, he noticed, were children.

Duncan, a Tae Kwon Do instructor and small-town deputy fire chief, a father of young children, forced himself to walk slowly down the center aisle, looking left and right for survivors. Near the front, he paused beside a stack of bodies. He felt a slight tug on his pant leg. In the charnel house where he stood, it startled him.

Looking down, he saw the pale hand of a small child reaching out from under a woman's body. Pinned beneath the mother who had died trying to save him, little Ryland Ward was alive, critically injured, but alive.

Chapter Nine

"When the Holy Spirit calls out a demon,
it has to follow instructions."

TERRIE SMITH AND HER companion, Lorenzo Flores, lived just up the road from the Valero station and convenience store that Terrie managed. On Sunday morning, November 5, they were dropping off equipment and leftovers from a catering job the night before. Their longtime friend and occasional employee, Joann Ward, had stopped by a few minutes earlier with her kids, but they had missed her. She had gone on to church.

Lorenzo noticed the man first. "Terrie, look at that," he said, staring across the highway at the church. He pointed toward what looked like some sort of soldier, maybe a police officer, dressed in black tactical gear. He had stepped out of a pearl-colored Ford Expedition in a parking space beside the church, leaving the driver's-side door open. He had a military-style rifle in his hands. He was wearing a visored helmet and bulletproof vest.

"So here's this guy dressed up like GI Joe," Lorenzo was thinking. "What's he doing at a church?"

Lorenzo knew that a sheriff's deputy lived nearby. Could he have dropped by the church for some reason? Maybe some kind of training exercise? To Lorenzo, the man with the rifle appeared hesitant initially, like he was debating with himself.

The hesitation didn't last long. He began walking toward the white frame chapel, firing as he walked. From their vantage point about a hundred yards away, Terrie and Lorenzo could hear the staccato bursts of gunfire. They watched him crouch as if in battle (or a movie). They watched him shoot out windows as he made his way around the corner of the building toward the front door.

"It was just *bam-bam-bam,* the sound when a dude keeps his finger on the trigger," Lorenzo would recall.

Suddenly realizing that something terrible, something inconceivable, was happening, Terrie fell to her knees on the service station pavement. Hands to her face, she wailed, knowing that Joann and her kids—Rihanna, Ryland, Emily, Brooke—were inside that building. Lorenzo helped her up, and they locked themselves inside the store. (A few months later, Terrie would lose a nephew in the Parkland, Florida, school shooting.)

Motorists had pulled up to the pumps for self-service gas. "Run!" Lorenzo yelled. A man fueling a power company truck dropped to his hands and knees and crawled across the pavement toward the front door. Two customers crouched behind their cars.

Seconds later, they watched through the store's barred plate-glass windows as a second man appeared from around the corner of the church. Wearing civilian clothes, he was running, stumbling, looking over his shoulder. He was headed their way, across the highway toward the station. Was he another gunman? Had he done something horrible inside the church? Was the guy in militia gear chasing him?

The running young man made his way across the highway and banged on the front door, begging to be allowed inside. Lorenzo and Terrie recognized him. It was Kyle Workman, shirt bloodied but seemingly uninjured.

Lorenzo unlocked the door and let him in. Kyle fell to his knees, got up, and ran to the back of the store. He crouched behind the last row of shelves. His face was "ablaze with fear," Lorenzo would remember. He could barely get his words out. "Somebody went in and shot everybody!" he cried. "My family's in there! My family's in there! Everybody's been shot!"

Lorenzo started praying for him. "I was pissed," he would say later. "I didn't have a gun. I didn't have anything but words to say."

Suddenly, Terrie saw the man in black they had seen earlier. He was running away from the church. At the same time, they heard a different timbre of gunfire. They assumed some sort of battle was raging. And then it was quiet.

"I gotta go over," Lorenzo said.

"No way," Terrie said. "We don't know if there's another shooter."

When they finally crossed the highway twenty minutes or so later, they found Rihanna Tristan, Joann's nine-year-old stepdaughter, standing in the churchyard. Her shoes were filled with blood. "She looked so blank, and then they took her," Terrie recalled. "We couldn't find Joann."

Kevin Jordan, a slender, dark-haired medical assistant, lived across the road from the church with his wife and two-year-old son. Jordan, thirty, was changing the oil in his Ford Focus, parked in front of his house. He was getting the car in shape for a family trip. He heard shots.

Glancing across the road, he saw a man in military gear walking toward the church and firing what appeared to be an AR-15. The man was shooting as he walked. A black mask covered his face.

Jordan ran for the house. The gunman, fifty yards or so away, noticed him and fired. A bullet crashed through the front window, a couple of feet from where his son was standing. The little boy screamed and began to cry. Frightened and enraged, Jordan snatched up the child and grabbed his wife by the arm. They barricaded themselves in the bathroom. He called 911.

They heard volleys of gunshots for the next several minutes. When they began to hear shots that didn't sound like the gunman's, Jordan peeked out the bathroom window. He saw his neighbor firing toward the shooter with an AR-15.

Stephen Willeford, who had worked in plumbing construction for thirty-four years before retiring, would have been in church himself on most Sunday mornings, but not in Sutherland Springs. He and Pamela would have made the forty-five-minute drive into San Antonio to the Oak Hills Church of Christ, their church for nearly three decades. On this Sunday morning, he decided to stay home and rest up for the hard week ahead. He knew he would be at the mercy of his beeper, on call as a contract plumber at San Antonio's University Hospital. More often than not, he would be roused out of bed in the middle of the night to deal with a hospital emergency of the nonmedical type.

He went back to bed, drifted off to sleep. A few minutes before eleven thirty, the Willefords' oldest daughter, Stephanie, came into the bedroom and woke him up. "Dad, do you hear that?" she asked. "Does that sound like gunfire to you?"

He could hear something, but in his bedroom it wasn't loud enough for him to tell what it was. Stephanie had heard the noise from the kitchen, where she had been washing dishes. He pulled on a wrinkled brown T-shirt and a pair of loose-fitting jeans and walked into the living room, where the walls were less insulated. Now, he could hear what attracted Stephanie's attention. There was no doubt. Someone was shooting, and it wasn't far away. He recognized the rapid-fire sound of an assault rifle.

Stephanie jumped into her car and drove around the block to scope out what was happening. Moments later, she was back. She was shaken. She told her dad she had seen an armed man wearing black tactical gear at the church.

His wife, Pam, was five miles away, installing drywall for the house she and Stephen were building for their youngest daughter, Rachel, and her husband. Rachel was almost three months pregnant at the time. Stephen called his wife, told her there was an active shooter at the church, told her not to come home.

"Don't go over there!" she pleaded. He could hear the fear in her voice. He hung up on her.

"I knew you were going over there," she told him later.

"How could I not?" he said.

That's what he said, although several of his neighbors—gun people, as well—saw and heard what was happening and made the perfectly rational decision not to expose themselves to danger.

He grabbed an M4-style AR-15 from the gun safe in his bedroom. He had assembled the gun himself over the years and had used it only to shoot bowling pins, his method of target practice. He knew it was easy to handle, easy to aim. He scooped up a handful of ammunition, like they were peanuts, not wanting to waste time loading a full magazine. In T-shirt and jeans, no shoes, he bolted out the front door and hurried past a large dockside shipping container and a half dozen cars parked perennially in the Willefords' narrow front yard. He waded through knee-high grass and weeds that he never seemed to get around to mowing.

Stephanie followed. He looked over his shoulder and waved her back inside. He told her she needed to load a magazine for him. "I knew she would run in, get frustrated, and stay there," he said later. "I didn't want him [the shooter] to have my daughter as a target. I didn't want her to see me fail."

Barefoot, running gingerly on the pavement, he headed toward the church, rifle at the ready. He was scared. Despite all the years he had handled guns, he had never fired at a human being. And a human being had never fired at him.

"I had been on a pistol team, but that ain't real bullets coming at you," he told me. "One time we had a drill where you had to diaper a baby doll, throw it over your shoulder, and shoot. We called it competition, and it was fun."

What was unfolding was about to be competition, to be sure, but it was not fun. Stephen admitted to being terrified.

Approaching the church, he yelled "HEY!" Why he shouted at an armed antagonist or where the voice came from, he's not sure, to this day. He believes it was the Holy Spirit calling out evil inside the sanctuary, like the peculiar tale in the Book of Matthew where Jesus summons demons out of a herd of pigs. "When the Holy Spirit calls out a demon, it has to follow instructions," is the way Stephen interprets the story.

Survivors inside the church told him later they heard the shout—and so did the shooter. He stopped killing people and headed toward the door.

Stephen angled across Farm Road 539, the road that runs beside the Willeford house, to the front yard of his neighbors, Fred and Kathleen Curnow; their yellow frame house is directly across the street from the church. At that moment, a person wearing black body armor and a visored helmet stepped into the sunlight. He noticed Stephen, who ducked behind the front tire of Fred's Dodge Ram. The gunman in black raised his pistol and fired three times. One bullet went through the bed of the pickup. Another hit the house. A third hit Fred's Dodge Challenger parked behind the truck.

Stephen raised up just enough to steady his AR-15 across the hood of the pickup. Through his thick, black-rimmed glasses, he peered through the telescopic sight. He focused his eye on the holographic red dot homed in on the man's chest. He fired twice.

"I was perfectly calm, which was surreal to me," he said later. "I could see the pistol, the rounds firing. I don't know where I hit him in the body armor, but a bullet will break ribs through the armor. Basically, it was like I was punching him with it."

Stephen may or may not have hit him during the initial volley—later, it was determined that the shooter had contusions on his chest and abdomen consistent with getting shot while wearing body armor—but regardless, the gunman lowered his weapon and ran for his SUV, still idling about twenty yards from where Stephen was positioned across the street. As the shooter rounded the front of his vehicle, Stephen saw that the man's vest, similar to a life preserver, protected only the front and back, the panels attached with Velcro; he was vulnerable on each side. Stephen fired twice more. This time, there was no doubt. He hit the shooter in unprotected spots—in the thigh and below the arm, the bullet likely burrowing into a lung.

"Any hunter knows those are long shots—one in the side, one in the legs, one in the hip," Stephen said later. "I got two of them."

The man leaped into the vehicle, slammed the door, and fired twice with a pistol through the driver's-side window. Stephen placed the red dot where he thought the shooter's head would be. He pulled the trigger, and the window shattered. The Expedition sped away, heading north on 539. Stephen ran into the road and got off another shot. He saw the rear window shatter.

The SUV raced through the highway stoplight, past the post office and the Valero station. Crossing the bridge over Cibolo Creek, the vehicle roared up the hill and out of sight.

"I was just panicking, seeing him leaving," Stephen recalled. "He shot over seven hundred rounds, every shot aimed at one of my neighbors, one of my friends." As we talked over lunch at Baldy's, he removed his glasses and wiped tears from his eyes.

Should he run back to the house, jump behind the wheel of his powerful Ford Mustang and give chase? Take the time to call the cops? Punch in 911? As he quickly considered his options, he noticed to his left a late-model Dodge Ram pickup, navy blue, idling at a stop sign on a nearby cross street.

Almost without thinking, he ran to the truck and tapped on the raised window. "That guy just shot up the church!" he shouted at the young driver. "We need to stop him."

Stephen heard the click of doors unlocking. He climbed in.

On a weekday morning months later, I was sitting at one of two round tables near the cold-beer refrigerator in the Valero gas station and convenience store. I was drinking coffee, reading the weekly *Wilson County News,* and glancing now and then at the steady stream of customers who walked through the door to buy their breakfast tacos from Terrie. She knew most of them; most took a minute or so to talk.

A young man walked in, bought a couple of tacos and a Big Red soft drink, and sat down at the table next to mine. He was an interesting-looking fellow—tall and exceedingly slender, wearing baggy shorts, a T-shirt, and a baseball cap, sunglasses perched behind the bill. His forearms were thickly tattooed, almost as if he were wearing long sleeves. Handsome, with green eyes and dirty-blond hair, he had a tattoo of an eagle, wings spread, on the front of his neck, the majestic bird partially obscured by a scraggly beard.

Terrie walked back to our tables. "Do you know who this is?" she asked me. I didn't.

"This is Johnnie," she said. "The young man who chased the shooter that morning."

I turned my chair toward his. We shook hands and talked a bit about his lottery ticket purchase. I mentioned that I had read a couple of days earlier about a man who had bought a carton of orange juice at a 7-Eleven, took it back because his wife, unbeknownst to him, had brought home a carton at half the price, and on the spur of the moment had bought Powerball tickets instead. One of the tickets, he found out a few days later, was worth $316 million. Terrie told us she'd had a $10,000 winner at her store.

Johnnie Langendorff, twenty-seven, said he was a welder, that he worked on a ranch and had grown up in Seguin. I told him about my *Houston Chronicle* columnist friend Lisa Falkenberg, who had grown up in Seguin. "She won a Pulitzer a couple of years ago," I said.

"What's a Pulitzer?" Johnnie asked. He said he didn't like Seguin.

I asked him about that Sunday morning in November. He took a sip of Big Red and in a soft, laconic voice started in on his story.

On weekends, he said, he did construction work on the side with a friend, but on that Sunday he didn't feel good. "Stomach gurgling, just didn't feel right; I felt anxious," he recalled. He thought about staying home but then decided to get up and go, even though it bothered him that he was getting a late start. "Two things I pride myself on," he said. "Getting to work on time and finishing whatever job I started."

After working a couple of hours, he wasn't feeling any better, so he decided to quit for the day and go home. He lived with his girlfriend, now fiancée, Summer, just outside Sutherland Springs. They planned to marry in about a year.

He pulled up to the stop sign near the church and heard POP-POP-POP! He couldn't believe what he saw: two men walking parallel to each other on opposite sides of the road. One was wearing black combat gear and firing a pistol; the other, a stocky, gray-haired man in jeans and a T-shirt, barefoot, was wielding an AR-15. They were shooting at each other. He punched in 911.

Johnnie sat in his truck and watched the man in combat gear scramble into a light-colored Ford Expedition. He watched the gray-haired man fire at the Expedition, saw the window shatter, and then saw the man running toward his truck.

I asked Johnnie if he was scared, if he wondered what a barefoot guy running toward him with a loaded and lethal AR-15 was up to.

"I wasn't scared," he said. "It was like time stood still." He thought his reaction might have had something to do with his difficult upbringing. He and his two sisters grew up in a violent household, a household so dysfunctional that Child Protective Services took him away on two occasions. He lived for two weeks in a foster home that was worse than his own home. For a month he was in a mental hospital and managed to get out and get back home by threatening suicide. He was twelve. Those experiences, he said, taught him to protect himself, to think through things rationally, to avoid getting emotional.

As Johnnie negotiated the winding, two-lane blacktop, the speedometer flirting with ninety-five on the straightaways, Stephen was in a panic. He managed to get a 911 dispatcher on his phone but was too distraught to communicate where they were, so Johnnie took the phone from him and explained they were on 539 headed north. He kept the dispatcher informed each time they passed a marked road. Stephen, the AR-15 propped between his knees, kept hitting the dashboard with the flat of his hands. "Sir, could you not do that?" Johnnie asked.

At least three police cars passed them, lights flashing and sirens blaring; they were headed southward to the church. Johnnie hoped they would notice he was way over the seventy miles per hour speed limit. Ignoring yellow no-passing stripes, he pulled out and passed several cars as the road wound through rolling live oak–dotted pastureland, past scattered suburban houses. A few miles beyond Whitehall, the imposing Polley mansion, they rounded a bend and spotted the Expedition about a hundred feet ahead.

Stephen still didn't know his companion's name, but he realized that if they caught up with the shooter, he'd be putting the young man in danger. "I'm thinking to myself," he said later, "'this guy's a nut,' but he was calm, cool. Redneck-style."

Stephen glanced at Johnnie. "If we catch him, we may have to use your truck to put him off the road," he said.

"I already figured that," Johnnie said. As he drove, he was multitasking: trying to stay in touch with the 911 dispatcher, trying to "keep the gentleman calm," and trying to stay in sight of the Expedition. They were gaining on it. As they approached the Wilson–Guadalupe county line— not far from where Stephen's parents had been killed years earlier—the Expedition began weaving back and forth across the center line. Stephen figured the driver's lungs were filling with blood because of his side shot at the church; he probably was losing consciousness. Suddenly, the Expedition veered off the road into a ditch and came to a halt. Johnnie pulled up about five yards behind.

Stephen, staring through the windshield at the SUV, knew that he had only two rounds remaining, not enough to survive a shootout if it came to that. He wrapped his right hand around the AR-15, his eyes riveted on the driver's side of the Expedition; with his left, he reached across for the door handle. Just as he got one bare foot nearly out of the truck, the Expedition roared off, taking down a road sign as it clambered back onto the pavement. Stephen slammed the door shut, and Johnnie hit the gas. The SUV traveled only a few hundred yards before missing a curve and veering off the road again. It tore through a barbed-wire fence on the opposite side. Eleven miles from where the chase began, the vehicle came to a stop about thirty feet inside a field dotted with cylindrical-shaped hay bales, near a sign pointing the way to Post Oak Community Cemetery.

Johnnie braked to a stop on the shoulder, about fifty yards from the Expedition. Stephen, telling his companion to duck under the dashboard, slowly stepped out of the truck and posted up behind the front tire. For the second time that morning, he steadied his rifle on the hood of a pickup.

"Get out! Get out!" he yelled at the driver, calling him every obscenity he could think of. (For a godly man, there weren't many.) Five minutes passed. Then six. Then seven. Except for his shouting, it was country quiet beside the road. "Where are the police?" he was thinking to himself.

"I can tell you," he said later, "holding a man at gunpoint for five to seven minutes is an eternity."

Johnnie stepped out on the driver's side, the shooter's side, and ran around the back of the truck to take cover. He suddenly noticed a line of cars headed their way, so he dashed into the middle of the road, exposing himself again, and waved his arms to stop traffic. The cars stopped, and he ran back to where Stephen waited beside the front tire. The SUV's rear brake lights blinked on and off.

Minutes later they heard the voice of a police officer using a PA system. "Driver! Put down your weapon and come out with your hands up!" they heard. When the officer repeated the command, Stephen laid his rifle on the hood and turned toward the squad car that had pulled up on the shoulder, several yards behind Johnnie's truck. He raised his hands.

"Not you!" the officer shouted. Johnnie and Stephen saw that two police officers—one with a rifle about fifty yards away, one with a pistol maybe a hundred yards away—had the Expedition in their sights. A Wilson County Sheriff's Department SUV advanced slowly toward the vehicle, almost as if it was coasting. An armed deputy walked beside the vehicle, using the open passenger door as a shield.

Johnnie was videoing with his phone, had been videoing since the chase began, his phone sticking out of his shirt pocket. He and Stephen stayed beside the tire for at least half an hour. "What are we waiting for?" Stephen grumbled. The pavement was hot on his bare feet.

Johnnie's video shows Stephen responding to basic questions from a Wilson County deputy about who he is and what had happened. His hands are shaking, his voice breaks; adrenaline is obviously still pumping. He still doesn't know Johnnie's name.

"I was scared to death," he was not ashamed to admit, scared from the moment he ran out the door of his house until the ordeal was over. Standing beside a guard rail on the road, he asked the deputy if he could call his wife and family.

More officers arrived—SUVs from the Wilson County Sheriff's Department, Guadalupe County Sheriff's Department, Texas Rangers, state troopers, at least a dozen officers from various jurisdictions pulled up. Stephen and Johnnie were unaware the police were waiting for a drone to inspect the vehicle rather than rushing it.

It took about an hour before a Wilson County sheriff's deputy arrived with the small surveillance drone. Homing in like a hawk from high in the sky, the drone descended until it was hovering at the driver's-side window. The camera showed that the shooter was dead in the driver's seat. Officers cautiously converged on the Expedition. Peering through the window, they could see that the fatal wound was a self-inflicted gunshot to the head. Stephen remembered feeling a sense of relief. He had not killed a man, after all.

He and Johnnie stayed on the scene about four hours that afternoon, telling their story to sheriffs from three counties, officers from Alcohol, Tobacco, Firearms and Explosives, and Texas Rangers. (They would talk to the FBI and the Department of Homeland Security later that evening.) After about an hour, Pam drove up, vastly relieved her husband was okay. She brought him a pair of shoes. Crocs.

Tambria Read, the high school art teacher and local historian, was not a member of First Baptist at the time, but she attended services occasionally and knew most members. She had taught several of their kids over the years. When she heard the horrific news, she immediately texted her friends Karla and Bryan Holcombe. "Please tell me you're all right," she had texted. (Telling me that story months later, she cried, recalling that moment.)

She drove into town from her country home a couple of miles away and unlocked the museum so first responders would have access to the copy machine. She drove to the Community Building three blocks from the museum, where volunteers and first responders were getting organized to help family members of people killed or wounded. When she drove up, family members, anxious and distraught, had just received wristbands so law enforcement could identify them.

As she stood outside talking to the Wilson County sheriff, the county judge, and the county attorney, Michelle Shields walked out. She already knew that her mother, Lula White, was among the dead.

Michelle saw Tambria. The two women knew each other, but not well. Michelle was Tambria's regular bank teller in Floresville; Tambria had known Michelle's kids at school. Tears flowing, they embraced.

Michelle stepped back and looked at Tambria, then at the county officials. Her face was almost as pale as her snow-white hair. "I know who did it," she said, her anguish so intense she almost choked on the words.

"Have you told the FBI?" the county attorney asked.

"Not yet," Michelle said.

In what would be his final Facebook posts, Devin Kelley complained about headaches and lingering neck pain from a motorcycle accident in 2014. "Damn, my heads been hurting for three days now," he wrote. "Ah fuck. I'm a wreck," he added in another.

Driving from New Braunfels toward Sutherland Springs thirty-five miles to the southeast, he called his parents. He asked them to walk over to the barn apartment he had left a few minutes earlier. Danielle needed their help.

Mike and Rebecca Kelley found their daughter-in-law bound to the bed, the two youngsters crying. They got her untied, helped soothe the children, and tried to figure out what in the world was going on. They knew the young couple had been having trouble, but this…

Danielle's cell phone rang. It was Devin. She put her husband on speaker phone so his parents could hear. He had done "something horrible," he told them. In a frenzied burble of words, they heard him say, "I just shot up the Sutherland Springs church."

The three huddled around the phone. They were numb, in shock. They pleaded with him to stop whatever it was he was doing, not knowing that he was wounded, that he was sitting in his SUV in a field beside the road, that two men were watching him from a pickup truck on the shoulder nearby, that one was aiming an assault rifle at him. They could not have imagined that a few minutes earlier he had slaughtered twenty-six people, including Danielle's grandmother, and wounded twenty more.

He told Danielle and his parents he wasn't going to make it home. He said he loved them. Through their tears, they told him they loved him too. After eight minutes, the call ended.

Sitting behind the wheel of his vehicle, staring through the windshield into an empty field, twenty-six-year-old Devin Patrick Kelley raised a gun to his head, aiming just above his right ear. He pulled the trigger.

Chapter Ten

"I thought we were done."

FRANK POMEROY WAS IN Oklahoma City that particular weekend, because it was the only time the National Rifle Association offered the muzzle-loading classes he needed to qualify as an instructor at a Baptist youth camp scheduled for July. On Saturday, beginning at eight in the morning, he was sitting in the classroom all day with fellow muzzle-loading enthusiasts. On Sunday, he would be on the range qualifying.

Had he been at church that morning, in the pulpit, armed, he might have gotten off a shot with the pistol on his hip. More likely, a shooter with an AR-15, the element of surprise on his side, would have targeted Frank first. Frank acknowledged the odds would have been in the shooter's favor.

Shortly after eleven Sunday morning, he was signing papers for his "quals" when his cell phone pinged. Glancing down at the phone, he saw he had a text message from John Holcombe. "There's an active shooter at church," he read on the small screen in the palm of his hand.

"I know John doesn't have much of a sense of humor, but that wasn't very funny," Pomeroy recalled. "I told him so. He texted back: 'It's true.'"

He heard nothing more from John, still at the mercy of the shooter, so he started trying to reach other church members, trying to think as he punched in numbers who would have been in church that morning. Sherri, no. Grandkids, maybe. Annabelle, yes.

Everyone he tried to call was in church, under siege. Finally, he reached Rod Green, who rarely missed but was running late that morning. He told

Frank he and Judy were ten minutes away. He soon called back. "Frank, it's bad," he said.

Knowing what Rod had experienced in Vietnam, Frank knew his friend wouldn't be exaggerating. He braced himself. "What about Annabelle?"

Rod answered: "She didn't make it, Frank."

By noon, Frank was in his truck barreling down I-35, every mile a rolling kaleidoscope of memories, every hour the same torturous thoughts looping through his mind: *I should have been there. Maybe I could have stopped the shooter. Who else is gone? What do we do now?* And, again and again, Annabelle, the smile, the laughing brown eyes, the love she felt for her church family. He remembered dropping her off at school on Friday. She was happy, excited about the singing and speaking part she had gotten in a school production of *Elf, the Musical.* They were joking with each other as Frank pulled up to the curb at school. "See ya Monday," he told her as she gathered up her backpack and scrambled out.

ABC News started trying to reach him before he cleared Oklahoma City. He knew he had to reach Sherri. He didn't want her to hear the news on TV. He also didn't want to share the unbearable over the phone. When they finally connected, he told her Annabelle had been hurt, that she had been hit.

Across the rolling plains of rural Oklahoma and then the Red River, negotiating the interstate maze through Dallas and the clotted traffic of Austin, he began to separate out the feelings of pain and desperation that threatened to overwhelm him from the practical steps he knew he had to take in the next few hours, the next several days. He had been forced during his early home life, and in the military, to focus on the task at hand, ignoring emotions of the moment; he had never experienced anything so painful. What would God have him do? Was there a biblical character to emulate?

"I have seen so much death in my life, I have learned to compartmentalize my emotions," he recalled months later. "I tell myself I'll deal with the emotions later."

It was dark when he got to San Antonio.

*　　*　　*

Sherri had been on the job as a FEMA contractor all of two weeks when she got the call to go to Florida, still recovering from Irma, a Category 4 hurricane that displaced thousands of people in the Miami area. Her job was to interview Floridians who had lost their homes, helping them determine their eligibility for FEMA assistance. In years past she had worked as the La Vernia school cafeteria manager and more recently as the church secretary. She enjoyed the new job, enjoyed helping those in need. She liked being out in the world and having an identity separate from the church.

With twenty dollars in the pocket of her red Bermuda shorts, she dropped by the Fort Lauderdale field office to see if there was any more work to do. If not, her plan was to hit the beach before flying back to Texas. She chatted with her supervisor about Annabelle, "which was odd for me to talk to a stranger," she said later. Work done, she happily headed out, eager to see how a Florida beach compared to the Gulf Coast beaches she knew back home.

"I saw I had a call from Frankie, so when I got to the elevator I called him back," she recalled. "He said, 'Sherri, listen to me.' I knew it was serious, because he doesn't call me Sherri, usually Baby or Hey."

He told her there had been a shooting at the church. He told her Annabelle had been hurt. She screamed. Unlike her husband, she had no practice compartmentalizing emotions.

Hanging up, she rushed back to her Miami hotel room and started frantically trying to find a flight home. When she found one departing Fort Lauderdale that afternoon, she headed to the elevator, leaving everything in her room. Her new boss drove her to the airport. Waiting for the plane, she called the hotel and asked that they pack her belongings and ship them to her. She confessed to stealing a towel.

"I was bawling, squalling, getting calls from reporters," she recalled. "I knew that Annabelle had been shot. That's all Frankie told me. I remember sitting at a metal table talking to Frankie again [by phone]. 'Just tell me,' I begged him. He said, 'Annabelle didn't make it.' I don't know how I got on a plane from there."

She was in the air headed to South Carolina—or was it North

Carolina?—the first leg of a meandering journey home, when she realized to her horror that their son's mother-in-law was keeping the grandchildren for the weekend and likely had taken them to church. Nish usually got them dressed and out the door on Sunday mornings when she and her husband, Darrell, kept them. The youngsters often sat in the front pew.

Sherri learned later that Nish had looked into the refrigerator that morning and noticed she had eggs that needed eating, so she fixed a late breakfast for the grandbabies. They didn't make it to church.

Landing in South Carolina (or maybe North Carolina), a flight attendant helped her off the plane ahead of the other passengers. Waiting for the next leg, she called Frank again. He told her about the others, and she realized that she had lost not only her daughter but also her two best friends, Lula White and Karla Holcombe. "I didn't know the depth of it until then," she said. "I wasn't watching the news."

The flight home from Florida took ten hours.

Frank got to the San Antonio airport just as Sherri's plane was landing. Airport security allowed him to meet her as she stepped off the ramp into the waiting area. Escorted off the plane before the rest of the passengers, she collapsed into his arms. He half carried her down the long corridor to the lobby. "We walked forever and forever," she recalled.

All she had with her was a book and a work bag. Her computer and most of her clothes were back in the Miami hotel room. They drove to their son Kaleb's San Antonio home, where the rest of the family, twenty in all, had begun to gather. It was close to eleven at night. Making a pallet on the floor, they tried to sleep for a few hours. During that brief, dark night tossing and turning on the hard floor, despair threatened to overwhelm both of them. How could they go on, they asked each other through tears. They had lost their beloved daughter, a little girl adored by everyone, a child who had transformed their lives. They had lost nearly half the congregation they had served for fifteen years, including most of the church leadership team. Frank doubted that whatever remnant of the church that still existed could afford to pay a preacher's salary, however modest. He wondered whether the church could survive. "I thought we were done," Frank said.

At the church earlier in the day, at least thirty ambulances, an AmbuBus, and a half dozen helicopters converged to ferry survivors to area hospitals—nine to University Hospital in San Antonio, three to Connally Memorial Medical Center in nearby Floresville, and eight to Brooke Army Medical Center in San Antonio. Both San Antonio hospitals have superb trauma centers.

Joe Tackitt Jr., a former peanut farmer who was first elected Wilson County sheriff in 1992, was in the tiny community of Black Hill for an annual turkey dinner. He and his wife had bought tickets and were waiting in line for their plates when a deputy called to report an active shooter at Sutherland Springs. The couple got their food to go, and the sheriff headed toward the church, thirty-five miles to the northeast. "It took me a while to get there," he recalled. "I took my wife by the house first."

Tackitt, seventy at the time, resembles the quintessential Texas sheriff. Tall and slender, he usually wears jeans, a white hat, and a sheriff's silver star pinned to a white western shirt. Belying the stereotype of the belligerent southern lawman, he's easygoing, modest, and soft-spoken. He wears a pistol in a brown leather holster on his hip.

Speeding toward the church, Tackitt tried to imagine what he would find in the little community he knew well. He recalled a Labor Day weekend in 1993, shortly after being elected sheriff. On Friday night of that weekend, a family of five near Stockdale burned up in a house fire set by the father, who had shot them all and then shot himself. On Saturday night, a young couple died when a car veered into their lane and crashed into them head-on. On Sunday night, he got a call about a traffic accident on FM 539. An emergency medical services (EMS) technician met him at the scene as he got out of the car.

"You're not going over there," she told him.

"Yes, I am," he said. "I'm the sheriff."

"You're not going over there," she repeated, this time more insistently. "These are people you know."

A drunk driver had hit two people on a motorcycle, killing them instantly. They were Stephen Willeford's parents.

Nearly twenty-five years later, that horrific weekend stood out because it was so unusual. Wilson County has drug crime and drunk driving, domestic abuse and meth-related crimes. A portion of the county is inside an oil-boom area, so itinerant oil field workers cause problems. It has the occasional homicide. Mostly though, it's like any other rural part of Texas; peace and quiet are more the rule than the exception. Now, Tackitt was headed toward a crime scene that would dwarf anything he or his law enforcement colleagues had ever experienced.

"Get all the EMS you can get, all the Life Flight you can get," a deputy at the scene told him as he was driving. The deputy was one of two who had arrived about four minutes after the first 911 call got through. Another deputy headed up FM 539 and was among the first to find Devin Kelley dead in his vehicle. Texas Parks & Wildlife officers and officers from the La Vernia Police Department also were arriving about the time Tackitt pulled up to the church. So were Texas Rangers and FBI agents, whose first task was to figure out what they were dealing with. A hate crime? Terrorism? A mass shooting?

"They started trying to do triage on the wounded," the sheriff recalled. "I kept asking myself, 'Is this really happening?'"

He saw John Holcombe sitting on the steps of the church. The two knew each other well because John handled IT for the county, including the sheriff's department. "I don't know if he even knew who I was," Tackitt said. "Just the week before he was asking where he could find a twelve-passenger van, because they were fixin' to have a baby."

What the veteran lawman saw inside the sanctuary would haunt him, he suspects, for the rest of his life. He and all the other first responders had seen crime scenes, had worked fires and car crashes and natural disasters, but they had never seen anything like the ravaged interior of the little church, the bodies scattered around the room, many sprawled atop each other. Veteran cops staggered out of the building in tears. It was the children who got to them.

"Grown-ups I can deal with; kids I have trouble with," said Harold

Sherri Pomeroy rests at the grave of daughter Annabelle after pulling weeds around her gravesite. When Annabelle accompanied her father, Pastor Frank Pomeroy, to funeral services he conducted at the rural cemetery, she liked to pass the time by playing with cows, ducks, and other animals who came for water at the stock tank across the fence.

Following a women's retreat seven months after the shooting, Sarah Slavin summoned the strength to tell the Sutherland Springs congregation that the loss of nine family members had left her feeling "shattered."

Rod Green, a longtime member of the First Baptist Church of Sutherland Springs, walks past the original church, now a memorial, with his granddaughter Hali Rose Honigbaum. Green and his wife, Judy, who run the church's food pantry, were late for services on that tragic Sunday.

Stephen Willeford, the NRA-certified shooting instructor who became the quintessential "good guy with a gun," tries out an AR-15 rifle made especially for him by Stephen Oliver, a firearms manufacturer and dealer. Willeford, who owns an arsenal of various types of firearms, believes that churches are foolhardy if they don't rely on armed guards for protection at all services.

Tears stream down the face of Danielle Kelley, the widow of gunman Devin Kelley, as Stephen Willeford prays with her following the first church service she attended after the mass shooting. Willeford shot and wounded Danielle's husband as he fled the massacre, shortly before Kelley killed himself.

David Colbath, who proclaims that his faith has grown stronger since the shooting, attends a Sunday service with his daughter Olivia.

Charlene Uhl decorates the memorial cross dedicated to her daughter Haley Krueger, who was sixteen when she was killed at the church. Uhl has continued to decorate the cross almost every week since the shooting. Like other family members of the deceased, she's struggled with grief daily.

Sylvia Timmons (left) comforts her sister, Sherri Pomeroy, and Sherri's grandson, Lee Pomeroy, during a Sunday service on October 21, 2018, which would have been the fifteenth birthday of Annabelle Pomeroy, one of the twenty-six who lost their lives in the mass shooting. After services that day, church members held a balloon release in Annabelle's honor at the country cemetery where she's buried.

Prosthetist/orthotist Jesse Rettele fits Kris Workman, paralyzed in the shooting, with custom orthotics while Workman's wife, Colbey, watches and their daughter, Eevee, entertains herself at the University of Texas Health Science Center. The orthotics are designed to help Kris, the church's praise team leader and former race car driver, stand and eventually walk with the aid of a walker or cane. The Workmans are among several church members who have had to retrofit their residences to accommodate the physical needs of survivors.

Haley Ward, eight, looks at the chairs dedicated to her family members during "Remembering Sutherland Springs: One Year Later at First Baptist Church of Sutherland Springs," a memorial held on Sunday, November 4, 2018.

The praise team, larger and more exuberant in the weeks and months following the shooting, rehearses in the temporary modular building where services were held for a year and half, in preparation for the opening of the congregation's spacious new building.

Pastor Frank Pomeroy speaks from the pulpit during a private service for church members, survivors, and victims' families on May 19, 2019, the Sunday the congregation moved into its new building. Pomeroy urged the congregation to be "a city set upon a hill."

Schott, a Wilson County justice of the peace who got to the church early. He had been a San Antonio cop for three decades, but no amount of experience could have prepared him for Sutherland Springs. Even the most hardened among the first responders sought counseling and therapy, he said. A longtime police psychologist he knew in San Antonio stayed busy for weeks and weeks.

Justice of the peace Sara Canady lived in Floresville and had just gotten out of church when she and her daughter stopped for gas. On the other side of the pump was a pickup truck with the radio playing loudly enough for her to hear, something about a church shooting. A woman in the passenger seat was crying. When Canady found out it was Sutherland Springs, she started crying, as well. Although she was a member of the Baptist church in Floresville, she often drove over to Sutherland Springs because she enjoyed Pastor Frank's sermons. She dropped her daughter at home, told her to lock the doors and call her father, and headed toward Sutherland Springs on a back road. Although she wasn't on call that morning, she figured she could help.

The highway was already blocked off when she got there, and a helicopter had landed in the field behind the church. A body lay on the front lawn. Sheriff Tackitt met her at the end of the sidewalk outside the church. "Judge, it's not good," he said.

They ducked under the police tape and stepped inside. What she found, she said, was not only utter horror but what looked like utter chaos. No one was following official procedure, and in the absence of leadership, Canady was irritated to see that FBI agents had taken charge (as in countless movies where the locals resent the feds big-footing it).

Canady got a call on her cell phone from a justice of the peace in Central Texas who was considered the state's mass-fatality expert. He had handled the Branch Davidian siege, the West fertilizer plant explosion, and a mass shooting among bikers at a Twin Peaks "breastaurant" in Waco. He had information and experience to share. No one wanted to hear it, Canady said. She did what she could.

* * *

One summer afternoon months after the shooting Windy Choate was working in the church office when a tall woman with long, blonde hair stepped through the door. She had been an emergency medical technician that day, she told Windy. She held out her badge, and as she started to introduce herself, she began to tremble. Tears rolled down her cheeks. She couldn't talk.

Windy waited while the EMT composed herself. The woman explained that she and she alone had been ordered to carry out the bodies of the children—because she was single and had no children of her own. In and out of the church she walked, a broken, precious child in her arms each time she exited the building. Since that day, she had never returned to the church.

Windy, in tears herself, walked her across the yard to the sanctuary. It had been transformed into a memorial. Seeing the cleansed space made her feel a bit better, the woman told Windy.

Mark Collins, Frank Pomeroy's predecessor at First Baptist, was in the pulpit at the Baptist church in Yorktown, a little town fifty miles south of Sutherland Springs, when his daughter stepped up to the lectern, stopping him in midsentence. The tall, gray-haired minister leaned down while she whispered in his ear. She told him she had just gotten a call about a mass shooting in the little church where she had grown up, where they still knew almost everyone. Collins stepped down from the pulpit and hurried to his car. He got to Sutherland Springs in less than half an hour.

With helicopters circling overhead, police vehicles surrounding the building, traffic on 87 backed up in both directions, and knots of distraught people gathering beyond the yellow police tape, Collins parked near the small frame house next to the church that serves as the community food pantry. He hurried over to the grassy area beside the sanctuary and stood near a long-broken concrete picnic table beneath a hackberry tree. Laid out on the grass was a body beneath a yellow plastic tarp. Uncovered at one end was a pair of scuffed work boots.

Two weeks earlier, Collins had attended a Baptist association luncheon meeting in the nearby town of Gonzales, where he sat at a table with his old friend Bryan Holcombe. He was surprised to see the man who favored loud Hawaiian shirts wearing a dark suit and tie—and scuffed work boots. Collins kidded him about the boots. Holcombe took it good-naturedly.

"I knew it was Bryan lying there," Collins said later. "That's when it hit home to me."

Shortly afterward, he got a call from Frank. "Buddy, I don't know if you've heard, but there's been a mass shooting at the church. Can you be my eyes and ears?"

Collins assured him he would do just that. As Frank's representative, he was allowed inside the building. In the little sanctuary where he used to preach, he stared at the bullet-riddled front doors, the overturned pews, the blood-soaked Bibles scattered on the floor, the bullet holes in the walls, splatters of blood staining the walls, the floor, the pulpit, even the ceiling. Once he had been on a mission trip to Kenya at a time when there had been a massacre in a small church. The odor inside the Sutherland Springs sanctuary, "the sour-sweet smell of blood," took him back.

As first responders went about their grim task inside the church, law enforcement personnel began to get control of a chaotic scene. To separate out family members from townspeople, casual onlookers, and members of the media who were showing up, a Texas Ranger directed them to the Community Building three blocks away.

Kati Wall was among them. Her grandparents, Sara and Dennis Johnson, the two people who had raised her, had been inside the church. The Johnsons were among those members who had failed to set their clocks back, so they got to church an hour early. At home in the little town of Poth, Kati's mother heard a report on the radio. She screamed.

Kati and an uncle had jumped into a car and headed toward Sutherland Springs. They made the twenty-mile drive from Poth in less than fifteen minutes. "We were frantic. It felt so surreal," she recalled. "We get there, and it's chaos. People are everywhere. We run toward the church. I saw John Holcombe sitting in an ambulance. He said he didn't know what had happened to my parents."

*   *   *

Haley Krueger told her mom she loved her when she got out of the car that morning. The sixteen-year-old got to church early so she could help prepare breakfast for the congregation. That's the last time her mother, Charlene Uhl, ever saw her. She found out about the shooting on social media. "I just ran up there and watched all the helicopters, in and out, just waiting. Nobody would answer," she recalled.

A police officer sent Uhl and other family members to the Community Building. They were among the first, but when they got there the doors were locked. Alice and Oscar Garcia, who lived a block and a half from First Baptist, had a set of keys. They had been in church in La Vernia when they started getting text messages. As they rushed home, a stream of ambulances, sirens wailing, passed them. They went to the church first, saw the bodies laid out on the grass, and then rushed to the Community Building and unlocked the front door.

Without really knowing what needed to be done, the Garcias began setting up tables. Other volunteers showed up bearing food and drinks. Red Cross representatives arrived and arranged a staging area for first responders. Governor Greg Abbott showed up and prayed with the people gathered there.

It quickly became obvious that the small, un-air-conditioned community center, with only one men's and one women's restroom, wasn't adequate to deal with the immensity of the tragedy. Texas Rangers announced that everything would be shifting to the civic center in Stockdale, eight miles away. The families mutinied. We're not going to Stockdale, they told the Rangers.

Pastor Paul Buford of River Oaks Baptist Church, a couple of miles to the north of Sutherland Springs, had already offered his church's newer, larger facilities but had been ignored. After the mini-rebellion, the Rangers took him up on his offer. At River Oaks, they would have private rooms available when they had to inform family members of their loss (or losses).

Representatives from the American Red Cross and the Southern Baptists of Texas Convention arrived, as did the Baptist Emergency Management Service, a capable organization with disaster-relief experience around the world. The state Crime Victims Assistance Fund sent representatives, as did FBI Victim Services. The FBI representatives, including an agent who specialized in helping children, flew in from Las Vegas, where they had been assisting families and survivors of the Mandalay Bay Resort mass shooting.

"When I felt better was when somebody called and said FBI Victim Services was coming," said Katie Etringer Quinney, the lone victim assistance coordinator with the district attorney's office in Wilson County. "When I saw her walking up, she could have had a white light behind her, just to know she and her team had come from doing all that in Las Vegas."

Quinney, a talkative and relentlessly cheerful former public relations professional, is a victim assistance coordinator because of what had happened to her son a dozen years earlier, when he was five years old. That traumatic experience showed her how important it was to have someone besides law enforcement looking out for the child.

Her older son went into law enforcement because of what happened to his little brother. A Victoria resident, he was visiting his mom in Sutherland Springs that weekend. Grabbing up his gun and in jeans and T-shirt, he drove to the church three miles away. He came back not long afterward. "Don't go over there," he told his mom. There were tears in his eyes.

She went anyway, first to the church and then to the Community Building before ending up at River Oaks, where she stayed until two thirty in the morning (her routine for the next two weeks). Someone found floral-decorated tape at the nearby Dollar General store, and Quinney and other volunteers made identification bracelets for family and friends who were gathering at River Oaks. The make-do bracelets made do until the Red Cross arrived with plastic wristbands.

Counselors arrived from the Ecumenical Center, a San Antonio–based counseling service chartered in 1967 by Jewish, Episcopal, Catholic, and Methodist hierarchies. Counselors, therapists, and psychologists from the center would be on hand for months.

"Trauma of this nature and severity takes a long time to resolve," said Mary Beth Fisk, CEO and executive director of the Ecumenical Center. Her organization set up two counseling centers in Sutherland Springs, one specializing in children's play therapy. A third office, known as the Center for Healing and Hope of South Texas, opened in La Vernia.

Fisk got to the River Oaks church a couple of hours after the shooting. "We need help," a San Antonio police chaplain told her as she walked up. "It was an excruciating time," she said.

With victim identification continuing into the early hours of Monday morning, Fisk began setting up a crisis counseling effort, a team to help children and families and counselors to help first responders deal with the horror they had seen. She also brought therapy dog Sadie, an English bulldog. All services were free of charge.

From the beginning, Fisk was impressed with the faith of the Sutherland Springs people. "It's a great deal of strength these people have shown when they rely on their faith," she said. "It's very helpful in the healing process."

Floresville funeral director Gail Uhlig and her husband, Edward, live a couple of miles from the River Oaks church. She set up a table for people inquiring about funerals. The people who approached were friends and relatives.

Still not knowing anything about their loved ones, Kati Wall and her uncle drove to the bigger, better-equipped church. Wearing plastic wristbands, they waited for word as other family members joined them, among them Charlene Uhl.

Like Kati's family, like so many other families, Charlene waited. The hours passed. "I was trying to remain positive, hoping [Haley] got away and was able to run off," Uhl said. Late that evening, she got word. "A piece of me is gone," she said. "We'll never be the same."

"That was the worst, not knowing," Kati recalled. "We waited thirteen hours. I called hospitals, but they didn't have them. I kind of had a feeling it was not good. I saw a Texas Ranger, a beautiful young woman. She looked very distressed, but she held herself together.

"We were the last family that was called. There was a cacophony of wailing. Nanny's best friend of thirty-one years, she was there. We had to call an ambulance for her."

*　　*　　*

On San Antonio's East Side, the trauma team at Brooke Army Medical Center got the alert shortly before noon that mass casualties were headed their way. BAMC (known as Bam-See) and University Hospital in San Antonio are the nation's only civilian-military hospital partnership, and the only Level I trauma centers in the San Antonio region, an area of twenty-three thousand square miles. Tracing its history back to frontier Texas, the huge military hospital also is the sole verified Level I trauma center within the Department of Defense.

BAMC is the stateside hospital that receives the young Marine who steps on an improvised explosive device (IED) in Afghanistan and loses a leg, it's where an infantryman blinded in Iraq by a mortar comes for long-term rehabilitation and recovery care. Through its Center for the Intrepid unit, the hospital has been responsible for advances in amputee care, prosthetics integration, and functional restoration for patients undergoing limb salvage. David Colbath, arriving at BAMC with eight bullet holes in his body and a hand that no longer functioned, would get to know the Center for the Intrepid well.

The two hospitals had completed a joint mass casualty drill six months earlier. In the hypothetical scenario, sixty people had been shot and needed care. Army Col. (Dr.) Kurt Edwards, chief of trauma at Brooke Army Medical Center, told *USA Today* that at the time he thought the number was "ludicrous." He never imagined the casualty count from a mass shooting would be so high.

When the hospitals completed the exercise, the most recent real-life episode had been a mass shooting in July 2016 in downtown Dallas, where a gunman shot twelve police officers, killing five. The shooting at the Harvest Music Festival in Las Vegas, the deadliest mass shooting in modern American history, killing fifty-eight people, wouldn't happen until October.

Alerted that a mass shooting had occurred in a little town nearby, BAMC prepared ten operating rooms and called in thirty surgeons and physicians from various departments to help. The patients came in two waves and were taken immediately to the operating room or were treated in the trauma bay. All the victims who came to BAMC survived.

Edwards, whose experience included seven deployments to combat zones, told *USA Today* about his experience treating ten wounded soldiers with limited resources as part of an Army Forward Surgical Team. This time, he said, he had the staff and supplies he needed to save lives, but he couldn't come to terms with the circumstance.

"I've taken care of the same kind of injuries in combat that we had to see here, but these are volunteers wearing body armor and they get shot like this," Edwards said. "To have to take care of civilians who are sitting in church? Old ladies? I don't know where we've gone as a society that it's gone like that."

Although the trauma center at University Hospital had successfully completed the mass casualty drill earlier in the year, most of the staff had never treated victims from an actual mass shooting. Eight patients, five adults and three children, arrived within the hour. Many were bleeding from multiple gunshot wounds. Others had bullet fragments lodged in their bodies. One child had been trampled.

The first to arrive was Ryland Ward, his arms and legs tied with tourniquets to stop the bleeding. The pale five-year-old resembled a limp rag doll, make-do cords holding together a toy that had been torn and ill-used.

The little boy's femur was broken, bullet fragments were buried in his abdomen, and a blood vessel in his arm had been severed. He was confused, struggling to understand where he was and what had happened.

Dr. Lillian Liao, director of the pediatric and burn program, worked for hours to repair the severed blood vessel in Ryland's arm. Another doctor treated his abdominal injuries. When they finished, Liao left the boy with an orthopedic surgeon who tended to his broken leg while she went to check on two other pediatric patients.

Ryland's seven-year-old stepsister, Emily Garcia, arrived with severe abdominal injuries. "She was very unstable," Dr. Ronald Stewart, director of trauma at the hospital, told *USA Today*. Stewart rushed to help with the girl's surgery after coordinating the arrival of patients.

"When I went to the operating room, it was clear that the probability of her survival was low," he said, "but we have patients who survive all of the time with a low probability of survival, so I think we were focused on doing everything we could to fix her problems."

When Liao checked on the seven-year-old girl, Stewart asked her to scrub in and take the lead so he could speak with the girl's father and relatives. By then, the surgical team had exhausted nearly all treatment options.

"When you have a patient on the table—it doesn't matter if it's a kid or an elderly person or a young person who is dying in front of you—it's hard not to think about the fact that they're going to die," Liao told *USA Today*. "You then have to step back and run through all of the steps, to be sure that there's nothing else I can do for this person."

There was nothing else. After hours of surgery, unit after unit of blood, and multiple resuscitation attempts, the little girl who idolized the Tejano entertainer Selena, was dead of gunshot wounds. Like her idol.

Emily was the only person from the church to die at a hospital. Her stepsister Brooke, a five-year-old who dreamed of dancing onstage as a ballerina, who danced in the aisle at church, had died in her mother's arms.

Gunny Macias, shot five times and near death, was one of the first adults to arrive at BAMC. He was put in a medically induced coma to help his body recover from the extensive surgeries and to stop the hemorrhages. Months later, he would be one of the last patients to leave the hospital.

BAMC doctors told David Colbath that bullets were falling out of him as they performed surgery. They rebuilt his arm during the initial surgery, repaired damage during multiple surgeries in the first few days, and left lodged in his side the bullet that hit a rib in front of his heart. In the months to come, he would work to rehabilitate alongside wounded combat veterans.

The first task for doctors treating Kris Workman, the praise team leader, was to stop the bleeding, before sending him into surgery to resect his small intestines. He was placed in an induced coma, as doctors prepared for spinal surgery later in the week. He would eventually undergo five surgeries and weeks of therapy.

Dr. Liao was one of several trauma surgeons who attempted to explain to the *New York Times* the devastation assault rifles cause to the human body. She was initially clinical, the reporters said, as she described what the Sutherland Springs wounds had done. "Muscles and skin and fat surrounding skin can be sheared off," she said. "We saw holes in intestines and bladders."

Then, the reporters asked her about the emotional impact of the killings, and she said she thought she had moved on. "Then came the Parkland shootings," they wrote, "and the horror came flooding back."

"The tissue destruction is almost unimaginable," said Dr. Jeremy Cannon, who served with the Air Force in Iraq and Afghanistan. "Bones are exploded, soft tissue is absolutely destroyed. The injuries to the chest or abdomen—it's like a bomb went off."

Dr. Martin Schreiber, a trauma surgeon with the Oregon Health & Science University, was an Army reservist who served in Iraq in 2005 and in Afghanistan in 2010 and 2014. "What makes injuries from these rifles so deadly," he told the *Times*, "is that the bullets travel so fast. Those from an M16 or AR-15 can depart the muzzle at a velocity of more than 3,000 feet per second, while bullets from many common handguns move at less than half or a third that speed."

The result, Schreiber explained, is that "the energy imparted to a human body by a high-velocity weapon is exponentially greater than that from a handgun. You will see multiple organs shattered. The exit wounds can be a foot wide. I've seen people with entire quadrants of their abdomens destroyed."

Dr. Jeffrey Kerby of the University of Alabama at Birmingham was formerly an Air Force surgeon. He told the *Times* he never forgot the first victim of a high-velocity bullet wound he treated when he was serving in the southern Philippines. The soldier had been shot in the outer thigh, and Kerby's first thought was that the wound did not look so bad. There was just a tiny hole where the bullet went in. Then he looked where the bullet had exited. The man's inner thigh, he said, "was completely blown out."

As Kerby explained, the high-energy bullet creates a blast wave around the bullet. The bullet starts tumbling, causing even more destruction.

"Organs are damaged, blood vessels rip and many victims bleed to death before they reach a hospital," the *Times* reported.

Here's another description, from *Rolling Stone* writer Tim Dickinson: "The AR-15 assault rifle was engineered to create what one of its designers called 'maximum wound effect.' Its tiny bullets—needle-nosed and weighing less than four grams—travel nearly three times the speed of sound. As the bullet strikes the body, the payload of kinetic energy rips open a cavity inside the flesh—essentially inert space—which collapses back on itself, destroying inelastic tissue, including nerves, blood vessels, and vital organs."

Dickinson quotes another trauma surgeon, Dr. Peter Rhee, a retired Navy captain: "It's a perfect killing machine."

The surgeons' descriptions make it easier to understand why Emily Garcia's life could not be saved, and even harder to understand how her brother Ryland's life could.

The little boy would eventually undergo two dozen surgeries to repair injuries to his arm, leg, pelvis, and abdominal organs. He would undergo hours and hours of intensive physical and occupational therapy to help him regain the use of his left arm and leg. And he would meet with a child psychiatrist, who helped him process his ordeal. He would be in the hospital for two months.

"It literally took an entire hospital system to save his life," Dr. Liao told the *San Antonio Express-News*.

Chapter Eleven

"We are the remnant."

WHEN THE SUN CAME up on Monday morning, Frank and Sherri Pomeroy folded up the pallet they had slept on at their son's house and drove the thirty miles to Sutherland Springs. Whatever misgivings they had about the future of the First Baptist Church, whatever aching need they felt to grieve the loss of their daughter—not to mention arrange her funeral—it was distressingly obvious as they pulled into the church parking lot that their broken community needed them as never before. Twenty-five friends and loved ones had lost their lives the day before, twenty-six counting Crystal Holcombe's unborn child; they needed help and consolation. A pastor who knew and cared about those broken people needed to preach their funerals. Twenty of their friends and loved ones were in area hospitals, some still fighting for their lives; they needed visiting and their families needed consoling. One victim remained unidentified, her wounds so destructive no one recognized her. Frank had to perform that heartbreaking task when he arrived at the church. He recognized Joann Ward by the tattoos on her body.

On a sunny Monday morning, with reporters from around the world thrusting microphones and cameras into the faces of the grieving couple, clamoring for their attention, and angling for the shot that best captured their sorrow, Frank held a press conference in front of the church. Days later, he barely remembered what he said, but he did remember that an extremely tall black man, impeccably dressed, had slipped under the police tape and stood with him and Sherri. To Frank, he looked African he was so black; no one seemed to know who he was.

"It was amazing to me," Frank recalled. "He prayed with us. He told us, 'I know you don't know what's going on right now, but whatever you do, you have to lift Christ. You have to lift Christ.'"

As the mysterious visitor spoke in a voice so quiet only he and Sherri heard, Frank glanced down at the man's black dress shoes. They were polished to such a high sheen, they looked like patent leather. And then, in the chaos and clamor of that morning, the man disappeared, faded into the crowd. Had he come from God? Frank wondered. Was he some kind of angel?

Although the Pomeroys didn't get his name, a photo exists of him embracing them both. He was Dimas Salaberrios, a former drug dealer turned pastor and street preacher for a church in the South Bronx. In the photo, the tall, slender man from the Bronx wears a black suit, black tie, and crisp white shirt.

"I made a commitment," Salaberrios told reporters, "that if there's a church shooting and I can get there, I'm going to go. We did this with the Emanuel Nine," he said, referring to the Charleston church massacre in 2015.

"The pastor's faith and his wife are incredible," Salaberrios said. "He is a true shepherd. Pastor Frank is focusing totally on ministering to others. But we all know that if we don't lift him up in prayer there's going to be a point where he cannot escape the reality that he lost his daughter and he lost a beloved congregation."

Frank spoke briefly to the massive media gathering. "We had a long night with our children and grandbabies we have left," he said. "I don't understand, but I know my God does." His voice broke as he introduced Sherri, still wearing the red shorts and white top she had on when she had left Florida the day before.

"Frank and I want to say thank you to all the outpouring of love for our family from family friends and complete strangers," she said, her girlish voice strong. "I especially wanted to say thank you to American Airlines, who took great care of me all the way from Florida, and my angel flight buddy, Chris, wherever you are. News media have been bombarding us with requests to share and comment and appear to celebrate Annabelle's life; however, as much tragedy as that entails for our family, we don't want to overshadow the other lives lost yesterday.

"We lost more than Belle yesterday," she continued. "One thing that gives me a sliver of encouragement is the fact that Belle was surrounded yesterday by her church family that she loved fiercely, and vice versa. Our church was not comprised of members or parishioners; we were a very close family. We ate together, we laughed together, we cried together and worshiped together. Now most of our church family is gone, our building probably beyond repair and the few of us that are left behind lost tragically yesterday. As senseless as this tragedy was, our sweet Belle would not have been able to deal with losing so much family yesterday. Please don't forget Sutherland Springs. Thank you."

The Pomeroys needed time and space to grieve, but Frank was still pastoring a church that also needed time to heal, with his help. Two of Frank's closest preacher friends understood that. Kevin Cornelius, pastor of the Baptist church in nearby Karnes City, and Mark Collins, Frank's predecessor at First Baptist, dropped what they were doing and devoted themselves to easing their friend's almost unbearable burden. For the next several weeks, they became his chauffeurs, media spokesmen, and secretaries, responding to hundreds of messages, calls, and texts daily.

"I was just so busy," Frank recalled later. "The kids felt like they lost Sherri and me—Sherri emotionally and me physically. I was blessed to have Kevin and Mark beside me. There was so much that had to be handled that I wasn't capable of handling."

Among numerous chores and obligations, the two pastors helped him deal with elected officials who wanted to demonstrate their concern beyond the ritualistic "thoughts and prayers." Governor Greg Abbott was one. He visited with Kris Workman, a visit that took the nearly sixty-year-old governor back to the day when he lost the use of his legs at age twenty-six.

"When I entered the room I saw Kris on the bed to my left with all types of medical devices and equipment in his body, and his mother was on the right in a semi-inconsolable state, completely uncertain about what future was ahead for her son, who was now in this condition," he said. "Having seen my own mom in that very same situation, decades ago, I knew once again I needed to summon some way to provide a sense of hope to Julie Workman for her son. Knowing that her son had been injured like I had, the only thing I could think of was to tell Julie it is great to come and get to meet a young man who may be a future governor of the great state of Texas."

Months later, the Workmans would tape a poignant political ad in support of Abbott's reelection. (He didn't need the ad to trounce his Democratic opponent, Dallas County's lesbian Hispanic sheriff, Lupe Valdez.)

Vice President Mike Pence and his wife, Karen, visited patients at BAMC and then stopped by the church, where the vice president described talking with several survivors. "We just met Gunny Macias, who is recovering from serious injuries, shot five times," he said. "But I was told despite his injuries that Marine stood up and was triaging the scene, barking out orders. And we think of Joann Ward, who laid down her life shielding her children, ultimately saving her son."

So many people came to see David Colbath the first couple of nights—including the Pences and Governor Abbott—that visitors had to wait in line in the hallway. "It was an amazing experience," Colbath recalled, "but I wanted them to see God, a part of God when they walked in, not just see David. I didn't want them to think that I was helpless and hapless but that I was blessed and happy."

Frank's own visit to David and others lifted him up as much as it did those who were fighting to recover. "To a one, they said they felt joy," he recalled. "They said they felt privileged to suffer for His sake."

Kris Workman told him, "I can't wait to see the new normal the Lord has in store for me."

"That snapped Frank out of it," Collins recalled. "We were walking out of the hospital about midnight Tuesday night, and he said to me, 'You know, we still have a church.'"

"Every one of the people that I spoke to that day I went to encourage them was excited and could not wait to express to me how they could not wait to get out and share how blessed it was to be persecuted in the name of the Lord," Frank said.

"We are the remnant," he told Collins, borrowing a venerable word from Old Testament prophets referring to Jews who returned to Israel from Babylonian captivity. "We have to go on," he said.

The church had lost most of its leadership team, so most major decisions were on Frank's shoulders, including what to do about the battle-scarred old building, a sanctuary invaded and violated in the most grievous way imaginable. His initial response was to tear it down. There was history in that humble, little building, to be sure, but he just couldn't imagine spending time in a room where his daughter had been shot to death, where so many of his friends and loved ones had lost their lives. He toyed with the idea of razing the building and replacing it with a prayer garden.

Other communities that had become mass shooting sites had confronted the same vexing question. After the shooting at Columbine High School in 1999, parents, students, and administrators considered tearing down the modern building but ultimately decided on extensive remodeling. A one-room Amish schoolhouse near Lancaster, Pennsylvania, was torn down in 2006 after a gunman took children hostage and shot and killed five girls, ages six to thirteen. In Newtown, Connecticut, Sandy Hook Elementary also was torn down after a gunman killed twenty children and six adults inside the school. A new school was built on the same site.

Every time Frank talked to reporters, the fate of the sanctuary was surely one of the questions. "They were just driving him crazy," Collins recalled.

Collins is a tall, former basketball player in his late fifties who wears his long, gray hair gathered in a ponytail. He resembles images of George Washington, and the Father of the Country has, in fact, become his alter ego. He has played Washington in a National Geographic Channel miniseries and a Discovery Channel miniseries and has appeared as Washington at Mount Vernon and Williamsburg and at various political gatherings. His business card shows his face next to a plaster mask of the first president, made when Washington was fifty-three. They look identical.

Collins's Yorktown board of deacons also had driven over to Sutherland Springs and then to San Antonio that Sunday afternoon. Six of the nine are retired military and, with their wives, were able to get inside security-conscious BAMC and find out the status of the Sutherland Springs patients. "It was amazing," Collins recalled. "They came back with the best information."

That evening the chairman of the board of deacons found Collins at the Community Building and called him aside. "We just had a meeting," the deacon said, "and we want you to know you're fired."

For a split second Collins was taken aback—until the deacon added, "You have no responsibilities in Yorktown until Frank doesn't need you anymore."

The Yorktown youth pastor took over his pulpit and pastoral duties, and Collins spent most of the next six weeks in Sutherland Springs. On Monday, a day spent helping shield Sherri Pomeroy from intrusive reporters, squiring around Senator Ted Cruz, and visiting hospitals with Frank, the tall, angular preacher slept at the church on three squishy beanbag chairs he pulled together in the toddlers' room. "I was so tired, I slept really well," he recalled (perhaps channeling General Washington at Valley Forge).

After visiting hospitals again on Tuesday, he drove home to Yorktown, arriving about one a.m. Wednesday morning. He got out of his church clothes, showered, and set his alarm clock for seven thirty. Kneeling beside the bed, he asked God for wisdom, for discernment, so that Frank would know what to do about the sanctuary. "Show us a way out of this mess," he prayed.

At about four thirty in the dark of night, a vision of sorts jarred him out of his deep sleep. Someone was walking him through the unscathed front doors of the violated sanctuary, but it was a sanctuary transformed into a vision of white. The walls, the floors, and the ceiling were stark white. Twenty-six white folding chairs indicated where in the sanctuary the members who lost their lives had been sitting, a long-stemmed red rose on each chair.

"It was just as real as if I was walking through the church," he recalled. "It's the only time in my life something surreal like that has happened."

The next morning Collins told Frank what he had in mind. The FBI, its investigation completed, had turned over the sanctuary to Frank and the elders the night before. Blood was still everywhere.

"I'm having trouble seeing it," Frank said, "but I trust you, you're the artistic one. Let's do it."

Collins called Brad Beldon, CEO of a San Antonio–based construction company, and told him what he envisioned. "Consider it done," Beldon said.

A paint company in New Braunfels and a general contractor in Dallas both were eager to help. A Beldon employee found twenty-six chairs that met Collins's vision specifications at an Ikea in Round Rock, Texas, a hundred miles north of Sutherland Springs. A San Antonio calligrapher agreed to paint twenty-six names on the twenty-six chairs. Her hue of choice was a pale gold.

As Collins imagined the redeemed space, each white chair would carry the name of one of the shooting victims on the front and a red cross on the back. Visitors walking through the main doors at the back of the church would see the red crosses against the white backdrop, and the crosses would seem to be floating.

The crime scene became a construction site; the room would have to be almost totally rebuilt. Workers carried out bullet-riddled pews, ripped apart splintered walls, tore out blood-stained carpet, and replaced damaged ceiling tile. A biohazard team came in and completely cleaned the sanctuary.

The volunteer construction crew—as many as thirty men and women plus a Red Cross crew providing refreshments—filled in the bullet holes in the outside wall, replaced the bullet-riddled wooden front doors with new doors and the broken colored window panes with translucent vinyl tiles resembling those still intact. They refreshed the weathered, old building with a coat of white paint.

Collins was pleased to see that a large wooden cross that stood to one side of the altar was unscathed, as was a family Bible owned by Dr. John Sutherland Jr., the early settler and community namesake. A recording of Scripture readings from past services played on a loop.

Once the walls were replaced and the carpet and pews removed, the crew painted everything in the room—walls, floor, ceiling, and altar—a glossy white. Collins's vision had become reality. In the days to come, some would call it a vision of heaven; others, a minimalist art installation.

Collins invited John Holcombe to come in and see the transformation.

"Does this honor God and the people who died, John?" he asked. "Is there anything you think needs to be changed?"

Words failed the quiet man whose loss was immeasurable. He simply stared at the stark-white space and shook his head no. Nothing else was needed.

The sanctuary was ready for visitors the Sunday after the shooting. Collins was pleased. It looked exactly like his dream, he said.

Meanwhile, shocked and grieving families all over Wilson County—the Bradens, the Johnsons, the Wards, the Marshalls, the Rodriguezes—were laying their loved ones to rest. Floresville funeral director Gail Uhlig arranged nineteen funerals within a week.

One of her first tasks was to find forty-two pallbearers and seven hearses for the combined Holcombe family funeral. Ten members of the family, including an unborn child and three youngsters, would be commemorated. Uhlig knew the pallbearers would be distraught; she had to give them something to do to feel useful, to get them involved in the service.

"The last thing they could do for that child," she explained, "was to carry that child to his final resting place. This was part of the healing process. These were uncles, cousins, friends." (She, too, was related by marriage.)

The thousand-seat Floresville Event Center on the edge of town was filled to capacity that weekday morning. As friends, relatives, neighbors, and strangers settled into their seats, they looked toward colorful caskets—red, blue, purple—lined up before a stage overflowing with floral arrangements. It was quiet inside the cavernous building.

Eighty-six-year-old Joe "Papa" Holcombe walked slowly to the microphone to open the service with a prayer. The retired teacher, a mentor to many, was known throughout the county, as was his wife, Clarice, also a retired teacher.

"This is a blessing, because these people are home with You now," he prayed, the caskets bearing the remains of his son, daughter-in-law, grandson, pregnant granddaughter-in-law, and four great-grandchildren arrayed before him. "They are receiving the rewards that they deserve."

The family patriarch also prayed for the family of Devin Patrick Kelley, no doubt raising eyebrows under bowed heads. The twenty-six-year-old who took his life after killing so many others had been cremated a few days earlier.

"If we can't forgive this person that's done all of this evil, God can't forgive us," Joe Holcombe said. "We hold nothing against the shooter. He is also getting his reward."

Throughout the two-hour service, relatives read the favorite Bible passages of their loved ones. They played songs and showed photographs of the boisterous extended family. Throughout the service those in attendance were reminded to lean on their faith—"the best way to honor these saints lying before you," Pastor Frank reminded them.

"Neither of my parents were afraid to die," Sarah Slavin told the audience, adding that her parents had spoken to her before about dying. "They both thought it was worth it to further the kingdom of God."

Sarah also spoke about Tara McNulty, thirty-three, who had lost her own parents at age ten and had come to live with the Holcombe family. She and Tara became close friends—like sisters, Sarah said.

Danny Holcombe's coworkers recalled the kindness and generosity of the thirty-seven-year-old jack-of-all-trades. They noted his deep love for Jenni and Noah Grace.

Audience members laughed as friends recalled the Holcombes' legendary Christmas gift exchange, where holiday wrappings might conceal a scratched-off losing lottery ticket or an expired can of sardines. The laughter quieted as John Holcombe stepped to the microphone.

A big man in his early forties with thinning brown hair and a close-cropped beard, John is soft-spoken, reserved. Unlike his father, who loved to share his faith with friends and fellow church members—not to mention a corny song or a good joke—John was content on Sunday mornings to stay behind the video camera at the rear of the sanctuary. As he stood at the mic, gathering himself for the task ahead, members of the large audience were no doubt praying that God would give him strength.

In a quiet voice, he opened his Bible and read Scripture for his wife, unborn child, and his three stepchildren, and then he began sketching verbal portraits of the loved ones he had lost forever just a few days before.

His voice catching, he told his listeners that Crystal was so good at bringing plants back to life that he only bought her wilted ones at the nursery. He knew they would thrive under her care. She looked after the family vegetable garden and her homeschooled children. She looked after him.

"She could take a broken man like me and make me whole again," he said softly.

With the hint of an embarrassed smile on his face, he recalled how in 2011, as male suitors hovered near a widowed Crystal at church— her husband, Peter Hill, had died of a heart attack at age thirty, six years earlier—women in the congregation would sidle up and urge him to go sit with her and her children. They wanted him "to shield her" from the others. He wasn't quite ready for five stepchildren, he said, but gradually he began to realize that they all were becoming inseparable.

The couple wed in 2012 in a ceremony after Easter Sunday services. It didn't take long for John to become a second father to Crystal's children.

He told his rapt audience about nine-year-old Megan Hill, who loved drawing and karate and cats. He recalled how she had trouble saying the letter r; he loved hearing her pronounce the name of her cat, Pur-Pur. He called her "Megacute," explaining that "if there was one word you had to use to describe Megan, it was cute."

Eleven-year-old Emily Hill, he said, also enjoyed karate. She had been perfecting magic tricks and recently had won third prize in a cooking contest for her quesadillas.

At home John might glance outside and see thirteen-year-old Greg Hill in the midst of a solitary sword fight, using a stick for his slashing sword. The youngster loved Star Wars, video games, cooking, and karate. "He had an incredible imagination," John said.

The day Crystal learned she was pregnant, the couple found a six-toed kitten with a broken tail, diarrhea, and ringworm. Crystal, ever the healer, managed to nurse the little creature back to health, John said. Of course, she and the kids also developed ringworm.

The new baby was a surprise, John said, but the whole family could hardly wait for its April arrival. If the kids had their way, they'd call the new baby Billy Bob. Crystal and John passed on Billy Bob, agreeing instead on Carlyn for a girl or Carline for a boy. At eighteen weeks old, the baby was killed before they knew the gender, so John settled on "Carlin Brite." Carlin, he explained, meant "small champion" and was similar to Karla, his mother's name. Brite, he said, was the last name of Crystal's grandparents.

As the service continued, funeral director Uhlig recalled the numerous distraught family members—Holcombes and others—who had begged her for the opportunity to see their loved ones one last time. "Just let me touch their hands," they would ask. She had to gently and firmly tell them no.

Earlier in the week Uhlig had asked John Holcombe if there was anything in particular he needed for the upcoming funeral service. First Baptist had just conducted its first worship service after the shooting—in a large tent on the Sutherland Springs baseball field. Uhlig noticed him standing alone on the field after the service.

"I need the bagpipes," he told her. "Dad told me, 'You're not going to need them for a long time, but we want the bagpipes to play at my funeral.'"

Uhlig arranged for a twelve-member bagpipe group from San Antonio to play at the funeral. The leader of San Antonio Pipes and Drums was distantly related to Dr. John Sutherland, and the group had played a few weeks earlier at the annual Old Town Sutherland Springs celebration. The keening bagpipe rendition of "Amazing Grace" filled the auditorium, while pallbearers slowly rolled the caskets out of the building to a convoy of white hearses waiting to take the victims to a private burial.

"It was the longest performance of 'Amazing Grace' I've ever heard," Uhlig recalled. "The bagpipers played it through the whole casket procession."

All around the county, through tears and through laughter, people were mourning, remembering. They told stories over coffee at the Valero station, at the big H-E-B in La Vernia when they ran into a neighbor, at school waiting to pick up their kids, at receptions after funerals. So many funerals.

"She was bold," Terrie Smith recalled, talking about Joann Ward, the dark-haired young woman she thought of as her daughter. "You had to get to know her, but once you were in her heart, there was nothing holding Joann back.

"She'd have these ridiculous garage sales now and then. Her dad got ill with cancer. Her and her daddy were very, very close. She sold stuff and held benefits. He died two months later."

"My mother loved life to the fullest," Michelle Shields said at Lula White's funeral. "She was a clown."

Family members talked about how she loved the Gulf Coast, how she loved sitting in her beach chair in the water and taking the grandkids fishing. She loved dancing to oldies music, loved playing Mexican Train dominoes, pinochle, canasta.

"Her husband was sick for ten years and she was devoted to him," Michelle said. "He had congestive heart failure ten or fifteen times. She'd do anything for you."

She died trying to save the life of a young girl who loved her.

"She was funny. She was tough. She always had some smart-ass comment. She picked on people," said Kati Wall, talking about Sara Johnson, the grandmother who adopted her, the grandmother Kati thought for years was her mother. "She took care of everybody."

She always carried a pocketknife, Kati recalled. When she picked up the occasional hitchhiker, she kept the knife on the car seat under her thigh. She also carried a .38 Special. "If there was a noise outside at night, she's the one who would go out to investigate in her nightgown."

In La Vernia they buried Bob and Shani Corrigan, Michigan natives who settled in South Texas after Bob retired from the Air Force. The Corrigans traveled widely and had three sons during Bob's thirty-year military career. One of their sons, twenty-five-year-old Scott, had committed suicide a year earlier. Their two surviving sons were active-duty military.

One of their last tours was Offutt Air Force Base (AFB) in Nebraska, where Bob was superintendent of the 55th Medical Group.

"This hits a little too close to home for me. Airman Robert Corrigan reported to Wurtsmith AFB (Michigan) as his first duty station and was assigned to the obstetrical unit. I was his charge nurse," Jeanette Sunie Splonskowski wrote on Facebook. "He was 51. My heart is breaking."

"He was one of those rare souls who sincerely cared about the people he worked with," Cecilia Shifflett wrote, adding, "Chief, please look down from the heavens and know you and your wife are honored, respected and truly missed."

"He was a Yankee country boy," said Sherry Kay, a cousin who grew up with both Corrigans in Michigan. "He grew up on Johnny Cash in Michigan." Shani, she said, "was a bubbly character, always animated."

In a small brick church in La Vernia, Frank and Sherri Pomeroy and their extended family commemorated the life of "our brave child," Annabelle Renee Pomeroy. They reminded each other that she loved animals. That she was learning sign language. That she had a friend at school who was blind.

She was laid to rest in the country cemetery outside Sutherland Springs. The cemetery director told Frank no one wanted the grave site in a corner overlooking a duck pond, a place where cows from an adjacent farm occasionally congregated just across the wire fence.

"That's because God was saving it for Annabelle," Frank said he told the man. It was where she would go when she accompanied her father as he conducted graveside rites. After her burial, when he dropped by to trim the grass or replace the flowers, he sat on a small bench and watched ducks waddle into the pond, cows and calves amble over. He thought about her love of animals.

In Floresville two days after the Pomeroys buried their daughter, they watched the procession of caskets bearing the Holcombes being loaded into the hearses. "These are some of my best friends," Frank commented. "They were living for the Lord. Now, they are jumping and leaping and praising God."

Chapter Twelve

"Without faith, I don't know
how anyone makes it."

IN HIS CLASSIC *The Faith of a Heretic,* the late philosopher and theologian Walter Kaufmann offers a quick tour through recorded history and religious thought as he explores humankind's struggle to resolve the age-old problem of suffering. He offers three "pseudo-solutions" that various religious traditions and belief systems have proposed through the ages. One involves "asserting, in flat defiance of experience, that everybody gets precisely what he deserves—no better and no worse: if Anne Frank suffered more than Heinrich Himmler, that proves that she was much more wicked."

The notion is shocking, of course, but no more shocking—or bewildering—than what happened at Sutherland Springs, Texas, on an autumn Sunday morning in 2017. As Kaufmann points out, all attempts at explanation by questing, yearning humankind are inadequate (for people of faith and for everyone else). They're inadequate, he notes, "unless either the traditional belief in God's boundless power or the belief in his perfect justice and mercy is abandoned. Short of that, only pseudo-solutions are possible."

The other "pseudo-solutions" are no more adequate than the third, Kaufmann maintains. One involves a belief in the existence of some sort of evil deity, created by God, who has the power and inclination to resist his creator's goodness. The Bible calls him Satan, which, as Kaufmann notes, literally means accuser or slanderer.

Yet another involves the belief that the soul lives on after death without a body and retains some sort of consciousness. A variation on the immortality of the soul is that our bodies will be resurrected in the unforeseeable future, and we will come back to life to be judged by a just God who rules the universe.

"What matters in the present context," Kaufmann concludes, "is that no doctrine of immortality or resurrection can solve the problem of suffering. Suppose that Anne Frank enjoys eternal bliss in heaven: should an omnipotent god have found it impossible to let her have eternal bliss without first making her a victim of the Nazis and without having her die in a concentration camp? If you treat a child unfairly, it may possibly forget about it if you afterward give it a lollipop, but injustice remains injustice. Faith in immortality, like belief in Satan, leaves unanswered the ancient questions: Is God unable to prevent suffering and thus not willing to prevent it and thus not merciful? And is he just?"

Kaufmann offers one more solution—also spurious, he contends. This fourth explanation rests on the notion that suffering is a necessary component of free will. According to Augustine and most other early Christian theologians, God created man with the ability to do what he pleased, to choose his own course, but man, like a rebellious teenager, misused his free will. His disobedience made suffering inevitable.

Kaufmann dissents. If suffering is "the inevitable consequence of Adam's sin—or if this is the price God had to pay for endowing man with free will—then it makes no sense to call him omnipotent. And if he was willing to pay this price for his own greater glory, as some Christian theologians have suggested, or for the greater beauty of the cosmos, because shadows are needed to set off highlights, as some Christian philosophers have argued, what sense does it make to attribute moral perfection to him?"

In the wake of excruciating tragedy in their midst, the people of Sutherland Springs were not—as far as I know—pondering Zoroaster and the religion of Egypt, Plato and the poem of Job, or Nietzsche and Nathanael West's novella *Miss Lonelyhearts,* as did Kaufmann in the chapter of his book entitled "Suffering and the Bible." Still, their suffering and their soul searching were nothing if not profound—and profoundly in the tradition of humankind's age-old dilemma. They distilled the ancient existential questions into one agonizing word, the word long-suffering Job uttered in the midst of his inexplicable agony: Why? Their answer—or rather their un-answer—could be distilled into one word, as well: Trust.

In the months following the massacre, I don't know how many times I heard, in sermons, prayers, and supplications, in interviews and conversations, some version of the following: We don't know why it happened, but we trust that God has a plan, and someday we'll understand. A plan. A story. A dance, of sorts, "choreographed." Those were the images that seemed to offer comfort to the survivors.

At first, I found it incredible, almost infuriating, that a young woman who had watched the life drain out of her child could tell me, calmly, that she believed in a God who willed—or allowed—such a terrible thing to happen. And that she placed her trust in that God.

I suppose I expected her—and everyone else who expressed such benign acceptance—to be angry. Angry at God. Angry at the shooter. Angry at society. Angry at somebody or something. Angry enough to take action so that something so horrendous never happened again. But they weren't angry. Or at least they didn't profess to be.

And yet who was I to question the depth and sincerity of their belief— and their grief? I could only listen and try to understand.

So, what would have happened if members of an upscale Protestant church—say All Saints Episcopal Church in Austin, the historic church near the university—experienced a mass shooting? That was my question for Greg Garrett, a novelist, religion professor at Baylor University, and lay Episcopal minister.

The response would have been similar, he said, although the metaphors might have been more sophisticated, not so literal. Hope is the bedrock, the essence of the Christian faith, he pointed out, expressed in multitudinous ways.

In addition to several novels, Garrett is also the author of *Entertaining Judgment: The Afterlife in Popular Imagination*. One passage in particular about how Christians portray heaven seemed pertinent to the Sutherland Springs tragedy.

"Human beings long for the beauty manifested in paradise, but we also seek safety and security, another iteration of heaven that appears in this longing. We live in a world in which airplanes can be crashed into skyscrapers and tsunamis can kill thousands, a world where a deranged man can walk into a school or a movie theater and open fire, or an explosion in a fertilizer plant can level a town. In such a world, not even faith can make us feel safe. The desires to keep and bear arms, to hoard possessions, to keep ourselves and those we love from harm are expressions of our desire for sanctuary, and are as strong as our desires to eat, pray, and love."

We paint pictures, using the palette and the brushes we've been given. We imagine. We create. Or we surrender. Mute surrender to the mystery was the response of the philosopher Nicholas Wolterstorff to the loss of an adult son in a skiing accident.

"I did not shy away from taking note of the gaping void in me that his death caused," he writes in an article about his book, *Lament for a Son.* "I did not shy away from voicing my lament over his death. But I could not bring myself to try to figure out what God was up to in Eric's death. I joined the psalmist in lamenting without explaining. Things have gone awry in God's world. I do not understand why, nor do I understand why God puts up with it for so long. Rather than Eric's death evoking in me an interest in theodicy, it had the effect of making God more mysterious. I live with the mystery."

His loss and his anguish did not result in the loss of his faith. He did not give up on God, he reported. "When I consider the stupendous immensity and astonishing intricacy of the cosmos, and the miracle of human consciousness and intelligence, I find that I cannot believe it all just happened," he writes. "A being of incomprehensible wisdom, imagination, and power must have brought it about—or rather, is bringing it about. I have come to think of God as performing the cosmos. I look out the window of my study on this autumn day in western Michigan, at the deep blue sky and the gorgeous colors of the leaves. This is a brief but glorious passage in God's performance of the cosmos.

"The words wisdom, imagination, and power do not describe; they point. They're the best we can do. Something like our wisdom, something like our imagination, something like our power—yet infinitely beyond. The God who became more mysterious to me has also become more awesome, awesome beyond comprehension."

The people of Sutherland Springs, people who suffered loss beyond imagining, would likely say "Amen."

"Without faith, I don't know how anyone makes it," Sherri Pomeroy said on a weekday morning at her personal sanctuary, the church fellowship hall. She was keeping busy, on this day helping prepare lunch for a group of Michigan teenagers who had come to Sutherland Springs to build ramps for the disabled, install skirting on mobile homes, and remodel houses for church members with long-term injuries. Keeping busy, I've heard her say several times, is her way of coping with unbearable sorrow, despite her faith.

"You have to be strong enough to believe truth," she said, laying out rows of cookie dough on a baking pan, the dollops of moist dough studded with dark-brown chocolate chips.

I could believe in Sherri's chocolate chip cookies. The fragrance as they came out of the oven was tantalizing (and they tasted even better than they smelled). I had trouble with the intangibles that manifested themselves in the kitchen that morning—hope, yearning, an unyielding faith that shaped the lives of church members.

"God was right there," Julie Workman told me one morning after church. "You just had to open your eyes and look for him." With her own eyes wide open, she saw her adult son instantly paralyzed. She saw children she had known and loved since their birth, children she had taught in Sunday school—she saw them disintegrate.

"Yes, it sounds horrible," she added. "Twenty-six people lost their lives that day. No! Twenty-six people went home to Jesus."

"I don't like calling it a tragedy, because so much good has come of it," Julie's son Kris told me. As we talked, the sturdy young man with the close-cropped beard sat in a wheelchair. Behind us was the wooden ramp constructed for him and others who were no longer able to negotiate stairs and steps.

"I came to realize," he added, "that life is fragile. We at the church know that with a bit more intimacy. We have to have faith in God. We have to love each other and to realize that we are all broken people."

Any regrets? I asked.

"I guess, not being able to run and play with my daughter," he said. (Eevee was three at the time.)

"We had a contingency plan at Sutherland Springs," Pastor Frank told James Dobson on Dobson's nationally syndicated radio show *Family Talk*. The plan, he said, relied on church members who were concealed carry holders. Rod Green was one of those concealed carry holders who got to church late that morning. "We are not going to let evil interrupt our faith," he said. "We will not bow down to it."

"I'm okay," Jenni Holcombe told me, seven months after losing her husband and their little girl. "Danny and Noah are gone, but I know where they are. I walked out of that building that morning, because God needed me here. The hope we have is the big thing that keeps us going. This isn't permanent. We know that we'll see our family again. Maybe we can help someone else."

"Satan got thrown out of heaven once," David Colbath told his class one Thursday evening, channeling Dante. "If he tries to get back in, God can throw him out again. It's like watching a movie. I don't know all the stuff in the middle, but I know how it's going to end. I know that I know that I know."

"These twenty-six are more alive today than they were before November fifth," Mark Collins told a crowd gathered under a big white tent on the six-month anniversary of the shooting. "They're dancing in heaven. Second Corinthians chapter five, verse eight tells us that to be absent from the body is to be present with the Lord.... Those twenty-six are not that far away from us."

"God prepares us if we're aware," Julie Workman said. "He doesn't promise us streets of gold. It's how we respond that's important. I heard God tell me, 'This has nothing to do with you; it has everything to do with your response and whether you turn away from me.'"

"We lost a lot of good people here, a lot of people we loved, but we don't know God's plans," said Michelle Shields, the shooter's mother-in-law. "I think about how Karla Holcombe would walk the property [next door to the church] and pray that we could afford to buy it. And now, we're going to have a new church."

"The blood was shed here for a reason," funeral director Gail Uhlig told me as we sat at her kitchen table on a hot summer day. Her husband, Edward, was on his riding mower out front, cutting tall grass under a stand of post oaks. Her grandson sat on a couch in the den watching TV.

"I've already seen a lot of good works," she said. "The new building is going to serve Wilson County. The food pantry is going to be larger. We'll have a place for teenagers to go, couples having marital problems. We will see growth from this. We will always be on the map for this, but this building will be used."

As I was leaving, she had another thought she wanted to share about the mystery of God's handiwork. "All this didn't hit me until January," she said. That's when she got a call from one of her adult sons. They hadn't spoken in twenty-two years. She had never seen her two grandchildren. He called after the shooting to see if she was okay, and now they talk regularly. God moves, it seems, in mysterious ways.

Gail Uhlig and most Christians, despite their stabbing efforts to explain, interpret, or understand, ultimately live with the mystery. Some translate their belief into action.

Dave Cullen, the journalist who wrote the definitive book about the Columbine shooting, found the same sort of trust, confidence, and equanimity among evangelical parents coping with the shooting tragedy that befell them in 1999. Cullen quoted Lynn Duff, who was assisting families as a Red Cross volunteer.

"The way that those families reacted was markedly different," she told Cullen. "It was like a hundred and eighty degrees from where everybody else was. They were singing; they were praying; they were comforting the other parents, especially the parents of Isaiah Shoels [the only African American killed]. They were thinking a lot about the other parents, the other families, and responding a lot to other people's needs. They were definitely in pain, and you could see the pain in their eyes, but they were very confident of where their kids were. They were at peace with it. It was like they were a living example of their faith."

Duff, a liberal Jew from San Francisco, bore witness to belief and to experience lived—"belief incarnated," to borrow the words of theologian Sallie TeSelle (*Speaking in Parables*). It's belief in action that even non-believers can admire; Albert Schweitzer, Dietrich Bonhoeffer, Dorothy Day, and Martin Luther King Jr. come to mind. Most, of course, are anonymous, including an elderly married couple who drove to Sutherland Springs from their home in Upstate New York, where they are longtime members of an intentional Christian community called the Bruderhof. Renouncing private property and sharing everything in common according to the tenets of their faith, the couple came to Texas to volunteer their time, effort, and modest means. They ended up spending much of their weeks-long stay guiding visitors through the sanctuary transformed into a memorial.

The Bruderhof couple believe—and seek to live out their faith. So does Stephen Willeford, who wielded a gun that Sunday morning. So, too, do his fellow parishioners, who would shoot to kill, as well, if they thought it necessary to save lives. It's a difficult notion, a disconcerting notion.

Chapter Thirteen

"I'm not really mad at the
guy who did this."

ON A SUNNY OCTOBER morning in 1991, Dr. Suzanna Gratia, twenty-nine, left her chiropractic clinic in the small Central Texas town of Copperas Cove and picked up her parents, Al and Ursula Gratia, for lunch at Luby's Cafeteria in nearby Killeen, the larger of the two towns that border sprawling Fort Hood. She had just finished her meal—chicken tetrazzini, coconut cream pie, iced tea—when a Ford Ranger pickup seemed to explode through the front window of the cafeteria. Coming to a halt completely inside the building amid jagged sheets of shattered glass, toppled tables, and people sprawled on the floor, the truck was still gyrating up and down on its shock absorbers when Gratia suddenly heard a gunshot. The driver had stepped out of his truck and was firing a pistol. One of his first victims was a diner rushing over to see if the driver was injured and needed help.

Crouched with her parents behind their table, balanced precariously on its side, Gratia assumed they were witness to a particularly outrageous robbery in progress, something out of Hollywood—until she peeked over the top of the table and saw the shooter strolling from one person to the next, taking aim and pulling the trigger. Armed with two pistols, the gunman was calmly executing people. He circled the dining room several times, pausing only to reload.

As the gunman rounded the front of his truck, his right shoulder toward Gratia, she suddenly realized, "I've got him!" She reached for her purse on the floor, next to the splattered chicken tetrazzini. He was fifteen feet away. She had no doubt she could hit him with the small revolver she carried wherever she went. Then she realized: her gun wasn't in her purse. Aware of state law at the time that prohibited concealed weapons, she had tucked the weapon behind the passenger seat of her car; it was a hundred yards away from where she and her parents and dozens of other terrified diners were under siege. Get caught carrying a concealed weapon during a routine traffic stop, and she might lose her chiropractic license. That's what she was thinking. In a memoir published in 2010, Gratia called it "the stupidest decision of my life."

Facing inevitable death if someone didn't act, Al Gratia bravely rose to confront the shooter. His daughter and wife watched in horror as the seventy-one-year-old man immediately took a bullet to the chest and died instantly. Shortly afterward, Suzanna managed to flee through a broken window, thinking her mother was behind her. Instead, Ursula Gratia had crawled to her husband, looked up at the gunman, bowed her head, and took a bullet in the skull at point-blank range. "All women of Killeen and Belton are vipers!" the gunman shouted.

Al and Ursula (Suzy) Gratia were among twenty-three people who died that day. In ten minutes, the gunman shot fifty people, most of them women, out of approximately eighty in the cafeteria, before killing himself.

His name was Georges (George) Pierre Hennard, a thirty-five-year-old resident of nearby Belton. His mother was a housewife, his father an orthopedic surgeon who worked at various military hospitals, including White Sands Missile Range Army Base. Hennard grew up near the base in Las Cruces, New Mexico, and was known in high school as "completely introverted." Conforming to an evolving stereotype, he was a young, introverted white male who during childhood had been subjected to emotional abuse, if not worse, from his father. After graduating from high school, he joined the Navy and later served in the merchant marine, working chiefly in the Gulf of Mexico. His family had moved to Belton in 1980 when his father was assigned to Fort Hood.

Hennard was arrested for marijuana possession in 1981 and got his seaman's papers suspended the next year when he engaged in a racial quarrel with a shipmate. "He hated blacks, Hispanics, gays," reported a man who briefly shared an apartment with him. Acquaintances reported later that his behavior grew increasingly paranoid and bizarre during the last few years of his life. He quit his job with a Copperas Cove cement company a month before the massacre.

Hennard's thirty-fifth birthday dinner was a cheeseburger and fries at a small hamburger joint outside Killeen. Eating alone, he watched the evening news on TV, and, as the manager recalled, became infuriated at coverage of Clarence Thomas's Supreme Court confirmation hearing. Watching an interview with Anita Hill, he started screaming, "You dumb bitch! You bastards opened the door for all the women!"

The next day he left his house in Belton just before dawn. Armed with two legally purchased semiautomatic pistols, a Ruger P89 and a Glock 17, he eventually drove the fifteen miles to Killeen, arriving at Luby's shortly after noon.

At the time, the Luby's massacre was the largest so-called spree killing in American history. It wasn't the first. That dubious honor goes to another Texas horror—in Austin on a hot summer day in 1966, when a twenty-five-year-old engineering student, Eagle Scout, and former Marine named Charles Whitman murdered his wife and mother and then climbed to the top of the twenty-seven-story University of Texas tower and began sniping from the observation deck with an arsenal of high-powered rifles. For the next ninety-six minutes he fired down on people walking across campus and on an adjacent street known as "the Drag." Whitman killed fourteen people that August day and wounded dozens more before three Austin police officers and a civilian ascended the tower to the observation deck, where Officer Ray Martinez shot him to death.

"Whitman, it seems, had set a fashion and signaled permission among the disaffected and disturbed," Austin writer Carol Dawson has observed, noting the increasing number of such spree killings as the years went by.

Except for longtime Killeen residents, friends and family members of the deceased, and survivors, the Luby's massacre gradually faded from national consciousness (particularly as similar events kept erupting across the country with ever-greater frequency). What makes Luby's of continuing significance is the effect it had on Texas gun laws—laws that may serve as a prototype for American gun laws. Although the deconstruction of gun regulation may have occurred anyway, the cafeteria massacre served as a touchstone.

In 1996, Suzanna Gratia Hupp relied on her Luby's notoriety to win election to the Texas House of Representatives, where she quickly became an ardent and outspoken crusader against anything that smacked of gun control. A few years earlier, she had told her Luby's story to a US Senate committee considering gun legislation. "I'm not really mad at the guy who did this," she told the lawmakers. "That's like being mad at a rabid dog....I'm mad at my legislators for legislating me out of the right to protect me and my family."

Long-running efforts to scrub away laws to control or limit the ownership and use of weapons in Texas had intensified during the legislative session immediately before Hupp arrived, starting with laws that prohibited concealed weapons. In her memoir Hupp wrote that she didn't like the idea of concealed-carrying licensing, because "requiring people to jump through hoops and receive a permit to be able to exercise a right strikes me as counterproductive....But I am a pragmatist. I recognize we have not lost those American rights all at once. They have been slowly nibbled away while we were not looking. I believe restoration of those rights will probably happen incrementally as well. So anything that moves the bar in our favor is something I am likely to support. That is why I generally support concealed-carry permit legislation."

The concealed carry bill passed the state house and senate in 1994, only to be vetoed by Governor Ann Richards, a Democrat facing a tough reelection battle against Republican George W. Bush. To underscore her Second Amendment bona fides, Richards had gone dove hunting during her 1990 campaign for governor, but gun rights absolutists merely sneered at the made-for-media event. The veto confirmed their disdain.

"To this day," Hupp wrote, "I believe her decision to veto played a major role in eventually putting George W. Bush in the White House. You see concealed-carry permitting was a huge issue in the following gubernatorial race that pitted the two against each other. Bush made it clear: if the

Texas legislature could get a similar bill to his desk, he would sign it. That declaration rallied the troops, and the pro-gun, pro-self-defense people came out of the woodwork at voting time. Of course, Bush won."

The Copperas Cove chiropractor went to Austin committed to kneading the kinks out of the Second Amendment, state-imposed kinks that, she believed, constricted law-abiding gun owners and prevented Texans from carrying a machine designed to kill wherever they happened to be— in schools, in the home, in churches, in places of business, in a cafeteria. Hupp had no doubt that we lived in a dangerous world—a "rough country," so to speak—and to defend ourselves, we needed to be armed at all times. As the woman who survived a senseless massacre that killed her parents, she embodied that belief. On the floor of the Texas House, on TV and radio talk shows, and in her memoir, she brooked no argument.

Hupp served for a decade in the legislature, where she gained a reputation as a stubbornly doctrinaire conservative and a tenacious true believer in unfettered Second Amendment freedoms. In her crusade against "the stupidity of gun-control laws," laws leading her fellow Americans to their demise "like sheep to a slaughter," she and her legislative cohorts—mostly Republicans representing rural and suburban districts—were stunningly successful. The US Supreme Court helped, of course, with its 2008 ruling that gun ownership was a constitutional right.

Concealed carry was the beginning. Next was open carry, the right for Texans to display their handguns on their hip where everyone could see or on their shoulder if long guns were their preference. With guns carried in the open in toy department aisles at Walmart, in line at McDonald's, in churches, Texas towns and cities would be even more gun dependent and gun aware than frontier Tombstone and Dodge City (ironically, both of these wide-open, shoot-'em-up towns of lore imposed gun restrictions). Never mind polls showing two-thirds of Texans opposing the measure. Never mind that an overwhelming majority of Texas police chiefs were against open carry. On January 1, 2016, a decade after Hupp left the legislature, open carry became legal in Texas.

Public buildings could opt out of the law, although legislative gunsters required signs barring weapons to be as obtrusive as possible. The font of the wordy no-guns-allowed text in English and Spanish—red letters on a white background—had to be at least an inch high.

Guns are still banned from schools and hospitals, but not in many places where they were previously banned, including state universities and state mental health treatment centers. In Austin at the state capitol—a venerable domed building that before 9/11 was totally open twenty-four hours a day—a class of first graders on a tour will wait in line as a state trooper guides each child's backpack along an X-ray machine conveyor belt. Then the child must go through a metal detector. Meanwhile, those who are licensed to carry a firearm are waved through, pausing only long enough to sign their name. (A number of statehouse journalists who go in and out of the Capitol several times a day have gone through firearms training to qualify for their concealed carry license. They never expect to fire a gun or even carry one, but the license allows them to avoid waiting in line to get into the building where they work.)

Gun rights crusaders kept pushing. In the years following the 2007 mass shooting on the campus of Virginia Tech—thirty-two killed, seventeen wounded—campus carry became the cause célèbre. Most students said no. Professors and administrators, including the chancellor of the University of Texas System, William McRaven, said no. McRaven was the former Navy admiral who as head of the United States Special Operations Command had directed the operation that killed Osama bin Laden. Campus carry, he insisted, would make campuses less safe, not more.

On June 13, 2015, a gunman in an armored van assaulted police headquarters in downtown Dallas. That same day Governor Abbott went to a gun range in an Austin suburb and signed into law a bill requiring public colleges and universities to allow handguns on campus and in dormitories. The bill went into effect on August 1, 2016, fifty years to the day after the UT Tower shooting.

Lawmakers kept pushing. In 2015, 2017, and 2019, state representative Jonathan Stickland, a young Tea Party Republican representing a suburban district near Fort Worth, filed a bill that would allow so-called constitutional carry. Under Stickland's bill, any Texan who legally owned a handgun would be able to carry it openly or concealed without first getting a permit. Current law required Texans to undergo training and pay a fee before they were granted a license to carry.

"It is a major legislative priority for the Republican Party and very popular with my constituents," Stickland told the *Fort Worth Star-Telegram*. "I think there's a real need for it."

In the Texas Senate, the chief gun maven was Brian Birdwell, a retired Army colonel who represented a rural district southwest of Fort Worth. On 9/11, he was in his office at the Pentagon and was gravely injured when the plane crashed into the building. Listening to his calm, soft-spoken gun peroration on the Senate floor, I would be thinking that there must be more worthy causes for a man of his abilities and experience than pervasive gun proliferation. I simply did not understand it—and still don't.

In 2016, I wrote an editorial envisioning Birdwell, Stickland, and other Second Amendment absolutists portrayed in bronze. "Hands outstretched," I wrote, imagining their statue on a leafy Texas campus, "they proffer to young Texans, not a diploma but a gun. That will be their legislative legacy."

The state's elected officials were in thrall not only to their conservative beliefs and inclinations but also to the National Rifle Association and to guns in general. As Texan writer Lawrence Wright has pointed out, even if we could conclusively prove that stricter gun laws in the state would make us safer, our current crop of politicians is not going to allow such a thing to happen. Maybe someday, when urban interests overcome rural advantages hardwired into the legislative system, but not yet.

In his book *God Save Texas: A Journey into the Soul of the Lone Star State,* Wright notes, "There's a locker-room lust for weaponry that belies the noble-sounding proclamations about self-protection and Second Amendment rights."

He recalls then-governor Rick Perry in 2010 boasting of killing a coyote that was menacing his daughter's Labrador retriever. Perry was jogging through a suburban Austin neighborhood at the time and—as strange as it seems—packing somewhere on his person a Ruger .380. Legend has it that he dispatched the wily canine with a single shot. My wife, Laura, prefers to recall how she had encountered Perry—whom she had covered as a journalist—on the jogging trail a few years earlier, when he came to the rescue of her stubby-legged black pug. Noticing an off-the-leash shepherd mix bounding toward them as they chatted, the gallant future governor scooped up little Dash and held the dog above his head while the large dog clawed at his chest with muddy paws. Apparently, Perry wasn't packing heat that afternoon.

Wright also points out that Texas, with more than a million residents licensed to carry handguns, is actually far behind Florida, with 1.7 million.

"I'm EMBARRASSED," Abbott tweeted in 2015. "Texas #2 in nation for new gun purchases, behind CALIFORNIA. Let's pick up the pace Texans. @NRA."

Such was the atmosphere in Texas in the early decades of the twenty-first century, an atmosphere even more gun-obsessed than Fightin' Jack Potter's frontier Texas, one that encouraged Pomeroy and his elders to openly carry weapons in the sanctuary; that encouraged Stephen Willeford—the quintessential good guy with a gun—to amass an arsenal of weapons in his home, including at least seven AR-15s; that encouraged his Sutherland Springs neighbor, Mike Jordan, to amass an even bigger arsenal. Their gun collections were perfectly legal.

Several weeks after the Sutherland Springs shooting, Jordan volunteered to patrol the church perimeter on Sunday mornings, although he wasn't a church member. He often wore a black T-shirt with the message in white block letters across the chest: "Buy a Gun / Annoy a Liberal." His son Kevin was the young man Devin Kelley shot at on his way into the church, almost hitting Jordan's two-year-old. The prevalence and popularity of guns in the small community where the Jordans and the Willefords and their gun enthusiast neighbors lived were in no way out of the ordinary. You have to assume that small-town and rural Texans, unlike residents of the English village near Cambridge where my daughter lives—and unlike residents of most other towns and cities in developed nations around the world—are armed and ready to fire.

Whatever the cause-and-effect connection between public safety and laws that accommodate gun ownership, the spree killings continued, in Texas even more frequently than elsewhere. Good guys with guns, to appropriate the NRA-invented label, weren't able to stop them:

- On September 16, 1999, a man named Larry Gene Ashbrook walked into a midweek youth service at the Wedgwood Baptist Church in Fort Worth armed with a semiautomatic handgun, two hundred rounds of ammunition, and a pipe bomb. Ashbrook fired on the group and killed seven people, including several teenagers. He killed himself before law enforcement arrived at the church.

  Having covered the incident as a stringer for the *New York Times,* I remember how quiet and unremarkable the suburban neighborhood was—"How could this happen here?" I heard more than once— and how accepting of God's will the minister and his parishioners professed to be. It was a bewildering expression of faith and acceptance that I would hear again nearly two decades later in a small country church, where I would still find it bewildering.

- On November 5, 2009, gun violence returned to the Killeen area when Major Nidal Malik Hasan, an Army psychiatrist, brought a semiautomatic pistol to nearby Fort Hood. Opening fire at a processing center on the base, an area for soldiers returning from deployment and those preparing to deploy, Hasan killed twelve service members and one Department of Defense employee while wounding more than thirty others. Hasan's rampage was the deadliest mass shooting in history on an American military base.

  Hasan was shot by police and survived but was paralyzed from the waist down. In 2013, he was found guilty of the murders and sentenced to death. He still awaits execution.

- On April 2, 2014, again at Fort Hood, Army Spec. Ivan Lopez used a .45-caliber pistol to kill three people and injure at least twelve others when his request for leave was not approved. Lopez died from a self-inflicted gunshot to the head.

- On May 17, 2015, in Waco, a shootout erupted at a Twin Peaks restaurant, where members of several motorcycle clubs had gathered for a regularly scheduled meeting to discuss political rights for bikers. Waco police, including a SWAT team, had gathered to monitor them from outside the restaurant and opened fire after the shootout started. Nine bikers were killed and eighteen others were injured.

- On July 7, 2016, Micah Xavier Johnson ambushed a group of police officers in downtown Dallas, killing five and wounding nine others. Johnson started shooting near the end of a mass protest against recent killings of African American men by police in Baton Rouge, Louisiana, and Falcon Heights, Minnesota. After a standoff that lasted into the early hours of the next day, police killed Johnson with a bomb attached to a remote-control robot.

- On May 18, 2018, seven months after the worst church shooting in Texas history, seventeen-year-old Dimitrios Pagourtzis, a student at Santa Fe High School, near Houston, walked into his school and started firing at people with a pump-action shotgun and a .38-caliber revolver. He killed ten—eight students and two teachers—and wounded thirteen others before being subdued by police.

Responding to Santa Fe, Governor Greg Abbott and other Texas officials called for arming teachers and administrators, just as Texas attorney general Ken Paxton had said on Fox News a few months earlier that the best way to prevent church shootings was to arm parishioners. In Sutherland Springs, Stephen Willeford and most of the parishioners heartily agreed with their calls for gun profligacy.

In September 2018, nearly a year after the Sutherland Springs shooting, the *Texas Tribune* convened a panel of four people whose lives had been forever changed by a mass shooting. Sitting on the speaker's platform of a Presbyterian church in downtown Austin were Chris Grady, a survivor of the Marjory Stoneman Douglas High School shooting in Parkland, Florida, where a gunman murdered seventeen students and faculty; Nicole Hockley, mother of a six-year-old boy killed at Sandy Hook Elementary School in Newtown, Connecticut, and cofounder and managing director of an organization called Sandy Hook Promise; Pastor Frank Pomeroy, still grieving the loss of his daughter; and Suzanna Gratia Hupp, still crusading more than twenty-five years after her parents' death in Luby's Cafeteria for the right of ordinary citizens to carry guns for self-defense.

Responding to an opening question from moderator Pam Colloff, a Texan writer for the *New York Times Sunday Magazine,* Grady, eighteen, sought to explain the political movement he and fellow students launched, alternately known as March for Our Lives and Never Again. "Our goal," he said, "is to take guns out of the hands of people who would cause harm to others. I don't think that's really a divisive thing to say. We're trying to stop random and senseless acts of cold-blooded murder."

Pomeroy, resorting to preacherly jargon, sought to explain his congregation's post-shooting emphasis. He looked inward, spurning politics or a political movement. "We're still hoping in the Lord—coming together, building together, and strengthening together," he said. "This event does not define us; it is a part of who we are now, but we're focusing on the future, how we're going to strengthen through this, how we are going to build through this, and how we are going to continue to give God the glory."

"I tried to turn my rage and grief into action," Hockley said. "I started talking about change one week after Dylan's death, at his funeral. One month after the shooting, I launched Sandy Hook Promise, to save someone else's life, because I couldn't save my son."

"You either do something or go crazy," Hupp said.

Hockley told the Saturday morning audience that her group quickly concluded the nation wasn't ready to resolve the policy debates that arise after each mass shooting, whether requiring universal background checks or banning so-called assault weapons. The group decided to shift the focus to learning to recognize the early-warning signs teenagers who may be in trouble exhibit.

"We studied social change," she said. "As a country we have had difficult issues and have found common ground, everything from marriage equality back to civil rights, so what are the levers we need to pull to engage that change?"

The answer, she said, was to "take the gun out of the conversation and focus on how do we ensure we're getting help for someone long before they pick up a weapon and hurt themselves or someone else."

Hockley's group speaks to students, teachers, administrators, and parents about recognizing signs of at-risk behavior, whether it's bullying, eating disorders, cutting, social isolation, or any number of indications that a child is in trouble. "How do you ensure," she asked, "that when people do come forward and say something's wrong here that it's not ignored, that it's fully case-managed?"

Grady agreed that solutions start with mental health, but the focus of his Parkland group was on legislative change, he said. The fed-up teenagers he helped organize quickly became one of the most recognizable gun reform advocacy groups in the country. The group managed to persuade reluctant Florida lawmakers and a Republican governor to ban bump stocks and raise the age for buying a gun from eighteen to twenty-one.

Pomeroy told the gathering he saw no need to "politicize" the issue. He preferred "defending the rights that are already there. I quote Thomas Jefferson: 'I prefer to live in a dangerous freedom than a peaceful slavery.' Therefore, we tend to believe that true protection comes from carrying the Second Amendment and looking out for one another.... We did not find anyone who wanted to pursue limiting the Second Amendment or anything of that nature. For that reason, I think, Sutherland Springs fell out of the limelight very quickly—because we refused to be politicized."

Hupp, a combative true believer, had chosen to politicize herself by serving in the Texas legislature, but she took basically the same tack as Pomeroy. "I teach my boys that evil exists," she said. "We can talk about mental health issues, and I think that some people are reachable and we might prevent them from doing this, but I also think some people are evil. That's why I want to be able to protect myself and my friends and my parishioners. I want to change the odds, that's all."

Adam Winkler's 2011 book *Gunfight* is pretty much what the title suggests—an exploration of this nation's long and contentious debate about the place of guns in law and the culture. He focuses on *District of Columbia v. Heller,* the landmark gun control case the US Supreme Court decided in 2008, with the late Justice Antonin Scalia writing for the 5–4 majority. *Heller* afforded the court the opportunity to rule on the constitutional issue of whether the frustratingly murky Second Amendment— "A well regulated militia, being necessary to the security of a free state, the right of the people to keep and bear arms, shall not be infringed"— protected militias primarily, and not necessarily individuals, or whether it guaranteed every American the right to own a firearm. No decision of the Supreme Court had ever reached the latter conclusion, while others had upheld restrictions—the government's right, for example, to restrict machine guns.

Dick Heller was a security guard at the Federal Judicial Center in Washington, DC, who lived across the street from a crime-ridden public housing complex. He was required to carry a firearm at work, but DC law prohibited him from registering a weapon to keep at home. Scalia, writing for the majority, ruled that the District was wrong. The Second Amendment did, in fact, protect Heller's right to own a firearm, he wrote, thereby resolving a two-hundred-year-old dilemma.

Scalia, a so-called originalist on the court, said that he relied on history to reach his conclusion. Winkler, a UCLA law professor, relied on accounts of the nation's past, as well. He uncovered ancient British antecedents that suggested support for an individual rights' reading of the Constitution, noting that in early America, federal law not only allowed for possession of individual weapons but also in some cases required it. He also reminds his readers that gun restrictions in various forms were as old as the Constitution.

"The right to bear arms in the colonial era was not a libertarian license to do whatever a person wanted with a gun," he writes. "When public safety demanded that gun owners do something, the government was recognized to have the authority to make them do it."

Gun owners were barred from selling guns to Native Americans and blacks—and to those who refused to swear allegiance to the Crown. Communities in the so-called Wild West required residents and visitors to check their weapons. More recently, supporters of gun control included the Ku Klux Klan, which saw it as a way to disarm blacks. Gun control laws in Texas, dating back to the Reconstruction era, were among the more restrictive in the nation. Fear of guns in the hands of freed slaves and ex-Confederates was the primary motive.

Although the Scalia-led majority found a Second Amendment sancti-fication for private gun ownership, the court also allowed for a number of exceptions. Governments still could ban guns in schools or government buildings, and they could bar persons with mental illness and ex-felons from owning guns. Second Amendment absolutists were not pleased. They vowed to go further.

One year before the Sutherland Springs massacre, Donald Trump won the presidency with the enthusiastic support of the National Rifle Association and other ardent gun rights groups and individuals. Within months, the new president had appointed conservative-leaning justices who shared his expansive Second Amendment views, prompting Winkler to suggest that as Texas has gone, so goes the nation.

"The view of the right to bear arms that has governed Texas over the last 30 years…that same attitude, I think is shared by several of the justices," he said in a 2019 interview. "And they may find that laws that are more restrictive than the laws in place in Texas…are too onerous and too restrictive of Second Amendment rights, and that Texas is the model for America."

If Winkler's theory about Texas as the prototype for guns unleashed in America bears out, the gun rights victors might look back to Killeen, Texas, a lunchtime tragedy, and an indefatigable gun rights true believer setting the pace. Arguably, that's where their triumphant march began.

Chapter Fourteen

"Thank you to God . . . for the NRA."

ON A SUNDAY MORNING in August, nearly ten months after the shooting, Stephen Willeford and I stood chatting near the front of the sanctuary. On the platform behind us, Kris Workman and his praise team had just concluded the service with a hard-driving gospel song powered by electric guitar. As we talked, once the music quieted down, I glanced down at Stephen's small pistol, nestled in a leather holster—a Kimber, he told me, "the highest quality stuff, real expensive." It rested on his right hip beside a small beeper hooked over his belt. The gun is for one kind of emergency, the beeper for another. He never knows when his client, University Hospital in San Antonio, might call with a leak or a blockage in the innards of several large buildings.

Short and stocky, with gray hair that fluffs away from a high forehead, Stephen, fifty-six, almost always wears jeans to church—jeans and a T-shirt or jersey, untucked. "I'm never tucked. It's not a fashion statement," he told me one morning, lifting the tail of a maroon Texas Aggies jersey to reveal the pistol underneath.

Occasionally, he wears a forest-green T-shirt bearing the image of a stubby, gold-colored .45-caliber bullet on the back. The slogan in white letters below the image reads, "BECAUSE SOMETIMES SHORT, FAT AND SLOW WILL GET THE JOB DONE." The double entendre is obvious: Stephen, not tall and not slender and not quick, got the job done on that awful Sunday morning in November.

A few weeks earlier, I had been talking to his longtime friend Joe D. Tackitt Jr., the Wilson County sheriff. In his small Floresville office behind a cell block in the county's Justice Center, Tackitt told me that in all the years he had been sheriff—he was first elected in 1992—he had never had to use his gun. I was surprised.

"I hate guns," the soft-spoken sheriff drawled, surprising me again, this time with his candor. "The fact is, though, Stephen Willeford is a hero. If he hadn't had a gun, and if he hadn't come outside that morning, the shooter would have killed everyone in that building."

The Hero. The label attached itself almost immediately after the shooting to the modest, unassuming plumber from Sutherland Springs, Texas. He was "The Hero" who confronted "The Shooter," an unlikely Gary Cooper in *High Noon,* Alan Ladd in *Shane,* Glenn Ford in *The Fastest Gun Alive,* Clint Eastwood in *Man with No Name.* That wasn't Stephen's perception of himself, but it became the public's. He was the quintessential "good guy with a gun," embodying the label coined by Wayne LaPierre of the NRA. "The only thing that stops a bad guy with a gun is a good guy with a gun," LaPierre had said in 2012, responding to the slaughter of twenty schoolchildren in Newtown, Connecticut. Stephen, despite his fear, had been brave enough to respond.

His newfound notoriety brought him honors, acclaim, and opportunities to travel around the country talking about God and about church security. He told me about meeting with the elder of a San Antonio megachurch, a congregation with some five thousand members. He said he told the elder that the church needed to hire armed guards and to control entrances. The man politely demurred. He told Stephen the congregation chose to respect its tradition of openness. He and other church leaders didn't want members to have to pass through a security system to enter the large sanctuary.

Stephen said he reminded the elder that Sutherland Springs lost half its members that November morning. "What if your church lost half its members?" he asked, the disturbing math implicit in his question. "What if it lost twenty-six members? What's a life worth?"

For Stephen, the questions were rhetorical, however unconvinced the elder might have been. "You can't any more say it's not going to happen here," he reminded the man. "Was there any place more unlikely than

Sutherland Springs? Are you willing to say you can sacrifice half of your congregation to an open church building?"

Stephen shook his head and looked down at the floor of the sanctuary. "The truth is not always easy to take," he said.

The Hero is a modest man. As far as he's concerned, his notoriety is about as unlikely as a country church in South Texas becoming the site of a mass killing (a church across the road from his house, no less). He remembers waking up the morning after and for a fleeting moment wondering whether what had happened the day before was merely a dream.

He could never have imagined the president of the United States praising him during a press conference and later shaking his hand. He could not imagine spending time with Vice President Mike Pence, US senators Ted Cruz and John Cornyn, and other notables. When Cornyn's office called to arrange a meeting, he happened to be wrestling with a leaky steam pipe at the hospital; Cruz and Stephen's local congressman, Henry Cuellar, called shortly afterward. Cuellar was inviting him and wife Pam to be his special guests at the 2018 State of the Union Address.

The conservative *Washington Free Beacon* named him "Man of the Year." A few months later, he opened the pages of *Texas Monthly* magazine and read an admiring profile of himself. Everywhere he went he was offered gifts—all-expenses-paid trips, business opportunities, and expensive guns, usually handcrafted AR-15s. He pondered book offers, maybe movie deals.

"Who'll play you?" I asked him as we stood in line for barbecue at church one Sunday.

He stared off into the distance for a moment as fragrant barbecue smoke wafted around us. "Maybe George Clooney," he said. He was joking (I think).

A few months after the triumphal visit to the Capitol for the State of the Union, he was the NRA's guest of honor at its national convention in Dallas, where he delivered a memorable speech to a crowd of thousands. "We are the people that stand between the people that would do evil to our neighbors," he said, a black (not white) wide-brimmed hat jammed down on his head. "I'm nothing special," he said, speaking in a calm, assured drawl, without notes. "Look at you guys. Every one of you would do what I did. And I love you all."

He described himself as a sheepdog, a metaphor become meme among fundamentalist, gun-loving Christians. He said he first heard it from police officers eager to express their gratitude for what he had done. A sheepdog, he explained, protects the community—the sheep—from wolves. "I took care of my community that day, and I would do it again," he said, wife Pam standing at stage left, his audience listening intently.

"Being a sheepdog," he said, "we all need to understand that we can't do it alone. There's always a shepherd that takes care of the sheepdog. And what the shepherd does is, the shepherd makes sure that his sheepdogs have food, water, and a warm place to sleep at night and rest. And a shepherd will take care to brush the thorns and thistles out of a sheepdog's coat. And when too many wolves come down on one sheepdog, he sends other sheepdogs to help or steps in himself to protect his sheepdog.

"I'm here to tell you today that Jesus Christ is my shepherd," Stephen said, as a few people in the audience began to clap at the mention of Jesus, and then a few more began to whistle, the applause spreading until it threatened to drown out his remarks. "And what happened in Sutherland Springs was all Him, and it's His glory. And thank you for my God, for His son that paid the price for us. Thank you to God for protecting this great nation and thank you for the NRA."

Audience members were on their feet as Stephen concluded, many with tears in their eyes, their applause and whistling and shouts of encouragement washing over the gray-haired man in black-rimmed glasses and a big black hat. It was a masterful performance. In that moment I saw the fierceness and intensity of Stephen Willeford's belief—in God and in guns. I saw the intensity of a rapt audience, several thousand people listening to The Hero—the short, stocky, heroic Everyman, as it were, who embodied a cherished way of life, a way of life they believed was threatened, despite their guns.

Stephen told *Texas Monthly*'s Michael Mooney that he ordered room service for the first time in his life later that evening, while staying in a block of Omni Hotel suites the NRA reserved for him and his family.

Everywhere he went that weekend people wanted to shake his hand, engage him in conversation, take photos with him. He had his own picture taken with Trump.

"I think I could meet Trump tomorrow and he wouldn't recognize me," he told Mooney. "But Mike Pence would. And Ted Cruz knows me well."

Later, he was a guest speaker at the Republican State Convention and was honored on the floor of the Texas Senate during the early days of the 2019 legislative session. Governor Abbott appointed him to the Texas Private Security Board, a seven-person body that regulates the private security professions—security guards, armored-car couriers, guard-dog trainers, locksmiths, and the like.

Stephen Willeford loves guns almost as much as he loves Jesus. He collects guns, tinkers with them, assembles them, trains with them. He likes the feel and heft of them, their history and their craftsmanship. Along with muscle cars and motorcycles, they are his hobby; target practice at a range property he owns in the country is his way of relaxing. As a long-time NRA member—now an official "lifetime member"—gun people are his people.

He also respects what guns can do. He reminds me, when I use the wrong term in his presence, that guns are "firearms," yes, but they're not necessarily "weapons." They're tools, he likes to say, like a high-powered hole punch (his metaphor), to be used for specific purposes.

He's been around guns since he was five, when his dad set up a row of Coke cans in the backyard and handed him a bolt-action .22 rifle. As he grew older, he became a competition shooter and got to where he was outshooting police and military teams. By his mid-thirties, he could hit the string tied to a bobbing balloon from a hundred yards away. For years, the Bible study group at his church in San Antonio met each week to shoot for a few hours before delving into God's Word. For years, he's been an NRA-certified instructor.

He and Pam have three children, ranging in age at the time of the shooting from twenty-three to twenty-nine. He taught them to respect guns and how to use them. "By the time they were seven or eight, they were trained," he said. "If somebody was trying to come through that door that didn't belong here," he said, nodding toward the front door of the house, "they'd know what to do."

Every experience he's had with guns, he now believes, was God-ordained preparation for what happened at the church—the extensive training, the practice, even the discussions he had in years past with a police officer friend about the best place to aim when you're firing at a moving target who's wearing body armor. He never imagined he would use the advice, but it came in handy when he made the disabling side shots between the Velcro-connected armor panels.

I asked Stephen at church one Sunday for a gun tutorial. I told him I didn't want to make any mistakes about gun usage, gun names, or shooting technique. I had read enough angry letters to the editor and outraged comments from gun aficionados—some addressed to me—to know to be as accurate with the pen as Stephen was with a gun.

I showed up at the Willeford house across the road from the church at the appointed time one weekday afternoon, but no one was home. I waited twenty minutes or so before Stephen in his white Mustang with the blue racing stripe whipped into the yard. He had been at the Capitol attending a Private Security Board meeting. Governor Abbott had appointed him. As we walked into the house, he was complaining about being outvoted 4–3 on a request from a locksmith who had a felony conviction when he was seventeen and failed to include the information on his license request. He didn't believe the man deserved a second chance. Stephen was wearing a black suit, charcoal-gray shirt, and blue tie; I had never seen him in anything but jeans and a T-shirt or football jersey.

"Training is everything," Stephen said, as we stood in the cluttered living room. The unloaded AR-15 he used that Sunday morning leaned against the backrest of a rose-pink rocking chair. "It's easy to shoot children and women," he said, "but when I started shooting back, he [the shooter] started running for his door. All my years and years of training mattered."

Each time he brought out a gun (not a weapon) from a backroom, he had me inspect it and assure him it wasn't loaded. He had to remind me not to "index"—in other words, don't put my finger on the trigger until I was ready to fire.

I looked more closely at the pistol he carries, an Ultra CDP Kimber brand, a .45, "hand-built, very accurate, very nice." Rod Green's pistol, he said, was an old Colt officer's model called a 1911, referring to the year when the federal government adopted the Colt as a sidearm. "It's the gun that won the West," he said. Frank Pomeroy, he said, used a Kimber, Micro 9, an American-made gun.

"Whatever you choose to carry," he said, "you're saying, 'I bet my life on this gun.'"

The AR-15 he used against the shooter was an M4 style that he assembled himself, customizing the gun until he had just what he wanted. The M4, he said, "takes down insurgents at two to three hundred meters. It's very light, very tactical." He had me lift the dull-black gun to my shoulder (after I assured both of us it wasn't loaded). It felt heavy to me.

"People think I'm this redneck who ran out of his house and confronted a shooter," he said. "The fact is, I probably have more training than most police officers."

Stephen has helped Pastor Frank organize and train a twelve-person emergency response team at First Baptist, the team part of a security regime that includes multiple cameras and locks on doors. Some team members are armed, some are not. As Stephen and I talked about their training, I remembered a conversation with Frank about the SRT, safety response team. Several team members are retired military who remain at war internally with PTSD.

"I don't want people who feel they couldn't take a life with firearms if need be, 'cuz they're the ones who end up causing more mayhem and trouble, trying to protect them," Frank said. "We call it the hero syndrome. They don't want to do it, they force themselves to do it, and they could end up hurting themselves or hurting other people, whereas someone who's calm would stay on the sidelines and try to talk this out."

Without hurting their feelings, you give them something else to do, Frank explained. He was not talking about Stephen.

"The United States is awash in a sea of both faith and firearms," sociologist David Yamane has written. Yamane, who studies guns, religion, and their connectedness—who also owns guns and enjoys target shooting at gun ranges—notes that civilian Americans own more than 270 million firearms, including handguns, rifles, and shotguns. That's one firearm per person, although ownership is far from evenly distributed. Most Americans don't own even one gun, while gun owners frequently collect an arsenal. Yamane points out that we have the most guns in the world, and, of course, we are one of the most religious countries in the world.

Stephen Willeford's reverence for guns isn't unusual in rural and small-town America. Nor is it unusual at the First Baptist Church of Sutherland Springs. Even among members who saw their children die at the hands of a madman, whose lives were changed forever by a gun in the hands of a man who should never have had one—even those people remain gun enthusiasts.

"I love 'em," David Colbath told me one evening after Bible class. "It's a crying shame people blame guns." David, a big-game hunter, has been charged by a lion in Africa. He took his second wife hunting in Tanzania a year or so before their divorce; he thought the trip might help their marriage. She killed a cape buffalo, but they still divorced. Part of the right-hander's rehabilitation at Brooke Army Medical Center was a weekly session shooting with his left hand at the hospital's Center for the Intrepid's Firearms Training Simulator. He shot at bad guys—electronically, of course.

"David knows more about guns than anyone I know," Frank Pomeroy said, laughing. "Knows about their caliber, knows about their weight, which ones are best for what."

Julie Workman has a gun of her own, a 9-millimeter pistol, but it happened to be dirty the morning of the shooting and she hadn't gotten around to cleaning it. "I wish I'd had one," she said. She also has two AR-15s registered in her name, although she's never fired them. "I own guns, because we live in the country," she said. "We have snakes; we have coyotes."

Julie the nurse offered a comparison from her profession: "Guns are a tool, like a scalpel in the operating room. They can be used for good; they can be used for bad."

"I wouldn't change anything about guns in this country," Julie's son Kris said, "except for better enforcement of the laws we have."

James Dobson, the popular fundamentalist minister and founder of the organization Focus on the Family, hosted the Pomeroys and David Colbath on his nationally syndicated radio show *Family Talk*. He devoted two episodes to the Sutherland Springs story, including an extended conversation to conclude the second show on guns and church security.

David told Dobson that any type of armed confrontation, whether in a church or in a school or in the workplace, needed to be met with armed confrontation. "Why doesn't anybody go into a police station with a gun?" he asked rhetorically. "Because everybody's got guns in there. So, they're not willing to attack that, but yet all our schools are gun-free zones. Of course, the guy that's going to attack them knows there's no opposition."

Dobson reminded David that their listeners probably included people who strongly disagreed with his gun enthusiasm. They want schools to be gun-free, whether a university or a kindergarten.

"Those that don't want armed teachers and armed personnel in there, then you're going to tell me as a school district or whoever you are that you don't want people that are armed protecting our kids, then you protect them," David said. "You show me how you're going to protect them. Your way is not working. Gun-free zones, only people with guns that are bad come through there. So your way's not working."

Frank spoke up. He told Dobson that armed members weren't in church that morning—because God "choreographed" it that way.

"We had a contingency plan at Sutherland Springs," he said. "We have people who were concealed-carry holders that were armed on Sunday mornings in our church, but we need to also remember that God is the great choreographer, and He choreographed it where all of us who normally would have a side arm were not there that day at the church, so it is God who makes the final stand. That's why, if He doesn't want the firearms in there, He'll make sure they're not there. However, unless He says otherwise, then we should be taking every implement that He has given us, and every tool in our arsenal should be there to protect the sheep and share the gospel."

Frank continued: "Someone once asked me, didn't I feel as though it was wrong, and what would I say to those who felt it was wrong to ever utilize a firearm in the church, and I said that firearm didn't do any damage. It was the person holding it. It's a machined piece of equipment just like the machined pieces of equipment in emergency rooms that save lives. If you choose not to use this one to save lives, then why would you choose to use these to save lives? They're just machines."

In a town called Nacogdoches, in the sanctuary of a small Baptist church nestled among the tall pines of deep East Texas, a couple of dozen congregants have gathered on a Saturday morning to discuss church security. They sit in folding chairs in a circle, their two-hour discussion directed by a retired psychologist named Bob. Their congregation, Austin Heights Baptist Church, is a few blocks from a large state university; a sizable portion of the membership has university connections. Most of those in the circle—indeed, most members of the congregation—consider themselves progressives. "Fightin' Frank" Pomeroy and his armed posse would be welcome, but their reliance on weaponry would make these particular Baptists uncomfortable.

I discovered Austin Heights when I read an article published by its minister in the venerable *Christian Century*, a progressive Christian magazine founded in Chicago in 1884. *Christian Century* was an unlikely outlet for a Baptist minister, but Kyle Childress, the congregation's pastor since 1989, is himself unusual, as is Austin Heights. The Saturday morning gathering, Childress told me, was an exercise in seeking "discernment" on a complex issue. For his own spiritual discernment, he's more likely to look toward the likes of Dr. Martin Luther King Jr. or the late Rev. William Sloane Coffin, a peace activist, Yale chaplain, and senior minister at New

York City's Riverside Church (a church affiliated with the American Baptist denomination, more-progressive cousins to Southern Baptists). Despite his differences with Jerry Falwell Jr., Franklin Graham, and other outspoken fundamentalist figures with far-right views on politics and social issues, Childress considers himself as much a Baptist as they are.

Early in the discussion, several members of the Saturday morning group admitted that, however they felt about guns, they had come to feel uneasy whenever they're in crowds, including church services. Jerry, a professor of sociology at the university, sought to reassure them. He mentioned that the odds of their church being attacked were about 1 in 4 million.

"For me as a Christian," a woman named Jane said, "I don't believe in us being armed or shooting someone or hurting someone, but it doesn't seem wrong to be prepared."

"It's proper to be concerned about it," the professor responded, "but the risk is infinitesimal for us. A lot of churches are caught up in a culture of fear. It's similar to the eighties and nineties when people got caught up in a mass panic about children being abducted by strangers. It changed how we lived, even though the risk was infinitesimal."

"I'd rather be a victim than carry a gun with me every day," a middle-aged woman said. "I'd rather be a martyr."

"I agree with that," a woman sitting near her said, "but I don't want my grandchildren to be martyrs. I'd stand in front of them, and I'd shoot."

"I do recognize that we live in a society that is becoming ever more violent, and more and more people wielding guns are likely to try to be a hero," Bob the psychologist said. "Can we take steps to be prepared for the almost statistically impossible event? A little bit of awareness and prevention can make a difference. Preparedness is good. Awareness is good."

"I don't want this to suck us into a culture of fear," an older woman named Toni commented. "I had a break-in at my house recently. They stole a [clothes] dryer, of all things, and I have found pry marks on my door where somebody was trying to break in. I refuse to live in a culture of fear. I used to not lock my door, although now I do."

Jerry the sociologist mentioned that his sister had been murdered, with a gun, on the streets of Los Angeles in 1985. "Her death changed the way

I saw the world for a long time," he said, "but the fact is, statistically, things are much, much better than they were thirty and forty years ago.

"I don't want to go to a church where I'm surrounded by guns," the sociologist continued. "It reminds me of Archie Bunker, back when skyjacking was such a big thing. The solution is simple, Archie said. Hand out guns to every passenger when they board; take them up when they get off. We don't want to live in a culture of fear, because that's not who we are."

"Looking at the life and ministry of Christ, how do we minister to the culture of fear?" Toni asked. "I look at the life of Christ, and that doesn't resonate with carrying weapons. Those who live by the sword shall die by the sword. Isn't that what Jesus said?"

Steve, a deacon who serves as chairman of the Church Safety Committee, reported that the congregation had begun researching and instituting safety measures a year and a half earlier. The measures included having greeters at the front door "who try to get a gut feeling about someone coming in." A panic button in the pulpit, something similar to bank tellers' alarms, might be worth considering, he said, although in its half century of existence the church had never had an intruder, armed or otherwise.

"We are not a church that meets violence with violence," Steve said from behind a full gray beard. "I'm not waiting in the lobby to attack someone. My first response is to dissuade. Our response so far is welcome and openness and love. As Christians, our story all along is that there is another way; there is a better way. It's not in Smith & Wesson we trust; it's in God we trust."

The group agreed to continue the discussion at a later date. Listening to the thoughtful observations and the probing questions, I tried to imagine Stephen Willeford in their midst. Like a battle-scarred soldier home from the war, he no doubt would shake his head at the dangerous naiveté of his fellow Baptists in East Texas. Like them, he believes in praising God. Unlike them, he believes in passing the ammunition.

Pastor Childress is a former high school quarterback who has put on a few pounds since he was flinging passes for the Stamford High School Bulldogs, a West Texas gridiron powerhouse, during his playing days in the 1970s. Baptist seminary–trained, Childress likes to do pastoral counseling on the back porch of his home, preferably with a shot of dusky bourbon within reach and an aromatic cigar in hand. His informality reflects the southern good ol' boy spirit of his mentor, hero, and friend, Will Campbell, the late Baptist preacher, iconoclastic author, and civil rights provocateur.

Like most Texans, particularly small-town Texans, Childress grew up around guns. He and his brother went bird hunting with their father and grandfather. But when dove season or quail season was over, the shotguns were put away in a closet. No one paid any attention to them.

"Now, though, for me as a pastor to raise a question about why someone carries a firearm on his belt while professing to be a baptized follower of Jesus Christ is to invite outright, in-your-face hostility," Childress has written. "It provokes defensiveness that far exceeds expectations. One of the rare times I've been screamed at was after I said something in a sermon against guns."

Childress acknowledges that the gun issue is complex for Christians. "The choice is not between naiveté and reality," he told me. "The option is witnessing for Christ. The integrity and witness of the church is important. Historically, there are certain places that are sacred. You don't bring weapons into these places. Can you do church safety that's nonviolent? That's the question."

He began noticing a more pervasive "culture of fear" in the church as well as the community as mass shootings seemed to proliferate. Perceived threats seemed to be just outside our doors waiting to burst through. He was surprised to see some churches, in response to Texas's new open carry law, erect signs proclaiming, "Guns Welcome Here." An informal survey he conducted around town suggested there were more pistol-packing preachers in Nacogdoches than he would have guessed.

"A close friend who is a dental hygienist and a devoted Catholic is considering going through handgun training so that she can become licensed to carry," Childress wrote in a 2016 *Christian Century* article. "As she says, 'Who knows if someone might barge into the dental office and start shooting?' Down at the barbershop I've discovered that my barber is armed. Now I'm anxious about getting a haircut. Maybe I need a panic button like the ones that the church with the armed ushers installed throughout the building. Church members can sound an alarm if they feel threatened."

For Childress, the issue of guns in the church is ultimately not about safety and security. It's a faith issue, a moral issue.

"I keep asking myself where the witness of Christ is in all of this," he wrote. "Many of the pastors who are carrying guns teach and preach a version of the gospel that's different from what I know. It is a gospel of everyone looking out for himself or herself, a gospel that says, 'It's a dangerous world, so get them before they get you. I'm protecting me and mine, and furthermore it is God's will and biblical teaching to do so.' Loving your neighbor as yourself, loving enemies, suffering servanthood, forgiveness, the Sermon on the Mount, living and dying like Jesus—I'm hearing much less about that."

Scott Bader-Saye is an Episcopal theologian who literally wrote the book on a Christian's response to a "culture of fear," the term that came up several times in the Austin Heights meeting. In *Following Jesus in a Culture of Fear,* he reminded his readers of a radical pacifist tradition that hearkens back to Christian martyrs going to their gruesome deaths willingly, even happily.

Bader-Saye explores Taize, heir to that tradition. Taize is a religious community founded in 1940 in southern France as a sanctuary for Jews, refugees, and non-Jews during World War II. Over the years it's grown into an ecumenical monastic community of more than a hundred brothers, both Catholic and Protestant. Those who make pilgrimages each year to the small French town see themselves as making a "pilgrimage of trust on earth," a phrase coined by Taize's founder, Brother Roger.

In 2005, Brother Roger was stabbed to death during a prayer service. While the worshippers sang and the brothers knelt, a mentally unstable Romanian woman emerged from the congregation and murdered the ninety-year-old founder and prior. The community was not only shocked and saddened but also deeply perplexed (like Sutherland Springs). How could the community sustain its mission when the radical trust that was at the heart of the mission had been broken and betrayed in the most violent way imaginable?

As Bader-Saye reports in his 2007 book, there was no security before the shocking murder; there was no security afterward. There were no metal detectors in the community's Church of Reconciliation, no screening process, no surrender to what most of us would consider measures of caution and common sense. At Brother Roger's funeral service, there were expressions of forgiveness for the murderer.

"Like the parables of Jesus," Bader-Saye writes, "this band of brothers functions to subvert our easy expectations about how the world works."

We continued the conversation in his comfortable book-lined office at the Episcopal Seminary of the Southwest. A picture window framed a venerable spreading live oak just outside.

"More and more people these days thrive on apocalyptic fear," he said, "whether it's the government or a natural disaster or dangerous individuals. They plan for it, spending all sorts of time and energy on something extremely unlikely to happen."

We journalists were partly to blame, he said. Our "fear-based reporting" fed the paranoia of people disposed toward conspiracy.

Bader-Saye knows what Sutherland Springs experienced. He wasn't applying the paranoid label to Stephen Willeford and his armed church friends, but he contended that guns, weapons of destruction in a place called "sanctuary," robbed the word of its meaning.

"If we start arming ourselves, it changes the way we do church," he said. "The very thing we do to prevent something could end up causing it. Every single gun you bring into the sanctuary creates a different dynamic."

The First Baptist Church of Sutherland Springs is, like Taize, a close-knit faith community. Unlike Taize, it's a community whose leaders believe that protection and security are paramount, even if protection and security come at the point of a lethal weapon designed solely to devastate a human body. Indeed, it's almost impossible to imagine not shooting back, not trying to kill, when a madman invades a sacred space and starts slaughtering men, women, and children. But what about preparation for that possibility? Can preparation and reliance on firearms pervert the message? For the Christian, it would seem, the vexing question remains.

Childress would be the first to admit that he had not been tested the way the people of Sutherland Springs had been tested. He did not witness half his own small congregation slaughtered by a psychopath. He had not had to minister to survivors whose lives were changed forever. Nevertheless, he worried that our penchant for protection and our fascination—if not obsession—with guns had led American Christians down a dark path.

"This gun thing is about God, and it's about the power of death," he has written. "[William] Stringfellow said that only as we immerse ourselves in God, the God of the resurrected life, can we hope to resist the power of death. This is also why I rarely get into discussions about the Second Amendment but I talk a lot about the first commandment. And Jesus."

I encountered three people involved with Sutherland Springs who offered any kind of criticism of America's gun culture. Two of them surprised me.

One was David Colbath, who has a personal arsenal of between thirty and thirty-five guns (he says he needs to sell a few). Speaking to a round-table discussion organized by Governor Greg Abbott's office in the wake of the mass shooting at Santa Fe High School, David said law-abiding gun owners need to resist the NRA's all-out obstinance.

"Why can't people like you and me, why can't we force the NRA to back off?" he said, glancing at survivors, family, and community members among the forty roundtable participants. "I love the NRA, by the way, and I love guns."

Earlier, he had told me that he believes some people should never be in possession of a gun, including the shooter at Sutherland Springs.

The other member willing to at least consider what he would call sensible gun regulation was Frank Pomeroy himself. Controls are worth debating, he told NPR's *Here and Now,* although he saw no reason to debate taking away the right to own a sidearm.

"I am one of the few that do believe that there's not much use for automatic weapons in the hands of civilians," he said. "I understand there is the hog populations and such, where they utilize those kinds of weapons. But I also understand, too, the fear of that being a first step if folks was to say, 'Oh yes, we're gonna relent and allow the semiautomatic weapons to be taken from us. The next step is going to be our sidearms.' I don't really buy into that mantra. Therefore my personal opinion is that we probably do not need the military, assault-style rifles. That's coming from a hunter. I have twenty-three rifles, different styles, and I do not own an assault rifle. I see no point in it for me."

And then there was Kati Wall, who lost "Nannie" and "Pa," the grandparents who raised her, Sara and Dennis Johnson, whom she refers to as her "parents." She wrote an opinion piece for the *Dallas Morning News* in the form of an open letter to the governor, describing herself as a "secondary victim" of the shooting. "There is a massive crater blown in my life and in my children's lives by their loss," she wrote.

"I remember your visit, Mr. Governor, and how it felt surreal, like none of this could be happening," she wrote, "the way it still feels most moments. I remember the words you said about strength and love in the hearts of Texans and I remember feeling raging frustrations, because I didn't know if my parents were alive or dead and I wanted news more than anything in that moment. But all I received were platitudes and 'thoughts and prayers.' I waited 13 hours hoping and constantly shaking with fear and anxiety to finally be informed that both my parents had perished in the church."

Kati told the governor she had two issues she wanted him to consider: gun control and mental health. "Stay with me," she urged. "I know gun and control are two words that tend to upset people on either side of the aisle. This is NOT me saying that we need to just round up all the guns and call it a day. Consider our country's approach to driving. We recognize that a vehicle in the hands of someone who is untrained, impaired, or under age can be a deadly and destructive tool. While accidents will happen, regulation discourages reckless behavior. It is my opinion that we should take a similar approach to guns."

She called for more strenuous background checks, bipartisan

cooperation to combat the influence of gun lobbies, and "common sense conversations that shut down extremists."

"I saw the pain in your eyes that night in Sutherland Springs, and I know you actually care about us," Kati told the governor. "I am asking you personally to share this with every Texas politician, no matter their leanings. We need to require gun training, psychiatric evaluations, medical and mental history, background checks, and secure storage for every gun owner, and we need to enforce this consistently and hold rule-breakers painfully accountable. We need to shut down private gun sales and gun shows. Every gun needs to be traceable to a licensed owner who can be held accountable should the weapon be used in the commission of a crime. This is too serious an issue to continue to have a wait-and-see attitude about."

She reminded the governor that Devin Kelley had a long history of mental health issues and violent criminal behavior. Acknowledging there were no clear-cut solutions, she urged better training about risk factors and antisocial behavior in schools and hiring more counselors. She called for destigmatizing mental illness.

"The pain this tragedy has caused my family is indescribable and only beginning," she concluded. "There is a very long road to our recovery ahead. It would make my parents' deaths meaningful to see improvements that prevent these things from happening. I look forward to seeing what develops in Texas and beyond, thanks to the open minds and hearts of our officials."

A couple of months after her op-ed appeared, Kati and I were talking over lunch about guns, God, and what she planned to do with her life in the wake of the tragedy. She wasn't sure that day about future plans, although she would ultimately leave—her job, the church, her home in the little town of Poth where she and her husband, Jason, had lived near her grandparents and other family members. They wanted nothing more to do with a place that had brought such pain.

"Stephen Willeford is the kind of man who *should* own a gun," she mentioned the day we talked. "Except my parents are still gone."

Chapter Fifteen

"Look, Dad! Look how far I walked!"

MAGGIE VIDAL WAS ONE of the luckier survivors (if that's not a contradiction in terms). The diminutive, dark-haired woman and long-time church member, shot once in her right knee and once in the back near her spine, got to leave the hospital within days—although she had to endure eight surgeries and couldn't return immediately to her small frame house a couple of blocks from the church. Instead, she was transferred to Floresville Residence & Rehabilitation Center, where, like each of her fellow survivors, young and old, she began the slow and arduous process of putting her life back together. While doctors fought an infection in her leg wound, she spent weeks getting around in a wheelchair and relearning how to use her leg again. Two months after the shooting, she told a San Antonio TV reporter that certain noises could trigger emotional trauma. If she saw scenes and sounds of guns on TV, she switched the channel. "I just try to keep strong," she said.

Kris Workman, unlikely ever to walk again, was in the hospital for two and a half weeks, where he underwent numerous surgeries. From the hospital, he was transferred to outpatient rehab for another two and a half weeks of grueling work. There he began relearning day-to-day activities, from a wheelchair. He got home the day before Christmas and got back to work at Rackspace, a San Antonio computer company, a few days afterward.

Twenty people of widely varying ages had similar experiences, had ongoing visits to hospitals and doctor's offices and rehabilitation centers. Twenty people, and their families, had to grow accustomed to a vastly different way of life.

The next-to-last survivor to be released from the hospital was Gunny Macias, the retired Marine who finally made it home to Sutherland Springs after two and a half months convalescing. With an IV drip slung over his shoulder, he shuffled into church on a Sunday morning in the spring, leaning on a walker. His wife, Jennifer, and support dog, Belle, accompanied him. Week after week, church members could see a palpable change for the better in their old friend, although the symptoms of PTSD were never far from the surface, as David Colbath discovered when he walked up behind Gunny in a Starbucks line and slapped him on the back. Briefly, the old Marine was back in combat mode, fearful and ready to fight.

David was still in recovery, as well, both physically and mentally, but he tried to stay optimistic. Hope was essential to his faith. "My ankles, arms, and fingers hurt. My buttocks hurt. But my cup runneth over," he told me on a Thursday night several months after the shooting. Before being wheeled through the doors of Brooke Army Medical Center on a stretcher, the fifty-six-year-old had never been a hospital patient. He spent three and a half weeks at BAMC and underwent five surgeries. As the hospital public information office reported, surgeons used a vein from his leg to reconstruct one of two blood vessels in his right forearm to restore blood flow to his hand. Following the reconstruction by the vascular team, an orthopedic surgical team performed nerve reconstruction in the same area and rotated muscle over the vascular and nerve reconstruction to prevent infection and allow his arm to heal. Every survivor was the recipient of similar complex treatment.

As the wounds began to heal, David rehabbed two to five days a week alongside wounded warriors at the Center for the Intrepid. Seeing those who had been grievously wounded on the battlefield, seeing how they worked every day to get better, kept him motivated, he said. "It's kind of hard to look over at a wounded warrior who's lost a leg and two arms and want to slough off when they're doing their part to get better," he told a San Antonio TV station.

Occasionally, it seemed, David's life verged on the tragicomic. On his third day in the hospital, he turned on the TV and saw his father's San

Antonio house explode. The elder Colbath had been smoking in bed and tossed the cigarette butt into a bathroom waste basket. A TV news crew that had come out to interview him about his son had just finished up in the front yard, although the camera was still recording. Suddenly, a bright orange flash lit up the screen. Ammunition inside one of the rooms had exploded. The house burned to the ground.

"He has no home. His insurance was minimal," David told me weeks later. "So typical of my dad. So, so typical. Just forgetful, not thinking, smoking in bed."

"It's been a helluva week," one of David's nephews told reporters.

Zoe Zavala, seven years old at the time of the shooting, saw her grandfather die and her grandmother nearly die. Zoe, shot in the hip and left with a shattered pelvis, nearly died herself. After three surgeries and six weeks in the hospital, she took her first steps on a visit to her first-grade classroom in La Vernia. As the weeks went by, the lively dark-haired little girl got to be a familiar sight running around the churchyard after services. Often she was chasing her friend Ryland, or he was chasing her. Except for a brace on one leg, her life appeared to be just like it used to be.

"Anytime I'm feeling down, I go by and see Zoe and Ryland," Sheriff Tackitt told me one afternoon.

Doctors weren't sure Zoe would walk again, much less run. They weren't sure Ryland would live. Even after he was stabilized, doctors were worried that he might lose his arm. Then they worried he might lose his kidney. High-velocity rounds had blasted away tissue and muscle on Ryland's left arm, damaging a radial artery and nerve and leaving a craterous wound. A large section of his left thigh bone was splintered, and his pelvis was fractured. Bullets had burrowed into Ryland's abdomen, injuring his bladder and intestines. Blood had pooled in his lower abdomen. Bullet fragments peppered his pelvis and abdomen. The bullets so devastated his small body that doctors couldn't be sure exactly how many times he'd been shot. They estimated that he lost at least half the blood in his body.

"Most child gunshot victims treated at the hospital have suffered a single wound, often the result of an accident. Ryland had been shot multiple times in multiple areas. His wounds looked like those inflicted in war zones," *San Antonio Express-News* reporter Lauren Caruba noted in a comprehensive report on Ryland's treatment and recovery.

After leaving the hospital, the just-turned-six-year-old spent several hours each day in physical and occupational therapy at a rehabilitation facility for children to regain the use of his left arm and left leg. He met with a child psychiatrist who gently, patiently helped him process the ordeal.

Ryland's rehab sessions began the day after Christmas. He struggled at first. Even simple tasks like sitting up for five seconds left him in tears. Sometimes, Caruba wrote, he would cry through entire sessions. Once the little boy got comfortable with the routine and with his rehab team, he progressed quickly. Sometime around the New Year, he took his first halting steps after being bedridden for weeks. One of his therapists remembered him calling to his father as he rounded a corner: "Look, Dad! Look how far I walked!"

Ryland was required to complete three hours of rehab a day, six days a week. Those appointments had to be scheduled around surgeries and medical procedures, nursing care, time with family, psychotherapy, and lessons with a teacher who visited Ryland at the hospital.

On January 11, 2018, Rusty Duncan, the firefighter who had rescued a little boy close to death, brought him home in a big, red fire truck. A procession of at least a hundred fire trucks, police cars, and other emergency vehicles followed, a procession that got longer as it approached Sutherland Springs. Sirens and horn blasts signaled their arrival. Cars stopped on the shoulder. A contingent of motorcycle officers lined up and saluted.

As the procession approached the church, people cheered and waved signs or Texas flags. They hoisted balloons. Six-year-old Vivian Salinas welcomed home her friend Ry-Ry with a sign that read, "Good to See You." Perched on the front seat, the blond-haired little boy in a light-blue dress shirt smiled and waved through the open window. He looked a bit dazed at all the hoopla.

Terrie Smith, manager of the Valero station, cried tears of joy. Ryland's stepmother, Joann Ward, had been her best friend. She considered Ryland a grandson. "It's just a beautiful blessing from God to have him home and well," she said.

"He's one happy little boy right now. He got to ride in a fire truck and talk on the radio and he was a captain for the day," Edwin Baker, chief of the Stockdale Volunteer Fire Department and Wilson County's fire marshal, told reporters afterward. "He was a little bit overwhelmed by the enormity of it, but he's very ecstatic to be home."

The procession continued through town and into the winter-brown countryside toward the farmhouse where Ryland's grandparents lived. Their house would be his for a while. Before the shooting, the Wards lived in a five-bedroom, three-bath house near the church, but Chris Ward, Ryland's father, could not bear to go back there.

Young Ryland and his fellow survivors came home to a church community that had captured the heart of the world. Thousands of cards arrived daily, many with money enclosed. Several GoFundMe pages sprang up, including one that raised $160,000. The Southern Baptist Texas Convention took over paying Pastor Frank's salary. The Ecumenical Center donated long-term counseling.

Companies contributed goods and services. H-E-B, the San Antonio–based supermarket chain, set aside $150,000 to help retrofit survivors' homes, pay their bills, and provide them gift cards for gas and groceries. H-E-B also raised an undisclosed amount at checkout stands and online.

In a rural community where finances already were stretched thin, where the family breadwinner was gone or unable to go back to work anytime soon, where insurance wouldn't cover needed remodeling or equipment (if they even had insurance), where long-term childcare or nursing care would be needed, those donations and contributions were a godsend. (The people of Sutherland Springs would take that throwaway term literally, of course.)

At a press conference in San Antonio in the spring, Pastor Frank announced that the North American Mission Board, a division of the Southern Baptist Association, would coordinate the construction of a new sanctuary and education building on the two-acre highway-frontage property adjacent to the church. The site, unaffordable in years past, was purchased and donated to the church after the shooting (just as Karla Holcombe had always prayed it would be). Renderings that Pomeroy unveiled showed a handsome building of cut stone with seating in a high-ceilinged airy sanctuary for 250 people and an adjacent education center—about fourteen thousand square feet in all. A memorial prayer garden would fill the space between the two buildings. Atop one of two towers would be the old bell from the original church; atop the other would be a light. The stone walls would be thick, Pastor Frank said. A security team would be on the alert and cameras would be watching. He wanted worshippers to feel safe and secure inside. The project was expected to cost about $3 million.

"We are in the midst of a celebration week. This is the week leading up to Easter," Pastor Frank told reporters. "And what better way to celebrate the resurrection of the Lord than the resurrection of a new church? I think God choreographed that."

He added that the congregation had more than doubled in number since the shooting and that baptisms had "increased exponentially."

"God is going to use the blood of those twenty-six martyrs and those survivors to bring forth revival into the land," he said. "Any time the church was persecuted, then God backed that up with a magnification or a multiplication of his people."

On a cool, cloudy first day of April in Sutherland Springs, about sixty members and visitors met outside for an "Easter Son Rise" service on the empty lot where the new building soon would begin to rise. Pastor Frank, wearing sunglasses, a tan sport coat, and jeans, leaned on a crutch because of recent knee surgery.

"Our path is based on the resurrection of Jesus Christ defeating death, hell, and the grave," he told the congregation. "If you do not know Jesus as Lord and Savior, you're blinded, and you're going to face eternity in a place you don't want to be."

"At the cross, at the cross where I first saw the light, and the burden of my heart rolled away," the praise team sang. The sun broke through, turning the patchy clouds pink.

Pastor Frank continued: "Satan tried to intervene and take our joy, but because our Lord is still large and in charge, we celebrate this resurrection. Don't allow the memories of our past to steal our joy. Satan tried his best to shut us down and make the world think God wasn't in His house....He is alive, He arose and because of his resurrection, we have been resurrected. He lives."

The sun broke through that Easter morning, and yet clouds would linger during the coming days and weeks. Money, a strange kind of madness abroad in the land, and the enduring pain of loss would make sure of that.

Given human nature, rancor over money was probably predictable, even among people who seek to be godly. Questions, suspicion, and skepticism that had been rumbling under the surface for weeks broke into the open with the church's announcement of the new building. The church's inexperience with handling large sums of money contributed to the rancor.

How could a church whose members had such urgent needs spend $3 million on a fancy new building? That was the question skeptics raised. It took a while for word to get out that the building was a project of the North American Mission Board. Money donated to church members' immediate needs was not involved.

The congregation was overwhelmed with donations: cash, checks, in-kind contributions. It took Pastor Frank and the elders who survived the shooting months to sort through it all and arrange a system for distribution.

Meanwhile, some family members of the victims began questioning who was getting the money and why. They began attacking the Pomeroys, the elders, and each other online. The attacks became so bitter and personal that the Sutherland Springs Facebook group, created to support those affected by the shooting, had to be frozen. Words like *cult* and *greed* popped up. The skeptics were accused of being a "lynch mob" or conducting a "witch hunt." It became verboten around the church to mention the names of families and individuals questioning the church's motives or its methods. They had been written out of the fellowship.

Pastor Frank appealed for unity. Sherri Pomeroy broke down in tears. "Emotions are running high," she wrote on Facebook on April 5. Mentioning her daughter, she said, "We lost Belle. While yes it was tragic and unfair and devastating, my financial loss does not compare to someone who lost their breadwinner.

"Some people believe that we can just simply divide all money that was donated strictly to 'victims' or 'survivors,'" she added. "They just don't understand how complicated that is."

She also posted a long Facebook entry from a local county commissioner, who wrote that he was trying to clarify misconceptions and misinformation. "Most have never been involved in this type of process and aren't familiar with the guidelines and legal issues for conducting a moral, ethical, legal relief effort of this magnitude," he wrote and then listed a number of "reputable sources providing services to victims."

The commissioner assured his readers that the Pomeroys were not making decisions about who received assistance. "While they do meet with families and collect info, they forward it to the Restoration Committee or HEB or the insurance company. Once received, those groups validate the requestor and requests and determine the appropriate response," he wrote.

"I ask that people not reinforce rumors that the Pomeroys are rejecting needs. Anyone stating this should be directed to the contacts listed above. Examples of assistance provided so far include: Food, medical care, lost wages, counseling, retrofitting homes to make them wheelchair accessible, roof repairs, damaged phone replacement, tree removal, fence repairs, yard work, transportation needs, wheelchair ramps, to name a few. Additionally, Christmas gifts received by the church have been distributed through a bunch of different events. None of the victims have complained directly to any of the organizations providing help....Responses to requests received are being responded to as quickly as possible. If anyone feels that assistance is needed, they should contact the resources listed above. If the right people are not contacted, then people are not equipped to assist."

The commissioner expressed his appreciation for those trying to help their neighbors, but he said he was disappointed that others were taking to social media to criticize those who were helping "organize and distribute the donations without knowing the entire story or circumstances involved in the process."

Lisa McNulty, whose daughter Tara was killed that Sunday, was one of the more outspoken skeptics. "This has gotten way out of hand—way out of hand," she told reporters. She accused the church of holding on to donations designated for her family. "There's some greed going on, and it's wrong," she said.

McNulty, fifty-four, told the *San Antonio Express-News* that before losing her daughter she had been hoping to retire but had become the sole caregiver for two grandchildren, who also were wounded that day. She said she worried about providing for them but hadn't requested money, because she didn't want to provide personal information.

"My grandson fell down the stairs the other day. I had to take him to the emergency room to make sure that the plate in his leg hadn't been jostled and moved," she said. "Am I supposed to go to the church for $20 for gas and wait two weeks? And I'm sure as heck not going to give them my account numbers."

She said she was worried about long-term expenses—her grandson needing braces in a year, her granddaughter going off to college in two years. How would she afford those future expenses? Would the church with all its donations be able to help?

The church also helped Kati Wall with expenses she incurred when she took off work after losing her parents. She complained that it took her months to get a response and when she did, she had to prove she was unable to get the money elsewhere. "The process is the thing that really bothers me," Wall told the *Express-News*. "What if you need help right now?"

The church paid specific victims' expenses if they could provide proof of need—copies of bills and prescriptions, for example—and also required confidentiality "by all parties." The church also modified its application for funds, according to forms posted on Facebook, by removing prohibitions on requests for money "to relieve the consequences of sin, such as bail bonds, drug/alcohol issues." It also rescinded limits on how many requests could be made per year.

Some victims thought each family would be getting a lump sum of money whether they were survivors or victims' family members. That's what happened after the Las Vegas shooting. Patrick Dziuk, a no-nonsense chemical engineer who headed the church's Restoration Committee, said the IRS required the church to use a needs-based system.

Dziuk and his wife, Christy, were from Karnes City. They made the hundred-mile round trip to Sutherland Springs several times a week and had basically embedded themselves in the church immediately after the shooting, faithfully attending almost every service. Pat occasionally preached and applied his business expertise to the church's ongoing financial challenge.

"How do you put a value on someone who's been killed versus someone who's wounded? How do you do that?" he asked rhetorically in an interview with the *Dallas Morning News*.

"You may have some victims who have very protracted needs, like Kris (Workman) or Zach (Poston), they'll have medical expenses for years. Then you have some folks like us, who lost Annabelle," Pastor Frank said. "And how incredibly sad that is, but we have no needs like they do. It's not fair for us to take the same amount of money."

Overwhelmed church leaders said they were working as hard as they could to distribute funds to victims and their families. They were following the law, they insisted. "There are going to be some people who are not going to be satisfied no matter what," Dziuk said. "God bless them. I know they're hurting and I'm sorry, but we're not going to make everyone happy."

A *Dallas Morning News* analysis of dozens of online funds as well as individual and corporate donors confirmed that at least $3,023,675 had been given since the shooting: More than $1.4 million was raised through GoFundMe.com for specific families. An additional $405,000 was donated to various general victims funds, and more than $1 million in cash and in-kind donations was raised to rebuild the church. The $3 million total did not include several other pots of money the *Morning News* was unable to assess, including the church's victims fund, money raised by H-E-B, and potentially dozens of private or unpublicized relief accounts.

"The one big question that everyone is asking," Dziuk said, "is, 'You're building this big church. Are victim funds being used for that?' The answer is absolutely, positively no way."

Two years earlier, similar tensions had arisen in Charleston in the aftermath of the Mother Emanuel shooting. Donations poured in from strangers across the country and around the world. Mail arrived in giant bags and boxloads day after day; most contained money of varying amounts. Many of the letters were addressed to the church, but others contained more precise instructions about how the sender wanted the money to be spent. People across Charleston held countless fundraisers; various local entities created funds, including the city of Charleston. Millions of dollars poured into the funds.

"Two months after the shooting, the families still hadn't heard from [the interim pastor] how or when the church planned to divide up the funds," Jennifer Berry Hawes wrote in her account of the Charleston shooting, *Grace Will Lead Us Home.* "As families and survivors waited, bills piled up and tensions grew. So did suspicions. Why all the secrecy?"

Both churches were overwhelmed not only by the tragedy but also by the aftermath. Both struggled to get on top of the challenge. Two months after the Sutherland Springs shooting, Terrie Smith, the Valero gas station manager serving as president of the Sutherland Springs Community Association, told reporters tensions in the community still could be resolved. "It's not too late to fix it. Everything in this world is fixable," she said.

For the most part she turned out to be right, even though a few disgruntled members walked away and never came back. On an April Sunday, Pastor Frank presided over an informational meeting after the morning service. He revealed that $2.91 million in donations had poured in since the shooting. "That looks like a lot of money, but with the medical conditions and the things that are going on...that can burn away really quick," he told the congregation.

He handed out a one-page spreadsheet showing the balance in various relief funds and the broad purposes donors had designated. The donations were sent to the church, a Wells Fargo relief fund, and two PayPal accounts. Nearly 29 percent of the sum donated—$840,000—was designated for "victim relief," according to the spreadsheet. Pastor Frank said that money was being distributed to survivors and victims' family members, although he said he didn't know how much had been disbursed to date.

Almost $2 million was undesignated, for the church to use as it wished, he said. He said that for any expenditure above $1,000, "the church is going to vote on it." The rest of the money—about $130,000—was designated by donors for a memorial at the shooting site, the church's food pantry, and funerals, among other purposes.

Maybe the disclosure wouldn't quell concerns, Pastor Frank said afterward, but at least the information was out there. "I'd rather be transparent and let them make up their stories as they want, and that way I have nothing to hide. It's just a matter of honesty," he said.

Not everyone was happy, but the grumbling and complaints gradually died down. Pastor Frank and his parishioners had more vexing issues to confront.

Chapter Sixteen

"Don't let anybody tell you it's time to get over it."

WEEKS GO BY. MONTHS. Autumn becomes winter, or what passes for winter in South Texas. Winter becomes spring, and black angus graze in fields turned Irish green. Bluebonnets and Indian paintbrushes burst forth along roadsides. Life goes on.

Milestones come and go. They are painful. The first Thanksgiving, just weeks after the shooting. The first Christmas. A loved one's birthday. An anniversary. Life goes on, yes, but the grinding pain of grief hardly seems to ease.

Nicholas Wolterstorff, a philosopher and writer whose adult son died in a skiing accident, calls it a "gaping wound."

"When someone to whom we are attached dies or is destroyed, we are cast into grief. That tells us when grief befalls us, not what the thing itself is," he writes. "Grief, I have come to think, is wanting the death or destruction of the loved one to be undone, while at the same time knowing it cannot be undone. Grief is wanting the loved one back when one knows he can't come back. Tears and agitation are typical expressions of grief, but they are not the thing itself. My grief was wanting intensely for Eric to be alive when I knew that could not be."

Sherri Pomeroy suffered from that gaping wound. She was more open about the pain she felt—that all survivors and family members felt—than her husband was. He felt an obligation to be strong for his flock and in public, at least, often resorted to what sounded like preacherly clichés. Sherri was more expressive. She cried, she questioned, even as she circled back to traditional expressions of faith.

"Tonight was too hard," she shared on Facebook about three weeks after the shooting. "I got physically sick, because it hurt so bad. I have moments that I cry so hard I can't breathe. I have feelings so deep I feel like my body is cut in half. Thankfully, they don't last forever, even though they feel like they do. I know there is joy in the morning, but this night has been four weeks too long."

When people asked her, "How are you doing?" she had a standard response. Months after the shooting she would say, "It's not one day at a time; it's one breath at a time. Every morning we start new."

Ridiculous little things intruded, also a sign of grief's hold on a person. Another Facebook entry from Sherri a few weeks after the shooting: "We stopped at the SS Express about 10 pm tonight to get gas. When we got home, Frank couldn't fund [sic] his wallet. We drove back and have been searching all over. Please be on the lookout."

Next entry: "Found it all scattered down [Highway] 539. Thank you God."

She and Frank had always done up Christmas big, both at home and at church, but they couldn't bear to decorate their tree. Their children came from out of town to make sure the house wasn't bereft for the holidays.

Every Christmas the family watched *Annabelle's Wish* together. The 1997 movie is about a mute boy and his friendship with a calf who wants to be a reindeer.

"She just loved that her name was in a movie," Sherri told Silvia Foster-Frau of the *San Antonio Express-News*. "It was about a special Christmas wish and the hope of Christmas. It was about giving."

Months later, she described how she hated to hear the school bus stop outside the house every afternoon, knowing Annabelle wouldn't be getting off and coming through the front door. "We are all so fragile," she said.

The extended Holcombe family also was having a hard time. Jennifer Holcombe showed Foster-Frau the Christmas stockings for her husband and their infant daughter on the mantel of her home. Both gone. A cup on the sink still had a small toothbrush, and children's bath toys were stuck to the bathtub walls.

"This is my home. All my memories are here. I couldn't just pack up and leave," Jennifer said. "That's what I have now, the memories. I need them."

Brother-in-law John also had holiday items laden with memories around the house. While Foster-Frau looked on, he rummaged through a box full of ornaments he was trying to preserve—a pink My Little Pony that was nine-year-old Megan's favorite; eleven-year-old Emily's unfinished ornament, a gift to her mother, with beads glued to only a quarter of it; seven gingerbread men, a gift to the family in 2013, each with the names of John's family members. Only three of those loved ones were left.

"It's a lot more quiet than it used to be," he told Foster-Frau. "There's this knot in my chest," he said, searching for a word to describe the feeling. "There's a spaceyness."

Jennifer Holcombe put it this way: "Everything I did, I'm not doing anymore. Everyone I had, now I don't."

On a Thursday evening in March, the conversation after supper and before David Colbath launched into Bible study drifted into the topic of stress. David told how he had been getting regular therapy at the Center for the Intrepid, the psychological services unit made available to Sutherland Springs survivors at Brooke Army Medical Center. He told us that he was in tears earlier in the week, and he had apologized to his therapist.

"Let me tell you something, David," the therapist said. "Some of the toughest soldiers in the world have sat right there in that chair where you're sitting. And they were in tears. So why shouldn't you be?"

"I was offered counseling immediately after I woke up," David said. "I attribute God to being with me and Christ leading me, but I also got good PTSD help, good counseling from total professionals that have helped our warriors. I got the same help they did."

Sitting by himself at a table in the corner, an older man with a grizzled beard and wearing a battered gimme cap raised his hand. I had seen him occasionally on Thursday evenings but had never met him. His name was Doug, and he was the owner of the junkyard adjacent to the church property. His neighbors tended to avoid him, because he always seemed to be in a bad mood. He came on Thursday evenings now and then for the meal and company but wasn't a church member. David called on him.

"I've had PTSD since I left Vietnam," he told us in a quiet voice. "The doctors have been working on me for thirty-five years. What happened here put me back in it again....I sleep in the dark. I walk around in the dark. My windows are boarded up. There's no light in my house except for one window. I used to have panic attacks you couldn't believe. I thought it was a heart attack. I have to stop and think through in my mind: It was just imaginary. Every hour and every minute of the day I think about God. I think about Jesus. I talk to God all the time."

David had to gently interrupt Doug, who seemed to be ambling through an extended reverie of his own. David had told me about similar symptoms he had experienced: waking up breathless in the middle of the night, heart pounding, feeling the hovering, threatening presence of someone in the room. The Center for the Intrepid, he said, had given him coping mechanisms.

The PTSD symptoms were becoming more common, Windy told me, as the holidays came and went, the media spotlight dimmed, and life became more routine. Even though Windy missed church that Sunday morning, she knew about PTSD. She had seen her dad, seven years a prisoner of the Viet Cong, struggle with its debilitating symptoms when he came home.

She herself knew what it felt like in her own life. Her son Blake had committed suicide in 1996 at age twenty. "I don't tell 'em it's going to get better," she said. "It's not. You'll have that scab, and every once in a while you'll hit it against something and break it open. There's nothing anybody can say that will magically make them better. Don't let anybody tell you it's time to get over it."

As the weeks passed, I saw people laugh and joke and enjoy themselves. I saw children and adults come to church one Sunday morning dressed like pirates, greeting each other with a fearsome "Aargh." At the annual Fall Fest, the first since the shooting, the biggest problem Pastor Frank had to deal with were the quizzical looks his Halloween costume elicited.

He and Pat Dziuk both wore black suits, skinny ties, shades, and black narrow-brimmed hats. To their disappointment, no one knew who the Blues Brothers were.

I saw happiness break through often. And, just as frequently, I saw sadness. I saw people wander down the aisles of the sanctuary on a Sunday morning and suddenly stop and embrace someone, tightly, in tears, for minutes at a time. Most who had been church members on that Sunday in November did not go away. Sunday after Sunday, week after week, they stayed with family, their church family.

Mary Beth Fisk also had experienced the gaping wound. She had lost an adult son to cancer. As CEO and executive director of the San Antonio–based Ecumenical Center for Education, Counseling and Health, she arrived in Sutherland Springs a couple of hours after the shooting. She stayed until two the next morning; her team never left.

"This is a very faith-filled community," she reminded me one morning as we talked in her office near the University of Texas Health Science Center in northwest San Antonio. "The church is like a family. Everybody knows one another. They have shared life events together—the faith they share, their shared ideals, worship, fall festivals, Bible study."

Their connectedness and their faith were good things, Fisk said. They were tools for coping with tragedy. "They see themselves as happy, fulfilled, blessed. They're amazing people," she said.

Fisk has counseled people over the years who are ashamed to seek help for trauma. Often they're ashamed of their symptoms. She had to help them understand that trauma is normal. Months after the shooting, survivors and family members were still coming in for the first time.

"Trauma is an emotional response to a terrible event. Could be an accident. Could be rape, a natural disaster. Immediately after the event shock and denial are typical," Fisk said. As time goes on, she added, they're likely to deal with flashbacks, strained relationships, and physical symptoms, headaches and nausea, for example. Failure to address the trauma could lead to more long-term chronic diseases.

I was surprised that many in Sutherland Springs were willing to take advantage of services the Ecumenical Center offered. I thought they might be suspicious of worldly consolation and assistance, instead of relying solely on God. Most weren't reluctant at all, and those who didn't take advantage of professional help were often the subject of prayers on Thursday nights. First responders also took advantage of counseling and therapy. So did high school kids in Floresville, Stockdale, and La Vernia, where school counselors were alert to their needs.

Those who seek help can emerge into a phase called post-traumatic growth, Fisk said. "It involves life-changing shifts in thinking and relating to the world that contributes to a personal process of change that is deeply meaningful."

The Ecumenical Center still had six counselors in the area, including one at the church, months after the shooting. There's no time table, Fisk told me. "The memories are never going to go away, but healing could take years."

The world beyond Sutherland Springs intruded. "Once you think you're at some place of normality, here comes an announcement of another shooting," said Terrie Smith one morning in February. "It's hard."

The announcement came from a place called Parkland, Florida, a sunny, upscale suburb, where a teenage gunman armed with a semiautomatic rifle similar to Devin Kelley's attacked Marjory Stoneman Douglas High School. The former student killed seventeen people and injured more than a dozen students and staff.

It was an achingly familiar story, although this time the aftermath was different. The young survivors, self-confident, politically sophisticated, and media-savvy, were sick to death of "thoughts and prayers" as a cynical palliative. Unlike the Sutherland Springs survivors, who turned inward and relied on their faith for healing, the Florida youngsters reached out to a wider world. They pushed for political change. They got together on the night of the shooting and resolved to organize. Amid the grieving and funerals, they began speaking out. They organized marches and traveled to Tallahassee to prod a balky Florida legislature toward tightening the state's gun laws. As their movement began to take hold, they traveled to Washington, DC, and to cities around the country, finding creative ways to keep the spotlight on the nation's gun crisis.

Emma Gonzalez, a Stoneman Douglas senior who became one of the familiar faces of the movement, explained at a rally shortly after the shooting, "Every single person up here today, all these people should be home grieving. But instead we are up here standing together, because if all our president can do is send thoughts and prayers, then it's time for victims to be the change that we need to see."

The Sutherland Springs survivors were not politically inclined. Most of them, I suspect, were not regular voters (and if they were, they voted for fierce protectors of the Second Amendment). A few of them—Stephen Willeford, the Pomeroys, and David Colbath, primarily—were pulled into politics by candidates and elected officials who sought to use their pain and public witness to aid their unrelenting legislative efforts to loosen gun regulations. The Sutherland Springs survivors became public advocates for arming teachers and administrators and hardening church security with armed guards. They were willing advocates, but politics was not their primary concern.

The Parkland students were not pulled into politics. Instead, they pushed into the political arena smartly and aggressively, and for at least a year captured a fickle public's attention with their #NeverAgain movement and March for Our Lives. Teenagers still in school, they raised millions of dollars from around the country, gave speeches and interviews, and wrote op-eds. They stood toe to toe with Second Amendment absolutists and pro-gun politicians and used their social media skills to respond to critics, some of whom accused them of being "crisis actors," not students who had watched their friends die.

Their efforts resulted in modest early success legislatively, in addition to huge success raising awareness. Oregon lawmakers were inspired to tighten up some gun restrictions, while in the students' own state—a state as NRA-friendly as Texas, if not more so—lawmakers grudgingly agreed to impose a higher age limit and a longer waiting period for purchasing semiautomatic rifles like the one used at Stoneman Douglas. They pushed for a broad ban on semiautomatic rifles, but Florida lawmakers voted against even debating the issue.

During the summer, a troop of Parkland students on a nationwide "Road to Change" tour spoke to an overflow crowd at an inner-city Methodist church in San Antonio, on a weekday afternoon, no less. No one from Sutherland Springs attended, and the Parkland students had no plans to visit Sutherland Springs, thirty miles away.

Cameron Kasky, a survivor of the Parkland shooting, told the audience they were continuing to call for gun reform because they went to school one day, not knowing a terrible tragedy was about to happen. "We are all here because of the worst possible thing that could have happened," he said.

I talked to a young Houston woman traveling with the Parkland group about Stephen Willeford, the "quintessential good guy with a gun." "A good guy with a gun can easily be turned unintentionally into a bad guy with a gun," she said. "We should pass legislation that helps us prevent shootings before they occur."

The next intrusion into Sutherland Springs' ongoing recovery, the next mass shooting, occurred close to home. On May 18, 2018, just after seven thirty on a Friday morning, a young man carrying a Remington Model 870 shotgun and a .38-caliber pistol opened fire on an art class at the high school in Santa Fe, Texas, a town of about thirteen thousand in the southeast Houston suburbs. He killed eight students and two teachers and injured thirteen others. Taken into custody by police, he was identified as Dimitrios Pagourtzis, a seventeen-year-old student at the school. The guns belonged to his father.

"You could almost conjure the whole scene in your mind without visiting the place, the aftermaths of school shootings having become so familiar," Houston journalist Mimi Swartz wrote in the *New York Times*. "The only thing that made Santa Fe different was the hypocrisy of major Texas politicians—the ones who have never wavered in their push for more guns on college campuses, showy open carry laws, and laws that have made it easier for the mentally ill to buy guns."

Actually, there were slightly nuanced differences. Politicians had been so shamed and ridiculed for their "thoughts and prayers" mantra that many of them strained to say something else, without saying too much else. Texas lieutenant governor Dan Patrick, a Tea Party icon and talk-radio host, suggested reducing the number of school-building entrances and exits to prevent more shootings. He also opined that divorce, abortion, and video games had something to do with the shooting. Governor Greg Abbott promised to "do more than just pray for the victims and their families," by holding roundtable discussions to stop the violence. He also promised to speed up background checks and keep guns away from those who pose "immediate danger."

Vice President Mike Pence told the students, "We're with you." President Donald Trump said that "this has been going on too long in our country" and promised "to do everything in our power to protect our students."

Bisected by tree-lined bayous, with subdivisions sprawling across a low coastal plain, Santa Fe looks and feels like the Deep South. The town votes like the South, too. In the 2016 election, nearly 80 percent of Santa Feans supported Donald Trump. Santa Fe was last in the news in 2000, when Santa Fe High School students sued the school district over the venerable Texas custom of opening football games with a prayer. The case made it to the US Supreme Court, which ruled in favor of the students. Most public events still open with a prayer.

A handful of Santa Fe students took part in a March for Life demonstration, but they were made to feel ostracized, said Megan McGuire, a tall, dark-haired junior who was not among the victims of the shooting. Most of her cohorts, she told me, were satisfied with gun laws as they were. So were their parents.

The shooting was on Friday. On Sunday, three thousand people gathered at a mosque outside Houston for the first student funeral. Sabika Sheikh, a seventeen-year-old exchange student from Pakistan, had been in Santa Fe for the school year and was scheduled to fly home to Karachi in a few weeks. Her host mother, Joleen Cogburn, wore an embroidered crimson hijab that Sabika had given her on Mother's Day. She repeated something Sabika had once told her: "I want to learn the American culture, and I want America to learn the Pakistan culture, and I want us to come together and unite."

Fifteen-year-old Jaelyn Cogburn told the audience that she had bonded with Sabika because she, too, was a newcomer at Santa Fe High School. She had just begun her first year at public school after being homeschooled. With tears flowing, she said that the two had grown close and that on a recent night she had begun to cry, realizing that her friend would soon be returning to Pakistan. "She leaned in and said, 'I love you and I miss you.' Even though we were always together, I don't know why she said she'd miss me."

That same day, seniors and their families gathered for a baccalaureate ceremony at a Baptist church near the school. With Governor Abbott in the audience, seniors wearing their forest-green graduation gowns and mortarboards took their seats in the wooden pews. A senior named Aaron Chenoweth spoke about what the class had endured during the school year: Hurricane Harvey, freak snowstorms, a false alarm two weeks after Parkland that resulted in a school lockdown, and, of course, the shooting. "Storms, snows, threats, you name it," the young man said. "One thing I've always found and trusted in is God."

The church's interim senior pastor, Jerl Watkins, told the congregation that Jesus taught "that as long as we live on this Earth, we are going to have trouble, we are going to face tragedy, but if a person is in Christ, then he can have a peace in spite of their tragedies."

Sutherland Springs residents promptly sent a supportive banner to Santa Fe. Banners, in fact, were becoming popular Hallmark-style expressions of a grim American tradition. A banner from residents of Las Vegas, where fifty-eight concertgoers were killed by a gunman, hung on the fence outside First Baptist. "#VegasStrong sends wishes of strength and healing to Sutherland Springs, Texas," it read.

Santa Fe victims also remained on the Thursday night prayer list for many weeks. "Sutherland Springs and Santa Fe are members of a tragic fraternity, brothers and sisters in suffering," Pastor Frank reminded his flock.

David Colbath led a small group of church members on a visit to Santa Fe and reported back that members of the community were divided and unhappy. Many, he said, blamed the school board and school administrators for not doing more to arm teachers and hire guards. Because the shooting took place at a large high school, with a highly diverse student body, Santa Fe, as David saw it, couldn't rely on the cohesiveness and sense of community—not to mention belief—that had strengthened Sutherland Springs. "We are fortunate," he said.

"It's not about guns. It's about a change of heart," Pastor Frank preached on the Sunday after the shooting. "We should try not to take a political stance on this. We need to make Christ the forefront of the conversation. We should be lifting them up in prayer during this period of grief, heartache, and pain, in the midst of this hard, hard trial they're having to face."

Hard, hard trials kept on coming: A gunman forced his way into the office of the *Capital Gazette,* an Annapolis, Maryland, newspaper. He killed five people...In Pittsburgh, a gunman burst into the Tree of Life Synagogue during Shabbat services and killed eleven people. He wounded six more, including four police officers. It was considered the largest attack on Jews in American history. An arsenal of twenty-one weapons was registered in the shooter's name...In Thousand Oaks, California, a man entered a bar on "college night" and killed twelve people, including a police officer. At least twelve were injured. The gunman then killed himself.

Those were the spectacular mass shootings. In small towns and large, in workplaces and homes, the plague of pain, grief, and yearning that afflicted Sutherland Springs spread across the nation. It was an American epidemic.

Chapter Seventeen

"Opening wounds and pouring salt in"

IN A SPEECH TO the Knight Foundation Media Forum in Miami in early 2019, renowned technology scholar danah boyd recalled discovering that, before about noon on November 5, 2017, the number of times the words "Sutherland Springs" had appeared in searches on Google or Bing during the previous two years was zero. Not one person in the world had either reason or curiosity to investigate a nondescript little town in the shadow of San Antonio.

"Even if you're in Texas, you might not know about it," said boyd (who eschews capital letters for her name). "It's not a popular town; it's very small."

When journalists and the curious began searching that day, all they got initially was automatically generated content—information from the real estate site Zillow, US Census basics, and assorted generic content available for every town in the country. "Google had already pulled that information as part of its infrastructure, trying to find something that was there; YouTube had absolutely nothing relevant at all," boyd said.

Exploiting the brief vacuum, groups and individuals boyd labeled "adversarial actors" rushed in to shape and manipulate the information landscape. They did what they've done with every mass shooting since at least Sandy Hook Elementary School in 2012: they flooded the sites with misinformation that lays the blame for the shootings on "antifa"—short for antifascist—a protest movement made up of autonomous groups affiliated by their militant opposition to what they consider fascism and other forms of extreme right-wing ideology.

"They want to stage a false equivalency to say that there's a group that's so much stronger than white-supremacist and white-nationalist groups," boyd said. "By staging that at scale, by creating fake antifa accounts all over Twitter, they can actually shape the discourse."

The truthers homed in on Sutherland Springs within hours of the shooting. Writing for *Fast Company* the day after the shooting, a reporter named Cale Guthrie Weissman found "a conspiracy-laden dystopia of alternative facts at your fingertips" on sites like YouTube. When he typed in "texas shooting," the first suggestion that filled in automatically was "texas shooting antifa," which produced numerous videos falsely tying the shooter to the antifascist movement. The first to show up on Google's search engine after typing in "Devin Kelley" was "Devin Kelley antifa." Other videos popped up describing the massacre as a "false flag," a term used to describe a staged event meant to distract from the truth.

It was predictable. On countless websites, in chat rooms, and on message boards the world over, the truthers propagate bizarre conspiracy tales about "psy-ops" and 9/11 as an "inside job." They contend that the slain children at Sandy Hook were child actors in a scheme pulled off by gun control zealots out to destroy the National Rifle Association. The Parkland students who organized the March for Life Movement were "crisis actors." The shooting never happened. David Hogg, a survivor of the Parkland shooting and a prominent spokesman for the student-led movement, felt compelled to go on Anderson Cooper's CNN show to announce, "I'm not a crisis actor."

Believers in these theories are an unsavory mix of gullible rubes, obsessive antigovernment extremists, fantasists, kooks, and the mentally disturbed. A steady diet of the outrageously repugnant Alex Jones, Rush Limbaugh, and other right-wing media figures fed their insanity. They were annoying and infuriating.

When they did more than rant and rail on websites, they could be dangerous. They took it upon themselves to act, to set the record straight. It was a shotgun-wielding truther who in 2017 responded to "pizzagate," driving from North Carolina to Washington, DC, to rescue children

Hillary Clinton and other prominent Democrats were supposedly holding hostage as part of a child prostitution ring at Comet Ping Pong, a neighborhood pizza joint near the National Zoo. On a day when the restaurant was crowded with kids and families, the truther accidentally fired shots into the wall before police arrived and took him into custody.

They harassed Sandy Hook parents, sent them threatening letters, and issued death threats. A Florida woman went to prison for threatening a Sandy Hook couple who had lost their son.

They also showed up in person in Sutherland Springs, alighting like noisome locusts shortly after the shooting. Their first stop was Terrie Smith's Valero gas station. "These conspiracy idiots showed up here and said I was part of an FBI conspiracy, that it was theatrical," Smith recalled. "They wouldn't let me out of my car!"

The "conspiracy idiots" who arrived in Sutherland Springs were Jodie Marie Mann and Robert Mikel Ussery, small-town Texans who proclaimed on Ussery's website, Side Thorn Journalist, that the mass shooting never happened, that it was staged by the Department of Homeland Security. They insisted that neither the victims nor their graves were real. They also demanded proof of Annabelle Pomeroy's birth certificate.

Mann and Ussery and other truthers had been harassing church members for months online, but when the couple showed up in person at the church, that was the last straw for Pastor Frank. It was a Monday morning in March, and as he arrived at church in his car he noticed two people, Mann and Ussery, writing in large, loopy letters on a poster attached to a fence for well-wishers to sign. They were writing, "The truth shall set you free." Frank recognized them. Church members had posted their pictures on a Sutherland Springs community Facebook site as a warning for members to be on the lookout.

On his own website, Ussery included a video he made at the church sometime before confronting Frank. In the video he starts to go inside the sanctuary and is met by an elderly couple who had come to Sutherland Springs from a Bruderhof peace community in Upstate New York. The man listens politely to Ussery's rantings about the thirty-three fake events, including Sutherland Springs—"How do you know it's real?"—

and then takes a brochure Ussery hands him. He walks away with Ussery still ranting.

Once Ussery and Mann recognized who Frank was, they started yelling and threatening him. Ussery told the pastor he was going to hang him from a tree and pee on his body while he was hanging. He yelled, "Your daughter never even existed. Show me her birth certificate! Show me anything to say she was here!"

Ussery had a camera on his chest and was taping the confrontation as he had done with the Bruderhof couple. Mann was recording it, as well— to be added, presumably, to the website filled with homemade videos purporting to prove that the Parkland school shooting, Sandy Hook school shooting, Las Vegas massacre, Charleston church shooting, and Boston Marathon bombing were all fake. They claimed the events were all false-flag operations organized by the federal government and then mourned by "crisis actors" with political motivations. They posted a video contending that the Parkland shooting was "100% proof of crisis actors." Ussery offered a $100,000 reward "for proof of death in any of the listed staged events. They are all drills using crisis actors that were sold to the public as real. NO DEAD, NO WOUNDED."

"He was armed at first," Frank said, telling the story later. "When he walked around to his truck, he stuck the sidearm under a floor mat or something. What I saw is, when the constable got here, his holster was empty. At that time I didn't know what happened to it. I was more worried about her. I was thinking maybe she had it now. She was out moseying around too. She scared me way more than he did. One, she was crazy, and, two, I didn't know what happened to that sidearm."

Frank was armed, as well, and so was Rod Green, who pulled up in his pickup shortly before the truthers started yelling. Green, Vietnam veteran, church elder, and member of the congregation's safety team, called the police. The pastor was trying to keep his eye on Ussery, who continued to yell at him to his face, and on Mann, who might have been carrying a gun. At the same time he was urging his friend Rod not to do anything rash.

"I had to keep telling Rod, 'Rod, just stay behind me,' because he was baiting Rod, and Rod's temper was, shall we say, getting there. And Rod was armed, and I was worried about Rod doing something bad....I'm not going to say I wasn't stressed, but I'm able to compartmentalize it and stay calm in those types of situations and think my way through them. I grew up on the streets, I rode with the Bandidos a little while, and you learn to watch what people are doing. You learn to watch for stupidity."

Rod begged to differ with his pastor. "I knew exactly what I was doing," he told me one cold, wet afternoon before heading out to fill up a trailerload of hay for his cattle. "I was trying to bait the son of a bitch and get him to do something. He kept telling me he was going to take me up the road somewhere and take me out. I learned in law enforcement you have to confront people like that. They'll back down 99.9 percent of the time."

A county constable arrived and arrested the fifty-six-year-old woman and her fifty-four-year-old boyfriend without incident. She was committed to a psychiatric facility, and he went to jail on charges of being a felon in possession of a gun. When the feds raided his home in a nearby county, they found ten guns, including a .50-caliber rifle, two assault-style rifles, two shotguns, and nearly a thousand rounds of ammunition.

"A nightmare," Sherri Pomeroy called the harassment. "They're just opening wounds and pouring salt in," she said. "We've already had to deal with one person that lived in an alternate reality," referring to the shooter, Devin Kelley.

Pastor Frank managed to defuse a potentially dangerous situation on the church lawn that day, but I could tell the encounter got to him. He brought it up several times. How could they believe that stuff, he wondered. Did they believe it?

It's a bizarre wormhole, to be sure, where true believers insist that up is down and truth is fiction. They spend countless hours in a never-ending echo chamber confirming their twisted confabulations with each other. To most of us, their beliefs—assuming they are beliefs—are as incredible as Pastor Frank's beliefs must be to nonbelievers. The pastor, of course, doesn't harass.

Months after Side Thorn and Conspiracy Granny were in custody, Frank appeared on a panel with three other people whose lives have been affected by mass shootings. Asked by the moderator about the confrontation with Ussery, he had to pause and compose himself as he told the audience about how "he made it personal about Annabelle."

"In my mind," he said, "I was thinking, 'he has to know, she has to know, that what they say is lunacy.' But when I had him nose to nose and he was yelling, he was screaming, he was being very profane, I could see in his eyes he believed what he was saying. Being a praying man, I was praying in my heart and I was standing my ground. I wasn't going to allow them to hurt the others there—around my church, people like to say, 'he wasn't always a preacher'—but the real scary part was when I looked in his eyes and realized he truly believed what he was saying."

Asked by the moderator what ought to be done about the truthers, Frank mused briefly but ultimately had no answer. "I think it's insane to try to explain insanity," he said.

Another panelist, Nicole Hockley, who lost her six-year-old son in the Sandy Hook massacre, told the audience that she and her organization initially ignored them. "Don't feed the trolls," they told themselves. "If you don't give them air, their fire doesn't burn. That's hard when you're constantly being attacked," she said.

After Parkland, she said, they decided that ignoring them wasn't enough. They decided "it's time to shut this down." They started filing lawsuits. "We have to protect our kids," Hockley said. "We have to protect future victims. We have to say there is a consequence to trying to make money off of conspiracy theories, and we will destroy you."

Chapter Eighteen

"No valid reason"

Because the USAF did not submit Kelley's fingerprints and final disposition, he was able to purchase firearms from federal firearms dealers, which he used during a shooting at the First Baptist Church of Sutherland Springs, Sutherland Springs, Texas. (From the Department of Defense Inspector General's *Report of Investigation into the United States Air Force's Failure to Submit Devin Kelley's Criminal History Information to the Federal Bureau of Investigation*)

ON DECEMBER 6, 2018, the inspector general for the Department of Defense released a comprehensive report detailing how the Air Force on six separate occasions failed to submit records to the FBI that would have barred Devin Patrick Kelley from buying the guns he used at Sutherland Springs. The 131-page report provided details confirming what already was known. For survivors and family members who chose to read it, the report offered sickening confirmation of what might have been.

The report concluded that on at least four occasions during and after the criminal proceedings against Kelley on charges of violence against his wife and infant stepson, the Air Force should have submitted the airman's fingerprints to the FBI Criminal Justice Information Services (CJIS) Division. On two other occasions, it should have submitted to the FBI the final disposition report of his court-martial. In each instance, the fingerprints were not submitted.

If the Air Force had simply followed protocol during Kelley's almost five years in the service, he would have walked away empty-handed in years to come after picking out a gun at a military PX or a sporting goods store in Texas. The information about his court-martial would have been recorded in the interstate identification index, and a gun store clerk would have seen it come up in the National Instant Criminal Background Check System (NICS) when Kelley tried to make a purchase. Federally licensed firearm dealers are required to use NICS. Kelley might have ended up buying a gun on the street or from an individual, but not from a licensed dealer.

Because of the Air Force snafu, because of the bureaucratic bungling, Kelley's name never showed up in NICS, despite his 2012 court-martial conviction. He legally bought four guns, three of which he used to slaughter twenty-six churchgoers and wound nearly two dozen more.

The inspector general's report was tediously thorough and at the same time maddening to read, knowing the end result of the Air Force's failure. The excuses investigators were able to uncover were innocuous— and infuriating. Inexperienced federal agents. Individual personal issues at the time. Leadership gaps. A "high operations tempo." Agents and security forces who had not been taught how to take fingerprints. Did not understand the policies. Could not explain why he did not submit Kelley's fingerprints.

These factors "provide context" but "do not excuse the failures," the report acknowledged, concluding there was "no valid reason" for the Air Force's mistakes.

The Air Force should have been on alert about Kelley in 2011–2012, when he was accumulating the various administrative punishments that ranged from the trivial to the more serious—everything from wearing headphones while in uniform to lying to a female supervisor about calling her a derogatory name. He obviously was having trouble. Someone— his commanding officer, a base psychologist, someone—should have flagged him.

That's also the same time period that the Air Force Office of Special Investigations suspected child abuse, after Kelley's eleven-month-old stepson was hospitalized twice in one week. At the end of an interview with special agents about the situation, Kelley's fingerprints and a DNA sample were taken—but were never submitted to the FBI. That was the first missed opportunity.

Not long after the child was placed in foster care, Kelley voluntarily checked in at the mental health clinic at Holloman Air Force Base, where he told a staff psychologist that he was unable to cope with work stress because Child Protective Services had taken his stepson away. From September 2011 to February 2012, Kelley was treated seventeen times at the mental health clinic, but the notes his psychologist made did not flag any alarming behavior, the report found.

The inspector general's report concluded that Kelley's treatment at a mental health facility did not meet the criteria of a "prohibited person" under the Gun Control Act of 1968. Mere treatment was not enough. He had to be involuntarily committed or deemed mentally defective to be prohibited.

Tessa Kelley left her husband in February 2012 and told investigators that he had abused her emotionally and physically for months. The Air Force issued a no contact order, and investigators tried to interview Devin Kelley about the abuse allegations. Declining to speak to them, he requested legal counsel. The report concluded that the Air Force should have collected fingerprints and then submitted them on this occasion, as well. It didn't happen. That was the second missed opportunity.

During the next several months, Kelley was in and out of Holloman's mental health facility frequently, his behavior becoming more serious. When he left the clinic without permission one night and headed to El Paso, where authorities apprehended him as he was trying to leave town on a Greyhound bus, his commander ordered him into pretrial confinement on grounds that he had become a flight risk and a danger to himself and others. According to Air Force Corrections System policy, he should have been fingerprinted as he was being processed into the confinement facility.

Maybe he was and maybe he wasn't. The inspector general couldn't make a determination, because the facility closed in May 2016 and all its records were apparently destroyed. Investigators were able to determine that his fingerprints never made it to the FBI. Regardless, the report doesn't include this incident as one of the four missed opportunities to file Kelley's fingerprints.

The third protocol violation occurred during an interview at the confinement facility. According to the interview record contained in his case file, special agents collected Kelley's fingerprints when they were finished speaking with him, but the inspector general's office did not find his fingerprints in the file. Investigators were able to determine that the FBI never received the fingerprints.

On November 7, 2012, Kelley was convicted of assaulting his wife and stepson. He was reduced in rank to Airman Basic, sentenced to twelve months of confinement, and given a Bad Conduct Discharge. When he was returned to the confinement facility where he had stayed before his trial, facility personnel should have collected his fingerprints and submitted them to the FBI, along with his final disposition report. They did not.

Investigators could not determine whether the facility collected the fingerprints, because the case file had been destroyed. What could be determined, yet again, was that the FBI never received the information.

When Kelley's case was closed in December 2012, the Air Force had a final opportunity to ensure that his fingerprints and final disposition made it into the FBI CJIS Division database. Once again, it failed. The special agent overseeing the investigation certified in the Air Force's Office of Special Investigations database that Kelley's fingerprint cards and final disposition report were submitted to the FBI. "This was not accurate," the report stated. In fact, the fingerprint cards were left in the investigative file, and the checklist for closing cases was left incomplete.

Even after his discharge from the Air Force, Kelley's run-ins with the law should have landed him in NICS. The animal cruelty incident in Colorado and the sexual assault allegation in New Braunfels were both serious enough to block a gun purchase. Authorities didn't pursue an investigation into the latter. "An error," the local sheriff conceded.

Kelley wasn't the only one whose misdeeds slipped through bureaucratic seams over the years. As part of its report, the inspector general's office audited 70 investigations that had been conducted by the Air Force Office of Special Investigations detachment, including 25 that were investigated in the same time frame as Kelley's case. In 45 of those cases, fingerprints and the final disposition should have been sent to the FBI. Air Force investigators collected fingerprints from 45 of the 49 subjects, but 10 of them—or 20 percent—were not submitted.

The Air Force's recalcitrance prompted US senator John Cornyn to visit Sutherland Springs in March 2018, bringing with him a flag that had flown over the Capitol and what he called "something that would actually save lives." The Texas Republican was referring to legislation he cosponsored—along with US senator Chris Murphy, D-Conn.—that was designed to close the loopholes in the background check system that had allowed Kelley to purchase guns. The bill's nickname was "Fix NICS."

"It's not just mere symbolism," the tall, white-haired lawmaker said, standing in front of the church on a spring morning.

Frank Pomeroy, his handgun in a leather holster on his hip, thanked Cornyn for a law that will "make us all feel a little safer." He added that self-protection is part of American culture. "I've always been a proponent of carrying," he said. "God's called some of us to run toward the fight, not away from it."

Cornyn called Fix NICS "a solution" but "not a complete solution" to the problem of gun violence. Separating himself slightly from many of his GOP cohorts, he proposed penalizing would-be gun owners who lie about their backgrounds to purchase firearms and praised President Trump's efforts to regulate bump stocks (an effort that eventually got lost in the perpetual gun control feud).

In addition to strengthening reporting procedures, Cornyn's bill created a Domestic Abuse and Violence Prevention Initiative. The objective was to ensure that states had adequate resources and incentives to share all relevant information with NICS showing that a felon or domestic abuser was excluded from purchasing firearms under current law. Kelley, of course, would have been a prime target.

Asked about additional gun control measures, including a ban on assault rifles, Cornyn gestured behind him toward a man wearing a black cowboy hat. "He stopped the shooter from killing more people," the senator said, referring to Stephen Willeford. "It's not the gun itself, it's the person who's using it."

Willeford stepped to Cornyn's side and praised him as "a tireless protector of our Second Amendment rights."

"I met him [the shooter] with the very same gun that he had," Stephen said. "There's only one thing that stops a bad guy. That's a good guy."

Cornyn's Senate Bill 2135, the Fix NICS Act, was folded into a $1.3 trillion spending bill, which President Trump signed into law on March 23, 2018.

The inspector general's report buttressed legal claims against the federal government that lawyers for survivors and family members began filing in the summer of 2018. Among the first were Joe and Claryce Holcombe, the couple in their eighties who lost nine members of their extended family— adult children, a daughter-in-law, grandkids, and an unborn child. Their lawsuit claimed damages of up to $25 million.

The family's lawyer, Houston-based attorney Rob Ammons, contended the Air Force failed to provide conviction and discharge information to the FBI that would have prevented Devin Patrick Kelley from buying a gun. "The shooter had a storied history of problems with law enforcement…while he was in the Air Force, and the Air Force didn't report him into the system," Ammons said.

"[John Bryan] Holcombe's death was caused, in whole or in part, by the institutional failures of the United States Department of Defense, including, but not limited to, the U.S. Air Force, in that these entities negligently, recklessly, carelessly, and/or egregiously failed to report pertinent criminal arrest and conviction information of the shooter into a federal database, as required by law and which would have prevented and barred the shooter from purchasing, owning, and/or possessing the firearms that he used in the shooting," the suit claimed.

The Holcombes were among more than sixty family members and survivors who had filed administrative complaints against the Air Force six months earlier but received no formal response. Ammons said the federal government "has done nothing but ask for more information from the Holcombe family."

The attorney noted that Kelley was able to purchase an AR-15 from a San Antonio–area sporting goods store. "Under a 1996 law preventing spouse and child abusers from possessing firearms, the service's Office of Special Investigations should have entered that conviction into an FBI database," he wrote. "The office didn't, the Air Force has admitted. What's more, the acts Kelley pleaded guilty to—breaking his baby stepson's skull and hitting and kicking his then-wife—were punishable by imprisonment of more than a year. That qualifies them as felonies, which must be entered into the database."

Jennifer Holcombe, who lost her husband and their infant daughter in the shooting, did not join in the lawsuit. It was her belief, she said, that lawsuits would not honor the memory of her loved ones.

Maggie Vidal and her grown children also sued the Air Force and the Defense Department, as did the grown children of Sara and Dennis Johnson, including Kati Wall. Like the Holcombes, the two families alleged that the US government was negligent and could have kept Kelley from possessing guns if the Air Force had properly managed his military records. The attorney representing both families, Jamal Alsaffar, said the government had six months to respond to a notice of claim requesting it take responsibility for failing to report Kelley's conviction, but didn't.

"Despite acknowledging that it failed to protect this community and many others, the government did nothing the past six months to try to right the wrong. So the family had to file a federal lawsuit to ensure that the government is held accountable for its negligence and to make this and other communities safer," Alsaffar said.

One morning Alsaffar and I were sitting in his sleek office in a modern multistory building on the western edge of Austin. Behind his desk an expansive picture window afforded a postcard-pretty view of the cedar-cloaked Texas Hill Country.

"Have you seen some of their houses?" he asked, referring to his Sutherland Springs clients. "I'm hitting my head on the ceiling inside some of them. You ought to see some of the bathrooms that they're trying to retrofit. There are trip hazards, fall hazards."

The shooting left some of them with lifelong medical needs, he said. Some already had preexisting conditions. "They deserve the best, not just the cheapest," Alsaffar said. "The best wheelchairs. The best au pair care. They deserve being made a little more comfortable for the rest of their lives, whether or not they're experiencing actual physical pain. All they're asking is to be fully compensated. That's really what justice is."

Alsaffar acknowledged that it was difficult to prevail in a lawsuit against the federal government, despite the Air Force's admission of wrongdoing. The government was likely to claim that no matter how blatant the mistakes, those responsible were shielded by governmental immunity. The doctrine of sovereign immunity made it nearly impossible to sue the federal government, although under the Federal Tort Claims Act, people could seek damages in limited cases if they could prove direct negligence.

In February 2019, a year and a half after the shooting, Alsaffar's clients were among fifty-six Sutherland Springs survivors and family members who filed a newly consolidated lawsuit against Academy Sports & Outdoors, the Texas-based sporting goods store that sold Kelley the AR-15 and thirty-round magazine that he used in the mass slaying. They based their claim on Kelley's use of a Colorado ID to buy the weapon. Colorado bans the sale of any magazine with a capacity of more than fifteen rounds. Kelley presented a Colorado ID card when he purchased the firearm, the thirty-round magazine included with it and another thirty-round magazine. He paid cash.

The filing included a copy of Academy regulations stating that "the seller is presumed to know the applicable state laws and published ordinances in both the seller's state and the buyer's state."

In an earlier hearing to determine whether the case could proceed and eventually go to trial, Academy argued that the definition of a firearm didn't include its magazine. The company also argued that the Air Force was at fault for failing to notify federal authorities about Kelley's previous felony convictions. Janet Militello, Academy's lawyer, referred to a federal law called the Protection of Lawful Commerce in Arms Act. The law shields firearms makers and dealers from being held liable when their products are used to commit crimes. The only exceptions are in cases of negligence or if the dealer knowingly broke federal or state laws when the weapon was sold.

"There was a horrible tragedy," Militello told the judge. "Nobody thinks that this should be ignored. But Academy is not responsible."

Militello contended that even though Kelley was a resident of Colorado, where the thirty-round magazine is banned, Texas law allowed Academy to sell high-capacity magazines. She added that the "magazine" was not included in the definition of "firearm."

The families' lawyers contended that federal law prohibited sales to residents from out of state unless the buyer met them in person and the sale "fully" complied "with the legal conditions of sale in both such states." Academy was grossly negligent, they said, when it sold Kelley the Ruger AR-556 and high-capacity magazines.

"Academy is the gatekeeper to protect people from buying guns who shouldn't have them," attorney Jason Webster said. "When you have a guy who's 850 miles from his home and paying cash…that kind of raises some flags."

As the *Dallas Morning News* reported, attorney Webster turned away from the judge and pointed out the Sutherland Springs families present in the courtroom, including the mother of Joann Ward, who died trying to shield her four children. He also acknowledged family members of Dennis and Sara Johnson, both of whom were killed. In one hand, Webster clutched an AR-556. In the other, a magazine. One doesn't work without the other, he said, so arguing that "magazine" and "gun" are two different things is like arguing a car isn't a car without its wheels.

"If Academy were to have followed the law, that gun would not have been in his hands," Webster said. "If anybody deserves their day in court, it's these families here."

Bexar County district judge Karen Pozza ruled that the case should proceed. The families were asking for millions of dollars in damages for physical and mental anguish, disfigurement, and medical expenses.

Pastor Frank counseled his parishioners not to file suit. He didn't forbid them to go to court—he doesn't have that power—but he reminded anyone who asked that the congregation itself would not be filing lawsuits.

"My personal stance," he told me one fall afternoon in his office, "is that we shouldn't take our faults before a government. You should take your faults to the Lord. It stays among brothers."

I must have looked confused, so he reached for a Bible on his desk and turned to 1 Corinthians 6:1–8. In the passage, the apostle Paul is admonishing members of the church at Corinth who are feuding among themselves. "Dare any of you, having a matter against another, go to law before the unrighteous, and not before the saints?" Paul writes.

The saints will judge the world, judge the angels, Paul reminds them. How can they rely on outsiders to solve their internal disagreements? "Now therefore, it is utter failure for you that you go to law against one another," he writes. "Why do you not rather accept wrong? Why do you not rather *let yourselves* be cheated?"

Pastor Frank didn't expect his brethren to be cheated, necessarily, but he didn't expect the legal system to solve the problems that church members faced. "My idea to this," he said, "is, I need to take any issue to the Lord and to my brother rather than to the world. A lawsuit would not help us in our situation."

A number of the pastor's parishioners felt otherwise.

Chapter Nineteen

"The way it used to be"

LISA KRANTZ, AN AWARD-WINNING photographer for the *San Antonio Express-News,* stayed with the Sutherland Springs story for months, long after most reporters had moved on to the next natural disaster, the next mass shooting. She got to know the people of the congregation well, and they knew her. And trusted her.

When a church member we both had come to know told Lisa months after the shooting, "I wish we could all go back to the way it used to be," she was referring specifically to journalists hanging around, but Lisa knew not to take her remark personally. We nosy, intrusive reporters, with our cameras, our notebooks, our insistent questions, were just a symbol. Our friend longed for the BJE—Before Journalist era, so to speak—a happier time when things were normal, when most people had never heard of Sutherland Springs and its tiny church, had never even imagined the worst church shooting in American history. She knew, as Lisa and I knew, that the way it used to be could never be, even as time passed and horribly vivid memories of an awful event slowly faded. Still, she could wish.

The first anniversary was coming up. Members were hoping it would be not just a commemorative moment and a milestone but also a punctuation that marked a fitting end to mourning and those ever-present memories. They would never forget, of course. Their pain would never completely dissipate, but they were tired of ritual reliving. It was time—time they "turned to their affairs," to borrow from an affecting Robert Frost poem about a beloved young man's sudden death.

* * *

The six-month anniversary in May had been a kind of preview. It was a ground-breaking ceremony for the new church that would rise from the vacant lot adjacent to the old building (that for the foreseeable future would remain as a memorial). For the survivors and their families gathered under a large, white tent amid an audience of two hundred or so, the day was an ordeal. Six months on, their emotions were still raw. The prayers and politicians' speeches, the pastoral words of comfort from preachers and Baptist leaders, the ground-breaking itself—complete with ceremonial golden shovels—were well intentioned, but words and good intentions were losing their force. Plus, the journalists were back—scribbling, taking photos, asking questions, hovering like moths to a lamp.

"We're counting the blessings, we're counting the good that has come from it. But it doesn't make it easier," said Deborah Braden, who was shot four times and who lost her husband in the massacre. Her granddaughter was wounded but survived.

The ceremony wasn't easy for her. She told the *San Antonio Express-News* her emotions were "up and down." Being on the site and intentionally remembering the dead intensified the pain she constantly felt but could sometimes ignore.

"Everything is so different. I mean my life was shattered and torn apart," she said, speaking through tears. "We would be celebrating our thirty-fourth anniversary at the end of the month. It's just so unfair."

The Saturday morning ceremony began with a consecration of the ground itself, at each of the four corners of the building-to-be. Karla Holcombe's old friends remembered how she used to walk the grassy lot when the property belonged to someone else, praying to God as she walked that someday, somehow the church would be able to acquire it. A few weeks after the shooting, a San Antonio businessman bought the land and donated it to the church. Karla's prayer had finally been answered.

Sherri Pomeroy, her face drawn and wet with tears, stepped to the mic. "The six-month anniversary has been especially tough, to remember how they lived, not to dwell on how they died," she said. Her voice trembling, she began reading the names of the twenty-six who were lost that day, steeling herself against breaking down as she spoke the familiar names of friends and loved ones: "Lu White. Robert Marshall. Karen Marshall. Annabelle. Bob Corrigan. Shani Corrigan. Peggy Warden. Dennis Johnson. Sara Johnson. Keith Braden. Joann Ward, with Emily and Brooke. Haley Krueger. Therese and Richard Rodriguez. Karla and Bryan Holcombe. Tara McNulty. Danny Holcombe, and Noah. Crystal Holcombe, with Greg and Emily and Megan. And Carlin Brite 'Billy Bob' Holcombe."

US senator Ted Cruz stepped up. "One hundred eighty-one days ago this community saw the face of evil," he reminded the audience, "and yet beyond the evil this community saw so much more. You saw love, you saw strength, you saw courage, you saw compassion."

The Texas senator and 2016 presidential candidate, an alumnus of Houston's Second Baptist High School and the son of a fiery evangelical preacher, exhibited homiletic skills that had come in handy with conservative Christian voters during his senatorial campaign. In what was basically a well-wrought sermon, he told his audience that he didn't know why God allows evil to happen.

"You will always mourn the precious twenty-six souls that were taken from you that morning," he continued. "They saw the love and peace and strength of Jesus that in worldly terms makes no sense. This town has been forged in fire. This community is a special community. Use the grief. Use the mourning to touch others."

"We are the survivors of Sutherland Springs, and evil will not overcome good," Sherri Pomeroy said, voicing hope and intention that sometimes buckled under the weight of grief.

Six months later, the survivors gathered yet again, this time for the first anniversary of the tragedy. They marveled that it had been a year. Physical wounds were healing for most of them. Emotional wounds lingered. Many were still in therapy—and would be indefinitely. They were getting on with their lives, as best they could.

The little ones, Ryland, Zoe, and Evelyn, were back in school. So was nine-year-old Rihanna. Zach Poston, whose grandmother sacrificed her life to save his, had begun his freshman year in college a few weeks earlier. Twenty-one-year-old Morgan Harris, her leg still healing from the wounds she suffered while in the sound booth that morning, had married Kyle Workman, the young man who managed to race out the door when the shooter was distracted. Kyle's older brother Kris, still the church praise leader, was back at work at his old San Antonio computer firm. He was intent on acquiring—and driving—a dirt-track race car with hand controls. He continued to insist that he wasn't suffering from depression or PTSD, that he had no regrets. "I don't like calling it a tragedy, because so much good has come of it," he said.

Governor Greg Abbott, taking a quick break from the campaign trail, reminded the anniversary audience that he and Kris shared a special bond, one he discovered when he visited the young man in the hospital a few days after the shooting. He told his listeners, as he had told reporters six months earlier, that the vertebra where Kris had been injured was exactly the same location where he had been injured when, at age twenty-six, a tree limb had fallen on him while he was out jogging. He reminded the audience of what he had said to Julie Workman, Kris's mother—"that it was great to come in and get to meet a young man who may be a future governor of the great state of Texas."

As Abbott wrapped up his speech, he told Sutherland Springs residents it was normal to question how such a tragedy could befall them. "You have to ask, 'God, why did this happen? God, how did this happen?'" he said. "But I know because of the strength of your relationship with God that you are seeing exactly what I experienced, and that is because I kept reaching out to God. The reality is that after my accident, it actually brought me closer to God than before my injury. I know the same thing is happening to you because God wants you. God is reaching out to you every single day."

Photographers clamored to take pictures of the two smiling wheelchair-bound men—one young, the other in late middle age—sitting side by side in the churchyard. "God is working, God is big, and if he decides that I'm going to walk again, I'll walk again," Kris told reporters. "And if he doesn't, that's OK too. You know, it doesn't matter, because whatever I'm intended to do, it's not a surprise to God, and if that includes me being in a wheelchair, that's OK."

David Colbath was on hand for the commemoration. He still was making occasional talks in churches around the country, giving his testimony about his fervent belief in God and guns. He had been to Tanzania for a big-game hunt and was gradually getting strength back in his hand, although the injuries to his backside still gave him trouble. A bullet remained in his chest.

He sent me an audiotape he had made one afternoon from the deck of a hotel on the Florida coast, after speaking to a church in the area. In the background, I could hear the shouts and squeals of children playing in the surf.

"Watching the boats and the people and the water," he mused, "I sit and I think about what this shooting has done to my life. Has it made me more compassionate? Has it made me more caring? Has it made me more understanding? Has it made me a man that wants to follow God more? Has it made me a man that doesn't look for arguments and fights? Has it made me a man who wants to do more than just go along and get along, however that saying goes?"

The answer, he said, was yes, although he was resigned to the fact that he was just a man and would always be a work in progress. "Yes, I have to work at it," he said. "Yes, I have to think about it. Yes, it's not second nature, but it's still a life and a lifestyle I want to lead."

Colbath also shared some thoughts about his old friend Frank Pomeroy. "I saw him cry and shed tears one time in fifteen years, over the death of the family dog," he said. "Now he knows how to shed tears of empathy and sympathy. He has compassion. He didn't know how to show it before. He's always been a great pastor; now he's a great preacher. And he's a man of God to go with it."

The Pomeroys considered selling their house in Seguin, the house where their kids had grown up. It was just too painful to walk by Annabelle's room, to step into the realm of a typical teenager—where everything was purple, Belle's favorite color—and imagine for a fleeting moment that she would be coming through the door from school in just a little while. Even the two dogs, the two dogs she loved romping with in the backyard, made them sad. She would have been fifteen on October 21.

Frank mentioned to Silvia Foster-Frau that if he were independently wealthy, he and Sherri would sell the house, buy a big RV, and hit the road for a year. They didn't, of course. They stayed—in the house and with the church.

A year after the tragedy, Stephen Willeford was still on beeper alert for plumbing emergencies at the hospital, thankful that his life and his family's were slowly getting back to normal. He was still The Hero, maybe always would be.

He insisted he preferred the country-boy anonymity of his life before the event, and yet his status afforded him potential opportunities that he couldn't ignore—starting a security business, consulting with churches, writing a book, making Hollywood connections. He also announced that he was running for a county commissioner's seat. I got the feeling, despite his protestations, that he had come to enjoy the notoriety a bit, and yet I had no doubt that he and Pam would exchange all of it for "how things used to be," when their grown children and their beautiful grandbabies were the focus of their existence.

He told *Texas Monthly*'s Michael Mooney that he sometimes worried about Pam, who usually stood quietly, just beyond the spotlight, when the focus was on him telling his story to enraptured audiences. She preferred being in the background but said she felt like she was still in a fog. She had trouble sleeping.

She told Mooney about begging her husband on the phone that morning not to go across the street and then driving back into town from the house in the country that she and Stephen had been remodeling. She knew that something horrible had happened; she didn't know whether her husband had gotten himself involved.

She and daughter Rachel had rushed across the road to the church; Stephen was eleven miles away, with Johnnie Langendorff and police officers. In the churchyard Rachel comforted one of the Holcombe children, a little girl who minutes earlier had been shielded by her wounded mother before the woman died. The child had lost not only her mother but also her three siblings. The two women noticed matted blood in her long, blonde hair. Rachel and the dazed little girl sang songs from *Moana*, the youngster's favorite movie.

Pam told *Texas Monthly* she was unsure what she and her husband were supposed to do next. They were looking for direction. That's what they prayed about the most.

One Sunday morning after services, Stephen spent a few minutes in the back of the sanctuary talking to a young woman who hadn't been to a service in a long time, even though she had grown up in the church. In the weeks and months since the shooting, she had been afraid to attend. She wasn't sure how she would be received.

Her name was Danielle Shields Kelley. She was the young widow of the shooter, the man who, in the old sanctuary just a few feet away, had slaughtered twenty-six people, including her grandmother. She assured Stephen she didn't blame him for shooting her husband; he did what he had to do. Stephen held her hands while they prayed together. He told the tearful young woman not to blame herself.

Michelle Shields worried about her daughter, who said she intended to keep her husband's name forever because she still loved him. Who insisted he wasn't a monster. Who believed that he was sick during the last months of his life.

Michelle listened but was not convinced. She believed he still had Danielle under his spell, even from the grave.

Some months after the shooting, Danielle had another child. The father of the child looked a lot like her late husband. Her mother feared she had lost her way.

Michelle and Ben Shields, who would have been prime targets had they been at church that morning, felt lost, as well. After the shooting, they decided it was best to retire—Ben from the lumber yard where he had worked for years, Michelle from the Floresville bank where she knew everybody and everybody knew her. It was hard to do her work when everybody who came in to the bank wanted to talk about the shooting. She and Ben were thankful for the church. They tried not to be bitter about their lives beyond the church.

Michelle told me about a brief conversation she had with Devin Kelley's father, when he dropped by the house one afternoon to pick up the grandchildren. "He never said anything like 'I'm sorry for your loss,'" Michelle recalled. "All he said was, it took him two weeks to find someone to do the cremation. I was thinking it took us two weeks to find someone to bury my mother, because your son killed so many. I wanted to say it, but I didn't."

The anniversary day had begun with a crowd overflowing the temporary building and spilling into the yard. In a few months they would no longer need the prefab building. The new structure was out of the ground, the concrete blocks, like gray Legos stacked atop each other, were looking more and more each day like a double-steepled church. On the hill above the healing springs of Cibolo Creek, it could be seen for miles around. A light would shine from one steeple, a bell would ring from the other.

It was big. Michelle Shields hoped it wasn't too big. She didn't want the congregation to lose the feel of the small country church that had nurtured her and her family for so many years.

Kris Workman got the morning service started. "We are a full church right now," he said. "I know a lot of you are guests. Spend the day with us, celebrate with us, love on us." Strumming his royal-blue electric guitar, the bullet hole in the neck now repaired pro bono by the Nashville manufacturer, he and the praise team launched into "Amazing Grace." The congregation joined in.

Pastor Frank stepped to the rostrum and read a letter from Vice President Mike Pence. "Faith is stronger than evil, and your faith has inspired the whole country," Pence wrote.

Ted Elmore of the Southern Baptists of Texas Convention was the guest speaker for the morning. "Nostalgia is wishing for a day that's long gone. A memorial gives it meaning," he told the audience. "There will be a generation here that does not remember," the white-haired preacher continued. "They will not know....We remember. We remember the lives. We remember the stories. There are forty years from generation to generation. This generation was lost. We remember."

Frank, wearing on this special day a gray suit, turquoise shirt, and a blue, red, and yellow speckled tie, again stepped to the podium. Whether he had his pistol on his hip, I couldn't tell. "We remember our loved ones, but they're never fully gone," he said. "Those are twenty-six I don't have to worry about. I know their salvation was true. They chose to serve Jesus Christ. They had faith....As we proceed into this new year, as we proceed into our lives, I can continue with joy in my heart, with tears in my eyes."

On a weekday afternoon a few days before the anniversary, I was looking for a workshop on a country road south of Sutherland Springs. When I found myself circling the historic Wilson County Courthouse in downtown Floresville, I realized I was lost. A phone call to Sarah Holcombe Slavin got me straightened out, and a few minutes later I was pulling up before an old frame military-surplus building set among a grove of tall, straight post oaks. Sarah, she of the violet-colored hair, met me at the door of her dad's business, American Canvas Works.

For more than three decades Bryan Holcombe had made custom canvas covers for trailers, trucks, and boats, as well as canvas awnings, oil field windbreaks, and auto upholstery. Inside the cluttered building were heavy rolls of various-colored canvas leaning against walls; large, specially adapted tables that Bryan himself had invented; and several industrial-sized sewing machines, their clickety-clack hum quiet.

I knew about Bryan's ministry, at church and at the Wilson County Jail. I had watched the video of the sermon he preached a few weeks before the shooting, the sermon where he ruminated about the Las Vegas shooting. I knew that Karla Holcombe, who loved jokes and laughing and kids, had run the church's Vacation Bible School. Their abiding faith, I assumed, explained the large timeline of the Israelites' Old Testament history tacked across one wall, above a scribble-marked chalkboard that suggested the building once was a classroom. Stacks of clothes were laid across one of the worktables. Atop another was a large cardboard box with ukuleles and fiddles sticking out. Bryan's instruments, they were scuffed and well-used.

He was a collector, maybe even a hoarder—of ukuleles, old clothes, kitchen food mixers, and, for some reason during the last few months of his life, shoes. Sarah laughed, but she wasn't sure what to do with all the stuff. Or the shop. Or her parents' house. She had been gradually cleaning out and organizing the shop for the past several weeks, perhaps to sell it, perhaps to reopen the family business one day.

"The decision making is one of the hardest things, for me," she said. "I've always been indecisive anyway, because I worry about how my decisions will affect others. It's very freeing to be able to give them up to God and truly feel He really cares about them and will provide an answer when it's time. It takes a lot of the weight off, but I still get very overwhelmed with it all."

Toward the back of the workshop, Elene, her dark-haired three-year-old, was entertaining herself in "the baby jail." Elene was the reason Sarah couldn't stay down for long. Laughing Elene wouldn't let her.

Sarah had taught high school math for a year. Despite the example of her grandparents, who had been longtime respected teachers in the Floresville public schools—not to mention her husband, Rocky, a university computer science professor—she had decided a year was more than enough.

Bidding the classroom adieu, she went to work in the shop with her father. For six years, she sewed, welded, and hemmed beside him. She always had been close to her mom, she said, but those six years with her dad were special. They even developed a shorthand language they used as they worked together.

Everyone in Wilson County knew Bryan Holcombe as a round-faced, red-bearded man with a perpetual smile and an irrepressible sense of humor, but Sarah learned he could be a taskmaster, as well. She described the frustration she had experienced one afternoon a couple of years earlier trying to sew together two pieces of bulky canvas, yards and yards of heavy material that would stretch tightly over a cattle trailer. Time after time she tried to line up the pieces, but she just couldn't get it right.

"I've been sewing since I was nine years old," she said, "and it was so frustrating."

Fingers growing numb, patience wearing thin, she gave up and called her dad over. He sewed the pieces together in about five seconds. They lined up perfectly.

"Why can't I do that?" she asked him.

"Because you're not a master," he said matter-of-factly. "I've been doing this for thirty years. You should have come to me sooner, because redoing weakens the seam."

He said something else that stuck with her: The tarp they were working on had his name stenciled on it. He had to be sure the work she was doing measured up to his high standards. His customers expected nothing less.

And now he was gone. Her mother was gone. Her brother was gone. A sister-in-law and her unborn child. Her infant niece. Three of another brother's stepchildren. Like the two pieces of canvas her dad helped her connect, she had been trying ever since to thread her life back together.

We could hear the chirpy voice of Elene, happily playing a game of her own invention in the baby jail. Otherwise, it was quiet in the building. Quiet but haunted, it seemed to me, with watchful ghosts. Sarah, I suspect, would call them angels.

"Before November, I used to go out to my dad's shop and work with him on automotive upholstery or canvas three or four days a week or so," she said. Sometimes, Crystal would be there working, too. Often, all the cousins would be there, in and out of the shop. The farm was always full of life."

After November, when she got bogged down with tasks and decisions, she occasionally called Jenni, whose infant daughter Noah Grace had died in her arms that Sunday, alongside her husband, Danny. Maybe they would run errands or work together cleaning out the shop. It helped to stay busy.

They would talk about their kids—one lost, one very much alive. After years of fertility treatments, Jenni and Danny had considered Noah's birth a blessing from God.

"We joke she never slept because she had too much life to put into that little bit of time that she had, that she had to just get everything she could out of it," Jenni told Silvia Foster-Frau, laughing through her tears.

"Before November, Jenni and I would often take our daughters to the zoo or the park or story time or some other fun toddler thing," Sarah recalled. "Now, I still go to the farm regularly. But instead of being with those people, they are gone. Instead of doing canvas or upholstery work, I'm working on my parents' estate arrangements. Or tackling new problems that come up, or trying to somewhat maintain the property."

Slowly, gradually, Sarah was sewing her life back together—with help, she would tell you, not from her father anymore but from her Father. (That's her poetic conceit. I think she was proud of it.)

John, Sarah's older brother, suddenly had to learn to be a single parent to a teenage son and a lively little girl. Philip was not at church that day; Evelyn was. Her "favorite father," as Evelyn called him—her biological father had died of a heart attack—John had to learn how to cook, how to brush a little girl's hair and gather its honey-golden strands into a ponytail. With sisters no longer around to play with, he had to learn to keep her occupied when the house suddenly went quiet. Jenni and Sarah dropped by the house and helped him as often as they could.

Jenni was sewing her own life back together, as well. She became more active at church. Helping organize Vacation Bible School and Fall Fest, she assumed roles her mother-in-law had taken on. When she had trouble sleeping, she got out of bed and posted photos and videos of her daughter and husband on Facebook.

Before marriage and motherhood, she had worked at Macy's. Now she wondered what life held in store for her. "I can't go work at McDonald's," she said with a laugh. She prayed she would recognize the right path when it appeared.

Scott Holcombe, Sarah and John's younger brother, had perhaps the most difficult sewing task. At thirty-one, he had been living with his parents and looked forward to Sundays when he would have the house to himself. At the very moment his parents were dying, he was at home, high on methamphetamine. After his parents' deaths, he ended up in jail for a while, weaned himself away from drugs and alcohol, and began pulling himself together.

In 1972, in a West Virginia coal-mining community called Buffalo Creek, a makeshift dam broke and millions of gallons of coal-infused black water and debris roared down a narrow mountain hollow, destroying everything before it. One hundred thirty-two people died; hundreds were left homeless.

When Yale professor and sociologist Kai T. Erikson arrived in Buffalo Creek to explore "the human wreckage left in the wake," he found a once–tightly knit Appalachian community struggling to find strength in the sharing of grief—struggling because no community was left. As Erikson revealed in his classic *Everything in Its Path*, the "loss of communality" was almost as devastating as the disaster itself. A once hardy and resourceful people—people he would come to know and respect—had been rendered apathetic, fearful, and disoriented. Like the men and women of Sutherland Springs, most were God-fearing, but their faith had been sorely tested. "People are much more suspicious of God's justice," an old Baptist minister told the inquiring sociologist.

I thought I might find similar fissures in the wake of tragedy in the Sutherland Springs church community (a word that comes from the same root as *communion,* Erikson points out). I did not. Members of the church had their problems, both before and after, but their community, their "communality," held firm. Even Pastor Frank, their stalwart and trusted spiritual guide, had initial doubts after losing half the congregation, including his own daughter. And yet the community was resilient; the community lifted him up. "The remnant" found strength in its faith and common purpose.

I could not share their tenacious belief. But as I came to know them during the weeks and months after their loss, I could only admire how they bore the unbearable. As the therapist Mary Beth Fisk said, "They are amazing people."

I thought of Elaine Pagels, the renowned author and theologian who shortly after losing her young son to a congenital heart defect lost her husband in a climbing accident. As she recounts in *Why Religion? A Personal Story,* she grieved, deeply, and for months felt lost and undone. She recovered.

"However it happens, sometimes hearts *do* heal," she writes, "through what I can only call grace."

As Sarah Slavin and Sherri Pomeroy and David Colbath and every other member of the First Baptist Church of Sutherland Springs will tell you, it had been a slow, uneven process, with two or three steps forward over the ensuing weeks and months and then a couple of steps back. Like Pagels, they were recovering. Like those in years past who journeyed to the Cibolo to "take the waters," they expected to heal.

Still, as life returned to a semblance of normal for survivors of the deadliest mass shooting in Texas history, a worrisome question lingered— for me, for a gun-loving Lone Star State, for America. How long would we accept our nation's epidemic of gun violence, the kind of gun insanity that ripped apart a small country church?

No other civilized country on earth tolerates in its midst lethal weapons, battlefield weapons that ravaged the body of a small child in her mother's arms on a Sunday morning. No other nation accepts the death of innocent men, women, and children as collateral damage in the name of an abstract ideal.

Columbine, Virginia Tech, Aurora, San Bernardino, Charleston, Orlando, Las Vegas, Sutherland Springs, Parkland, Santa Fe, Jacksonville, Pittsburgh, Thousand Oaks, and whatever unlucky locale that next finds itself under fire have become, in the words of *New Yorker* writer Adam Gopnik, "ritual sacrifices to be greeted, as all ritual sacrifices are, with prayer."

Try to imagine a similar roll-call reading of slaughter sites elsewhere— one that includes, let's say, Halifax, Toronto, Windsor, Calgary, Vancouver, or, across the Atlantic, London, Cambridge, Birmingham, York, Norwich, and maybe a little country church in the Cotswolds. When it comes to guns, Canada and Britain are not obsessed, not infatuated. Guns are not fetishized.

The mass killings, in Gopnik's words, "have become essential to the demonstration of the power of guns…to a fantasy view of 'liberty' that involves the destruction of another person."

Or twenty-six persons, with at least twenty more still living but torn apart physically and emotionally.

The people of Sutherland Springs, Texas, are living exemplars of courage, grace, and resilience. They bear living witness to their faith—in God, the Giver of life, and in guns, precision instruments of death. Two faiths irreconcilable, it seems to me. With due respect to their awful experience on that Sunday morning in November, I would argue that we need them—this nation needs them—to take the side of life. Without guns.

I know how Stephen Willeford, Frank Pomeroy, and other gun enthusiasts in Sutherland Springs would respond. They are kind, conscientious people who love their community, and they would insist they stick to their guns as an expression of their deep affection.

I'm persuaded there's another way. From faith communities like the First Baptist Church of Sutherland Springs, we need not a reflection of a troubled culture but a brave and life-affirming countervision.

Epilogue

LET'S SAY YOU'RE DRIVING eastward out of San Antonio these days, toward Victoria and the Gulf Coast on US Highway 87. Fifteen miles out, you pass the big H-E-B and the Dairy Queen in La Vernia and a few miles farther on, always-busy Baldy's Diner on the left and the cowboy church on the right. You're coming up on a little Texas town that has shed its decades-long anonymity. Heading up the incline where once you might have noticed the yellow warning light at the intersection of Farm Road 539 and not much else—unless you have a hankering for Terrie Smith's breakfast tacos at the Valero station—you'll see beside the road a towering double-steepled church building clad in beige-colored Texas limestone. Looming over the now-iconic little sanctuary where twenty-six people died, the impressive new home of the First Baptist Church of Sutherland Springs is visible for miles around.

More than six hundred worshippers dedicated the building on a warm spring morning in 2019. They crowded into a soaring, sunlit sanctuary and spilled over into an adjacent classroom to give thanks to God and to sanctify the handsome edifice that now dominates the small community. They heard a governor and US senators, Southern Baptist officials and church leaders christen the new building as a testament to a community's refusal to be defined by tragedy. They joined young Kris Workman and his praise team in the opening hymn "It Is Well with My Soul." As the lyrical music wafted upward in the acoustically sensitive sanctuary, parishioners waved their outstretched hands in praise, sang along with the words on TV screens, and dabbed their eyes with tissues.

From his wheelchair, Governor Greg Abbott reminded his listeners yet again that he could identify with survivors as they struggled to regain control of their lives. "I know what it's like to face a life-altering tragedy, to lose the ability to walk," he said. "I know the tears that have been shed, I know the angst you have suffered. But I also know what it's like to make it through the other side of the abyss, and I know you know that, too."

Pastor Mark Collins, the man who transformed the old sanctuary into a memorial, read the names of the twenty-six people who were killed in the massacre. A bell that had been transferred from the old church belfry was rung for each name.

Earlier, in a private morning ceremony, Pastor Frank spoke about the joys of moving into a new building, and the steep price the congregation had paid for it. "The dedication has been costly to many of us," he said. "Physically, mentally, emotionally. And for twenty-six of our precious friends and family, it cost them everything."

Earlier, the church's twelve-member security team, all volunteers, had practiced active-shooter training. They learned how to use heavy flashlights to disarm attackers and developed defense tactics tailored to the contours of the new building. Team members familiarized themselves with security cameras, keyed access, and other modern devices designed not only to prevent another shooting but also to provide comfort and assurance to a group of traumatized people whenever they came together in the building.

Most members seemed pleased with the new edifice. Waiting in the crowded lobby to make our way into the sanctuary, I heard expressions akin to awe as they took in the clean lines, high ceilings, and stark beauty of the $3 million structure, a building that had arisen almost miraculously on what had been a vacant field beside the highway for as long as most Sutherland Springs residents could remember. John Holcombe, who had lost so much, called it "a new beginning," a fitting tribute to his martyred mother Karla, who had prayed for years that the church could somehow acquire the property and construct a new building.

A few expressed reservations. Some worried that the large structure was out of proportion for such a small, unprepossessing community. Others weren't quite used to the contrast between old and new. Julie Workman told the *San Antonio Express-News* the new church was dismayingly different. She said she mourned for the old one.

"We've made no memories in here. It's very stark. And until we start having memories, it's not going to feel like our church," she said. "In the old building, we always felt comfortable putting duct tape on the walls, nailing holes in the ceiling, decorating it however we felt. But in this building, I don't have that comfort yet."

To Julie, the new church was not yet home, not yet a place where, as in the old building, longtime friends, loved ones, and fellow Christians gathered regularly. "There's lots of faces I don't know," she said. "And after what happened…that makes me nervous."

The old church, as Julie sought to express, was intimate, a bit insular. Its people prayed together, ate together, played together. It's where they supported each other during times of trouble, even before the massacre. They were an extended family in that old building.

Their small country church was no longer small. "The remnant" that remained after the massacre had more than doubled in size. The challenge in the years to come would be to retain the intimacy and connectedness of that old country church, in a new setting. Members would have to nurture and sustain those ties that had bound them to each other in the first place.

Pastor Frank was aware of those disconcerting feelings; he felt them himself at times. But he reminded his listeners that the new building was "just brick, stone, wood, glass." The real church is "the people, the heart of the people."

He anticipated great things for his people. The new building would be "a beacon on a hill to Wilson County," he liked to say. The venerable congregation would be known for turning evil into good, for its good works among the community. When he spoke—prophesying, if you will—his people responded as one with a hearty "Amen!"

Pastor Frank anticipated a new beginning for himself. One Sunday after church, three months after the new building was dedicated, he called a special meeting in the sanctuary for anyone interested in an announcement he had to make. Wearing a charcoal-gray suit, white shirt, and patterned tie instead of his Donald Duck favorite, he told those gathered in the pews before him that he would be a candidate for the state senate. Although he rarely spoke of politics from the pulpit and had never been politically active, he told friends he had been pondering such a move for at least a dozen years.

"If I can bring civility and godliness and help stymie the downward spiraling of the great state of Texas, that's what I'm choosing to try to do," he said. "I feel as though that morality and integrity is disappearing rapidly and I feel as though the direction Texas goes—if Texas falls, the country falls."

Running as a Republican in a solidly Democratic district against a popular and powerful incumbent, he was up against strong odds. In biblical terms, his effort would be something akin to Gideon leading the outmanned Israelites against the mighty Midianites or Joshua fighting the battle of Jericho.

The district he sought to represent stretched from liberal Austin southward to the heavily Hispanic Rio Grande Valley. It wrapped around San Antonio, jutted out to the Corpus Christi area, also heavily Hispanic, and took in the border city of Laredo. His opponent, a self-proclaimed pro-life Democrat named Judith Zaffirini, had easily defeated Republican opponents in the past and had faced no opposition in her 2016 reelection campaign. She announced that she definitely planned to run again.

Frank admitted he was a babe in the political woods, but he said he was relying on professionals, "people who will shape me and mold me." He expressed confidence that his faith would guide him to victory in the November 2020 election. "This is totally out of my wheelhouse, but I'm totally trusting the Lord to show me how to do the things I need to do," he said.

So, why was he running? Why was he turning his attention to secular concerns rather than maintaining his steady focus on matters of the spirit? Some suggested he had grown accustomed to the limelight and was looking for another venue as attention waned. Others saw the hand of Governor Abbott in his decision or the influence of Suzanna Gratia Hupp, the former state representative and gun rights advocate who lost her parents in the 1991 Luby's shooting. Still others, Frank himself acknowledged, would likely accuse him of using the tragedy "as a springboard as much as it is something God used to put me in a position to do what He had called me to do."

He insisted that public service, not self-service, impelled him to run. In the spirit of his hero Teddy Roosevelt, he insisted he wanted to climb into the arena and do his part, not watch from afar.

His listeners applauded his decision. They assured him they had his back. They prayed he would succeed.

The Texas legislature meets for six months every other year, so a victorious Pastor Frank would not have to give up his pastorate. During the 2019 legislative session, the first after the massacre, Frank made regular trips to Austin, consulting with lawmakers and serving on various roundtables the governor had appointed to address gun issues.

As a direct response to the Sutherland Springs shooting, Texas lawmakers in the 2019 session passed eight new bills *loosening* Texas gun laws. One allowed licensed handgun owners to legally carry their weapons into places of worship. Of course, guns were already in churches—on Pastor Frank's hip—but the legislation dispensed with a provision in what had been the current law that said handguns were not allowed in "churches, synagogues, or other places of worship." Places of worship would still be able to prohibit licensed citizens from carrying firearms on their premises so long as they provided oral or written notice. The bill sponsor was Republican state senator Donna Campbell, an emergency room physician from New Braunfels, the shooter's hometown.

"The existing statute is confusing and clunky and has kept law-abiding Texans from exercising their second [Amendment] rights where those with evil intentions have tragically targeted innocent lives," Campbell told the *Texas Tribune*. "This bill provides clarity of the Legislature's intent to treat churches and houses of worship in the same manner as other privately owned establishments in Texas."

Other legislation prohibited property owners' associations from banning storage of guns on rental property; provided a legal defense for licensed handgun owners who unknowingly entered an establishment that banned firearms as long as they left when asked; prohibited landlords from banning renters and their guests from carrying firearms in lease agreements; loosened restrictions on the number of school marshals who could carry guns at public and private schools; allowed Texans to carry handguns without a license during hurricanes or other natural disasters; prohibited school districts from banning licensed gun owners from storing guns and ammunition in their vehicles in parking lots; and allowed certain foster homes to store guns and ammunition together, not separately, in a locked location.

On February 14, 2018, in Parkland, Florida, three months after the Sutherland Springs massacre, a nineteen-year-old who had been expelled from Marjory Stoneman Douglas High School for disciplinary reasons returned to the campus armed with a semiautomatic rifle and opened fire. He killed seventeen students and staff members—seven of whom were only fourteen years old—and wounded at least a dozen others. The shooter was ultimately arrested without incident. The attack surpassed the 1999 Columbine High School shooting as the deadliest shooting at a high school in US history.

On May 28, 2018, at Santa Fe High School, southeast of Houston, seniors had just picked up their caps and gowns and were a few days from graduation. At seven thirty on that Friday morning, a seventeen-year-old junior walked into the large suburban school with a shotgun and a .38-caliber revolver he'd taken from his father and began spraying bullets. He killed ten people and injured thirteen more. He ultimately surrendered and was arrested.

On June 28, 2018, a thirty-eight-year-old man who had obsessively harassed journalists at the *Capital Gazette* in Annapolis, Maryland, burst into the newspaper's offices with a 12-gauge shotgun and killed five staffers. Police arrested him at the scene. The paper's staff put out a paper: the next day. On the front page: "5 shot dead at The Capital."

On October 27, 2018, a truck driver with a history of posting anti-Semitic material on social media entered the Tree of Life Synagogue in Pittsburgh's quiet Squirrel Hill neighborhood and killed eleven people and wounded six others. He was armed with an assault rifle and three handguns and wounded four police officers before being shot and taken into custody. According to the Anti-Defamation League, it was the deadliest anti-Semitic attack in US history.

On November 7, 2018, a former US Marine burst into the Border-line Bar and Grill in Thousand Oaks, California, on a night when it was jammed with dancing college students. He tossed a smoke bomb into the space and proceeded to open fire with a .45-caliber handgun. Twelve died in the attack and eighteen were injured, including a Ventura County sheriff's deputy. The twenty-eight-year-old gunman killed himself at the scene.

On February 15, 2019, a forty-five-year-old factory worker in Aurora, Illinois, killed five coworkers at the Henry Pratt Company manufacturing plant in suburban Chicago during a meeting in which he was fired. One other coworker was also wounded, as were the first five police officers to arrive at the scene. The shooter was able to acquire the .40-caliber handgun he used because a background check didn't turn up a prior felony conviction for aggravated battery in Mississippi. After a ninety-minute manhunt inside the plant, he was killed in a shootout with police.

On May 31, 2019, a forty-year-old civil engineer for the Public Utilities Department in Virginia Beach, Virginia, burst into a municipal building in Virginia Beach and killed twelve people before police shot and killed him. The shooter, described as a disgruntled employee, used two .45-caliber pistols in the rampage, both apparently purchased legally.

On August 3, 2019, a gunman opened fire at a busy Walmart in El Paso, killing twenty-two people and injuring twenty-six, among them a US Army veteran and Mexican nationals. The gunman had penned an anti-immigrant manifesto before driving four hundred miles from his home near Dallas to the Walmart near the Mexican border. The El Paso shooting was the third-deadliest in Texas history, behind the Sutherland Springs shooting and the Luby's shooting in Killeen.

The day after the El Paso shooting, a gunman killed nine people and injured an estimated twenty-six in Dayton, Ohio. Police arrived within minutes and killed the twenty-four-year-old gunman, armed with a .223-caliber rifle and wearing body armor, as he tried to enter a crowded bar to slaughter more people. Among the dead was the shooter's sister.

Less than a month later, on a Saturday afternoon in Odessa, Texas, a thirty-six-year-old man armed with an AR-type assault rifle drove along the highway between Odessa and nearby Midland shooting people at random, including a postal worker he gunned down during a carjacking. Police officers fatally shot the man outside a movie theater after he sped toward a barricade and an officer in an SUV rammed the stolen US Postal Service mail van he had commandeered. He killed seven people and injured twenty-two.

Since the day after the shooting at Sutherland Springs, the chain-link fence beside the old church had been festooned with cards, banners, stuffed animals, Mylar balloons, wooden crosses, paper hearts, and other expressions of sympathy. A long canvas banner expressing support for the people of Sutherland Springs stood out among all the items. It was from the people of Las Vegas, Nevada, where on October 1, 2017, a sixty-four-year-old gunman high up in a hotel room fired down on people attending a country-and-western concert. He killed fifty-eight people and wounded more than five hundred more.

After the Santa Fe High School shooting in early 2018, Tambria Read and Terrie Smith organized an effort among their fellow Sutherland Springs residents to design a banner in support of those who grieved in the Houston suburb, just as the Las Vegas people had done for them. They took the banner to Santa Fe just before the opening of the 2018–2019 school term.

After the El Paso shooting in the summer of 2019, they prepared another banner, simply altering the name and adding at Pastor Frank's request the message "Evil did NOT win."

The incidents kept coming. In response to the Odessa shooting a month after El Paso, the good people of Sutherland Springs decided to send sympathy cards instead of a banner.

Acknowledgments

"'Tis a fearful thing to love what death can touch," the esteemed Hebrew poet Judah Halevi wrote in the twelfth century. Nearly a millennium later, the good people of Sutherland Springs, Texas, are living exemplars of the poet's words of wisdom.

I admire and appreciate the members of the First Baptist Church of Sutherland Springs, men and women who were willing to share with a journalist their heart-rending experience, their deep faith, and their prayerful hope for lives of meaning in the wake of profound tragedy. I'm grateful to Frank and Sherri Pomeroy, Stephen and Pam Willeford, Oscar and Alice Garcia, Ann and Ted Montgomery, Rod and Judy Green, Windy and Stormy Choate, Juan "Gunny" Macias, Fred and Kathleen Curnow, Sarah Slavin, Jennifer Holcombe, John Holcombe, David Colbath, Elizabeth Briggs, Pat and Christy Dziuk, Julie Workman, Kris Workman, Ben and Michelle Shields, Kati Johnson Wall, Gail Uhlig, and others who entrusted their stories to me.

Thanks also to Pastor Mark Collins (aka George Washington) of the First Baptist Church of Yorktown, Texas, and Pastor Ted Elmore of the Southern Baptists of Texas Convention.

Thanks to a number of good people I got to know in and around Sutherland Springs. Tambria Read, a veteran high school teacher and the indefatigable director of the Sutherland Springs Historical Museum, is a font of information, freely shared, about her beloved hometown. Thanks also to Tambria's museum cohorts—Beulah Wilson, Fred Anderson, and Eileen Anderson, as well as members of the Wilson County Historical Society: Maureen Liles, Shirley Grammer, and Pat Jackson. Barbara Wood taught me a lot about the history of the First Baptist Church of Sutherland Springs. Thanks also to Terrie Smith and Lorenzo Flores, Sutherland Springs residents who care deeply about their community.

I'm grateful for the cooperation of Wilson County officials: County Judge Richard "Dicky" Jackson, Sheriff Joe Tackitt Jr., justices of the peace Sara Canady and Harold Schott, District Attorney Audrey Louis, and victims' advocate Kate Etringer Quinney.

Thanks also to Mary Beth Fisk, director of the Ecumenical Center of San Antonio, an invaluable resource for the people of Sutherland Springs and for so many other South Texans needing emotional support. For thoughts and ideas about gun policy, I relied on the good work and dedication of Gyl Switzer and Frances Schenkkan of Texas Gun Sense.

I'm grateful to Robin and Keith Muschalek, who are painstakingly restoring Whitehall, the historic Polley mansion just north of Cibolo Creek. The Muschaleks gave me a place to stay when I was in town and with patience, good humor, and thoughtful insights helped me think through everyday life and faith in small-town Texas. I value their friendship.

Thanks also to Pastor Kyle Childress of the Austin Heights Church in Nacogdoches, Texas. As we sat by the fire on his back porch on a cool East Texas evening, a bottle of Woodford Reserve Kentucky bourbon close at hand, the old Stamford Bulldogs quarterback talked about faith and works and his heroes, Will Campbell and Wendell Berry. Thanks also to Kyle's wife Jane and to Professors Katie Day of the United Lutheran Seminary and David Yamane of Wake Forest University. Jane, Katie, and David also sat on the Childress porch one weekend and shared not only libations and snacks but, more important, their profound thoughts about God and guns.

Thanks to my old friend Robert Abzug, an esteemed historian at the University of Texas at Austin, who helped me sort through ideas and notions and who read an early version of the book. Thanks to Professors Greg Garrett and Scott Bader-Saye of the Episcopal Seminary of the Southwest, Barry Hankins of Baylor University, and Robert Wuthnow of Princeton University. I also relied on Richard McCaslin's superb history of Sutherland Springs.

Thanks as usual to Jim Hornfischer, who is not only a smart, hardworking literary agent but also a fine writer and military historian. Thanks to Paul Whitlatch, my former editor at Hachette Book Group, and Brant Rumble, who succeeded Paul. Both are keen-eyed and thoughtful professionals.

I appreciated the encouragement and support of my fellow journalists. Award-winning photographer Lisa Krantz and talented staff writer Silvia Foster-Frau, both of the *San Antonio Express-News,* spent months in Sutherland Springs working to tell a difficult story fairly and with sensitivity, while earning the trust of church members. We talked often in the churchyard on Sundays or over lunch in San Antonio or La Vernia or Floresville. Not only were their tips, observations, and insights invaluable, but it was also inspiring to watch true professionals at work. Lisa and Silvia are credits to our beleaguered profession.

Thanks also to freelance writer Eva Ruth Moravec, reporter Lauren McGaughy of the *Dallas Morning News,* and Houston photographer Lauren McFalls.

I'm grateful, as well, to the young reporter who showed up in Sutherland Springs that first night wearing a "Democracy Dies in Darkness" T-shirt. Covering the tragedy for the *Washington Post,* my son Peter Holley not only wrote his own superb stories but also patiently listened to his dad muse and ponder in the ensuing months. He offered valuable insights and suggestions. As a proud father, I'm happy to say that he too is a consummate professional. (Pete's siblings—Heather Holley, Rachel Austin, and Kate Holley—also listened patiently and offered encouragement.)

And, of course, Laura—wife Laura Tolley. (It's obvious why we don't hyphenate our names.) A former Associated Press reporter and an exacting editor at newspapers in San Antonio and Houston, Laura understood intuitively what I was trying to do during the weeks and months in Sutherland Springs and then afterward during the weeks and months at the computer. She listened, questioned, encouraged, and offered valuable insights. Maybe most important, she lifted me out of the darkness on those Sunday afternoons when I came home with stories almost too heartbreaking to tell. I love you, LT. I could not have written this book without you.

Bibliography

BOOKS

Atwood, James E. *America and Its Guns: A Theological Expose* (Eugene, OR: Wipf & Stock, 2012).

———. *Gundamentalism and Where It's Taking America* (Eugene, OR: Cascade Books, 2017).

Ault, James M., Jr. *Spirit and Flesh: Life in a Fundamentalist Baptist Church* (New York: Knopf, 2005).

Bader-Saye, Scott. *Following Jesus in a Culture of Fear* (Ada, MI: Brazos Press, 2007).

Barton, Barbara. *Pistol Packin' Preachers* (Lanham, MD: Taylor Trade Publishing, 2005).

Bowler, Kate. *Everything Happens for a Reason and Other Lies I've Loved* (New York: Random House, 2018).

Carney, Timothy P. *Alienated America: Why Some Places Thrive While Others Collapse* (New York: HarperCollins, 2019).

Edmondson, J. R. *The Alamo Story: From Early History to Current Conflicts* (Lanham, MD: Republic of Texas Press, 2001).

Erikson, Kai T. *Everything in Its Path: Destruction of Community in the Buffalo Creek Flood* (New York: Simon & Schuster, 1976).

Fea, John. *Believe Me: The Evangelical Road to Donald Trump* (Grand Rapids, MI: Eerdmans, 2018).

Garrett, Greg. *Entertaining Judgment: The Afterlife in the Popular Imagination* (New York: Oxford University Press, 2015).

Graves, Rev. H. A. *Andrew Jackson Potter, Fighting Parson of the Texan Frontier: Six Years of Indian Warfare in New Mexico and Arizona: Many Wonderful Events in His Ministerial Life on the Frontier Border of Western Texas, During a Long Term of Evangelical Toils and Personal Combats with Savage Indians and Daring Desperadoes, Including Many Hair-Breadth Escapes* (Nashville, TN: Southern Methodist Publishing House, 1881).

Haidt, Jonathan. *The Righteous Mind: Why Good People Are Divided by Politics and Religion* (New York: Vintage Books, 2012).

Hankins, Barry. *American Evangelicals: A Contemporary History of a Mainstream Religious Movement* (Lanham, MD: Rowman & Littlefield, 2008).

———. *Jesus and Gin: Evangelicalism, the Roaring Twenties and Today's Culture Wars* (New York: St. Martin's, 2010).

Howe, Ralph E. *The Voice out of the Whirlwind: The Book of Job* (San Francisco: Chandler Publishing, 1960).

Hupp, Suzanna Gratia. *From Luby's to the Legislature: One Woman's Fight Against Gun Control* (San Antonio, TX: Privateer Publications, 2010).

James, William. *The Varieties of Religious Experience.* Abridged with an Introduction by Robert H. Abzug (New York: St. Martin's, 2013).

Junger, Sebastian. *Tribe: On Homecoming and Belonging* (New York: Twelve, 2016).

Kaufmann, Walter. *The Faith of a Heretic* (New York: Signet, 1959).

Kidd, Thomas. *Who Is an Evangelical? The History of a Movement in Crisis* (New Haven: Yale University Press, 2019).

Lenz, Lyz. *God Land: A Story of Faith, Loss, and Renewal in Middle America* (Bloomington: Indiana University Press, 2019).

McCaslin, Richard B. *Sutherland Springs, Texas: Saratoga on the Cibolo* (Denton: University of North Texas Press, 2017).

Morrow, Lance. *Evil: An Investigation* (New York: Basic Books, 2003).

O'Gieblyn, Meghan. *Interior States: Essays* (New York: Anchor Books, 2018).

Pagels, Elaine. *Why Religion? A Personal Story* (New York: Ecco, 2018).

Phares, Ross. *Bible in Pocket, Gun in Hand: The Story of Frontier Religion* (Lincoln: University of Nebraska Press, 1964).

Robinson, Marilynne. *What Are We Doing Here? Essays* (New York: Farrar, Straus and Giroux, 2018).

Seierstad, Asne. *One of Us: The Story of a Massacre—and Its Aftermath* (New York: Farrar, Straus and Giroux, 2013).

Wiman, Christian. *My Bright Abyss: Meditation of a Modern Believer* (New York: Farrar, Straus and Giroux, 2013).

Wood, Barbara J. *A Time to Seek the Lord: 1926–1996* (Sutherland Springs, TX: First Baptist Church of Sutherland Springs, 1996).

Wright, Lawrence. *God Save Texas: A Journey into the Soul of the Lone Star State* (New York: Knopf, 2018).

Wuthnow, Robert. *Rough Country: How Texas Became America's Most Powerful Bible-Belt State* (Princeton, NJ: Princeton University Press, 2014).

ARTICLES

Carey, Greg. "New Book on Trump and Evangelicals Gets It Mostly Right." *Religion Dispatches,* April 16, 2018.

Childress, Kyle. "Texas Tough: A Review of *Rough Country,* by Robert Wuthnow." *Christian Century,* December 29, 2014.

Fortini, Amanda. "What Happened in Vegas: The Days, Weeks, and Months After the Worst Mass Shooting in Modern American History." *California Sunday Magazine,* May 22, 2018.

Froese, Paul. "American Values, Mental Health, and Using Technology in the Age of Trump." *Baylor Religion Survey, Wave 5,* September 2017.

Holley, Joe. "Six Months After 'the Incident,' a Little Texas Town Copes." *Houston Chronicle,* May 5, 2018.

Jacobs, Alan. "*Evangelical* Has Lost Its Meaning." *The Atlantic,* September 22, 2019.

Kilbey-Smith, Nannette. "Giving Names, Respect, Dignity to the Victims." *Wilson County News,* May 16, 2018.

Lingle, Brandon. "Remembering Sutherland Springs." *American Scholar,* April 9, 2018.

Mooney, Michael J. "Stephen Willeford Still Grappling with the Sutherland Springs Mass Murder." *Texas Monthly,* October 2018.

Reed, Katherine. "The Mars Shooter and the Media." *The Investigative Reporters and Editors Journal,* fourth quarter 2018.

Yamane, David. "Awash in a Sea of Faith and Firearms: Rediscovering the Connection Between Religion and Gun Ownership in America." *Journal for the Scientific Study of Religion,* January 6, 2017.

Index